Madoc took Wynne by the hand now and led her to a large white sheepskin rug that lay on the floor before the fireplace. Gently he drew her down so that they knelt facing one another. Taking her face into his hands, he kissed her mouth, gently at first, then a bit more fiercely as his ardor rose. Her arms had been quiet at her side. Now she lifted them and, palms smoothing slowly up his chest, she slid them tightly about his neck, drawing him down with her as she lay back upon the soft sheepskin. His lips never left her all the while, and he thought that she was wonderfully brave in her innocence. . . .

A MOMENT IN TIME

Bertrice Small

BALLANTINE BOOKS • NEW YORK

Copyright © 1991 by Bertrice Small

All rights reserved under International and Pan-American Copyright Conventions. Published in the United States of America by
Ballantine Books, a division of Random House, Inc., New York,
and simultaneously in Canada by Random House of Canada Lim-
ited, Toronto.

Grateful acknowledgment is made to Alfred A. Knopf, Inc. for
permission to reprint excerpts from *The Prophet* by Kahlil Gibran.
Copyright © 1923 by Kahlil Gibran. Copyright © renewed 1951
by the Administrators C.T.A. of Kahlil Gibran Estate and Mary
G. Gibran.

Library of Congress Catalog Card Number: 91-91862

ISBN: 0-345-39079-2

Manufactured in the United States of America

First Trade Edition: September 1991
First Mass Market Edition: September 1994

10 9 8 7 6 5 4 3 2 1

In memory of my friend, Tom E. Huff:
Tom, who was always Tom,
except when he was busy being Jennifer.
Till we meet again, darlin'.

A Guide to Pronunciation

Wynne of Gwernach	Winn of Garnock
Owain ap Llywelyn	Owen ap Lew-el-in
Enid	E-nid
Caitlin	Kate-lyn
Dilys	Dill-is
Dewi ap Owain	Dewey ap Owen
Mair	Mare
Rhys	Reese
Madoc of Powys	May-dock of Pow-is
Nesta	Nes-tah
Brys of Cai	Brice of Kay
Einion	Eye-none
Rhiannon	Ree-an-non
Pwyll of Dyfed	Powell of Dif-id
Angharad	Ann-har-id
Bronwyn	Bron-win
Eadwine Aethelhard	Edwin Athal-hard
Caddaric Aethelmaere	Kad-er-rick Athal-mare
Baldhere Armstrang	Bald-air Armstrong
Eadgyth	Edith
Aeldra	Eldra
Ealdraed	Eldred
Berangari	Bear-an-gary
Dagian	Dag-e-an
Aelf	Elf
Haesel	Hazel
Ruari Ban	Rory Ban
Aelfdene	Elf-dean

Love gives naught but itself and takes naught but from itself.
Love possesses not nor would it be possessed;
For love is sufficient unto love.

Kahlil Gibran
THE PROPHET

SOMEWHERE IN TIME

*A*ngharad, Queen of the Fair Folk, appeared suddenly in the Great Hall of Dyfed in an ominous cloud of violet mist. Her entry was preceded by a rather portentous thunderclap that shook the carved rafters of the building so hard, those within the hall looked fearfully up to be certain that the roof was not collapsing upon them. The clearing haze revealed to them a woman of uncommon beauty, although Angharad was not as lovely as her sister, Rhiannon, who was wife to Dyfed's prince. The queen's gown shimmered with the mysterious iridescence of mother-of-pearl. Her long golden hair was plaited into seven braids, each one of which was interwoven with pearls and multicolored gemstones that glistened with the subtle movement of her head as she looked slowly about her, her silver-blue gaze observing all within her view.

Teirnyon, the lord of Gwent, and his sweet-faced wife, Elaine, stood with the child, Anwyl. Angharad's eyes softened briefly as they passed over the little boy. They hardened once more as they rested upon Bronwyn of the White Breast who sat boldly next to Pwyll, Dyfed's prince. There was no shame in Bronwyn. She graced her half of the ruler's bench as if she actually belonged there, glaring defiantly at the queen of the Fair Folk for being the unwelcome intruder that she was. Pwyll, to give him credit, looked the shamed and broken man he now was.

"*Sister.*" The voice was gentle, yet insistent.

Angharad turned and embraced her elder sibling. A small smile of triumph touched her lips as she looked at Rhiannon. The Cymri had not destroyed her, although God knows they had tried. If anything, Rhiannon's beauty had but increased despite the unjust treatment meted out to her over the past four years. The time had come for retribution.

"*Be merciful, sister.*" Rhiannon had not spoken aloud, and yet Angharad heard her.

3

"I might have had they shown you any mercy," the queen of the Fair Folk responded in kind.

"There were some who were thoughtful of me in my distress," Rhiannon replied.

"I know them, and they shall not feel my wrath," Angharad said, and turning away from her elder sister, she spoke aloud. Her words were deliberate and carefully chosen. Upon those who had aided Rhiannon she disbursed blessings and unequaled good fortune that would descend down through their families for a thousand generations to come. To those who had calculatingly and purposefully planned deleterious and ruinous hurt to Rhiannon, the queen of the Fair Folk laid upon them a curse of terrible proportions. The silence in the Great Hall of Dyfed as she spoke was so thick it was almost visible.

Then Angharad glared at her brother-in-law, who sat upon his seat of office, his head within his hands. Fiercely she willed him to look up at her, and when he did, she spoke again. The anger was gone from her voice now. Only a deep sadness remained.

"Pwyll of Dyfed," she began. "When you came to wed with my sister, Rhiannon asked but two things of you. That you give her your complete love and your complete trust. This was all she demanded of you in exchange for the great sacrifices she made in order to become your wife. You have betrayed Rhiannon on both accounts. You could not trust her in the face of your people's condemnation of her because she was not of the Cymri, and therefore her credence was to be doubted; but even that the Fair Folk might forgive you had you remained true in your heart to her. You have not, Pwyll of Dyfed. Your love for Rhiannon has wavered as surely as your faith in her has wavered. Even knowing the great concessions my sister made for you, you left her helpless, unable to defend herself and caught between two worlds. For this, Pwyll of Dyfed, you will be punished."

Then Angharad, Queen of the Fair Folk, pronounced Pwyll's fate; a fate so severe it left all within the hall breathless and in awe of its subtlety. It was a harsh judgment. As the full meaning of it penetrated Pwyll's brain, his eyes widened with horror, even knowing as he resisted his punishment that he fully deserved it.

Then, before the astonished eyes of the assembled court of

Dyfed, the hall began to fill with a silvery smoke. There was another monstrous thunderclap which immediately cleared the haze, revealing to all that Angharad and Rhiannon were no longer amongst them. Bronwyn of the White Breast whimpered, finally fearful, and piteously clutched at Pwyll's arm. Furiously he shook her off, and opening his mouth, he cried after his wife.

"Rhiannon! Rhiannon! Rhi-an-non!"

There was no answer, and as Pwyll's voice echoed and died within the Great Hall of Dyfed, a deep, sad silence descended upon all there.

Part 1

WYNNE OF GWERNACH

WALES, 1060

If in the twilight of memory we should meet once more, we shall speak again together and you shall sing to me a deeper song.
                    Kahlil Gibran
                    THE PROPHET

▪Chapter 1

Wynne of Gwernach stared down at her father's grave. A month had passed since Owain ap Llywelyn had met his death in a freak accident. The grass was already beginning to grow and thicken upon the burial mound which would soon look like her mother's grave. As if it had been there for a hundred centuries. As if there was nothing beneath the mound at all but the earth itself. She felt a tear begin to slide down her cheek and impatiently brushed it away. She had not cried at her father's demise. Tears were for weaklings, and she could not be weak like other women. Other women did not have the responsibility of a large, productive estate that must be kept safe for its boy heir. Other women did not have the liability for the safety of that little brother or three sisters.

"Father," Wynne said aloud. " 'Tis a hard task you have left me," and then she sighed deeply.

Owain ap Llywelyn had been a tall, handsome man in the prime of his life. Although he held one of the richest estates in all of Morgannwg, there was none who begrudged him it, even the king, Gruffydd ap Llywelyn, his distant cousin. In warlike Wales he was regarded as a man of peace, although Owain ap Llywelyn had been known to pick up his sword when the occasion merited it. Still, he preferred his lands and his cattle; his wife and his family, above all else; and he would do nought to jeopardize those things.

For his entire life Owain ap Llywelyn had been considered fortunate in all things. At the age of twenty-two he had taken to wife a girl considered the greatest beauty in all of Wales; Margiad, called *the Pearl*. She had given him four daughters and a son before dying in childbirth; but even so, Owain ap Llywelyn was still thought to be a lucky man. His children were all healthy, and he could certainly marry again. He was considered a prime catch; but Owain did not remarry. He had loved his wife greatly, and mourned her loss deeply. Those who knew Owain ap Llywelyn best noticed that he did not laugh quite as easily, or as frequently after Margiad's death. He named the daughter she had died birthing Mair, which meant *sorrow* in the ancient Cymri language. He loved the baby no less than he had loved her siblings, for he was not a cruel man, but he was never again the same man; the man that he had been before Margiad the Pearl's death. Now he drove himself relentlessly, as if seeking to escape the reality of his widowhood.

Never an overly prideful man, he thought nothing of picking up a scythe and working in the fields with his serfs and his slaves. Indeed, on the day that Owain ap Llywelyn had died, he had suddenly decided to help in the rethatching of his barn. The spring rains would be upon them, and the winter had taken its toll of that vital structure's roof. A load of thatch upon his broad shoulder, he had lost his footing and fallen from the roof into a pile of hay below. A pitchfork, left carelessly in the hay, had pierced Owain ap Llywelyn's heart, killing him instantly.

The heir to Gwernach was ten years old and, although technically the estate was his, he was much too young to manage it. That task had fallen to his eldest sister, Wynne, who was fifteen, there being no male kin available. Fortunately the orphans of Gwernach had their paternal grandmother, Enid, to look after the management of the household, leaving Wynne free to oversee her little brother's large inheritance. There were other things that needed settling, though, and Wynne feared she was not capable of doing these things.

As the lord of Gwernach, her little brother was a valuable marital catch; but Wynne was not certain it was wise to betroth Dewi ap Owain to a wife until he was considerably older. It was not unusual for boys of ten to be married; but the truth of the matter was that should Dewi not survive his childhood, a child wife's family could place a claim on the rich lands of Gwernach in the widow's name. Then what would happen to the rest of them? Standing by her father's grave, Wynne frowned, for she knew the answer to her question. She, her sisters, and their grandmother would find themselves displaced and penniless. It was all so complicated. Husbands had to be found for Caitlin, Dilys, and Mair. How was she to go about that? She didn't even have a husband herself.

Caw! Caw!

Wynne turned at the sound of the harsh voice and the noisy flapping of the wings that accompanied it. A great black raven stood eyeing her from a nearby tree. He cocked his head almost as if to ask what the problem was that kept her here on this bleak hilltop in a rough wind that smelt most distinctly of rain. A small smile touched Wynne's lips. The raven was an old friend. He seemed ageless, having been about her whole life. Her father had always teased her that the bird must certainly be the oldest living raven, for ravens, he said, were not particularly long-lived; but Wynne knew that this bird now looking at her was the same bird she had always known.

"Hello, Dhu!" she called, feeling strangely comforted by his presence. "I've no bread on me to share with you today. Sorry."

The bird looked aggrieved at her words and made a small crackling sound in the back of his throat.

"Ohh," Wynne said gently, "I've hurt your feelings, haven't I? You didn't come for bread at all, but to comfort me, old Dhu. Well, my problems are surely bigger than yours today." Then she laughed softly. "And wouldn't the world think me mad or a witch to be talking to a raven? And yet we're old friends, aren't we?"

The raven appeared to bob his head.

Wynne chuckled, amused. "Well, I'd best be off, old Dhu. I'll not solve my difficulties standing here chattering to you. Take care of yourself and don't steal too much seed when we plant next week." Then she was off down the hill from the grave site, while behind her the raven continued to watch her, perched comfortably on his tree; but then as the first drop of rain began, the bird flew off, grumbling, to seek shelter.

Wynne pulled her woolen shawl up over her head as she hurried down the hill. Spring rains could be treacherously deceptive, and she didn't need a chill. At least the house would be warm. It was strange, but despite its proximity to the river, it was always comfortable. As a child she had wondered about the ancestor who had built their house upon a promontory overlooking the river. As she grew in wisdom she understood that by doing so the house was only vulnerable on one side; and that side was surrounded by a thick stone wall allowing entry only through heavy ironbound oak gates which were closed and barred at sunset and in times of danger.

Within those walls were the estate's main dwelling; main barn; blacksmith's forge; cook house; stables, kennels, dovecote; well; and kitchen gardens. The house, which was constructed of both stone and timber, had a thatched roof with several smoke holes for the fire pits which indicated that it was a wealthy man's home. Inside, the main floor consisted of a hall that extended almost the entire length of the building and soared two stories high. Above the portion of the hall that was single-storied was a second floor consisting of a solar and a single small chamber which had been Owain ap Llywelyn's private sleeping place for himself and his wife. This, in itself, was unique, for generally the lord and his family slept in the same room, curtains drawn about each bed being the only privacy available.

Wynne dashed through the gates of her home as the skies opened in earnest, gaining the house with a gusty sigh of relief. She shook the droplets from the heavy fabric of her shawl, rendering it almost fully dry, and wrapping it about herself, moved into the hall. The two fire pits were both blazing merrily, and as usual, the place was snug and dry. Her green eyes skimmed over the room, taking in her grandmother, Enid, as she instructed the servants bringing in the evening meal; to her brother, Dewi, who was happily rolling about in the rushes with the latest litter of puppies and their baby sister, Mair; to her next two sisters, Caitlin and Dilys, who sat idly gossiping as usual. Seeing her entry, Dilys jumped up and ran to her elder sister.

"Where were you?" she whined. "We were afraid! We've had word Irish slavers are raiding our coast again. What if you had been taken? What would happen to us?" Her pretty mouth had a petulant cast to it.

Caitlin joined them and said in superior tones, "She was at the grave again, weren't you, Wynne? Why you go there is beyond me. There is nothing there. Father is long gone; but Dilys is right. The Irish are raiding. It would behoove you to be more prudent in your wanderings."

"Thank you for your concern, *dear sister*," Wynne said dryly, "and how do you know about the Irish? There's nought to fear from them. We are too far from the coast for the Irish to bother with us."

"A messenger came!" Dilys burst out. "While you were gone!"

"Was I gone so far that you could not have sent for me?" Wynne answered sharply. "I was, after all, in sight of the house. I saw no rider."

"You saw no rider because you were probably daydreaming again," Caitlin replied. "The rider came, and he departed as quickly, for he was ordered by his master to return immediately. Rhys of St. Bride's needs every man he has until the danger is over, I would think."

"Rhys of St. Bride's sent to us to tell of Irish slavers?" Wynne was puzzled. " 'Twas kind of him, but quite unnecessary, I believe."

"No! No!" Dilys giggled inanely, dancing about her eldest sister, her golden-brown braids swinging madly.

"Be silent, you silly wretch!" Caitlin ordered her sibling. "I will tell Wynne the message." She turned to her elder. "Rhys of St. Bride's would come to visit us. He would speak to you on a matter of some importance," Caitlin said loftily, "which can only mean he wants to marry you! I told the messenger to tell his master that you would be pleased and honored to receive him at his convenience. If you wed Rhys of St. Bride's, then we will be able to find rich husbands too! What an opportunity for us all! Are you not pleased, Wynne?"

Wynne, however, looked at first astounded by her sister's news and then disturbed. "No," she finally said, choosing her words carefully. "No, I am not pleased at all by the prospect of being courted by Rhys of St. Bride's. I shall have to refuse him should he ask, and refusing him while keeping his friendship will not be an easy thing, Caitlin."

"*Refuse him?* Why would you refuse him?" Caitlin shrieked. "You will ruin us all, you selfish creature, before you are through!"

Wynne sighed. "Caitlin, think a moment. Why would a powerful warlord with a great castle want me to wife? Oh, my dowry is good, but our name is not great. Rhys of St. Bride's can have both in a wife, so why would he want me?"

"Who cares why he wants you?" Caitlin said petulantly. "Don't you understand anything, Wynne? With Rhys for a brother-in-law, and our comfortable dowries, we shall have our pick of good husbands. Besides, we are related to the king."

"Our connection to Gruffydd ap Llywelyn is so slender as to be almost invisible," Wynne said matter-of-factly. "If Rhys of St. Bride's is to come courting me, it is because of our brother."

"What has Dewi got to do with it?" Dilys asked, her pretty forehead wrinkling with her puzzlement.

"Our brother is young. Should anything happen to him before he is grown, wed, and a father, Gwernach would be mine. We are fortunate we have no close male relations else they threaten Dewi for his inheritance. You can be certain that that is what is in the back of Rhys of St. Bride's mind as he comes courting me. Dewi's possible demise. I should not put it past him to hurry our brother into the next life that he might gain Gwernach through me. The line of descent in the matter of Gwernach is quite clear. It is first through the male line to the third degree, and then through the female line beginning with the eldest daughter. Rhys of St. Bride's has never even seen me. I might be bald and snaggle-toothed, but he would have me to have Gwernach."

"You're mad!" Caitlin said, but she could not look at her sister as she spoke.

"Nay," their grandmother said, joining them and entering into the conversation. "She's probably right, and yet I do not feel we should judge Rhys of St. Bride's harshly until we have heard him out. Perhaps his offer will be a genuine one. Wynne is a practical girl. She clearly sees her main attraction for a powerful lord is the fact that, though Dewi is Gwernach's lord, she is Gwernach's heiress until Dewi has fathered a son of his own. Still, my girl," Enid said, putting a comforting arm about her eldest grandchild, "Caitlin did the correct thing when she told the messenger that you will receive the lord of St. Bride's."

"Let us hope the Irish keep him busy for several months," Wynne muttered. "The last thing I need about Gwernach right now is a suitor. The corn and the hay must be planted if I am to feed the cattle next winter. It is hard enough, as you well know, to wrest grain from this soil."

"Four more cows calved today," Dewi said coming up to his

sisters. "Old Blodwen had twins again, and one of them is a wee bull, Wynne."

She smiled down at him, pulling the straw from his black hair and ruffling it affectionately. "A wee bull," she repeated. "Well, if he's half the stud his sire is, he'll prove valuable to us."

Dewi grinned, pleased, but Caitlin glowered darkly.

"Cows and bulls!" she said irritably. "Is that all you can think about, Wynne?"

"One of us must think about such things if this estate is to survive—*if your dowry is to survive*—until I can marry you and Dilys off," Wynne told her.

"My dowry is *my* dowry," Caitlin said firmly.

"Your dowry," her sister replied, "is part of this estate, and Gwernach comes first."

"And there's another reason that you should marry Rhys of St. Bride's if he asks you," Caitlin insisted stubbornly. "No woman is competent to manage an estate. I don't even understand why you won't do it. Better you wed and let Rhys handle Gwernach before you lose everything for us!"

"Wynne doesn't have to marry anyone she doesn't want to, you selfish cow!" Dewi told his older sister, his blue eyes flashing at Caitlin in his defense of Wynne. *"I am lord of Gwernach, and I have spoken!"*

"Lord of Gwernach! Lord of Gwernach!" mocked Dilys, for she and Caitlin were close. "You're nought but a little runt!"

"I'm as big as you are," Dewi replied spiritedly, reaching out to yank at one of Dilys's long braids and grinning with satisfaction at her shriek of pain.

Caitlin smacked at her brother in an effort to defend Dilys, but he eluded her hard hand and aimed a well-placed kick at her shin. Caitlin howled with outrage as his foot successfully met its mark.

"Missed me! Missed me!" he laughed at her, capering about Caitlin who was bending to rub her sore leg.

Wynne grasped her little brother by the scruff of his neck and held him fast. "Apologize to your sisters," she said sternly to the wiggling boy.

"I'm sorry," Dewi said in sugary, repentant tones, but his eyes were dancing devilishly. If Wynne could not see his look, Caitlin and Dilys could.

Caitlin's cold blue eyes warned her little brother that he
would fare badly should she catch him alone in the near future.
Caitlin respected but two things: gold and power. As far as she
was concerned, Dewi had neither of these at this point and,
consequently, was vulnerable to her vengeance. Dewi, however, could count on Dilys's forgetful nature. Though selfish
and self-absorbed, Dilys rarely held a grudge, unlike Caitlin.

Outside the wind was beginning to pick up and the rain was
beating strongly against the shuttered windows. A gust blew
down the chimney hole, sending a shower of sparks into the
air, but they fell harmlessly back into the round stone fire pit.

"Come," Enid said firmly, "the evening meal is getting cold
while we stand here arguing a matter about which we have not
all the facts. Perhaps Rhys of St. Bride's but wishes to purchase cattle from us."

"It is well known that we do not sell our cattle," Caitlin said
impatiently.

At the table, Father Drew sat patiently awaiting the family.
He was a gentle little man with twinkling brown eyes who was
their only near male relation, but as a man of the cloth, he was
exempted from inheriting Gwernach. He had lived there his
entire life but for the years he spent in an English monastery,
returning several months after Wynne was born, when
Gwernach's former priest, another cousin, had died. His stomach rumbled hungrily, but he held his peace until his relations
had seated themselves. Then he quickly mumbled a blessing
upon the bounty they were about to receive, reaching for his
cup even as the "Amen" died upon the others' lips.

Enid restrained a chuckle, nodding to the servants to serve
the meal. No one, she knew, appreciated his food like Drew,
and yet he was but a wisp of a man. A stew of mutton, onions,
carrots, and cabbage was ladled onto the individual trenchers
of bread. It was a tasty dish, well-flavored with sea salt and
peppercorns, for Enid, in charge of the kitchens, had a sophis-
ticated palate and disliked bland food. The sea salt was easily
obtainable, but the peppercorns were a luxury imported from
some far place, she knew not where. There was cheese and
bread baked this morning upon the table as well as a pitcher of
ale, the sides of the vessel frosted.

The room was quiet as they ate, Wynne silently admonish-
ing Dewi with a severe waggle of her eyebrows to use his

spoon and not his fingers. Though there was more than enough to eat for everyone in the household, it was a simple meal, for they were but country folk. When they had at last finished and the servants had cleared away the last remnants of their supper, a bowl of wizened apples was brought. In cold storage all winter long, these last of the past year's harvest had seen better days.

"Take them away," Enid commanded, "and stew them for our breakfast."

"Do not forget to sweeten them," Caitlin called after the departing servant.

"If she ate all the honey in the world it wouldn't help her disposition," Dewi muttered beneath his breath.

Wynne shot her brother a warning look, but she was unable to restrain her mouth from turning up slightly at the corners, and he grinned mischievously back at her.

"*What* did he say?" Caitlin demanded.

"Nothing that concerns you," Wynne said with finality, firmly blocking the avenue to additional discord.

"I wonder when Rhys of St. Bride's will come courting Wynne," Dilys said.

"Must we speak of the lord of St. Bride's?" Wynne replied irritably.

"What is the matter with you?" Caitlin snapped at her eldest sister. "You act as if the devil himself is coming to woo you. Rhys of St. Bride's is said to be a fine figure of a man, not much past thirty. He's still young and vigorous. He's only had one wife, and there are no children from that marriage. It would be your son who would inherit St. Bride's! A rich and powerful man is coming to pay you suit, Wynne! By the blessed Christ, I wish it were me he were coming to see!"

"So do I," Wynne said quietly. "I have no wish for a husband at this time."

"Then you're a fool!" Caitlin raged at her. "You're fifteen, sister, and not getting any younger!"

"If you feel that strongly," Wynne replied, "I shall suggest a match between you and Rhys of St. Bride's, if it is indeed a wife that he comes seeking here."

"He won't have me," Caitlin said matter-of-factly and sounding extremely irritated by her own honest assessment of the situation.

"Nay, he will not," her sister answered, "*and* we both know why, don't we, Caitlin? It is for *that* reason that I will not wed *any* man until Dewi is grown and a father himself."

"*But what about us?*" Caitlin wailed. "Are we to be condemned to be old maids because you choose that path for yourself? That is selfish!"

"Enough!" Enid interjected sternly. "For shame, Caitlin! When have you ever known Wynne to be selfish? You are the selfish one in this family, and selfish enough for all of us, I might add. Between us, Wynne and myself, and our fine young lord of Gwernach, you and Dilys shall have good husbands."

"I do not want a good husband," Caitlin told her grandmother stubbornly. "I want a rich and powerful one!"

Wynne burst out laughing. "By the blessed rood, Caitlin, you are blunt."

"Good men are usually dull," Caitlin noted.

"But if he were a rich, good man," Wynne teased her, "would it make him more palatable for you?"

"She'd probably drive him to an early grave," Dewi noted sagely.

"Ahhh," Wynne chuckled, "then she would be a rich widow and could do just what she pleased. Would that not make you happy, Caitlin?"

"Only if I might take a lover," Caitlin said.

"*What?!*" Enid looked shocked. "What talk is this, granddaughter? What mischief have you been up to, my girl?"

"Oh, Grandmother, do not fret," Caitlin replied in bored tones. "I shall not throw my virginity away for a mere moment's passion when I can sell it to the highest bidder. Nonetheless, I am certain I shall very much appreciate the carnal relationship enjoyed by a husband and a wife. So much so that if I am widowed I shall not want to do without it. I am not like Wynne. All cool and distant. I am a creature of fire!"

"You are a bold baggage," Enid said, and she slapped Caitlin sharply on her cheek, but the girl just laughed mockingly at her grandmother as she rubbed the sting from her pretty, petulant face.

Dilys giggled foolishly at the exchange and was also slapped for her trouble. Her great blue eyes filled with tears that spilled down her pink cheeks.

"Go to your beds," Enid said wearily to the two girls. "You also, my precious boy," she told Dewi.

Without another word Caitlin arose and stalked proudly from the hall, Dilys hurrying in her wake. Dewi, however, arose from his place and kissed his eldest sister and his grandmother lovingly before taking his departure.

"She will come to a bad end," Enid predicted darkly of Caitlin.

"Nay, Grandmother," Wynne said gently. "It is just that she has suddenly discovered she has a woman's feelings within her. She wants to be her own mistress in her own home."

"But you do not," Enid said. "Why is that, my child?"

Wynne shook her head. "I dare not marry lest I endanger my brother," she said.

"You may fool the others with that tale," Enid said, "but you do not fool me. What is it? What is it that keeps you from seeking a husband, Wynne? I will not deny you that Rhys of St. Bride's motives in courting you are perhaps not as honest as we would have them; but there are others who would wed you for yourself and not Gwernach. Before my son died in that foolish accident, there were two who sought your hand in marriage, yet you would not have them. *Why?*"

Wynne sighed deeply, her long fingers worrying at the fabric of her tunic dress. "Am I a fool, Grandmother, to believe in true love in a world that makes marriage contracts based on rank, and wealth and expediency?" she said softly. "I cannot, it seems, be comfortable with the idea of giving myself to a man I do not love or respect; and yet that is not how things are done in our world, is it? Caitlin chides me with good reason, but I cannot change how I feel, and I do not believe I should have to, for marriage is a sacrament between God and man. It should be taken seriously, but how can I take it seriously if I marry simply to marry, and I am unhappy in my decision?"

Enid nodded understandingly. "I have had two husbands. The first one my father chose. Your grandfather was a wonderful man and I loved him. When he died I thought my world had ended. I remarried that your own father and mother not be burdened by me. That marriage was a mistake, and had Howel ap Merredydd not died of natural causes, I think I would have hastened his departure from this earth. He was a cruel man.

You will get no argument from me, my child. If you would wed but for love alone, then follow your heart, say I!"

Wynne slipped from her chair to hug her grandmother, and the old woman stroked her hair lovingly. "You always understand me, Grandmother. You always have. Better than anyone else. Why is that?"

Enid chuckled. "You are like me, child. I see myself in you each day in so many ways." A small bubble of laughter escaped her. "You but see me as a white-haired old lady, but once I was young as you are young; and filled with the same fiery juices that you are filled with, though you are not yet aware of such things."

"Caitlin is, though she be younger than me," Wynne noted.

Enid made an impatient little noise. "Hummmph," she said. "Caitlin was born all-knowing. There are some women like that though they be few in number. They seem to understand certain things without even being told. Do not change! You, my child, are a true innocent and pure of heart."

Her grandmother's wise words pleased Wynne, although she did not really understand why. Still, they comforted her in the following weeks when the unceasing rains made it almost impossible to plant the grain; and then washed the first planting away entirely, making it necessary to replant.

"You see," Caitlin carped. "We need a man to run Gwernach."

"Do you think a man could force the rains to stop?" Wynne mocked her sister. "Do not be a fool! If you would be helpful, Caitlin, I suggest that you pray that the good weather holds until the grain has grown enough to withstand a heavy downpour."

Caitlin sent her sister a scathing look. "Better I pray that Rhys of St. Bride's makes his appearance soon," she retorted.

"Perhaps we should pray he doesn't find a more suitable bride," Dilys said fatuously.

"Or that he breaks his bloody neck before he can come to bother our sister," Dewi said wickedly, and Wynne burst out laughing.

"You stupid little toad," Caitlin said angrily, "can you not understand the value to us if Rhys of St. Bride's weds our eldest sister?"

"I understand the value to *you*," Dewi replied, "but if Rhys gains Wynne, there is no certainty that he will help you or Dilys. There is no need for our sister to marry if she does not choose to marry. I will not force her to it, and I will not allow you to do so, Caitlin."

"What if she falls in love with him?" Caitlin demanded.

"Then she will have my blessing," the boy answered. "I would have my sisters happy in their marriages."

"I shall be happy with a rich and powerful husband only," Caitlin told them.

"So you have said, my sister, on numerous occasions," Dewi returned. "I should not say it too loud, however, Caitlin, for a man would be desired, I think, for more than his name, his rank, or his wealth."

"Even as a woman would," Wynne replied.

"What a pair of fools you both are," Caitlin said. "A man seeks many things from a woman. More gold to fill his coffers. More power for his family. Sons. He cares not if a woman loves him if he has these things. We have little gold and no power to speak of, but we have beauty, which has a certain value, and our mother was a good breeder, which also has value. Couple this with a sister wed to a powerful coastal lord. . . ." Her blue eyes glittered with pleasure at the thoughts she no longer voiced.

Dewi shook his head. Though he was young, he understood Caitlin far better than she would have imagined, or even liked; and he knew as he had always known that he did not like her. He pitied the man that she would eventually entrap and marry. Caitlin had a heart of stone, if indeed she had any heart at all. There was nothing in her for anyone but herself. She was cold. "A man would be loved, Caitlin," he told her, knowing even as he said it that Caitlin was incapable of loving anyone, perhaps even herself.

"I repeat, little brother, you are a fool!" came the harsh retort. "Men care not if women love them. Power! Gold! Those are their only goals. You will see that I am right one day when you grow up and stop believing in the fairy tales our grandmother and eldest sister so love telling."

"I will marry for love alone, Caitlin," the boy told her quietly. "What good is a fat dowry in a house that is riven with discord between its master and its mistress? What kind of children do such poor souls breed? Gold can never ease a sore heart."

Before Caitlin might argue with her brother further, Wynne held up her hand. "There can be no agreement between you on this subject," she said, "and so I would bid you both to cease your childish bickering. When Rhys of St. Bride's finally arrives, we will listen to him with courtesy, whatever he may have to say."

The siblings nodded their agreement of Wynne's words, though each thought separate thoughts from hers. Caitlin believed that when Rhys of St. Bride's offered their sister a proposal of marriage, she would prevail upon Wynne to accept him, thus ensuring golden futures for herself and Dilys. She smiled a most smug smile at them all.

Dewi's eyes narrowed almost imperceptibly as he regarded her distastefully. Caitlin reminded him of a nasty cat eyeing a helpless mouse. She would not have her way if he had anything to say about it, and he would. His rights as the master of Gwernach would be upheld. He might be young, but Dewi knew if he did not begin to exert his influence now, he would have a hard time making those around him take him seriously later on in life. He would not exhibit any weakness, if only for Wynne's future happiness.

"For your sake, sweet sister," Dewi told Wynne, and touched her cheek lovingly with his small hand.

Caitlin glowered. She did not miss the significance of either his gesture or his words, but she held her peace. In the end it would be her words that prevailed in the matter and not some unfledged boy's.

The weather improved, and within a short period of time the fields were green with new growth. Wynne, with Dewi at her side, rode out daily to inspect the estate. They were a familiar sight to the serfs and slaves belonging to Gwernach, the young master upon his fat dappled grey pony; his sister upon her gentle black mare. Though it frightened them to have a boy for a master, the people of Gwernach trusted the lady Wynne to make certain that all would be well. In the years before the old master had died so suddenly, the lady Wynne would accompany him upon his daily rounds. Even as a child they had known that there was something special about her, and indeed, as she grew, their collective instinct had been proven correct.

Wynne of Gwernach was a healer, but it was not just her knowledge of medicines, herbs, potions, and poultices that made her so special. It was her healer's touch, a rare ability granted to few. So they trusted the young master's sister to keep them safe.

It was a good spring. The cattle grew fat in meadows grown to lushness from the early rains. They lost no calves either in the birthing, or to illness, or to predators. The demand for their cheese was greater than ever before, not simply for its quality, but due to the fact they could only produce a certain amount which in turn drove up the price, filling Gwernach's coffers with new gold. As she rode over the estate early one afternoon with her brother, Wynne thought their life perfect.

"Caitlin no longer complains that we need a man to run the estate," Dewi noted. "Allowing her her fill of cloth and small treasures from that passing peddler seems to have soothed her fretfulness." He chuckled.

"Caitlin is merely distracted by her new acquisitions," Wynne told him wisely. "She considers everything she was permitted to purchase her rightful due."

Dewi laughed aloud, and then he grew serious. "We have heard no more from Rhys of St. Bride's, my sister, but having said he will come, I have no doubt that he will. What shall you do if, indeed, he does bring you an offer of marriage?"

"I shall refuse him, Dewi. I have told you that I will not leave Gwernach until you are grown and wed. Our parents would, God assoil their good souls, want it that way. As soon as it is possible, we will arrange marriages for Caitlin and Dilys, although Dilys alone is a harmless and simple soul. Caitlin, however, needs a husband. Her spirit is a restless one, and she sows discord in our house because of it. It will not be so when she has her own hall to rule."

"She would not like it that you know her so well, sister," Dewi said.

"Then we shall not tell her, little brother," Wynne replied with a smile, "but your instinct is as sharp as mine, is it not?"

"I think you may be too wise a woman, sister," the boy said mischievously, but then his eye was distracted and he cried, reaching for his slingshot, "Look! It is that black beggar who steals the seed!" Delving into his pouch for a stone, he fitted it quickly into the sling and launched it even as Wynne cried out.

"No, Dewi! 'Tis my raven! Do not shoot him!"

His aim, usually true, was not this time, or perhaps the raven was simply quicker. With an indignant squawk it flew directly above them, scolding angrily.

Wynne laughed. "One does not need to speak the raven's tongue to know that he is cursing you quite heartily, little brother," she teased the boy.

"Mistress! Mistress!" The voice called across the hillside and they were quickly joined by Einion, a house slave. He was a large man, so tall that his legs practically touched the ground as he rode his horse. Broad of shoulder, with sinewy arms and legs, a leonine head of fiery red hair that fell to his shoulders, he was an impressive and fearful sight. Off his horse, however, Einion limped badly, and it was that injury that had resulted in his enslavement. He had been captured after a battle with the Irish and sold by them into slavery. He was, he had told Owain ap Llywelyn, a Norseman from the far north country of Norway. Though his gait was ungainly and awkward due to his injury, Einion had incredible strength in his upper body. Owain ap Llywelyn had liked the man immediately and trusted him instinctively. Removing the slave collar from Einion, though he did not release him from bondage to the family, Owain had assigned him to protect his children, who, at the time of Einion's arrival into the household, had consisted of an infant girl called Wynne.

"The lady Caitlin sent me for you," Einion said. "The lord of St. Bride's is near and requests your permission to stop at Gwernach."

"Permission our sister undoubtedly sent," Dewi said irritably.

Einion grinned. "Yes, master," he said, and then he added, "she would not have even given the poor messenger so much as a drink of water, in such a hurry was she, but that your grandmother spoke up."

"What a pity we cannot match Caitlin with Rhys of St. Bride's," muttered the boy. " 'Twould serve him right!"

"Dewi!" Wynne laughed. "You will not shame us with bad manners, my young lord of Gwernach. Rhys of St. Bride's must be welcomed and treated with courtesy, no matter that I will refuse of his suit."

"What if you love him?" the boy said.

"I would still not accept an offer of marriage that would endanger you," Wynne told her brother quietly. "Not for the love of a man, Dewi. For love, sworn to most passionately, can turn and change until it disappears entirely. Nay, dear one, I shall never base any important decision I make in life upon love."

The boy nodded, content. All he understood of Wynne's words was that she would not leave him or place his existence in jeopardy; but Einion's brown eyes were troubled. The lady Wynne was much too young to have so acute a knowledge of life, particularly as she lacked the awareness of men and women. It was not the first time she had spoken thusly, and each time she did, he peered at her curiously, seeing someone else. Yet it was she and no other who always stood before him. He shook his great head, puzzled, and kicked his horse to follow along after them.

They arrived back at Gwernach to find Rhys of St. Bride's there just ahead of them, his troop of men and horses milling about in the courtyard as the stable serfs struggled to gain control of the situation. Their relief was almost palpable as Wynne arrived; the chief amongst them ran to take her horse's bridle.

"See to our guests," Wynne gently instructed him. "I am capable of managing my own mount."

As the serf backed off, his place was taken by a man of medium height, richly dressed. "I shall not have to kill those who have told me that Wynne of Gwernach is a beautiful girl," he said, "but perhaps I should, for they did not praise your beauty enough, lady."

"And I had not heard it said that Rhys of St. Bride's was a flatterer, my lord," Wynne answered, looking down upon him.

The face that looked up at her was pure Celt. The head was large and oval. The face from forehead to cheekbones, broad, narrowing slightly as it moved downward to the well-barbered, dark, short beard and moustache that encircled a sensuous mouth. The nose was straight and the eyes now engaging hers light grey. The physique was battlehard as evidenced in the thick, bull-like neck. His close-cropped hair was a rich, deep brown.

Wynne did not lower her gaze from his. To do so would

have given evidence of weakness on her part. Wynne did not think it wise to allow Rhys of St. Bride's to believe she could be manipulated or bullied.

"Let me help you from your horse, lady," he said, and without waiting for an answer, lifted her down, his strong fingers firmly grasping her about the waist, loosening slightly as her feet made contact with the ground.

Wynne stepped away, brushing the dust from her clothing, casually shaking an imaginary wrinkle from her yellow tunic dress. "Thank you, my lord," she said. "Will you come into the hall for refreshment?" Turning, she moved away from him.

For a moment Rhys was nonplused. He had been told that Wynne of Gwernach was an untried and innocent maid. Yet this girl seemed quite strong and confident. Though his experience with young girls was not great, he did not somehow feel her behavior was correct. Still, he had no choice but to follow after her, which he did.

Wynne's heart was beating perhaps a bit more rapidly than normal. So this was Rhys of St. Bride's, she thought, attempting to marshal her thoughts logically. He didn't look like an easy man, but neither did he look cruel. Rather, he appeared to have a look to him that reminded her of the tenacity of a hunting dog. If he wanted Gwernach, she was going to have a battle keeping it from him, but keep it from him she would. Gwernach belonged to Dewi ap Owain, and Wynne intended that her brother grow to manhood, marry, and pass Gwernach on to his descendants.

They entered the hall and Caitlin and Dilys came forward, simpering their welcome to the lord of St. Bride's as Wynne introduced him. Each girl was wearing her second-best tunic dress. Caitlin's was rose-colored with silver and black thread embroidery which complemented her fair skin. Dilys's was a pale blue with darker blue and pink thread embroidery. They giggled and lowered their eyes modestly as Rhys's frank gaze swept over them.

"Your sisters are fair," he said bluntly.

"They are young yet, my lord," Wynne replied, signaling a house slave to bring wine.

"We are both certainly old enough to marry!" Caitlin said boldly.

"Sister!" Wynne spoke sharply. "What will my lord of St.

Bride's think of such impudence? Please to be seated, my lord. It is an honor to have you stop at Gwernach."

"I did not just *stop*, lady, and well you know it. Did I not send to you weeks ago a message saying that I would come? Your sister speaks a truth. She is old enough to wed, as are you, and hence, the purpose of my visit."

Wynne turned to Caitlin and Dilys. "Leave the hall," she told them, "and send our grandmother to me." She turned her back to Rhys of St. Bride's. "I beg you bridle your tongue, my lord, until my sisters are gone and the lady Enid come to us."

He nodded, well pleased. She had manners, and more important, she was discreet. Beauty, manners, discretion. A man could do worse, and it soothed his uneasiness over her forward manner.

Caitlin and Dilys left the hall. Disappointment was written all over their faces, even as Wynne smiled briefly and said, "They would gossip, my lord, and our business must, I think, remain private."

"Not for long," he told her confidently.

Wynne held her peace for the moment and set about being the good hostess; offering her guest more wine, freshly baked bread and some of their own Gwernach's Gold cheese, over which he smacked his lips appreciatively.

Enid came into the hall to join them. Her greying hair was braided into a coronet atop her head, which added to her height, giving her stature. Her under tunic was red; her outer tunic dress was a rich indigo blue embroidered with silver threads on the sleeves. A square of sheer fabric sewn with silver threads and anchored by a gold headband served as a headdress. She had garnets of an excellent quality in her ears, and an enameled cross worked with garnets and pearls hung from a heavy gold chain upon her breast.

"My granddaughter has seen well to your comfort, my lord of St. Bride's," Enid said by way of greeting. "I am the lady Enid of Gwernach and I bid you welcome to our home."

He had arisen from the high board at her approach, and now he kissed her hand before seating her. "The lady Wynne seems to know well the duties of a good chatelaine." He sat next to her, between grandmother and granddaughter. "Her good reputation and the fame of her beauty have reached me at St.

Bride's. Such attributes in a woman please a man in search of a wife."

Wynne colored, saying nothing, but Enid said calmly, "You are in need of a wife, my lord?"

"I am," he said bluntly. "I'm widowed several years now, and it is time I took myself another bride. A man of my stature needs legitimate sons to follow him."

"You have illegitimate sons?" Wynne said quietly.

He was startled by her bluntness, assuming a young girl of good family would not know of such things. "Aye," he said slowly. "I have several sons. The eldest is seventeen. They cannot inherit, however, as you must surely know."

"Your honesty is commendable, my lord," Enid said, and she lifted her cup to her lips to hide her smile. How typical of Wynne to disconcert this great coastal battle lord. The girl's appearance was so deceptive. Her smooth-skinned, pale, serene face gave an appearance of meekness. Until she opened her mouth to speak, Enid thought wryly, placing her cup back upon the high board. "Why have you come to Gwernach, my lord?" she asked him. Best to get back to the business at hand.

Rhys of St. Bride's cleared his throat noisily, and then taking a deep breath, said in a resonant voice that rumbled up from his chest, "Lady, I wish to have your granddaughter for my wife."

"You refer, of course, to Wynne," Enid replied calmly. "Not Caitlin or Dilys."

"It is the eldest one I seek," was the reply.

"We are honored, of course," Enid began, only to be interrupted by the proposed bride.

"I thank you, my lord of St. Bride's, for the great honor you do me, but I cannot be your wife," Wynne said plainly.

"*Cannot?* Whyever for, lady? Are you already promised? Or perhaps it is the church for which you have a calling?" Rhys demanded.

"Nay, my lord, I have no wish to cloister myself, but I do have a duty to my family. To my brother, Dewi ap Owain, who is Gwernach's lord, though he be too young; and to my parents, may God assoil their good souls, who would expect me to stand by Dewi until he is grown and capable of managing on his own. I cannot leave Gwernach until my duty to my family is done, which will be many years hence. So, my lord, I thank you again for your most kind offer, but I think it best you seek a wife elsewhere," Wynne concluded politely.

"It is not another I want, lady. It is you," Rhys said gruffly.

"My lord! You do not know me. My family is slight compared to yours, and my dowry, though adequate, not at all what your great name could expect."

"You have nought to be ashamed of, lady," he told her. "Are you not the heiress to this estate? Gwernach is famed far and wide for its herbs and cheese. It is a goodly inheritance and one that is worthy of my wife."

"I shall never inherit Gwernach, my lord," Wynne said firmly.

"You cannot be certain, lady," he told her bluntly. "Your brother is young. It will be many years before he comes to manhood and sires sons of his own. Anything could happen before then."

"It will not as long as I am here at Gwernach to defend and protect him, and I will be, my lord. That I promise you," Wynne told Rhys of St. Bride's.

"And what of your younger sisters, lady? Will you keep them at Gwernach too? Do they not deserve to be wed?"

"All of my granddaughters will be wed to proper husbands in time, my lord," Enid said.

"If you will be my wife, Wynne of Gwernach," Rhys replied, "I will see your sisters married to men of wealth and stature. I have two cousins seeking wives. They are young and each has a fine estate. You cannot possibly find husbands of such stature for your sisters as I can. The weddings can be celebrated even before you wed me. An act of good faith on my part, if you will."

"I have a younger sister as well," Wynne said, wondering what his answer to that would be. "Her name is Mair and she is six."

"The child who killed your mother with her birthing? She should be settled in a convent after our marriage that she may spend the rest of her days atoning for her sin," he answered.

"Never!" Wynne gasped, furious. "That my mother died in giving life to Mair is unfortunate, but surely no sin of the child's. I shall never incarcerate her in a convent, unless, of course, she wished to go to one. If those be your plans for Mair, I shudder to imagine what plans you have for Dewi."

"The boy would be raised at St. Bride's," Rhys said. "I have several fosterlings in my charge. He could learn his battle skills with them. They are a fine, rough and tumble troop of lads."

"Dewi's place is here at Gwernach, learning how to manage his lands and care for his people; not at St. Bride's learning how to kill people!" Wynne told her suitor indignantly.

He looked at her and his eyes narrowed as if he were reconsidering her worth as an opponent. Then he said, "Lady, you are obviously overwrought by the magnitude of my offer. I could go to our king, Gryffydd ap Llywelyn, who is the head of your family, and request your hand in marriage and the fostership of your brother and his lands. What do you think his answer would be, lady? When I explained to him the seriousness of the situation, do you think he would leave Gwernach and its little lord in the hands of an unfledged girl?

"I should prefer, however, that you accept my offer of your own free will. I shall be a good husband to you, and I shall look after all of your interests with care, that you may feel free to concentrate on bearing me legitimate sons who will, in time, inherit my own holdings. What say you, lady?"

"I must have time to think," Wynne told him. "What you say has merit, my lord, but I must still rest easy in my mind that I am doing the right thing. I know you will understand my feelings, though I be but a mere girl."

Rhys of St. Bride's smiled, showing a row of short, even white teeth. "Tonight is the first night of the new moon," he told her. "When the moon is full again, I will come for your answer, lady mine."

"You will stay the night?" Wynne asked, hoping he would refuse her, but he did not.

Instead he nodded. "Aye, I will bide here tonight that we may get to know one another better."

"Grandmother," Wynne said, "I must see to the evening meal. Will you entertain our guest?"

"You have taught her well, lady," the lord of St. Bride's said approvingly. "Does she know the duties of a wife as well as she knows those of a chatelaine?"

"She will upon her wedding day," Enid said, her tones slightly tart. "Such knowledge is best saved, my lord, lest a maiden become too curious before the proper time."

"Aye," he agreed, and he smiled broadly. "Teach her well, lady, for I am a man of vast appetite where female flesh is concerned. I will accept girlish modesty upon our wedding night, but after that I will have no coyness or disobedience. Be sure your granddaughter understands that. I will mate with her often, and not just to get a child upon her, but because I enjoy the act."

Enid was astounded by his frankness. "I hope," she told him as directly, "that you will be as honest with your wife as you have been with me, my lord."

He laughed. A rich, deep sound that filled the hall. "Aye, I will, lady. I am not such a fool that I believe all women to be alike. Weak, helpless creatures without a thought beyond their halls and children. Most are so, but some, like the lady Wynne, are not. Your granddaughter is intelligent, I can see. I will not hold it against her, for it is an asset to me. It means that should I have to go to war, I can entrust the safety of my castle and my lands to her. She will not steal from me as would one of my male relations."

Now it was Enid's turn to laugh. Rhys of St. Bride's reasoning was, to her amusement, both astute and sound. She understood Wynne's reluctance to marry anyone at this time, but certainly her grandchild could do worse than to have Rhys of St. Bride's for a husband. Though she would not put it above him to dispose of Dewi ap Owain should the opportunity present itself, she did not believe he was a truly wicked man. "I shall not oppose your suit for Wynne's hand," she told him.

"Thank you, lady," he answered.

Dewi now came into the hall, and Enid was pleased to see he had changed his clothing. He was wearing a red-orange tunic decorated at the neck with gold embroidery, and his hose, which was yellow, was cross gartered. His father's heavy gold chain hung from his neck. He strode up to the high board, joining them and saying as he did so, "As lord of Gwernach, I welcome you to my home, Rhys of St. Bride's."

Rhys noted that a well-trained house slave placed a goblet almost immediately in the boy's hand. His elder sister obviously saw that the lad was deferred to by their people. "Thank you, Dewi ap Owain," he said. "You will undoubtedly want to know the purpose of my visit."

The boy nodded.

"I wish your sister, Wynne's, hand in marriage. Will you give me your permission to wed with her?"

"The decision must be my sister's and hers alone," Dewi said. "Marriage, my lord, is a serious step for a woman to take. Should she be permitted to choose well, she gains a lifetime of happiness. Should she be forced to it, she faces many years of bitterness and sorrow. I love Wynne too well that I would force her to any marriage but one she chose herself."

"If your sister wed with me, Dewi ap Owain, you should come to St. Bride's castle with us and learn all the skills of a knight. Would you not like that?" Rhys tempted.

"A lord of Gwernach's place is at Gwernach," Dewi replied, "not at St. Bride's. I have no burning desire to be a warrior, my lord," and then seeing his grandmother's stern look, he amended, "but I thank you for your offer."

Caitlin and Dilys reentered the hall and hurried to join the others.

"Do not be such a baby, Dewi," Caitlin said, her sharp ears having overheard her brother's remark. "The lord of St. Bride's has offered you a fabulous opportunity, and not one that is offered to just any lad. I have heard it said, my lord, that you do not accept all the boys whose families would have you foster them. That you choose only the bravest and the strongest. Is it true?"

"Aye," he said shortly, still somewhat put out by Dewi's answer. What kind of a boy didn't want to be a warrior?

"Will we live at St. Bride's too when you wed with our sister?" Caitlin asked coyly.

Her question penetrated his conscious and he smiled slightly. This was an opportunistic wench, he thought, but she would be an excellent match for his weak-kneed cousin, the lord of Coed. There had been too much inbreeding in that particular branch of the family. This girl would take his cousin in tow and bear strong sons for that line. "If your sister, the lady Wynne, will marry me," he told Caitlin, "I will give you my cousin, the lord of Coed, to be your husband."

"And my sisters?" Caitlin demanded.

"The child, Mair, is too young to marry, but I have another cousin, the lord of Llyn, who will do for the lady Dilys. Both these men are young with rich estates. Would that please you, my lady Caitlin? My lady Dilys?"

"Aye!" Caitlin said. " 'Twould please me mightily, my lord! We will plead your cause with our sister, I assure you."

Dilys giggled vacuously.

The house slaves now began to bring the table service to the high board, laying well-polished pewter plates before each diner, and matching goblets. Trenchers of bread were placed on the plates. Frosty pitchers of ale and crocks of sweet butter; a small round of Gwernach's Gold upon its own board were set forth upon the table.

Wynne joined them, saying, "I apologize, my lord, for the simplicity of our meal. Alas, we did not have enough notice of your coming."

She signaled the servants, who began to place upon the table serving dishes of all sizes. There was a platter of broiled rabbit, and others containing trout, capons, and venison. There were two pies filled with game birds cut into chunks and swimming in a rich gravy of red wine. There were bowls of carrots, braised lettuce, and one of spring peas, as well as loaves of bread fresh from the ovens and warm enough yet that the butter melted upon it.

"You have directed your cook well in the seasoning," Rhys of St. Bride's noted. "Are you capable of instructing your kitchen churls in more intricate fare, my lady Wynne?"

"Indeed she is," Enid said quickly. "Wynne is skilled in all manner of household arts including the making of medicines, poultices, and potions. Caitlin makes fine fragrances and soaps. The best I have ever known."

"And the lady Dilys?" he asked.

"Her nature is sweet, my lord, but we have yet to find a skill at which she excels," Enid admitted honestly.

When the last course, a cake soaked in sweet wine, covered with clotted cream and dotted with small wild strawberries, was served and eaten, Rhys of St. Bride's sat back, a smile of contentment upon his face. "Lady," he said, looking at Wynne. "I will enjoy your *simple* meals when you reign at St. Bride's as my wife."

"My lord," she reproved him gently. "I have not yet said that I would accept your suit."

"You are a woman who understands the meaning of the word *duty*, lady. You will do your duty to Gwernach and to your brother; to your sisters, Caitlin and Dilys. To your little sister, Mair," Rhys said, "whom I suppose I can find a suitable husband for one day."

"We are to be promised to the lords of Coed and Llyn," Caitlin told Wynne. "They are young and rich!"

Rhys's laughter rumbled through the hall. "Surely, lady, you will not disappoint this greedy wench who is your sister," he teased her gently.

Wynne fixed him with her green gaze. "You do not play fair, my lord of St. Bride's," she said disapprovingly.

He grinned at her mockingly. "Love, lady, is as much a battle to be won as is war."

"I was not aware, sir, that *love* would have anything to do with a marriage between us," Wynne said sharply.

"It can," he said, suddenly serious, "if you will but allow it, lady."

"Love, my lord, is an illusion, I fear, ofttimes confused with passion or lust. Once they have fled a marriage, love goes as well," Wynne told him.

"My sister does not believe in love," Dewi told Rhys of St. Bride's.

"But I do," he answered quietly.

"You surprise me, my lord, for I would not have thought so fierce a man capable of such foolishness," and Wynne arose from the high board. "My grandmother will show you to your sleeping place, my lord. You must excuse me, however, for I am weary. I will be up in time to bid you farewell come the morrow." Curtsying to him, Wynne walked from the hall.

"She is far wiser than a maiden should be," Rhys of St. Bride's noted suspiciously, suddenly wondering what man had soured the girl's outlook on love; wondering if she were indeed a virgin. His wife must be a virgin. He wanted no man to have traveled the path before him. He wanted no doubts about his son's paternity.

Before Enid might defend Wynne's good name, however, the heretofore silent Dilys spoke up brightly. "Wynne has always been like that, my lord. When we were children and our mother would tell us fairy stories, Wynne would not believe. She said our father and mother were unique in their love for one another."

"Did she?" Dilys was obviously so innocent that Rhys could not help but believe her.

"Aye," Dilys answered him simply.

"And what of you, my lady Caitlin?" Rhys asked. "Do you believe in love, or like your elder sister, do you think it an illusion?"

"Will your cousin, the lord of Coed, be good to me?" Caitlin countered his query with her own.

Rhys looked at the pretty girl before him with her silky, dark brown hair and her bright blue eyes. "Aye," he told her. "He'll no doubt make a fool of himself over you, lady."

"Then I shall love him well and long," she answered.

Rhys laughed again. "You are honest, lady, though I have not a doubt it surprises you as much as it surprises me." He stood and said to Enid, "Show me where I may rest, my lady Enid. I must leave for St. Bride's at first light."

She led him to a large, deep bed space set within the stone walls of the hall that was nearest to the largest fire pit. A straw mattress covered by a featherbed, which was in its turn piled with furs, was offered him.

"You should be quite comfortable here, my lord," Enid said politely. "Shall I send a woman to you?"

"My thanks, lady, but nay. Methinks I will forgo my own pleasure tonight that I not offend your granddaughter," he told her.

"As you will, my lord," Enid said. "I will bid you a good night then. Einion will help you with your lorica." She hurried away, and Rhys noticed the giant of a man he had previously seen with Wynne and young Dewi standing by his side.

"You wear no slave collar," Rhys said. "Are you a serf, or are you a freed man?"

"I am a slave, my lord, but Owain ap Llywelyn removed my collar from me the day I came to Gwernach. My chief duty over the years has been to guard the children. It is a task yet unfinished, but allow me, my lord, to help you." Einion's supple fingers moved to undo the straps holding Rhys's lorica, a cuirasslike garment of leather and gilded scales of bronze, together. "There, my lord," Einion said, removing the lorica. He then pulled Rhys's boots from his feet, placing them with the lorica by the bed space. "Good night, my lord," he said, and departed.

Rhys watched the large slave go, and then shrugging, removed his full-skirted outer tunic. He would be warm enough in his under tunic and sherte beneath the furs of the bed space. Climbing into it, he found himself most comfortable. There seemed to be no lice or fleas in the bed space. Wynne was obviously a good housekeeper.

The hall had grown quiet. He dozed, coming alert as he heard a footfall within the hall. Turning his head, he saw Wynne. He smiled to himself. Like the good chatelaine she was, she was checking to be certain that everything was as it should be for the night; that fires were banked. He watched through slitted eyes as Einion joined her. They spoke in voices too low to hear. Then the big slave bowed, and both he and Wynne departed the hall.

Rhys of St. Bride's felt his body beginning to relax, a state he rarely allowed himself to enter. There was peace and comfort to be had here at Gwernach. These things were Wynne's doing. He looked forward to the day when she would bring the same peace and comfort to his great castle at St. Bride's, and she would. She really had no choice in the matter. A smile of pleasure upon his face, Rhys began to snore most contentedly.

Chapter 2

Wynne of Gwernach watched with palpable relief as Rhys of St. Bride's departed her home. Although she did not sense cruelty in the man, he had a personality that could best be described as forceful, and it irritated her. He was determined that she would be his wife, but Wynne, for all her delicate appearance, was equally determined she would not. She did not choose to marry. At least not at this moment in time. Yet how was she to refuse Rhys without offending him? And what if he did go to the king? The great Llywelyn would hardly object to such a match between an unimportant relation and a powerful coastal lord. He would, as Rhys had so bluntly put it, prefer a man to hold Gwernach in trust for Dewi ap Owain than to allow a girl such as herself to carry on those duties.

"A pox on all men!" Wynne muttered as she kicked at a pebble irritably, and then seeing Rhys turn in his saddle to wave a final farewell, she returned his salute unsmiling. Above the lord of St. Bride's the waning moon hung in the dawn skies, reminding Wynne that she had but a few weeks in which to find a solution to her conundrum, if indeed there was another resolution to her problem.

She needed to work. She needed the benefit of hard, physical labor to help clear her brain, and, like her late father, Wynne was no stranger to the kind of work that sent her sisters into fits of hysteria. She followed a wagon into the meadow, and when it stopped, she grasped a pitchfork and began filling a hayrack with hay, for there was not yet enough new grass to satisfy the cows. She worked steadily and rhythmically, trailing in the wake of the wagon as it made its way from hayrack to hayrack across the field. When the wagon was empty, she rode back to the barns with the driver and, climbing into the high loft, began to pitch down a second load of dried grass. The armpits of her tunic dress were now stained damp with the evidence of her effort, and she hiked her skirts up, baring her legs in an attempt to facilitate her labor. Descending from the hayloft, she followed the wagon back out into the fields.

For the next few days Wynne worked from dawn to past dusk in the company of Gwernach's serfs. Still she could find no answer to her problem, and it did not help that her sisters chattered incessantly in the hall each evening about their bright futures as wives to Rhys of St. Bride's cousins. Caitlin and Dilys were so self-involved that they did not notice their elder sibling's distress; but Dewi did, and their grandmother did.

"You do not have to marry him, Wynne, if you do not choose to," the boy told her earnestly one evening. "Have I not said it before, and am I not master here?" But his voice was low, that his other two sisters did not hear him and begin to harp at Wynne again.

"I seem to have no other choice," Wynne admitted reluctantly. "He will go to Llywelyn if I refuse him. I know it. No man of honor wants a bride who must be dragged to the altar. Will he not resent me if I shame him like that? If I must wed him, I would hope to make him like me, brother."

Enid nodded. "You are wise, child. It is not good to antagonize a husband who will have the power of life and death over you. You must reconcile yourself to your fate before Rhys comes again, that you might greet him next time with a smile."

Wynne sighed deeply. "I do not want to marry," she said. "I hold no grudge against Rhys, for all I suspect his motives at wanting me to wife. Though he might dream of possessing Gwernach some day, I think, Grandmother, that you and I are clever enough to outwit him in his desires. I do not sense him to be a wicked man, and yet if the choice were really mine, I should refuse him."

Enid had often heard her eldest grandchild voice her objections to marriage, but it had never occurred to her until now to ask Wynne why she did not wish to wed. "What is it that frightens you, child?" she inquired gently. "Would it make it easier if I explained the mysteries of the marriage bed to you now? Marriage is a good and natural state for a woman. There has always been marriage between men and women since time began. Does not the Church teach us that?"

"It is not the marriage bed I fear, Grandmother," Wynne answered honestly. If the truth be known, she thought wryly, that

was the one aspect of marriage of which she was most curious
to learn about from personal experience.

"What is it then?" Enid asked, unable to understand why
Wynne would want to refuse Rhys's offer if she didn't dislike
him, wasn't afraid of the physical aspects of marriage, or
didn't have a religious calling.

Wynne considered for a long moment, and then she spoke
slowly, as if she were carefully evaluating each word individ-
ually. "I do not wish my fate to be in anyone else's hands but
my own, Grandmother. Since Father died I have been free to
control my own life with no man to gainsay me. Would Rhys
of St. Bride's understand my feelings? I do not think so. He
would be shocked with such a wife and beat her into submis-
sion, or at least try to force her to his will. Oh, Grandmother!
That is not the kind of life I want to live! Perhaps someday I
will find a man who will understand these feelings within me
and love me in spite of them, but until then, I would prefer not
to marry."

The two women sat by the fire, Dewi now virtually forgotten. Enid leaned forward and took Wynne's hands in hers,
squeezing them sympathetically. "My poor child," she said,
and her eyes were damp with her emotion. "What you want is
a virtual impossibility. Women do not live as you suggest.
They wed with either a man or the Christ. To that fate you
must resign yourself. There will be nothing else for you,
Wynne, and you must face it."

The girl said nothing, and so Enid continued. "Rhys is a
rough fellow, but I sense kindness in him as well. An impatient
man would not have given you these weeks in which to accept
your future. This man will love you if you will but give him
the opportunity. Not that love is necessary to a marriage, but it
does make a marriage better. By plighting your troth to Rhys,
you will provide for at least two of your sisters. This is no
small thing, child."

"And Dewi?" Wynne said quietly.

Enid chuckled. "You are deep, child, but in this instance you
must be clever as well. Rhys will be happy if you willingly betroth yourself to him, but you need not wed him for at least a
year. Tell him you wish to marry on Beltaine next. He will be
satisfied. Then we will petition Llewelyn for his permission to
the match, and at the same time Dewi will request he not be

forced against his will to leave his lands when the lord of St. Bride's holds his fosterage. Dewi will go with Father Drew himself to the king to plead his own case. The king has a soft spot for his own kin, no matter how distant. Dewi's determination coupled with his passion for Gwernach will impress Llywelyn, and Rhys will not be there to make a case for himself. The king will certainly grant Dewi's request. Rhys dare not dispute him, I suspect, lest his motives for doing so appear questionable."

Wynne nodded. "It is a good plan, Grandmother, but I still cannot bring myself to accept this fate." As each day passed, she felt more and more like a beetle in a trap. Helpless and unable to find a way out.

"You must, child," the older woman said. "What other choice do you have? For almost two weeks now you have worked as if you yourself were a serf. No other answer has come to you but this one. There is, however, one last thing you might try. Go to the forest tomorrow and free your mind of all its turmoil. The forest has always been your favorite place. Wander about it and enjoy the wonders of this new springtime. Perhaps another solution to your problem will come to you there. I know not what else to advise you."

"Yes," Wynne said thoughtfully. "I will go to the forest! I will take my herb basket along. Einion says the streams are already growing cress. I could use some capers if I can find them. I am low on toothache remedy and need them to make more. We seem to have more toothaches this spring than in past years."

Just before the dawn on the following morning, Wynne crept from the house barefooted and dressed in an almost outgrown green tunic dress. The dew on her feet was cool and, as she slipped into the nearby forest, her cleverly chosen costume rendered her almost invisible but for the natural-colored under tunic showing beneath the green. The birds were just now beginning to awaken, calling to one another despite the fact the sun had not yet penetrated the wood. This was the time she loved best of all. Those brief minutes before sunrise.

Following an almost imperceptible track, she made her way through the soaring oak and beech trees to a small glen where a lacelike waterfall tumbled down from a height of rocks into a clear, sandy-bottomed pool. With a smile Wynne put her basket down, shed her garments, and stepped into the water, shivering at its first touch, then quickly diving beneath it only to resurface almost as quickly, sputtering and laughing. She swam slowly about the pool, her long dark hair floating behind her, fully awake and quite clear-headed. Despite her dilemma, she felt more at peace now than she had in days.

Paddling into the shallows, she stood spotlighted in a single shaft of sunlight that had worked its way into the forest and wrung her hair free of excess water. A light breeze springing up raised a faint pattern over her fair body, and the nipples of her small, young breasts were puckered with the chill. Naked, Wynne sat upon the mossy bank allowing her skin and her hair time to dry. She sat very still, barely breathing, willing herself to become one with the woodland. Soon a family grouping of red deer stepping from the trees on the other side of the pond and drinking their fill departed. A fox appeared to take his morning drink and, seeing Wynne across the water, sat observing her curiously for a few minutes before going on his way.

Suddenly Wynne felt as if she were being observed, and looking quickly about, she discovered a raven in the tree near her. "Is that you, old Dhu?" and she laughed. "For shame! Fie! Spying upon a lady in her bath!" Wynne sprang up and shook her finger at the raven in admonishment. The bird cocked his head and eyed her with such an admiring look, or in her confusion so it appeared, that Wynne blushed and reached for her chemise, feeling quite foolish even as she did so. Still she felt somehow uncomfortable and redressed herself quickly before hurrying off, her basket in her hand.

The bird kept her company throughout the day, occasionally flying off upon his own business, but always returning to her side as she made her way. Wynne loved the forest near Gwernach, but if you had asked her precisely why, she could not have given an answer that made any real sense. To Wynne the forest felt familiar, as if it were home. There was nothing about it that she found threatening, or a cause for fear; even in the fiercest weather or the dark of night. There were those who avoided the forest at certain times, calling upon old legends and stories about the woods to substantiate their fears and superstitions about spells, and pixies, and the Fair Folk, a magical people said to have inhabited the forests of ancient Wales long ago in another time.

She found a patch of tender young capers and gathered them quickly, for they were best picked in the morning before the dew was dried upon them. The trees began to thin out, opening finally into a sunny meadow in full bloom. Wynne gathered the pale lavender and white blossoms of the yarrow. Yarrow flowers made a fine spring tonic as well as an excellent ointment for wounds. There were those who said it could also be used in magical potions, but Wynne knew nothing of that. She saw some pink comfrey and dug it up by the roots. Comfrey root was good for the kidneys, and its flowers, when properly distilled, made a wonderful lotion for the skin. Further on she spied dandelion and dug up several of these plants as well. The young leaves were good for eating, the flowers made a pleasant wine, and the root a tonic that toned the liver.

As Wynne moved back into the forest she stopped to pick a large bunch of violets. Candied, the flowers made a delicious treat. Boiled, the distillation was good for headaches and choleric humors. Even just smelling them was supposed to make you feel better, but she did not feel better. Following a narrow path, she hurried along until she came to a small stream that tumbled merrily over a jumble of lichen-covered rocks. There was watercress growing in the stream, but Wynne decided not to pick it until she had eaten the bread and cheese she had brought with her. She sat down, an oak at her back, and, digging down into her basket, removed a carefully folded napkin. Opening it, she spread the bread and cheese wrapped in it out upon the cloth.

The raven, perched upon a nearby tree limb, eyed the food expectantly and made soft noises in the back of his throat.

Wynne chuckled. "So, old Dhu, you're hungry too, are you? Well, you've kept me good company this morning, and I'm willing to share my meal with you. Here!" She tossed a piece of the bread in the large black bird's direction.

Flying down to the ground, the raven picked up the bread and then returned to his tree to enjoy it.

Wynne sighed, her mood suddenly solemn. "Oh, what am I to do?" she cried. She looked to her companion as if he might supply her with another answer than the one she already had. Indeed, in moments of whimsy she had contemplated the possibility that the raven was a shape-changer. One of those magical beings spoken of in hushed whispers that had existed amongst her people since the earliest of times. Oh, the Church forbade such teachings, but these things went deeper than the Church. "If you are a shape-changer, old Dhu ... if indeed you are a magical being ... please! Oh, please help me now! Rhys of St. Bride's is not an evil man, but he is hard and he will have me to wife whether I will or no! I don't want to marry him! *I don't!* If only you could help me!" She put her head into her hands and sobbed.

The raven observed her curiously and, catching the pathos of her mood, cawed softly as if in sympathy.

Wynne felt its eyes upon her, and looking up, saw just a large, black bird, its head cocked to one side. She laughed aloud, but the sound held no mirth. Rather it echoed the despair in her heart. "Poor Dhu," she said. "How can you possibly understand? You are nought but a bird. Birds fly free as I would do. They choose their own mates as I would do." She sighed again. "There is no other road open to me. I must marry Rhys of St. Bride's though I love him not. I must wed him that my sisters Caitlin and Dilys may obtain rich husbands. So my brother and grandmother may live in peace and safety while I hold Rhys at bay. That little Mair may someday be provided for in a more generous manner than I can provide for her."

Then Wynne began to weep bitter tears. "How will I bear it? Oh, how will I bear it?" she sobbed. "Yet I have no other choice. I do not believe the religious life is for me, and if I fled Rhys to a convent, who would care for my brother and sisters? Who would keep Gwernach safe for Dewi? Not Caitlin or Dilys! I must marry the lord of St. Bride's. And, I must learn to accept my fate before he comes again. The moon already waxes, and in another few days it will be full. He will come for his answer, even knowing what it must be, and I dare not greet him with tears, but rather with smiles."

Wynne brushed her tears away and reached for a piece of cheese. What good were her tears? Tears accomplished nothing. Mechanically she chewed on the cheese and a small piece of her bread. The food was tasteless and stuck momentarily in her throat before finally sliding down into her stomach, where it seemed to lay in a sodden and undigested lump. She crumbled the remaining bread and cheese and spread it beneath the tree for the birds and small animals to have, for she had no appetite of her own left. She felt exhausted, almost drained of all emotion, and before she realized it, she was dozing beneath her tree by the rushing stream.

From the vantage point of his perch the raven watched her silently. She dreamed. The same confused dream she had always had from earliest childhood. Colors and images, none of them distinct, surrounded and enveloped her, yet they did not threaten her. Rather there was a feeling of great and deep sadness. A melancholy despondency so deep that when she inevitably awoke, sensing the sound of a name she could not quite distinguish being frantically called, her face was always wet with tears. Wynne's eyes flew open and for a moment she thought a large, dark man stood before her, but then as she focused she could see it was just the tree facing her, and her friend, old Dhu, patiently waiting in its branches.

With a shaky little laugh, she scrambled to her feet, noting by the position of the sun that it was late afternoon. Then remembering the watercress, she knelt by the stream and picked a fat bunch which she added to her basket before arising and moving off through the forest. Despite her nap, she did not feel rested, nor was she really comfortable with her decision, but she could see no other way out of her dilemma than to marry the lord of St. Bride's. She would spend the next few days before the full moon adjusting herself to that hard fact. Rhys's motives for wanting her as his wife might not be as flattering as a man in love's might have been; but he would have no cause to feel cheated by his choice. She would be a good wife to him even if she did intend seeing her brother grow safely to manhood that Rhys not inherit Gwernach through her.

Stepping from the forest, she saw her home and a soft smile lit her features. It was not a castle, but she loved it with all her heart. The old stone and worn timbers with its green ivy mantle spoke to her of the love and fidelity of several generations. It had always been a happy house upon which the sun showed no hesitation about shining. That she would miss it she had not a doubt, but she had always known in that part of her brain which was sensible that she would one day leave Gwernach. As long as her brother lived to father another generation, she would be content to do so.

She had paused to consider it all a final moment, and looking for Dhu, she found him now sitting amid the tangle of a nearby bush. "Well, old friend, as I have no choice but to accept the lord of St. Bride's offer of marriage, I will," she told him.

"Caw!" answered the bird.

"I know, I know!" Wynne smiled ruefully. "But you have no other answer to give me, my friend. I would wed for love of a man, but it is not the way of the world in which I live. How my sisters mock me for my beliefs, and who is to say they are not right? I should be selfish to refuse Rhys. He will see to my sisters' well-being, and I think Grandmother and I are clever enough to keep Dewi safe from Rhys's greed. And if we are not, I still have not the luxury of a choice; but oh, if I did! I should refuse Rhys of St. Bride's! *I would!*"

"Caw!" the raven replied, and then he flew off, circling the house once before heading into the nearby hills.

"Farewell, Dhu!" Wynne called after him, and feeling a bit sad that he had forsaken her company, she entered the house, handing her basket to a house serf as she did.

"Where have you been?" demanded Caitlin, her pale cheeks flushed with her irritation. "You have been gone the whole day long!" She glared at Wynne from her place near the fire pit, even as she combed her long dark brown hair with an ivory comb.

"Did you have need of me then?" was Wynne's reply. "I was in the forest. Grandmother knew."

"How can you bear to wander about those dank and dreadful woods?" Caitlin shuddered delicately and, putting her comb aside, braided her hair in two neat plaits.

"Someone must gather the herbs for the poultices, the tonics, and the medicines needed here," Wynne told her sister. "You will be expected to do such things in your husband's house, Caitlin. I have tried to teach you, but you show no interest. A good chatelaine knows how to care for her people."

"My husband will be rich," Caitlin replied. "I will have serfs to gather the herbs and serfs to make these concoctions you are always babbling about."

"I will too!" Dilys piped up.

Wynne sighed. There was no arguing with either of her sisters. Their thoughts did not extend beyond their own needs.

"Have you made up your mind then to accept Rhys's generous offer and cease behaving like a fool?" Caitlin asked.

"Not that he will not have you if he wishes it; but if you fight with him, he may not give us our husbands."

"I will accept the lord of St. Bride's with as good a grace as possible, Caitlin, though if I had another choice, I should take it," Wynne told her sister bluntly. Caitlin's preoccupation with herself was particularly irritating today.

"Then perhaps, my child, that is the answer you sought for," said Enid, overhearing Wynne as she entered the hall.

"There seems to be no other," Wynne agreed, "but I had hoped to marry for love, Grandmother."

"You are incorrigible," Caitlin told her older sister, and her tone was decidedly unsympathetic. "You do have, however, a saving grace in that you are sensible to a fault in the end. Now that you have finally come to terms with yourself, having given us all a most difficult time, be certain that you gain the marriage contracts for Dilys and for me from Rhys before you wed him, lest he try to cheat us out of our due."

"Yes, Wynne," Dilys added. "You must not sell yourself cheaply, but gain the best price for us all from Rhys."

"I will do better than you desire," Wynne told her sisters. "I will insist you are both wed first and well-established in your husbands' households before I marry Rhys. Does that not please you?" she said, and her tone was slightly mocking, but Caitlin and Dilys did not notice it.

"Aye!" Caitlin smiled broadly at her eldest sibling. "That is most practical of you, sister!"

"Aye!" Dilys echoed.

"Will I have a husband one day, sister?" little Mair, who had been listening to their exchange unnoticed, asked.

"Aye!" Wynne smiled at the youngest of them all. "You shall have a fine young lordling who will ride into Gwernach and sweep you away to be his bonny bride."

"What nonsense!" muttered Caitlin.

"I want lots and lots of babies," Mair announced.

"And you shall have them, my lambkin, if that is your desire." Wynne laughed, ruffling Mair's light brown hair with its pretty golden lights.

"See!" Mair stuck her tongue out at Caitlin, who was in too good a mood now to be bothered by the child.

"You have come to your decision just in time," she told Wynne. "Rhys will certainly be here tomorrow."

"Nay," Wynne answered. "He will not come until the full moon."

"Tomorrow," Caitlin replied. "You have lost count of the days, sister."

For a moment Wynne had a sinking feeling, but then she drew upon her deep well of courage and laughed weakly. "If tomorrow night is the full moon, Caitlin, then I have indeed lost track of my time."

"Well, I have not," Caitlin said tartly. "I long for the day when I may be married to Rhys's rich cousin and leave Gwernach for my own home. That time cannot come quickly enough for me."

"And me," echoed Dilys.

Wynne shook her head sadly. She could think of nothing harder for her than having to leave Gwernach behind, and yet her sisters were eager to do so.

"Do not think badly of them, my child," her grandmother said quietly as Caitlin and Dilys turned back to their own pursuits. "You are the eldest and it is only natural that you love Gwernach better than they do. They know that it is unlikely that either of them will ever inherit these lands. It, therefore, has no hold on them, and they are anxious to have a place that they may call their own."

"But I will not inherit Gwernach either," Wynne noted, "and yet I love it."

"With God's blessing, child, you will not inherit, but there is always that chance that Dewi may not reach his manhood, or not produce heirs. If that should happen, then you will be Gwernach's mistress. That is a possibility, but the chance of both you and Dewi dying and leaving Gwernach to Caitlin is slight. Your sister is no fool. A shrew, perhaps, but no fool."

"And speaking of that scamp brother of mine," Wynne said, "I have not seen him since my return from the forest. Where can he have gotten to, Grandmother?"

"He said he was going birding this afternoon," Enid answered.

"Did Einion accompany him?"

"Nay, child, it was not necessary. Dewi would have been deeply insulted by such a gesture. You are overprotective of your brother, Wynne. He may yet be a boy, but he is lord of Gwernach nonetheless and should be treated as such. Besides,

Einion was giving Mair her riding lesson, and the child would have been heartbroken had she not been able to have it. She loves that fat pony of hers greatly," Enid finished with a smile. Her youngest grandchild was her admitted pet.

Wynne glanced through a window in the hall and frowned. It had become overcast and, although she could see no sunset, the sky was already darkening with impending night. "Einion," she called to the big man as he entered the hall. "Have you seen my brother?"

"Nay, lady, not since he departed, but I shall go into the courtyard and ask. He may be in the stables." Einion returned the way he had come.

"I know it is foolish of me, Grandmother, and I realize I am oversolicitous of Dewi's well-being, but he is my responsibility! If anything should happen to him before he reached his manhood, I should feel that I had failed my parents in my duty to Gwernach. I cannot bear the thought that I should profit at my brother's expense. Can you understand that?" Wynne's usually serene features were distorted with her distress.

"I do understand, my child," Enid assured her granddaughter, but in her heart she was angry at the unkind fate that had burdened this young girl with so much accountability at so young an age. And she was angry at her late son, God assoil him, for Wynne had been his favorite and he had instilled in her a passion for Gwernach that could never be satisfied. It was a hard world in which they lived, and children died easily. That Owain and Margiad had produced healthy children was both a blessing and a miracle; but Dewi and Mair were yet young and vulnerable. If accident or disease took them before their maturity, Wynne could not hold herself responsible, and Enid told her so, squeezing her granddaughter's hand as she spoke to reassure her, but she could see in Wynne's foresty green eyes that although the girl nodded her agreement, she did not really accept Enid's attempt to set her mind at rest.

Einion returned, saying, "The young lord is not yet back, lady."

Wynne paled and, looking again to the window, said worriedly, "Night has fallen. What if something has happened to Dewi? What if he is lying injured and frightened? We must send out a search party to seek him immediately!"

"Lady," Einion told her gently, "the night is dark and thick with clouds. Were it not so, the young lord could walk home himself once the moon had risen, and should the overcast be dispelled in the next few hours, he may very well do so. I do not believe him injured, for he is a careful lad when climbing, though you may not think it so, knowing him otherwise."

"But he is so little," Wynne fretted. "He is alone and in the dark. We must find him!"

"Einion is right, my child," Enid said matter-of-factly, but in her secret heart she worried too. Still, it would do Wynne no good to know that. Enid signaled the servants to begin serving the evening meal, and shepherded her family to the high board.

Caitlin and Dilys chattered endlessly on as the food was served.

"Do you think," Dilys ventured, "that the lord of Llyn is a handsome fellow? Oh, I hope he is handsome! I cannot bear that which is ugly."

"What difference does it make?" Caitlin snapped. "If his purse is full, if he is generous to you, and if his lance is mighty and he gives you pleasure, what care you if he is handsome? In your marriage bed in the dark it will make no difference, you silly goose."

"But if he is disfavored, sister, even in the dark I will know it," Dilys persisted.

"Then you are a greater fool than I ever believed possible, Dilys," Caitlin said unkindly, not even noticing the hurt tears that sprang into Dilys's soft blue eyes. "I care not if my lord of Coed is as plain as mud, or has the wit of a flea, as long as his purse is endless and he denies me nought."

"How can you say such a thing, Caitlin?" Wynne said angrily. "Our mother, God assoil her sweet soul, and our grandmother have certainly not taught you so."

"Margiad's mother, your other grandmother," Enid said dryly, "was even more selfish than Caitlin is. I remember her well. She bore her husband three sons and two daughters, both of whom were sweet-natured by some miracle. Dilys is very much like your mother's sister, for whom she is named. She died at eleven. That Dilys was also a younger sister who lacked intellect, but the sister she followed was a better influence than Caitlin is to Dilys."

"Your words cannot distress me, Grandmother," Caitlin said. "I will be shortly wed and gone from here."

"How can you think of yourself at such a time?!" Wynne raged at Caitlin. "Do you not care that Dewi is missing? What if he is injured or dead?"

"The deed is already done, whatever it is," Caitlin said bluntly. "My chatter cannot change anything, Wynne. You fret too much. Dewi has been caught by the dark and is sheltering somewhere. That is all there is to it, as you will see in the morning."

She arose from the table. "Come, Dilys. We must get our beauty sleep. I would not want Rhys of St. Bride's to regret his decision when he comes."

Wynne put her hand over her mouth to keep herself from shrieking as her younger sisters traipsed from the hall. If marrying the lord of St. Bride's meant getting free of Caitlin and Dilys, then perhaps it was not such a bad bargain she was making. Little Mair, wide-eyed, was unable to refrain from giggling as she eyed her eldest sibling, and Wynne, her hand dropping away from her mouth, grinned at the child, ruffling her hair affectionately. "They make me so angry," she said.

"They are very mean," Mair noted. "I know I should love them, but I do not." She glanced half fearfully at Father Drew. "Will God send me to burn in Hell's fires for that, Father? I know it is sin not to love Caitlin and Dilys, but I just can't!"

The priest swallowed hard, his own feelings warring with his conscience. "It is wrong to hate, Mair," he told her, "but I do not think God will condemn you to damnation because you do not like your sisters, Caitlin and Dilys. Our lord understands feelings like that." He patted the child's head reassuringly and then muttered softly beneath his breath, "Besides, it would take a saint to love those two."

"Time for bed, Mair," Enid said, rising from her place, her voice quavering with her need to laugh, for she had overheard the priest's remark. Taking her little granddaughter's hand, she led her from the hall.

"Are other priests as human as you are, Father Drew?" Wynne asked him. She too had overheard, and her eyes were dancing with merriment.

The priest's own brown eyes twinkled back at her. "It has been so long since I've been with other priests, Wynne, I cannot remember," he said honestly. "My world is Gwernach, and I am its only priest. My many years in the monastery were

spent in study, preparing myself for the priesthood that I might
return one day to Gwernach and, in serving my God, serve it
and its people as well. My memories of that time are no longer
clear. I can but recall two things. Study and prayer."

"No friends?"

"One," the priest said slowly. "Like myself, destined to
eventually return to his family's lands to care for the spiritual
well-being of his people. What was his name? Aelfric, I think.
He was a Saxon from somewhere near Winchester."

"And what do you remember about him?" Wynne inquired.

Father Drew's brow furrowed a moment as he thought, and
then he smiled. "I remember, my dear, that Aelfric loved to
laugh, and even our harsh life in the monastery could not
change that in him. We were both called home at the same
time. I have not seen him since."

"You rarely speak of yourself," Wynne said, "and yet I find
your tales interesting when you do."

"It is not my duty as a priest, Wynne, to speak of myself.
Besides, what is there to say about Drew ap Daffyd? I am the
only child of your father's youngest uncle, who is long deceased. You know that."

"I think there is more to you than you would admit," Wynne
teased him, and then she sobered. "I am doing the right thing
in marrying Rhys, aren't I?"

"Your grandmother and I will keep your brother safe,
Wynne, never fear. I realize that is your greatest concern in this
matter. Rhys of St. Bride's will get a better wife than he undoubtedly deserves, but he will not get Gwernach, I promise
you," Father Drew told her. Then he chuckled. "And we will
be rid of Caitlin and Dilys too!"

Wynne smiled at him, but then as she looked to the windows she frowned. "The moon should long be up, Father, but
the overcast is still thick and it does not break through. Poor
Dewi! I pray he is safe."

"Go to bed, my child," the cleric advised her. "You cannot
help Dewi with all your concern. If the lad does not return
home first thing in the morning, then I will lead the search
party myself. We will leave at first light."

"I will not sleep a wink!" Wynne vowed, but she was tired.
Her day in the forest as well as the strain she had been under
these last few weeks were taking their toll now that she had fi-

nally reached her decision. She made her usual rounds, checking to be certain that all was secure for the night, and then she climbed the stairs to the family solar. Softly she tiptoed across the floor to her own bed. Caitlin and Dilys shared a bed, and their snores from behind the drawn curtains were loud. Wynne smiled to herself thinking how horrified they would be to be told that they snored.

Mair slept on the trundle of their grandmother's bed. Wynne smiled down at the youngest of them, her little cheeks flushed with her good health, the tendrils of soft brown hair curling about her face, the little thumb that was half in, half out of Mair's tiny rosebud mouth. Then turning away, she began to undress, carefully folding her under tunic and tunic dress away in her chest; drawing out the garments she would wear on the morrow and laying them out neatly over the chest. Sitting down upon her bed, she drew off her soft boots and set them aside. Reaching for her brush which was beneath her pillow, she slowly brushed her long, dark black hair free of its one thick braid. Then with a sigh she drew the bed curtains shut and slipped beneath the coverlet.

For some time she lay awake, her mind a jumble of mixed thoughts that would not be silenced. Then firmly, but not without difficulty, she pushed her thoughts away, clearing her head of everything but her prayers. As they came to an end, Wynne found herself slipping into a relaxed sleep. Dewi would be all right. Her initial panic over, she allowed her instincts to guide her and she felt no threat to her little brother. Indeed, she sensed now that he was quite safe. *And not alone.*

Wynne sat up, suddenly fully awake. Why had she thought that? Yanking the curtains open, she discovered that the dawn was already beginning to lighten the edges of the sky beyond the windows. It was near to morning, and she had obviously been sleeping for several hours, although it did not feel as if she had. What had awakened her? She could not remember, and lay very still listening for the sound that had surely stirred her to consciousness; but everything was quite still. Caitlin, Dilys, and her grandmother were all snoring now. Mair continued to sleep peacefully on her trundle bed. There was no sound from the hall below. Even the birds had not yet begun their early song.

It was obvious that she was not going to go back to sleep,

and so Wynne arose quietly, shivering in the cool air, for she wore only her sheer, soft linen chemise. She walked across the solar to a small stone alcove that held an earthenware basin and a pitcher of water. In the winter the water often froze overnight, but in late spring it was simply icy cold. Pouring some of the contents of the pitcher into the basin, she washed her face and hands, and scrubbed her teeth with a piece of rough cloth, dipping the cloth in a mixture of pumice and mint she kept for the purpose. Rinsing both her mouth and the cloth, she opened the small window in the alcove and threw the dirty water away. The day looked to be fair, though there was a mist right now.

Moving back to the trunk at the foot of her bed, she began to dress. First an under tunic of indigo-blue with long, close-fitting sleeves that fell to her ankles, and then a shorter knee-length overtunic of bright green with long sleeves embroidered in pretty bands of gold thread on the wide cuffs which ended at her narrow wrists. It was her best gown, and Wynne girded the overtunic with a belt of gilded leather with a silver-gilt buckle set with a particularly fine piece of crystal that had just the faintest blush to it. Opening her trunk, she took out a pair of soft leather shoes made to follow the shape of her narrow foot. Today she would do Rhys of St. Bride's honor by looking her best when he came for the answer she knew she must give him.

Digging deeper into the trunk, Wynne drew forth a small carved box and, opening it, removed a pair of pear-shaped crystal earrings which she affixed in her ears. Sitting herself upon her bed, she brushed the tangles from her hair and carefully braided it into the single, thick braid she favored, tying the end with a small piece of green ribbon. It was custom that young girls wore their hair loose and flowing, restrained only by a ribbon band until marriage; but Wynne had taken to braiding her hair in an effort to appear older when she found herself responsible for her family and having to do business with strangers. She was proud of her thick, long hair which, when loosened from its woven confinement, blossomed about her like a night cloud. It was, she was certain, her best feature; and she was relieved that the unpleasant custom of cutting one's hair short immediately after a first marriage to show servitude to the bridegroom had finally been discontinued. Cut her beautiful tresses? *Never!*

She removed a final item of jewelry from her little box. It was a particularly beautiful circular gold pendant, enameled in greens and blues and attached to a heavy red-gold chain. The design was Celtic. Both the chain and pendant had come from Ireland. Her father had received it in exchange for a large shipment of cheeses many years before, when Wynne was but a child. The pendant had fascinated her, and, even though it had been an extremely valuable piece, Owain ap Llywelyn had gifted his eldest child with it simply because she loved it. It was rare, he noted to Margiad, that Wynne desired anything of earthly value. The girl treasured the pendant, but even more now that her father was gone. She always felt that Owain was with her when she wore it, but more, she had always felt the pendant belonged to her from the first moment she had seen it.

Ready to face her day, Wynne departed the solar. Below in the hall a few household serfs were bestirring themselves and lighting the fires in the fire pits. Through the open door of the house she could see smoke rising from the bakehouse chimney and nodded, pleased. Rhys would have to be asked to dinner, and judging from his last visit, he was a big man with a bigger appetite. They would need all the breads and cakes her baker could produce this day.

Einion spoke at her elbow. "It will be a fair day, lady, and as the young lord has not yet returned, the holy father and I will gather together a party of men that we may seek him out and bring him home."

Wynne felt a momentary surge of guilt. She had completely forgotten Dewi! "Aye, and I shall beat him well for this," she told Einion firmly. "Lord of Gwernach or no, he is still a lad of ten and under my rule. He has shown a deplorable lack of feeling for us all with this prank! Tell him to expect to feel my hazel switch on his bottom once Rhys of St. Bride's is gone. I will not embarrass the lord of Gwernach before another, but he will be punished."

"Who will be punished?" Dewi ap Owain stood just within the doorway of the hall.

"Dewi!" Wynne shrieked, and racing across the floor, gathered her little brother into her arms, hugging him soundly until he fought his way free of her embrace. "Thank God, and His

blessed Mother, and our own St. David, that you are alive and well!" Wynne half sobbed.

"Who will be punished?" Dewi repeated, shaking himself like a puppy.

"*You!* You thoughtless scamp!" his eldest sister told him. "You have given us a terrible fright and a worse night worrying about you. How could you go off like that, Dewi! I was terrified!"

"I went birding," Dewi told her calmly. "I have been going birding by myself since I was six. There's a merlin's nest nearby, and I've been watching it, for I intend taking one of the hatchlings to train for you as a wedding gift."

"Oh, Dewi!" Wynne's eyes grew teary, but then she said heatedly, "But why did you not come home last night?"

"Because I was so fascinated watching the merlin's hatchlings that the night overtook me," he said somewhat irritably, sounding as if she might have certainly figured it out by herself without him to tell her. "Do you think I enjoyed my night in the damp and chill, sister? If it had not been for Madoc I should have gone hungry as well."

"*Madoc?*" Wynne sounded puzzled, and then she realized that a man stood next to her brother. As her startled gaze met the stranger's, Wynne felt her body suffused by a fiery heat, and for the longest moment she could not seem to draw a breath.

It mattered not, however, for all attention was drawn away from her by Enid, who hurried down the stairs from the family solar, her saffron and violet robes billowing about her as she came. "Dewi! My child! Praise God and St. David you are back safely."

"Good morrow, Grandmother," the boy said. "May I introduce my friend, Madoc of Powys. We met last night," the boy said wryly.

Enid hugged her grandson and then she looked up at his companion, studying him carefully for a long moment. "You are Madoc of Powys Wenwynwyn, my lord, are you not?" she said finally.

"I am, lady."

"I thank you for seeing to the safety of my grandson, and I welcome you to Gwernach, my lord prince, even as my granddaughter, Wynne, would have done."

"Prince?" Wynne had regained her ability to breathe and to speak, and her eyes again met those of Madoc's; but this time he refused to allow her to look away.

He had wonderful eyes, oval-shaped and a deep blue with black, bushy eyebrows, and thick black eyelashes that any woman would have envied, but yet there was nothing feminine about them. For a moment she felt as if she were drowning in the depths of those blue eyes. She could not look away, and, finally in desperation, she closed her own eyes, feeling faint, her heart hammering violently even as her legs began to give way beneath her.

"Wynne!"

She heard her grandmother's voice from a long distance, and then she was lifted up and her head fell against a hard shoulder. For a moment she floated in a nothingness, and then as she began to regain use of her body and her senses once more, she realized she was seated on a bench near the main fire pit. Opening her eyes, she saw a man's hand attached to an arm, gently, but firmly, girding her waist. Wynne gasped, and almost immediately strength flowed into her limbs.

"Are you all right, lady?" she heard a voice inquire.

"Poor child!" Wynne heard her grandmother say. "She has been so worried about the lad and his wee adventure." Enid knelt before her granddaughter. "Are you all right now, my dearie?"

Wynne's senses and mind began to function normally now. "Aye," she replied slowly. "I cannot imagine what happened to me, Grandmother. I am not a maid given to swooning as a rule." She glanced nervously again at the arm about her and immediately it was removed. Was he reading her mind, Wynne thought uneasily, remembering that it was Madoc's piercing gaze that had tumbled her into a faint. She arose from the bench and was amazed to find that her legs were functional once more. It made her nervous to think she must face him squarely again, but she had no other choice.

"My lord," she began, carefully keeping her eyes lowered modestly, "I thank you with all my heart for keeping the lord of Gwernach safe last night. Had I but known of his good fortune in finding so protective a companion, I should not have fretted so. Will you break your fast with us after the mass?"

"Gladly, lady," came the reply. The voice was deep, yet there was no roughness about it. Indeed, it was almost musical.

"So!" a voice interrupted them, "the brat is back!" Caitlin, in her best gown, a scarlet silk tunic embroidered with gold, a dark blue under tunic beneath it, came down the stairs from the solar. Behind her Dilys, also in her best, a pink and silver brocade tunic over an under tunic of deep rose, and Mair in her everyday sky blue, followed.

"Dewi is safe, Caitlin," Wynne said sweetly, but there was a faint sharpness to her tone. "Why are you both attired in your very best, I would ask?"

"Did you think we would not do Rhys of St. Bride's honor when he comes to claim you? Besides, we do not want him to forget that he has promised us husbands as well, sister." Her glance turned to Madoc, whom she eyed thoroughly, taking in the full-skirted tunic of blue-green silk brocade he wore which, although edged in a rich brown marten, was decorated simply at its neck and on its long sleeves. Still, the fine leather belt encircling his narrow waist, with its beautifully worked gold buckle richly decorated with amber, indicated a man of certain stature. "And who is this, pray?" Caitlin asked archly.

"My lord, these are my younger sisters, Caitlin and Dilys," Wynne said. "Sisters, I would present to you Madoc, a prince of Powys. He found our brother last night and sheltered him until this morning."

"Have you business at Gwernach, my lord, or are you just passing through our lands?" Caitlin demanded, asking what no one else had thought to ask.

Madoc of Powys smiled slowly, recognizing in Caitlin a possible adversary. "I have business here, lady, *but not with you*," he answered.

Wynne wanted to laugh, for Caitlin looked extremely put out. Instead she said, "It is time for the mass, and we have much to be thankful for this day. Our brother, Gwernach's lord, has been returned to us safely."

"*And,*" Caitlin put in, "the lord of St. Bride's comes to claim you for his wife and give us rich husbands. Aye, I thank God for that!"

Madoc of Powys looked toward Wynne and saw that her lovely face darkened when Rhys of St. Bride's was mentioned. He smiled, almost to himself, and then followed the family from the hall to the church which was outside the walls encircling the house. Father Drew, a brown-eyed elf of a man, smiled broadly seeing Dewi, and sang the mass particularly well, to Madoc's pleasure, for the prince loved music. He complimented the priest afterward on the church porch as they were introduced, and smiled to see the old man's flush of pleasure at his words.

Wynne looked at Madoc less fearfully now, pleased by his kindness to Father Drew. He smiled back at her, and she wondered why she had had such a strange reaction to him earlier She still had to admit that this prince made her flesh burn with an unaccustomed fire, her heart beat faster, her toes and the soles of her feet tingle mysteriously. She had never before felt this way, and she wondered why Madoc had such an odd effect upon her. Still, he did not seem like a wicked man.

"Come," she said, remembering her duties as mistress of Gwernach, "let us return to the hall and break our fast."

"Right gladly, sister," Dewi said. "Remember that I had no supper last night and I am famished!"

"Serves you right," Caitlin said meanly. "You frightened us badly."

"What?" Dewi mocked her. "Do not tell me that you gave me a moment's thought, Caitlin, for I will not believe you. You think of no one but yourself, and if you did by chance think of me, it was merely that my premature death would put you in mourning, forcing you to wait to make a rich marriage."

Briefly, Caitlin looked outraged, but then to her credit, she laughed. "Aye," she said. "You are probably right, brother."

"I prayed to St. David for you, Dewi," Mair lisped softly.

"So 'twas you who kept me safe, my little dearling," Dewi said generously, ruffling his smallest sister's soft hair. "God always hears the prayers of the good."

"But I prayed to St. David!" Mair said firmly.

"And St. David prays to God," Father Drew replied, settling the matter for the child.

"Ohh," Mair answered, her eyes wide.

They were all so enchanted by the child as they walked toward the house that they did not hear the sound of approaching horses until the beasts were practically upon them.

" 'Tis Rhys of St. Bride's!" Caitlin whispered excitedly. "Blessed Mother, he is eager for your answer, though he knows what it must be! Do you think the lord of Coed and the lord of Llyn are with him? How do I look, Dilys? Is my hair neat? My gown graceful?"

"In the name of heaven, Caitlin, try not to simper at the man this time," Dewi said, and then turning, he said loudly, "Welcome back to Gwernach, my lord of St. Bride's. You are just in time to join us at our morning meal."

"Having undoubtedly timed his arrival for just that purpose," murmured Wynne softly. "Pray God the baker has enough loaves to satisfy my lord's monstrous appetite."

Dilys and Mair giggled and Enid forced back a smile.

Rhys of St. Bride's, however, had eyes only for Wynne. His grey gaze took her in hungrily as he stopped his great black horse next to her and looked down. His beard and moustache were newly barbered and had been perfumed with a scented oil that hung in the damp morning air. The fragrance of damask rose emanating from the facial hair of this rough warrior was almost humorous, had anyone dared to laugh.

"I have come for my answer, lady," he began bluntly, "even as I promised you I would. It is the first day of the full moon. I now ask you a final time. Will you be my wife?" Rhys's stallion danced nervously at the sound of his voice, and the horses behind him carrying his men-at-arms moved as restlessly.

Wynne took a deep breath, and then the voice of Madoc, Prince of Powys, spoke in her stead.

"Wynne of Gwernach cannot be your wife, my lord of St. Bride's, for she is promised to me and has been since her birth."

Rhys leapt from his horse to face his rival and growled angrily, "And who might you be . . . my lord?"

"I am Madoc of Powys," the prince said quietly, and yet Wynne felt there was a faint threat to his words.

Rhys's slate-colored eyes widened imperceptibly. "The lord of Wenwynwyn?" he said slowly, and Wynne instinctively felt that her suitor was hoping that Madoc would deny his heritage.

"Aye," the prince said, his mouth, which was long and narrow but for a slightly wider underlip, twitching faintly in his effort to restrain his amusement.

Why, wondered Wynne, was Rhys fearful and Madoc close to laughter? And more important, what did Madoc mean when he told Rhys that she was betrothed to him and had been since her infancy? This was the first she had heard of such a thing! Then to her great surprise, Rhys, whom she had believed fearless, began to babble hysterically.

"My lord prince! I meant no disrespect! I meant no offense to you! The maid did not tell me she was betrothed to another! She did not tell me she was betrothed to so great a lord!" He turned to Wynne. "Tell him you did not tell me, lady! *Tell him!*"

"Of course I did not tell you, my lord," Wynne answered him. "How could I tell you what I did not know myself?"

"*What!*" Rhys's small eyes narrowed suspiciously, giving him the appearance of an angry boar contemplating a charge.

"Might we discuss this matter in the hall?" the prince said reasonably, looking down to find several chickens scratching about his booted feet.

"Aye," Wynne said before her duties as chatelaine of Gwernach took over completely. "I think we must certainly discuss this matter, and now; but we must also break our fast. Serious matters are best settled on a full belly. Come, my lords!"

They followed her into the hall of the house, where the servants had lain out the first meal of the day upon the high board. Wynne noted with satisfaction that her house serfs had set enough trenchers of new bread upon the table for her guests. Without asking, a hot barley cereal was ladled into the hollowed-out trenchers. Wynne sent a smile of approval at Dee, the chief house serf in the hall, as the good silver spoons with their polished bone handles were placed by the cereal-filled trenchers. Pitchers of fresh, golden cream, dishes containing newly churned butter, pots of honey, several fresh cottage loaves, and a bowl of hard-cooked eggs followed. Brown ale was poured into fine silver goblets. Madoc, Rhys, and Dewi began to eat hungrily.

"What is going on?" Caitlin hissed at her elder sister. "Have you destroyed our chances for rich husbands? I will never forgive you!"

"Be quiet!" Wynne snapped. "I do not know what is going on, but I intend to find out once our guests have satisfied their appetites. Would you have me violate the laws of hospitality to pacify your greed?"

"Are you not hungry, lady?" Madoc murmured softly so that only she might hear his words.

Wynne sent him a fierce, quelling look. "Eat your fill, my lord, but do it quickly. I would not seem inhospitable, but since you have dared to set my life upside down, I would have an explanation of you, and quickly!"

He grinned engagingly at her, and pulling a piece of the nearest cottage loaf, buttered it lavishly, and slathered it with honey before popping it in his mouth. The tip of his tongue swirled swiftly about his lips, recapturing errant crumbs and several beads of clear gold honey as he chewed and swallowed the bread. Once again Wynne found herself growing briefly light-headed as she found herself staring at him, fascinated. She was unable to understand her behavior.

Dragging herself back to reality, she found him holding out a similarly prepared morsel to her, but when she accepted it, his fingers would not release her fingers even as she raised them to her mouth. Awkwardly Wynne pushed the bread between her lips, fearful of making a scene, yet conscious of her lips touching his skin. She tried to pull free from Madoc, but with a knowing smile that reached all the way to his blue eyes, he drew her hand to his own mouth and licked the honey from her fingers, sucking slowly upon each digit before releasing it.

Once again she was being consumed by a terrible heat that sought out every crevice of her body and burned with an unrelenting fire. She was aware of feelings sweeping over her she couldn't even comprehend, for she had never had them before. They were the only two people on the face of the earth.

"I like the taste of you," Wynne heard him say low.

"Let go of my hand," she heard herself reply in equally low tones, although where she had gotten the courage to defy him she did not know. He did not argue with her. Looking guiltily about, Wynne saw Rhys and her family eating busily, not the least conscious of what had just transpired between herself and Madoc. Indeed. What had transpired? She wasn't even certain herself, and, reaching for her goblet, swallowed her ale greedily, finding herself almost painfully thirsty.

Rhys of St. Bride's, having devoured his cereal, trencher and all, gobbled down four eggs and finished off a cottage loaf by himself. The house serfs refilled his goblet at least three times. Now belching appreciatively, he pushed himself slightly back from the high board and fixed his gaze on Madoc. "I would respectfully request an explanation of you, my lord," he said in softly placating tones. "I seek the hand in marriage of Wynne of Gwernach. You claim to be her betrothed husband, yet she claims no knowledge of this fact. You will certainly understand my confusion." His gaze benign, Rhys picked several crumbs off his black and gold brocade tunic front and then smiled as engagingly as he knew how at Madoc.

"Indeed, my lord, I should myself appreciate being enlightened as to how I became, without my consent, betrothed to a man I have never before in my life laid eyes upon," Wynne said sharply. She was strangely irritated by this turn of events, even though the unexpected but timely arrival of this prince was obviously going to save her from a marriage with Rhys. Better a devil one knows than a devil one doesn't know. The thought popped uninvited into her head.

"You are not the priest who was here when Wynne was born," Madoc began by addressing Father Drew. "Where is he?"

"Long dead, my lord," Father Drew said, "may God assoil his good soul."

"His name was Father David, was it not?" Madoc asked the priest. "And he was a fat little man with a bald head, but for a small fringe of white hair about his pate, and the bluest eyes I have ever seen, which were particularly startling on one so old. He had a deep, booming voice that almost bounced off the walls of this hall, did he not? And a large pink mole the size of a pea upon his left cheekbone."

"You have described my predecessor exactly!" Father Drew said excitedly. "He was my cousin, and it was because I loved him so well I became a priest, that I might be like him."

"When the lady Wynne was born," Madoc continued, "I came to Owain ap Llywelyn and asked for his child's hand in marriage. I was newly come into my inheritance then. My mother had been twice widowed and I did not feel I could marry until I had raised my sister, Nesta. I sought a maid of good family, but one who would not be ready for marriage for many years. It was Father David who drew up the betrothal agreement." Madoc drew a tightly rolled parchment from beneath his tunic and handed it to Father Drew.

The priest carefully unrolled the document, smoothing it

flat, and scanned it carefully. Finally he looked up at them and said, "It is all in order, my lady, and the hand is that of Father David. I know it well."

"But why was I not told of such an arrangement?" Wynne demanded.

Madoc smiled at her. "You were not to be told for several reasons, lady. I wanted no child wife, but a girl grown who could oversee my house and bear my sons. I wanted a maid I might lovingly court, not one unwilling and perhaps in love with another. It was agreed that I should come to Gwernach the summer of your sixteenth year to woo you and hopefully to wed you. If you found another before then, you were to be told of this betrothal, but allowed the final choice in the matter. I only recently learned of your father's untimely death and, knowing that he had probably not informed you of this arrangement else you would have sent for me, I came to Gwernach to tell you myself."

"And found yourself amidst a love triangle," Enid said quietly.

"If it is Rhys of St. Bride's you love, lady, then I will step aside," Madoc said. "I would not have you unhappy."

"No!" Wynne said in a strangled voice, and then she blushed to the roots of her hair, turning to Rhys and saying, "I mean you no offense, my lord, but if my father, God assoil him, arranged this match for me, I feel I must honor his wishes, even as I have honored them in caring for Gwernach and my family."

"You have showed us your copy of the betrothal agreement," Rhys said a trifle sourly, and not quite willing yet to give up the rich plum that Wynne represented. "Surely Owain ap Llywelyn also had a copy of this agreement. I would see it before I release my claim on this lady." He could have almost bitten his tongue off even as the words poured forth from his mouth. Was he mad, Rhys wondered? He knew full well the reputation enjoyed by Madoc of Powys. The princes of Wenwynwyn were a race of sorcerers whose power it was said was a gift from the great Merlin. Rhys silently cursed himself for a fool. If Madoc took offense, and sorcerers were notoriously short-tempered it was said, his own race could end now when Madoc turned him into a beetle to be squashed beneath his foot!

Madoc, however, smiled as his eyes met the openly nervous ones of Rhys. The smile seemed to say, I understand and I will be merciful. "An excellent idea," the prince replied to Rhys's request. "I know that Owain ap Llywelyn had a copy of the betrothal papers because I remember signing two copies." He turned to Wynne. "Tell me, lady, would you know where your father would have kept such a document?"

"He had a locked box in his bedchamber," Wynne said slowly, "which I removed after his death. I have the key, but I have not yet opened the box. He kept the estate records and copies of all his transactions regarding the sales of Gwernach's excess cattle and cheese. I have not had time to go through it all."

"I'll get the box," Dewi said eagerly. "I know where it is!"

He raced off up the stairs before anyone might gainsay him and was quickly back, almost tottering beneath the weight of a carved oak box. Dewi set it upon the high board with a thump and looked to his eldest sister.

Reaching for a ring of keys that hung from her belt, Wynne found the one she sought and, inserting it in the lock of the box, opened it. She raised the lid even as Rhys tried to shove her aside.

"You do not know how to read," he said. "I will find the document."

Angrily Wynne shoved him away. "Indeed, my lord of St. Bride's, I most certainly do read! And I write a fine hand as well. How do you expect I have been able to keep the estate's accounts since my father's death?" She began to rifle through the papers carefully.

"You read, and write, and keep documents?" He almost moaned the words. This was a treasure of a woman he was losing. He could have profitably spent all his time at war with his weaker neighbors knowing that his wife, whose interests would of course be his own, was at St. Bride's overseeing everything. With Wynne as his mate he could have added considerably to his own holdings. The pain of that loss was almost too much.

Wynne's fingers quickly sifted through the parchments, and finally, at the bottom of the box, she found what she sought. Drawing it forth, she compared it to Madoc's copy and then, looking up at the assembled group, she said quietly, "It is identical. My father did indeed betroth me to Madoc of Powys when I was but six weeks old. There can be no question now of a marriage between Rhys of St. Bride's and myself."

Rhys groaned low, one fist clenching and unclenching in his disappointment and frustration.

"I cannot allow you to depart Gwernach my enemy, my lord," Madoc said, to Rhys's surprise.

"Your enemy?" Who was he to make an enemy of a sorcerer, Rhys thought bitterly. Was the prince mocking him? But he could see he was not.

"You need a wife," Madoc said quietly, "but not just any woman will do, for the mother of your heirs must be, like my Wynne, a rare pearl. You did not know that this maid was promised to me, but by my timely arrival I have, in a sense, stolen a bride from you. Let me replace that bride with my own sister, Nesta, who is as fair a girl as any you might find, and well-tutored in the arts of housewifery."

"Your sister?" Rhys knew he must appear an utter fool at this moment, repeating everything the prince said, but he did not care. Nesta of Powys was famed for her beauty! It was rumored that she had more than a passing acquaintance with magical arts. He would be allied by marriage to Madoc! What did it matter that he had lost Gwernach! He would have Nesta of Powys and her powerful family for relations! Rhys almost shouted with his joy.

"My sister is seventeen," Madoc continued, "and has told me she is ready to wed. She has placed her welfare in my hands. If you will have her to wife, then I will feel that I have settled this matter between us to everyone's satisfaction. What say you, my lord of St. Bride's?"

"I say aye!" Rhys answered him enthusiastically, a pleased grin splitting his face.

"But what of us?!" Caitlin burst out, unable to contain herself any longer. Wynne was to have a prince, and the prince's sister was to have Rhys. What of her? And Dilys? "What of the husbands you promised my sister and me, my lord?" Caitlin demanded.

"This changes nothing, lady," Rhys said, feeling expansive in his own good fortune. "We will be related by marriage, no matter that I wed another woman, and my cousins of Coed and Llyn need pretty, young wives to keep them warm and happy

this winter, and always. I have promised you husbands, my ladies, and rich, young husbands you shall have of me!"

"And when will we be wed?" Caitlin was not entirely certain she should trust Rhys now.

The lord of St. Bride's turned to Madoc. "I must defer to
you in this matter, my lord," Rhys said politely. "Gwernach is
now your responsibility."

Dewi ap Owain leapt upon the table and glared angrily
down at the two men. "Nay, gentlemen, I must protest," he
said fiercely. "I am Gwernach's lord, though I be yet a boy
Gwornach is *my* responsibility and no other's!" He stood, legs
apart, his hands balled into fists and set upon his hips, his dark
blue eyes flashing with his youthful outrage.

"My young brother-in-law is absolutely correct," Madoc
said in kindly tones. "You and I, Rhys, have been guilty of a
serious breach of good manners." Madoc looked up at Dewi
and smiled. "Come down, my lord. You have gained our attention now. If we do not settle the matter of your sister's wedding day, however, I fear the lady Caitlin may be driven to
violence." He held out his hand and helped Dewi down. "What
say you to the sixth day of September after the harvest, my
lord of Gwernach?"

"Not before?" Dewi sounded disappointed.

"I believe your sisters will need the summer months to finish preparing their dowries. Then too," Madoc said, "there is
my sister to consider. I thought I would bring Nesta to
Gwernach to meet her intended husband when the ladies
Caitlin and Dilys wed. With your permission, of course."

"Aye, my lord, it is a good plan!" Dewi agreed, although secretly he had hoped to rid himself of Caitlin and Dilys sooner.

"I will not meet the lady Nesta before September?" Rhys
said, sounding almost like a young boy with his first love.

"The betrothal papers must first be drawn up and my sister's
dowry settled between us," Madoc said. "Our late mother had
always wanted Nesta to have Pendragon, her ancestral home,
of which she was its last heiress in the direct line. I will, of
course, honor my mother's wishes in that matter; but then too
there is the gold I would settle upon my sister, and she will
need time to prepare her trousseau. I think we might set the
wedding date at the Winter Solstice, my lord, if that suits you.

Send me a priest to see to the legalities of the matter as soon as you can."

Rhys of St. Bride's head was reeling with the good fortune that had just been heaped upon his shoulders. Gwernach's loss was easily and quickly forgotten in the light of his acquisition of Pendragon, a small but most strategically placed castle on the coast near him. He had always coveted Pendragon, which was impregnable to attack. Like his neighbors, he had been forced to ignore it, believing there was no other sensible choice open to him. With Pendragon, his holdings would be more than doubled, for though the castle was insignificant in size, the lands belonging to it were vast and quite rich. With his marriage to Nesta of Powys, he would certainly become the most powerful of the coastal lords. He was exchanging a slight possibility for an absolute certainty. Rhys pulled a gold signet ring from his little finger.

"Give this to your sister, my lord," he said gravely. "It is my token and pledge to her."

"Your thoughtfulness will please Nesta," Madoc told him. "She is a girl with a gentle heart who appreciates elegant gestures. You will win much favor with her by the giving of this ring."

Rhys flushed, quite pleased by Madoc's words. His simple courtesy would delight Nesta. How different a maid she must be from this cold girl of Gwernach he had almost allied himself with in his effort to protect these lands from marauders who might otherwise have tried to steal them from young Dewi ap Owain.

He stood. "I will return to St. Bride's then," he told them all. "You will hear from me soon, my lord prince!" Rhys signaled to his men, who had been stuffing themselves with Gwernach's freshly baked bread, famous cheese, and nut-brown ale. "To horse!" he commanded, and they all clumped noisily from the hall behind him.

"Well," Caitlin said shrewishly, her blue eyes narrowing suspiciously, "I only hope he will keep his word and not try to trick us in this matter of his cousins. I should be happier were my marriage day coming sooner."

"There will be no delay in your wedding, my lady," the prince assured her. "Remember, Rhys cannot wed with my sister until you and the lady Dilys are safely wed to his cousins.

There is no malice in Rhys's heart. You need have no fears. Now, with your brother's permission, I would ask you and your younger sisters to leave the hall as I have business with Gwernach's lord that does not concern you."

With a swish of her skirts and, surprisingly, not another word, Caitlin left the hall followed by Dilys, who led Mair by the hand.

"Would you have us gone also, my lord?" Enid asked politely.

"Nay, lady," he answered her with a warm smile. "This business that Gwernach's lord and I must discuss concerns the lady Wynne. I think she should be here. You as well, for you are wise by virtue of your years, and I believe your grandchildren respect your opinion."

Enid returned his smile, thinking as she did that he was a most charming man for all his family's reputation. She looked to her eldest granddaughter, but Wynne's serene face gave no hint of what she was thinking, which Enid knew was not a good sign. "Well, my child," she said in an effort to elicit something from the girl, "you prayed to be saved from Rhys, and so you have been."

"Indeed, Grandmother, I have been saved from Rhys, but to what end?" Wynne burst out. "Why did you not tell me of this betrothal?"

"Because, my child, I did not know," Enid replied honestly. "Remember, I did not return to Gwernach until you were almost a year old. When my second husband died, I had no wish to remain in his house, a helpless widow to be ordered about like a common serf by Howel's brutal son and his vicious wife. I preferred to return to Gwernach to help your mother with her growing family, and Margiad welcomed my return. There was a babe started and as quickly lost between you and Caitlin. Margiad was happy for my company and my experience. Never did your father mention any betrothal, but such reticence was like him. He rarely discussed anything of importance with your mother, or with me, unless it directly concerned us and was imminent. He was no different with you, dear child. As his death was an accident and he was a relatively young man in good health not expecting to die, it is most unlikely he would have mentioned this betrothal to any of us until your sixteenth birthday. If you had fallen in love with another, you would have, according to the terms of the betrothal, been expected to make your own choice. We are fortunate that Madoc heard of Owain's death before you wed with Rhys." She paled. "Such a marriage would have been bigamous in the eyes of the Church, and the children born of it, bastards."

"Do not fret, good lady," Madoc soothed her. "All is well now."

"When will you marry my sister, Wynne?" Dewi asked bluntly.

"On Beltaine next, if it suits her, *and* if she will have me," the prince said quietly.

"I have no wish to marry now," Wynne replied, wondering where she got the strength to say it when she was suddenly feeling weak and helpless with the relief of her narrow escape from Rhys.

"Are you of a mind to join your life with that of the Church, lady?" Madoc asked her, and when Wynne shook her head, he continued, "Then eventually you must wed. Since I am your betrothed husband and no other suits you, then you must wed with me." Reaching out, he took her slender hand in his and, startled, she could feel the strength flow from him directly into her body. "Do I displease you so then, lady?" he said gently, his marvelous eyes searching her face.

"How can you displease me, my lord, when I do not even know you?" Wynne said, carefully averting her eyes from his.

"That is precisely why I have affixed our wedding day almost a year from now, dearling," he told her, and what his look had been unable to accomplish, the sweet sobriquet he gave her did. Heat began once more to race through her body.

"It is more than fair," Dewi said, much to his sister's surprise. "It is most generous. Since you have no passion for the Church, then you must honor this betrothal our father made and wed Prince Madoc, Wynne."

"Did you not swear to me that the choice would be mine?" she insisted almost angrily.

"Aye, and I will not go back on my word, sister, *but* if not Madoc of Powys, *who*? You will be sixteen in December, and you have already refused several suitors of good family and reputation. You are not in love with anyone to my knowledge, and now we learn you are betrothed to this man. I know I need not fear for my life with this husband of yours, as I felt I must fear Rhys of St. Bride's. Madoc does not seek to have my lands. Indeed, his family's reputation will keep me safe from those who might otherwise dare to wrest Gwernach from me."

Wynne was astounded by her younger brother's knowledge and firm grasp of the situation. Yesterday he had been but a naughty boy gone birding. Now he spoke with mature dignity and logic. She did not know how to fight him under these circumstances. Everything he said was true, even if he was but a child. "And if in getting to know you, my lord," she addressed Madoc, "I find we do not suit . . . you will set me free?"

He nodded slowly. "I want no unwilling woman to wife, lady. After the harvest and your sisters' marriages, I will take you with me to my home at Raven's Rock. You will keep my sister Nesta company until the Solstice, when we celebrate her marriage to Rhys. In that time we will get to know one another. Come the long winter when we are alone, we shall truly see if we are suited. Will that please you, Wynne of Gwernach?"

"But to leave Gwernach!" she protested.

"Come, sister!" Dewi said a trifle impatiently. "Surely you cannot expect the prince of Wenwynwyn to remain here courting you. You will go to Raven's Rock Castle with him after the harvest and begin to familiarize yourself with your new domain. And now that that is settled, I would change my clothes. I am still damp to the bone from my adventures." He arose from the table. "Come and help me, Grandmother."

"Your eyes have the look of a netted bird," Madoc noted as they watched Dewi and Enid depart the hall.

Wynne turned, startled, surprised that he could read her so easily. "My brother likes you," she said, avoiding his reference, "and because he does he will see that our marriage takes place whether I want it or not, no matter he tells me the choice is mine. For the first time since our father's death he is behaving like a true lord of Gwernach despite his youth and inexperience."

"You have taught him well, lady, but have no fears. My pride is not so overweening that should you refuse me I will suffer, or Gwernach will suffer. The choice is truly yours. I swear it!"

"Why can no one understand that I simply do not wish to wed?" Wynne said despairingly.

"Why do you not wish to marry, lady?" he inquired gently. "Have you some dislike for men?"

"I do not think so, my lord," Wynne said. "No! I do like men."

"Then what is it that makes you struggle like an animal in a trap against the inevitable, lady?" he probed.

"I would be free!" she said. "No man's possession! My own mistress!"

"And so you shall be when you are my wife, Wynne of Gwernach. Far more free than you are now, dearling, for now you are caught in a snare of your own making. You have woven it tightly using fear and ignorance, but you shall escape this pitfall soon, dearling, for I shall give you the greatest weapon of all with which to fight your own fears."

"What is it?" she almost whispered, his words sending a small thrill through her veins.

"*Love*," was the simple answer. "Love is the greatest weapon known to man, Wynne. You will see, my dearling. You will soon see!"

Chapter 3

The harvest was adequate. Husbanded carefully, there would be enough to feed both Gwernach's cattle and Gwernach's people in the coming winter. The summer had been wet, but not as wet as previous years. There had been enough sunshine to ripen the grain and dry the hay. The growing season over, the weather had become sunny and mild. The grass was thick and lush on the wooded hillsides where Gwernach's milk cows grazed peacefully. The apples hung in the orchards, growing plumper and sweeter with each passing day.

In the hall, Wynne, Enid, and little Mair oversaw the many preparations for the double wedding to be celebrated in three days' time. Dewi and Einion had gone hunting a final time in an effort to add to their larder. The bridegrooms, accompanied by Rhys, would not arrive until the night before the nuptials. Madoc and his sister, however, were expected tomorrow.

He stayed at Gwernach but one night those three months ago, and he had not come since. He had written to her—some letters sweet, some of a more practical nature—several times over the past weeks. He had sent her gifts that had had Caitlin pea-green with envy, for her betrothed had sent but one item, an ill-fashioned necklace that even Wynne had to agree was ugly. There was an ivory box that had contained half-a-dozen beautiful gold hairpins set with creamy pearls. A fine chain of Irish red-gold. A necklace of garnet and one of amethyst, each with matching earrings. A willow cage containing a pale green finch who sang more sweetly than any Wynne had known had arrived one day. Soft-hearted, she had attempted to free the little creature, but though it flew about the hall and the gardens, each night it returned to its cage, where it tucked its tiny head beneath its wing to sleep most soundly until first light.

A month after Madoc had left them, his messenger had arrived with several bolts of fabric: brocade, silk, fine soft wools,

72

sheer delicate linens, and jeweled ribbons in every hue of the rainbow.

"With my lord's compliments," the young page had said as his men-at-arms brought this sudden and unexpected bounty into the hall. "He suggests that perhaps you might find amongst his offerings something that would please your sisters to wear upon their wedding day."

With a single and unabashed shriek of delight, Caitlin and Dilys fell upon the fabric and were instantly embroiled in a violent quarrel over who should have which.

"Please thank my lord Madoc for his kind thoughtfulness," Wynne replied, offering refreshments to the page and his men before they left. She then turned her attention to her sisters. "Cease your bickering immediately," she threatened them, "or you shall have nothing. I would remind you that the fabrics are mine to do with as I please. Grandmother shall have the first pick, then Dewi and Mair. Only then will I allow you your choice."

"That's not fair!" Caitlin protested. "We are the brides! We should choose first!"

"Argue further with me," Wynne said darkly in a threatening tone, "and you shall find yourself wed in your shift, your hair cut to show the lord of Coed your true spousal servitude."

"I am content to wait my turn," Dilys said quickly, dropping her grip upon a swatch of brocade, her hand going to her long brown-gold hair as if to assure herself it was still there. It was her best attribute, for she was a bony girl with sharp features, whose bosom was only just beginning to soften her shape.

"You would not dare," Caitlin hissed menacingly, clutching a bolt of silk she particularly fancied to her breasts and glaring defiantly at Wynne.

"Nothing, sister mine, would give me greater pleasure," Wynne softy assured Caitlin, "but remember that first impressions are important. If you hope to rule your husband, and I know that you do, Caitlin, then you must bind him to you in those first moments. Can you do that if I shear your head like Einion shears the sheep?"

The bolt of silk slid from Caitlin's grasp and she pushed it away irritably. "The color did not suit me anyway," she said sourly.

Wynne smiled. "I would not know, but perhaps you are right. Your taste in these matters is always good."

In the end Caitlin had had her first choice. Enid had chosen for herself a fine indigo-blue fabric that complemented her silvery-white hair and a rose-colored silk. Dewi had taken a yellow and black brocade, leaving a coppery-colored and black silk brocade for Caitlin, who found it unusual and elegant. Dilys had chosen her favorite, a pale blue silk that matched her eyes and was embroidered with tiny silver stars. Enid had insisted that the rest of the fabrics belonged to Wynne, and had several fine new tunic dresses and under tunics made for her eldest grandchild. Still, there had been enough fabric left over for her sisters to make additional gowns.

"I do not know why you insisted on having so many things made for me," Wynne protested to Enid. "I already have enough to wear. More than enough!"

"Child, you have never been away from Gwernach," Enid counseled her. "Although I have never been to Raven's Rock Castle, I know it to be a place such as you cannot imagine. Madoc has done you a great kindness in sending these fabrics that you might make a new wardrobe for yourself. You will need it and more once you are his wife. Wait and see! I am right, for I have lived away from Gwernach. I know."

Her grandmother's words had touched a chord within Wynne, but she did not know why. How provincial would she seem to those who lived at Raven's Rock? What if they did not like her? She had always been liked by all who knew her, but all who knew her were of Gwernach, not strangers with strange ways in a strange place. The thought had nagged her ever since. Now tomorrow was upon her. Madoc and his sister would be here. In just a few days time she would be leaving the only home she had ever had. The only place she ever loved.

Wynne was angry at herself for what she deemed her own cowardice. Madoc, for what little she knew of him, was a kind man. Surely his people would be kind. If she was inexperienced in the ways of living in a fine castle, she would quickly learn new ways and correct any deficiencies in her knowledge. She would make friends. She had never had a friend. Only her sisters. No, that was not right. Einion was her friend, but he must remain behind to protect Dewi and Mair. And Madoc's sister would soon be leaving Raven's Rock for St. Bride's. Perhaps that singular similarity between them would make Nesta her friend, but would there be others? She felt uneasy in her heart, but as she was not a girl to dwell on what she considered foolishness, Wynne put these disturbing thoughts from her mind.

"There is nothing left to clean," Enid said, her voice replete with self-satisfaction. "There isn't a thing in this hall that hasn't been scrubbed twice over and polished within an inch of its life." She looked about her, smiling as she saw the relief etched into the faces about her. They had worked hard, and they had worked the house slaves equally as hard.

"If the bridegrooms ask," little Mair said mischievously, "shall we swear this is all Caitlin and Dilys's doing?"

Her grandmother and elder sister chuckled aloud.

"Fortunately," Wynne said, "the bridegrooms are young, Mair, and their first interest will be in the beauty of their brides. As our sisters are pretty girls, I think we may safely say our new relations will not be disappointed."

"Caitlin and Dilys have done nothing these past weeks but perfume themselves and rub their bodies with that wonderful cream you make from rendered lamb's fat and rose water," Mair said.

"There is more to my cream than that," Wynne laughed. "I had better teach you how to make it before I go, else I not have the chance again."

"Aye," Mair agreed, "you had better, sister, for Caitlin and Dilys have secreted all the jars of cream that you stored up in their chests and there is none left!"

Enid shook her head. "What will they do when it is no more, I wonder, since they were not interested in learning how to make it," she said.

"They will send to me at Raven's Rock," laughed Wynne, "demanding a supply instantaneously." Then she looked down at her little sister. "I have some of my cream hidden away where neither Caitlin nor Dilys knows, and tomorrow we will make more!"

"But not for Caitlin and Dilys!" Mair said firmly.

"No," Wynne responded. "Not for Caitlin or Dilys."

And the following day when she was looking, she was certain, her absolute worst, Madoc and his sister arrived early.

Wynne was in her pharmacea with Mair in her oldest tunic dress, a garment well-faded, not quite long enough, and with stains beneath the armpits, when Dewi came to get her. There was no way to the solar but through the hall. No way, therefore, of escaping the scrutiny of the prince and his sister, a dainty fairy of a girl whose eyes widened at her first sight of the barefooted Wynne of Gwernach.

"Could you not have sent a messenger ahead with a warning of your coming?" Wynne said irritably in greeting.

"But you knew we were expected today," Madoc replied, confused.

"But not when!" Wynne answered spiritedly. "I was in my pharmacea teaching Mair how to make my special body and face cream, for Caitlin and Dilys have depleted my stock entirely. What must your sister think of me to greet you both so and looking as I do?!"

Nesta of Powys burst out laughing. "Ohh," she said, gasping with her mirth. "I am so pleased you are not in awe of Madoc! I was so fearful of leaving him with some meek and mindless little thing who would jump with his every breath. If that cream of yours is responsible for your marvelous complexion, then I want to know how to make it too! Can we go back to your pharmacea now, sister? My brother is quite capable of fending for himself."

Sister. Nesta of Powys had called her sister as easily as if they had known each other their whole lives. Wynne felt a prickle of tears behind her eyes and swallowed hard, a smile creasing her lovely face as Madoc's sister slipped her arm through hers. They were going to be friends.

"You need not fear that my sister is docile and retiring," teased Dewi. "She is afraid of no man . . . or so she assures me. I have not, however, gained my full growth yet."

"Scamp!" Wynne chuckled, swatting affectionately at the lad.

She then led Nesta to her pharmacea, where Mair was carefully adding rose water to the creamy mixture. Introducing Madoc's sister to her own, Wynne set about to instruct both girls in the fine art of making her beauty cream. With three pairs of hands, her little stone crocks were soon filled, sealed carefully with beeswax covered with linen, and set upon a high back shelf where neither Caitlin nor Dilys would be apt to find them. Mair then ran off while Wynne and Nesta remained to restore order to the pharmacea.

"Tell me about Rhys of St. Bride's," Nesta said. "He was your suitor, wasn't he?" She washed the mortar and pestle Wynne had been using.

"An unwanted one," Wynne replied as she slowly dried the utensils.

"Why?" Nesta's light gold eyes were curious. "Do you find him physically repugnant?"

"An unwanted suitor only because I do not desire to wed at this time," Wynne explained to Nesta. "As for his features, I believe you could call them attractive. Rhys is of medium height and every inch of him is a warrior. I sense that his physique is a hard one. There seems to be no softness about him. His neck is bull-like. He exudes fierceness." Wynne wiped the stone counters clean.

"Yet you were not fearful of him," Nesta noted.

"I did not show my fear, but aye, I was fearful. Perhaps not so much of him as that he might take me away from Gwernach, that he might be a danger to Dewi. His motives in seeking me out for a wife were not of a romantic nature. My brother is young and not yet grown to manhood. If he dies, then I am next in line to inherit this land. I think my attraction for Rhys was Gwernach. He is an ambitious man."

"There is nothing wrong with ambition," Nesta said thoughtfully, "but I can understand your fears for your little brother; and you are wise to follow your voice within, sister. Tell me more of Rhys. What color are his eyes? His hair? He is quite faceless to me."

"Are you not afraid?" Wynne asked. "Your brother has promised you to someone you don't even know if you will like."

Nesta smiled. "I feel no calling to the Church. Therefore, I must, of necessity, wed. There is no one whom I love. I trust Madoc to choose wisely for me, and I believe he has. My mother's home, Pendragon, is my inheritance from her. I cannot have it without a husband. Had Madoc chosen a man with holdings inland, what good would Pendragon be to him or to me? Rhys's castle is quite near my own— But tell me more of the man!" Nesta removed the apron Wynne had given her to cover her gown.

"He is a Celt in face. His eyes are light grey, almost silvery, and his hair is a rich dark brown. He has a beard, and it is, I think, his one vanity, for it is beautifully barbered, with a moustache that encircles his mouth running into the beard. His mouth is large, and his lips are thick and sensuous. Yes, he is an attractive man. I do not think he will disappoint you, but as to his character, I know little except that he is stubborn."

Nesta laughed her tinkling laugh again. "In other words, you could not frighten him off," she said.

Wynne shook her head ruefully. "I could not. Had your brother not appeared when he did, I do not know what would have happened to me."

"Madoc is clever that way," Nesta replied. "He always appears when you need him the most."

"Is it true what is said about your family?" Wynne queried Nesta, curious, and yet almost afraid of what the girl would answer.

Nesta smiled. "Aye," she answered simply, "but some are more skilled than others."

"Madoc?"

Nesta nodded. "He is a clever man, Wynne, but I have never known him to use his powers unfairly or with malice. If the truth be known, I do not even know the extent of his wisdom."

"And your skills? Are they as great? Forgive me, but I need to learn what it is I must face at Raven's Rock. I have never known any world but Gwernach. I must sound so childish to you," Wynne finished as she gave the stone counter a final wipe.

"Nay, you are not childish. Your concerns are natural ones, sister." Nesta put her arm through Wynne's once again. "My skills are little more than yours. You see, I am Madoc's half sister. Our fathers are different, and the lords of Wenwynwyn inherit their powers through the male line, not the female. Most people do not know that and assume otherwise. Madoc and I have another brother, Brys, who shares a father with me. Brys allows people to believe that he too has powers, although he really does not."

"I did not know you had another brother!" Wynne said.

"Brys is estranged from us. He has his own holding at Cai," Nesta said shortly. "You need not concern yourself with him.

Now tell me. When will Rhys arrive? I am most anxious to meet him."

"He will not come until the night before the weddings," Wynne told her as they made their way back to the hall. "He escorts the two bridegrooms who are his cousins. I have invited him to remain for several days after the celebration, however, for I thought that you would want the time to get acquainted."

"Perhaps we will even allow him to return to Raven's Rock with us. I do not know what St. Bride's Castle is like, but I think it only fair that Rhys know my home is an elegant place, that he may have time to prepare for my coming after our marriage," Nesta said proudly.

Wynne nodded. "Aye, you are wise, *sister*." She flushed with her use of the word, but already she felt quite close to Nesta, who was so easy to talk with, and who was so candid in her opinions. "Rhys has been a bachelor for a long time, with no wife or mother to rule his hall. If he is like most men, it is probably a pigsty!"

In the hall, Madoc was comfortably settled talking to Enid. Wynne noted that her grandmother looked happier and more at ease than she had in many months. It was obvious that she liked the prince. If only I could be certain, Wynne thought, then blushed as Madoc looked up, gazing directly at her as if she had spoken aloud instead of within her mind.

"Do not do that!" she told him angrily. "You have not the right."

He had the good grace to flush guiltily, and said, "I beg your pardon, dearling. I am so attuned to you that it is hard not to hear."

"Then you must teach me how you do it that I may have the equal advantage," Wynne said, mollified slightly.

"What is it?" Enid asked, confused by their words.

"Nothing that should fret you, Grandmother," Wynne told her.

"Take your betrothed for a walk in the garden overlooking the river," Enid instructed her granddaughter. "He has spent all his time entertaining an old woman this afternoon while you toiled in your pharmacea. Did you replenish your supply of cream?"

"Aye, and I've hidden it where Caitlin and Dilys will not

find the jars. It was thoughtless and greedy of them to take all of the cream without asking first," Wynne said.

"But so like your sisters," Enid replied. "Go with Madoc, child. I will take Nesta to the solar that she may refresh herself. She will share your bed with you while she is here."

"Tell me of this garden overlooking the river," Madoc said, taking Wynne's hand as they departed the hall into the sunny afternoon.

"It is little but a patch of ground," Wynne said, smiling. "My mother and my grandmother insisted upon planting it and tending it. The house is built, as you will see, on a high promontory that juts out into the river below, and it is well walled. It is impossible to gain access to the rear of the house but from the house itself, for the walls prevent it on two sides, and the cliff is much too sheer to climb up from the river."

She waved her hand gracefully. "So here is our wee garden, my lord. There is no great deal to it, but grandmother loves it."

"And so do you," he noted, and she nodded.

"Aye, I do. I like to sit here on our one little bench and look to the hills beyond. It is peaceful. As you can see, there is little need for a wall where our garden thrusts out over the river, but mother planted roses there that no one might come too near the edge and fall."

"Rosa Damacena," he said knowledgeably. "I love their fragrance."

"You know the Rose of Damascus?" Wynne was surprised.

"There are beautiful gardens at Raven's Rock, dearling, and they eagerly await your gentle and clever touch," Madoc told her. "They have been somewhat neglected since my mother's death two years ago. You would have liked my mother. Nesta is very much like her."

"Nesta tells me that you have a brother too," Wynne said.

A shadow passed over Madoc's face. "Brys of Cai. Aye, but we are not close. I regret it, of course, but Brys has a restless and troubled spirit. He could be dangerous if I would let him, but I will not. You grow sweet herbs in your garden, I see," Madoc noted, deftly changing the subject. It was obviously one upon which he chose not to dwell.

Curious, but respectful of his wishes in the matter, Wynne plucked a piece of lavender and, crushing it between her fingers, put it beneath his nose. "My lavender is a special one I have bred as one might breed a cow. I think it more fragrant than other lavenders, and I shall bring seeds with me to Raven's Rock to plant."

He sniffed appreciatively, and then taking her fingers, kissed them. "Sweet," he said.

Her heartbeat quickened momentarily. "The lavender or my hand?" she said. "You seem to have a penchant for fingers, my lord," and though her look was grave, her green eyes twinkled.

Releasing her hand, he said, "You are a puzzle to me, Wynne of Gwernach. I am not certain how to behave with you lest I frighten you or offend you by my actions. One moment you're as prickly as a sea urchin, the next as shy as a doe. Yet I cannot help myself and I act on instinct alone with you. What else am I to do?"

"What is it you want of me, my lord?" Wynne asked him bluntly. "It is more, I sense, than just my hand in marriage."

"For now, dearling, I would simply have your love," Madoc answered, evading her cleverly, for the truth was too potent a brew for her to drink at this moment in time.

"I do not know if I can give you love, my lord. I love my brother, and Mair, and my grandmother. I think I may even harbor a small tender emotion for Caitlin and Dilys. I loved my parents, and I love Einion, who has watched over me since I was an infant. I even have an affection for a large raven I call old Dhu, but what I feel for these good souls is not what you would have me feel for you, I sense. Having never felt *that* particular elusive emotion, Madoc of Powys, I do not even know if I am capable of it. Besides, is that emotion we call love real?

"It seems a dangerous thing to me to entrust one's heart and being to another. Circumstances change as life passes, and what was certainty yesterday may not be tomorrow. To love, I think, means you must have certitude and faith in another. You must rely totally upon them. I do not know if I dare allow myself the luxury of what you call love."

"You tell me you have never loved a man, dearling, and yet you speak as a woman of experience who has been deeply hurt by another," he replied.

"Do I?" Wynne look genuinely surprised. "How strange," she told him, "yet I have told you the truth, and I have felt this way from my earliest years."

"Perhaps in another time and place," he said casually, "you gained this sad knowledge that has lingered on to plague you in this time and this place."

She nodded slowly. "Perhaps," she agreed.

Madoc found it interesting that she did not discount his words, and he wondered if she understood the theory of reincarnation. It was a wisdom as old as time itself; understood and believed by their Celtic ancestors, and once even taught by the Christian faith. It was a simple doctrine, and the sacrifice of the Christ had made it even clearer to those who believed.

The immortal soul, a gift from the Creator, would be reborn again and again in human form as it struggled to purify itself. The human soul, like an uncut gemstone in its earliest stage, constantly working to cut and polish itself to perfection that one day it might move on to the next plane of spiritual existence. The Church had ceased teaching reincarnation many centuries before. The early mass of the faithful were simple people who misunderstood the doctrine. For them reincarnation was an excuse to indulge their vices with the reassurance that they would return to repent those sins in another life. As this was not the purpose intended, the Church simply ceased the teaching of higher spiritual attainment; but the knowledge constituted an integral part of many other faiths.

Madoc was a Celt in his heart and soul. He knew that Wynne's reluctance to wed stemmed from another life. It certainly had not come from anything that she encountered in this time and place, but he knew from where it did come. It was a problem that she must work out for herself. He could do nothing to help her. He could love her and he could reassure her. Perhaps in time she would be content. *Or perhaps she would remember.* Though he welcomed that possibility, he also feared it.

"When your sisters are wed," he told her, "we will return to Raven's Rock. There we will come to know one another. Mayhap you will even learn to love me. Come Beltaine next I will take you for my wife, Wynne of Gwernach."

"Will you learn to love me, Madoc?" she asked him.

"I think I already do, dearling. Do not forget that I have known you since your infancy."

"How is that possible, my lord? I but became cognizant of you three months ago! Are you a flatterer then?"

"In time," he promised her, "you will know everything, Wynne, but much of it you will have to learn for yourself. I shall only tell you part, and then only when the moment is right."

She laughed. "You speak in riddles, my lord of Powys, but at least you are not pompous or dull."

Madoc plucked a late-blooming damask rose from its hedge and tucked it in Wynne's thick, dark braid. "Am I so transparent then, dearling, that you see through me?" he teased her, smiling.

"I am not sure I see the real you at all, my lord," she replied wisely.

He chuckled. "It is an advantage I shall savor for now, my dearling, for it is not an advantage a man is able to keep on longer acquaintance with the lady of his heart."

Wynne burst out laughing. "Why, my lord, I would almost feel pity for you, did I not know better."

"I shall have no mercy from you, lady, I can see that," he said.

"None," she cheerfully agreed, surprised that she was beginning to like this man.

Caitlin and Dilys did not appear at the evening meal, sending word that they needed their beauty rest before the exhausting festivities of their wedding.

"I should understand better," muttered Enid, "had they accepted any responsibility for the preparations involved in these weddings, but they have not. They have spent hours soaking themselves in the oak tub and creaming themselves until they must surely be as slippery as eels."

"Come, Grandmother," Dewi said, his blue eyes twinkling devilishly, "would you really want Caitlin and Dilys *helping* you? We have all been far better off without them. I for one am grateful for their absence."

"Dewi!" Wynne chided him. "What will the prince and the lady Nesta think of you that you show such lack of filial love for your sisters?"

"There are some siblings," Nesta said quietly, "who are not easy, nay, they are impossible to love. We cannot love a relation simply because he or she is a relation, I fear."

"You see!" Dewi crowed. "The lady Nesta understands even if you do not, Wynne."

"What I see is that the lady Nesta has better manners than the lord of Gwernach, brother. She puts you at your ease, but you make us all uncomfortable."

Dewi quickly understood his elder and, with a blush, he said, "Your pardon, my lord and my ladies."

The next two days passed quickly, and Gwernach was in a fair uproar with preparations for the weddings. Dewi had declared a holiday in honor of the two brides, and his serfs would be excused from the fields that day, although the cows must be milked twice daily no matter the festivities. It was hoped the day would be fair, as the celebration was planned for outdoors. Although they had no family left and few near neighbors, for Gwernach's lands were vast, Rhys would travel with his great troop of men, and the bridegrooms would certainly bring some relations with them, but no word was received from Rhys until he and his party were but an hour's ride from Gwernach.

Wynne scanned the missive. "The lords of Coed and Llyn bring their widowed mothers, and there is at least one sister in the group, although Rhys does not say whose."

"There are beds stored in the cow barn nearest the house," Enid remembered. "I'll send some men to fetch them, and we will set them up in the solar." She turned on Caitlin and Dilys, who were creaming each other's hands. "There are hangings and mattresses stored in the trunks in the nook at the end of the hall. Fetch them and make up the beds for our guests."

"But we will ruin our hands," whined Dilys.

"If you do not do it," their grandmother said, "it will not get done. Do you think the mothers of these men will let you wed them if you cannot even be bothered to make them comfortable? But if you prefer to remain here, old maids, I will not stop you."

Without another word of protest, Caitlin and Dilys arose from their place and hurried off to do her bidding. Enid smiled archly.

Rhys and his party arrived, and when finally the horses had been stabled and everyone brought into the hall, the introductions were made between all parties.

Arthwr of Coed was a lanky man with a large Adam's apple. His stringy hair was nondescript in color, and his eyes, which peered intently, a pale shade Wynne could not put color to, try though she did. He grinned, pleased, showing bad teeth, when presented to Caitlin, grabbing her and placing a wet, noisy kiss upon her perfect cheek.

"By the rood, cousin," he said to Rhys as if Caitlin were not even there, "this is a pretty pigeon you've placed in my nest! Right gladly will I fill her belly with my seed." His arm was tight about Caitlin's waist, and he did not look as if he would soon release her.

Caitlin flushed, an angry look springing into her eyes, but before she might vent her outrage, her husband-to-be was introducing her to an enormously large woman whose tiny eyes were almost lost in the folds of fat that made up her face. This was his mother, the lady Blodwen. Wynne flashed a warning look at Dewi lest he blurt out that one of their prize cows was named Blodwen.

"What a pretty child you are," the lady Blodwen said in a honied voice. "I am so glad my son is to have you for a wife and that you will come to Coed to look after me. I am of a most delicate constitution, as you must surely know."

Before Caitlin might say a word, Rhys was dragging forth his other cousin, Howel of Llyn, to introduce him to Dilys. He was a most beautiful young man with fair skin, dark brown eyes, and bright blond hair. He peered at Dilys critically and then whined, "She is not as pretty as the other, Rhys. Why should Arthwr have the prettier one? What do you think, Mother?" He addressed his last question to a woman who might have been his twin. She did not look like a mother.

"She will do quite nicely, Howel. Not everyone can be as fair as you are, my darling boy. She is pretty enough that you may take your pleasure of her without disgust, but not so beautiful that another man will covet her. With this one you will be certain that your sons are your own. Kiss her now, Howel, lest the lady think I have taught you no manners."

Dilys was, despite their words, ecstatic. Howel of Llyn was the most handsome man she had ever seen. "Ohhh," she whispered softly, "how beautiful you are, my lord!"

Pleased by her homage, Howel kissed her and, standing back, smiled at Dilys. "I will give you beautiful sons, lady," he told her.

The lady Gladys, for that was the name of Howel's mother, then introduced her daughter, Gwenda, a proud girl of eleven. She had brought the child along when she had heard that

Gwernach's lord was not yet promised to any maid. Gwenda
was as fair as her parent and her sibling, but her personality reminded Dewi too much of his sister Caitlin to attract his serious interest, but as the lady Gladys was not aware of that, her
hopes were high. Though she deemed Dilys unimportant, she
did not want to remain at Llyn forever. Gwernach would be a
fine place to end her days, and the old grandmother could not
live forever.

The betrothed couples moved off in tandem. Enid offered
wine to the mothers and made them comfortable by the fire,
thinking as she did how attractive Madoc and Wynne looked
standing together. Rhys shuffled his feet nervously and tried
not to look about too obviously.

"You will find my sister Nesta in the garden beyond the
hall," Madoc told him. "She did not want to take away from
Caitlin's and Dilys's excitement." He smiled, and Wynne did
too. "Go to her, my lord."

Rhys made a mighty effort not to appear too eager, but he
could scarce keep himself from running. As he entered the
small garden his mouth fell open in wonder. The most ravish-
ing girl he had ever seen in his entire life, surely the most exquisite girl in the entire world, stood awaiting him, her hands
outstretched in welcome. This, he realized, shocked as the
thought penetrated his consciousness, was the woman he had
been waiting for his whole life long; and until his first glimpse
of her, he hadn't realized it. Behind her a hedge of pink damask roses bloomed their last, a wild and tangled background
for her dark red hair with its coppery lights that seemed to
float all about her almost like a garnet mist.

The girl's face was a perfect heart with a straight, little nose,
a rosebud of a mouth on either side of which were deep, single
dimples, and the most beautiful gold eyes Rhys had ever seen.
She was garbed in a blue-green and gold brocade tunic dress
with a blue-green silk under tunic. A narrow gold band encircled her forehead, just barely containing her wonderful hair. In
its center was a moonstone.

"Welcome, my dear lord of St. Bride's," Nesta of Powys
said in her clear, musical voice, and she stepped forth to greet
him.

Rhys of St. Bride's fell to his knees and kissed the petite
girl's tiny hands. This wonderful creature was his! He felt sud-

denly humble, and almost shouted with his joy were he not so close to weeping. What had he, a great, rough man, ever done to deserve such a perfect treasure of a wife? "Lady," he finally managed to say, the fact he must appear the fool not distressing him in the least.

Her fingers closing about his, she urged him to his feet and said admiringly when he stood again, "You are so big! I do not think I have ever known so big a man; but you are gentle too, I can tell though you would hide it lest some think you weak." She stood as tall as she might upon her tiptoes and, drawing his head down, kissed his mouth warmly.

To his surprise, Rhys felt a single tear slide down his bearded cheek.

Nesta smiled full into his face and with one finger, she brushed the tear away. "It will be all right now, my dear lord," she told him. "We have found each other and nothing will ever part us." Then she kissed him again. Rhys shuddered, closing his strong arms about her, fearful that he might unwittingly hurt her, for she was so delicate a little creature.

Wynne, watching with Madoc, shook her head in wonder. "She is not in the least afraid of him, yet I was. I do not understand it."

"He was not the man for you, my dearling," Madoc said.

"And you are?" she answered, smiling slightly.

"Aye, I am," he responded quietly, his arm tightening about her. Then his fingers gently took her chin in their grasp and, turning her head just slightly, he put his lips briefly upon hers.

Wynne's green eyes widened in surprise as she felt the warmth of the contact.

Madoc smiled down into her eyes. "You do not know how to kiss," he remarked, surprised.

Hearing amusement in his voice, she said sharply, "Of course I do not know how to kiss! I have never done it before. Surely you would not have a wanton wife!" Then she stamped her foot at him. "You will teach me to kiss properly, Madoc. There must be great pleasure in kissing, for people seem to enjoy doing it, I have noted."

"I shall gladly teach you, my dearling, and I will give you as much pleasure as you desire, I swear it!" he promised.

"Good! We shall begin tonight after the meal, when my duties are concluded for the day. Though we be pledged to one another, you must court me if you are to win me. Kissing is part of courting, is it not, my lord?" Her cheeks, he noted, were flushed pink.

"Aye, very much a part of courting," he told her.

Hand in hand they turned back into the hall. Wynne would not allow her own curiosity to override her province as Gwernach's mistress. She did not find either of Rhys's cousins to her liking, but her sisters had no complaints at all. After her initial shock of being treated like a brood mare had subsided, Caitlin had skillfully set about to win over both Arthwr and the lady Blodwen. Her betrothed husband would respond, she concluded, to flattery regarding his masculinity, and so she had immediately set about adulating him, allowing him outrageously bold liberties that included passionate kisses and naughty fondlings in the shadows of the hall where none could see.

"Ohhh," Caitlin cried softly as Arthwr squeezed one of her plump breasts hotly. "You set me aflame, my lord! I am a virgin, but I sense you will be a mighty lover. I shall never want another but you!" She pushed herself against him, her lips wet and parted, her hand reaching out to fondle him daringly. She almost laughed at the glazed look upon his face, seeing she had easily enslaved him, and now certain as she received his wet kisses that she would have her own way in their marriage.

As for that fat old cow, the lady Blodwen, Caitlin was swift to realize that all her new mother-in-law would desire to be content was flattery, an unending supply of sweetmeats, and the leisure to pursue absolutely nothing. She hoped that Coed had a competent staff of house slaves. If they were not competent, Caitlin would soon see they were, for she knew her home must run smoothly, although she preferred not to be involved herself. She had learned a great deal watching her eldest sister. Because she didn't choose to lift her hand to menial tasks did not mean she wasn't aware of how something should be done properly. Caitlin was well-satisfied with her bridegroom.

As was Dilys. Dilys was not clever like Caitlin, but instant and innocent adoration of Howel of Llyn won her his immediate favor. The handsome Howel was vain beyond most men, a condition encouraged his whole life by his mother. Dilys was obviously not going to change anything in their lives. She would, like the lady Gladys, heap praise upon her beautiful spouse. She was immediately welcomed into her new family. Her mother-in-law was particularly tender toward Dilys, for she hoped to cajole the girl into influencing Dewi to look favorably upon her daughter Gwenda, not realizing that Dilys had no leverage at all with the young lord of Gwernach.

After the evening meal the women departed for the solar. The twin marriages would be celebrated with the first mass of the new day. Then the brides and their grooms would be feted until the noon hour, when they would depart. Gwernach had not the facilities for two simultaneous bridal nights. The newlyweds would have to return to their own separate homes in order to consummate their marriages. Wynne personally saw to the comfort of her female guests. Two additional beds had been set up to house the mothers-in-law. Gwenda would sleep with her mother, and the two serving wenches who had accompanied these ladies would sleep upon trundles belonging to the beds. There was plenty of water for washing.

In the hall below, Enid saw to the comfort of the gentlemen, assigning bed spaces, making certain that there were enough coverlets, that the fires were banked, the men-at-arms settled in the stables, the doors bolted securely. Noticing Madoc glancing toward the staircase, Enid said quietly, "She must get her rest, my lord. All of tomorrow's preparations rest upon her shoulders."

"We had planned a tryst, lady," he admitted.

Enid shook her head. "Not this night, I think."

He bowed politely. "As you will, lady. Will you tender my regrets to Wynne?"

"I will," Enid promised, and patted his cheek. "There will be plenty of time to get to know my granddaughter after tomorrow."

He smiled at her and said, "I can see from where it is Wynne gets her strength of will, lady."

Enid chuckled. "Perhaps," she agreed, "but Wynne is also very much herself, my lord. Never forget it."

"I suspect she will not allow me to, lady," was his response, and Enid nodded even as she turned to ascend the staircase to the solar. There she found Wynne, free now of her obligations, preparing to descend.

"No child," she told her granddaughter. "I have told Madoc that you must have your rest this night. Tomorrow will be a fiercely busy day for us all, but most of the obligation will fall upon you. I am simply too old for it."

Wynne was disappointed, but she knew that her grandmother was correct. Besides, she was eager to hear what Nesta had to say about Rhys. Curious as to how Madoc's petite sister had so easily enslaved the big man, for it had been obvious from the moment the two had returned to the hall in the late afternoon that Rhys of St. Bride's was touchingly in love with the radiant Nesta of Powys. Removing her clothing but for her chemise, Wynne washed herself, as was her custom, and then climbed into her bed.

"I thought you were to meet Madoc," Nesta said, surprised.

"Grandmother said I must get to bed, for tomorrow will be busy," Wynne answered. "Tell me about Rhys? You must certainly possess some sort of magic to have so easily tamed so fierce a man."

Nesta's laughter tinkled softly. "There is no magic involved, Wynne, I swear it!" She rolled upon her side and looked into Wynne's beautiful face. "Ever since I was a tiny child I have dreamed of marrying a man like Rhys. A great bear of a man with a heart as tender as an egg."

"Rhys? *Tender-hearted?*" Wynne whispered unbelievingly.

Again Nesta laughed. "Aye," she said. "Tender-hearted! I vow it is true, Wynne, but of course he dare not show such a face to the world. You can understand that, can't you?"

Wynne nodded. "Do you love him?" she said.

"Not now," Nesta said honestly, "but I am going to once I get to know him better." She smiled. "When your sisters are wed and gone, we will have such a good time! We will take bread, your fine cheeses, sweet wine, and we will picnic in the hills near Gwernach."

"If the weather holds," Wynne answered practically.

"It will," said Nesta with a deep certainty, "but go to sleep, sister, for the lady Enid is right. You do need your rest."

It was the best night's sleep that she had had in many weeks, and when the head house slave, Dee, touched her shoulder to awaken her in the hour before the dawn, Wynne rose refreshed. It was too early for her to dress in her fine garments, but she pulled an ancient, well-worn tunic from her trunk and, belting it, hurried downstairs barefooted. She was pleased to see that the fires had already been rebuilt from their embers and were blazing merrily. Unbolting the door to the hall, Wynne hurried to the bakehouse to find the baker was even now removing a second baking of fresh breads from the ovens. With a smile of approval and a wave, she moved on to the dairy to find the cows being milked and the cheeses to be eaten at today's feast set upon the stone counters, awaiting transportation to the hall.

In the cook house, Gwyr, the cook, his spoon badge of office waving, directed his minions in a number of duties both inside and outside the building. Outside spits had been set up for the two great sides of venison, the two sides of beef, and the four young lambs that were now turning over open fires. Inside, the cook fires roasted capons, ducks, and a young boar. Wynne almost collided with a lad carrying a tray of game pies to the bakehouse to be baked.

Gwyr, a fussy fellow, shrieked aloud. "Drop those pies, you clumsy oaf," he threatened, "and I'll mince you up to take their place!"

The boy tossed the cook a saucy grin, not in the least fearful of the threat. "You'll have to catch me first, Da!" he laughed.

"Is there to be fish?" Wynne asked.

"Aye, my lady! Sea trout stuffed with mullet stuffed with oysters. It's to be steamed in wine and herbs and served with carved lemons on a bed of fresh watercress."

"You are an artist," Wynne told him. "Are the sweets made?"

"Aye! Harry, the baker, has made a sugar cake for our brides, and we have molded rose jellies and candied violets as well as an apple tart."

"You have all done your work so well, there is little left for me to do," Wynne complimented Gwyr and his staff.

"You must make yourself beautiful for your prince," Gwyr said with a sly smile.

Wynne laughed. "I shall have no time for my lord Madoc until I have seen to the safe departure of my sisters."

Gwyr said nothing, but a voice from somewhere in the cook house said quite distinctly, "Which cannot come too soon, lady!"

"For shame!" Wynne answered, shaking her finger at the unseen culprit, but she was hard-pressed to contain her laughter. Neither Caitlin nor Dilys had ever been popular with the servants, and with good cause. They were both demanding girls who were never content with the service rendered them.

Wynne next hurried to the church to find Father Drew directing several young girls who had just arrived bearing fresh flowers, still wet with the dew, and branches of greens, newly picked, with which to decorate the church. Unlocking a long, narrow box in the vestibule, Wynne drew out fresh beeswax candles and gave them to the priest. Moving on back to the hall, she found the men already stirring and, catching Einion's attention, said, "Make certain that the lords of Coed and Llyn bathe before they wed. I suspect neither has seen water in several weeks, for I noted that both were rank yesterday when they came. Perhaps, though, it was just the hot ride."

"I'll bathe them myself, lady," Einion said, a grin upon his face, "not that your sisters deserve the kindness I do them. The prince will help me. He's a man who likes his water."

"Take them to the river and then see the oak tub is filled as quickly as possible so the ladies may wash."

The large oak tub used for bathing was quickly set up in an alcove of the solar and filled with hot water. Wynne woke her guests first, but both the ladies Blodwen and Gladys looked horrified at her suggestion they might like to bathe.

"I shall be chilled to the bone if I bathe," Blodwen protested in weak tones. "I would surely catch my death of cold and be abed for months . . . if I survived."

"I only bathe in my own tub," the lady Gladys said loftily, "and I did so last month. I certainly do not need another bath yet."

"Mother! Do I have to?" Gwenda whined petulantly.

"Of course not, my treasure," Gladys told her daughter.

"As you will, my ladies," Wynne said politely, and woke her sisters.

Seeing the large tub set up, Caitlin and Dilys began to argue as to who should bathe first.

"Caitlin is the eldest," Wynne said, settling the argument.

"You are the eldest," Mair piped up.

"I will go last, as any good hostess would," Wynne said. "Let our brides wash themselves before the rest of us; and Caitlin is the eldest of the brides."

Several maidservants came up to the solar to help with the preparations, and to Wynne's amazement, they were all ready in the few minutes before the first mass of the morning was to begin. Wynne silently blessed Madoc's generosity, for she, her grandmother, Dewi, and her sisters looked wonderful. They had no need to feel ashamed before their guests.

Caitlin was elegant and almost beautiful in her copper and black brocade tunic dress with its under tunic of shiny copper silk. The outer tunic was girded with a belt of hammered copper circles enameled with a black design. Caitlin's shoes were a soft brown leather that followed the shape of her foot, and about her neck she wore a long strand of pearls, while from each of her ears dangled a large, fat pearl earring. Her long, dark brown hair, the color of ripe acorns, flowed unbound down her back, contained by a gold band decorated with small pearls.

Pretty Dilys wore equally lovely wedding garb. Over her pale blue silk under tunic she had a sky blue silk tunic dress embroidered with dainty silver stars and belted with a twisted silver rope. Upon her feet were silver kid slippers, and about her neck she wore a long strand of pearls similar to her sister's. Her earrings, however, were aquamarine drops set in silver, which matched the oval aquamarine centered in the headband restraining her brown-gold hair, which, like Caitlin's, was unbound.

"Your sisters are remarkably well-dressed," the lady Gladys noted sharply, feeling slightly put in the shade by the youthful loveliness of the two brides. "I would not have believed it possible, for you are simple, country people."

"Gwernach is not a poor place, lady," Wynne said softly. "My sisters are well-dowered and well-dressed, as befits the sisters of the lord of Gwernach."

"What fine pearls they wear," noted the lady Blodwen, peering intently at Caitlin's strand.

"My late son gifted his wife with a strand of pearls with each daughter she bore him," Enid replied. "I thought it appropriate that when their daughters wed, they each have one of those strands."

"Father Drew will wonder where we are," Wynne told them. "Let us go to the church so our families may be united at last." She stood graciously back, allowing their guests to go ahead, but Nesta hung back.

"Warn your sisters not to be intimidated by either of those

two harpies," she said. "They covet the pearls, but if Caitlin and Dilys remain firm in their intent to keep them, those witches will eventually cease in their efforts to obtain them."

"You need not worry about Caitlin," Wynne replied. "The lady Blodwen will not get anything of hers no matter how hard she tries. In fact, I suspect that good lady's days at Coed are numbered. I can tell from what she has said that she thinks to have a daughter-in-law who will wait upon her hand and foot. She will quickly learn that Caitlin's sole concern is for herself. Dilys, however, is a different matter. I will see my brother makes certain that the lady Gladys does not impose upon poor Dilys. If he can manage to contain his dislike of her daughter Gwenda long enough for Dilys to work her way into her husband's affections, I think it will be all right. Away from Caitlin, Dilys is not quite so bad. She is not a quick girl, but she does have a sweetness about her."

"I think we are far more fortunate in our mates," Nesta said, and Enid smiled to herself, overhearing.

As much as Enid liked Madoc, she also liked his sister, who appeared to be the same sensible sort of girl that Wynne was. Nesta even had Rhys eating out of her hand, something Enid had never thought to see. She smoothed the fabric of her tunic dress, pleased with the richness of the indigo blue silk brocade which was shot through with silver threads. Aye, Rhys had turned from a lion to a lamb before their very eyes, and Nesta of Powys was entirely responsible. If that wasn't magic, she'd like to know what was.

Enid breathed deep of the warm late summer air, feeling a deep contentment envelop her as she did. If six months ago you had told her that everything at Gwernach would be so good by autumn, she would have considered the teller mad. She looked to the hillside where her son was buried. Ahh, Owain! she thought. The fates have dealt kindly with us indeed. Caitlin and Dilys are marrying well today and will be gone from here. Wynne's betrothed husband has come for her and will protect Dewi's rights. We need not fear his motives as we might have feared others. I believe we are safe, though I should not have thought it so without you, my son. If only Wynne were happier about her own impending marriage, but ahh, 'tis just maidenly concerns. Some have them and others do not. It will be well. I know it will be well.

The old woman stood smiling in the little church at Gwernach as Father Drew united in the holy sacrament of marriage her granddaughter Caitlin to Arthwr of Coed, and her granddaughter Dilys to Howel of Llyn. She nodded, pleased, as she saw Madoc of Powys reach out to take Wynne's hand in his, and Wynne not frown or pull away. Ah love! Ah youth! And yet, she thought wisely, there was a great deal to be said for age. Far more than youth could ever know. With age came acceptance, and sometimes, as in her case, peace. It was good to arise in the morning despite one's aches and pains, secure in the knowledge that one had survived to live another day. It was equally good to lie in one's featherbed at the end of a long day, warm and safe, and allow sleep to overtake one's thoughts. Enid smiled once more. If God would but allow her the time to see the others safe, she thought; and then little Mair was tugging at her hand.

"Come, Grandmother! The mass is over," she said brightly. "It is time to celebrate!"

"Aye," Enid responded. "It is certainly time to celebrate!"

⬛Chapter 4

She was in the woods, and about her a faint mauve mist blew through the trees like pieces of shredded silk gauze. The world was frozen in time, yet above her a raven cried.

Remember!

She sensed the word rather than truly heard it, and she struggled to comprehend its meaning.

Remember! The word was whispered softly, urgently, in her ear.

Once more the raven sounded its harsh, raucous cry.

Remember? Remember what? She didn't know what. Then as always a terrible sadness began to wash over her. She heard the name being called, but she could absolutely not make out that name. Stirring restlessly, Wynne suddenly awoke. She was drenched in perspiration. As she came to herself, she was grateful that Nesta was now sleeping in the bed that had once been Caitlin's and Dilys's. The recurring dream was not something she wanted to share with anyone. It confused her and it frightened her.

Pushing the bed curtains back, she slipped from her sleeping place. Outside the window she could see light beginning to creep up the horizon. In the dark blue sky above, the morning star blazed brightly like a perfect crystal. Opening the chest at the foot of her bed, Wynne drew out her favorite old green tunic dress and slipped it on, not bothering to belt it. Then splashing some cold water on her face, she moved softly down the stairs, across the hall to the entry. Drawing the bolt back as silently as she could, she opened the door and stepped outside.

She padded barefooted across the courtyard, nodding at the sleepy sentry who opened the gates for her. At Gwernach they were used to the young mistress's early morning wanderings. Halfway across the field opposite the gates, Wynne stopped suddenly as a great fifteen-point buck stepped daintily and silently from the forest. Wynne pulled a handful of green grass and held it out to the buck. Her heart was beating wildly in her excitement, but drawing several deep, slow breaths she managed to quiet it, thereby lowering the tempo of her life force so that she would not seem hostile to the big deer.

The beast eyed her curiously for what seemed like several very long minutes. Then he snorted softly, tossed his head and pawed the ground gently, all the while watching her to see what effect his actions would have upon this human. When Wynne giggled low, the deer stepped nervously back a pace or two.

"Shame on you," she said in a soft voice.

The deer's ears pricked at the sound of her words, a definitely nonhostile sound.

"Why you're twice my size," Wynne continued, "and you're afraid of me? Don't be silly! Come and take this fine meadow grass I've picked for you. 'Tis sweet and the dew's yet on it."

As if he understood her words, the buck came slowly forward, curious and lured by the delicious scent of the grass. He stretched his neck out as far as he could, reaching for the greenery, yet hoping to keep a goodly distance between himself and this human. Wynne leaned forward a tiny bit to facilitate the animal, who now began to chew upon her offering and, thus distracted, did not notice the slender girl moving forward just slightly toward him.

An arm sliding about her waist would have startled her terribly had not Madoc's voice whispered in her ear, " 'Tis only me, dearling. I see you have tamed Hearn to your hand."

"How can you be certain it is Hearn?" she demanded of him.

"How can you be certain it is not?" he replied. Reaching out, he rubbed the muzzle of the big buck with the knuckles of his hand.

The great deer, finished eating, raised his head to stare directly at them both. Then turning gracefully, he moved off slowly across the meadow, browsing casually on choice tidbits here and there as he went.

Madoc turned Wynne about so that she was facing him and smiled down at her. "You are clever that you can entice the beasts of the forest to your side."

"There is no trick to it, my lord. I merely concentrate on not being threatening to them," Wynne told him, and she shifted nervously in his arms. It was happening again. She could feel the heat beginning to pound through her veins. Why did he have this odd effect upon her?

Madoc could plainly see her discomfort, but he appeared in no hurry to release her, and Wynne would not ask him to do so. "I believe I was to give you a lesson in kissing the other night," he said quietly. "As we were not able to meet then, I think now as good a time as any." He tipped her face up to his. "Open your lips slightly."

"What?" She found the request startling

"To kiss properly you must part your lips," he explained seriously, struggling very hard with himself not to laugh. Teaching a maid to kiss seemed a strange occupation. Most girls appeared to come by it quite naturally.

"Like this?" Wynne, obviously very intent on getting it just right, pursed her lips adorably.

"Close your eyes," he said.

"Why?" she demanded.

"I believe it's considered more conducive to kissing to close one's eyes," he told her.

Her beautiful green eyes shut obediently, the thick, dark lashes fanning across her pale skin like smudges of black dirt. For a brief moment Madoc stared down at her in rapt awe. She was really incredibly beautiful. Who would have guessed that the pudgy infant he betrothed himself to those long years ago would have turned out to be so fair? Then he smiled to himself. He had always known. His mouth closed over hers without further delay, savoring the sweetness of her, the tenderness of her flesh.

Had her soul left her body? For a brief moment Wynne was entirely certain, for she seemed to soar, but then the heat consumed her as never before. Her stomach seemed to clench and unclench over and over again. Her heart beat a wild tattoo, and as passion, that hitherto unknown sensation, caught Wynne in its firm grasp, she became intoxicated with the intensity of her feelings. She was kissing him back, suddenly knowledgeable, a student no longer. She pressed herself against Madoc with an eagerness that caused him to gasp with surprise. She could not possibly understand the cravings she now felt; nor even those she engendered in him. All Wynne knew was that kissing was a most marvelous pastime, and she was filled to overflowing with her enthusiasm.

Madoc, however, knew that if he did not stop her now they would shortly be rolling about in the sweet green grass of the meadow, consummating their union in a manner Wynne could not possibly even imagine. Not that he could not teach her to enjoy that too, but it was far too soon for such revelations. He broke off the kiss and set her firmly back from him, smiling to show her that he was not displeased. "Dearling, you are as apt a pupil as any man could want," he assured her.

"Again!" she said, launching herself at him, lips at the ready. "I like kissing you!"

Swiftly he brushed her lips with his and then said, laughing, "And I like kissing you, dearling, but there is more to love than just kissing. It is too soon for us to explore other things, and I would enjoy courting you slowly, that we may first be friends."

"Is it possible for a man and a woman to be friends, my lord?"

"Aye, and the best of friends, Wynne, make the best lovers, I promise you," he told her.

"Kiss me," she wheedled him. "I feel there is a storm within me and only your kisses can calm the tumult."

"But your kisses awaken the turmoil within me, dearling," he returned. "Trust me and let us go slowly that our first union be all the better for the waiting."

Her cheeks grew rosy with his words, and she was suddenly shy of him again. "What must you think of me, my lord? I have been most bold with you." She turned away from him.

"Look at me, Wynne," he begged her, tipping her face back up to him. "I adore your boldness; but there are so many degrees of passion that I would have you experience first. Let me guide you in this as in other things. Do you not understand that I want you to love me?"

Wynne looked distressed. "Ohh, my lord, I have told you that I do not believe I am capable of such an emotion. I dare not be owned!"

"To love is indeed a possession of sorts, Wynne," he admitted, "but when one truly loves, it sets you free. I want you to love me, but if you do not believe you can, then I will be content to have you for my wife and my friend. Now you must call me by my name, for I will not have you sounding like a stranger or a servant."

"Who are you, Madoc of Powys," she asked him, "that you are so patient with me? I do not think Rhys of St. Bride's would have been so considerate of my feelings."

"Rhys was not meant for you. He did not love you."

"Nesta, however, is another matter," Wynne said with a smile. "Oh, Madoc, I want to laugh when I see him with her! He is like a great bear trying too hard to be gentle and tender of your sister. She says she has no magic about her, but I do not believe it so!"

"She has certainly bewitched him," Madoc agreed, "but it is love with which she has ensorceled Rhys. Nothing more, I vow."

"And you, Madoc," Wynne said boldly. "What sort of magic do you use? Your family's reputation precedes you. I admit to being curious. Most curious!"

"But not afraid," he noted, amused. "Well, dearling, I shall tell you all you need to know once we have returned to Raven's Rock, but for now I am ravenous for my breakfast! Since I will not allow myself the pleasure of feasting upon your sweet flesh, we must return to the house for more conventional fare."

"You are wicked!" she accused him, blushing scarlet at his words.

"Nay, good!" he told her with implied meaning. "Only good, I swear it, Wynne!"

"I dare not think otherwise, Madoc," she answered him, and taking his hand, led him back to the hall.

The next few days were probably the most idyllic Wynne could ever remember. The weather remained warm and fair. The two pairs of lovers strolled the meadows, the hills, and the forest, happy to be in each other's company. They picnicked by swiftly flowing woodland streams and sat upon the benches by the main fire pit in the evening, taking turns singing while one or another of them played upon a small stringed instrument.

Wynne, who had adored Nesta from the first moment they had met, now found herself looking at Rhys through different eyes. To her surprise she found she liked him. He was a bluff, honest man with a strong sense of morality in him; and he had a most marvelous sense of humor which delighted her. Wynne always believed you could trust a man with a sense of humor. Obviously and hopelessly enamored of Nesta, he now treated Wynne with the gentle courtesy of an older brother. She wondered had they wed if she would have found the true man within him, but thought not. Gwernach would have always stood like a wall between them.

She considered how incredible her own luck had been to send Madoc to Gwernach just in time to prevent her from pledging herself to Rhys. *Madoc.* Wynne smiled dreamily to herself. There had been many lessons in kissing since the morning in the meadow, although both of them acknowledged that Wynne needed no more lessons in that art, especially after Madoc had shown her just how sweetly two tongues could cavort. She had never imagined that a tongue could play a part in lovemaking, but he assured her it was so.

Now Wynne faced the moment of her departure from Gwernach, and she was overwhelmed with a plethora of mixed feelings. How could she leave the home she loved so deeply? How could she leave her aged grandmother, Mair, and especially Dewi? How would they survive without her to look after them?

"Must I go with you now?" Wynne asked Madoc for the hundredth time. "We know each other now, and I do not resist at the idea of becoming your wife any longer. They need me here!"

"We do not!" Enid contradicted her quickly and bluntly. "You think a few kisses have shown you the merit of this man, my child? Ohh, how much you have to learn about him. If you are wed a thousand years to him you will not learn the entirety of it."

"Do not fear for your family, dearling," Madoc reassured her gently. "Among my people is a man called David. He was once a bailiff for one of my family's estates. He has been unhappy ever since the heir came into his own and sent him back to me. I have already arranged to send him here to Gwernach to guide Dewi in his responsibilities. He is a kind and wise man. He will teach your brother well."

"Begone, sister!" Dewi half teased her. "I weary of hanging onto your pretty skirts! I would truly be master in my own house, and I cannot be until you are no longer here."

"You will remember all I have taught you?" she persisted. "You will treat our grandmother and Mair with love and courtesy? You will defend them? You will administer justice with a blind eye and a firm hand among our people? You will oversee them with loving kindness?"

"Aye! Aye! And again aye!" he said wearily.

"I will miss you all," Wynne said tearily.

"It is Gwernach that is your first love," Dewi said intuitively. "As a final gift from me, I am sending Einion with you to keep you safe from all harm."

"But Einion must stay with you to protect you and Mair!" Wynne protested, growing teary. "Father chose him to watch over the children."

"He goes with you, sister," the lord of Gwernach said firmly. "I am the lord here now and I will look after Mair. My brother of Powys can have no objection, can you, Madoc?"

"Nay, Dewi ap Owain, I have no objection to this gift you would make your sister, but do you not think me capable of defending my own?"

"As I am defending *my* own," the boy replied, much to the prince's amusement.

Madoc bowed elegantly, acknowledging that the subject was closed. Taking Wynne by the hand, he led her outside to where Nesta and Rhys already awaited them. He lifted her onto her horse, a gentle white mare he had given her.

A brief panicked look entered Wynne's eyes for a moment, but Enid, coming to her side, patted her hand comfortingly. "We will be fine, my child. Write to me when you can, and remember that I got on quite well in the world before you entered it! I imagine I will continue to survive quite nicely even though I be here and you there."

Her grandmother's pithy remarks were enough to ease Wynne's tension and she laughed. "It is an adventure, Grandmother, isn't it?"

"Aye, my child, and every young girl should have some adventures before she settles down to the dull business of being a wife and a mother! It is the natural order of life for women, having been given the gift of life bearing, to organize their homes and bear children; but such a life is not always the most interesting."

Father Drew stepped forward to bless them and to bless

their journey. As he made the sign of the cross over them, Wynne felt the tears she was unable to contain finally slipping down her cheeks. It wasn't that she was unhappy. She wasn't. But she was sad to be leaving Gwernach. As the horses moved away, the sight of her grandmother and little Mair etched itself in her heart, even as her brother, with a cursory wave in her direction, quickly disappeared around the corner of the manor house, intent on his own business. Suddenly the sadness drained from her.

"Dewi is certainly eager to be rid of me," she noted with a watery chuckle.

"He is anxious to be his own man," Rhys said wisely. "You cannot fault the lad, Wynne. With good further guidance he will do well for Gwernach. We'll have to put our minds to finding him a good wife in a few years, but not my cousin Gwenda of Llyn. I could see he took a right dislike to the wench, although her mother entertains high hopes, I doubt not."

"She reminds him of Caitlin in her manner," Wynne replied. "Dewi has never liked Caitlin."

"We know many lovely young girls who would make your brother a perfect wife," Nesta said.

Madoc laughed at them. "Give the boy time," he counseled. "He is only just free of his eldest sister, and he needs to first grow up a bit *and* then to sow himself a few wild oats."

"Ahh, wild oats!" Rhys grinned appreciatively.

"And have you sown many, my dear lord?" Nesta asked sweetly, her lovely face deceptively bland, her gold eyes twinkling devilishly.

"Enough, I believe, that you will not find me wanting in our bedchamber," he responded boldly.

Nesta, taken by surprise at his answer, blushed prettily.

Rhys chortled, satisfied. "You've bewitched me, my fair Nesta," he admitted, "but always remember that I am the man!"

"I shall never again forget," Nesta replied promptly, but even as she spoke, Wynne felt she meant something far different than her words implied to her besotted lover.

The distance between Gwernach and Madoc's home at Raven's Rock Castle was one of several long days' duration. They were not always fortunate enough to find shelter in a convent or a monastery guest house; or with some noble family, or well-to-do manor farmer willing to put up with so many mouths to feed. Two nights they camped out in the forest, keeping fires going to frighten away the wild animals and a strong watch posted to keep away the violent robbers that preyed upon careless travelers and were far more savage than the beasts of the wood.

Rhys escorted them but part of their way, for he could not be away from St. Bride's too long a time lest some unwise fool challenge his authority. Early one morning a large party of armed men approached them shouting the prince's name. Madoc rode forth to meet them, smiling and waving a greeting.

"I will leave you now, lady mine," Rhys told Nesta, "and return with my men to St. Bride's that I may make it perfect for your coming."

"The time away from you will seem an eternity," Nesta told him. Tears sprang into her golden eyes as she leaned from her mare to catch his hand and press it to her cheek.

Wynne was forced to turn away, for the look on Rhys's face was heartbreaking. It was so obvious he could hardly bear to leave Nesta, nor she him. To love like that, Wynne thought, and on such short acquaintance. It was as if they had known each other their entire lives instead of just having met so short a time ago. Why could she not feel at least half of the love for Madoc that Nesta felt for her betrothed husband? Nesta's feelings for Rhys of St. Bride's were far different than what she felt for Madoc. Wynne was wise enough to recognize it. Not that her passion for the prince was an unpleasant thing, but Wynne instinctively felt that there should be more. She remembered her parents behaving as Nesta and Rhys behaved. Would these other feelings eventually come?

She was startled from her reverie by Rhys's voice saying, "I bid you fond farewell, Wynne of Gwernach."

"And I you, my lord. May God and St. David keep you safe until we meet again," she replied. He smiled at her, and Wynne realized that he was a handsome man. "I thank you for giving my two sisters such fine husbands, my lord."

Rhys's laughter rumbled in his barrel chest. "I think we have both done well by that transaction, Wynne. Do you not think so also?"

"Aye," she admitted, beginning to laugh, realizing that he

had been as eager to get his less than admirable relatives wives as she had been to get the shrewish Caitlin and the foolish Dilys husbands.

"And we shall rarely, if ever, have to see them." Rhys chuckled.

"If that be the case, my lord, then I shall indeed owe you a favor," Wynne told him, giggling.

"You are both dreadful!" Nesta scolded them, but her own mouth was turned up in a smile.

Madoc rejoined them and offered his hand to Rhys in parting. "Come two days before the Solstice, brother, to claim your bride. She will be awaiting you. You had best bring a large troop of men with you, for her dowry and all her possessions are great. Be warned, Rhys. This woman never disposes of anything that comes into her grasp. She still has clothing from her childhood."

"Which I have carefully stored away, and which will serve nicely for my daughters," Nesta said primly. "I do not believe in waste, Madoc. I have not your resources."

"Why, wench, you will carry away half of Raven's Rock, I vow!" he teased her.

"I deserve it all for putting up with you these many years," she teased back spiritedly.

Rhys grinned at Madoc and shook his hand. He saluted Wynne politely. Then leaning forward, he kissed Nesta heartily, leaving her rosy and breathless. "Farewell, lady mine. Magic the time between us away, my love. Until we meet again!" He turned his horse and called out a command to his men to follow.

Madoc's party sat on their horses a minute watching Rhys and his men go, and then, at Madoc's signal, they moved off in the opposite direction. Wynne was silent for most of the rest of their journey. Having never been more than a mile or two from Gwernach, she was awed and fascinated by their travels. There was such a variety of countryside. They moved through dark forests, across wide, meadowlike plains edged in marshes, over hills both gentle and steep; and always the mountains rose before them, beckoning them onward.

Madoc's castle of Raven's Rock, or Bran's Craig as it was called in the Celtic Welsh tongue, was located in the Black Mountains of Powys. When she first saw it, Wynne thought she must be dreaming, for never before had she seen anything like that which arose before her now. It seemed to spring from the mountainside itself. Indeed, it appeared to be not just a part of the mountain, but one with it.

"It is a magical place," she said softly upon her first sight of her new home.

"Is it?" he said.

"Do not toy with me, my lord," Wynne said sharply. "Your family's power is said to stem from Merlin himself. Did not Merlin help Arthwr to fashion Camelot? How else could you carve a castle from the mountainside?"

"Raven's Rock merely looks as if it is one and the same with the mountain. That is because it is built of the same granite the mountains are made of, dearling. My ancestor thought it a good camouflage."

"I admit to being ignorant where castles are concerned, but I have never seen a place such as Raven's Rock," Wynne said. "It looks almost foreign in its design."

"It is," he told her. "It is a mixture of styles not yet common to this island of Britain upon which we live. My ancestor brought back his ideas from his travels. He spent many years traveling the world. The original part of the building is a round tower."

"There are four towers," Wynne noted.

"Look closely," he told her as their horses carefully traversed the steep trail across the gorge from Raven's Rock. "Two towers are round and two square. It is the tower on the west that is the original one."

"Where are your gardens?" she asked.

"The open areas that are walled upon the edges of the cliffs are called *terraces*, Wynne. There my gardens are set, and they are most fair to the eye. I have already sent word ahead that my gardener open a place for you to plant your herb cuttings. That way they will settle themselves into the earth before the winter comes. It will be good to have a woman's touch in the gardens again. They have not been quite the same since my mother's death. The earth responds well to a woman's touch. My sister Nesta could not bring herself to plant in our mother's garden. She said it made her sad."

"Women understand the earth, my lord, for the earth gives life even as women are capable of giving life."

The trail that they followed wound down into the gorge which was traversed by a swiftly flowing small river. A sturdily built stone bridge spanned the river. They crossed it to the other side, where they followed another narrow road up the mountain to the castle gates. Raven's Rock had no moat. It needed none, for the road to it was but one horse in width. It was truly impregnable to anyone foolish enough to seek to attack it.

"It appears a mighty and terrifying place approaching it for the first time," Madoc said to Wynne, "but once you have passed beneath the portcullis, you will find yourself in a gracious and beautiful world."

"It appears so black and so fierce as we grow nearer," Wynne told him, gazing up at the dark soaring towers and sharply etched parapets of the castle.

"To frighten our enemies," he answered.

"Do you have enemies, my lord?"

"Few men are without them, I fear, my dearling," he said, but no more.

A loud cry arose from the men at arms upon the walls of Raven's Rock. They shouted the prince's name over and over again by way of greeting him. *"Madoc! Madoc! Madoc!"*

"Do they love him so?" Wynne inquired of Nesta.

"Aye, they do," Nesta said. "There is something about the princes of Wenwynwyn that binds men in loyalty to them. They say Madoc's father, Prince Gwalchmal, was very much like him."

"What happened to Madoc's father?" Wynne asked. "I know so little of this family into which I am expected to wed."

"No one really knows," Nesta said. "Prince Gwalchmal was found at the foot of the mountain one early spring day, his neck broken. It is believed he fell, although no one knows how or why it happened. He was a man in his prime, which made it all the more confusing. Madoc was seven at the time. Our mother, Gwenhwyvar, remarried with a haste that some might have thought indecent; but she felt she needed to protect Madoc. He was a child incapable of protecting himself. She took for her second husband the twin of her first husband, Cynbel of Cai. Madoc's father had died in March. Gwenhwyvar wed Cynbel in May of that same year. Our brother, Brys, was born the following February."

"A twin brother!" Wynne said, amazed. "At Gwernach a serf woman gave birth to two daughters at the same time. No one could ever tell them apart, for they were that alike."

"Madoc's father and mine, although born at the same time, did not look at all alike," Nesta told Wynne. "Madoc is said to be his father's image; dark hair, fair skin, and those wonderful blue eyes. Gwalchmal looked like all princes of Powys-Wenwynwyn do; but my father, Cynbel of Cai, favored our grandmother's family, who are fair of hair."

"Then your father raised Madoc?"

"Aye," Nesta said shortly, and when Wynne looked questioningly, she continued in a low voice. "My brother Brys is just like our father. Beautiful to the eye and charming beyond all, but wicked! It is said that Gwalchmal and Cynbel almost killed their mother at their birthing, for each was determined to be the first into the world that he might inherit Raven's Rock. It is said that when Gwalchmal, the firstborn, pushed forth from his mother's womb, Cynbel's fist was grasping his ankle tightly as if to hold him back."

Wynne's eyes widened in shock.

"The twin brothers fought constantly throughout their childhood and youth," Nesta continued. "They were always in competition with one another. There was nothing that Gwalchmal did that Cynbel did not try to outdo. When our maternal great-grandfather died, he had no surviving male heirs. His castle at Cai was inherited by Gwalchmal and Cynbel's mother. Cynbel was sent to Castle Cai in order to separate him from Gwalchmal. It was feared that they would kill each other, leaving the line of the princes of Powys-Wenwynwyn extinct. The strain of birthing her sons had been too great for my grandmother. She had no other children. Nonetheless, she lived to a great old age."

"Stop a moment," Wynne said. "You told me you had no powers, Nesta, for the powers of Wenwynwyn are inherited through the male line and you and Madoc had different fathers. Now I learn that your father and Madoc's were twin brothers. How can it be that he has powers and you do not? And what of your brother, Brys of Cai?"

"My grandfather, Caradoc, when he saw the wickedness of his son, Cynbel, cast a mighty spell upon him, removing the powers he might otherwise have gained when he grew to maturity. That spell also included Cynbel's descendants, a thousand generations hence. I usually find it easier when I am in a position to have to explain my situation to simply say Madoc and I have different fathers and the gift comes from Madoc's father's line."

"Why are you closer to Madoc than your brother, Brys?" Wynne asked.

"Is it so obvious?" Nesta looked distressed. Then she explained, "Brys is three and a half years older than I am. When I was not quite six years of age, Brys attempted to use me as a man would use a woman. I fought him, for I knew what he desired of me was wrong. Our father came upon us, and I ran weeping to him, for protection. Instead of punishing Brys, our father laughed. He was pleased with his son's burgeoning manhood and he said to him, 'Nay, lad, you are doing it wrong. No wonder you have not succeeded in your attempts. I will show you how.' Then he reached for me. He was quite drunk at the time.

"And indeed he would have committed the sin of incest with me had not Madoc arrived on the scene. One look told him the deviltry my father and my brother were up to, and his anger was awesome to behold. He caught me up in his arms, thus protecting me. My father had never been truly kind to Madoc, but he was never allowed the opportunity to harm him, for the castle servants were vigilant and Madoc was clever. Still, my father hated the fact that it was Madoc who was the prince of Wenwynwyn and not he. My father shouted at Madoc that he had no rights in this matter. I was his daughter to do with as he pleased. Madoc, who was now virtually grown, replied that it was he, Cynbel, who had no rights at Raven's Rock. He forthwith banished him and Brys to Cai. The castle servants were more than happy to obey Madoc and eject my father and brother from Raven's Rock. Father died two years later. He is said to have fallen into a vat of new wine."

"And your mother? Did she not go to Cai with him?"

"No. Mother was relieved to have Cynbel gone. She was not a woman of great personal strength, I fear. She was a gentle woman who disliked controversy and was afraid of much in life about her. She wanted peace, and she wanted protection from the world at any price. My father really forced her into their marriage by making her believe Madoc's life was in danger and telling her she needed a strong man to hold Raven's Rock. He was very handsome in his youth, before he began to live on wine and ale. His beauty, however, was a mask. He was a cruel and wicked man who grew more cruel and wicked by the day. Only my grandmother's strong presence kept him from serious violence toward Madoc. I believe she was the one person living whom my father truly feared. She died almost immediately after my father drowned. It was as if she didn't dare leave us until he was dead and gone," Nesta said.

"And your mother? She is but recently dead?"

"A little over a year ago," Nesta replied.

"Has Brys lived at Cai alone all these years? I'm surprised that your mother did not go to him after your father's death," Wynne noted.

"She offered to, but Brys did not want it, nor would he return to Raven's Rock, for Madoc invited him back for mother's sake. When he refused to come, Madoc sent a strong and trusted bailiff to oversee Brys. The day Brys turned eighteen, he returned David to Madoc saying he no longer had a need of him and inquiring after my mother's health."

"You have not seen him recently?" Wynne was frankly curious.

"Not since that dreadful day he attempted to rape me. I do not want to, and Madoc did not want me to see him."

"Now I understand why you and Madoc are estranged from your brother," Wynne said. "I shall hope for a more peaceful life."

"And no twin sons," Nesta said with a small smile. "Ahh, we are home!"

And indeed they had passed beneath the portcullis of Raven's Rock Castle. Wynne's eyes widened in surprise. They were in a huge courtyard that bustled with activity. She could see stables, a farmyard, an armory, and a water supply with just one quick glance. Servants ran to take their horses, their faces friendly, their gazes frankly curious. Einion was immediately at her side. Gently he lifted her down from her mount, setting her firmly on her feet.

The big man glanced around curiously. " 'Tis bigger than Gwernach, that's for sure," he said, "but I see no unfriendly faces, lady."

Wynne smiled upon him. "There are never unfriendly faces where you are concerned, my Einion. How many broken hearts did you leave behind at Gwernach? Already I see several wenches casting their eyes in your direction."

Einion grinned. "A woman is part of a man's life, lady. 'Tis the natural order of things."

"Come," Nesta said, taking Wynne by the hand. "I will show you where we live." She led Wynne up a small flight of six steps and through a stone archway.

"Ohh, my!" Wynne gazed around her, totally surprised. Before her stretched a garden planted upon several levels, and directly ahead of her at the far end of the gardens was a landscape of mountains. She ran down several steps, across a stretch of garden, down several more steps. She scarcely knew where to look next, for it was all so beautiful. Finally she ascended three wide marble steps to a terrace that extended the width of the gardenscape. Beyond the balustrade was a sheer drop into a wooded mountain glen below. The view was wild, and wonderful, and totally breathtaking. Raven's Rock, Wynne now realized, sat upon the spine of a mountain dividing two valleys.

Wynne turned to find Nesta smiling at her. "I must seem a fool to you," she said, "but never before in my life have I seen anything so . . . so . . . so magnificent!"

"I'm so glad you like it," Nesta said, "but I will tell you a secret, sister. Although I have lived with this beauty my whole life, it still has the power to enchant and overawe me too. There is no place in the world like Raven's Rock."

In the blue sky above them there was a sudden cry of a bird and both girls looked up.

" 'Tis old Dhu!" Wynne cried. "I am certain of it! He has followed me here!"

"Old Dhu?" Nesta looked surprised.

"My raven." Wynne laughed. "He has been at Gwernach my whole life and he is my friend! Ohh, I cannot believe it! It is an omen. A good omen! He was not at Gwernach when we left, you know. I looked and looked for him in the days before we left, but old Dhu was nowhere to be found."

"We have many ravens here at Raven's Rock," Nesta said with calm logic. "How can you be certain that this is the same bird?"

"I just know," Wynne replied with absolute certainty.

Nesta laughed. "Another Celtic mystic," she said with good humor. "You and my brother will get on very well, I think. Come. Let us go indoors. I am beginning to feel a chill in the air as the afternoon wanes."

It was as Nesta spoke that Wynne realized the beautiful gardens in which she stood were surrounded on three sides by the castle itself. The living quarters of Raven's Rock were totally separated from the bustling courtyard. The only way into this area was through the archway. Closed off, the residents of the castle were not simply impregnable, they were totally and utterly impregnable. Wynne followed Nesta back across the gardens. To the right of the archway where they had come in was a gracious set of six steps leading up to the main entrance of the living quarters.

Inside, servants hurried forward to take their cloaks, and Wynne followed in Nesta's wake. They entered the Great Hall built of stone and timbers. Silk banners hung from the rafters. There were four large fire pits, and yet they were not fire pits, for they were set into the walls like bed spaces. Still, fires blazed merrily in them and they did not smoke. Behind the high board was a large, tall arched window that looked out on the mountains, offering a similar view as Wynne had seen in the garden. There were smaller arched windows set high on the east and west walls.

"What do you think of our Great Hall?" Nesta asked Wynne.

"It's wonderful," came the answer. "I have never seen anything like it before. How do you get rid of the smoke from your fire pits, Nesta? I've never seen any like them."

"We call them fireplaces, Wynne. Instead of the smoke going up and out a smoke hole in the roof, there is a tunnel in the walls for the smoke to escape up. It is called a chimney."

"I do not think you will find such wonderful luxuries at St. Bride's," Wynne said honestly. "How can you bear to leave Raven's Rock?"

"When Rhys sees how we live here," Nesta laughed, "I do not think I will have any difficulty in persuading him to make some little improvements for me. Come along now and I will show you to your own quarters. I stink of horse and long for a hot bath."

They exited the hall the way they had come and hurried up a wide flight of stairs. The stairs were stone, Wynne noted, and not wooden as at Gwernach. At the top of the staircase they turned right into a hallway lit by many torches.

"This is the darkest part of the house," Nesta told Wynne. "That wall," she waved her left hand carelessly, "is the courtyard wall, and as such, has no windows for safety's sake. The rooms on this side"—Nesta waved her right hand—"overlook the gardens."

They came to the end of the hallway, and Nesta turned right once more and opened a carved oak door. "These are the family apartments," she told Wynne. "My chamber is here and yours will be in the prince's quarters there." She pointed.

"We each have a single room to ourselves?" Wynne was amazed, for at Gwernach only the lord and his lady had had such privacy. Then she blushed. "I cannot sleep in Madoc's room, Nesta. We are betrothed, but we are not wed yet."

Nesta laughed her tinkling laugh. "My brother's apartments have more than one room, Wynne. Come and look!" She opened another set of doors and led Wynne through. "Madoc has a room for sitting by the fire and reading. Another for bathing. One for sleeping. Of course, there is the chamber of the prince's wife, not to mention rooms for clothing and servants. As you are to be Madoc's wife, it is only fitting you have the proper room."

"I have only come to Raven's Rock to see if Madoc and I can like one another," Wynne protested nervously. "I am not to be held to the betrothal if I do not choose to be."

"Oh, Wynne, if you do not wed with my brother, what will happen to you?" Nesta asked her, distressed.

Before Wynne might answer Madoc's sister, however, the door to the chamber of the prince's wife opened and a pretty girl came forth. She had nut-brown hair and warm brown eyes, and she wore a simple tunic dress of pale blue. "Welcome to Raven's Rock, lady. I am Megan, and I am to serve you," she said in a sweetly melodious voice.

"Well," Nesta said, sounding slightly relieved, "I will leave you in good hands if Megan is to be your servant, dear sister. I am off to have my bath."

"You will find Gwyn has already drawn it, my lady Nesta," said Megan.

Nesta hurried out without so much as a backward glance.

"I have taken the liberty of arranging a bath for you also, my lady Wynne," the servant girl said. "Let me help you with your garments. You must be weary after your long ride from Gwernach."

Wynne allowed herself to be led into another room, where a great oak tub bound with large bands of polished brass sat steaming with the evidence of its hot water. Megan swiftly aided her new mistress to remove her clothing and then helped her into the tub.

"Ohhh," Wynne said as the warm water touched her skin. "That's wonderful! Thank you, Megan, for being so thoughtful."

"You will find a stool to sit upon, my lady, and while you enjoy the water I will take your clothing to the laundress."

Only when she had hurried out did Wynne realize that for the first time in days she was totally and completely alone. It was quite a lovely feeling. She glanced about the room. *A bathing room.* It was a most novel and yet practical idea. The tub obviously remained in it all the time and did not have to be put out of sight in some cabinet. Where did the water come from? Wynne wondered. Then as she looked about her, her eye fell upon what she had at first thought to be a stone sink. It was not, however, for about it hung a bucket. This bathing room had its own well for water! The idea was simple and yet so obvious. And, of course, the water was heated in the large fireplace that took up almost an entire wall of the room, for there was a large cauldron hanging to one side away from the flame now. And the fireplace heated the bathing room as well! There was even a window through which she could see those wonderful mountains. It was all most marvelous!

The gardens. A bathing room. The mountains. It wasn't going to be very difficult to be happy here at Raven's Rock. It was, of course, much larger than the manor house at Gwernach had been. She hadn't seen the cook house yet, or the bakery, or met any of the servants, but there was plenty of time for that. It amazed her that the castle was in such good order, considering that Madoc's mother had been dead for several years. Nesta must be an excellent chatelaine, and she had but three months to learn from her all she needed to know about the domestic arrangements if she were to do as well.

Wynne's thoughts came to a screeching halt. What on earth was she thinking? She didn't want to marry, yet here she was considering all she would need to know regarding the concerns of Madoc's home. She was in a trap, and the trap was slowly closing about her. She was being wooed by Madoc's charm and patience, and now by his wonderful castle. It wasn't fair. Everything was conspiring against her, and yet . . . She stemmed the tide of her anger. She must be coolly logical about this situation in which she found herself. What exactly was wrong with it? Why had she been so determined all her life not to marry?

She reviewed the facts in her mind. Her father had betrothed her to Madoc. She was to be free to refuse the marriage if she chose. Madoc had agreed to it. Her father would not have made the match if Madoc were not a good man. Owain ap Llywelyn was not a man to be swayed by wealth and prestige. Madoc was attractive, albeit in a mysterious way. He was kind, thoughtful, and patient. He said he was in love with her and that he wanted her to love him. He offered her a life of comfort and happiness. Logically, she could find nothing wrong with any of this.

Even she, in her sheltered life at Gwernach, had heard of a woman for whom a man's touch was unpleasant. Such was not the case with her. Indeed, she found Madoc's kisses most delightful; and she was quite curious to learn more of passion between a man and a woman. They were long past the time when the Celtic tribes roamed the earth and her people considered physical love between men and women a natural thing to be enjoyed with whomever and whenever the spirit moved one. In these times people were not quite as enthusiastic or open with one another; but passion was not an emotion of which Wynne was afraid. Certainly a woman was free to enjoy the physical aspects of love with her betrothed husband.

A time long past. The words slid unbidden into her consciousness. The ancient Celts had believed in reincarnation. It was not a teaching of the Church, and yet Wynne had often wondered why the Church did not teach it. There was nothing in reincarnation, as the Celts had believed it, that was at odds with Christ's teachings. *Reincarnation.* It was not talked about a great deal, and yet many still believed. Did she? Was that the reason behind her unexplained antipathy to marriage? And if it was, why?

Had Wynne of Gwernach and Madoc of Powys known each other in another time and another place? And if they had, what had happened that she was so opposed to marriage? She was certainly not opposed to Madoc. Indeed, she was increasingly attracted to him, but it did not seem to be enough. What unfinished business lay between them? Or was she being a fool? Was her aversion to marriage actually fear of the unknown, and was she placing greater importance upon it than it deserved? She determined to put it all, her worries, her curiosity, from her mind. She would concentrate upon accepting her marriage instead of struggling so futilely against what was in reality a most pleasant fate.

The door to the bathing room opened and Megan hurried in, chattering as she came. "I apologize, my lady, for taking so long a time with the laundress." She picked up soap and a cloth and began to wash her new mistress. "Well, actually it wasn't the laundress that kept me. It was that big handsome fellow with the game leg who is your servant. Insisted upon knowing precisely where you were. He's most protective of you."

Wynne laughed. " 'Tis his task, Megan, to watch over me. He has ever since I was a baby. My brother sent him with me to Raven's Rock; but you'd best beware of Einion. He's a merry rascal who loves a pretty wench. *All* pretty wenches for that matter."

"Oh, I could see he has a roving eye," Megan said, her brown eyes twinkling, "but I've a roving eye myself. Now, let's get that beautiful hair of yours washed, my lady. It is filled with the dust of the road!"

Einion, Wynne thought as Megan washed her long hair, had possibly met his match. It would not be a bad thing, for as Einion was to remain at Raven's Rock for the remainder of his days, it was probably time for him to find a wife and settle down. Wynne smiled to herself, wondering what her beloved protector would think of her thoughts, and knowing, even as she began to chuckle over it.

❧Chapter 5

*H*er intellect had decided one thing. The voice within disagreed; but Wynne would not listen. She thrust her instinct as far away from her conscious mind as she could and concentrated upon resigning herself to a life at Raven's Rock as Madoc's wife. She began that first night, entering the hall garbed in a beautiful tunic dress of violet silk brocade embroidered with silver flowers. Going directly to Madoc, she had knelt before him, publicly subjugating herself to her lord's will.

The prince, more attuned to Wynne than she could have imagined, quickly raised her up and presented her to his assembled retainers and servants. "I submit to you Wynne of Gwernach, the future princess of Powys. Those of you within her domain will do her bidding without question, and all will render their respect," Madoc said in a strong voice.

"Wynne! Wynne! Wynne!" came the cry from a hundred throats as she looked out, smiling over the hall.

"You will never kneel to me again, dearling," he told her. "As my wife you are my female equal, my other half." Then he put a goblet of wine in her hand, kissing it as he did so.

They sat at the high board and Wynne said, "There are so many men, my lord. Are there no women here at Raven's Rock but Nesta and the servants?"

"None," he replied. "My mother had no liking for strangers. As she and Nesta were content, I was content. If it displeases you, however, you may invite the daughters of other houses to keep you company."

"When Nesta goes to St. Bride's I shall be alone, my lord. Perhaps my brother will allow my little sister, Mair, to come to us."

"Your grandmother will be lonely without Mair. I can see she quite dotes upon the child," Madoc remarked.

"My mother died quite unexpectedly giving birth to Mair,"

Wynne told him. "Grandmother has raised Mair, and she is more a daughter to her than a grandchild."

"Your grandmother could come to Raven's Rock if you desired it, my dearling," Madoc offered.

"Grandmother must remain with Dewi," Wynne reminded him. "My brother cannot oversee Gwernach without guidance."

"I promised you that I would send someone to aid the boy, Wynne. Tomorrow you will speak with the man I have chosen to be your brother's bailiff. His name is David. He is a loyal and clever man. When my brother Brys went to Castle Cai, I sent David to be the bailiff. My stepfather was incapable of managing his estate, and Brys was too young and inexperienced. He was, in fact, just Dewi's age. David tells me that they got on quite well. If your instincts warn you otherwise though, you must tell me and I will choose another. If David and Dewi do well together, I think your grandmother would enjoy coming to Raven's Rock. We could offer her great comforts in her old age, and in our house Mair could aspire to a more important family from which to choose a husband than she could at Gwernach. What say you, lady?"

"You are so good, my lord," Wynne answered him ingenuously. "You seem to have a care for my feelings at every turn. I do not know if I shall ever be able to match your solicitude. Yes, I should like to have my grandmother and sister here with me at Raven's Rock if I could be certain my brother was safe."

"David, with your permission, will go to Gwernach shortly; and if all is well with the arrangement, then the lady Enid and Mair will come to live at Gwernach after our marriage," he told her.

"Not before?" Her disappointment was quite evident. "Nesta will be wed at the Solstice. I shall be alone the whole winter long."

He smiled. "I want that time for us, dearling, that we may truly learn to know one another with no other distractions. You will not want for entertainment, I promise you," he said, and his look was suddenly smoldering.

She felt her bones turning to jelly in an all now familiar pattern, and she knew that he knew it. Her breathing was suddenly quick and her tongue flicked out to moisten her lips, which had gone dry. "What is this magic you do, my lord?" she said low.

He smiled a slow smile and, leaning forward, kissed her lips in a leisurely fashion. Wynne found she could not pull away. She wasn't even certain that she wanted to pull away.

"I think the time has come for us to progress past kissing," he told her softly.

"When?" she asked breathlessly, and then blushed, wondering what he must think of such unmaidenly, such unseemly eagerness.

"Very soon," he promised.

"What comes after kissing?" she inquired.

"Caressing," he told her.

"Who caresses whom?"

He chuckled. "I caress you, dearling, and you caress me."

"How do I caress you?" she demanded.

"I will instruct you most thoroughly in the art, you charmingly shameless wench," he said, laughing now.

"Oh, Madoc," she said, and his heart quickened, for she so rarely used his name, "is it wrong for me to be curious and eager? I truly am and I cannot help it. When you kiss me I find I am beset by feelings I do not understand, but I also find I want to go forward that I may learn what follows. I have had no mother to teach me, and Grandmother has said little regarding the relations between men and women."

"Ahh, dearling," he said, and his voice was tight with his own emotions, "I am glad you have *feelings* for me, even if you do not understand them. They are not wrong, and I am glad you do not fear me."

"Madoc, my brother," said Nesta, breaking into their conversation, "I think it is time that Wynne and I retired. We have not slept in a decent bed in several days, and she must be as exhausted as I am."

Wynne arose from the high board and, seeing her do so, Gwyn and Megan left their places at the table, below the salt, to follow their two mistresses from the hall.

The two girls kissed each other good night, and Nesta, yawning copiously, entered her own sleeping chamber gratefully. Wynne had not paid a great deal of attention to her own chamber earlier. Not in the least sleepy, she looked with interest about the room. There was a fine fireplace in which a good blaze now burned, and the room was quite warm and toasty. Beautiful tapestries woven in soft roses, blues, greens, and a natural cream color showed gentle landscapes filled with flowers, birds, and butterflies. They hung from ceiling to floor, covering much of the cold stone walls. Wynne had never seen anything like them.

Her windows opened onto a mountain and garden view. There were three fine-carved chests for her belongings, a table, a chair with a woven seat and a cushion, and a large, beautiful bed with pale rose curtains that appeared to have been spun from a spider's web, although actually it was simply a delicate sheer wool. Wynne was enchanted by them, for she realized they would keep her bed quite draft-free and yet they were exquisite. The bed was piled high with a featherbed and the most beautiful fluffy white furs she had ever seen.

Megan helped her from her elegant garments, taking even her chemise, to Wynne's surprise; but she quickly replaced it with a loose-fitting garment with long, billowing sleeves. The gown was of the finest sheer linen. "Your sleeping robe, my lady," Megan said as she laced it shut with silken ribbons that ran from navel to neck.

"I've never had one," Wynne admitted. "It's lovely."

"You'll find many things here that exist nowhere else in our land," Megan told her. "Our lord prince has traveled as far as Byzantium." She then walked over to a small door set in the wall and opened it. "Your necessary, my lady," she explained.

Peering in, Wynne saw a small stone bench set between the walls with a neat round hole carved in it. On a shelf above it a bronze oil lamp burned. Next to the seat a pile of neatly folded cloths had been placed. "This is truly amazing," Wynne said.

" 'Tis but one of a thousand things that will astound you, my lady. Raven's Rock is truly like no other place." She shut the door to the necessary and said briskly, "Let me brush out your beautiful hair and then I'll help you into bed, my lady. You must be exhausted with all your travel." She undid the single, heavy braid Wynne favored, untangling it with supple fingers, brushing the hair until it shone like a swatch of black silk, then pinning it up so her mistress could sleep more comfortably.

"There's a bed space for me in the little chamber where I

hang your garments, my lady. Your Einion will have his bed space with the prince's body servant, Barris, in our lord's dressing chamber."

"But are you warm enough? Surely the hall would be warmer for you."

Megan was touched by Wynne's concern. "Do not fret, my lady Wynne. The fireplace from my lord's reading chamber backs up against the bed spaces. We are all quite comfortable. The prince would have it no other way. He is a good master and there is none better!"

Wynne had seen this loyalty all day long since their arrival at Raven's Rock; Megan's easy assurances and her obvious devotion to Madoc were all such good signs, Wynne thought after the servant had left her alone. Everything was going to be fine once she accepted it and stopped fretting at every turn.

Wynne tried to sleep, but she couldn't. She was simply too excited by her arrival here and all the wonderful things she had seen this day. Impatiently she arose from her bed, throwing back the lavender-scented sheets and the warm furs. Walking over to her windows, she gazed out. There was a wide crescent moon hanging in the heavens, but it was not so bright that she could not see the myriad stars scattered so generously by the celestial hand across the dark night skies. It was all so beautiful and so magical that she sighed with the pure pleasure of just viewing it. An arm slipped about her waist, and Wynne leaned back against the man who held her in his tender embrace.

"You are not surprised that I am here," Madoc said, and it was a statement more than a question.

"Nay," she answered him quietly, "for I knew that you were as eager for the caressing as I was, my lord."

He laughed low. "Do you always say exactly what you think, Wynne?"

"Aye, the truth is best, I have been taught."

"Are you not curious as to how I came into your chamber, my dearling?" He bent to kiss her shoulder.

"There are three doors within this chamber, my lord," she told him. "One leads into your reading chamber. One to the necessary. The other, I assume, leads to your sleeping chamber. This is the room of the prince's wife. Logic dictates there would be a way from your chamber to mine."

"You are quite observant," he noted, his fingers skillfully unlacing her sleeping robe, even as he planted little kisses along the column of her neck.

"What are you doing?" Her voice sounded high in her own ears, and her heart was beginning to flutter quite rapidly.

"Does not logic tell you that to caress you properly I must undo your robe?" he teased her.

"Can you not caress me through the cloth?" she asked him, catching at his hands.

"I could," he agreed, "but it would not be half as pleasurable for either of us, dearling." He gently pushed her hands away and concluded his task.

Wynne's sleeping robe fell open from belly to throat. Madoc gently slipped the gown over her shoulders and it slid quickly to the floor, leaving her quite naked. "Ohh," she cried, surprised, for she had not expected him to bare her. It was the first of several shocks, for as he drew her back against him, she realized that he too was without a garment. "Ohhhh!" she said a second time. And "Ohhhhhhh!" a third time, as his hands slipped beneath her small breasts to cup them gently within the palms of his hands.

"Don't be afraid, sweeting," he murmured, kissing her ear as he spoke and then nibbling on it gently.

"I'm not," she replied somewhat breathlessly, "I just did not expect *this*. Not so soon." She drew a deep breath and, releasing it, sighed luxuriously. "I like your hands, my lord."

He fondled her flesh with a light touch, his thumbs softly teasing at her nipples, which contracted themselves into taut little buds. She murmured her approval, unconsciously pressing herself back against him. Madoc drew a sudden sharp breath, for he found his betrothed wife far more delicious than he knew he should at this point in their relationship. Bending, he kissed the point where her neck and her shoulder met, savoring the sweet, clean fragrance of her.

Wynne's eyes had closed, seemingly of their own volition, at the onset of his caress. She relaxed, thoroughly enjoying his touch and the delightful feelings engendered by his skillful hands. Her arms lay limp by her sides; her head lay back against his shoulder. It was lovely, and she almost purred, cat-like.

Madoc released one of her breasts, and his hands swirled

downward, brushing in circles over the flesh of her torso and belly. Wynne gasped softly and stiffened beneath his touch now. "Nay, dearling," he crooned low, "I'll not hurt you."

His fingers were sending rather sharp darts of excitement through her veins. "When," Wynne said, her voice slightly shaky, "when, my lord, do I learn to caress y-you?"

In answer he turned her about so that they were facing one another, and his mouth swooped down to find hers in a deep, burning kiss. "Now!" he almost groaned against her lips.

With trembling fingers she ran her hands over his muscular shoulders as he continued to kiss her, softly now, nibbling on her lower lip until, confused, she half whispered, "Stop, I beg you, my lord!"

He instantly ceased and stood silent.

Half shyly, half boldly, Wynne slid her hands over his smooth skin. Her touch was like a wave flirting with a beach. It came and then it fled back, unsure, never venturing farther than his waist. Madoc cupped her buttocks in his hands, and Wynne then followed his lead, her small hands fondling him with now daring abandon. "Does it pleasure you, my lord?"

"Perhaps too much so, dearling," came the answer, and he released his hold on her bottom, sliding his arms about her waist to draw her even closer to him.

She could feel his male organ pressing against her leg. She had not dared to gaze upon it yet, but it seemed quite hard and very big. Her palms flattened themselves against his smooth chest and she moved them with growing assurance in small circles over his skin. "I should like another kiss, Madoc," she told him, and he most eagerly complied, sending new flashes of heat racing through her body. "Ahhhhh, my lord," she said, "kissing and caressing together gives one even greater pleasure! Is it the same for you?"

The blood was thundering in his ears. What in the name of all common sense had ever made him think he could do this without wanting to make total love to her? Was he receiving pleasure as she was? Dear God, aye! But it was all he could do to refrain from taking her here and now. He forced himself to answer her. "How could I not receive pleasure from so soft a hand and such sweet lips, Wynne?" Releasing her, he bent and, slipping her sleeping gown back over her delightful little body, laced it with shaking fingers.

When he had stepped back she had seen his state and, reaching down, she took him in her hand.

Madoc groaned as if in dire pain.

Another woman might have drawn away, but she did not. Instead she caressed him gently, saying as she did so, "How strong and mighty is this lance of yours, Madoc of Powys. Why do you cry out? Does my touch hurt you?"

"I ache to possess you, dearling," he told her. "There is no fault in you."

"I am not ready yet to give myself totally to you," she replied.

To which he answered, "I know. I thought I might teach you of pleasure tonight, but I find I cannot touch you, Wynne, without wanting you."

"I desire you also, Madoc," was the surprising answer, "but again I say I am not quite ready to allow you possession of my body and my soul." She withdrew her curious hand.

"No one can ever possess another's soul, dearling," he said.

"Yet there is a meeting of souls when two lovers truly love one another, isn't there, my lord?"

He nodded slowly, again surprised by her intuitiveness.

"We have been lovers in another time and another place," Wynne said. "Have we not?"

"Aye."

"Tell me, for you know, I am certain of it!" Wynne said.

"I cannot, dearling. You must remember. It is part of our fate that you do. I can tell you nothing that you do not learn for yourself." He put his arms about her and drew her close.

There was a scent to him, Wynne realized, as she pressed her cheek against his shoulder. Unable to help herself, she kissed the skin beneath her lips. "Since my earliest memory, I have had a dream, Madoc," she began. "I have never understood this dream, but now I think it may have something to do with us."

"Tell me," he begged.

She rubbed her face against him. "There is little to tell. It is always the same and there is no sense to it."

"Tell me!" His plea was urgent now.

"I am in mist. There is much sadness. I can feel it all about me. It permeates the very air. I hear a voice calling, and above me a raven soars, crying the word, *Remember*. Then I awaken weeping. It is always the same."

"What does the voice say to you, Wynne?" he asked her gently.

"It calls out a name," she answered him, "but I cannot make out the name, Madoc, try as I will."

He held her tightly and said, "It is a start."

"Do you understand my dream?" she asked, drawing away and looking up at him.

"Aye, I do." His face was sad.

"But you cannot tell me," Wynne said.

He shook his head. "You must learn for yourself, dearling."

"*How?*" she demanded.

"I am not certain yet, but perhaps there is a way to unlock your memory, Wynne. Helping you to learn what you must know is not, I believe, like telling you. I must think on it else we find ourselves at an impasse, and that I cannot allow." Their talk had cooled his passions, and he kissed her upon her forehead. "You really must rest, my dearling. These last few days have been tiring for you." He picked her up and, carrying her across the chamber, settled her gently in her bed.

"It is a very large bed," she noted. "Lie by me for a while, Madoc."

"Nay, my love, for if I do, I will finish what I so foolishly started tonight. You must trust me when I tell you that the time is not yet right." Then before she might protest, he was gone from the room through the door into his own chamber.

For several minutes Wynne lay silently in the dark. It was so confusing, and yet it was also fascinating. And passion. She smiled to herself. The more she learned of passion, the better she liked it. Madoc's touch had been a revelation. Shyly she touched herself, feeling her nipples grow tight, and yet it wasn't the same. Pleasurable, but not the same. Suddenly she found herself most sleepy. There was so much to see and to learn here at Raven's Rock. She sighed and was asleep.

In the days that followed, Wynne learned all she needed to know about the functioning of Raven's Rock Castle from Nesta. There were many innovations here that she would have never dreamed of, although she found them most practical. There was no cook house. The kitchens were instead located within the castle itself on a lower level. There was a kitchen garden within the main gardens set comfortably against a castle wall. They grew lettuce, peas, carrots, beets, marrows, and parsnips, Nesta told her, as well as simple kitchen herbs like parsley, rosemary, sage, and thyme. There was a small orchard with apple, peach, and cherry trees.

The servants were pleasant souls, eager to please her. From the morning after her arrival, she found she was expected to give the cook the menus for the day. He was a large, jolly man who shared his kitchens with his younger brother, who was the castle's baker. When Wynne admitted she was unused to so large a home, both the cook and the baker told her, smiling, that she would soon be used to it all. In the meantime they would help her to cope.

"You'll have no difficulties," Nesta assured Wynne. "You ran Gwernach quite well. Raven's Rock is only a matter of getting used to the greater number of people to care for, and I will help you."

"Where does Madoc's wealth come from?" Wynne asked Nesta one day.

"There are several sources," Nesta said, "for our family has always thought it unwise to put all one's hopes on one thing. The glens below us open out into a large single valley. It is ours. We graze our cattle there. There was a period after my father died that Madoc left Raven's Rock and traveled to Byzantium. Our family has always been involved in trading."

"But Raven's Rock is not near the sea," Wynne said.

"It doesn't have to be," Nesta replied. "Here is where the princes of Powys-Wenwynwyn live; but our trading houses are located in the cities along the coast of our own Wales, of England and in Ireland as well. We have factors in the land of the Franks and in cities along an ancient sea that one sails to get to Byzantium; and we have a great trading house in Byzantium itself. Then, too, my brother makes investments in other trading ventures. Caravans that travel to Jerusalem and beyond. It is all quite complicated. I don't really understand half of it, but if you are curious, ask Madoc. He loves to speak on his own cleverness, and will go on for hours if you allow him."

Wynne laughed. "I do not think that is kind, sister," she said. "I think Madoc must be very clever to be so rich."

The autumn months waned as the hills grew golden with passing time, finally fading into December. Now the only colors to be seen were the green of the pines and the grays, blacks, and browns of the winter hillsides. The Solstice was upon them, and with it, Nesta and Rhys's wedding.

Rhys arrived at Raven's Rock as Madoc had instructed him, two days before the marriage was to be celebrated. He came with a party of a hundred men; and accompanied by his cousins, the lords of Coed and Llyn; their wives; the young lord of Gwernach, his grandmother, and his sister. Madoc had sent David the bailiff to Gwernach several weeks after Wynne had come to Raven's Rock. She had interviewed the man and found him to be everything that Madoc had said he was.

"I realize my brother is young," Wynne had told David, "but unless you are absolutely certain that he is wrong, you must defer to him in all things. He will not learn otherwise, and his pride is great."

"Not unlike the pride of most men, my lady," David replied, a twinkle in his eyes, and Wynne liked him even more for it.

With David overseeing Gwernach, Dewi ap Owain was free to come to Raven's Rock to attend Nesta's wedding to Rhys. His eyes widened at the wonders he saw, but as impressed as he was with Raven's Rock, he could not help but say most bluntly, "I still prefer Gwernach."

"And so you should," Wynne agreed. "It is your home."

"A fool never changes," Caitlin muttered to her brother. "This place is paradise, and you prefer that dung heap from which we sprang forth? I'd sell my soul to Satan himself to have all this!" And she gestured broadly about the hall with her hand.

"Are you not content at Coed then?" Wynne questioned her sister.

" 'Tis a fair enough place, but much like Gwernach, to be honest with you," Caitlin replied. "I've had more than enough to do to put it in order to suit me, but now that I've gotten the lady Blodwen out of the house, 'twill be easier. There is much I see here that I can adapt to a smaller home, but perhaps I shall just enlarge it instead." She looked thoughtful.

"What has happened to the lady Blodwen?" Wynne asked, more than curious to learn how Caitlin had rid herself of her mother-in-law.

"Oh, she's gone to St. Frideswide's Convent, where she will

end her days. She's quite comfortable, but she is out of my hair at last," Caitlin said in a pleased tone.

"And just how did you get her to leave?" Wynne demanded. "The truth, Caitlin!"

Caitlin laughed smugly and then lowered her voice. "I would not want Arthwr to hear, for I promised the fat old cow I would keep her secret from her son in return for her voluntary departure." Caitlin's voice dipped lower. "I caught my dear mother-in-law in the bakehouse, her skirts bunched up about her waist, bent over a table stuffing her face with cakes and sweetmeats while the baker, his rough hands grasping her fleshy hips, pumped her full of his own cream. It was not the first time I had seen her thus, but I waited to expose her until I was certain it was a regular occurrence. Old Blodwen is lewd beyond all, although to look at her one would not guess it. She visited the bakehouse at least four times a week, and at her age too!" Caitlin finished, sounding just the tiniest bit aggrieved.

"So you forced her from her home and into a convent?" Wynne exclaimed. "Was that not harsh, sister?"

"I cannot have such a creature about to debauch my children with her shamelessness," Caitlin said primly, her hands touching her belly for the briefest moment. "Her behavior was inexcusable, and she would not have changed it had I allowed her to remain. Really, Wynne! A discreet lover of our own class I could have forgiven, but sister, she was swiving the baker!"

"And what happened to the baker?" Enid asked, curious.

"I told Arthwr that he had offended me, and I had him well flogged. He got off lightly, Grandmother, and the baker is no fool. He took his whipping and went back to his ovens. I could have had his life."

"But to do that," Wynne noted, "you would have had to expose the lady Blodwen, and then you would not have had such a good bargaining chip. Perhaps she would not have gone willingly at all."

Caitlin nodded. "Do not frown so at me, Wynne. Blodwen is as comfortable at St. Frideswide's as she was at Coed. Arthwr has seen to that, for he loves her well. She will have an unending supply of sweetmeats."

"And just what excuse did you give your husband for shipping his mother to a convent?" Enid said.

"Well," said Caitlin, sounding smug again, "the old cow

was forever going on about the delicate state of her health, and
so she told Arthwr that being in the house with a squalling infant would be more than she could bear, even if the infant was
her grandchild."

"You are expecting a baby?" Wynne looked closely at her
sister.

"Of course!" Caitlin replied. "Can you not tell? Arthwr says
I bloom more beauteously every day his son grows within
me."

"My child," Enid scolded her, "you might have told me!
When is your baby due?"

"In the month of June," Caitlin answered her grandmother.
"I conceived my son when we returned to Coed, immediately
after our marriage. Arthwr is a lusty lover."

"I conceived my son on my wedding night." Dilys spoke up
quite suddenly. "Howel is most pleased with me. He says I
have all the earmarks of being a good breeder," she finished
proudly.

Enid shook her head in wonder. "And when is your child
due to enter the world, Dilys?" she asked dryly.

"Certainly before Caitlin's," was the self-satisfied reply. "It
is I, dear grandmother, who will give you your very first great-
grandson."

Wynne looked to Nesta, who was as near to laughter as she
herself was. Distance had made the pettiness engendered by
her sisters seem quite funny. Like her brother, Wynne could
not like her next two siblings, try as she might. The entire time
they were at Raven's Rock they were never still. They prowled
about inspecting every intimate detail of the castle, its possessions, its workings. They were openly envious of their elder
sister, jealous of Wynne's good fortune, which each assured all
who would listen really belonged to her.

Wynne was too busy, however, to pay a great deal of attention to her sisters, as the burden of Nesta's wedding had fallen
upon her. The wedding feast would be one that was worthy of
the sister of a prince of Powys. There would be over three
hundred people, retainers included, to be fed, but Wynne was
now confident in her ability to provide enough food. There
were to be twelve tubs of oysters that had been brought from
the coast set in tubs of cracked ice and snow off the nearby
mountains. Four sides of beef packed in rock salt were to be

roasted in the great spits in the kitchens. There would be a whole ox and two roe deer, as well as hams, geese, ducks; rabbit stew flavored with onions, parsley, and carrots; partridge pies; platters of quail roasted to a golden turn; and a peacock stuffed with dried fruit, which would be presented with all of its beautiful feathers intact upon a silver salver. There was trout that had been caught in the local streams, to be broiled in butter and lemon; salmon upon cress; and cod prepared in cream and sweet wine. There would be tiny green peas, little boiled beets, and new lettuce steamed in white wine with leeks and capers.

The bakers had worked overtime to produce all the fine white bread that Wynne demanded of them, to be eaten by those served above the salt. For those below there would be cottage loaves and good brown bread. There was butter and honey in abundance, as well as several different cheeses, among them six wheels of Gwernach Gold brought by Dewi ap Owain. There were sugar wafers, and both candied angelica and violets as well as several large apple tarts that would be served with heavy cream. A bridal cake of spun sugar and marzipan was to be the final delight to be enjoyed by all the guests; and all the tables would contain bowls of apples and pears.

To drink, there would be beer and October ale and several varieties of wine. Madoc's cellars were deep, and Wynne made certain that no one would go thirsty. As a special treat she had arranged for those at the high board to have mead, a festive and most deceptively potent drink made from honey. Mead was known to make the blood flow hotly and was said to be a great stimulus to an eager bridegroom.

On that account Rhys of St. Bride's certainly qualified, for his three months' absence from Nesta of Powys had only served to increase his ardor for her. It was a passion that Nesta fully reciprocated. To see them together was to understand the meaning of the word *love*. It was unfortunate, Wynne thought sadly, that seeing it, she could not herself feel the same emotion. Nesta and Rhys seemed to be bound by some slim and invisible thread. They could scarce wait for their wedding day, for they longed to be united in marriage.

Madoc had calculated the very moment of the Winter Solstice, and it was at exactly that moment that the bridal couple were formally united in marriage. Nesta, as radiant as the winter sun itself, was garbed in gold, a fitting background for her dark red hair and her creamy skin. Her tunic dress was made of gold silk, sewn all over with pearls and gold thread. Both the hem and the wide sleeves were edged in rich brown marten. Her under tunic was of cream-colored silk, the material having been woven with narrow bands of pure beaten gold. The tunic dress was belted with a loose-fitting rope of twisted gold with pearl tassels. A gold torque enameled in green and blue was fastened about Nesta's slender neck and sat upon her neckbones above her rounded neckline. She wore pearls in her ears, and a gold and pearl band encircled her head, holding her long, flowing hair in place. Upon her feet were dainty gold kid slippers.

Rhys was as resplendent as his beautiful bride. He was garbed in a full-skirted kirtle of red and gold brocade, the open neck of which was decorated with garnets and pearls. The tunic was belted with links of gold. As his kirtle was long, only his boots showed, but they were boots such as the guests had never seen. Of red leather! The bridegroom carried no sword. To come armed into his own wedding would have been considered an insult of the highest order.

They were a handsome couple, and when the priest had pronounced them man and wife, Rhys kissed Nesta heartily to the cheers of all the guests. The music began almost immediately. There would be dancing after the feasting was over. An ancient minstrel entertained them, singing in a voice that was incredibly sure and sweet for one so old. Once the minstrel had roamed the world singing his songs, but now he lived out his years in comfortable retirement at Raven's Rock. The knowledge of the minstrel's history had endeared Madoc to Wynne a small bit. She appreciated this new evidence of Madoc's kindness to others.

"You have done well," Madoc complimented her as the evening progressed. "I can find nothing that has been overlooked. You have more than honored my sister and her husband. I am grateful, dearling."

Wynne flushed with pleasure at his words. Never before had she overseen so large a gathering, and toward the end, as her wedding day approached, Nesta, attacked by bridal nerves, had been virtually useless. "It is good, my lord," she agreed. "All our guests seem to be enjoying themselves. The mark of my great success is that not once has my sister Caitlin complained this evening. She seems satisfied with her place at the high board, the food, the music, everything! Do you think that impending motherhood is mellowing her?"

"More likely she is at a loss for words," Madoc replied, and then he murmured low so that only she could hear, "how beautiful you look tonight, Wynne. Green and gold are surely your colors. How I wish that this were our wedding feast, but alas, we must wait until Beltaine."

His words set her heart to racing. Madoc of Powys was a very romantic man, as she was beginning to learn. She found that she was anxious to be alone with him. She would be very glad when all her guests had departed to their own homes. He had been correct when he said that they needed time together. They did. She wanted to know him better. Wanted to learn what it was that bound them together, yet made her fearful of linking her life with his once again. She suddenly knew that she wanted to overcome whatever barrier it was that lay between them.

Wynne looked up at her betrothed husband and saw that he was smiling. "Villain!" she accused, rapping his hand lightly. "You have been intruding upon my thoughts again." She sighed deeply. "Madoc, you are incorrigible!"

"I love you," he said simply, as if that should excuse him.

Wynne laughed. "What am I to do with you, Madoc of Powys?"

"Love me, dearling," he told her. " 'Tis all I desire of you."

"No," she answered him, suddenly serious. "There is more, but it will come, I know. I feel myself changing here at Raven's Rock."

The bride and groom were put to bed with much good-natured teasing and ribaldry. The guests all found their own assigned sleeping spaces. In the morning, from the window of Nesta's chamber, a crimson-stained sheet was hung, bloodied proof of her virgin state and of Rhys of St. Bride's masculine prowess. The guests, well-breakfasted, began to depart. Wynne, returning to her bedchamber to change her shoes, for the ones she wore chafed her, was surprised to hear Nesta's voice coming from Madoc's chamber. Curious, she moved across the room, not really meaning to eavesdrop, but unable to help herself.

"You are happy?" she heard Madoc say.

"Aye," Nesta replied, "I am very happy, but I fear for you, my brother. Brys came yesterday, I know it. Did you think you could keep it from me?"

"He got only as far as the bridge that spans the river before I sent him away. He will not bother you again, Nesta."

"Oh, Madoc, 'tis not me he seeks to hurt, but you! He feels for you the same hate our father felt for your father, Gwalchmal. The same bitterness. The same envy. It seems to breed deep within him. It's a terrible curse, my brother. Black and evil."

"He cannot hurt me, Nesta," Madoc reassured his sister. "He knows the extent of my powers."

"He knows that despite your powers you are a soft-hearted soul. A man loath to destroy any living thing. If Brys had your powers, he would willingly and eagerly destroy you, and he would take pleasure in it. Perhaps you yourself are not vulnerable, Madoc, but you are vulnerable now through your love for Wynne."

"Brys knows nothing of Wynne."

"He knows!" Nesta said positively. "Oh, perhaps he did not know that you betrothed yourself to an infant those long years ago, but you may be certain that he now knows your betrothed wife resides within this castle! He is a part of it, Madoc! An important part of it! Has Wynne had no glimpse of memory yet?"

"She has had a dream since childhood," Madoc said, and then he related her dream to Nesta, "but there has been nothing else."

"She has to know the truth, Madoc. Particularly lest Brys try to destroy your happiness once more," Nesta said firmly.

"I cannot tell her, Nesta, and you know it. She must remember herself," Madoc told his sister.

"You can help her, Madoc, without telling her, and well you know that!" Nesta responded hotly.

Wynne was absolutely fascinated by the conversation between brother and sister. What did it all mean? She hoped against hope that no one would come into the prince's apartments and discover her listening. She wanted to hear more.

"I had hoped," she heard Madoc answer, "that being here with me at Raven's Rock, she would begin to remember on her own."

"You have little time left, brother. Your marriage is scheduled for the first of May. *Help her!* I cannot go to St. Bride's and be content, knowing of the dangers you both face from Brys, unless this matter between us is resolved once and for all. I love Wynne, Madoc. As she once was, she is again, the sweetest of souls," Nesta said, her voice filled with emotion.

"I will take your advice, sister," Madoc answered, "but now you must find your husband and depart, for I am eager to be alone with my own fair lady."

Wynne fled swiftly into her room, hearing his words. She would have been very embarrassed to have been caught listening to what had been a very private conversation. Changing her shoes, she returned to the Great Hall just in time to bid Nesta and Rhys a fond farewell; escorting them along with Madoc out into the main courtyard of Raven's Rock Castle, where their horses and their men awaited them.

Nesta, radiant with her own happiness, hugged Wynne warmly. "I shall come for your wedding in the spring," she promised.

"I wish you did not have to leave so soon," Wynne said.

"There is a storm coming," Nesta predicted, "and we would be wise to be well out of the mountains before it strikes."

"But the Christ's Mass is in just a few days," Wynne fretted. "You will still be on the road."

"Then we will celebrate it on the road." Nesta laughed. "I long to be in my own home. From the look of Rhys when he first arrived, I shall have much to do to make St. Bride's Castle habitable." She hugged Wynne a final time and kissed her upon the cheek. "Take care of Madoc, Wynne, and should you meet our brother Brys, beware of him. He has the look of the angels, but he is the devil's spawn."

"Wife!" roared Rhys, looking mightily pleased with himself and quite happy, "will you linger all day gossiping with our sister in the courtyard? To horse, I say!"

"Aye, my lord," Nesta answered meekly with a small wink at Wynne, and he lifted her into her saddle, putting her reins in her hands.

Madoc put his arm about Wynne. Together they waved the

lord and lady of St. Bride's off, standing at the entrance to Raven's Rock until their guests disappeared from sight around a bend in the road. "And now, dearling, we are alone," he said, smiling into her face.

"I am content with that, Madoc," Wynne replied serenely, and she smiled back as they turned to reenter the castle.

Chapter 6

Nesta, who Wynne had learned was weather sensitive, had been correct about the coming storm. Late the following afternoon after a still, grey day, the snow began to fall. It fell throughout the night. Delicate little crystallized flakes that clung to whatever they touched, until the castle and the land about them was frosted entirely in white. The windows were rimmed in icy patterns of beautiful design. And the storm had brought with it a deep stillness that penetrated even into the castle.

They were alone in the Great Hall, and it seemed so large with the servants gone to their beds. Fires crackled in the four big fireplaces, sparks occasionally shooting from the burning logs with a noisy pop that invariably startled. They had ridden the previous afternoon, after the last of their guests departed. Madoc agreed with his sister about the coming storm and said they should take the opportunity to get out while they still could. Today Wynne had overseen the servants as they restored Raven's Rock to normality following the celebration.

They sat most companionably together, enjoying a rich, sweet wine, and for a time Madoc played upon a small reed instrument. Suddenly he put it down and, looking directly at her, said, "What is it that frets you, Wynne? I can feel your distress."

"It came to me," she replied, "that I had not seen old Dhu, my raven, in several days. I had not thought to look for him, with all the last minute preparations for Nesta's wedding. We rode all yesterday afternoon and he did not appear. Now with the storm upon us, I worry that he is all right. He is quite old for a bird, Madoc."

"And does this ugly black creature mean so much to you, Wynne, that it would trouble your slumber?"

"He is not ugly!" Wynne defended the bird. "I consider him most handsome for a raven."

Madoc laughed. "Why does this beastie mean so much to you, dearling, that you would safeguard him against even me?"

"Old Dhu has been my friend my whole life," Wynne said softly. "I believe that he keeps me safe from harm, even though I know such a thing is not possible."

"Perhaps it is," he told her.

"I do not understand you, Madoc."

"Close your eyes but a moment, dearling," he said quietly.

She trusted him enough by now that her green eyes closed most obediently, and it was then she heard the flap of wings. Wynne's eyes flew open and she was hard-pressed to believe what it was she saw. Soaring about the room was old Dhu, who swooped amid the rafters of the Great Hall, cawing triumphantly.

Wynne burst out laughing and clapped her hands together gleefully. "*I knew it!* I suspected it all along! I just didn't know it was you," she cried. "You're a shape-changer, Madoc!"

The great black raven flew directly toward her, and in the second that Wynne blinked, Madoc stood before her. "You are not afraid?" he said.

"No! I want to learn how to do it! Will you teach me? Ohhh, Madoc! It was you all those years watching out over me. It was you to whom I poured out all my secrets. *It was you!*"

"Aye, Wynne, it was me. I never meant to intrude upon your privacy, dearling. At first I was merely curious as to how you were growing. I wanted to make certain that you were healthy and happy. Then it became more. I needed, it seemed, to be near you. I could not be happy unless I was. There were times when my own concerns kept me from you for days and weeks on end, and I would grow irritable with my need for the sight of you. And the year I went to Byzantium! It was torture! After several months I was so desperate for the sight of you that I feigned illness in order that I might have the time and the solitude to cast a powerful spell enabling me to see you for a few brief minutes."

"There was a year in which the raven was missing," Wynne said thoughtfully. "I was eight, I think." She looked at him. "Has this always been a part of you? The magic, I mean. In other times?"

"Nay," he said. "Only in this time and place."

"But how did you learn it? You were only a child when your father died." She took his hand and led him to a bench before the fire.

As they sat down he said, "My father was murdered, Wynne. It was his brother's hand that struck him down, no accident. My uncle was seen perpetrating the foul deed. The witness was my grandmother, but my grandmother was only a woman. She could do nothing, and so she told several trusted servants and swore them to secrecy. Then she spent the rest of her life protecting me from Cynbel.

"I had the knowledge to destroy when I was seven, but my father had taught me that life is sacred to the Mother and the Father. I had gone with him into his pharmacea from the time I could toddle. When he died I taught myself from his secret books which were hidden from my uncle, who would have taken them for himself, even though they would have done him no good. He always believed if he could find those books he could change the fate his own father had ordained for him and for those of his descendants who followed him."

Madoc sighed. "My uncle was such a warped soul, Wynne. He married my mother in order to have Raven's Rock, but he could not. After Brys was born, his madness—for it was madness—grew even worse. He was determined his son should have what was mine. He taught Brys early how to hate. The envy and jealousy that oozed out of him was absorbed into Brys's very pores. Of course, with my grandmother and the servants watching over me, my uncle had no chance of harming me. He turned my brother against me for nought, but once the deed was done, there was no changing it. Brys attempted his rape of Nesta because he knew how very much I loved our sister. In his warped mind her violation was to be a mortal blow at me."

"But once again he failed," Wynne said softly, "and in failing, found himself exiled from Raven's Rock, which but increased his bitterness and his anger toward you."

Madoc nodded sadly. "After that there was no real hope of a reconciliation between us, although I did try for our mother's sake that once when Brys's father died."

"Has he married?" Wynne asked, curious.

Madoc laughed harshly. "Nay! He has found what he believes to be the perfect avenue of revenge. The Church. Brys took orders several years ago, and then when the old bishop of Cai died two years ago, my brother shamelessly bought his office. He is one of the youngest bishops in the Church. He attempts to destroy me by claiming my powers come from the devil. There are some fools in King Gruffydd's court who fear my influence and would like to believe it so."

"Then your marriage to me cannot fail but be an advantage, as I am related to the king," Wynne said thoughtfully.

" 'Tis not why I betrothed myself to you, dearling," he replied.

"I know that," she answered him. "I have no fear of your motive, Madoc. I trust you, but enough of your brother! I want to become a shape-changer as you are."

He chuckled and said, "Why, I believe that you love me for my knowledge of magical arts, Wynne. I am not sure I should not be offended."

"I am not certain why I love you, Madoc," and the words out of her mouth, Wynne looked even more astounded than the man by her side did. "Ohhhh!" she said, her green eyes wide with her own surprise.

"You love me?" His voice was slightly strangled.

"I seem to have said so, haven't I." Wynne bit her lower lip in vexation and then continued carefully, "I suppose I *do* love you, Madoc. I should not have said it otherwise, but I was certainly not aware of it until the words popped unbidden from my mouth. When could such a thing have happened? I acknowledge that I desire you, for I surely do, but love you? Well, I *have* said it, and I seem to feel no great desire to deny it, so it must be. It does not change, however, whatever it is between us from that other time and place which must be concluded. Perhaps now, though, we will be able to settle our past difference, as my heart obviously has a tendre for you."

For the first time in his life Madoc of Powys found himself at a loss for words. He knew he should say something, but he feared if he did, whatever it was he said would drive her away again. Wynne quickly solved the problem for him.

"Now that we have agreed on that, my lord, tell me when you will begin to teach me how I may learn to change my shape as you do."

Somehow he managed to find his voice. "It is a simple matter, Wynne, but it can be dangerous. The world in which you and I live is no longer the world of our Celtic ancestors. I am called a sorcerer by many, though my reputation exceeds my actual deeds. Yet the knowledge I possess was once greatly respected and appreciated by our people. There is no evil to it except in the hands of evil men, but that has ever been so. Now, however, that knowledge I possess is said to spring from the devil. So I must conceal what I know for the most part from those around us, lest I be considered the devil's disciple. Still, my reputation persists because of the history of the princes of Powys-Wenwynwyn. A history forever being reinvented and embroidered upon by my brother, Drys, for the delectation of the ignorant, the foolish, and the superstitious."

"The knowledge you have must be passed on, my dear lord," Wynne told him quietly. "It is a part of who we are. Not just yesterday, but today and tomorrow."

"Perhaps today, but I am not certain about the morrow, dearling. Nonetheless, I will endeavor to teach you what I know. However, before I teach you the secret of changing one's shape, you must learn other things. You had a small pharmacea at Gwernach. I have one here within the castle. Tomorrow we will adjourn there together. I will see how far you have gotten with your potions, and then I will teach you what you must know. We will have to work very hard, Wynne, and I warn you I am not an easy taskmaster."

"Nor I one to be satisfied with poor work, Madoc," she told him.

He smiled at her pride and, taking her hand, drew her to her feet. "It is late, dearling. Past time that we sought our beds." Then he kissed her mouth lightly.

In the morning, when Wynne had arisen and washed herself, Megan came to her with a tray upon which was a freshly baked cottage loaf, a bowl of hot barley cereal, a slice of ham, a crock of sweet butter, a honeycomb, and a goblet of sweet, watered wine. "When you are ready, my lady, I am instructed to take you to the prince."

As excited as she was, Wynne ate slowly, and she ate everything upon the tray. She did not know how long they would remain in Madoc's pharmacea this day, or when she would have the opportunity to eat again. When she had finished, Megan brought her a basin of scented water that she might wash her hands and face again. Then she held out a garment of grass-green to her mistress.

"What is this?" Wynne asked, for the gown was quite foreign to her.

"The master asks that you wear it to please him," Megan responded.

Wynne put it on and found the garment to be a floor-length gown of silk with a simple round neckline that followed the shape of her body. It had fitted sleeves to the wrists. Over it she added a grass-green brocade robe with three-quarter-length sleeves that ended just below her elbow. The robe lay open from neck to hem. A three-inch band of gold embroidery done in a swirl of Celtic design descended from the top of the garment to its bottom, around its neckline edges, hem, and sleeve cuffs.

"If you will sit, my lady," Megan said, "I will do your hair."

Wynne sat upon a stool while Megan carefully removed the sleep snarls from her long black hair, brushed the ankle-length tresses until they shone, and then braided her mistress's thick hair into the single braid that Wynne favored. When she had finished, she placed a plain, narrow circlet of Irish red-gold about Wynne's forehead and, kneeling, slipped soft felt slippers upon Wynne's feet.

"You are ready, my lady. If you will follow me, I will take you to Prince Madoc." Megan arose and moved with fluid grace across the room and through the door.

Wynne followed her maidservant as they moved swiftly through the castle, down the corridor lit by flickering torches, and up a flight of stone steps into a tower. At the top of the staircase was a door, and Megan stopped before it.

"Knock once and enter, my lady," she said.

"You come no farther?" queried Wynne.

"Nay, my lady. No one in the castle but the prince is allowed into this room. It is a special place, sacred to the old ways of our people. For someone such as I to violate that chamber's sanctity would be a great sacrilege. You, however, are one of the special ones like the prince. We all know it, else he would not have chosen you for his wife."

For a long moment Wynne stood silently before the oak door listening to Megan's footsteps as they echoed and retreated down the narrow staircase. Finally raising her fist, she knocked once. His voice came quite clearly through the thick wood, bidding her to enter, which she did.

"Good morning, dearling," he said to her as she stepped into the room. "I trust you are ready to work hard." He smiled.

He was garbed even as she was, but that his costume was violet. About his neck he wore a heavy silver chain from which hung a silver pendant in which was imbedded the largest moonstone she could ever remember seeing. It was fully as big as one of the small apricots Madoc had sent her as a treat the previous summer. The silver diadem that restrained his unruly dark hair was studded with moonstones of a smaller size. He somehow seemed larger than life in this place, and Wynne suddenly considered that she should possibly be just a little afraid of him.

She bowed politely to him, never revealing that thought and hoping he had not read it. "I am ready to learn all you would teach me, Madoc, if in the end you will teach me how to change my shape as you do."

"In time, dearling. Do not be impatient with me," he told her.

Wynne looked about her with frank interest. "Where are we?" she asked him.

"This is the east tower of Raven's Rock," came the reply.

"It is one of the round towers," Wynne returned. "The original tower of the keep, I would venture." She looked about her. In the curve of the wall was a small fireplace in the shape of an inverted U. A peat fire burned brightly upon its hearth. There was a large L-shaped, slate-topped table and a similar table formed like a T within the room. Set on each table was a stone mortar and a pestle.

There were shelves hollowed from one wall, and upon them were an assortment of vials, bowls, and beakers of various sizes, shapes, and colors, as well as glass and stone jars holding quivering liquids, pastes, and other dried substances whose origins she could not fathom at this point. There were several charcoal burners set upon each of the tables, and from the walls of the room hung bunches and sheaves of all manner of herbs, roots, and dried flowers.

It was actually very much like her own little pharmacea at Gwernach, where she had mixed her own medicines and salves to help doctor her people. The room was very well-lit by small torches affixed in their iron holders which were set into the wall. They were quite necessary, as through the tower window she could see the day was grey and overcast. Set upon a tall, three-footed stand beneath the window was a thick manuscript.

"This is a wonderful room," she said with sincerity.

"You will note," he said with his dry humor, "there are no small horned demons lurking in the corners ready to do my evil bidding; nor is there a single cat, black or otherwise, that I use as my familiar. I am afraid I should greatly disappoint those who consider my arts to be those of the devil. I seem to lack all the necessary accoutrements."

"I suspect that if such things were really necessary to your talents, Madoc, that they would not be readily in evidence for all to see," she mocked him. "It is a strange world in which we live that denies such a wonderful part of our heritage. Still, I understand the need for caution and will act accordingly."

He nodded. "It is sad, Wynne, that we who were once the lords of this earth have had to learn the fine art of compromise. Compromise is confining and stifles the fires of talent. Still, we must survive within this new and righteous world in which we find ourselves. . . . But enough of this idle chatter, dearling. You have come to learn, and I will teach you. First, however, I must ascertain just how much you actually know. Use the L-shaped table and show me how you would make a love potion. You do know how to make a love potion?"

Wynne raised her eyebrows at him. "I would not be much of a healer if I did not know how to make a love potion, Madoc." Then she turned to face the storage shelves and, seeking carefully amongst the jars and beakers, removed precisely the ingredients she needed, placing everything neatly upon the table. Skillfully she measured out amounts of each substance, placing the ingredient first into the mortar, where she ground it to the desired fineness before adding it to a larger bowl, into which she would finally combine the mixture. When she had finished, Wynne looked expectantly toward Madoc. "Well?" she demanded.

"How do you administer it?" he asked her, neither approving nor disapproving her work.

"A pinch in a goblet of wine usually does the trick," she said.

"It would do even better if you added . . ." He paused, his

dark blue eyes flickering quickly over the shelves until, finding
what he sought, he drew it forth. "Three violet flowers ground
medium-fine. Remember, 'tis the flowers, not the leaves you
want; and a pinch of orris root. The potion is far more binding
and, therefore, more effective with these two elements added.
Made like this, you can also infuse the entire potion into red
wine. It should be heated just to the boiling point, but never
beyond," he cautioned, "for it loses its strength then. The
treated wine can then be stored safely for some months in a
stone bottle and not lose any of its potency. Just one small
spoonful mixed into a goblet of cool wine or into a cup of ale
will work quite well.

"Come, we will grind your ingredients into a fine powder.
Then I will show you just how much wine to use and demon-
strate how to heat the mixture properly. Once you have done
it successfully, you will not forget it."

"Can I trust you with so potent a potion, Madoc?" Wynne
teased him.

"I need no love potion to bind me to you, dearling. My devotion is one that has endured through the centuries. Soon, I
hope, you will remember that."

Wynne grew pink with the compliment, but said nothing
more. Instead she set to work pestling the mix she had made
into a smooth powder; while Madoc lit one of the small charcoal burners and set it near him on the slate-topped table. They
worked together, side by side, for some time; he, requesting
one compound after another; Wynne, showing him what she
knew, and her knowledge was vast for a girl so young. She had
gained her learning early from her own mother, a skilled
healer. When Margiad had died, Enid had completed Wynne's
education. Wisely, Wynne had never been loath to listen to the
remedies offered by some of the old women at Gwernach. The
elderly had a vast fund of wisdom and it was foolish to discount it.

Now as she worked with Madoc she realized how much
more she could learn. It was another bond she hoped would tie
them together and perhaps even help her to remember the past
that had separated them. Sometimes, as with the love potion,
he improved upon her own mixture. Other formulas he left
alone, nodding quickly in approval of her methods before dis-
posing of some of the mixtures and storing others.

The hours sped by quickly and the day waned. Finally Madoc called a halt to their labors, saying, "This table and this room are open to you whenever you desire to come here to make medicines and salves for our people."

She nodded and then said, "Tell me why, of all the beautiful birds in the world, you chose to become a raven?"

A slow smile altered his serious features. "It is true that I might have been something else, but think, Wynne. The raven is a plain and common bird. People pay little, if any, attention to it. In flight it has no enemies, for the birds of prey will not bother a raven who minds his own business. The raven is like an ordinary face in a crowd of people. One is very much like another. On the whole it is a safe bird to be. When I alter my own shape, it is not to put my life in danger."

"What is the secret to changing?" she begged him.

"Not yet, dearling. You have more to learn, and as I would not put myself at risk, I will certainly not put you at risk. Eventually I will teach you magic, but not yet."

She sighed but wisely accepted his decision.

"Are you tired?" he asked her solicitously as they returned to their apartments.

"Aye," she nodded, sighing.

"There are but the two of us, dearling. Let us bathe and rest and then have our supper here in my reading room before the fire. Would it please you?"

"Aye, I should like a bath and the informality of our chambers," she admitted. "Have the meal brought and set by the fire to keep warm. Then dismiss the servants, for we do not need them. I will serve you, my lord."

Megan, as efficient as ever, had already drawn Wynne's bath. She undid Wynne's braid, brushed it free and then, wrapping hanks of her mistress's hair about her hand, pinned the loops atop Wynne's head with her golden hairpins. Disrobing her lady and helping her into the great oak tub, Megan was surprised to find herself dismissed for the evening.

"I can wash myself," Wynne told her. "Spend your free time driving my Einion to distraction, as you seem to have been doing of late. It is a most humbling experience, and actually quite good for him I believe." Wynne chuckled. "He quite has his own way with the ladies as a rule."

"Well, he'll not with me, my lady," Megan said pertly with

a grin. "I'm not one of those kiss-me-quick lasses he's used to pursuing." She curtsied prettily. "If you're certain it's all right to leave you, my lady, then I'll bid you good night."

"Run along," Wynne told her, smiling as Megan almost flew out the door. There was a definite romance brewing between Einion and Megan. She snuggled down into the big round tub, murmuring with pleasure as the hot water soothed her tired shoulder and neck muscles, which were sore from bending over her work all day. Fragrant wildflower steam arose from the water, perfuming the room. The fire crackled comfortably while outside the winter winds howled and sighed about the castle. Wynne closed her eyes and relaxed. Suddenly from behind her closed eyelids she sensed she was not alone.

"Do you wish to join me, my lord?" she asked, not even bothering to open her eyes.

"It would not distress you?" he queried her.

Now Wynne did open her green eyes, and she looked directly at him. He was naked and he was beautiful. She had never seen a grown man naked, and yet she was neither surprised nor distressed by the sight. His body matched his fiercely handsome face. It was all bone and muscle. His legs were hairy, but the rest of his body was smooth, except for the thickly tangled thatch of dark curls springing from his groin where his manhood lay framed.

Wynne swung her look back up to his face. "Our ancestors saw nothing wrong in intimacy, Madoc. You are my betrothed husband. I am your betrothed wife." She smiled encouragingly at him. "Come, the water is delightful. Bring the brush and I will scrub your back."

"Once again you surprise me, dearling," he told her, and she laughed.

"Our marriage will be celebrated on the first day of May, my lord. I have been at Raven's Rock over three months. Yet although I find my desire for you grows daily, and I have indeed grown to love you, it is not enough. I must remember that which was between us before we marry. You admit that we were once lovers. Perhaps if we are lovers again, my memory of those times past will be returned to me and we may complete what is uncompleted between us before formally rejoining our lives once more."

"Wynne," he began, "do you know what it is you are saying?"

"Deny me not in this, Madoc," she replied seriously. "I am not afraid to become a woman. Does it displease you that I would be one?" He had entered the tub, and she now moved to face him, winding her arms about his neck provocatively. "Tell me you are not angry with me, Madoc." Her small, firm breasts pressed against his chest.

Lost. He was totally and completely lost in the depths of her forest-green eyes. Her mouth shimmered before him, coral-pink, berry-sweet, and ripe for kissing. They called him sorcerer, and yet it was Wynne, Wynne in her innocence and ancient instinct, who was a sorceress, beguiling and enchanting him until he could no longer resist. Madoc knew he had the power to renew the deep, secret memories of their past which she had repressed within her heart and mind; but right now all he wanted to do was to make love to her. She lured him on. He could feel her hand against the back of his neck, drawing him down to her deliciously tempting mouth.

"I won't be able to stop," he whispered desperately against her mouth in a final attempt at sanity.

"I would not start this if I expected you to stop, Madoc, my love," she murmured back, nibbling at his lower lip. "I am no coy maid to tease a man onward only to cry off at the crucial moment. I am yours!"

With a groan he surrendered. His mouth took hers in a hard, almost brutal kiss. The power of victory sang in his ears. *She was his!*

Wynne returned his passion kiss for kiss. The time for maidenly modesty was long past. Her own blood ran hot with her desire to be possessed completely by this man. *To learn how to possess him in return.* In this aspect of their relationship everything was perfect. She parted her lips as he had taught her and tasted his tongue mingling with hers. Her lithe body pressed against him as their mouths mashed together frantically and wetly.

Jesu! He had to regain control of the situation before he took her right here in their tub. She was a virgin. She deserved better than that her first time. He pulled his head away from her and drew several breaths to clear his senses before setting her firmly back from him. The hurt in her eyes astounded him.

"What is wrong?" Wynne begged.

He smiled to reassure her and then said, "There will be times, my love, when I may make love to you here in our bath; but not this time. Tonight it must be perfect for you. At least as perfect as I can make it. It is every woman's right when she gives up her virginity, and I will not take that from you. Now scrub my back, Wynne, and we will adjourn to my bedchamber, where I will endeavor to give you the sweet pleasure all women should have."

With trembling hands Wynne scrubbed him, rinsing him off with a soft cloth; and then to her surprise he did the same for her. "You speak of pleasing me, Madoc," she said low, "but I would learn how to please you."

"I will teach you, my dearling, but tonight, Wynne, I alone will be the master of our pleasure, for to give you joy, my love, is to receive it myself. You cannot quite understand that at this moment, but within a short time you will." He kissed her softly, stroking her jaw lightly with the back of his hand. Then stepping from their deep oak tub, he lifted her out, setting her upon the warm stones of the floor. Madoc reached for a piece of rough toweling and began to slowly rub her dry.

"You will catch cold," Wynne said softly, taking another piece of toweling and imitating his actions.

"I'll be hot soon enough," he teased gently, sliding to his knees before her, rubbing, rubbing, rubbing.

Trembling just faintly, Wynne bent slightly over to dry his broad shoulders, gasping with surprise as, reaching up, Madoc caught one of her breasts in his hand and, fastening his lips about the nipple, began to suckle her. "Ohhh!" Her little cry was almost a squeak. "Ohhh!" It came again as the prince transferred his attentions from the first small breast to the second. The sensations generated by the actions of his mouth were delicious, she thought, but why did she also have a tingling sensation in the secret place between her thighs?

Madoc stood up, putting his arms about her as he did, and drew her close against him. Wynne looked up unafraid into his face, her hand reaching up to stroke his cheek; a single finger moving softly over his fleshy underlip. Gently he bit that finger, his deep blue eyes holding her green eyes captive now, daring her onward. She lay her cheek against his shoulder, rubbing it softly with her head; and Madoc, in answer to her unspoken words, bent down to lift her up into his arms. He carried her from their bathing room to his own bedchamber, setting her down upon her feet for a moment while he poured them two goblets of rich, red wine which he placed upon a low table near the fire.

Wynne looked quickly about the room, for she had never been in it before. It was large and spacious, with a great fireplace which burned brightly, warming the room most comfortably. A great bed was set upon a raised dais. It was covered in a deep blue silk coverlet with a wide hem embroidered with gold thread and small jewels. Behind the bed, hanging from the ceiling to the floor, was a large, colorful tapestry depicting purple mountains and green forests filled with animals, both real and fabled, as well as birds that fluttered and flew about the scene. Windows looked out onto the mountains; she could tell by their direction, although those mountains were now obscured by both the night and the storm. There were beautifully carved chairs, and tables and chests of warm golden oak set about the room, which for all its elegance was simple.

Madoc took Wynne by the hand now and led her to a large white sheepskin rug which lay on the floor before the fireplace. Gently he drew her down so that they knelt facing one another. Taking her face into his hands, he kissed her mouth, gently at first, then a bit more fiercely as his ardor rose. Her arms had been quiet at her side. Now she lifted them and, palms smoothing slowly up his chest, she slid them tightly about his neck, drawing him down with her as she lay back upon the soft sheepskin. His lips never left her all the while, and he thought that she was wonderfully brave in her innocence.

He was careful not to put himself atop her lest he frighten her. Instead he slid himself sinuously down alongside of her. Kneeling back on his haunches, he took one of her slender feet into his hands. He kissed the top of her foot, nibbling playfully at her dainty toes, cradling the foot in his warm palms, massaging it gently before paying equal court to its mate. Wynne could not help but giggle, for the sensation against her skin was deliciously tickly.

"First you would gnaw on my fingers," she whispered, "and now my toes. Do all men love their ladies so, Madoc?" Then she gave a little squeal, for his tongue was licking the arch of her foot and the feeling was most sensuous.

"A wise man," he said, nuzzling her ankle, "loves a woman from the soles of her pretty feet to the top of her head, Wynne. To do less would be tragic. A woman is more than simple surcease for a man's randy cock." He fondled her calves with strong, warm fingers.

This was something she had most certainly not known, Wynne thought. His hands were so skilled, and they sent such wonderful little shivers of pure pleasure throughout her body. It was quite a delightful revelation. She stretched and purred her contentment of his continued actions, then giggled again as he kissed her rounded knees. "You are mad, my lord!" she half laughed.

He kissed them again, murmuring, "Poor little knees. They tell me that they have never been kissed before, but they quite like it." Then to her great surprise, he turned her quickly over onto her stomach and began caressing her buttocks with soft hands that pressed gently into her flesh and fingers that teased her skin with feathery touches.

She felt his mouth on her, kissing. His tongue, warm and stroking. A shiver raced through Wynne. *This was different.* Very, very different from the previous teasing caresses. Kisses were being placed all along her backbone to be slowly followed by the wet warmth of his stroking tongue. She squirmed nervously against the soft sheepskin rug as she felt him lay half atop her. His teeth nipped gently at her ear, and he murmured hotly into it, causing her to shiver again.

"Don't be frightened of me, dearling. I love you," he reassured her. "Remember, there is nothing for you to do this night but enjoy my attentions. Later on I will teach you how to pleasure me even as I now pleasure you." His lips found the soft sensitive back of her neck, and when he had paid it the homage he felt it deserved, he rolled Wynne over again onto her back. "Tell me."

She knew at once to what he alluded, and answered, "I am assailed by a plethora of emotions that buffet at me like the winds in a storm buffet this castle."

"You do not say if they are pleasant or unpleasant, dearling."

"More pleasant, I think. What unnerves me is what I find unfamiliar," she replied thoughtfully.

He caught her hand and, turning it over, kissed the palm

passionately. "Are you brave enough now to continue on without further explanation, trusting that I will not harm you, my love?" he asked her. The look he gave her was a tender one, yet she could see the banked fires in his eyes.

My love. How those two simple words thrilled her. Her own wisdom told her that when the dawn came she would once again begin to wonder exactly what it was that really bound them together in time; but for now she did not care. "I would be your wife, Madoc, in every sense of the word. Rid me of my dreaded virginity that we may explore new worlds together," Wynne told him. Then she pulled his head down to her and kissed him fiercely.

She was forever surprising him, he thought briefly as he began to return her kisses; drinking greedily from her mouth; scoring the straining flesh of her throat with his burning lips; his own lips and his hands finding her sweet young breasts. Tenderly he caressed her, his mouth fastening over each sentient little bud, drawing upon it sensuously until her nipples were sore with an undefined longing.

Wynne sighed deeply and arched her body up to meet his mouth, aching all over with the pure pleasure he was giving her. She protested when his lips began to once again move away from her swollen, tender breasts and wander down her torso. Still, his kisses and the gentle tonguing he employed were beginning to send her senses reeling. The tip of his tongue teased at her navel. She murmured nervously again as his head brushed against her closed thighs, which had instinctively pressed themselves tightly together.

"No, dearling," he scolded her gently. "You must open yourself to me. I would prepare you fully for our joining."

Wynne forced herself to relax. Her slim thighs fell apart even as he rubbed his cheek against her belly. She started edgily as his fingers grazed her nether lips, then gasped as they penetrated gently between them. *"Madoc!"*

"It's all right, Wynne," he reassured her. "Trust me, dearling."

A finger touched that most particularly sensitive nub of her and she gasped again. Never before in her life had she felt anything akin to the sensations now beginning to build up in her. That single finger began to move in a tiny circle of flesh and she shuddered hard. Madoc moved himself between her trembling thighs. His mouth was, to her great shock, where that teasing finger had been but a moment before. She felt his tongue snake out to touch her and was unable to stop the soft moan that seemed to well up from the deepest part of her. His lips closed over that tiny bit of flesh and he began to gently suckle on her. Waves of heat suffused her body leaving her weak with a want she couldn't quite understand.

"I do not think I can bear this!" she cried out to him, but instead of ceasing the sweet torture, Madoc seemed to redouble his efforts. "Ohh, please!" she half sobbed, realizing with blinding clarity even as she pleaded with him that she did not want him to stop, and he knew it. She was wracked by a series of distinctly pleasurable bursts. Then suddenly he was astride her. It would have been so simple to simply drift off at that moment, but instead Wynne opened her eyes and, looking up at Madoc, reached forth to guide his lance into her well-prepared sheath. "Do not delay," she begged him, her gaze one of intoxicated passion. "I would be yours!"

With a groan he sank into her, and she was as sweet as a split peach. When he encountered her maidenhead and stopped a moment in his intent, Wynne thrust her young body up hard, encasing him fully within her ripeness. He kissed the silent tears upon her cheeks away. And then certain the initial pain of Wynne's deflowering had eased, Madoc began to move on her, pressing forward slowly, withdrawing as lingeringly to ensure her a full measure of pleasure.

The pain of his initial entry had exploded blindingly before her eyes and, unable to refrain from her cowardice, Wynne closed them. Then, as suddenly, the sting and the burning she had felt were gone. Wynne began to relax, deciding that Madoc's movements were really quite delicious. He had told her that she need do nothing but enjoy his attentions. Now free of her previous fears, she did. Whimpering with a need she still did not quite understand, her fingers kneaded at his shoulders, digging into his flesh more sharply and with greater urgency as she felt a rising tide of ecstasy sweeping up to overwhelm her.

Every new sensation assaulting her was an acute one. She could actually feel his manhood, warm and pulsing with life, within her own body. Each stroke of it seemed to push her further and further away from reality. Yet his hungry possession of her body was the greatest reality of all. Like a song bird she glided higher and higher, seeking a pinnacle she had never known. Then as suddenly she found it. Great shudders racked her from the deepest chasms of her body, even as rainbows of light burst wildly upon her from behind her eyelids. Wynne opened her mouth gasping for air, and having gulped some, expelled it almost immediately before fainting dead away, her last sensation being that of being flooded with total warmth.

Madoc groaned with satisfaction as his own passions burst forth at precisely the right moment. He rolled half off her as he shuddered a final discharge of ecstasy. For the first time in his life he was transported into a semiconscious state. Never before had he known such bliss with a woman as he did with this woman. Nothing had changed in that respect, he thought hazily. Then he allowed himself to float free for a few minutes, reveling in the sweet sensations that assailed him like an afterglow. As his mind grew clearer he began to realize that Wynne, an untried virgin, had galloped the entire course of passion in her first attempt. She was amazing and obviously had an incredible capacity for loving. This shadow between them had to be dissolved.

She began to stir beside him, and pulling himself up into a seated position, Madoc gathered his betrothed wife into his arms. He cradled her gently, smoothing her wonderful long black hair away from her face, for it had come undone and tangled with their love play. It was such beautiful hair, he thought. Soft, smelling of white heather and silky beneath his fingers.

Wynne opened her eyes and studied the fierce features, suddenly gentle with his open adoration for her. "Will it always be as wild between us, my lord?" she asked softly. "Will I die a little death each time you pleasure me with your skillful lance? Will you show me how I may pleasure you as greatly, for having opened such a wonderful world to me, Madoc, I now find I am in your debt."

"Your pleasure is my pleasure," he told her sincerely. "There is nothing more."

"No ways in which I may offer equal bliss?" she pressed him. "Did you not say you would teach me? Do not deny me the right to give you the same pleasure that you gave me!"

He smiled reassuringly into her distressed face. "I will teach you how to give delight with touches and kisses, Wynne, but my greatest pleasure does indeed come with your own pleasure. I swear it!"

"But I want to see your happiness even as you saw mine!" she protested.

"That is possible, for sometimes one lover may move more quickly than the other. Then, too, it is also possible to give and take multiple delights in a bout of passion," he told her.

"Oh, yes! Teach me that, my lord!" She almost wriggled with her excitement, very much like an eager young puppy.

Madoc laughed, charmed with her enthusiasm, which, in all his years of watching over her, he could have never guessed. Perhaps, however, he should have and would have had he not been so entranced with her. Wynne had a great capacity for life and for living. Then he sobered. This *experiment* in passion had been performed for the express purpose of jogging her memory. "Tell me, dearling," he questioned her, "have you remembered anything of times past now?"

Wynne considered and then shook her head. "It matters not," she said, dismissing his query airily. "I love you, Madoc, and that is what is important to me. What was between us is a time long gone. It is now that I care about."

"Nay," he said. "You must remember, Wynne. If you love me, you must remember for my sake, if not your own."

"Then help me, Madoc! Help me to remember what I must for both our sakes! For the sakes of the children I will surely bear you!" Then she smiled. "Perhaps we just need a little more time, Madoc. After all, this is the first time we have made love, at least in this life." She smiled mischievously at him. "I think we need to make love again and probably yet again before I will begin to remember."

He laughed. "You are a vixen, I vow, my adorable dearling! You may be correct though." He cupped a small breast within the palm of his hand and fondled it teasingly.

"I will do whatever my lord commands," she replied in dulcet tones, and turned her face up to his for a kiss.

Part II

THE LADY OF RAVEN'S ROCK

WALES, 1061

*Deep is your longing for the
land of your memories and the
dwelling place of your greater
desires*

> *Kahlil Gibran*
> *THE PROPHET*

Chapter 7

*I*n introducing Wynne to lovemaking, Madoc had opened a whole new world for her. It was a world in which she was completely comfortable. It was a world that she enjoyed more fully than he would have thought possible. She was an apt pupil in the arts of Eros. Indeed, she wanted to give him as much pleasure as he was giving her. As each day passed he could see her genuine love for him growing, along with her passion for him. That knowledge tore at Madoc, for despite all Wynne strove to give him, it would not be enough unless she could remember that fatal moment in time that had set the course of their mutual destinies.

January passed. Then February. In mid-March the springtime burst upon them and the hills were bright with colorful blooms. Wynne sensed his rising despair. "I did not come to Raven's Rock to make you unhappy, Madoc," she told him one evening as they lay together. "I came to be your cherished wife. Yet my very presence, for all our passion, breaks your heart. I can bear no more of it, my love!" She pushed back an errant lock of her raven's black hair. Her face was even paler than usual. "I have tried to remember, but I cannot! It is as if something is preventing me and I know not why. You cannot tell me what it is that binds us together you say; but I must still know if we are to be happy. Help me, Madoc! Help me to remember that other time since I seem so unable to do so myself."

Madoc sighed deeply and then he looked up into her beautiful face. "I will blend a special packet of herbs for you, dearling. When you are ready to make your journey in time, Wynne, mix them in a goblet of wine and drink it down. You will fall into a deep sleep. The herbs in the wine will free your mind to remember that past which you and I shared. The wine will relax you so that you have no fear."

"Have we not shared more than one past together, Madoc?"

she gently pressed him. Now that her decision was made, some deeper instinct was stirring within her.

He nodded in the affirmative. "We have."

"Why now and not before?" she wondered aloud.

"God has a great sense of both justice and humor, Wynne. The timing was never quite right. This is the first time we have been lovers since then."

She nodded and then asked him, "How can I be certain that I will remember that particular life which seems to trouble you so greatly?"

"Because that is the life that you wish to remember, dearling," he told her. "That is the door which will open for you. It is as simple as that."

"How long will I sleep, my lord?" She pushed nervously at her hair again.

"A few hours. A few days," he told her quietly. "It depends upon how much you choose to remember."

"I would know everything, Madoc," she told him resolutely. "Though I believe the past is best left behind, I can see that the pain of that past will not leave you until I have relived it, though I do not understand why. Still, I will do it for you because I love you! I want us to get on with the lives we now live. There is so much ahead for us to share, my love!"

"Pray God you are right, Wynne!" he cried wholeheartedly and, reaching up, he drew her down into his gentle embrace.

She snuggled against him for a moment and then said, "I will not get lost in time, Madoc, will I?" It seemed to be her one great fear.

"Nay, darling," he promised her. "You will only sleep. Your lovely body will remain precisely where you lay it down. You will awaken when you choose to awaken. You need have no terrors over it."

"Is there anything else that I need to know?" she fretted.

"Nothing." He paused and finally said, "When do you wish to do this thing?"

"Not for a few days' time, but blend your herbs, Madoc, for there will come one moment in which I shall be braver than in any other moment. It is then I will depart on this adventure, so be prepared."

He seemed relieved by her answer, a fact that Wynne found intriguing. Her curiosity was now more aroused than it had been before. He loved her. Of that Wynne had no doubt. Yet despite his love for her, despite that undeniable fact, Madoc was suddenly showing signs of fear; he obviously wanted her to go upon this journey in time. What was it that she would learn? It was a puzzle that was beginning to fascinate her more now than it had before.

During the next few days Wynne rested and studied with Madoc in his high tower chamber. His knowledge of ancient Celtic medicine simply astounded her, and he willingly passed on to her a great deal of this valuable knowledge. It was unfortunate that some of that lore would be useless to her because many of the ingredients, once so easily available for the taking, could no longer be found growing. They had simply disappeared. They were irreplaceable, of course, because no one knew with what to replace them in the formulae.

Once there had been a special parasitic mistletoe that grew only upon the sacred oaks so beloved of the Celts. It had been used for healing serious cancers, but the mistletoe now available was not the same plant that had been used in those long gone days. That particular growth, Madoc told her, had been lost along with their sacred hosts when the Romans, and those other conquerors of the island of Britain who followed after them, viciously destroyed the oaks in an effort to wipe out the Celtic culture.

Madoc would have taught Wynne certain forms of spells and bindings, but she would not let him. His special knowledge was a great temptation that she feared she might be unable to control. Wynne knew that if she had Madoc's knowledge of sorcery, no matter her good intentions, she might one day lose her temper and do a harm she might later regret and be unable to undo. She remembered a fairy tale her grandmother used to tell about an unhappy queen, stepmother to four beautiful children, the three sons and the daughter of a king called Lir. Jealous, the queen had used her knowledge of magic to turn the children into swans. Quickly regretting her hasty actions, the queen found she could not undo her spell, and her husband died brokenhearted.

There were other dangers in Madoc's knowledge. It made his neighbors and those who did not know him well fearful of him. If her own learning extended too far past mere medicine, and word of it got out, which it always did, she might attract the attention of those who would seek to use and control her for their own wicked purposes. As it was, there were some, particularly in the Church, who would feel her knowledge was too great for a woman. Women like that were always a danger. She had the children she would bear Madoc to consider. She must walk a fine line.

The weather had turned warm, perhaps too warm for late March. Wynne fretted that there would be no flowering branches with which to decorate the Great Hall of Raven's Rock when their wedding day arrived. She grumbled about this to Madoc as they rode out over the hills one afternoon, and he laughed.

"The warmth is but a brief thing, dearling. It will storm by nightfall and turn cool, I promise. There will be more than enough flowers and flowering branches when May first arrives," he assured her.

"If it gets too cold the buds will be frosted and ruined," she grumbled.

"There will be no frost," he replied.

"You are certain?" she demanded.

"I am," he chuckled. "Like Nesta, I am sensitive to the weather. It will rain for the next few days, I promise you."

"Then perhaps tonight," Wynne told him, "I will begin my journey in time."

"So soon, my dearling?" His blue eyes bespoke his distress.

"Madoc," Wynne said in the severe tone of a mother reasoning with an unruly child, "You want me to go, and then you do not want me to go! I no longer care! I do this for you. Tell me yea or nay, now! Then we will have no more of it!"

"You must go," he finally agreed, "though I fear your return even more than your going."

Wynne reached out and took his hand in hers. "I love you, Madoc of Powys. What has been done is done for me. It is the present and the future that I love and reach out for; not a past that seems to haunt you so."

"I pray it be so, dearling," he said squeezing her hand.

"Though I must do this alone, Madoc, I ask of one thing of you," Wynne said softly.

"Anything!" he vowed.

"Be there when I awaken, my lord. Let your dear face be

the first thing that I see when my eyes open once again upon this time and this place," she replied.

"I will be there, my love! I swear it!" he told her, and she was startled to see tears in his beautiful blue eyes.

Wynne reached out and touched his face with her hand, comforting him as best she could. Though the past meant nothing to her now, she had to learn the truth of what had once been between them for both their sakes. The sadness his face had taken on unnerved her. What was so awful that he feared for her to know it, and yet insisted that she did? "Let us hurry home, my lord, for I feel my nerve beginning to waver, yet go on this journey in time I must!"

When they returned to Raven's Rock, Wynne kissed Madoc in such a way that he knew she was saying her farewell to him. He could not remain within their apartments, and fled to his tower for comfort. Megan had prepared her mistress's bath, and Wynne bathed quickly, donning a soft silk chamber robe in her favorite grass-green, which was lined in an equally soft rabbit's fur. Megan was instructed to pour her lady a goblet of sweet wine. Wynne mixed Madoc's herbs into it.

"Go to my lord, Megan," Wynne told the girl, "and say that I have taken his sleeping mixture. When I awaken I shall know all. Remind him also of his promise to me." Then lifting the goblet, Wynne immediately drained it. She handed the vessel to Megan and lay back upon her pillows.

Almost at once her eyes felt abnormally heavy. Her entire being seemed to be sinking, but before she could even consider being fearful, Wynne fell into a deep slumber. She felt as if she were falling, falling, falling; and yet there was now a weightlessness to her body. She wanted to open her eyes, but she could not. There was no sound. It was as if she floated within a great nothingness. *I want to know!* she thought desperately. *I must know what it is that binds me to, yet separates me from Madoc! I must know!*

Then suddenly above her a raven cried. *Remember! Remember!* About her a faint mauve mist blew like pieces of shredded silk gauze, obscuring her vision. Then all at once the mists were gone. Wynne found herself in a thick woods. A voice was calling to her, and yet it was not she who answered—or was it? She could feel her own life force ebbing, even as another life force surged forward; but she was not afraid.

"Rhiannon! Rhiannon, where are you?!"

"Over here, Angharad. Oh, come and look! Do come!"

Angharad, catching sight of her elder sister at last, prodded her mount through the trees to the edge of the dark green and gold forest where Rhiannon sat upon her own horse, peering intently through the trees. "What is so interesting that you would not answer me?" she demanded. Though younger than her sister, Angharad had always felt older, wiser, and protective of her beauteous elder sibling.

Rhiannon pointed with a slender finger.

Sapphire blue eyes followed her sister's delicate direction. Angharad stared for a moment, and then she said in a disappointed tone, "It is only a party of Cymri huntsmen, Rhiannon. There is nothing particularly fascinating about them."

"Not all of them, silly," Rhiannon admonished her sister. *"Him!* Pwyll, Prince of Dyfed. Is he not the most beautiful creature that you have ever seen in all of your existence?"

Angharad looked again and, seeing nothing she thought unusual, she wrinkled her pretty nose. "He is Cymri," she repeated, as if that explanation should be enough for her sister's understanding.

"Ohhh, look!" the besotted Rhiannon cried out. "He is dancing upon the mound! Is he not amusing, sister?"

"He's drunk with mead," replied Angharad pointedly, "or else he would not dare to do it. The Cymri believe that those mounds are entries into the worlds below the earth. What foolish beings they are. I've heard it said that they think if they tread even accidentally upon those grassy hillocks that they will invite enchantment. What silliness!"

"Pwyll," called one of the huntsmen to the dancer. "Come down off that damned mound! Are ye courting trouble then, man? Ye'll bring a curse upon us all!"

" 'Tis naught but superstitious nonsense," laughed Pwyll bravely. "Come and join me, Taran! Or is the victorious warrior of a hundred battles afraid of the fairies?"

"I am not afraid of the fairies," laughed Taran goodnaturedly, "but I'm also not drunk enough to be foolish."

From her hiding place Rhiannon's eyes twinkled mischievously and she giggled. Turning to her younger sister, she said, "I think that the beautiful Prince of Dyfed lacks a proper respect, Angharad. Perhaps I can instill it in him."

"What are you going to do, Rhiannon?" demanded Angharad. "The Cymri are best avoided."

"Stay right where you are, little one. As your elder, I am responsible for you. You may watch me, however," came the gay reply as Rhiannon moved her horse forward out of the shelter of the trees. She spurred her mount gently forward into the clearing where the men were gathered, but the creature's dainty hooves made no sound as they touched the ground.

Taran saw her first as she appeared from amid the tangle of woods that surrounded the little area where he and his companions had stopped to eat and drink. His mouth fell open with surprise. Speechless, he could do nothing more than raise a hand and point. Amazed that their usually voluble companion had been rendered silent, Pwyll and the others followed the direction of that shaking finger to find themselves equally stunned.

At first they were not even certain what it was they saw glittering and shimmering as it came toward them. Was it some trick of the light amid the delicate leaves of the golden beech trees and the sturdier quivering branches of the deep green pines? Was it their half-drunken state that made them imagine that they were seeing something? Was it magic of some sort that they were witnessing? Then gradually their confused eyes perceived a young girl upon her horse.

There wasn't a man in that clearing who did not think that the girl was the most beautiful creature he had ever seen. A tall, slender maiden with a serene face, mounted upon a dainty black mare with an elegant high step, whose bejeweled red leather bridle tinkled with the sound of tiny silver bells. The girl's heart-shaped face was framed by a mass of thick hair which seemed to be spun of gold and silver mixed together. It poured down her back in a rippling wave, spreading itself out over the shining dark flanks of the horse. Her gown was a pearlescent garment that appeared to have been spun from cobwebs and moonbeams. It floated about her. Her beautiful, delicate hands with their slender, bejeweled fingers rested quietly upon the reins. She seemed to be almost one with her mare. Eyes focused ahead of her on some unseen path, she did not once look toward the huntsmen as she trotted by and vanished on the opposite side of the clearing into the forest as silently and as mysteriously as she had come forth from it.

Open-mouthed, they stared after her. Then Pwyll managed to recover and called to a young huntsman, "Gwyr! Follow her! Quickly! I would know who that lady is, *and* where she goes."

Galvanized into action by the sound of Pwyll's voice, the young huntsman raced to his horse and dashed off after the beautiful girl.

As they watched him go, Taran said, "I think we may have seen some magical creature from another realm, my lord. Perhaps you should not have danced upon the mound."

"Aye, 'tis magic we have seen this afternoon, my lord," spoke up another of the prince's friends, Evan ap Rhys. "I hope you have not offended one of the Fair Folk."

"The Fair Folk are not to be feared," Pwyll tried to reassure his men. "They are our friends."

"They are different from us, Pwyll," replied Taran. "Oh, I know you have had dealings with them before and all has been well; but none of us knows where they live, or even how they live. They simply appear and disappear at will. They are prosperous, and yet do any of us know how they come by their wealth? Such lack of knowledge makes me uncomfortable with the Fair Folk."

"Have you ever known the Fair Folk to do anyone a serious harm?" Pwyll countered.

Taran shook his head. "Nay," he admitted, "I have not."

" 'Tis more than we can say for our more familiar neighbors," Evan ap Rhys muttered.

The huntsmen returned home, and later that evening, as they feasted in Pwyll's hall, Gwyr arrived tired, dirty, and soaked through with the rain which was now falling outside. The young man was given a juicy piece of venison on a trencher of bread and a goblet of wine. His companions waited politely for him to finish his meal, that they might learn of his adventure.

Finally restored, Gwyr put down his goblet and said to Pwyll, "I regret, my lord prince, that I could not catch up with the lady."

"Was her horse so swift then?" demanded Pwyll.

Gwyr shook his head, and his glance was a troubled one. "I kept the lady in my sight for some time, but no matter how fast I drove my own horse onward, I could not catch up with her. She, however, appeared to neither slow nor hurry her beast. Then suddenly she was simply no longer there, yet I cannot recall seeing her disappear. I do not understand it, my lord," he finished with a helpless shrug.

" 'Tis magic he has witnessed," Taran said quietly.

"What magic?" The query came from the girl who was seated next to Pwyll. "What are you talking about? You have all been so mysterious since your return from the hunt this afternoon. You must tell all!" She smiled winningly up at Pwyll, her eyes soft and alluring.

"There is little to tell, Bronwyn," Pwyll replied. "We saw an extraordinary lovely girl in the forest today, and I sent Gwyr after her to find out who she was, as none of us had ever seen her before. She seems, however, to have eluded young Gwyr."

"Oh," laughed Bronwyn gaily. "Is that all?" Then she reached out and, bringing her goblet to her lips, sipped her wine thoughtfully as the men in the hall went back to their conversation. Bronwyn of the White Breast was the only daughter of Cynbel, lord of Teifi. Next to Pwyll's family, the family of Cynbel of Teifi was the most powerful in Dyfed. It had been assumed by all at court that he would one day make Bronwyn of the White Breast his wife. No formal betrothal had ever been arranged, however, and the ladies of the court all enjoyed flirting with Pwyll at one time or another, although none would have dared to aspire to becoming his wife. That place would belong to Bronwyn of the White Breast, or so it was believed by all at Dyfed's court.

Bronwyn was a pretty girl whose best feature was her milky white skin. Her eyes were dark brown, but perhaps they were a trifle too harsh in her pale face. Her hair was a golden brown. She wore it in two long, neat braids along either side of her head. Still, her features were attractive and in good proportion, if not outstanding or unique. Her teeth were small, white, and even. As she was expected to be Pwyll's wife one day, none would criticize her. Though Bronwyn presented a sweet and pleasant picture, there were those who had felt the sting of her temper, which bordered on the vicious when she was, or felt she had been, crossed. No one complained. She was Cynbel of Teifi's only daughter. She would be Pwyll's wife.

Now as she sat at Pwyll's high board, her goblet clasped

within her two hands, she carefully considered the events of today. Why had Pwyll sent after this mysterious woman? Why should he be so intrigued? Instinct warned Bronwyn of the White Breast that such a thing did not bode well for her. She had never considered the possibility that Pwyll might ever marry outside of his court, might ever wed someone other than her. And he would not, if she had anything to say about it. *He was hers!* Then she laughed softly at herself for being such a fool. The lady had disappeared. They should never see her again, but perhaps this was a warning she should heed. She would speak most firmly to her father about arranging her marriage to Pwyll as soon as possible. It was past time she became his wife. Possessively her hand reached out to touch his arm, and she smiled the contented smile of a well-fed cat.

Pwyll did not feel her touch. The Prince of Dyfed was genuinely troubled. He was neither faint-hearted nor superstitious, but like all about him, he acknowledged the existence of the Fair Folk. They were of a far more ancient race than his own. They rarely associated with the Cymri, for they held them somewhat in contempt, Pwyll knew; but when they did deign to associate with his people, it was very much at their own convenience. Even the proud Cymri acknowledged the superiority of the Fair Folk whose magic was legend.

Pwyll knew it was better to have the Fair Folk for friends rather than to have them for enemies. He had had previous associations with some of their powerful clans. It had been very much to his own good and those of his people. His drunken capering in the forest this afternoon may have offended them, Pwyll now realized. Although no one understood the mysterious mounds, perhaps the beautiful maiden was their guardian. Whoever she was, he knew that he wanted to see her again. Unaware of Bronwyn's clinging hand, Pwyll stood up and the hand fell away.

"I have dealt with the Fair Folk before," he began slowly. "The maid this afternoon was unknown to me, but from Gwyr's tale I believe her to be one of them. They are just people, but as I do not wish to offend the Fair Folk, I will return to the forest alone tomorrow to that same grassy mound to wait. Mayhap the same maiden will appear again. I will apologize to her for my foolish behavior and beg her most gracious pardon."

There were murmurs of approval throughout the hall, and Taran said, "Aye! It is a good thing, my lord, that you do so. The Fair Folk are known for their kindness of heart, and surely their men have, on occasion, been in their cups. I doubt you have committed any grave sin against them, but it cannot hurt to apologize."

"No!" The word was said loudly and sharply. All eyes swung about from Pwyll to Bronwyn. "You must not go, my dear lord," she cried, and her brown eyes brimmed with tears. "The Fair Folk are not to be trusted!" She clung to his arm as if his departure were dangerously imminent.

"Nonsense!" laughed Pwyll. "My dealings with the Fair Folk have resulted in nothing but good."

"They are not like us," Bronwyn said firmly. "They have lulled you into a false sense of security. They have built up your trust. Now suddenly this magical maiden appears beneath your very nose! Why? I think she has been sent to lure you to your doom, my lord Pwyll. What will happen to Dyfed if anything should happen to you?"

"Why, another should be chosen to be its prince, dear child. Probably your own father, Cynbel." He chuckled. "Dyfed's survival does not depend merely upon me, but you are sweet to believe it so, Bronwyn," Pwyll finished.

Now there were murmurs of dissent within the hall as some considered Bronwyn of the White Breast's words, and others supported their prince's decision to seek out the magical maiden again to apologize. Pwyll let them chatter for a time. Then he raised his hand for silence.

"I am still Dyfed's prince," he said quietly, closing the matter to any further discussion.

The following afternoon Pwyll eagerly spurred his beautiful white stallion into the deep forest that surrounded his small castle. Finding his way back to the grassy mound, he dismounted to await the return of the maiden. He could not even be certain that she would come, and yet in his heart he felt she would. She did not, however, nor for eight days after that, when he kept watch. On the ninth afternoon, just as he was about to give up in despair, the maiden rode forth from the tangle of forest into the clearing and past Pwyll. He stared after her open-mouthed, but then as his initial surprise subsided, Pwyll leapt upon his horse and galloped after her.

Rhiannon's heart was beating wildly. She had done a most brazen thing that first afternoon, as Angharad had later scolded her; but it had been worth it! It had not been the first time she had seen the Prince of Dyfed, although she had not known at first that he was a prince. Twice before, alone, she had spied upon him. Each time was like the first time when she had come upon him quite unexpectedly, schooling a horse in a meadow on the edge of the wood. Her heart had contracted most painfully in her chest that first time, and each time thereafter when she laid eyes upon him. This afternoon was no different.

Pwyll of Dyfed was even more handsome up close than he had been at a distance. His hair was as black as a raven's wing. He wore it clubbed back as the Cymri were wont to do. About his head was a band of gold which only served to accentuate the darkness of the hair. He was as fair-skinned, however, as she herself, but the color of his eyes she could not ascertain. She had never gotten that close to him. Besides, upon that fateful afternoon when she had first shown herself to him, she dared not stare. His features were strong but for his mouth, which had a softness about it. Still, she longed to kiss that mouth.

Pwyll hurried his horse after Rhiannon, keeping the same gait at first, and then spurring his horse into a gallop. There was no horse in Dyfed who could outrun Pwyll's, yet to his amazement, his straining animal could not lessen the distance between them, though the maiden's mount never appeared to increase its speed. Pwyll burst out laughing. This was powerful magic indeed. He slowed his panting beast almost to a halt and called out to the girl ahead of him, "Maiden, I beg you to stop that we may speak. I must know who you are!"

It was a mad thing to do, and she knew it. To play hide and seek with this Cymri was one thing. To become involved with him was not wise, but nonetheless, Rhiannon drew her own mount to a stop. When she turned about, it seemed to Pwyll that there had been no distance between their horses at all.

She smiled at the prince and cast a look of sympathy at the panting charger with its sweating, heaving sides. "Poor beastie," she crooned to the horse and, reaching out, stroked his neck. Then she looked at Pwyll, saying, "You did not have to chase me over half the forest if you wanted to speak with me, my lord. I would have stopped before if you had asked, Pwyll of Dyfed."

He was enchanted by the incredible sweetness of her smile, the lilting tone of her voice. Then it dawned upon him that she knew his name. *Of course she knew his name!* "Who are you?" he asked her, feeling both elation and despair even as he asked.

"My name is Rhiannon. I am the daughter of Dylan and Cornelia, rulers of the Fair Folk of this forest." Her voice was melodious; clear yet soft. "Why did you pursue me, Pwyll of Dyfed? I am told that you have returned to this place for many days now."

"I wanted to apologize for offending you," he began, wondering who had told her he had returned here.

"Offending me? How?" she asked him, amused.

"Are you not the guardian of this grassy mound upon which I danced?"

For a moment Rhiannon stared at him in surprise. Then, unable to help herself, she burst into laughter. The merry sound was that of water tumbling over stones in a stream bed, and he was not in the least offended that she found him funny. "My lord of Dyfed," she finally managed to say as she struggled to regain control of herself, "those grassy mounds have been here since time began. Even we of the Fair Folk do not know their true origins. It is really I who must apologize to you, for, knowing the superstitions held by the Cymri, I decided to play a jest upon you when I saw you dancing upon the mound the other day. I knew that should I appear before you without speaking and go silently about my way, you and your Cymri huntsmen would think it some great magic connected with the mound. My sister, who was with me, scolded me quite roundly for it, I might add."

"Then you are not angry with me?" Pwyll said, relieved.

"Nay, my lord, and I hope you are not angered with me," Rhiannon replied sweetly.

He shook his head. "I am not angry, princess. It is only just, however, that I claim a forfeit of you for your most mischievous behavior," he told her boldly. " 'Twas not fair to tease a mortal so."

A faint rose colored Rhiannon's pale cheeks. She looked directly at him and said, nodding, "You have the right, prince."

Staring into the most incredible pair of eyes that he had ever seen, Pwyll could not speak for a long moment. Surely it was enchantment. Never before had he beheld eyes the deep, rich color of woodland violets, but her eyes were precisely that color. He was quite happy to drown in their bottomless depths.

Rhiannon's thoughts were strangely similar. As he gazed into her eyes, she saw his for the first time. They were the same wonderful deep blue shade as the sea off the island where her maternal grandfather ruled. To Rhiannon they were the most beautiful eyes she had ever beheld. At that precise moment in time she knew why it was that she had sought him out. *She loved him.* She did not know why she loved him. Indeed, she did not even know him, but she loved him. Of that she was certain. She loved him and she would love him forever.

The silence between them seemed long, but finally regaining her senses, she gently encouraged him. "What would you have of me in forfeit, my lord of Dyfed?"

"Your company, princess," he said simply. Then dismounting from his own beast, he lifted her down from her horse.

The touch of his fingers about her slender waist seemed to burn through her delicate clothing to her sensitive skin. She shivered. His boldness was exciting, for boldness was not a trait amongst her own people, who were more controlled. Rhiannon watched in silence as he slipped the reins from both their animals over the branches of a rowan bush to keep the horses from wandering. At last she said softly, "Would you like to walk? There is a pretty pond nearby that I could show you."

"Aye, lady," he replied simply, and, taking her dainty hand in his large one, he let her lead him.

They walked through the forest. The sun slipping down through the trees crowned the tops of their heads with golden light and warmed their shoulders. At first they said little. Then at last they reached the pond. It seemed to Pwyll that there was no source for the pond's water, and yet it was filled full with liquid so crystal clear, he could see its sandy bottom and the little fishes swimming in it. He could not remember ever having been in this particular part of the forest before. *Or had he?*

Nothing seemed quite familiar to him. A frightening thought suddenly bloomed in his brain.

"Are we in my world or yours, lady?" he asked her half fearfully. He knew, as did any sane man, that the portals separating different worlds were ofttimes invisible. Had this magical creature led him astray? Had Bronwyn been right?

"My lord," Rhiannon said quietly, "it is all one world in which we live. It is merely a matter of seeing not simply with one's eyes, but with one's heart as well. Often we do not see the most obvious things because we are either too busy or think we are. Or, and this I think a great sin, we do not want to acknowledge that which is before us, for it may be a more complex solution than we can willingly admit. How much easier to accept the obvious."

He did not fully understand her, but he felt somehow reassured. "Where do you live?" he asked. "Is it a near place, or in some distant spot?"

"My father's castle is here in this forest," Rhiannon replied.

"That cannot be!" Pwyll cried. "I know this forest! I have hunted in it since I was old enough to sit on a horse. It is mostly a wild and impenetrable place."

"Have you ever seen this pond before?" she asked him.

"Nay, I have not," he answered her.

"And yet this pond has been here all along," she told him with calm logic. "You do not know this forest at all, my lord. You have never before seen this pond because you have not looked carefully enough. So it is with my father's castle. You have not seen it because you have not looked for it. I will show it to you one day, Pwyll."

"When?" Suddenly he was eager to explore these new worlds that Rhiannon was opening up to him.

"On the day you come to claim me for your bride, Pwyll of Dyfed," came the startling reply.

"What?" The word sounded foolish to his own ears, but Pwyll could not remember ever having been so surprised in his life as he was now. Among the people of Britain he was a well-known and highly respected ruler. He was no backward fool. He ruled over a land of seven distinct and separate regions, each with a minimum of a hundred farms and villages. While his father had still ruled Dyfed, Pwyll had gained a reputation as a mighty and valiant warrior, fighting for justice in

other lands. He thought he was long past the point where
someone could surprise him so completely. Yet this beautiful
maiden, whose name meant "Great Queen," had startled him
totally.

"Do you not wish me for your wife?" Rhiannon asked him
in all innocence. "I have watched you for some time now, and
as I have, my love for you has grown," she continued. "We of
the Fair Folk do not believe in being coy. That is a trait of
Cymri women. We are open, and time is precious to us. To
waste time is to us the greatest sin. I love you, Pwyll of Dyfed.
I would be with you forever. I would be your wife."

His head reeled. This was a king's daughter. And not just
any king. Dylan of the Fair Folk's daughter! She wanted *him*
for a husband! The most beautiful maiden he had ever seen
wanted him for a husband! *Bronwyn.* Her name slipped unbidden into his head. Everyone had always assumed that he would
wed Bronwyn of the White Breast. Even he had assumed it,
and yet he did not love her. Of that he was absolutely certain.
It had simply seemed politic to marry Cynbel of Teifi's daughter. Particularly as there was no one else who seriously took
his fancy. *Until now.* Yet he had made no promises to Bronwyn
publicly or privately. There was no betrothal between them.

It was an incredible honor being offered him, but he found
himself a little afraid. There had been stories of men and
women of the Cymri beloved of the Fair Folk. Few of those
tales had ended happily, he recalled nervously. Rhiannon was
so very beautiful. Far more beautiful than any maiden of the
Cymri, and with that beauty came a sweetness that would
surely disarm his own people, easing any fears they might
have of this exquisite magical maiden. Pwyll suddenly realized
that he had loved her at first sight. He did indeed want
Rhiannon for his wife. No other would do, and yet . . .

Rhiannon sensed his concern. "You think of the others from
our two different races who have loved. None were husband
and wife as we will be," she told him.

"Why were they not wed?" he asked.

"Because those of my race would never give up their ways
for the Cymri that they loved. *I will.* I shall become one of you
on the day that you wed me, Pwyll of Dyfed. We will live happily forever. In exchange for my hand in marriage, you must
give me but two things. I would have your complete love, and

I would have your complete trust. Do you think that you can give me those two gifts, my lord? Think most carefully on it before you answer."

"Nay, Rhiannon, there is nought to think about!" he cried passionately. "For love of you, my dearling, I could conquer the world!"

"If I have your love and your trust, Pwyll, I have the only world I desire," Rhiannon told him seriously, and then she laughed happily. "If we are agreed, my handsome Cymri prince, then I must go. In one year's time you will come for me at the same grassy mound where we first met. On that day I will take you to my father's court and we will be wed. Then I will return home with you to Dyfed forevermore."

He caught her hands in his, touching her for the first time, and was surprised at how vibrantly she pulsed with life. "If time is so precious to you, Rhiannon," he begged her earnestly, "why must we wait a year to wed?" She was so fragile and delicate a creature that he could feel the life force pumping through her very fingertips.

She drew him near and, looking into his eyes, said, "Time among the Cymri is different than it is for the Fair Folk, my love. Alas, there are other considerations to our marriage. It is the custom of my people that a woman has the absolute right to choose her own mate. So I have chosen you, but I will have to overcome the objections of my family and my people. You see, Pwyll, I am not merely a king's daughter. I was chosen by my people to be my father's successor one day, for we Fair Folk fade from the earth eventually, even as do the Cymri. When I wed with you, I must give up my rights as a member of my kind.

"There will be much distress and unhappiness at my decision. My people will need time to decide upon another heir to my father's place. I believe my younger sister, Angharad, is far better qualified to be the next reigning queen of the Fair Folk than even I. I must work to convince my people of it. They in turn, as is their right, will seek to prevent my going. That is why you must be certain, Pwyll of Dyfed, that you are capable of giving me your complete love and your complete trust no matter what happens in our lives. To wed you, oh prince, I must give up my heritage. I do it gladly for my love of you! Is your heart as brave and can it be true?"

He was stunned by her revelation, and humbled too. This incredibly beautiful maiden, chosen by destiny to be a queen, was willing, nay she was eager, to give up everything she knew and held dear simply to be his wife. "Ahh, dearling," he sighed sadly, "I fear I am not worthy of you."

"Do you love me, Pwyll of Dyfed?" she asked him quietly.

"Aye, Rhiannon," he answered without hesitation, and knew in his heart that he spoke the truth.

"Then surely," she told him, "there is nothing that can prevent our marriage or destroy our happiness."

And at that moment a little breeze blew through the clearing, ruffling the golden leaves of the beech trees even as Pwyll drew her into the deep comfort of his arms. He bent only slightly, for she was practically his own height, for all her delicacy. He touched her lips with his in a gentle, reverent kiss; but Rhiannon's soft mouth kissed him back with a fierce passion that both startled and pleasured him, and bespoke other delights to come.

He held her against him, an arm about her supple waist, his other hand caressing her silvery-gold hair which felt like thistledown beneath his roughened fingers. Her kisses tasted like strawberries to him, and he could not remember a time in his life when he had felt so happy, so fulfilled, so at peace with himself and the world about him. And everything he felt and sensed, Rhiannon felt and sensed too.

"Dearling," he murmured against her ear. "I will never cease to love you. *Ever!*"

The mauve mists swirled suddenly about them. A raven cried in the sky above. *Remember!* The sensation of his arms was gone, and she heard a voice calling her once more.

"Rhiannon!" It was Angharad's voice.

"Rhiannon, my daughter." It was her father who now spoke to her.

The mists cleared and she found herself in her father's hall, her family about her, looking unhappy and disturbed.

"Oh, Rhiannon! How could you do this to me! I do not want to be queen of the Fair Folk! Really, I do not!" Angharad protested. She rubbed the pale pink silk of her gown between her thumb and her forefinger as she was wont to do whenever she was distressed.

"You are the perfect choice, Angharad, though you be

young," Rhiannon soothed her sibling. "You will be a great queen one day. I know it, and I will be so proud of you."

In an uncustomary burst of emotion, Angharad threw herself into her sister's arms and sniffled. "Don't leave us, Rhiannon! I beg you do not leave us! I fear for your safety amongst the Cymri. Though some like Pwyll accept us, most do not. No matter how hard you try, you will always be a stranger among them. An object of curiosity and suspicion."

"Nothing matters to me," Rhiannon replied, "but that I be Pwyll's wife and the mother of his children, dearest little sister. I know that this all came as a shock to you, but you are simply not used to the idea yet. It has been assumed our whole lives that I should one day follow our father as ruler of the Fair Folk of this forest, but it is not to be. I always believed that my fate lay elsewhere."

"I do not want to be queen because I do not want all the responsibility that goes with it," Angharad said petulantly and with perfect logic. "To be Trystan's wife and the mother of our children is the only fate I desire."

Rhiannon laughed merrily. "It would never be enough for you, Angharad, and in your heart you know I speak the truth. You are one of those creatures who was born to mother the world. Our people will one day thrive under your rule. As for your Trystan," and Rhiannon chuckled, "he is so proud of you that if he does not dissolve in a burst of pure happiness, I shall be quite surprised."

Angharad could not resist a smile at her sister's words. It was true. Trystan was more than proud of her. He was adoring, and he had begun to fret that perhaps he was not a fit husband for a future queen of the Fair Folk. It would take all her powers of persuasion to soothe his fears, but soothe him she would, for she loved him, which surprised many. Like all races, the Fair Folk had their share of those who were wise and those who were not so wise. Trystan fit into this latter category, but Angharad knew what others did not. She knew that her beloved was kind and loyal and true. And he had a most marvelous sense of humor. Nonetheless, it seemed disloyal to her entire family, she thought, to take Rhiannon's place. "For all your words, sister," she finally said, "I am not happy with this decision you have made. To be queen of the Fair Folk will not be an easy thing."

"It is your duty now, my sibling," replied Rhiannon in that quiet voice of hers which all knew meant the discussion was ended. "The council has agreed, and so have all our people. Oh, Angharad! You are really far better suited to this office than I ever was. You are strong and sure in your ways. I am a risk taker who would follow her heart. No queen of the Fair Folk should be that way."

Now it was the sisters' mother, Cornelia, who spoke up. "Why can you simply not take the Cymri as a lover?" she asked her daughter. "That is what our people have done in the past. Why must you wed him and give up everything?" Her beautiful face showed great concern.

"Nay," Rhiannon said. "That is not what either of us wants. I would be Pwyll's wife, and, for our marriage to succeed, we must be as one. There is no way in which Pwyll can be a part of our world, but I can become a part of his world. Dearest Mother! You must be happy for me, for this is what I want most in all the world."

Cornelia's lovely violet eyes filled with quick tears. Rhiannon was her eldest child. Although she would not have admitted it aloud lest it be considered a betrayal of her darling Angharad, she did love Rhiannon best. She could not help it. The girl was so as she had once been. A romantic who believed the best of everyone. In the world in which the Fair Folk lived, that was not such a dangerous belief; but in the world of the Cymri . . .

Cornelia sighed deeply. Why, she wondered, had her elder daughter fallen in love with Pwyll of Dyfed? There was not an eligible man in their world who would not have given all he possessed and more for Rhiannon's hand in marriage. She might have been the daughter of the humblest of them, and she would have still been prized above all others. There was Gavin, Prince of the Fair Folk of the River Wye; the twin warrior princes, Cadawg and Cad-el, who came from her own island home in the West; and most distinguished of all, young King Meredydd, who ruled over the Fair Folk in the Southeast, whose kingdom might have been joined with theirs. He would be the most disappointed of all. Why could Rhiannon not have chosen amongst her own kind; but alas, she had not. Helplessly Cornelia turned to her husband for support.

Dylan shook his head. "We have argued over this problem

like an old dog that continues to gnaw upon a bone for marrow long gone," he told her sadly. "Rhiannon has made it quite clear that she will have Pwyll, Prince of Dyfed, a Cymri, for her husband, and no other. She has convinced both the council and our people of her intent. They have chosen Angharad to take her place as my successor. So be it."

He smiled at his younger daughter. "Though you protest this decision, Angharad, you already show a wisdom that will lead our people one day by your choice of your husband. Tell Trystan that we will celebrate your marriage to one another at the next full moon. I fully approve. I grow weary of my royal burden. I would pass my authority on to you within the next few years, that I may enjoy the remainder of my years in freedom and peace as my own father did. It is settled," he concluded, patting his wife's hand.

A tear slipped down Cornelia's cheek, which Rhiannon kissed away, even as Angharad's eyes met those of her father in agreement and acceptance.

At the next full moon the marriage of Angharad and Trystan was celebrated with much happiness by both their families. Trystan was a younger son of a powerful family from the Northeast. And at the wedding feast Rhiannon's four rejected suitors each attempted to claim her and override her decision, but she stood firm in her intent, to their great disappointment. Meredydd of the Southeast was particularly angry. Bitterly he took his leave of Rhiannon, saying, "The Cymri lord will certainly prove himself unworthy of you. They are a cruel race." Then he departed.

Dylan arose and said, "At the next full waxing of our sister, the moon, the Cymri year that Rhiannon gave her beloved is concluded. She will go to meet him and bring him to us, that we may celebrate their marriage. There is one condition to my acceptance of this match which they must both fulfill else I withdraw my permission. If either of them should refuse, there will be no marriage between them. Though it is your right, Rhiannon, to choose your own mate, it is my right as your king to forbid this match should my conditions not be met. That is also a part of our ancient law, and you must abide by it."

"What would you have of us, Father?" Rhiannon asked.

"I will not discuss it with you until Pwyll stands before me by your side, my daughter," King Dylan said with finality.

On the first morning of the next full moon, even as the sun was tinting the horizon with its arrival, Pwyll, prince of Dyfed, in his scarlet and gold wedding finery, arrived at the grassy green mound where he had first beheld Rhiannon. She was awaiting him with a warm smile of welcome, and happiness radiated from her very being at the sight of him. "Welcome, my beloved!" she greeted him, and then she smiled at the party of gaily clad gentlemen who accompanied the prince. "I bid you welcome also, my lords."

Those who had seen her before were again struck by her rare and flawless beauty, and those who had not seen her before were rendered dumb with their amazement, for they would not have believed so fair a creature actually existed. She seemed to be garbed in spun moonlight. When Pwyll had returned from his private meeting with Rhiannon a year ago to announce his marriage plans, there had been a terrible uproar in the council chamber of Dyfed. Some thought the prince bewitched by the maiden of the Fair Folk. They cried their outrage over the matter; but Pwyll calmed them. He was not bewitched. He was simply in love. Those who knew him best understood this and kept their peace, although it fretted them that their prince would wed with an outsider.

Cynbel of Teifi, however, was enraged by Pwyll's news and had to be restrained by those around him. Though he had never formally approached Pwyll; though there was no betrothal between his daughter, Bronwyn of the White Breast, and the prince of Dyfed; like everyone else he had assumed that one day his daughter would marry Pwyll. He had even planned to broach the matter with Pwyll shortly, as Bronwyn had strongly indicated that it was past time for a marriage to take place between herself and Pwyll. She was tired of waiting for Pwyll to come to her. Now there would be no marriage, and it would take a miracle to find a man whom Bronwyn would accept after wanting Dyfed's ruler all these years. Cynbel of Teifi was insulted, and his fury was difficult to calm.

Pwyll, unaware of all of this, filled with his enthusiasm and his passion for Rhiannon of the Fair Folk, spoke glowingly to his council of the girl he would make his bride. They loved him, and though it fretted some that he would take a foreigner to wife, in the end they were happy for him and agreed to it. All but Cynbel of Teifi, who considered how he might best take his revenge on Pwyll of Dyfed for this terrible offense to his daughter and to his family.

Now seeing Rhiannon before him, Pwyll's groomsmen were charmed by her beauty and her good manners. They followed her willingly into the dark forest, and only some were aware that the path that they followed through the deep bracken seemed to disappear behind them as they passed; or that the dense undergrowth before them opened mysteriously at the sight of Rhiannon's horse. Finally the forest began to thin and they entered a clearing upon the shores of a crystal-blue lake that none had ever known existed within the wood. They stared open-mouthed.

"We will leave our horses here," Rhiannon told them. "They will be fed and watered and well cared for by my father's people. The boats will take us the rest of our way."

"To where, princess?" asked Taran in a somewhat awed voice.

"Why, to my father's castle," Rhiannon laughed gaily, pointing.

They followed the direction of her finger and gasped with their surprise. As the rosy morning mists lifted from the surface of the lake, they saw a castle in its center. It was, however, a castle such as they had never imagined, built of pale grey stones with graceful towers that soared into the blue morning skies. It seemed to spring from the very depths of the water itself. There was a magical quality about it that brought renewed fear into their hearts. As their terror threatened to overwhelm them, the air about them was filled with bright blue and gold butterflies whose very appearance seemed to calm Pwyll's men, as their hearts were filled with a wonderful sense of peace and well-being.

Upon the sandy shores of the lake, six silver boats, each with a high dragon's-head prow of green, gold, and red enamel, sat neatly. Rhiannon gestured Pwyll and his party into the boats, placing herself alone with her chosen husband in the first boat, dispersing the others in the remaining five small vessels. Once afloat, the boats glided effortlessly, seeming to pilot themselves over the calm crystal surface of the lake. As they drew near to the castle, they discovered that it did not rise from the water at all, but was actually built upon a small island. As the dragon-powered boats slid upon the shore of the island, a group of gaily gowned and smiling young women came forth to greet them. They were all quite fair and carried garlands and wreaths of fresh multicolored flowers which they slipped around the necks and upon the heads of their Cymri guests.

"Come," said Rhiannon, taking Pwyll by the hand. "You must meet my family. Then we shall be wed in my father's hall. Your men will be happy with the ladies of the court. They are gentle and gracious hostesses. There is nothing for any of you to fear in my father's house."

Pwyll followed Rhiannon to a small, beautifully furnished chamber where her family awaited him. What amazed him most about the Fair Folk was that even those he knew to be the eldest among them looked young. There were two men and two women within the room. One was a tall, blue-eyed gentleman with wavy golden hair, wearing a jeweled diadem upon his head. This would be Dylan, Pwyll reasoned as he bowed low and was greeted politely in return. A lovely woman with silvery hair fashioned in a coronet of braids was introduced to him as his bride's mother. Again Pwyll bowed, sensing reserve, although she was most cordial to him. He could scarcely blame her, he thought.

"And this is my sister Angharad, and her husband Trystan, who are newly wed," Rhiannon said, bringing forward a young woman who very much resembled their father. Trystan, however, had a hint of fire within his rich blond locks.

They sat, and delicate little serving girls who seemed to dance across the floor brought a light golden wine which glittered in their crystal goblets. When the servants had left, the king of the Fair Folk did not mince his words. He looked directly at Pwyll and said, "Prince of Dyfed, are you certain that deep in your Cymri heart you love my daughter? Are you positive that you would have her to wife above all others of your own kind? Speak frankly and openly to me. No harm will come to you if you speak with candor and truth. If your heart is not true, however, I shall know it. I seek only happiness for my beloved daughter."

"I love Rhiannon more than I love life itself, sire," Pwyll replied. "I will have no other to wife but her. Ask those who accompany me. I did not know love until the day I first saw your daughter."

"And you will give her your complete love, and your complete trust, Prince of Dyfed? Again I beg you to think carefully before you answer!" Dylan said. "A marriage between a Cymri lord and a princess of the Fair Folk is serious business."

"I will give Rhiannon my complete love and trust," Pwyll answered in a strong and sure voice.

Rhiannon smiled happily at him. He was so very handsome and manly.

"You do understand, Pwyll of Dyfed, that when Rhiannon is your wife, the powers she possesses as one of the Fair Folk will be gone from her. To us she will become as you are. A Cymri. There are those among your race who would have a woman of the Fair Folk in their clutches merely for the powers we possess and not for love of them. Are you one of those?"

"Nay, sire. I love Rhiannon only for herself and for no other reason. I realize her powers will be gone, but it matters not to me, for it is the woman I want. Not her magic."

Dylan nodded and then turned to Rhiannon. "I ask you a final time, my daughter. Are you determined to wed with this man, even knowing that by this marriage you will forfeit your heritage?"

"I am, Father," Rhiannon said with determination. "I would be Pwyll's wife and nought else matters to me."

"Very well then," said King Dylan. "I will permit this union, but only upon one condition. If you find you cannot agree to it, then I shall not allow the wedding to proceed. Rhiannon, my daughter, and Pwyll, my son. I must insist that this marriage between you not be physically consummated for one full year."

"Father!"

"Sire!"

Both had spoken in unison, but Dylan gestured to them to be silent. "Hear me out, my children," he said in kindly tones. "I have but your interests at heart. You must understand that in all of our joined histories there has never been a marriage recorded between the Fair Folk of this forest and the Cymri of Dyfed. There have been lovers amongst our peoples, it is true, but those lovers have always been parted in the end. Alas, the differences that separate us seem great, although in truth they are not. Still, it is something we have not been able to overcome.

"My elder daughter, however, insists that she be your wife, and you have agreed. As her father I am fearful that Rhiannon's heart leads her into a world of darkness rather than one of light. But I must accept her wishes whatever I may feel, for that is our way. Nonetheless, I would protect my child as would any good father. If you consummate your marriage immediately, there is certain to be a child. We of the Fair Folk are noted for our fertility. Once there are children, Rhiannon is bound to you.

"If you are both wise and willing to wait for your pleasure, what do you lose? Even in the Cymri world, a year is not a great deal of time. It will give my daughter a chance to learn your ways. It will give her the opportunity to know for certain if she can really be happy among the Cymri, if the love you have for one another is strong enough to sustain you in the face of opposition; for I know, Pwyll, that there are those within your court who are not happy with this decision you have made to marry my child. A year will give Rhiannon time to win the Cymri of Dyfed over, to learn if your people will really accept her as one of you.

"Rhiannon gives up everything to be your wife. She has willingly forfeited her inheritance as our next queen. She has accepted the loss of her powers. Once she is completely yours, she cannot return to us. I think her sacrifice for the love of you is much too great, Prince of Dyfed. What can you offer her in return that is of equal value? Nothing that I can see. The risk is all hers.

"Therefore I ask that you both agree to these, my terms. Today we will celebrate a marriage between you, but there must be no consummation of that marriage for one year. If in a year you have decided that you cannot be happy together as man and wife, the marriage can be easily dissolved. Rhiannon can return to us, and although she has given up her rights to be my successor, it is within my ability to restore her powers to her. She may wed among our people and be happy, even as you may wed among your people and be happy.

"This pact will be between those of us within this chamber. No others need know, lest they use this knowledge to cause trouble between Pwyll and Rhiannon. Think carefully, my children, before you answer me; but for both your sakes, I beg you agree," Dylan concluded.

"It is ridiculous!" Rhiannon burst out. "Of course we will not agree! How can you even ask such a thing of us, Father?"

"Wait, my love," Pwyll said. "Do not be hasty in your anger, but consider what your father has said. You are very wise, my lord king, and I believe you correct when you say there is little risk for me in this marriage, but risk aplenty for Rhiannon. I would never willingly harm her."

"Do you not think I know that, Pwyll?" Rhiannon cried. "Still, it is not fair what my father asks of us! Nay, he does not even ask, he demands it as the price of his blessing upon our union! Let us leave this place and be wed in your castle this very day. I will give you a son before another year passes!"

Dylan and Cornelia looked to the prince, whose handsome face was serious and his tone grave as he spoke again.

"Rhiannon, I once told you that I did not feel worthy of one such as you. What your father asks of us is not so hard. It is the only way in which I may prove myself fit within my own mind to be your husband. Give me this opportunity, dearling, I beg of you! Let me show your father, your family . . . nay! Let me show all the Fair Folk that a Cymri prince is indeed a worthy husband for Rhiannon, the most perfect and beautiful princess of the Fair Folk of this forest." He knelt before her and, taking her hand in his, he kissed it tenderly.

Cornelia looked to her husband, and Dylan nodded his approval. They did not need to speak aloud to communicate their thoughts with one another. Pwyll's behavior was more than promising and boded well for the success of this marriage, they thought.

Tears, however, sprang into Rhiannon's violet eyes. They were tears of both distress and frustration. How could she deny this man whom she loved so dearly a chance to prove himself, not just to her own people, but in his own mind as well? She could not. "Stand up, Pwyll," she said, resigned. When he stood by her side she sighed deeply, and then looking at her father, told him, "I will agree to your terms, sire. I think it unfair of you to impose such a stricture upon us, but as my beloved lord has no objections, then I too must concur with your wishes."

Suddenly the mauve mists swirled about them and time dissolved around her, even as it raced by in its eager pursuit of the future.

"One year," she heard Pwyll say, and his breath was warm against her ear. "We have been wed one year this day. The time has flown by so quickly, Rhiannon."

She was in his arms and, looking up at him, she smiled, the year behind them now all quite clear in her mind. "We have met my father's foolish terms," she told him, "and tonight we may, at last, consummate our union. Our people grow quite anxious for an heir. Perhaps when I have given you one they will be less suspicious of me."

He kissed her pale brow. "You fret needlessly, my love. Our people both accept and love you," Pwyll assured his wife.

Rhiannon did not bother to reply, for she knew the truth of the matter, even if Pwyll refused to see it. The Cymri had been nervous and suspicious of her from the moment she arrived at Pwyll's castle. The women of the court were particularly unkind, though never before the prince. Led by Bronwyn of the White Breast, they ignored her when they were alone. They made disparaging remarks about her pale gold hair and very fair skin. They were jealous of her talent at weaving, which far surpassed their own.

"I could weave every bit as well as you," Bronwyn told her one day, "if I had magic in my fingertips as you do."

"There is no magic in what I do," Rhiannon exclaimed to her disbelieving audience. "I left my magic behind when I came to Pwyll as his wife."

"What lies she tells," mocked Bronwyn boldly. "As for Pwyll, he would have done better to wed with me as was intended. At least I should have given him a son by now."

Rhiannon held her peace as the women about her tittered meanly and, then rising, followed Bronwyn from the hall in a show of open rudeness.

"Why do you not tell Pwyll of their disrespect, my princess?" Taran of the Hundred Battles was by her side. His rough features were troubled. From the beginning he had set himself up as her champion.

"What could he do, Taran? Order them to like me? That is something that they must do on their own," Rhiannon told him serenely. "I will not distress Pwyll with this foolish pettiness. Do you think I do not recognize Bronwyn's bitterness for what it really is? I know that she would sit in my place. All her life she has assumed that she would be Pwyll's wife. Her family has encouraged her in this ambition, none of them considering for a mere moment whether that might be what Pwyll wanted also. Well, he did not, and Bronwyn, in love with my husband, or at least as much in love as she can love anyone other than herself, must blame someone for her disappointment. I am the logical choice. The other women, used to following her lead, continue to do so, though none of them dare to show me discourtesy before Pwyll."

"Bronwyn is right about one thing," Taran answered, and Rhiannon knew instantly to what he referred.

"Soon, Taran," she promised him. "Soon I will give our people the news they desire."

And soon, Rhiannon thought from the comfort of her husband's arms, was at last here. In the year she had been Pwyll's wife, she had not been entirely without allies. There were Taran and his friend, Evan ap Rhys, who, unlike the bluff warrior Taran, was a man of learning. It was he who had taught her all he knew of Cymri history, and Rhiannon in return had shared with him a chronicle of her own people. The simple people of Dyfed held Rhiannon in a great respect, for from the moment of her coming, she had gone gently amongst them as any good chatelaine would. She listened willingly to their problems and concerns, dispensing her own brand of common sense, which was considered magical wisdom by them all. She eased burdens grown too heavy when she could by her personal intervention. She healed through her knowledge of herbs and other medicinal poultices. She was generous with her purse.

All of this had kept her busy, but it had not been enough to make up for the lack of one woman friend with whom to share her secrets and her days. She missed Angharad, for her sister had always been her best friend. She wondered how her family got on, but heard nothing of them. On the day she had ridden from the forest with Pwyll as his wife, she had known that that was how it would always be. She was no longer Rhiannon of the Fair Folk, but neither was she considered a Cymri, because they would not accept her as such. *A child.* A son and heir for Pwyll, she thought. Perhaps then some of the women would begin to accept her, and the cruel influence wielded by Bronwyn of the White Breast would begin to lessen at last.

Slipping her arms about Pwyll's neck, she said huskily, "Why, my dearest husband, should we wait any longer to culminate our union? The year is over and the terms we agreed upon have been fulfilled. Among my people passion is not a thing confined to the dark hours only."

He laughed happily. "Dearest Rhiannon, my desire for you has only grown over this year, but alas, I am expected at a council meeting this morning. The matter of a trading agreement with the land of Gwynnd. I should, I assure you, far rather linger here. It has not been easy sharing a chamber with you these months past while denying what is natural and should have been between us. This afternoon, however, I shall be free."

"Do you remember the little pond that I showed you in the wood the first day that we spoke?" she asked him.

He nodded slowly.

"Do you think that you could find your way back there this afternoon, Pwyll? I will await you with a picnic feast, and we will allow nature to take its course between us at long last." Rhiannon smiled into his eyes meaningfully.

"I will be there," he told her softly, smiling back into those wonderful violet eyes of hers.

Rhiannon hurried to the kitchens of her castle, and the cook, with a smile, packed the picnic basket himself. He liked his master's wife, who had only recently cured his son of a horrible rash the boy had most of his life. It had left the child withdrawn and afraid. Now his son played happily with other children, and even spent part of his day in the kitchens willingly helping his father.

"There's a newly roasted capon, my lady," the cook told Rhiannon, beaming at her. "And fresh bread, and a good, hard, sharp cheese. Apples too! Crisp and sweet. And a flacon of wine to warm your blood should the afternoon grow cool."

She thanked him, asked after his son, and, satisfied with the answer she received, left the kitchen. The day was so fair that Rhiannon could not bear to remain within Pwyll's castle. Her *ladies* were in the Great Hall, clustered about Bronwyn like hens, and gossiping as usual. Few would miss her. Taking her basket of food, she hurried out into the sunshine and made her way on foot through the forest to her pond, where she found, to her great surprise, that Angharad was awaiting her.

The two sisters embraced and Angharad said, "I knew that you would come here today. You are ever the romantic, dearest Rhiannon!"

Rhiannon laughed. "How Cymri of me to be so predictable," she said.

"You will never be one of *them*!" Angharad replied, not without some bitterness. "They do not accept you, sister, nor do they treat you well. *I know.*"

"It has only been a year, Angharad, and I have no child with which to win them over. Before the next year is past that will all change, and so will their attitude toward me," Rhiannon answered. "But tell me of yourself and of the Fair Folk. Are Mother and Father well?"

"I have a son now," Angharad told Rhiannon proudly. "We call him Ren. He will rule our people one day when I decide to put my mantle of office aside. I will be crowned Queen of the Fair Folk on Samhein. Father is well, but he no longer wishes to rule. He and Mother desire to visit the island kingdom from which she came and spend some time with our grandparents."

"Aye, Mother spoke often about returning once we were grown. Our parents are very old now," Rhiannon noted.

"Return with me to our people, Rhiannon!" Angharad said suddenly. "Do not stay amongst the Cymri any longer, I beg you!"

Rhiannon put a comforting arm about her sister, saying as she did so, "No, Angharad, I cannot return with you, but I thank you for the asking. I love Pwyll more, if that is possible, than I did a year ago, despite the fact our marriage has yet to be consummated. And he loves me. Nothing else matters. Not the scorn of Bronwyn of the White Breast, nor the other women of the court. Nothing matters but our love for one another. I have some friends among the court, and the simple people know that I am good. It is enough for now. When I have given Pwyll half-a-dozen children, fine Cymri sons and daughters of which he may boast with pride in the hall among his friends, do you think Bronwyn's bitterness will still have any influence? I do not. If she is foolish enough to wait about for Pwyll to cease loving me, she will grow withered, and old and alone."

Tears of frustration sprang into Angharad's eyes. "I do not care for that Cymri woman, Rhiannon. 'Tis you for whom I fear!"

Rhiannon comforted her sister as best she could, but she knew that Angharad could never really understand how deep her love for Pwyll went. It was unusual for the Fair Folk to love so strongly. Even Rhiannon knew how rare and unique a love it was she felt for Pwyll. "I will be all right, little sister," she soothed her sibling.

"At least let me help you," begged Angharad. "I will put a spell upon that creature, Bronwyn of the White Breast, that she fall madly in love with the next eligible man to visit Pwyll's court! A foreigner who will take her far away!"

Rhiannon laughed. "Poor man!" she said. "What a dreadful thing to do to some poor unsuspecting soul, Angharad."

"You have lost your ability to see clearly, my sister," Angharad fretted. "Are you really unaware of how wicked a woman this Bronwyn is? She would not hesitate to destroy you if she believed that she might have Pwyll as reward for her deed."

"You will not interfere in my life, Angharad, no matter how righteous you believe your cause," Rhiannon warned her sister. "Promise me that!"

Angharad bit her lip with vexation. "I cannot promise you, sister, for I love you too much," she admitted honestly.

"Then at least swear you will let me attempt to remedy my own ills before you interfere. Remember, I am trying very hard to become the perfect Cymri wife in the eyes of all of my husband's people. It does my efforts little good to have you about, weaving spells on my behalf, Angharad, no matter how well-meaning you want to be! Were our positions reversed, I should respect your wishes, even as I expect you to respect mine. You cannot mother the entire world, my sister!"

Angharad sighed. "We will never come to an agreement on this point, Rhiannon," she said sadly, and kissed her sister on the cheek. "I can only hope the Creator will watch over you that you be kept safe from all harm. I must go. Your husband even now is making his way eagerly out of his council chamber that he may join you."

The sisters kissed once more, and then Angharad moved toward the forest, mingling with the afternoon sunlight and melting away even as Rhiannon watched her. When at last she was gone, the princess slipped from her tunic gown and chemisette, leaving them where they fell. Pinning her long golden hair up, she entered the pond, slipping gracefully into the sun-warmed waters of the forest pool just a moment before Pwyll entered the small clearing.

He stood for a long minute, entranced by the sight of her fair, rounded limbs, which until today he had never seen. She smiled and beckoned him to join her. He needed little encouragement and quickly shed his clothing. They met in midpond, feet upon its sandy bottom, the crystal water caressing their naked bodies. Rhiannon slid her arms about her husband's neck and, bringing her mouth to his, kissed Pwyll with a deep and burning kiss. Her round, full breasts pressed hungrily against his well-furred chest, and so desperate was his long suppressed desire for her that he became instantly aroused. His hands slipped beneath her buttocks and, lifting her up, he impaled her upon his raging manhood. She received him gladly, welcoming him as he plunged deep within her equally eager body.

"Ahhh, Rhi-an-non!" he moaned against her mouth, and again she found herself enveloped by the swirling mists of time and place, and she protested against the intrusion, even as she heard a voice saying,

"The princess has been delivered of a fair son!"

Chapter 8

*R*hiannon opened her eyes to find herself lying upon her bed, feeling both tired and happy. Turning her head slightly, she saw sleeping in the cradle next to her bed a fair-haired infant. She felt a kiss upon her opposite cheek and, turning, looked into the eyes of her husband. Pwyll's demeanor was one of pride, and he smiled happily at her.

"He is to be called Anwyl," she told Pwyll.

"Anwyl ap Pwyll," he gently corrected. "Anwyl, the son of Pwyll."

"Anwyl, meaning the beloved one," she answered softly. "Anwyl, our beloved son."

"He has your coloring," Pwyll remarked, "but he is sturdily built, as are all the Cymri, dearling. Our people are ecstatic with this next prince of Dyfed. Anwyl was worth the wait."

"I am cold," Rhiannon said. "Come into our bed, Pwyll, and keep me warm."

"I cannot, my love. It is a custom of the Cymri that for the next few months we be kept from one another. It is a good custom, for it will allow you to regain your strength, Rhiannon. I will sleep in the hall with my men while you remain here. You will have Bronwyn and the other women to wait upon your every need. They will also keep watch during the night that no harm comes to either you or to Anwyl," he told her.

"Not Bronwyn, Pwyll!" Rhiannon cried. *"I do not want Bronwyn about me!"*

"I cannot offend her father, my love. I know Bronwyn is difficult, but be patient with her," he said.

Rhiannon shook her head stubbornly. "I do not care if the lord Cynbel is offended or not, Pwyll! Bronwyn should have long ago departed our court for a marriage of her own, but she has not. She remains and continues to usurp my authority daily over the women of this court. There is not one amongst them that would obey me over her, my lord husband. Are you aware of that? I have given you your firstborn son, and in return I ask nought but that you do not inflict this embittered creature upon me. Will you deny me this little thing?"

Pwyll looked troubled. "I do not want to deny you, Rhiannon, but I also do not wish to offend Cynbel. What am I to do?"

"Tell Cynbel that I have requested that his daughter Bronwyn sit in my place for me, acting as your hostess in my stead while I recover from Anwyl's birth," Rhiannon told her husband cleverly. "Cynbel will feel his family honored, and I will be free of Bronwyn's company."

"My lady wife," he told her admiringly, " 'tis the most perfect solution! I thank you for it! Rest now, my love, that you may grow strong again and conceive another son for me."

"I shall not conceive a son again, my lord, until we share the same bed," Rhiannon pouted.

"Custom must be served," he told her, and then he grinned. "I will not keep from you one day longer than custom requires, Rhiannon. Had I known what a delicious armful you are, I should not have been so noble on our wedding day when I promised your father to keep from you for that very long year." His blue eyes twinkled. "You conceived Anwyl so quickly, there was scarce time for us to learn of each other. We have so much to look forward to, my sweet wife. Rest well!" He kissed her brow and departed their chamber.

Alone for a brief moment, Rhiannon reached for her son and, sitting up, lay him in her lap. Gently she undid the swaddling clothes in which they had wrapped the newborn and smiled, pleased, for he was perfect. As Pwyll had so proudly boasted, he was beautifully made. There was none of her delicacy about him, but she was pleased to note he bore upon the front of his left shoulder a small birthmark in the shape of a star. It was a symbol indicating that he was of her line as well as his father's. All members of her family bore that hallmark somewhere upon their bodies. Rhiannon felt a tiny burst of pleasure at the sight of that tiny star. Carefully she rewrapped her son, who had remained silent and watchful of her throughout the proceedings. Now the infant pierced her with a look so like his father that Rhiannon laughed and, kissing the downy head of her baby, set him back in his cradle.

A waiting woman whom she did not know entered her chamber bearing a goblet. "Your pardon, lady, but you must drink this healing draught now," she said, offering it to Rhiannon, who wrinkled her nose in distaste at the unpleasant smell. Nonetheless, she quaffed the beverage down and then, extremely exhausted with the ordeal of childbirth, fell back upon her pillows.

"Where are the women to look after my son?" she demanded sleepily.

The serving woman opened the door and half-a-dozen ladies streamed into the room, chattering and settling themselves.

"Guard my son well," mocked one of the ladies as Rhiannon slept. "Prideful bitch! It should be Bronwyn's son we watch over, not this foreigner's spawn."

"He is our lord's son too," another lady ventured hesitantly.

"Is he, I wonder?" the first woman said venomously. She peered into Anwyl's cradle. "Look at the brat! As pale as his wretched mother! What kind of a Cymri prince is that, I ask you?"

The others murmured in agreement, and the lone dissenting voice amongst them grew meekly silent, for she was no fool, no matter her good heart. She was but newly come to Pwyll's court, and though she found the princess a sweet, gentle lady, she was quickly coming to realize the lay of the land.

Rhiannon slept deeply throughout the entire night, never once awakening; but as the dawn began to peek through the windows of her chamber, she roused and, turning toward the cradle, reached for her son. To her great shock the cradle was empty! And worse! Her hands, those delicate hands that reached out for Anwyl, were covered in bright red blood. With a terrified shriek Rhiannon sat up, demanding of the unfriendly faces staring so avidly at her, "Where is my son! What have you done with my baby?"

"What have *we* done? We have done nothing, but you, woman of the Fair Folk, have killed the child! 'Tis his blood that even now covers your guilty hands!" said the chief of the ladies-in-waiting.

"Liar!" Rhiannon screamed at her. "You are a foul liar! Where is my little Anwyl? It is not a custom of the Fair Folk to murder their young! Whatever has happened in these hours that I slept is not my fault, but yours, because you were derelict in your duties. Did you fall asleep? Be truthful with me,

I beg of you! I will protect you, but be honest with me. Do not, I pray you, accuse me of some foul deed because you, yourselves, fear punishment!" Rhiannon was weeping now, not even aware of the tears that poured down her pale cheeks in her fright for herself and her son.

"Aye, we slept," admitted the woman. "You cast an enchantment over us all that we slumbered, and while we did, you murdered your child, Rhiannon of the Fair Folk! You wantonly destroyed a prince of Dyfed!"

Rhiannon staggered to her feet and slapped the woman with every ounce of her returning strength. Then taking up her chamber robe, she put it on and hurried from her chamber to find Pwyll. Her heart was hammering in her fear for Anwyl. Had Bronwyn's partisans killed her baby? If not, where was he? Hair flying in disarray, her chamber robe billowing about her, Rhiannon ran barefooted into the Great Hall to find her husband. Behind her came the waiting women, cackling with outrage to any who would listen.

"She has killed her child! She has killed her child!"

And those gathered in the Great Hall, seeing Rhiannon, her beautiful hands red with blood, drew back in horror as she fled by them.

"Pwyll!" Her anguished voice rang through the hall. "Anwyl is gone! *Help me!*" She flung herself at her husband's feet weeping. "I slept, and when I awoke our son was gone from his cradle. These women you set to watch over us did not." Her grief-stricken face gazed up at him helplessly.

"She lies!" cried the chief lady-in-waiting. "This woman of the Fair Folk bewitched us so that we slept, and while we did, she killed the infant! Look at her! Guilt is written all over her face, and her hands run with the blood of the innocent child she has murdered!"

"I have not killed my child!" Rhiannon cried, rising to her feet to face her accusers.

"Liar! Liar!" the lady-in-waiting repeated and turned from Pwyll to face the others. "What do we really know of this woman?" she asked. "She comes of a magical race whose customs are different than ours. Now she has proved herself a wicked witch of a woman! An evil sorceress! Our prince should never have wed with this black-hearted creature who has wantonly destroyed his son. Rhiannon must be tried and condemned for the murder of her son, Anwyl! Our prince must put this woman aside and wed with one of our own!"

There were murmurs of assent at her words, but Rhiannon declared vehemently once again, "*I have not harmed my son!* Whatever has happened to him is the fault of these lying women who slept instead of watching over us! I am innocent of this terrible thing of which you charge me!"

"Then why is there blood on your hands, woman of the Fair Folk?" a voice from the back of the hall demanded loudly.

There came an answering chorus of "Ayes!" and a great murmuring rose up against Rhiannon. Pwyll was in deep shock. He could not seem to find his voice in the midst of the dispute. His son was dead, and his wife was charged with the terrible crime. It was almost more than he could bear. Seeing his state, Taran of the Hundred Battles spoke up before someone less sympathetic took charge of the situation.

"There must be an investigation of these charges," he said sternly. "Evan ap Rhys and I will go to the princess's chamber immediately." Then he and his friend hurried from the hall.

Pwyll finally found his voice. "Bring my wife a basin of scented water that she may cleanse her hands free of blood," he commanded. He was reluctantly obeyed.

Rhiannon stood shivering in the early morning chill of the hall. She was yet weak with her labor of the previous day and terrified as to the fate of her infant son. The very air of the hall was ripe with evil. Looking up, Rhiannon's violet eyes met the triumphant ones of Bronwyn of the White Breast. In that moment in time the princess of the Fair Folk knew that Bronwyn was involved in Anwyl's disappearance; but unless she could prove her suspicions, she dared not accuse the jealous girl. For the first time in her entire life Rhiannon felt that most human of all emotions, despair.

Taran and Evan returned to the hall. Taking Pwyll aside, they spoke to him in low, urgent voices, gesturing passionately as they did. They appeared to be showing the prince something. Finally, when they had finished, Pwyll held up his hand for silence and the hall quieted.

"Taran and Evan have thoroughly investigated my wife's chamber. Both the cradle that contained my son and the linens upon the bed are free of blood. The only evidence of blood seems to be upon my wife's hands. Beneath the bed the bones and bloodied skin of a deer hound puppy were found. Taran has checked the kennels, and one of the pups born three weeks ago is missing. It would appear that someone has deliberately forged evidence in an effort to harm my wife's reputation." He turned angrily upon the chief lady-in-waiting. "*You!* I want the truth! What nonsense do you mouth about enchantment? Did you see my wife kill our child? Did any of you?"

The woman fell to the floor at his feet babbling hysterically. "Oh forgive us, my lord! There was no enchantment. To our shame we slept instead of watching as we were bid. When we awoke, the child was gone and the princess bloodied. We feared your wrath, and in our fear we assumed the worst! Forgive us, my lord! Forgive us!"

"Get from my sight, all of you! You are banished from Dyfed from this day onward!" Pwyll shouted angrily and the women fled.

"There is still the small matter of the infant prince's very mysterious disappearance," said Cynbel of Teifi. "Though the waiting women admit to being derelict in their duties, the child is still gone. Who can say for certain that Rhiannon of the Fair Folk is not involved? I, for one, think the child is dead. The evidence that Taran and Evan claim to have found may have been concocted by them to deceive us. Everyone knows that they have been under this creature's spell since her arrival to Dyfed. This woman is not one of us. How can we be certain she speaks the truth? How can we be certain Taran and Evan are not possessed by enchantment? If she is indeed innocent, let her produce the child!"

"Rhiannon, my lady wife," pleaded Pwyll, addressing her for the first time since the ugly incident began, "tell us what has happened to Anwyl, I beg of you!" Suddenly he could not quite look at her; all the warnings given him about marrying a foreigner surfaced in his brain. Had they been right?

"My lord," came the reply, "I know not where our son is, for I was sleeping that I might recover my strength after his birth. I have never lied to you, Pwyll. Why do you now allow me to be accused of such a heinous crime? Why have you not mounted a search for our child? Every moment that passes is a moment lost us. Send criers out through all the lands of Cymri telling of our son's mysterious disappearance that we may find him. Hurry, I beg of you!" Catching his hands in hers, Rhiannon looked into her husband's face and was devastated by what she saw. There was total confusion in Pwyll's look. He did not know whether to believe her or not. Her own heart plummeted.

The prince of Dyfed was caught helplessly between his council and his wife. He loved her, but that love could not override the fact that his son was missing under strange circumstances. The Cymri were a people of regular habits; *but*, a voice whispered in his head, *the Fair Folk are an elusive people whose ways are obscure and secret.* Perhaps Rhiannon had not been directly involved in Anwyl's disappearance, but the Fair Folk could be. Perhaps this was but another of King Dylan's conditions of their marriage. One that Rhiannon had feared to tell him. A firstborn son was a valuable commodity.

Then Bronwyn of the White Breast spoke up, and all turned to hear her words. "This is obviously some enchantment of the Fair Folk," she said, amazingly voicing Pwyll's concerns. "It has come upon not just you, my lord, but upon us all, for the baby, Anwyl, was the hope of Dyfed's future. It has come upon Dyfed because you insisted in wedding with this woman of the Fair Folk. A woman not of our own people. She has brought you, brought us all, bad luck.

"For two years we waited for her to produce an heir for Dyfed. Now, the very day after the child's birth, it is dead. This kingdom is without an heir. Who is to say that this horrible thing will not happen over and over again until it is too late for Pwyll to sire a child? What will then become of our fair land?

"The council has advised you well, my lord. They have said you should put this creature of the Fair Folk aside. Divorce her! You must choose a wife from amongst our kind and remarry as soon as possible." Bronwyn turned back to Pwyll and knelt before him. "I know, my dear lord, that there is no hope for me, for you do not love me; but please, I beg of you, choose one of our women for your wife, lest Dyfed wither beneath the curse this woman of the Fair Folk has brought upon us!"

"I will not divorce Rhiannon," Pwyll said, but his voice was uncertain and it trembled slightly.

"Nonetheless, my lord, she must be punished," said Cynbel of Teifi.

"*For what?*" demanded Taran of the Hundred Battles.

"The child is dead," was the answer.

"The boy is missing," snapped Evan ap Rhys. "There is no logical proof of his demise."

"The child is gone, my lord," Cynbel amended, "but he is as good as dead to us. This woman is obviously responsible. If she were not, she should produce her son that she might save herself. She has not, and therefore condemns herself by her inaction. She must be punished for this terrible crime!"

The other members of Dyfed's council nodded solemnly, in total agreement with Cynbel's words, and the lord of Teifi smiled, pleased. If Rhiannon were punished for the baby's loss, he thought, it would give them all time to convince Pwyll to divorce her and choose another wife. For all his daughter's self-effacing words, Cynbel knew her ambitions to be Pwyll's wife had not abated in the least. Pwyll must have a Cymri wife, and who better than Bronwyn of the White Breast; but it would take time. With Rhiannon in complete disgrace, they would have the time. Cynbel did not know what had happened to Anwyl ap Pwyll, but then he really did not care. It was very unlikely the child would ever be found.

"You must take command of this situation, my lord," he told Pwyll sternly.

Pwyll looked again to Rhiannon. He, who had always been so decisive, suddenly felt confused and afraid. Everything had been so perfect. Why was this happening to them? "Rhiannon, my love, I beg of you to end this bewitchment and to restore our child to us," he said desperately. He knew now that he was powerless to save her, and he had never felt more helpless in his entire life.

"Pwyll, my love," she gently reminded him. "When I left my father's castle to become your wife, I left magic behind. You know that to be the truth. Why have you lost your faith in me, my lord? Did you not promise me when I agreed to be your mate that you would always love and trust me without question? Why do you speak of punishment when I tell you and your council that you should be sending forth to all the kingdoms of the Cymri, and aye, to the Fair Folk as well, the word of this tragedy that has befallen us. Our child has been stolen away, Pwyll, but I am not responsible for his disappearance. Have I ever played you false? It is not within the nature of the Fair Folk to lie. What has made you doubt me? Why will you not defend me against these charges and slanders?"

Helplessly Pwyll looked from his wife and back to his council. His sea-blue eyes had filled with sudden tears as she pleaded with him. "I cannot put her aside," he half whispered to his council. "Whatever has happened, I love her!"

The council gathered together at one end of the hall, conferring in dark whispers. The courtiers clustered on another side of the hall, murmuring to one another and casting unfriendly looks in Rhiannon's direction. Taran and Evan spoke fiercely and urgently to the prince while Rhiannon stood proud and alone, silent tears slipping down her beautiful face. At last the council came before Pwyll once again.

Cynbel spoke the words of Rhiannon's punishment. "Rhiannon of the Fair Folk, it is my duty to sentence you now for whatever part you may have played in the disappearance of our prince Anwyl. For seven years, beginning on the morrow, you are condemned to sit before this castle, a horse collar about your neck. You must admit your crime to each passerby and carry upon your back into this hall any and all who wish to enter therein. Winter and summer, in weather fair and foul, you will sit before the gates. You will not be excused from this punishment for any reason short of death or an end to its term.

"At night you will be freed of your horse collar and allowed shelter in the farthest corner of this hall away from the warmth of the fire. Your sustenance will be whatever falls from the tables that you can retrieve before the dogs get it. It is forbidden that any speak with you lest your wickedness befoul the innocent, for you are evil incarnate. This punishment is a traditional one amongst our people, and should you survive it, Rhiannon of the Fair Folk, you will be banished from Dyfed afterward to go wherever you would choose; but as your crime will be broadcast amongst the lands of the Cymri, it is unlikely you will ever find shelter or kindness amongst our peoples again. This is as it should be, and is the final decision of the council," Cynbel of Teifi concluded, unable to keep a faintly spiteful tone from his voice.

Pwyll of Dyfed heard the sentence passed upon his wife with a breaking heart. He turned away from Rhiannon, unable to face her. He loved her in spite of it all, but he no longer knew what to believe. Anwyl was gone and Rhiannon refused to do anything about it. He simply could not believe that she did not still possess some powers of enchantment. *She had to!*

No one would really throw away such gifts just for love of another! He could understand a woman claiming to give up her most precious possession for him, but not really doing it. She must surely have retained her powers, so why did she refuse to use them to find her son? Unless, of course, she was indeed lying to him. Unless she was truly involved in this wickedness. Was it possible?

In the face of an armed enemy, Pwyll of Dyfed had known no fear, but now, suddenly he was very afraid. His hand visibly shaking, he reached out for a goblet of wine. Yesterday he had possessed all a man could want or desire. A beautiful wife, a healthy son, a happy kingdom. Now he had nothing. *Ashes!* It had all turned to ashes, and he did not understand why. Was his council right? Was he being punished for having wed a princess of the Fair Folk? Rhiannon had had powerful suitors among her own kind. Had one of them taken his revenge on Pwyll of Dyfed? It should not have happened had he married a woman of his own kind. He gulped his wine and groaned aloud.

When they attempted to lay hands upon Rhiannon, she took their hands off and walked proudly from the hall, never once looking back at her husband. She heard them lock the door to her chamber behind her as she entered her room, but she cared not. She could not believe the events of the past hour, and yet her son's cradle stood an empty testimony to the destruction of her marriage and her life. What a fool she had been to believe that love alone could conquer all obstacles to happiness! Had her family not tried to warn her? But she would not listen. She had deliberately and selfishly pursued her own desires.

Rhiannon had realized from the start that the Cymri did not accept her. At least Pwyll's court, with whom she must live, did not accept her. She had believed, however, that in time she would allay their fears of her origins, but alas there had always remained that suspicion of anything or anyone different from the Cymri. Bronwyn of the White Breast had seen to that, although on the whole the men had been kinder than the women.

The men had been fascinated by her fair beauty, so different from Cymri women. With them all, men and women alike, she had been modest, serene, nonthreatening. Never thrusting herself forward lest she irritate them. Never voicing unfavorable comparisons between her people and the Cymri. She had been kind to all, and yet they still would not accept her. How many times had she pretended not to see them staring at her? Whispering behind their hands and pointing slyly at her? She had borne it, all for the love of Pwyll. For love of a man who, in the face of mystery, had abandoned her.

He had never seen any of it, for she would not allow him to see their unkindness. Instead she had worked harder in an effort to bridge the gap between herself and the Cymri. She was skilled at weaving, but the exquisite cloth that spilled from her loom, finer in texture and more unique in its design than any they had seen before, only roused deeper jealousy amid the Cymri women. They seemed to delight in the differences between her work and theirs, criticizing sharply at every turn.

Among her own people Rhiannon was considered gifted musically, but because the Cymri loved their music, not once did she pick up her harp to play, lest she arouse their animosity further. Occasionally, for she could not refrain from it, she sang; but her sweet voice had an "other" worldly quality to it. It seemed eerily strange to her critics, and so she sang only to Pwyll in the privacy of their chambers when they were alone.

And without Pwyll she usually was alone. Because of Bronwyn, no woman of the court would dare to be her friend. Still, Taran and Evan ap Rhys had included her as much as they dared; but even they were careful in her company lest ugly rumors be started by Bronwyn and her adherents. Nothing had mattered to her because she was so certain of her husband's love. Now she wondered if she even had his love, having obviously lost his trust.

What had happened to Pwyll? He had always seemed so strong. His reputation as a warrior was more than well known. It was the stuff of which legends were made. Yet today, before the judgment of his council, he had crumbled before her very surprised eyes. Knowing full well there was no magic left in her, he had nonetheless pleaded helplessly with her to work enchantments she no longer possessed. Surely he did not think her like the Cymri who said a thing while not meaning it at all. He had judged her as he would have judged his own people. Knowing—surely he had known!—that it must be he who must save her, and in that moment in time Rhiannon's unbelieving heart had been quite broken.

She wept now as she sat by the window of her chamber and stared out into a new night. No matter what they did to her, she intended surviving. She had to survive in order to find her child. Anwyl was not dead. Her maternal instinct assured her of that certainty. She wept again, for she promised herself that she would not weep further after this night was over, until the day her son was returned to her. The Cymri would not rejoice over her tears.

In the hour before the dawn, she heard the sound of the key turning in her lock, and the door opened to reveal two tall and muffled dark figures. Rhiannon opened her mouth to scream, believing them to be assassins, but then Taran's voice whispered urgently to her.

"Princess, do not cry out! Evan ap Rhys and I come as friends."

"What is it you want of me?" she asked them.

"Princess, we believe you when you say that your son has been stolen but you know not by whom. We want to find the child, but we do not know how or where to start. Once your punishment begins it will be dangerous to attempt to speak with you. So when we must communicate with you, we will stand near you, apparently speaking to each other. Be most careful when you answer us, and do not give Cynbel of Teifi or his daughter any cause to punish you further."

"I know Cynbel would set his daughter in my place," Rhiannon told them.

Taran nodded. "He would, but she is not all that she appears to be, though some be fooled by her docile ways. But tell us how we may help you, my gracious lady?"

"You must speak with the women who were set to watch over my son and me before they depart the castle," Rhiannon said. "Surely one of them saw something but was too afraid to speak it for fear of retribution by Bronwyn. Do not speak with them together, but rather interview them alone. There is one, a new maid just come to court, who would have been kind to me had she not been afraid of the chief lady-in-waiting. Only after you have spoken with these ladies can I direct you further."

Taran nodded with understanding. "We will begin immediately, my lady, for these women will flee Pwyll's anger into banishment this very day, lest their deeds bring further disfavor upon their families."

"Princess," Evan ap Rhys said quietly. "We would spare you this punishment if we could, but we are helpless to do so despite the inequity of it. Do not fear, however, for we will allow no harm to come to you. This much I vow to you!"

Surprised by the deep passion in his voice, Rhiannon looked into Evan ap Rhys's eyes and saw something she had never suspected. She saw that he loved her, and the knowledge saddened her, for Evan, like herself, would love an unrequited love. Flushing, she touched his hand gently, thanking him and asking, "How is my husband?"

"He mourns," Taran said bluntly, "but for whom he mourns—you, himself, or the child—I do not know, my princess."

They left her then, and despite the bitterness facing her, Rhiannon felt stronger than she had in the past hours. To know that she was unquestioningly believed by these two stalwart men, and that she was not totally alone among the Cymri of Dyfed, was comforting in a time when there was little comfort to be had.

She washed her face and hands and bound up her long golden hair into a single braid. She chose from amongst her many garments a simple gown the color of lavender, which was girded about her waist with a rope belt of violet silk. The only jewelry she wore was her wedding band, and her dainty feet were bare.

As the first light of dawn touched the distant horizon they came for her. About her slender neck they placed a heavy leather horse collar which rested with brutal weight upon her slim shoulders and caused her to stagger as she was led outside to a stone mounting block before the castle's main gate. Those about her were all members of the council. Pwyll was nowhere in evidence.

"You will sit here, woman of the Fair Folk," said Cynbel of Teifi. He spoke her race as if it were a curse. "To each person who comes past you will say, standing, 'As I murdered my child, I am condemned to remain here for a term of seven years. Should you wish to enter the court of Pwyll of Dyfed it is my duty to bear you upon my back into the prince's hall. This is my punishment.' Do you understand, woman of the Fair Folk?"

"*I did not murder my son,*" Rhiannon said quietly.

"The child is gone. You will not produce him. It is the same thing. The council has judged you guilty of infanticide. If you do not speak the words assigned you, you will be punished further. You may expect no help or intervention from the prince. He has left you entirely in our charge," Cynbel said coldly. "Now let me hear you speak your part as I have told you, that I may be satisfied you know them."

"I will speak them," Rhiannon told him, "but your words cannot make so that which is not, Cynbel of Teifi."

Word of the cruel punishment placed on Rhiannon of the Fair Folk spread throughout all the lands of Cymri. Those who passed by or into Pwyll's castle would not suffer the beautiful, obviously grieving woman to bear them on her frail back. If anything, they were shamed by the treatment meted out by the council of Dyfed and astounded that Pwyll did nothing to clear his wife of the charges against her.

The common people murmured among themselves, suspicious of the quick judgment visited upon Rhiannon. They knew nothing but good of this princess of the Fair Folk. How, they asked themselves, could a woman not even recovered from the birth of an eagerly awaited child be party to a plot to harm him? *And why?* And once again the question of why no one sought to locate the lost infant. They were poor and powerless in the main, but they did not lack good sense.

When the third full day of her punishment had passed, and Rhiannon sat quiet and alone in the farthermost corner of the Great Hall of Dyfed, she heard Taran's voice near her.

"We have news, princess. On the night your child disappeared, wine was brought to the women watching over you and the babe. It came with the compliments of Bronwyn of the White Breast. After they had drunk it, your women fell into a deep sleep. All but one. The lady newly come to court did not drink the wine, for wine she told us, disagrees with her. She remained awake and saw what happened. She has been afraid to speak for fear she would not be believed. Then, too, she allowed herself to be involved in the chief waiting woman's lie. She is riddled with shame over her cowardice, and filled with remorse for her part in this affair. I discovered we are related, and so she is willing to speak to me, but she will say nothing to anyone else."

Rhiannon put her hands over her mouth, pretending to cough, and said, "Who stole my son?"

"The woman does not know exactly," Taran said, "but this

is what she told me. In the middle of the night she began to doze off, only to be aroused by the sound of the casement rattling violently. The window flew open and a great, huge arm ending in a large, clawed hand reached through and lifted the sleeping baby most gently from his cradle. The lady was terrified and did not know what to do. She fainted from her fear, she tells me, and when she regained consciousness, the child was quite gone. She closed the window and locked it tightly, telling no one of the incident until she spoke with me. She knows nothing more. Does any of this make any sense to you, my lady?"

"'Twas no mortal creature who did this thing," Rhiannon replied with certainty, "but as for what it was or who it was that has stolen my son, I do not know. The Fair Folk might be able to help us. I am unable to leave here Taran, but you must not go alone. It is too dangerous a trip for a lone Cymri, for by now my own people will have learned of Dyfed's judgment upon me. They will be angered, though we are a gentle people by nature."

Taran gazed down the hall to see if they were being observed and, relieved they were not, said, "Evan and I will go together."

"Aye, gracious lady," Evan ap Rhys replied, "but you must tell us how to get back to your father's castle, for well I recall your wedding day when the thicket opened before you as you came and closed behind us when we had passed."

"You must politely ask the forest to allow you to pass through," Rhiannon told them in low tones. "Say, 'For the sake of our lady Rhiannon who is sore pressed, let us pass, oh fair woodlands,' and you will find you are able to pass." Then she went on to quickly give them the directions they would need to find her sister's palace in the lake.

They left her then, and the following day she watched as Taran of the Hundred Battles and Evan ap Rhys set forth upon a quest that would keep them from Dyfed for many months to come. As they rode off she was overwhelmed with sadness, for they were her only friends within the court, but then a visitor approached the gates to Pwyll's castle. Rhiannon arose dutifully and said her pitiful little piece, not even bothering to look at the women before her until a sneering voice commanded,

"Come then, witch of the Fair Folk! Come nearer the block that I may mount you!"

Rhiannon's violet eyes met the belligerent gaze of Bronwyn of the White Breast. Dutifully she bent her body, and Bronwyn clambered upon Rhiannon's back, wrapping her arms in a choke hold about her victim's neck while her legs curled tightly about Rhiannon's slender waist.

"Go quickly then, witch!" Bronwyn said, cruelly digging her heels into the princess's sides. "Take me directly into the hall, witch! Others may feel sorry for you, but I do not. You have only gotten what you so richly deserve for stealing Pwyll from me by means of your vile enhancements, but magic cannot help you now! You are powerless, woman of the Fair Folk, but I am not!"

"What have you done with my son?" Rhiannon gasped.

Bronwyn laughed nastily. "You can prove nothing against me, else you would have already acted to save yourself; but I am not finished with you yet, woman of the Fair Folk. Long before your term of punishment is finished, Pwyll will be cajoled into divorcing you and putting you aside. He will marry me, and I shall reign by his side as Dyfed's princess. Our son, *my* son, a child whose blood will remain pure Cymri and free from any taint of foreign contamination that would defile it, shall rule Dyfed after us! Not your son with his mixed blood and odd ways. *My son!* And on our wedding night, mine and Pwyll's, you will be brought to our nuptial chamber bound and gagged to watch as Pwyll makes love to me, and I pleasure him as only I know how! You will know, for women, even women of the Fair Folk, are instinctive in that way, the very moment in which Pwyll plants his seed in me and it takes root!" And Bronwyn laughed all the harder, plying Rhiannon with her riding crop as the princess made her way into the Great Hall with the unpleasant burden upon her back.

Rhiannon said nothing, but she fought back her tears. What could she possibly say? She was, as Bronwyn had pointed out, defenseless. She could only bear her burden in patient silence. Each day for several weeks Bronwyn came and insisted upon being carried into the hall by Rhiannon. Then, as suddenly as it had begun, this particular form of torture ceased. Rhiannon overheard the servants in her husband's hall saying that Cynbel had forbidden his daughter her displays of open cruelty toward

Rhiannon. It did not do her cause with Pwyll any good, and only made the gentle Rhiannon appear a martyr in the eyes of all.

Bronwyn found other, more subtle ways to torment Rhiannon. She sat next to Pwyll at the high board regularly, fussing over the still-dazed prince, personally selecting choice bits from the serving platters to set upon his plate. She gave him wine to drink from her own cup, laughing up into his face in an effort to please him. At first her obvious little ploys seemed to have little effect upon Pwyll's state, but then a change, slow at first, seemed to come over him. If he was no longer merry, he at least responded to those about him, particularly Bronwyn. Rhiannon's heart ached, seeing their two dark heads together.

Pwyll was a somber, tragic man now. His laughter was no longer heard to echo through the hall, nor did he ever smile. Sometimes his eyes would stray to that dark, far corner where his wife sat upon a small wooden stool, shunned and alone with her thoughts; but more often than not as time passed, Rhiannon seemed to blend into the shadows and smoke of the hall until he could not even see her. It was as if she was not there, his golden princess of the Fair Folk, and Pwyll's heart seemed to shrivel within his breast.

In that far corner of the Great Hall of Dyfed was a little recessed alcove where Rhiannon slept at night. At first she did not even have a pallet, but one evening a small featherbed appeared upon her sleeping shelf. Forced to compete with the dogs in the hall for her food, she was near to starving, for the cruel among Pwyll's courtiers found it amusing to set the dogs afighting over choice morsels thrown upon the rushes, particularly when they saw the poor princess attempting to gather up a few crusts for her meal. Then one morning Rhiannon awoke to find a fresh trencher of bread filled with steaming barley cereal set within a small hollow in the stone walls by her sleeping shelf. She gobbled it eagerly, relieved to know she would not be nipped by the dogs that day. And in the evening there was more bread and an apple! Each day the food appeared; simple food; sometimes a piece of fowl, or game, or cheese; and always bread. She never knew who brought it, but she was grateful for the kindness, for lack of food, Rhiannon discovered, seemed to make her woes appear even greater.

Then the winter came and the days grew shorter. The air was bitter cold and the winds cut through the soft fabric of her gown, which had now grown quite faded and thin. One day a red-cheeked peasant woman approached Rhiannon, and she arose to say the words taught her. The woman, however, said in no-nonsense tones, "Now, my princess, ye'll not say such a lie to me, for I know it not to be true, whatever those wicked men may claim!" Then she removed her own long cloak, a thickly woven wool garment in a natural color and dropped it over Rhiannon's shoulders. "Ye'll not get through the winter without it, dearie," she said, and walked away in the same direction from which she'd come.

For the first time since she had been forced to sit before the gates of Pwyll's castle in punishment, Rhiannon wept. And it was not the only kindness that would be shown her. On another winter's day a young boy pushed a crudely carved comb of pearwood into her hand and, with a bob of his head, ran off. Rhiannon could not have been more delighted, for she had been forced to comb her hair with her fingers these many months.

But there was cruelty as well as kindness. One night Rhiannon watched, puzzled, as Bronwyn deliberately plied both her father and Pwyll with goblet after goblet of wine until Pwyll slid unconscious beneath the high board. Bronwyn then led the drunken Cynbel to that secluded place in the hall where Rhiannon now made her home and encouraged her inebriated parent, who had secretly lusted after Rhiannon since his first sight of her, to forcibly violate Pwyll's beautiful wife. Cynbel would not remember his bestial act come the dawn, but Bronwyn, her own hand silencing Rhiannon's cries for help, knew this final act of treachery would assure her her victory over Rhiannon.

In her pain the mauve mists swirled about her once again. *Rhi-an-non!*

How long had she sat here before Pwyll's gates, the heavy collar pressing its brutal weight upon her delicate frame? Four summers had passed since the birth and mysterious disappearance of her infant son. Four long summers when the dust from the road had almost choked her each time a party of merchants or other travelers passed by. Three long, cold winters when the icy rains, and finally the snows, had put chilblains upon her delicate hands and feet that would not heal completely until the warm weather had returned. She still wore the same gown she had worn from the first day, but it was now ragged beyond repair, and its soft lavender color had long ago faded to a dingy, pale ash-grey. Without the cloak she had been given, she would have never survived the winters, but she could not wear the wool garment throughout the summer, and wondered how she could obtain a new gown to cover her painfully thin form.

They had not broken her brave spirit, however. The common people had continued to be kind, and but for occasional cruelties from Bronwyn, the court ignored her entirely. As the featherbed had appeared so magically one day, and the food each morning and evening, so also did Rhiannon's silver hairbrush come into her possession after a time. She kept it with her wherever she went. Once each day she would sit before the gates of the castle, unbind her long golden hair and slowly brush it until it came alive with light. The Cymri people would come to watch her, enjoying the simple entertainment she offered. Seeing Rhiannon one day as she slowly stroked her golden hair with her silver brush, Bronwyn was enraged.

"Take the brush away from her!" she screamed at her father. "The bitch but draws attention to herself in an effort to gain the peasant's sympathy! Next, Pwyll will learn of it and take her back! All my work of the last few years will be for nought!"

"That, my dear Bronwyn, is your problem, not mine," Cynbel of Teifi told his furious daughter coldly. "If you cannot win Pwyll over, it is not my fault. He loves the woman of the Fair Folk yet, though not enough to overcome a suspicion of her which I have so carefully instilled in him. Be patient, and you will be Pwyll's wife, I promise you. Take Rhiannon's brush from her, and you will cause a spectacle. The peasants will turn against Pwyll, *and* against you. Be warned, my daughter! If Rhiannon's hairbrush should disappear, I will personally replace it."

They argued in the Great Hall and, though she could not overhear their words, Rhiannon saw the discord between them, and she was glad of this division among her enemies. As the shock of the injustice visited upon her had worn off, Rhiannon realized that though she would never return to Pwyll, neither could she allow Bronwyn to become his wife. Bronwyn was not fit to be poor Pwyll's wife. Besides, wherever Anwyl was, it was he who was the true heir to Dyfed.

The autumn came once more, and one afternoon as she sat upon the horse block before the castle gates, she saw three figures upon horseback coming toward her. As they drew nearer Rhiannon could see a man, a woman, and a small boy. She arose slowly and began her now familiar litany in a dull monotone. It was the only way she could manage to say the awful words without shrieking her frustration.

"As I murdered my child, I am condemned to remain here for a term of seven years. Should you wish to enter the court of Pwyll of Dyfed, it is my duty to bear you upon my back into the prince's hall. This is my punishment."

The man, who was obviously a wealthy lord, as the gold torque about his neck indicated, said quietly, "Rhiannon of the Fair Folk, I greet you. I am Teirnyon, lord of Gwent. This lady is my wife, Elaine, and the child is called Cant. We will take no part in a shameful injustice visited upon an innocent woman." The lord of Gwent was a tall man with a kind face. He reached out and carefully lifted the heavy horse collar from Rhiannon's slender shoulders. "Come with us into your husband's hall, princess."

"My lord, I am forbidden to leave my place until after the sun has set," Rhiannon said softly. The lord of Gwent's kindness was almost more than she could bear. It had been months since anyone had spoken to her, let alone spoken to her with kindness.

"You will never sit before these gates again, princess," Teirnyon told her firmly. "We are here to right the wrong done you four years ago by those who have only their own interests and not Dyfed's in their evil hearts. Only trust us and come." Then taking her hand, he led her into Pwyll's hall. Behind him Elaine and Cant followed.

It was the dinner hour. There were gasps of surprise and many a shocked face as the quartet entered the Great Hall of Dyfed and made their way to stand before Pwyll. Because of his great size, however, none attempted to stop the lord of Gwent or his little group, the crowd giving way before him as he strode through the hall, directly up to the high board.

"How dare you escort this felon into the center of the prince's hall?" demanded Bronwyn of the White Breast boldly from her place next to Pwyll on the prince's bench. "Has she not told you how she murdered her own newborn son? She is a witch of the Fair Folk, though her power has been rendered useless before honest folk as ourselves. Where is her collar? Whoever you are, you will answer for this outrage!"

The look Teirnyon cast in Bronwyn's direction was scathing in both its content and its brevity. "Greetings, Pwyll of Dyfed," Teirnyon began, addressing the prince directly and ignoring Bronwyn. "I am Teirnyon, the lord of Gwent, and this is my lady wife, Elaine of Powys."

Pwyll sighed deeply, but he focused his sad eyes upon his visitor. Gracious hospitality was the first law among the Cymri peoples. "You are welcome to my castle, Teirnyon of Gwent, and your family also," Pwyll responded. He deliberately ignored Rhiannon. Seeing her now was far too hard for him. She was so painfully thin, and yet her beauty seemed to glow as brightly as it ever had.

"Hear me, prince of Dyfed, for I have come to right a terrible wrong done your family. You have allowed your faithful wife, Rhiannon of the Fair Folk, to be unjustly condemned. Such behavior is unworthy of the prince of Dyfed."

Pwyll looked startled by this rebuke and more alert than he had in the past several years. "Can you prove my wife's innocence, my lord?" he asked Teirnyon hesitantly. "If you can, you will do what no other, even she, has been able to do."

Teirnyon nodded slowly and began his tale. "Several months ago there came to my court at Gwent, Taran of the Hundred Battles, and his companion, Evan ap Rhys. Although we had heard some murmurings of your misfortune, we had never heard the full tale which they told us the first night they were with us. They had gone from Dyfed with your wife's blessing to her own people. There they had learned that one of the lady Rhiannon's former suitors had, in his bitterness over losing her, sought his revenge against her, aided by one of your own people. Who this Cymri was, however, they could not learn, for the rejected suitor refused to tell them. He has been punished though by the high council of all the Fair Folk and will harm no one ever again," the lord of Gwent reassured his listeners, and then he continued.

"Taran of the Hundred Battles and his friend, Evan ap Rhys, had believed in the lady Rhiannon's innocence in the matter of your son's disappearance. On the morning after you allowed her to be so unfairly condemned, they spoke with the women who had been charged with watching over your wife and child. They learned that wine had been brought to the women by Bronwyn of the White Breast, and all but one drank it, only to fall promptly into a deep sleep. The single lady who remained faithful in her duty dozed lightly in the middle of the night, to be awakened by the sound of the casement being forced open. Terrified, she watched as a great clawed hand reached into the room and lifted your son from his cradle. The poor woman fainted, and when she regained her senses, the boy was gone. It was then the others awoke, saw the baby was missing, and fearing punishment for their dereliction of duty, attempted to make it appear that your gentle wife had murdered the child. That one woman who knew the truth was fearful of speaking out. She was new to your court and saw the others' animosity toward Rhiannon of the Fair Folk. She was afraid that no one would believe her tale, and thus allowed your poor wife to be accused unjustly. When Taran spoke with her and they learned they were related by blood, the lady admitted to what she had seen."

Pwyll's eyes widened in surprise at Teirnyon's words. "I have not heard this tale before," he said, but there was confusion in his voice. "Why have I not heard this tale?"

"Because it is undoubtedly a false tale!" snapped Bronwyn angrily, disregarding her father's warning look.

Teirnyon once again ignored the shrewish woman and said to Pwyll, "How many words have you spoken to your wife since you allowed her to be condemned, oh prince of Dyfed? She knew her babe was stolen away, but you, I am told, influenced by the prejudice of others, cut yourself off from her immediately. You did not grieve with her, or comfort her, or defend her innocence in any way."

A deep flush of shame stained Pwyll's face at the lord of Gwent's sharp words. "Ahhh, Rhiannon!" he said, speaking her name aloud for the first time in four years.

Rhiannon raised her violet eyes to him, piercing him with a look of such aching sadness that the prince cried out aloud as if in pain; but she spoke no word to him.

Teirnyon picked up his tale once more. "I knew of this creature that Taran and Evan sought, but I did not know what it was or where to find it. You see, my lord, I have a particularly fine mare among my herds that I love right well. For many years she foaled regularly, but there was a period of several years in which her newborn foals always disappeared under mysterious circumstances almost immediately after their births. Four years ago I determined that I should not lose the colt that my mare was about to drop, and so when she went into her labor, I brought her into my castle at Gwent for safety's sake.

"The foal was born and he was a beautiful one. As I stood admiring it, the windows in the room flew open and a huge clawed hand reached through and sought to take the newborn colt from its mother. I took my broadsword and hacked at that damned arm with its greedy, clawed hand! From outside, a terrible howl like a rushing, mighty wind arose. I dashed out into the darkened courtyard to do battle with whatever it was that was stealing my horses. I could see nothing in all the blackness, for there was no moon that night. Then suddenly I felt something being dropped at my feet and all was silent.

"I reached down and lifted the bundle up. Imagine my surprise when I found that the swaddling contained a healthy, newborn infant boy. I brought the child to my dear wife, Elaine, who is childless. We decided to call him Cant, meaning bright, for the hair on his head was shining and golden. We did not question our good fortune in obtaining a son to love and raise after all our years of childlessness. We even considered the possibility the creature left us the infant in exchange for the colt. We had absolutely no idea where the baby came from until Taran of the Hundred Battles and Evan ap Rhys arrived in Gwent some weeks ago with their tragic tale of Rhiannon of the Fair Folk, and Pwyll of Dyfed and the baby lost to them."

Teirnyon then looked down at the small boy by his side. "Show the lady Rhiannon the cloth you came wrapped in, Cant."

All eyes turned to the sturdy child with the hair of golden hue as he stepped forward and handed Rhiannon a length of green and silver brocade. Her tear-filled eyes devoured him eagerly, and the boy looked back at her with identical eyes. Her hands shaking, she took the fabric, though she did not really need to examine it. She had recognized it immediately. It was her own fine work, created upon her high loom during the months in which she carried her child. Her infant son had been wrapped in it the night he had been born. *The night he had been stolen away from her.*

Rhiannon fell slowly to her knees, sobbing. "I called you Anwyl," she said. "Anwyl, my beloved son!" And Rhiannon hugged the little boy who slipped so easily into her embrace and kissed her lovingly upon her wet cheeks.

Teirnyon bent and took the fallen brocade up once more. Handing it to Pwyll, he asked, "Do you recognize it, my lord? Is this indeed the cloth in which your son was wrapped on the night he disappeared?"

Pwyll took the cloth, fingering it with wonder. He nodded mutely, unable to believe his sudden good fortune. By some marvelous miracle his only son and heir had just been restored to him. "How can I thank you?" he asked the lord of Gwent thickly, his voice sticking in his throat.

"You cannot," Teirnyon told him bluntly. "By returning your son to you, I lose mine and I break my dear wife's heart. She has loved Cant and raised him with tenderness since the night he came to us. How can I compensate her for such a loss? There is no way, my lord. Elaine and I, however, learning the truth of our son's birth and seeing the stamp of both Dyfed and the Fair Folk upon his brow, could not in honor keep him from you, nor allow his sweet mother's name to be further besmirched."

"I indeed owe you a great debt of gratitude, Teirnyon, and my friends Taran of the Hundred Battles and Evan ap Rhys as well. Where are they?"

"We are here, my lord," came Taran's voice as he and Evan stepped forward from among the clustering crowd of courtiers.

"Whatever you want," Pwyll told them. "It is yours for what you have done for me and for Dyfed!"

"We did not do it for you, or for Dyfed, my lord," Evan ap Rhys said harshly. "We did it for the lady Rhiannon whom we love and honor."

Rhiannon now stood, lifting her son up into her arms as she did so. Seeing them together thusly left no doubt among those in the hall that they were mother and son. "Thank you, my friends," she told them quietly, and then she said, "Will you go with my son back to Gwent, Taran of the Hundred Battles and Evan ap Rhys? Will you teach him of his heritage and guard him until he comes of his manhood?"

"We will, lady, and right gladly," the two warriors chorused in unison.

Rhiannon then looked to Teirnyon and Elaine. "There is no need for you to lose your son, *our son*, Anwyl whom you call Cant. It is the custom among the Cymri, is it not, to foster out a prince's children? It is also a mother's right among the Cymri to choose the place for her child's fostering. My son now knows the truth of his birth. Taran and Evan will teach him all he needs to know of Dyfed. I return him to Gwent with you both until he is a man. You, Teirnyon, teach my son all he needs to know about ruling that he may one day rule in Dyfed with honor, having learned honor from an honorable man." Her meaning was brutally clear.

Both Teirnyon and Elaine were overjoyed, but they were curious as well. The lady of Gwent spoke softly to Rhiannon. "Having found your son, you would let him go again, oh princess?"

Rhiannon nodded. "Anwyl has never known any other parents but you two. I want my child to be happy, and I tell you that having lived six years among the suspicion and intolerance of this court, I know for certain that Anwyl's happiness, and indeed his very safety, are not to be found here in Dyfed. Here I will have no control over my son's fate. They would take him from me and seek to erase from his memory that half-heritage which comes to him through me. You surely knew by the very look of him that he was not entirely of the Cymri race, and yet you have both loved him without reservation."

It was then the child spoke. His little voice was high and piping. "I have but only found you, my other mother. I do not wish to lose you again."

"You will not lose me, Anwyl, my fair son. I will come to see you often in Gwent. Perhaps your father will come too one day."

"Then I will return to Gwent as you wish," the little boy said sweetly, and kissed her cheek again.

Outside Pwyll's castle thunder rumbled with an approaching storm. Lightning flashed beyond the windows of the Great Hall.

Pwyll arose from his place at the high board and looked directly at Rhiannon. "Rhiannon," he said, "will you return to me?"

Before she might answer, however, Bronwyn of the White Breast leapt to her feet as if she had been stung. Grasping at Pwyll's arm with talonlike fingers, she cried out, "*No!* You cannot do this to me, my lord! Send her away! She has only caused you misery, this woman of the Fair Folk. How can you really be certain that this boy is your son? This is some sort of enchantment of the Fair Folk against us! Surely you *must* see that!"

Pwyll shook Bronwyn's hand off. "Leave me be!" he told her angrily. "Your shrewish babbling confuses me."

"*Leave you be?*" she shrieked, her face pinched in her anger. "Leave you be? What is this you say to me, Pwyll? What of last night? What of the many nights before that when we lay together, two lovers? What of the promise you made to me this very day that you would at last divorce this creature and put her aside that you might finally wed with me? Dyfed needs an heir! A legitimate Cymri heir!" Bronwyn was flushed and almost ugly in her fury at being thwarted.

For a brief moment the old Pwyll reappeared from the shell of the man that now existed. "Dyfed has an heir, lady," he said strongly. "He is before us now!" His hand shot out and, grasping Bronwyn of the White Breast by her thick brown braids, he forcibly directed her head in the direction of Rhiannon and the child she still held within the shelter of her arms. "*Look upon my son, Bronwyn!* He may have his mother's fair coloring, but his face is mine. *His face is Dyfed's!* I have no doubts!" Pwyll's gaze swung toward his council and his court. "Are there any among you who have doubts as to the paternity of this boy?" he demanded fiercely.

"What of you, Cynbel?" Pwyll growled threateningly.

"The child is Prince Anwyl without question, my good lord," Cynbel of Teifi said silkily. "Dyfed's heir has most assuredly been restored to us, but I question the wisdom of allowing him to return to Gwent."

"Why is that, my lord Cynbel?" Rhiannon asked coldly. "Do you feel perhaps that *my* son would be safest in your gentle daughter's tender care, as opposed to the care given him by Elaine and Teirnyon?" There were snickers from those gathered, and sly looks were directed at Bronwyn as Rhiannon continued. "Your daughter may have Pwyll of Dyfed to husband if that is what they both choose, but she will *never* have care of my child. He returns to Gwent!"

"Where," Teirnyon told them all, "he will be zealously guarded and kept safe from all harm until the day comes that he inherits Dyfed from his father." The lord of Gwent smiled toothily at Cynbel and his daughter.

"It is the custom of my people," Rhiannon now said, "that a man or a woman unhappy in their marriage union may dissolve that union by merely releasing their partner from his or her vows. So I release you of the vows we made together in my father's court those six long years ago, Pwyll of Dyfed. I am no longer your wife. You are no longer my husband."

Pwyll nodded wordlessly, his shoulders slumping in a final defeat. "Our son, Anwyl, will have his inheritance of me nonetheless, Rhiannon," he promised her.

"What of *my* children?" hissed Bronwyn furiously. "Are they to have nothing so this half-breed may have everything?"

A monstrous clap of thunder shook the hall menacingly. A cloud of violet-blue mist sprang up directly in the center of the room and, with gasps of sheer fright, most of the court stepped back. The cloud dispersed as magically as it had appeared and a regal young woman whose golden hair was plaited into seven braids, each of which was woven with glittering jewels, and whose gown shimmered with light, stood before them.

Rhiannon could not help the faint smile that touched her own lips as her younger sister, now Queen of the Fair Folk, made a most dramatic entrance. Her heart swelled with joy to see her sibling once again, for she had never believed that she would.

"I am Angharad, Queen of the Fair Folk of the Forest and the Lake," Angharad announced in stentorian tones. Her cool gaze swept the room, softening as they passed over her nephew and his guardians; hardening as they encountered Bronwyn of the White Breast, who had the temerity to have attempted to take her sister's place. "You speak of *your* children, Bronwyn of the White Breast, but you will have none by any man, Pwyll of Dyfed or another. Your womb shrivels even now within you. You will be barren in this life, for to allow such evil blood to be passed on would be a crime against nature. This is the judgment the Fair Folk place upon you for your part in this matter of my nephew."

Bronwyn glared defiantly at Angharad, but the queen of the Fair Folk was through with her and looked to Cynbel of Teifi.

"For your secret crime, lord of Teifi, you are cursed, and all those of your blood who follow you for a thousand generations to come."

Cynbel of Teifi seemed to wither before their very eyes, and Rhiannon felt it incumbent to communicate with her sister. It was not necessary for her to speak aloud for Angharad to hear her. *Be merciful, sister.*

I might have had they showed you any mercy.

There are some who were thoughtful of me in my distress.

I know them, and they shall not feel my wrath, Angharad promised her sister as she fixed her gaze once more upon the court of Dyfed. "To those of you known or unknown who aided my sister by thought or deed, I disburse unequaled good fortune for you, and for your descendants for a thousand generations to come. We of the Fair Folk are not really so different from you of the Cymri. We live and we die. We love, and sometimes, though we try hard to control such negativity, we yet hate."

Angharad now turned to take in Pwyll. Poor Pwyll, she thought for a brief moment, and then she remembered the misery that this man had caused her sister.

You can take no more from him, Rhiannon silently told her sister.

But I can, came the hard reply.

Did you not promise me you would not interfere? Rhiannon gently scolded Angharad.

No, I did not, Angharad told her disbelieving sister. *Think back, sister. You asked me to make that promise, but I did not. Still, I stayed free of this controversy until Anwyl was found and your innocence proven beyond a doubt. I allowed you to endure terrible suffering that the name of our people not be further besmirched.*

Pwyll sat slumped in his seat of office, his head within his hands. He knew whatever fate Angharad of the Fair Folk pronounced upon him, he was more than deserving of it. Feeling her demand, he looked up at her.

All anger was gone from Angharad's voice now, and only a deep sadness remained as she sternly said, "Pwyll of Dyfed, when you came on your marriage day to wed with my sister,

Rhiannon, she asked but two things of you. She asked that you give her your complete love and your complete trust. It was so little in the face of the sacrifices she made in order to become your wife. But you were unable to keep faith with my sister, Pwyll. You betrayed her on both accounts. You ceased to trust her in the face of your people's false condemnations of her, simply because she was not of the Cymri race. Therefore, her credence was to be instantly doubted; but even that the Fair Folk might have forgiven you had you remained true in your heart to her, but you have not. You lay with Bronwyn of the White Breast, and your love for Rhiannon wavered as surely as your faith in her wavered. Did you ever once in all these years remember the great concessions my sister made for you, Pwyll of Dyfed? You left her helpless. You left her unable to defend herself. You left her caught between two worlds, and for that, Pwyll of Dyfed, you will be punished!

"Our people have watched agonized as Rhiannon was made to suffer because of you and your people. Even you, O foolish Cymri, cannot know the depths of her suffering! You were too busy wallowing in your own self-pity. It has been agreed by the high council of all the Fair Folk that Rhiannon be restored to her own kind. Though she has tried hard, she can never be one of you. To leave her caught between two worlds as you did was cruel. We are not by nature a cruel people. This, however, could not be done until the natural balance of things was corrected. With the restoration of my nephew, Anwyl, to his rightful place, it is. Rhiannon is once again one of us, and I have come to take her home."

"My powers . . . ?" Rhiannon whispered softly.

"Restored, dearest sister," replied Angharad. "It is as it was once before. You will never again be helpless before anyone!"

Her heart hammering joyously, Rhiannon smiled the first smile of genuine happiness that anyone had seen her smile in years. Kissing her son, she told him, "Go now with Teirnyon and Elaine. I will see you soon."

Anwyl put his arms about his mother's neck and hugged her hard as he placed another kiss upon her cheek. He did not protest as Rhiannon placed him back into Elaine's welcoming arms.

"I will keep him safe," Elaine promised Rhiannon, her

warm and loving gaze meeting the violet eyes of her foster son's mother.

"Let us go home, Angharad," Rhiannon said simply.

"Rhiannon!" Pwyll's anguished voice tore through the hall. "Rhiannon, you must forgive me! I love you! *I do!"*

Angharad reached out and placed warning fingers over her elder sibling's lips. "That, Pwyll," she said stonily and with great satisfaction, "is your punishment! For incarnations to come, though the paths your two souls may take will meet and cross, you will remember this moment in time, although Rhiannon's soul will not. You will know no deliverance from the guilt you now bear for your faithlessness against Rhiannon. You will remain frozen in time spiritually life after life after lifetime until another moment in time, somewhere in the future, when, if the soul now inhabiting my sister's body remembers this time and this place, *and* if she can find it in her heart to truly forgive you; then Pwyll, *and only then*, will you be given deliverance and fully exonerated of your crimes against Rhiannon. She must remember on her own, Pwyll. You cannot tell her. Until then, Pwyll of Dyfed, your own sad soul will suffer in unrequited anguish, even as you have allowed my sweet sister to suffer these past four years. And now, *farewell!"*

And before the astonished eyes of the assembled court of Dyfed, Angharad, queen of the Fair Folk, and her elder sister Rhiannon disappeared in another puff of silvery smoke and a thunderclap. Bronwyn whimpered, frightened, and clutched at Pwyll's arm once more, but he angrily shook her off.

"Rhiannon!" he cried after his wife. *"Rhi-an-non! Rhi-an-non!"*

The mauve mists. She was once again surrounded by the mauve mists, swirling about her furiously, even as the weightlessness overcame her once more, and she felt as if she were floating. Floating. Floating. *No!* Not floating. She was falling. Falling through time and through space at such a rapid rate that she feared she would be smashed down and totally destroyed. With a surprised gasp, Wynne of Gwernach opened her eyes and sat bolt upright in her bed, her heart hammering wildly in her chest, Madoc's handsome face before her.

Chapter 9

"*Y*ou know now," he said, his voice tinged with sadness. She nodded slowly. "How long have I slept, my lord?"

"Two full days and three nights, dearling. This is the third morning."

"How long have you been here, Madoc?" she gently asked him.

"Since Megan brought me your message. You dreamed?"

"I have known the legend of Pwyll and Rhiannon since I was a child at Gwernach; but the story always ended with Rhiannon forgiving Pwyll, and their living happily ever after," Wynne replied thoughtfully.

"A Christian ending to a Celtic tale," he said bitterly. "Our people were less forgiving in those far distant times, Wynne, than they have been since the coming of the priests."

"What happened to Anwyl?" she wondered aloud. "I cannot remember."

"The Fair Folk blessed Elaine and Teirnyon with a single child, a daughter. Anwyl grew into a fine man who ruled for many years after Pwyll's death in Dyfed, and also in Gwent by his wife's side. He took Morgana, the daughter of his foster parents, for a wife."

She nodded slowly. "It is good," she said.

"*Wynne?*" She heard the desperate question in his voice.

"Oh, Madoc," she said, looking up at him, her mind and her heart perfectly clear and suddenly filled with understanding, "of course I forgive you! With every ounce of my being I forgive you! What happened between Pwyll and Rhiannon was a series of wrongs on *both* sides. Don't you understand that? The Fair Folk were obviously of a higher order than the Cymri. It was most unfair of Rhiannon to ask poor Pwyll to give her his complete love and his total trust in exchange for her promise to wed him. It was equally foolish of the besotted Pwyll to give her that promise, for he could not keep it. But how often do we recognize our own weaknesses? But most of all, Madoc, my love, it was wrong of Angharad to place such a punishment upon Pwyll. Only the Creator has such a right, but once a curse is spoken, the Creator will not gainsay it. Rather, he turns his eyes upon the one who uttered the curse. Angharad was removed as Queen of the Fair Folk, for although she loved her sister well and had shown some restraint in the end, she proved herself too immature in her judgments."

"Who took her place?" he asked, relief pouring through every fiber of his being.

"Rhiannon did. It was her fate, though she had tried to avoid it. She did not remarry, however, and her nephew Ren ruled after her." Wynne smiled at him. "Do not ask me how I know these things because I cannot tell you, my lord. I simply know now." She sat up and stretched her limbs. "I am ravenous, Madoc!"

He laughed. "Then we must feed you, dearling. I cannot have it said that I starved my bride." Suddenly his face grew serious. "You are still my betrothed wife, my sweet Wynne, aren't you?"

"Aye, my lord, I am your wife now and forever. The past is finished for us, Madoc. Only today exists, and all the wonderful tomorrows to come," Wynne told him. "I have let go of the past. I would that you release it too, that we may, upon this bright and shining spring morning, begin our life together anew."

He took her hands in his and, raising them to his lips, he kissed them softly. "As Pwyll feared his worthiness with regard to his Rhiannon, so I fear my worthiness in regard to you, dearling. How can an innocent little country girl be so wise?"

Wynne pulled him close and kissed his lips. "I am hardly an innocent any longer, my love," she murmured, and then she chuckled. "As for the wisdom you attribute to me, Madoc, I think it is no more than common sense." She swung her legs over the side of the bed. "Send Megan to me, my lord. I must wash and dress. April is upon us, and we have a wedding to prepare for and scarce a month's time in which to do it!"

Madoc was astounded by her vigor and enthusiasm during the weeks that followed Wynne's return from her sleep journey. He had not been entirely certain of her ability to forgive him, and waited for a storm that never came. Finally he realized that she had indeed meant it when she told him that the past was finished and done for her. It was then he understood that having borne the knowledge of Pwyll's crimes throughout the ensuing centuries, he had become obsessed by them. His new awareness allowed him the final release he sought.

Wynne's excitement was contagious. Raven's Rock throbbed with activity as preparations for the wedding progressed. Wynne's family arrived from Gwernach, and she greeted them joyously. Dewi appeared to have grown much taller in the several months since she had last seen him, and Mair was more confident than Wynne had ever seen her shy little sister.

"Dear child!" Enid embraced her eldest granddaughter and, stepping back, her hands upon Wynne's shoulders, searched her face a moment and smiled, very pleased. "You are happy!" It was a statement of fact, and Enid said it in a most satisfied tone.

"Aye," Wynne told her. "I am happy."

"You are content to make this match, my child? There are no doubts lingering in the recesses of your mind?" Enid questioned her.

"There are no doubts, Grandmother. I love Madoc and he loves me. We will have a long and happy life together and, God willing, many children."

Enid nodded. "It is good then. I am happy for you both."

"Tell me of my sisters," Wynne asked Enid. "Are they well?"

Enid snorted with laughter. "They are living proof that the Devil takes care of his own kind," she replied. "Both bloom and are huge with child. They are very disappointed they cannot come to Raven's Rock for your wedding, but even they acknowledge 'twould be dangerous for them to travel now. Caitlin told me to tell you that she expects you will invite them to visit you this summer."

Now it was Wynne who laughed. "Oh no!" she said. "Even my patience has limits, Grandmother. However, both Madoc and I would be pleased if you and Mair would come to live at Raven's Rock."

Enid's face grew soft with her emotion and, blinking back her tears, she said, "My dear child, 'tis most kind of you to want us, but I think it better I remain at Gwernach a few more years. Dewi is not as grown as he believes himself, and still needs the guidance of an older woman in his life. I hope, though, that you will ask us again."

"I will," Wynne said, disappointed, but she smiled, that her grandmother not be made to feel uncomfortable.

Nesta arrived from St. Bride's, her adoring husband in her wake. "Ahh," she said, her eyes bright with pleasure, "you and Madoc have made your peace. I am so glad!" She hugged her brother and kissed Wynne's cheek.

"And you, dear sister," Wynne said gently to Nesta, "will in future think before you speak harsh words that may not be taken back."

"Then you know," Nesta said, not in the least nonplused.

"That the soul inhabiting your body once inhabited that of Angharad? Aye! Once I remembered, 'twas easy to recognize you, but tell me, Nesta. How is it that you knew and I did not?"

"It was only several years ago that I began having these dreams," Nesta began. "At first they frightened me, and I tried to ignore them. When I finally realized that I could not, I told Madoc. No sooner had I spoken to him than it all became quite clear to me in my mind. You can but imagine how awful I felt, knowing what I had done and being unable to help my brother, whom I loved best among all men. He reassured me that he held no ill will toward me, and that when he wed with you, all would be well, and it is!"

"Aye, it is, and now the past is done for us all," Wynne said.

"Thank God it is over," Nesta replied, relieved, and then she said happily, "I am to have a baby, dearest Wynne! Just before the feast of Christ's Mass."

"Should you be traveling?" Wynne fretted. "My sisters could not come to Raven's Rock because both are expecting their children soon."

"I have only just confirmed my suspicions myself," Nesta said, "but both Rhys and I agreed that we would not miss this wedding! I am no weakling to sit by the fire plying my needle for the next several months."

The princes of Wenwynwyn were an ancient family, and so Raven's Rock Castle filled with guests as the wedding day approached. Wynne had never seen most of the guests before. Madoc assured her she would in all likelihood never see them again. Still, they must be invited lest anyone important be offended. Wynne's distant kinsman, the king, Gruffydd ap Llywelyn, sent his regrets along with a pair of great silver candlesticks. The night before the wedding ceremony the Great Hall bulged with revelers who ate and drank and thoroughly enjoyed the Irish minstrels who had been brought to the castle for entertainment.

Wynne sat beside Madoc in the place of honor at the high board. Her scarlet and gold tunic dress flattered her fair skin and her dark hair. It was obvious to all gathered, from the looks that she and Madoc kept exchanging, that a love match had developed between them.

"My lords and my ladies," the majordomo's voice rang through the hall, "his lordship, the bishop of Cai."

"My God!" Nesta's hand flew to her mouth. *" 'Tis Brys."*

"He is not welcome here," growled Madoc, "and well he knows it, the devil!"

"My lord," Wynne put a restraining hand upon his arm, "you cannot send him away, else you create a scandal. Whatever has passed between you must be put aside, if only for a brief time."

"He has done this deliberately," moaned Nesta. "He has come publicly, and at a time when he knows we dare not send him away! Madoc, my beloved brother, you must beware!"

"Nesta," Wynne said, concerned by her friend's obvious distress, "is he really that bad?" She glanced down the hall to watch as Brys of Cai made his way toward them. He was an extraordinarily handsome young man. No, handsome was not the correct word. He was beautiful. "Surely he has reformed from the days of his youth."

"He is evil incarnate," Madoc said quietly. "Do not be fooled by his beauty, which is that of the angels, dearling. He will be charm itself to you, but he is wicked beyond mortal men. He is the youngest bishop in Christendom, it is said. He bought the office from a corrupt clergy. He has neither earned it nor does he deserve it." Madoc stood now and waited as his half brother approached the high board.

"Greetings, my brother, and God be with you," Brys of Cai said. He was the fairest man she had ever seen. Indeed, he might have been one of the Fair Folk of ancient times, Wynne thought. His hair glistened like pure gold, and his pale blue eyes were like a summer sky. Embroidered upon his white silk tunic was a gold and bejeweled Celtic cross.

"Why have you intruded here?" Madoc said quietly.

"What, brother? No polite speech of welcome for me?" The young man chuckled. "I had believed the omission of my name from your guest list an accident. Am I to assume 'twas not?"

"You know it to be so, Brys," Madoc replied coldly. "You are not welcome here. You will never be welcome here again."

"But here I am, dear brother, and here I intend to stay. I have come to personally perform the marriage ceremony for you and your lovely bride." His eyes turned benignly on Wynne and he smiled. "You do not dare send me away, Madoc. I have checkmated you quite nicely this time."

"Do not be cruel, Brys! Madoc has never harmed you," Nesta said.

Brys of Cai turned his eyes to his younger sister. "I came to see you wed last winter, but he would not let me in, Nesta. Did you know that Madoc kept me from your wedding?"

"I knew!" she said furiously. "I thanked him for it! You bring evil with you, Brys. It clings to your robes like the stink of a cow byre. You did not come to do Madoc and Wynne honor. You came to make trouble. If you are as honest as you claim, then wish them well and go back to Cai! You are not wanted here!"

"Such passion," Brys of Cai said softly. "I always knew you had passion, sister mine. I will not return to Cai, however, until after the wedding. If it displeases you so, I will not perform the ceremony, Madoc. But I will remain."

Madoc's look was a black one, but Wynne gently pressed warning fingers into his arm, and he threw her a despairing look of agreement.

"How politic the blushing bride is," Brys noted. "Are you a peacemaker then, lady?"

"Nay, my lord bishop I am a realist, however, and I can see you have come to sow discord as Nesta accuses you. Whatever difficulties you three siblings have encountered over the years, I am not a part of it. I will not allow you to spoil my wedding. Swear to me upon that cross you show so ostentatiously upon your chest that you will not ruin this happy time for us."

"And if I do not swear?" he mocked her. "What will you do, Wynne of Gwernach?"

"I will give orders to have you escorted from Raven's Rock no matter the scandal," Wynne told him firmly.

Brys of Cai laughed. "I believe you would, lady," he said. "Very well, I swear upon the Holy Cross upon which our Lord died that I will keep the peace during these festivities, but not a moment thereafter." He chuckled. "My brother, Madoc's marriage is something I never thought to witness. I should not like to miss it."

"Come join us at the high board then, my lord bishop, and tell me why," Wynne replied, and then turned to Dewi. "Will you give up your place to the bishop of Cai, brother?" The boy nodded, and Wynne instructed a servant, "Bring another chair for the lord of Gwernach."

Brys of Cai took his place next to Wynne and, having accepted a goblet of wine from another servant, said, "Do you not know of the reputation enjoyed by the princes of Wenwynwyn, lady? I would think a virtuous Christian maiden fearful of marrying into such a house."

"I do not believe in the nonsense mouthed by ignorant fools about Madoc and his family. I have known nothing but kindness from him. Besides, I am considered a healer among the people of Gwernach, and healers are frequently the subject of gossip."

"Do you speak sorcery, lady?" Brys of Cai purred in dulcet tones. His blue eyes glittered.

"I speak of herbs and healing, my lord bishop. I speak of medicine."

"Women should not be healers, lady," was the blunt answer.

"Why not?" Wynne demanded, the anger in her voice barely restrained.

"It is not a Christian thing, lady," he said. "Women have been given the task of bearing new life. That and the care of their families should be their sole interest."

"Does the family of a great lord not include all within his care?" Wynne said sweetly. "Does not care of one's family include ministering to their ills and healing them of sickness?"

"You are clever for a woman, Wynne of Gwernach," Brys told her. "Perhaps you are too clever. It is never wise to be too clever."

"Do not threaten me, my lord bishop," Wynne replied in low, even tones. "I do not fear you. I know all about you. Far more than you know about me, I will wager."

"Knowledge can be a dangerous thing, lady, particularly if you do not possess the power to use it skillfully, and you do not."

"Not yet," she retorted, and was pleased to see a startled look spring up on his face.

Quickly recovering his equilibrium, he laughed. "You are a most worthy opponent, Wynne of Gwernach."

"But how sad that we must be at odds, my lord bishop," she answered.

"We do not have to be at odds, lady," he told her.

"As long as you are Madoc's enemy, Brys of Cai, then you are mine as well. I am bound to Madoc by many ties, some of which you cannot even imagine. He is my lord, my life, and my love. I shall never betray him," Wynne said with certitude.

For the briefest moment a look of unbridled hatred sprang into Brys of Cai's soft blue eyes, and then it was as quickly gone. What startled Wynne most of all was the fact that the hatred had been directed toward her. How could Madoc's brother hate her so? He did not even know her.

"I am pleased," the young bishop said, and she knew it a lie, "that your loyalty is so firm, Wynne of Gwernach. It shows Christian virtue, and perhaps such virtue will reform my brother of his evil ways."

"I shall indeed be a good wife in all ways, my lord bishop," Wynne murmured piously in similar tones. "Will you have some roast pig?" she asked, suddenly the good hostess.

A servant hovered by Brys of Cai's side, a platter offered. With a grin the bishop snatched a well-crisped piece off the dish and sank his teeth into it. Those teeth, Wynne noticed, were his one facial fault. They were slightly yellowed, and the incisors had a feral look about them. He had turned away from her and was speaking with another guest, to her relief. It had been an effort to repel his evil. Nesta was right. Brys of Cai had an evil way about him that was not just a little frightening, although she would not have admitted such a thing to anyone.

The marriage of Madoc of Powys and Wynne of Gwernach was celebrated the following morning at the early mass. The ceremony was conducted by Father Drew, who had traveled

from Gwernach with Wynne's family. The only witnesses were
the immediate family, for the chapel at Raven's Rock was
small. The sun streamed through the small windows of the
chamber, making bright puddles of light upon the stone floor.
The candles twinkled golden upon the altar.

The bride was garbed in a cream-colored satin tunic dress
decorated with small pearls that had been sewn in abstract patterns all over the gown. Beneath it she wore an under tunic of
the same color, which was embroidered with little golden stars.
About her neck were the pearls her mother had left her. Upon
her feet were dainty kid slippers. Her single dark braid was
woven with pearled ribbons, and her head crowned with a
wreath of roses from a bush Madoc had potted the previous
autumn and brought to the castle, that he might have roses for
Wynne on their wedding day.

The bridegroom's full-skirted kirtle was of indigo blue silk
brocaded in gold and belted in gilded leather. His scarlet braies
were cross-gartered in gold, and he wore pointed red leather
shoes upon his feet. His dark hair was clubbed back and secured with a jeweled riband. About his neck was a heavy chain
of red Irish gold which matched the jeweled gold diadem he
wore about his forehead.

Nesta and Enid wept happily as the pair were united. Mair,
staring at her beautiful sister, dreamed of her own marriage
one day. Dewi was frankly bored. Weddings were always dull,
and he should have far rather been out hunting. Rhys clapped
a comforting arm about his sniffling wife and decided that
Madoc could never possibly be as happy with Wynne as he
was with his adorable Nesta. Einion wiped a tear from his eye
and then glanced surreptitiously about to see if anyone had noticed his lapse into sentiment. Brys of Cai glowered at his half
brother and his bride through narrowed eyes and decided that
he had never hated Madoc quite so much as he did this minute.
Why was it that Madoc got everything that he had ever
wanted? Raven's Rock Castle; a beautiful, loving bride. Why
was Madoc the favored one and not he? It would not end until
one of them was dead, Brys decided. Dead and buried deep.

The wedding celebration lasted the entire day long and into
the night. The wedding party entered the hall that morning after the ceremony to be greeted by the friendly cheers of all
their guests. The hearths in the Great Hall burned bright and

high, taking the chill of the May morning away. The hall itself was decorated in flowering branches of hawthorn and Maybud. There were flowers everywhere, and the servants raced to and fro carrying platters of food to the diners before it chilled.

Eggs, poached and served in a sauce of cream and sweet wines. Eggs, hard-boiled and sliced into a mixture of cheese and new peas. Eggs, hard-boiled and served cold with sea salt. There was ham, and roe deer, and salmon. Trenchers of hot barley cereal. Cottage loaves newly baked and fresh from the oven. Honeycombs and sweet butter. Wheels of Gwernach's Gold from the bride's own home. Everyone ate heartily, for the first entertainment of the day was to be a hunt in the forests surrounding Raven's Rock.

Wynne ate swiftly and then hurried to her apartments, where Megan waited to help her exchange her wedding gown for more suitable clothing for the hunt. In her garments of green and gold, the bride was selected to be the May queen that day. They spent the morning hunting amid the forested hills surrounding Raven's Rock, although their luck was not particularly good. At the noon hour the wedding party and their guests entered a clearing where a picnic had been laid out by the castle's servants. It was simple fare. Capon and small meat pies. Bread and several varieties of cheese. Tartlets of dried fruits. Bowls of tiny new strawberries and fresh, thick cream. There was ale and wine to slack the guests' thirst. After their picnic they returned to Raven's Rock, where archery butts had been set up in the gardens for their sport. A maypole had been erected as well, and Wynne led a number of ladies in the traditional May dance, moving with sprightly steps to the piper's tune as they danced about the pole, weaving their brightly colored ribbons of red, green, blue, and yellow until the pole was completely decorated. Some of the men stripped down and held a contest of wrestling skills.

There was an hour that followed when everyone returned to their chambers to rest and dress for the evening's banquet. As the sun sank with an orange-gold glow that stained the huge room with a barbaric light, the Great Hall at Raven's Rock began to fill once more with the wedding guests, refreshed by their brief hour and hungry again.

"How long has it been since these people have eaten, Madoc?" Wynne grumbled. "It is a good thing that they are going back to their own homes tomorrow, else they deplete our stores entirely." She had removed her hunting garb and was once again attired in her wedding gown.

Madoc, who had also changed back into his wedding finery, chuckled. "It is a testimony to your prowess as a hostess, my beautiful wife," and he kissed her on the cheek.

"It is a testimony to their appetites," she replied, but she smiled as she took her place at the high board with her husband.

Wynne had planned a wonderful final banquet for the wedding guests, and judging by the enthusiasm of her guests as each dish was offered, she had done very well indeed. A dozen barrels of oysters packed in ice and seawater had been transported from the coast for the meal. They were quickly set upon and devoured. Four sides of beef packed in rock salt had been roasted to a turn and were now being carved and placed upon platters. There was a whole ox and two roe deer, as well as several hams, geese, larks, capons stuffed with dried fruit, fat ducks dripping their juices; an enormous roast boar, several large partridge pies with flaky golden crusts, the steam rising from the pastry vents rich with the scent of red wine and herbs; and a cauldron of rabbit stew flavored with carrots and shallots. There were a dozen legs of baby lamb rubbed with garlic and rosemary.

There was trout broiled in butter, lemon, and dill; salmon steamed in seawater and sprinkled with parsley; flaked cod prepared in a sauce of cream and sweet wines; prawns and mussels boiled with fennel. New lettuce had been steamed with white wine. There were bowls of tiny green peas and little boiled beets. There was fine white bread in abundance, sweet butter, soft Brie from Normandy, and several wheels of Gwernach's Gold. There were beer and ale, and wines both red and white.

A cake had been baked and decorated with little figures and fruits of marzipan. There were several large tarts made of dried fruits and precious spices. Both violets and rosebuds had been candied and were served with tiny sugared wafers. There were bowls of small strawberries, although Wynne could not imagine where they had been found after the generous serving of the little fruits offered earlier in the day at their picnic.

The Irish minstrels entertained them with wonderful ballads

of love and songs of manly feats. There were morris dancers, and a funny little bit of a wizened man with a troupe of dogs that danced and jumped through hoops on their master's command. The guests ate until there was no more food, and drank until they could hold no more. Madoc and Wynne quietly excused themselves, for no one could leave until they did, and Wynne could see that both her grandmother and Nesta were weary. As for little Mair, she had fallen asleep in her chair, and Dewi, for all his bluster, was nodding off as well. Einion gathered up both children and took them from the hall.

Megan undressed her mistress and was dismissed. Wynne sat upon her bed brushing her long hair with slow even strokes as Madoc entered the chamber. Turning, she looked up and smiled at him. " 'Twas a fine day, my lord, but I am happy to have it over and done with."

He took her brush from her and, kneeling down, began to stroke her hair with it. "My wife," he said softly. "My beautiful wife. God, dearling! I cannot believe you are really mine!" He buried his face in dark scented hair and inhaled its subtle fragrance.

A lovely shiver ran up her spine, and Wynne twisted about to face her husband. Taking his face in her hands, she touched his lips with hers. "Aye," she murmured against his mouth. "I am yours, Madoc, but then so too are you mine, and I love you." Her lips softened and she kissed him passionately, her tongue swirling about his mouth, teasing and taunting his own tongue to do battle. Her hands left his face and tangled themselves in his own thick, dark hair. The hairbrush dropped from his hand, clattering to the floor.

Madoc pushed his face into the hollow between her sweet young breasts. He felt the steady beat of her heart beneath his lips as he pressed kisses on her soft skin. His hands, sliding beneath the mantle of her hair, moved down until they were encircling her small waist. Wynne arched her body, and Madoc's mouth found the sentient little nipple of a breast. Slowly he suckled on the tender flesh, drawing forth the sweetness first from one nipple and then the other until she began to moan softly in his embrace.

His tongue tormented her sensitive nipples, flicking swiftly back and forth as she threaded her fingers through his hair with growing urgency. His lips moved away from her now-swollen breasts and down her taut torso. Wynne shivered again, and her smooth skin was instantly embellished with a tapestry of tiny prickles. She squirmed and a small giggle escaped her.

"That tickles, Madoc!" she protested. She was beginning to feel hot with her desire for him.

"And we both know how ticklish you are," he responded, looking at her with a deceptively bland stare.

He reached for her, but Wynne was quicker and scrambled across their great bed. "Hah, my lord!" she mocked him. "You must be faster than that to catch me!"

He dove at her, and she squealed in sham terror as he grabbed out to imprison her. Together they rolled about their marriage bed like two young puppies, his fingers tickling her and her fingers tickling him. Finally weak with laughter, Madoc and Wynne collapsed side by side, wheezing and gasping for breath. When at last she felt the strength returning into her limbs, Wynne took the initiative, surprising Madoc by straddling him. Giving him a seductive smile, she tightened her thighs about his torso. Reaching up, she began to fondle her breasts, her tongue running swiftly over her lips. She looked down, sloe-eyed, into his face.

"Do you want me as much as I want you?" she demanded.

"Aye," he drawled softly and slowly, a single finger reaching up to trail down the valley between her breasts, down her belly, to worm its way between her nether lips. For a moment his finger rested atop her little love jewel, which he had found with unerring aim. Then he began to rub it with gentle insistence. "I want you very, very much, my beautiful bride."

A shudder ran through Wynne as he brought her to her first pleasure, and weakness coursed through her veins like hot wine. She wanted so to control the situation, she thought, but she had not yet learned how. All she desired right now was to have him take her, and she sighed gustily.

He smiled up at her and then, with deliberately languid movements, he began to smooth the palms of his hands up her body from her belly to her breasts. His hands moved in gentle little circles, caressing her lightly, stroking the fires of her desire. "You are so fair," he told her, and he fondled her breasts, squeezing them delicately, as with half-closed eyes she began to make whimpering noises in the back of her throat; her hips moving against him in jerking little motions.

"I want—" she began, and he placed warning fingers over her lips.

"Not yet, dearling," he said low.

"I want you!" she insisted and, leaning forward, kissed him passionately.

"I want you," he responded, and rolled her over onto her back, "but it is too soon, Wynne. Let us enjoy loving one another before the final culmination."

Wynne turned onto her side and, reaching out, she stroked him, reveling in the sensation of his body beneath her hand. He was a tall man, but unlike Rhys, Madoc was not as large-boned. Neither could he be called delicate, she thought. There was strength in him that belied his medium-boned frame. And his skin. It was so soft for a man. Especially a man whose appearance was that of an ancient Celtic warrior. She could feel the muscles in his shoulder and his arm, and, unable to help herself, she leaned over and began to lick his skin, pushing him onto his back. He groaned with pleasure as her little pointed tongue moved up his torso from his belly and encircled the nipples on his chest. There was a faintly salty taste to his skin that was not unpleasing.

Her long dark hair spread out over her shoulders and back and buttocks like a black silk mantle. He stroked her head, his whole body aquiver with her lovemaking. She nipped playfully at his shoulder and his throat; her little love bites followed almost immediately by a quick kiss and then the warm sweep of her tongue. Wynne's head began to move lower again on his torso, her tongue swirling over his sensitive skin, and he groaned again.

His manhood loomed ahead of her, stiff and straight. Wynne's fingers closed about it, feeling the life pulsing and coursing through the throbbing flesh. He had loved her with his tongue. Dare she do the same to him? Boldly she leaned forward and touched the tip of his manhood with the point of her tongue. Madoc gasped sharply. Her tongue encircled the ruby head of it with a warm and enticing motion. Losing her grip on him, she barely supported his lance within her hand as, moving closer to him, she licked the length of him with slow even strokes. He shuddered and then his body jerked violently with surprise as Wynne took him in her mouth and began to draw upon him until he feared his juices would burst forth.

Reaching down with his hand, he locked his fingers in her hair and gently pulled her away. "Dearling," he managed to gasp, "you will unman me and waste my seed."

Pulling away from him, she drew herself level with him and said softly, "When you taste of me, it pleasures me greatly. Do you not feel the same pleasure when I taste of you?" Her face was above his, and her hair fell like a waterfall to one side of her.

He reached up and caressed her cheek. "Wynne, my sweet wife, when your mouth and your tongue love in so intimate a manner, I die a sweet death; but my love, I also long to possess you more fully than you could ever imagine." He kissed her mouth swiftly and began to play with one of her pretty breasts which hung temptingly near.

"Do you think that only men feel such passion, my lord?" she demanded. "Women feel it too." A tiny dart of raw longing raced through her as he pinched her nipple, and then, raising his head just a bit, tongued the pain away.

In answer, he gently rolled her onto her back once more and swung over her. His fingers trailed teasingly over the tender inner flesh of her thighs. His deep blue eyes never left her mysterious green ones as he slowly pushed himself into her and then stopped. "I have never before desired a woman as I desire you," he said.

"Do not tell me of your other women," she teased him. "Tell me how much you love me, Madoc, my husband," and she wrapped her arms about his neck. He was so big inside her, she thought. He filled her full, and she almost rejoiced aloud as she felt him throbbing with life and love. Her head began to swim as pleasure engulfed her.

"Through all time and space have I loved you," he declared. "From a time that neither of us can remember until this moment in time, have I loved you, Wynne. I will never cease to love you, though we live, and die, and are born again in other times and places. You are my other half, dearling. There can be no real life for me without you."

"Oh, Madoc," she whispered, and her eyes were wet with her tears, "am I worthy of such a love?"

"Always, dearling!" he told her passionately, and then he began to move upon her.

"I will always love you," she promised him softly as she

gave herself up to the sweetness of the moment, letting it wash over her like water washing over a rock. Letting the moment take her until she soared like a lark, and the pleasure captured her in its grasp and kept coming, and coming, and coming until she died a sweet death, only to be reborn again new and eager.

And afterward they lay together in a loving embrace, stroking each other comfortingly and sharing tender kisses until they fell into a period of blissful slumber; awakening several hours later refreshed and renewed and ready to share their passion once more. Yet when the dawn broke, Madoc and Wynne arose happily to dress themselves and, like any good host and hostess, to see their guests off. If they shared secret looks and smiles in the completion of their duties, the departing wedding guests only found it charming. All but Brys, the bishop of Cai, who hid his hatred behind his charming facade and gaily departed for his own home as if he had been the most welcome of all the wedding guests.

"We will not have to see *him* again," Madoc said grimly as he watched his half brother and his small cortege make their way down the steep path from Raven's Rock Castle.

"It is not good that brothers are such enemies," Wynne answered. "His father molded him, but could we not change him, my love? I realize his attempted crime against Nesta was vicious, but he was but a boy. You saved Nesta. There was no serious harm done. Could we not at least try to mend this breach between you?"

"You are so innocent and so good," Madoc said. "You do not understand, Wynne. There can be no friendship between myself and Brys in this life."

"He is beyond redemption, Wynne," Nesta, who with her husband would be remaining at Raven's Rock for several days, said. "We have tried, both Madoc and I, to make our peace with Brys, to bring him back into the family fold. He wallows in his wickedness and cannot be weaned from it now, I fear."

"Perhaps you are both too close to the matter," Wynne said. "There is such bad blood between you, I think, that only someone like me, someone uninvolved in the past, can help to bring you all together once more. It is not good for families to grow apart. Even though I find my sisters, Caitlin and Dilys, aggravating beyond all, I do not cut them off from the family."

"I can deny you nothing, dearling," Madoc told her, "but we have just been wed and I am of a mind for feasting, and revelry, and frolic, not for discussing my brother. In time, however, I promise you that we will resolve the situation."

Wynne smiled up happily at her husband and, taking his hand, turned to go back into the castle, innocent of the meaningful look that passed between Madoc and Nesta, who were both of one mind in the matter of Brys of Cai. He was beyond the pale and would ever be.

≋Chapter 10

*A*lthough Dewi returned to Gwernach with Father Drew several days following the wedding, Enid and Mair had consented to remain for the summer months. Nesta and Rhys would also remain for a few weeks. Word came from Coed and Llyn that Caitlin and Dilys had been delivered of sons in the same hour of the same day. Both were filled to overflowing with maternal pride.

Enid laughed. "Though Caitlin was not due to have her child until next month, she would not suffer Dilys to gain a march on her. How typical of my granddaughter, but at least the children are healthy."

To celebrate her wedding, Wynne had released Einion from his slavery. "You are free to remain in my service or return to your own homeland," she told him.

"I'll stay," he said shortly.

Wynne smiled mischievously. "I think you should have a wife, my old friend. A wife settles a man."

"Perhaps," Einion agreed, smiling slightly.

"Would my maidservant, Megan, suit you?" Wynne asked sweetly.

"If she's willing, I'm willing," Einion replied shortly.

"Marry you?" Megan exclaimed when brought into her mistress's presence. She glared balefully at Einion. "So you are willing if I'm willing, are you? What makes you think I want to marry a great, ungainly, gimp-legged oaf like you?"

"Because you love me," Einion said blandly.

"Love you?" Megan's voice was slightly higher than it had been a moment ago, and her cheeks were flushed scarlet.

"Aye, you love me," Einion repeated, "and besides, who else would have a freckled-nosed termagant like you to wife? You've frightened all the lads for five miles hereabouts, Meggie, my lass. I'm all that's left to you. It's me or spinsterhood," he finished, grinning wickedly.

"And?" she demanded, glaring at him furiously, her hands on her hips.

"And what?" He pretended to be puzzled.

"And?" she answered, equally firm and insistent.

"And I love you," he said finally, with a shrug.

"Well," Megan allowed, "I suppose I could get used to carrot-topped children."

Wynne burst out laughing. "You are the oddest pair of lovers I have ever known," she said, "but may I assume 'tis settled between you? You may wed whenever you please."

"Tomorrow," Einion replied.

"I can't be ready by tomorrow," Megan raged at him.

"You can," he countered. "Lasses are always ready to wed at a moment's notice, or so I am told."

"Tomorrow will be perfect," Wynne said, stemming the tide of protest she saw rising to Megan's lips. "I have a lovely tunic dress that I seem to have outgrown, and 'twill fit you with just the tiniest bit of alteration."

So Megan was wed the following day to Einion, with their lord and lady looking on happily.

"He's so perfect for her," Nesta said afterward. "He's every bit as strong-willed as she is, and her equal in all ways."

"I am so happy!" Wynne said, twirling about the hall dreamily. "I want everyone about me to be happy too. Einion deserved his freedom and would not have asked Megan to marry had he not been given it. She was absolutely beginning to pine for him. I had to do something." She pulled up her skirts and danced a few steps. "Is not love grand, sister?"

Nesta and Rhys took their leave and returned home to St. Bride's the following week.

"You will come to us in December, won't you?" Nesta begged. "I want you there when I have my baby."

"I will try," Wynne promised her, "but I may not be fit to travel myself at that point."

Nesta's eyes widened. "Are you . . . ?" she began.

"Not yet," Wynne said, "but I pray daily for a child. I would give Madoc a son as quickly as possible."

Nesta smiled at her sister-in-law. "I know just how you feel," she admitted, "but I shall still hope that you can come."

"If I cannot, send for my grandmother. She is good at birthings and will be glad to come to be with you," Wynne replied.

"Would you, my lady Enid?" Nesta asked shyly.

"Of course, my child," Enid answered. "I shall enjoy a nice visit to St. Bride's, especially at the Christ's Mass feast, and I shall bring Dewi and Mair with me."

The summer passed. With the coming of the autumn, Enid and Mair returned home to Gwernach. They went happy in the knowledge that Wynne was to bear a child to her husband in the spring. While they had been with her, her grandmother and her sister had kept Wynne's mind from the breach between Madoc and Brys of Cai. Now, with nothing more than her household to oversee, Wynne began to think about how she might reunite the brothers in friendship. It would not be an easy task, for Madoc refused to even discuss the matter with her, although she had attempted to broach it with him several times.

"My brother chose to distance himself from his sister and me years ago," Madoc tried to explain to Wynne. "His actions toward us since the day he left Raven's Rock, nay, since even before that, have been consistently hostile."

"He attempted a dreadful act as a boy, I will agree with you and Nesta on that matter, but surely after all these years you can forgive him," Wynne said. "I cannot believe anyone is quite as wicked as you both insist Brys is. Surely there is some good in him."

"Wynne, my dearest wife," Madoc said patiently to her, "I know it is hard for you to believe that my brother is beyond decency. You have been so sheltered all your life, but even the spiritual maturity you possess cannot have possibly prepared you for someone like Brys. He is simply evil incarnate, and he revels in wickedness. There is absolutely no remorse in him, dearling. This is no sibling rivalry, Wynne. This is a battle between good and evil. Between the darkness and the light. You are not yet prepared to fight such a battle. I am."

For Madoc the matter was settled, but Wynne was not satisfied. The very early months of her pregnancy past, she was feeling full of new vigor. She wanted to believe everything that her husband said. After all, was not Madoc the wisest of men? Yet she could not quite believe Madoc in the matter of his brother. The thought niggled at the corners of her brain that Brys must surely have some redeeming qualities to him. If she could talk with him, understand his feelings about the estrange-

ment between himself and his family. Of course, she would not
be able to do it at Raven's Rock. She would have to go to Cai.

It would not be a long journey. The matter of a few hours
only. She was able to ride still, and she would take Megan
with her. *No.* Megan could not come. If she told Megan,
Megan would tell Einion, and he would tell Madoc. They
would stop her. The more Wynne thought about it, the surer
she became that Madoc was wrong in this one particular matter. Brys could not be as bad as her husband and Nesta painted
him. He had done a terrible thing as a boy, but he should not
be shunned by his family for the rest of his life for a single sin.
She smiled to herself. She would reunite the siblings, and her
children would grow up surrounded by warm and loving
relatives.

But when? When could she depart Raven's Rock unde-
tected? She did not want anyone guessing her intent and chasing after her; spoiling her chances to make peace between the
brothers. Wynne frowned. *When?* It had to be soon. Before the
winter set in and she was unable to ride her horse. She almost
shouted with delight when Madoc told her several days later
that he must go to the valley pasturelands below to check on
their herds.

"The shepherds report that some of the sheep are disappear-
ing," he told Wynne.

"Is it a wolf?" she asked him nervously.

"Nay, I think not, for no remains or blood have been found.
My neighbors to the north are not the most honest people. I
think it possible they have been stealing my sheep. If this is so,
I must put a stop to it immediately. Weakness is a character
flaw too easily taken advantage of, and I would not like to be
thought weak."

"How long will you be gone, my love?" Wynne said
sweetly.

"Three days, four at the most, dearling," he answered, and
kissed her brow tenderly. "I dislike being away from you,
Wynne, but there is no help for it, and you will be quite safe
at Raven's Rock." He reached out and placed a hand over her
belly. "Have you felt a quickening yet?"

"Not yet," she told him, smiling. "Perhaps in a few weeks."

"A child," he said. "Our child. What would you call him?"

"Anwyl," Wynne said softly, "and Angharad if *he* is a *she*."

Madoc chuckled. "I am not so pompous a fool to believe that my son could not be my daughter. It matters not. A healthy child is all I desire. A healthy child and a beautiful wife." Then his lips touched hers, and Wynne wound her arms about his neck, sighing with pure and perfect contentment.

On the following morning she bid her husband a fond farewell, but as the day was wet and overcast, Wynne decided to wait until the morrow before setting out for Castle Cai. When the following day dawned sunny, she knew she had been wise in postponing her trip. She had dismissed Megan the prior evening, telling her maidservant, who was also pregnant with Einion's child and extremely sick in the mornings, not to come to her until the noon hour. Megan gratefully thanked her mistress.

Wynne dressed carefully, sorry that her journey would necessitate a plainer garb than she would have otherwise chosen to wear. She did so want to make a good impression on Brys, that she might gain his sympathetic ear. She had sensed from their earlier meeting that he was as stubborn as Madoc. Still, Brys would certainly be far more interested in what she had to say than what she was wearing. Their brief bout of verbal sparring at her wedding had shown her that he was a very intelligent man. The dark green tunic dress she chose would blend in nicely with the woodlands she must traverse. She chose a sheer white veil to cover her head, affixing it with a simple gold band which was studded with dark green agate.

She chose the time of her departure well, going to the stable quite early, when the sun was just barely up. The grooms were still sleepy and, although one, older than the others, thought to remark that the master would not want her to ride alone, Wynne easily overcame their concern.

"I will not go far," she said with a smile. "Just to the bottom of the castle hill and perhaps across the bridge. It's far too lovely a day to be penned inside, and winter will be upon us before we know it. Besides," and she patted her belly with another smile at them, "soon I shall not be able to ride."

The stablemen chuckled, and then one of them helped her to mount her little mare. "Remember, my lady Wynne, no farther than the bridge," he cautioned with a gap-toothed grin.

Wynne turned her horse's head and rode serenely out of the courtyard, moving slowly down the castle hill. She knew the way to Cai, for the route was deceptively simple, although she had never before traveled that path. Nesta had told her about it during one of their conversations those long weeks back when she and Rhys were visiting at Raven's Rock. At the bottom of the castle hill the river ran swift, and, glancing up, Wynne looked to see if she was being observed, but to her relief she was not.

She trotted her mare across the stone bridge spanning the river. On the far side she turned right onto a narrow trail that moved around the base of the mountain and in the opposite direction from whence she had come to Raven's Rock from Gwernach over a year ago. Castle Cai was located around the other side of the mountain, Nesta had told her. It sat upon a promontory at the base of that mountain that jutted out over another valley. At least she would not have to climb her horse up another steep incline, Wynne thought, relieved.

The forest was thick with trees, and in some places the sun had a difficult time penetrating through the greenery. There were times that the trail she followed seemed to disappear, and yet Wynne felt no fear of her surroundings. High in the branches of a beech tree a bird sang, trilling notes of such clarity that it seemed almost unreal. When she came to a small stream that dashed over a bed of dark rocks, Wynne stopped her horse to rest and, dismounting, allowed her beast to drink. Tying the animal to a tree, she sat upon a bed of thick, soft moss and, taking a small flacon of wine from her saddlebag along with some bread and cheese, Wynne sat down to eat. She had been clever enough to obtain her picnic the previous evening after her supper. The servants thought she desired additional food to nibble on in her own quarters because of her condition.

She smiled to herself. Everyone at Raven's Rock was so good to her. Although she had always considered herself happy and content at Gwernach, she had never envisioned how absolutely blissful her life with Madoc would be. And it would all be better once she solved the estrangement between Madoc and Brys. She chewed her bread, noting that the cheese was her family's own. In the trees around her the birds sang, and several of them, curious, hovered on nearby branches. With a small chuckle Wynne crumbled the remainder of her bread and cheese and scattered it over the mossy ground for them. Arising, she relieved herself behind a thick stand of bushes. Then finding a nearby rock to use as a mounting block, she remounted her horse and, crossing the stream, continued on her way.

Another hour of gentle travel brought her around the other side of the mountain. The sun was now high in the late morning sky. The forest began to thin out and, ahead of her, Wynne saw Castle Cai. As Nesta had told her, it was perched on a rather narrow, high promontory that overlooked a misty blue valley. It was nothing like Raven's Rock. Rather it was a structure of greyish stone that seemed to cling precariously to the cliff upon which it stood. It was not large, yet it seemed very forbidding. A shiver took her, but Wynne brushed away her premonition and rode directly toward the castle. Reaching the lowered drawbridge, she hesitated a moment then moved across it. On the far side of the drawbridge she encountered a rather surly man-at-arms.

"Well?" he demanded. "State your business! His grace ain't in the market for a new woman today."

"I am the bishop's sister-in-law, the lady Wynne of Raven's Rock," she said in tart tones. "Have someone escort me to his grace immediately!"

The command in her voice impressed the man-at-arms, and he called to a companion beyond his post. "Here you, Will! This be his grace's sister-in-law come to see him. Help her off her horse and take her to him."

"Have someone give my mare a measure of oats," Wynne said. "She has brought me a goodly distance this day. And have her ready for me when I depart in an hour or so."

"Aye, lady," came the grudging reply.

The man-at-arms called Will lifted Wynne from her horse and, without a word, turned and headed through the portcullis into the courtyard, which appeared quiet and empty. There was an unnatural silence about the place. She followed Will up a broad flight of stairs into the castle and down a dark corridor into the Great Hall.

"You can find his grace there," Will said, pointing, and then he quickly disappeared.

The hall was not particularly large. It was smoky with poor ventilation, and dim from lack of windows. As Wynne focused her eyes, they grew wide with shock. In the middle of the room was a whipping post, and hanging from that post was some pour soul. Brys of Cai, informally attired in a pair of dark braies, his open-necked shirt hanging loose, began to ply a rather nasty-looking whip upon the bared back of his victim as Wynne stood horrified. A shriek tore through the hall, followed by another and another. Wynne, her heart pounding wildly, realized the offender was a woman.

"Brys!" she cried out. "I beg you to stop!" Then Wynne advanced into the hall, that her brother-in-law might see her clearly "Whatever this poor woman has done, surely she does not deserve to be beaten so cruelly." Reaching his side, Wynne put a restraining hand upon his arm.

"Wynne?" His eyes were slightly glazed, but then they cleared quickly. Tossing his whip aside, he demanded, "Wynne of Powys, what are you doing here? Castle Cai is certainly the last place I ever expected to see you." He took her arm and walked away from the whipping post, leading her up to the high board. "Bring wine for the lady Wynne," he called, and when she was settled he asked again, "Why are you here?"

"I have come to ask you to cease this quarrel that has existed for far too long between you and your brother, Madoc. I am with child, Brys, and I want peace in our family."

"Where is my brother? He certainly does not know you are here," Brys of Cai said with certainty. A crafty look came and went in his sky-blue eyes.

"No," Wynne admitted, "he does not. Our neighbors to the north were stealing sheep in the pasturelands below Raven's Rock. Madoc went to deal with them. I thought it a good time to come to Castle Cai and speak with you."

"I am surprised that you got here," Brys said. "Surely Madoc gave orders that you were to be carefully guarded. Yet somehow you have given your keepers the slip. I am quite impressed, belle soeur, by your cleverness."

"Oh, Brys, do not spar with me," Wynne told him irritably. "What you attempted with Nesta as a child was horrendous, but you are grown now. I cannot believe that you are as terrible as Madoc and Nesta insist. You are a man of the Church, Brys. Can you not help me to end this breach between you, your sister and brother? Is that not the Christian way?"

"I am no man of God, Wynne," Brys told her, amused. "I bought this bishopric for the power it could give me. Oh, 'tis true, I had to take holy orders, but I did not study, nor am I a priest. It was simply a formality insisted upon by those who wanted my gold." He chuckled. "There is much you do not know about me, for I know that my brother would not have distressed you with the whole truth."

"Do you not want to be reconciled with your family?" Wynne asked him.

He laughed bitterly. "Why should I want to be, belle soeur? Madoc, the great sorcerer-prince of Wenwynwyn, and Nesta, my sweet little sister, who perhaps loves Madoc more than she ought. What can they offer me that I do not have? I have power, and I have wealth. What more is there, Wynne of Powys?"

"There is love, Brys," Wynne said gently.

"Love?" He laughed again. "I can buy love!"

"To merely couple with a woman is not love, Brys," Wynne told him, shocked, ignoring his crude innuendo about Nesta.

"What else is a woman good for, belle soeur?" was the startling reply. "A woman is for a man's pleasure, and if he so desires, for bearing his children, and cooking his food, and sewing his clothing. There is no more. That illusory emotion you call love does not exist, for I have never experienced it, and God knows I have certainly allowed myself to run the gamut of every emotion available to man."

"Love most certainly exists!" Wynne cried. "It exists between a mother and her children. Between a man and his wife. Between siblings, Brys! Surely you have some feelings of love for Nesta and Madoc. For too long have you been estranged, and it is wrong! Nesta is to bear her husband a child sometime near the feast of Christ's Mass. My babe will be born in the early spring. I cannot feel content in my heart if you will not rejoin with your family, that the children Nesta and I bear may know their uncle."

"My God, you are so good!" he groaned. "I am surprised that Madoc has not already died of a surfeit of your sweetness!" He flung his wine cup across the room. "I have heard all I wish to hear, belle soeur. Allow me to return to the business at hand." He stood and glanced toward the woman at the whipping post. "The wench displeased me and will now suffer for it."

"*Brys!* I count at least five stripes upon the girl's back. Have mercy on her in the name of God! What can she possibly have done to merit such cruelty on your part?" Wynne pleaded with him.

Brys of Cai turned slowly and pierced Wynne with an intent look. His eyes, she noted, once again had a glazed, almost mad look to them. There was something familiar in the look, and yet she could not place it.

"Do you think I am cruel?" he asked her softly.

"I think you can be," she answered him honestly.

"Aye," he replied slowly. "I can be very cruel." He smiled at her, and she was once more struck by how handsome he was. As Nesta had said, he had the face of an angel. Nesta had also said his heart was black, and, as much as Wynne hated to admit that she was wrong, she was now beginning to believe Nesta had been correct in her evaluation.

"Let the girl go, my lord," Wynne said quietly. "If she truly displeased you, I will take her with me now and you will never have to lay eyes on her again. Serf or slave, I will pay her price."

Brys burst out laughing. "Wynne the Sweet, the Virtuous, the Good! You sicken me with your kindness! Barris! Where are you?"

"Here, my lord." A man-at-arms appeared from the shadows by the high board.

"Restrain the *princess* of Raven's Rock while I finish what I began earlier. If the bitch attempts to cry out, stifle her!"

Wynne leapt up. "Brys, how dare you!"

"Lady," Barris was by her side, "sit down. I will obey orders, but it would distress me to harm a woman."

Wynne reluctantly returned to her seat. She could see from the firm resolve in Barris's eyes that he would indeed obey his master's orders. She could but pray that her interference did not bode the worse for the poor girl who, seeing Brys approach once more, began to whimper fearfully. He added to his victim's terror by bending slowly and retrieving his whip, a nasty-looking instrument composed of half-a-dozen thin leather ribbons, each one of which was neatly knotted with tightly knit barbs intended to give additional pain.

With a slow smile of pleasure, Brys swished the whip in the air several times and then, with a grin, lashed out viciously at his helpless victim. Her shriek of agony echoed about the little hall, to be followed by cry after cry after cry as blow after blow after blow fell upon the girl's tender flesh until her back was bleeding, a raw mass of oozing welts. Still Brys's arm rose and fell unremittingly. He began to laugh as the girl tried desperately to turn, begging him to cease his torture.

Unable to stand a moment longer, and heedless of her own safety, Wynne leapt up. Eluding Barris's clumsy efforts to stop her, she ran around the high board, across the hall, and put a restraining hand upon Brys of Cai's arm. "In the name of God, stop!" she begged him. "The girl is near dead!"

His whip arm fell a moment, and he stared unseeing at her. Then a look of pure hatred poured into his gaze and, raising his arm, he hit Wynne a blow that sent her crumbling to the floor. As the darkness reached up to claim her, one thought leapt into her mind. *Bronwyn!* Then unconsciousness overcame her, and for a time she remembered no more.

When she finally came to herself again, she found she was in a dank and dark place. Wynne lay quietly, allowing her thoughts to carefully reassemble themselves. She was in a dungeon cell, placed rather carefully upon a pile of moldering straw. Although there was no light in the cell itself, the flickering of a torch was visible beyond the barred grate in the door. It allowed her a dim but distinct view of her surroundings. Her hands flew to her belly, and instinctively she knew the child was safe. A faint moan caught her ear. Scrambling to her feet, she reeled dizzily for a moment. Then as her head cleared she sought for the source of the sound.

She found the poor wench that Brys had beaten so brutally, face down upon another clump of straw. There was absolutely no doubt that the girl was dying. To increase her agony, salt had been rubbed into her many wounds. Wynne knew there was nothing she could do but render what small comfort her presence would offer. Kneeling, she took the girl's icy hand in her own and began to pray softly.

With great effort the dying woman turned her head that she might face Wynne. Her grey eyes were mirrors of her intense pain. "Thank ye," she managed to whisper. Then with supreme effort she grated out, "Yer in . . . more . . . danger . . . than me . . . lady!" and shuddering once, she died.

Wynne could feel the tears slipping down her cheeks. Poor creature, she thought, as the import of the woman's words hit her. What was she doing in this place? How did Brys dare to treat her in such a terrible manner? Then her memory began to stir. *He had hit her!* Without any care for her rank or her condition, he had hit her! Outraged, she rose to her feet and stamped across the cell to the door.

"Ho! The watch!" she shouted angrily, and she kept on shouting until Barris hurried around the corner into her line of vision.

"Lady, be silent," he begged her.

"Let me out of here this instant!" Wynne said furiously.

"I cannot," he said nervously, looking over his shoulder as if he expected to see something unpleasant.

"Why not?" demanded Wynne.

"His grace's orders, lady," came the reply.

"Do you know who I am?" Wynne asked the man. "I am Prince Madoc's wife."

"Lady, I cannot help you," said Barris desperately. Then he lowered his voice and stepped closer that she might hear him better. "I would if I could, but I cannot. Why did you come here in the first place? 'Twas a mad thing to do!"

Wynne laughed ruefully. "I came to try to make peace between my husband and his brother," she answered Barris.

The man-at-arms shook his head. "You should not have come, lady. Only God and His blessed Mother Mary can help you now; but God does not frequent Castle Cai." He turned to leave her.

"Wait!" Wynne cried after him. "The girl in here with me is dead, poor soul."

Barris stopped in his tracks and then turned back to her. "Are you certain, lady?" he asked, unable to hold back the tears that ran down his weathered face.

"Aye," she said softly. "I held her hand and prayed with her as she died."

"Poor Gwladys," Barris said sadly. "She were only fifteen."

"You knew her," Wynne said quietly. "Who was she and why did Brys beat her to death?"

"She was my youngest sister, lady," Barris answered. "She caught his grace's eye. He ordered her brought to him, and he forced her. Gwladys fought him, foolish lass, for she was to be married soon. It made no difference. His grace had his way with her. She told me he made her do terrible, unnatural things, and finally she couldn't stand it no more. She tried to run away, but she was caught. His grace said he was going to make an example of her so no one else would think they could disobey him. God assoil her sweet soul." He turned away again, saying almost to himself, "I must get permission to bury her, but not right away. His grace is still angry. He'd hang her from the battlements for the crows to pick at." Barris disappeared around the corner and was gone from her sight.

Wynne stood by the door grate for several long minutes and then she sank back down upon her pile of straw. She looked about, but other than Gwladys's body, there was nothing else in the cell. Not a bucket for a necessary, not a pitcher of water. She was below ground and so there was not even a scrap of window. She had absolutely no idea how long she had lain unconscious or what time it was. It certainly could not have been long. What was she going to do? Brys was obviously mad to believe he could keep her a prisoner. Aye. Brys was indeed mad.

Bronwyn. Once again the name burst into her consciousness. Wynne began to think. The look in Brys's eyes at one point had been familiar, but she had been unable to place it. Now she could. It was the same look Bronwyn of the White Breast had angrily cast upon Rhiannon of the Fair Folk on any number of occasions. It couldn't be! Yet why could it not be? If the soul inhabiting her body now had once belonged to Rhiannon; and Madoc's soul to Pwyll; and Nesta's soul to Angharad; why could not Brys's soul have once belonged to Bronwyn? It would certainly explain a number of things, including Brys's unreasonable hatred of them all, and his seemingly passionate desire to destroy their happiness. She had thought that the past didn't matter anymore, but oh, how wrong she had been! And what was she to do? In her own foolishness and pride she had put both herself and her unborn child in dangerous jeopardy. She struggled to keep from weeping, but could not. Finally exhausted, she fell into a troubled sleep.

Wynne awoke at the sound of a key turning in the rusty lock of the cell door. She struggled quickly to her feet, not wishing to be at any more of a disadvantage than she already was. The door swung open and a rough-looking woman entered.

"I'll take yer tunic dress and chemise," she said. "You can

keep the under tunic, his grace says, and gimme yer shoes too."

"Why?" Wynne demanded haughtily.

"Because his grace says so, wench! I don't ask no questions. I do what I'm told, and if you knows what's good for you, you will too," came the harsh reply. "Now hurry it up!"

Wynne pulled her soft leather shoes off her narrow feet and threw them at the woman, diverting her long enough so that she could thrust her gold chain beneath her under tunic neck-line. Then she quickly divested herself of her tunic dress and flung it in the same direction, turning her back angrily on the woman as she removed her under tunic and chemise and kicked the chemise across the floor. She heard the door creak shut as she drew her under tunic back on, the key turning in the old lock once more. Only then did it dawn on her that she still had no water, but she was too proud to call after the hag. Brys wouldn't let her starve . . . but perhaps he would.

She sat down. What on earth did they want with her tunic dress? She heard footsteps in the corridor again and scrambled to her feet once more. The door opened. Barris and another man entered the cell. For a minute the two looked down on the dead Gwladys, and Barris said, "This be Gwladys's intended, Tam, lady. We both thank you for trying to help our lass."

Wynne nodded and, as they began to remove the unfortunate girl's body from the cell, Wynne said, "I have no water, Barris, nor a necessary."

He nodded, but said nothing. The cell door was closed and locked. Wynne wondered if she would remain forgotten, but shortly Barris returned. He had with him a small wooden bucket, a flacon of water, and a wooden bowl which he word-lessly pushed at her. "Thank you, Barris," she said softly, but he was as quickly gone as he had come. Wynne put the bucket in a far corner, realizing she needed to use it very soon. She set the flacon in another corner so it could not be kicked over accidentally. She stared down into the bowl, which was filled with a hot potage of some kind that didn't smell particularly appetizing, and a heel of brown bread. With a wry grimace she ate the mess. She didn't know when she would see food again, and she had the babe to consider. The bread was stale, but she stuffed it in the pocket of her under tunic. She didn't need it now, but she might later. As an afterthought she removed the gold chain about her neck and her wedding band, stuffing them in her pocket as well. Then taking a drink from the flacon, she used the bucket to relieve herself and lay down to sleep.

"Lady! Lady!"

Wynne awoke, confused at first as to where she was. Reality quickly set in, and Barris was gently shaking her. "How long have I been sleeping?" she asked him.

"The night through, lady. His grace wants you in the hall now. You must come with me."

"Give me a moment's privacy, Barris, and I will be with you," Wynne said.

He nodded and drew the door shut behind him, but did not lock it. She could see the back of his head through the grating in the door. Quickly Wynne relieved herself once more in the bucket in the corner. Then taking a drink and rinsing her mouth, she used the rest of the water to clean her face and hands. Smoothing back her hair with her damp hands, she was able to bring some order to it.

"I am ready, Barris," she said, and he pushed open the door for her to exit. She followed him through a dimly lit corridor, up a flight of stairs and into the Great Hall of Castle Cai.

"Did you sleep well, belle soeur?" Brys inquired pleasantly as she made her way up to the foot of the high board.

"As well as I might, considering the poor accommodations, my lord," she replied sweetly. "If you would have my mare brought, I think it is past time for me to return to Raven's Rock." It was a bold bluff.

"Your mare, I imagine, has long been back at Raven's Rock, belle soeur," came the reply. He smiled charmingly at her. "You, however, will not be returning to Raven's Rock, I fear. You see, my dear Wynne, in your innocence you have given me the perfect weapon for destroying my brother Madoc. I have waited all my life long for such an opportunity. An opportunity I frankly never dared dream that I would get, and yet I have! You, Madoc's treasured wife, have unwittingly given me the knife which I shall plunge deep into his chest!"

"I do not understand you, Brys," she told him, but his very enthusiasm had already set her pulse pounding throughout her entire body. Dear God, he was evil! *Madoc!* She cried in her heart. *Madoc!*

"Madoc has always been too strong for me," Brys explained

in reasonable tones. "He was invincible, for he had no weaknesses through which I might strike out at him. Now he does. You, Wynne. You and the child you carry are Madoc's weaknesses. I shall destroy him through you! Your horse was taken back last evening to a point where it could not fail to find its way home, and it did, I am told. Already a search party combs the forest for any sign of you. Soon they will have it. Your torn and bloodied tunic dress will be found. Perhaps your shoes and chemise. It will be obvious to all that you have been eaten by wolves. Your loss, and that of your child, will destroy my brother. The knowledge that he did not protect you well enough, that you undoubtedly died in terror and fear, will break him! He will never recover. I shall be revenged on you both!"

"Why, Brys? Why do you hate us so?" Wynne probed.

"Why?" For a long moment Brys looked confused, and then he said, "Because I do! What difference does it make why? I simply do."

He did not know, Wynne thought. Instinct alone drove him. "You cannot get away with this, Brys," she told him. "What will you do with me? Kill me?" She felt far less brave than her strong words indicated.

"Kill you? Of course I will not kill you," he told her. "If I killed you, then your suffering would be over, belle soeur. No, no! I do not intend killing you. I want you to feel despair even as Madoc feels it. A broken man, he will grieve for you and the child that was to be, even as you live out your life in slavery somewhere with that child. A child who will be born into slavery and know no other life." Brys then began to laugh wildly as Wynne stared at him, transfixed.

"You cannot!" she cried. "I ask not for myself or for Madoc, Brys, but spare my child! I will do whatever you want me to do, but let my child be exonerated from whatever sin you believe Madoc and I have committed against you!" She fell to her knees pleading.

The laughter ceased abruptly, and Brys said, "It is useless to ask me for mercy. There is no mercy in me, Wynne. *None!* Now hear me well, for I will only say this once. If you want your child to live, you will keep your mouth shut while I do business with my friend, Ruari Ban. You see, belle soeur, there is always the slightest chance that if you are clever—and I believe you are—that one day you might escape the fate I have so carefully planned for you. If you attempt to interfere in my plans right now, however, I will personally rip the brat from your womb! Do you understand me?" His sky-blue eyes were cold, his voice uncharacteristically harsh.

Wynne rose to her feet and, looking defiantly at him, nodded. "I understand, Brys, and I damn you to Hell for what you are doing this day! Nesta once told me you were the Devil's own. I wish I had believed her when she said it, but to my discredit, I could not."

"Be silent now," he told her dispassionately, and turning to Barris, said, "Fetch in Ruari Ban."

Wynne watched as a tiny, wizened man entered the Great Hall. The top of his head was covered in a bristling thatch of bright red hair. His short legs almost danced their way up to the foot of the high board. His clothing was simple and dull, but there was an air of authority about him. His eyes were inquiring. They flicked quickly over Wynne and then turned themselves on Brys.

"Well, yer grace, and 'tis good to see ye again. I was just about to go over the hills into Mercia when yer message reached me. I hope 'tis worth my while, for I'd not intended to stop here." He gave Brys a brief little bow.

"When has it not been worth your while to visit me, Ruari Ban?" Brys demanded, laughing genially. "Come and join me. Wine for my guest!"

Ruari Ban clambered into a chair next to Brys and greedily quaffed down a goblet of wine. It was quickly refilled. "The roads are terrible dusty," he said, and then, "Well, yer grace? How may I be of service?"

"This wench," Brys said, his voice suddenly irritable, "I want to sell her to you, Ruari Ban. She was born right here at Cai, but she's been troublesome her whole life. There isn't a man-at-arms that takes her fancy she hasn't lain with, and now the wench has gone and gotten herself with child. And the lewd bitch doesn't even know who the father is! Unfortunately she is a beauty, as you can see, and the men persist in fighting over her. The few women slaves in the house dislike her for her proud ways. She's become more trouble to me than she's worth."

"Why not just marry her off to one of her men?" demanded Ruari Ban.

"And have her causing more trouble and cuckolding the poor fellow before she even gives birth? Nay! I want her gone from Cai. Make me a fair offer and she's yours. Surely you've some wealthy customer in Mercia or Brittany who'd have her."

"Well," the slaver considered, "let's see her wares, yer grace, and then I'll decide."

"Wynne! Remove your tunic!" Brys snapped.

She pierced him with a furious look, but the look Brys sent her back was ferocious. *The child, she thought. I must put my own anger aside and remember my child.* Wynne reached up, and loosening the neckline of the long under tunic, let it fall to the floor. Ruari Ban stared long at her naked form.

Finally he said, "I can sell her. What do ye want for her?"

"One copper," Brys said.

"Yer mad!" the slaver laughed. "*Sold!* Put yer gown back on, wench. Yer fate is sealed for this day." Then he turned to Brys. "Why so cheap, yer grace?"

"Because I want her gone from Cai immediately, my old friend, and because it pleases me to do you a great favor. You'll make a pretty penny on this piece of goods. One day I may want a favor from you. When that day comes, Ruari Ban, remember this day," Brys told the slaver.

"I will, yer grace, I will," Ruari Ban assured his host. Then he drank down his wine and, standing up, said, "We'd best be on our way. Though the day is new, it will grow old fast enough." He reached into the purse that hung from his belt and extracted a single copper which he handed to Brys. "Yer grace, payment in full." Then reaching into another bag hanging from his waist, he drew out a thin length of chain and, coming down from the high board, affixed it loosely about Wynne's waist. "We'll not be harming yer bairn," he told her. "Ye wear no slave collar, wench?"

"I didn't want to spoil her pretty neck," Brys cut in, "but you may have no choice, Ruari Ban."

"We'll see," the slaver said, and then, wrapping the length of chain about his hand, he nodded to Brys, saying, "Well then, we're off to Mercia, yer grace!"

"God be with you," Brys returned piously.

Ruari Ban cast him an amused look and then, yanking

lightly at the chain, drew Wynne with him. "God wouldn't come near this place," he murmured softly. "I suspect yer not unhappy to be going, eh lass? What's yer name? I heard him say it, but I don't remember."

"Wynne," she said.

"Wynne," he repeated. "It means *fair* in the Welsh tongue, doesn't it? Aye, it does. It suits ye, lass."

They had exited the castle and were now in the courtyard. She debated whether to tell him the truth now or to wait a bit, deciding that to wait was better. Best to be away from Castle Cai.

"Ye'll ride behind me, wench," she heard Ruari Ban say as a fat brown horse was brought. "Once we reach my caravan, ye'll walk with the rest of them, but until later today ye'll ride. Up with ye now!"

Her arms about Ruari Ban's ample waist, Wynne turned to look back at Castle Cai as they rode out from it and down into the misty blue valley below. For a time she had considered the possibility that she wouldn't escape Brys alive, but she had. It wouldn't take long to straighten out the situation she found herself in, particularly considering the fact that Brys had only sold her for a mere copper. Why, the gold chain in her pocket should buy her freedom easily.

"Sir," she said politely, "I would speak with you."

"What is it lass?" he answered her.

"It is not as Brys of Cai has told you," she began.

"I suspected as much," came the reply. " 'Tis his bairn yer carrying, I've not a doubt, and the devil didn't want you or it. He's a strange, cruel man, he is. Well, yer better off without him, and I'll find ye a good home, wench."

"I do not want you to find me a good home, sir. I have a good home. At Raven's Rock Castle," Wynne said. "I am Prince Madoc's wife, Wynne of Powys. My brother-in-law imprisoned me yesterday afternoon when I came to speak with him. If you will simply return me to my husband, you will be well rewarded."

"Now why would yer brother-in-law do such a thing, wench?" Ruari Ban did not sound particularly convinced by her brief explanation.

Wynne struggled to make him believe her. "Brys of Cai and his elder half-brother, my husband, Madoc of Powys, are bitter enemies. Because I am expecting our first child, I wanted the two brothers to be reunited in friendship. I waited until my husband was away and then I slipped away from Raven's Rock yesterday morning. When I arrived at Cai, it was to find Brys torturing some poor girl. When I tried to intervene, my brother-in-law struck me. I awoke to find myself in his dungeon, the dying girl with me. This morning Brys told me he was going to sell me into slavery. He said he had brought my mare back to Raven's Rock so that our people would find it riderless. He took most of my clothing from me, ripped and bloodied it, and left it in the forest for my husband to find. He feels by making Madoc believe I am dead, he will have his revenge on him. He threatened to harm my unborn child if I protested, and so I waited until we were away from Cai. If you will return me to Raven's Rock, my husband will reward you, Ruari Ban. Madoc loves me dearly, and this is his first child I am to bear," Wynne finished.

Ruari Ban sighed deeply and replied, "Now, lass, it may very well be that you are telling me the truth, but I cannot be certain. I have heard many tales far less plausible than yours over the years that turned out to be truth; and tales more plausible that were nought but lies. Of one thing, however, I am certain. The bishop of Cai is an evil man and an enemy who does not forgive a fault. I know little of Madoc of Powys, but what I know tells me he is as different from his brother as day is different from night.

"Brys of Cai sold you to me for one copper. It is obvious, whoever you are, that he desires to be rid of you. He has entrusted me with the business of carrying out his wishes. If I betray him, he will not rest until he has gotten his revenge on me. I have known some who tried to deal with his grace in a less than straightforward manner. All died, and it was a terrible death they suffered. Brys of Cai is a man who enjoys giving pain. The countryside hereabouts lives in fear of catching his eye or gaining his wrath. If I betray him, there is no place in this world where I shall be safe from his assassins."

"My husband will protect you, Ruari Ban. Madoc is the prince of Wenwynwyn, and that family is well-known for its sorcerers. Madoc will not allow Brys to harm you!"

"Your husband, if indeed he is your husband, sorcerer or no, could not protect you from Brys of Cai, wench," was the answer.

Wynne thrust a hand beneath the slaver's face. "Look at that hand," she demanded angrily. "Is that the hand of a slave woman? It is the hand of a lady! Do you not hear my speech? Is it rough or crude in either tone or its manner? I am not a slave born at Cai. I am the wife of Madoc of Powys. I insist that you take me home now!"

"Ye'd best curb that temper of yers, wench," Ruari Ban advised Wynne mildly. "There be some who won't take kindly to such a tone."

"I can pay you!" Wynne said desperately. "Gold! If you'll just take me home. What harm is there in it? If I'm not who I claim to be, you continue onward. But I am, and there'll be a reward in it for you."

He stopped his horse and turned about to look cannily at her. "What gold?" he demanded.

In that instant Wynne realized that to reveal to Ruari Ban that she possessed her gold chain and her wedding band would be foolish. This creature was a man who willingly associated and did business with Brys of Cai. He could not be trusted. He'd steal her jewelry and she'd be worse off than she was now. "I've gold at Raven's Rock," she told him simply, and then she smiled. "If you will but return me home, my husband will give you much gold."

The slaver grumbled, exasperated, "Shut yer mouth, wench! I've heard all I want to hear. Whatever the truth of the matter is, I don't want to incur the enmity of his grace, the bishop of Cai, who expects me to sell you off for a disobedient slave. If I don't, he will know and he will kill me. Now Madoc of Powys don't know old Ruari Ban at all. I've no quarrel with him. If yer indeed his wife and he don't know I've got ye, then I've still no quarrel with him, now do I? I'm not a bad fellow, but I'll listen to no more from ye. One more word and ye'll walk behind the horse."

Wynne wanted to shriek with outrage, but she restrained herself. Ruari Ban might be stubborn, but he was no fool. She understood his position, as difficult as that position was for her. Damn Brys of Cai for the dreadful villain he was! And knowing what a terrible person Madoc's brother was, why was she still questioning his motives? It was Madoc she should be con-

cerned about. Madoc who would believe her dead. She felt a
dull ache suffuse her heart at the thought that her actions
should cause the man she loved to suffer in any manner.
Madoc! She cried out to him with every fiber of her being.
Madoc! The child and I yet live!

She felt the tears slipping down her cheeks and, angry at
herself for such an open display of weakness, she brushed
them away. Her stomach growled noisily, and Wynne remembered the bread stuffed in her pocket. She drew it out, careful
not to disturb her gold chain and ring, which were hidden there
too. The bread was hard and dry, but she began to gnaw upon
it hungrily, moistening the crust with her saliva.

Ruari Ban turned his head about to look at her, saying,
"Have ye not eaten this morning, wench?"

Wynne shook her head, swallowing a mouthful of the dry
bread. "I was brought from my dungeon cell directly to the
Great Hall," she told him. "I saved the bread from last night's
meal, if indeed that disgusting mess I was served could be
called a meal."

"Be patient, wench," he counseled her. "Another hour and
we should catch up to my caravan. They're camped for the
day, and the cook fires will be going. I'll see yer well fed. 'Tis
not my policy to starve the merchandise. Any slaver who does
that won't make a fat profit. Besides, yer eating for two, ain't
ye? Ohh, ye'll bring me a fine profit, ye will, wench! Two for
the price of one, and yer not yet deformed with the bairn that
ye've lost yer looks either. I've got just the man in mind for
yer master too. A wealthly thegn with large moneybags who'll
pay well for a fertile lass like yerself for his childless son. Be
clever, m'dear, and 'twill be yer new master who ends up the
slave," he cackled, well pleased with himself.

When he had turned about again and was facing forward
once more, Wynne allowed herself the luxury of a few more
tears before finally growing calm. She had her gold chain and
her gold ring, and she did indeed intend being clever. Clever
enough to escape the fate Brys had planned for her. He would
not defeat her this time either!

Part III

THE THEGN OF AELFDENE'S WIFE

*And ever has it been that love
knows not its own depth until
the hour of separation.*
          Kahlil Gibran
          THE PROPHET

≋Chapter 11

Wynne quickly found that there was to be no easy escape for her from Ruari Ban, the Irish slaver. They reached his encampment, and she found herself chained to a tree with just enough length of links to move about comfortably, but that was all.

She was fed well and, in general, well-treated. The little Irishman did not believe in mistreating the slaves in his possession, for he was an astute businessman before all else. They remained the night. Then Ruari Ban's party, which consisted of close to thirty slaves and at least five other men to help with them, moved out along the roads leading across the hills from Wales to the Mercian town of Worcester.

Despite his threat to walk her, Ruari Ban seemed to have a soft heart where Wynne was concerned. Each day he took her up upon his horse, which did not particularly endear her to the other captives. Wynne did not care. Her mind was far too busy considering her situation and contemplating how she would escape. Ruari Ban, however, chattered away as they rode, telling her bits of history regarding the area through which they were passing.

When they had crossed over Offa's Dyke into Mercia he explained that the Mercian king, Offa, had built the earthworks to clearly mark his territory from that of Powys.

"But he built it on land belonging to Powys," Wynne noted.

Ruari Ban chuckled. "So he did, wench. So he did. Still, the lords of Powys allowed it, and the Mercian towns nearer the border have been the better for it. Both Hereford and Worcester have prospered mightily."

"Why are you taking me to Worcester?" Wynne asked.

"I have a buyer in mind for you, wench. The eldest son of a wealthy thegn called Eadwine Aethelhard. His sons are Caddaric Aethelmaere and Baldhere Armstrang."

"I do not understand these Anglo-Saxon surnames," Wynne said.

"It's not so difficult," Ruari Ban told her. "A man must earn his surname here in England. Aethelhard means noble and brave. Hence, Eadwine, the noble and the brave. He is descended from Offa and is known to be a very courageous warrior. As for his sons, Caddaric Aethelmaere is equally famed for his bravery, hence his surname, noble and famous; and the younger son, Baldhere Armstrang, gained his surname for a powerful and unflagging arm which is equally facile at throwing a spear accurately and using a broadsword to its greatest advantage.

"The sons are but a year apart and have spent their lives in constant competition. A competition at which the elder, Caddaric, held the edge until they married. Caddaric's wife, Eadgyth Crookback, has borne him no children in their eight years of marriage. Neither have any of his lesser women. Baldhere, however, has three daughters and a son by his wife Aeldra Swanneck; two little daughters by one of his lesser women; and his other lesser woman is, I am told, expecting her first child.

"Caddaric will inherit from his father, but unless he can father children, it is Baldhere's son who will inherit from him. Caddaric, you will understand, is desperate to have a child of his own. He is furious with his wife and his women for their failure to produce his children. It is to his great misfortune to have contracted the alliances he has with so many barren women. You, my pretty wench, are obviously a fruitful lass. I intend selling you to Caddaric so that he may get children on you once you have delivered of the babe you now carry. You will bring me a fine profit, wench!"

"Has anyone stopped to consider that perhaps this Caddaric is the barren one?" Wynne demanded. "How many lesser women does he possess, Ruari Ban?"

"Four, and a tasty lot of beauties they are," came the reply.

"This Mercian stallion plays the stud to five mares and he cannot get one of them in foal?" Wynne exclaimed. "I think you expect the impossible; from me or any other woman, Ruari Ban."

The slaver chuckled. "Eadwine Aethelhard used up a few wives before he got his two boys. Caddaric is like his da. Slow to start, but he'll be quick to finish with a hot-blooded, wild Welsh girl like you in his bed!"

Wynne shook her head in despair. This was all she needed. To be introduced into a household of jealous women, most of whom were barren, and one of whom expected her only son to inherit a rich estate, providing her brother-in-law had no sons. *Madoc!* She reached out to him with her mind as she had done ever since Brys's perfidy. *Madoc! I am not dead! Help me! Find me!* There was nothing. Could she ever reach him? She had to reach him! She didn't know what else to do.

Ruari Ban decided not to go to Worcester first, for he did not want to put Wynne up for public sale. If she was indeed who she said she was, word could easily filter back to Madoc of Powys. Ruari Ban would find himself with two powerful enemies to contend with. Madoc, because he had in effect kidnapped his wife; and Brys of Cai, for having failed the bishop. Instead he sent his people and his merchandise ahead to the market town of Hereford, where he would eventually catch up with them. Wynne he took directly to Aelfdene, the estate belonging to Eadwine Aethelhard.

They arrived close to nightfall, just as the gates were closing on the estate's courtyard. Ruari Ban and Wynne were shown into the hall, where the fire pits were blazing merrily, taking the chill off the autumn evening. The slaver had been wise enough to exchange Wynne's filthy and worn under tunic for a clean one of soft lavender silk which was belted simply with a twisted rope belt of darker violet. He had given her time to wash her hair in a nearby stream and rebraid it neatly. Indeed, Wynne had taken the opportunity to bathe her entire body, ignoring Ruari Ban, who had watched her most licentiously. Her gold chain and her wedding band were securely hidden in the pocket of her clean gown.

Wynne looked curiously up at the high board as they approached it. A huge Saxon with the obvious look of a warrior sat in the place of honor. He had a large leonine head. His hair was a fine ash brown, his beard of the same hue, well-barbered. His blue eyes were frankly curious. On either side of him sat a young man, obviously his sons from the look of them. Which was which? she wondered. Then Wynne noted that next to the sullen young man who had dark blond hair was a pinch-faced young woman with one shoulder slightly higher than the other. This then would be Caddaric and his wife, Eadgyth Crookback. To Eadwine's left was a darker-haired son with his wife, a pouty-mouthed girl with thick flaxen braids and a prideful look. Baldhere and Aeldra Swanneck, Wynne thought.

"Welcome to Aelfdene, Ruari Ban!" came the deep booming voice of Eadwine Aethelhard. "We have not seen you here in many months. I am told you travel only with this young girl."

"I have brought her for your son, Caddaric, my lord," replied Ruari Ban. "This beauteous Welsh wench is the answer to all his problems."

"Each time that my son has introduced another woman into my house, he has claimed her the answer to his difficulty, Ruari Ban. Why do you think this girl can succeed where the others have failed?" Eadwine Aethelhard looked curiously at Wynne.

"I have proof of this girl's fertility, my lord. She is with child by her former master. An odd sort who decided he wanted neither the woman nor the child she carried." Ruari Ban lowered his voice and spoke in a confidential tone. "He is a churchman of some prominence, my lord. You see the difficulty."

The thegn nodded and said, "Well, let's see her, my friend. I can tell little about her while she is clothed." He stood up and came down from the dais.

Ruari Ban quickly unlaced the neckline of Wynne's tunic. Pulling it off her, he allowed the gown to slip to the floor about her ankles. Wynne wasn't certain that she was even breathing. This was horrendous! To be exposed before a single stranger would have been bad enough, but to be presented naked before this Saxon's entire hall was almost more than she could bear. She had never before seriously considered the plight of a slave, for her family had always treated their slaves with kindness. Still, kindness was not enough if one could be manipulated against one's will. When I am back at Raven's Rock, she thought, I must tell Madoc of this. We will keep no more slaves!

Eadwine Aethelhard walked slowly about the naked girl, his eyes taking in every nuance of her. He lifted up one of her arms, running his hand along it, examining the palm. Kneeling, he ran his hands over the backs of her legs. Standing, he looked into her face. It was a beautiful face, but her eyes were deliberately unfocused, as if she had detached herself from the entire proceeding.

"Open your mouth," he commanded her. The eyes widened, startled, but she obeyed him. Her breath was sweet, her teeth sound, he noted. The thegn was no fool. This girl was obviously a captive and not slaveborn. Captives could be difficult. He cupped one of the girl's breasts in his palm, and her startled gaze immediately made contact with his. She blushed, the color staining her milk-white skin, but she said nothing and her green eyes again grew blank. He stood back from her now and saw the faint rounding of her belly, but was not surprised. Ruari Ban was an honest man and would not have lied about the girl's condition.

"*I want her!*" His son, Caddaric, was leaning across the high board, his eyes filled with lust. Next to Caddaric his daughter-in-law was looking dejected as usual. Eadwine Aethelhard wasn't surprised that Caddaric could not get a child on poor Eadgyth. She was a frail creature, but she had come to them with a dowry consisting of two and a half hides of land, and whether she lived or died, the land now belonged to them. Caddaric, however, had four strapping other women he used with vigorous regularity. So much so that the thegn had recently overheard them complaining of their lord's constant attentions. If his son were capable of fathering a child, something Eadwine had only recently begun to doubt, surely one of these other lasses could have given Caddaric a son or daughter.

"*I want her, Father!*" Caddaric's hoarse voice repeated. "Buy her for me!"

"You have too many women and can seem to do nothing with any of them," Baldhere teased his brother. "Now I have but two lesser women. I think father should buy this one for me."

"I do not intend buying her for either of you," Eadwine Aethelhard answered his sons. "I am going to buy her for me!"

"*What?*" Caddaric and Baldhere chorused in unison, and both of his daughters-in-law came to life, staring at him as if he had gone mad.

"Father," ventured Aeldra Swanneck nervously, "do you not think you are too old for a woman?"

"I am forty-three, Aeldra," Eadwine told her, amused. "I use the slave women and the female serfs belonging to this estate with great regularity."

"You do?" Aeldra Swanneck looked quite surprised. "I did not know."

"Well, daughter, now you do. I have had no woman in my life since my good Mildraed died three years ago. I want one, and this wench will suit me quite nicely," he concluded. He now turned his attention to Ruari Ban. "How much?"

"Five silver pennies, my lord. She's a rare beauty, and she will take good care of you in your old age," came the reply.

"Two silver pennies," countered Eadwine Aethelhard. "I am not so old yet, you Irish robber, that I could not get another son on this wench!"

"My lord Eadwine, you will beggar me, and after I have gone to all the trouble to bring this girl to you."

"You brought her to me, Ruari Ban, because you were afraid to sell her on the open market. This is no slaveborn girl, and I am no fool. She has the hands and feet of a well-born woman. I will ask you no questions, for I want her, but do not trifle with me. Two silver pennies!" the thegn said.

"Three, my lord, I beg you! Three! You are getting two slaves for the price of one," Ruari Ban wheedled pleadingly.

"The girl could die in childbed and I would lose them both. Three silver pennies make it a bad investment. Two and no more, or you can take her to Hereford."

"I will pay you three!" Caddaric shouted from the high board.

His father sent him a withering look. "You have nought but what I give you, Caddaric. Do not be a bigger fool than you already are, my son." He looked at Ruari Ban. "Well, slaver? What is your decision?"

Ruari Ban sighed dramatically. "You drive a hard bargain, my lord," he complained, "but I will accept. I can see the wench is taken with you already and would remain at Aelfdene."

Eadwine Aethelhard's deep laughter boomed through his hall. "The girl would rather be anywhere but where she is at this moment, you old robber!" Chuckling, he delved into his purse which hung from the wide leather belt girding his tunic and drew out two silver coins. "Here, and you are welcome to stay the night, Ruari Ban. Tell me, does my new slave speak our tongue?"

"She does, my lord," replied the slaver, hefting the coins within his palm to ascertain their weight.

"The weight is true." Eadwine Aethelhard chuckled, and turning to Wynne, said gently, "Reclothe yourself, lass, and tell me your name."

"My name is Wynne, my lord." She bent and drew her gown back up, fastening it neatly at the neckline, retying the rope belt about her waist.

"Are you hungry?" he asked.

"Aye, my lord. I have not eaten since morning," Wynne said quietly, and then she looked him full in the face.

"You won't go hungry here, Wynne," he told her. Then he looked about the hall and, finding what he sought, he called, "Ealdraed, to me."

An elderly woman hobbled across the hall. "Aye, my lord?"

"This is Wynne. Take her and feed her. Then bring her to the Great Chamber," Eadwine directed.

The old lady nodded and, smiling a toothless smile at Wynne, said, "Come girl. From the look of you I can see you need feeding up."

Ruari Ban took himself below the salt, accepting a plate of hot food and a goblet of ale from a servant. Eadwine Aethelhard was a hospitable man, and he'd sleep warm in his hall this night. His host rejoined his family at the high board and the conversation that followed was a heated one. The last thing Ruari Ban had expected when he had brought Wynne to Aelfdene was that the thegn himself would desire the wench. He shrugged and patted at the new weight in his purse. It was a fine profit! Brys of Cai had certainly done him a very good turn.

At the high board Caddaric Aethelmaere was working himself into a fine rage. He wanted to have the Welsh slave, and as it was rare that he had been denied anything in his life; he was not accepting his father's decision in the matter with ease or good grace. "You took her because you knew I wanted her," he grumbled half to himself.

"I took her because she is the first woman since your mother to genuinely stir my loins," the thegn told his eldest son. "I am not so old that a woman cannot arouse me. This one did it with a look. It is rare I want anything for myself, Caddaric. Something I cannot say for you or your women. I do not need to explain myself to you or to your brother. My will is law at Aelfdene, and it will be until I am dead. I expect to live a very long time, my sons, particularly now that I have such a toothsome playmate to amuse me."

Baldhere Armstrang burst out laughing. "You have surprised me, Father," he said. "I shall never again consider you predictable in your habits."

Eadwine chuckled. "You are wiser than your brother," he said.

"I know," came the reply.

"You may jest if you choose," Caddaric snarled, "but what if Father gets this slave with child? What then, Baldhere the Wise?"

"Why then, my dear Caddaric, we shall have a little sister or brother to amuse us. I find the prospect most delightful," Baldhere mocked his elder.

Caddaric arose from the high board and stamped angrily from the hall, his wife, Eadgyth Crookback, scurrying in his wake.

"Poor Eadgyth," said Baldhere. "She will have a hard night of it."

"Not Eadgyth," said Aeldra Swanneck in superior tones. "He will abuse the others in her stead. For reasons I do not understand, he respects Eadgyth. I am glad, nonetheless, Father, that you have given us each our own small hall. Haesel is particularly noisy when Caddaric beats her. At least the children will not be awakened."

"You have given your sons their own halls?" the slaver asked, surprised. "That is very generous of you, my lord."

"Generosity be damned, my friend," the thegn said, laughing. "Caddaric has a wife and four contentious lesser women. Baldhere has a wife, two lesser women, and six noisy little children, only one of them a boy. One of his women is pregnant with another child. They are welcome in my house during the day, but when the night falls, Ruari Ban, I have reached an age when I want my quiet. My grandchildren run about the hall shrieking. They are small, and so they fall frequently and then set up a howling that would wake the heroes in Valhalla. They poke at the dogs and pull at their ears and tails. When they are bitten for their pains, their mothers come whining to me about my hounds. I gave my sons and their families each a small hall of their own because it suited me to do so. There are some who call me foolish for it, and others who think I do not love my family, but I do. I simply want some peace and quiet of an evening."

"Yours is not a problem I have ever had to face, my lord, being that I have no real home and family. I am not sure if I envy you or not," the slaver replied.

"Get yourself a house, Ruari Ban, and find a good young woman to keep you content in your old age," Eadwine Aethelhard advised. "It is not such a bad life. And now I shall bid you good night." He arose from the high board and, walking across the hall, climbed up the stairs to the Great Chamber of the manor house.

The Great Chamber was the place where the family could retire from the hall for privacy in the manor house. Eadwine Aethelhard's home was somewhat more luxurious than many of his neighbors in that it was constructed entirely of stone but for its thatched roof. The Great Chamber extended over only about half of the hall below. It had once contained the sleeping spaces for the thegn, his late wife Mildraed, their sons, and later their sons' wives. The sleeping spaces were set into the stone walls, leaving the floor space free for table, chests, and benches.

Mildraed had even kept her loom here. He had given it to Eadgyth Crookback when she had died. By that time he had moved his sons out of his manor house and into their own halls. His desire for privacy was considered quite odd by most of his neighbors.

Ealdraed was waiting for him as he entered the chamber. "I put the girl in your sleeping space, my lord. You did not say to do otherwise."

He nodded, and she began to help him undress. "I want you to look after Wynne," he told the old woman. "She is not, I think, slaveborn. Put her to simple tasks during the day."

"Aye, my lord."

"Did she eat well?"

"Aye, my lord. Poor girl was very hungry, and her with child too. Most ladylike she was too, my lord, despite her hunger. Dainty with her food, unlike those women of your sons."

"Aye, you nosy old witch," he told her in response to her sly unasked question. "I'm taking this girl for my woman. Does that tell you what you want to know?" He chuckled.

"And about time too, my lord," she snapped pertly back at him, and then she eyed his naked figure boldly. "Yer still a young man, my lord. You should have your own woman and not have to go about tumbling serfs beneath the hedges."

"Is there nothing that goes on at Aelfdene that you do not know about, Ealdraed?" he demanded in mock outrage.

The elderly lady cackled merrily. "I do not think so, my lord. I do not think so," she told him. "What else is there for a woman of my many years to do but put her nose in everyone else's business?" She gathered up his clothes and began to fold them. "There is water in the basin, my lord."

He quickly washed his hands and splashed the water upon his face, brushing the droplets from his beard. "Good night, Ealdraed," he called, hearing her footsteps as she hobbled down the stairs. Then, turning, he walked across the room and climbed into his bed space.

Wynne lay as far away from him as she could, her back to him, next to the wall. He could tell from her breathing that she was not asleep though she attempted to feign it. He held the coverlet back admiring the graceful line of her back as it moved downward into her prettily rounded buttocks. She shivered suddenly and, softly chiding himself for his thoughtlessness, he drew the coverlet over them both.

"You are not asleep," he said.

"No, I am not," she answered honestly.

He moved himself next to her, rolling onto his side, reaching out to draw her into the curve of his body. His big hands cupped her breasts in a tender embrace. "Tell me," he said quietly. "You are not slave born. I would know who you are and how you came to me."

Wynne told him. She didn't know what else to do, even though she was uncomfortable in her present position. Eadwine Aethelhard seemed a kind man. When she had finished, she said, "Will you return me to my husband, my lord?"

"No," he told her, and when she stiffened in his arms, he continued, "this is the way of the world, Wynne. There are always captives who are sold into slavery. Perhaps the story you have told me is entirely true and perhaps it is not. I cannot trek

you across the countryside ascertaining the truth of the matter.
You have been sold to me as a slave, and I have paid for your
purchase. You will be safe with me, Wynne, and your child
too. I have not taken a woman since my wife's death. You will
have a place of honor in my household, and if after you have
borne the child you carry you give me a child, so much the
better. I should not be unhappy to have another child."

"You cannot mean to couple with me," she said, shocked.

"Do you dislike the act then?" he asked gently.

"No," she replied, "but I am a married woman!"

"No longer," he answered. "Whatever you once were, you
are no longer, Wynne. You are my wild Welsh girl, and I mean
to love you. What fine breasts you have," he noted, and he
fondled them.

With an agility that surprised even herself, Wynne squirmed
about so that she was facing him. "Eadwine Aethelhard," she
began, "if I must be your slave, I will be your slave. I will do
your bidding in all things, but please, I beg of you, do not
force me to couple with you. There must be other slave
women and serf girls who would be honored by your attentions, but I am a married woman."

"Slave women do not wed," he said patiently. "You are my
slave, Wynne, and you must accept it. A woman with child
should not fret herself so as you are doing."

"I will run away," she said defiantly.

"You will not be allowed the opportunity," he said with a
small chuckle.

"I will find the right moment," she persisted.

"Having found you, my wild Welsh girl, I will never let you
go," Eadwine Aethelhard told her. Then he leaned forward and
kissed her.

She realized his intent just a fraction of a second too late.
His mouth closed over hers warmly, pressing firmly, gently
coaxing a response from her though she strove to deny that impression. How could she feel anything toward this Anglo-
Saxon when she loved Madoc? *Madoc.* Why could she not
reach out to him? During the weeks she had traveled from her
home over the mountains and the hills into England, she had
not once seen a raven, let alone old Dhu. Did he really believe
her dead?

Eadwine Aethelhard sensed her sudden distance from him.

He pressed the woman in his arms back into the mattress and allowed his passions somewhat freer rein. This girl set his blood to boiling as no woman ever had. Not even his late wife, he thought guiltily. He knew as he kissed her that he wanted far more from Wynne than she was able to give him at this moment in time, but eventually she would give him everything he desired from her. For now, however, he must impress upon her the need for change, because whatever her life had been, it was now changed. In order to be happy she must adjust to that change. He wanted her to be happy.

She was not made of stone, Wynne thought, shamed as his lips traced a trail of kisses across her face and down the straining column of her throat. *"Don't,"* she pleaded with him, and she shivered. "Please don't."

"Your skin is so fine," he murmured against the throbbing pulse at the base of her neck. "It is like silk cloth." He tasted the flesh he praised with his tongue and his lips. "You smell of fresh air and the sun, my wild Welsh girl."

She wanted to fight him, but she feared his reaction should she seriously defy him. She had her child to consider. She had heard of warriors like this one going berserk in the heat of battle, and this really was a battle between them. As his hot kisses and his sensual caresses increased in ardor, Wynne was suddenly very aware of his big naked body pressing against her nude form. She had been so concerned with trying to divert him from his intentions, she hadn't even considered their mutual state. Now she was very aware of it and increasingly mindful of her own rising passions.

She had never expected to feel passion for any man other than Madoc, but she knew from her grandmother and from the women's chatter she had overheard in her childhood at Gwernach that such a passion was possible. A woman's body was a delicate and frail thing. It could be played upon like a lute, and in the hands of a skillful lover, it would respond. There was no doubt in her mind that Eadwine Aethelhard was just such a talented lover. If her heart and mind could not respond to him, her body surely could.

"My babe," she protested softly, hoping against hope to elude him.

His big hand delicately caressed the gentle, barely discernable mound of her belly, which was only beginning to swell with her child. "You are still able," he said softly, "and I will not hurt either you or your son." The hand slipped lower and pushed between her tightly clenched thighs.

"H-How can you be certain I carry a son?" she asked, and felt his fingers exploring the wetness of her. Her cheeks grew warm with her embarrassment.

"Because a woman like you would sire a son first," he said, and then he kissed her once more.

Her lips parted slightly beneath his. She simply couldn't help it. He was arousing her passions in a most masterful fashion. She felt his tongue move into her mouth and his breath was sweet. Finding her tongue, he caressed it adroitly, and Wynne could not contain the little moan that welled up in the back of her throat. The taut nipples of her breasts were tingling painfully; and all the while his fingers continued to play with the sentient flesh between her thighs. The heat of her desire was almost suffocating her, and she pulled her head away from his, gasping for breath.

"Look at me," he commanded her.

Wynne raised her eyes to him, surprised that in such an intense juxtaposition she should feel shy of this man with whom she was so intimately entwined. The pink in her cheeks, however, entranced him greatly. "Many men," he said softly, "will take a woman with no care for her own pleasure. I have found greater pleasure, however, in the knowledge that my lover is as well satisfied as I am. I know you fear for the child, Wynne. I am a large man and I could crush so delicate a creature as yourself if we did not take a care. I do not want you to be afraid." Then to her great surprise he turned her over onto her stomach and continued, "Draw your legs up, Wynne, and trust that I will not hurt you."

To her own surprise, she obeyed him, silently shocked by knowing that she wanted him. His clever ministrations had seen to her full arousal, and she shuddered as she felt his hands closed firmly over her hips. She bit back a cry as he carefully slipped between her thighs, and her back arched slightly as, finding her woman's passage, he pressed his manhood home, sliding deep into the dark warmth of her. She felt engorged by him as he delved and probed into the secret depths of her. Her face was hot with her shame as she felt the throb of his male organ, and then he began to move upon her; his fingers marking her white skin as he held her tightly in his grasp; his great lance thrusting and withdrawing, thrusting and withdrawing, until she could no longer contain her cries, and her own body plunged up and back with frantic impetus to meet his downward drive. Her head whirled in confusion at this assault upon her most tender senses. She tried desperately to block his final victory over her, but she could not stem the tide of pleasure that was beginning to wash over her.

He was groaning with intensity. The sound of a man close to his own crisis and well-pleased with his efforts, and yet he held back. She could feel it and realized that he needed the knowledge of her own pleasure to release his own satisfied passions.

"*No! No!*" she sobbed.

"*Yes!*" he countered fiercely and ground into her, immersing himself in her sweet flesh. "Yesss, my wild Welsh girl!" he shouted, triumphant as her despairing cry of defeat filled his ears, and he poured his hot love juices into her eager sheath.

Wynne burst into tears and found herself swiftly turned about and cradled in Eadwine Aethelhard's strong arms. "There, my sweeting," he crooned low to her. "There, my wild Welsh girl. Now you know to whom you belong. Do not weep, Wynne. Do not weep!"

But she could not stop at first. "I . . . I . . . I want to go home!" she sobbed.

"You are home, my sweeting, and I will keep you safe so that you need never be frightened or in danger again. This Madoc did not care for you well," the thegn said, and there was disapproval in his voice. "I will allow no harm to come to you, Wynne. You and your child will be safe with me." His blue eyes looked down upon her, and she saw the determination in them to do precisely what he said he would do. This was a strong man.

"My babe!" she said, and her hands flew to her belly.

"He is safe," Eadwine said with assurance. "In another few weeks I must leave you in peace for the child's sake, but for a short time we may enjoy one another." He caressed her dark hair. "You have hair the color of a raven's wing," he said. "It is so different from our yellow-haired Saxon women." Then he smiled down at her and she saw that his teeth were quite good. He was a handsome man.

"You are not a bad man, I think," Wynne told him.

The smile broadened. "No," he answered her. "I am not a bad man."

"You are a determined man, however," she said, and he chuckled. "I am a determined woman," Wynne told him.

"Then we are most admirably suited to one another, aren't we, my wild Welsh girl?" He kissed her mouth with a hard, quick kiss. "You make me feel like a stripling again, Wynne. I want to begin anew! I am sick unto death of my old life and all that comes with it. I want a new life, and I want you to be the centerpiece of that new life."

"What of your family?" she asked him. "Can you so easily cast them off, for that is, I suspect, what you desire to do."

"Caddaric and his women," grumbled the thegn. "Pah! They make me sick! My eldest son is a good fighter but a bad man, and I do not know how he got that way except perhaps my late wife, God assoil her soul, was too soft with him. Still, Mildraed was a good woman, and I cannot hold her responsible for the lad. My grandfather was very much like Caddaric. A hard, cruel man. Perhaps it is just as well he can whelp no pups."

"And Baldhere, my lord?" Wynne inquired.

"He will inherit his father-in-law's estates, although Aeldra casts eyes upon Aelfdene as well. Baldhere's wife is a greedy woman. How it would please me to get a son on you, my wild Welsh girl! A son of your body could inherit if I so desired it," Eadwine Aethelhard said. "Such a decision on my part could cause Caddaric to suffocate on his own choler, although Baldhere could find the entire thing amusing. He is basically a simple man with little ambition, although, like his elder brother, he too is a good soldier. He became one in order to survive his childhood with Caddaric." Eadwine chuckled.

Wynne giggled. She simply could not help it.

"Now there's a nice sound," the thegn said.

"It does not mean that I forgive you for forcing me," Wynne told him. "How could you? We don't even know one another."

Eadwine's eyes grew serious. "I wanted you," he said. "From the moment I set eyes on you, I wanted you. For now, I know that your heart and your mind resist me, Wynne. Your lovely, ripening body, however, does not. That will not always be enough for me, my sweeting, but for now I am satisfied.

We will come to care for one another as the months pass, I promise you. And after you have borne your child, I will take you for my wife and free you from your slavery."

Wynne shook her head sadly. "As long as Madoc of Powys lives, Eadwine Aethelhard, I can never be your wife, for I am his wife. This is a Christian land, my lord, and your sons have married their wives in the Holy Church despite the lesser women that they keep in the manner of the old ways. I cannot in good conscience wed anyone, for I am already wed. I have been kidnapped from my husband and my home, to be sold into slavery, but that cannot change the fact that I am a married woman. You may take my body, and you may arouse my passions, but I am still Madoc's wife."

"Yet he thinks you dead, you tell me," Eadwine countered.

"No, Brys of Cai has conspired to make Madoc believe that I am dead, but Madoc loves me. We are bound together through time and space. He will know that I yet live. He will seek me and our child out, and eventually he will find us," Wynne told the thegn in a firm and determined voice.

"He will never find you, my wild Welsh girl. You delude yourself if you believe that he senses you live," Eadwine told her. "If it comforts you to believe that now, then believe it; but in the end you will come to realize that I am right. Your prince will grieve greatly for you. That I understand, but he will eventually take another woman to wife, for he dare not allow his ancient line to die out lest the ghosts of his illustrious ancestors rise up and curse him. You are lost to Madoc of Powys, and he is lost to you forever."

"If it comforts you to believe *that*, Eadwine Aethelhard," Wynne replied, "then believe it, but in the end you will see that I am right."

He fell asleep quickly, his arm possessively about her. Wynne, however, despite her long and tiring day, lay awake. She was more than well aware of how fortunate she was in having been purchased by Eadwine Aethelhard. Another man would certainly have been less kind. *A slave.* No, whatever her legal position was in this land, she was not a slave in either her mind or her heart. She did not intend behaving like one either, or allowing anyone to make her feel less than that which she had always been. She was Wynne of Gwernach, wife to

Madoc of Powys. She was a freeborn woman, and she would behave as one no matter her position in this household.

Time. She needed time to assess her surroundings. To discover just where she was and how she might escape back to her own land. It was already November, and the winter would be upon them very soon. Did she have time to make her way home now, or should she wait until spring? But come the spring, her child would be born. It would be harder to travel with a baby than to travel with the baby unborn. Unborn, the child was safely sheltered within her body. She did not know what to do. For the first time in her life she was faced with a situation to which there seemed to be no right answer.

Sleep. She needed to sleep. Her exhaustion was making her fearful and indecisive. These were qualities she dare not indulge if she was to survive; if her child was to survive. *Madoc!* Her heart called out to him in the silence of the night. *Madoc!* Why could he not hear her? They had loved one another from the first moment of their first meeting somewhere back in the dim mists of another time and place. He had pursued her through the other times and places that had followed in order to gain her forgiveness, to regain her love. He had both those things now, but fate had separated them once more. Still she struggled to reach out to him. Why was he not reaching out to her? He could not believe her dead! No matter what Brys of Cai had plotted and planned! No matter what Eadwine Aethelhard had said. Madoc could not believe her dead!

Could he? And as if in answer to her question, Wynne felt her child moving within her for the first time. No, little one, she thought, her graceful hands protectively cupping her belly. Your father does not believe us dead. He will find us one day. *He will!*

≋Chapter 12

When Ealdraed woke her the following morning, it was, to Wynne's embarrassment, well past sunrise. "The lord wanted you to be well-rested," the old woman assured her. "I was told to leave you until now." She helped Wynne to wash and dress, giving her a dark green tunic dress to wear over her lavender under tunic. "The lord said you were to have it. It belonged to his late wife," Ealdraed said, and then took her downstairs into the hall.

There was no one at the high board when Wynne calmly seated herself to the left of the thegn's place.

"Yer a bold wench for a slave," Ealdraed noted.

"I am not a slave," Wynne said firmly, "though I have been stolen from my home and forced into this servitude. I will not behave as a slave."

Ealdraed cackled and hurried off, to return shortly with a trencher of freshly baked bread filled with a steaming barley cereal and a goblet of brown ale. "Eat," she said. "The lord has told me I am to show you Aelfdene and then set you to light tasks."

Light tasks? Wynne almost giggled, but she did not wish to hurt Ealdraed's feelings. Instead she ate her meal, thinking as she did that the cereal lacked flavor and the bread was tough. The ale, however, was excellent. When she had finished, she followed Ealdraed from the hall and out into the courtyard of Aelfdene.

"The lord has eighteen hides of land," the old lady told Wynne. "He is a very wealthy man."

"My husband has a castle and ten times as much land," Wynne replied, but Ealdraed looked disbelieving.

"Look back at the house, lass. Is it not a fine one? And stone too, not timber like so many of our neighbors'," Ealdraed bragged. "Did you see the posts supporting the roof, and the roof beams in the hall? Painted with designs, they are! And

278

three fire pits as well! 'Tis as snug and safe a house as any could want." She grinned a toothless grin at Wynne. "And see the walls about the manor house? And the iron-bound oaken doors and gates? There's none that could overcome us if they tried." Ealdraed was very proud of Aelfdene.

" 'Tis a fine house," Wynne agreed. "It is much like my girlhood home at Gwernach."

"The lord has a church," Ealdraed informed Wynne. "And a kitchen/bakehouse; and a bell tower to warn the countryside in case of danger!"

A church! "Is there a priest here for the church?" Wynne asked.

"Nay," came the disconcerting reply. "We had one once, but he died of a spring flux of the bowels some years back. There has been none since, and just as well, say I," Ealdraed muttered. "The old ways are strong here, for all the priests' teachings. Even Harold Godwinson keeps a Danish wife. Her children are honored among all, though the king disapproves. He is too saintly a man, King Edward."

"I would not know," replied Wynne. "My king is Gruffydd ap Llywelyn. My father was kin to Gruffydd."

"There are the halls the lord had built for his sons," Ealdraed said, ignoring Wynne's remark. "They are timber."

"You do not approve of Eadwine Aethelhard's sons, do you?" Wynne gently queried.

"No, I do not, though I be but a serf and should have no opinions," replied Ealdraed. "Baldhere, the younger, is not a bad sort, though his wife is overproud. Caddaric, however, now there is a wicked 'un." She lowered her voice. "I do not think he will ever get a child on any woman, and just as well!"

"I was told Eadwine Aethelhard had several wives before he fathered his sons," Wynne answered her.

"The lord was betrothed in the cradle and widowed at the age of five," Ealdraed told Wynne. "He was betrothed and widowed again before he was nine. 'Twas then the old master decided to wait until he was more of an age to consummate a marriage. The lord was a father first at seventeen and again at eighteen. After that the lady Mildraed miscarried five other children. Poor lady. She was a good soul. The lord, however, had no trouble getting his two sons on her. It is not so with his son, Caddaric. Now, the poor lady Eadgyth is too frail, as any

can see, to bear children, but look you there, Wynne. There are
Caddaric's four women now. The tallest one is Berangari. The
plump one is Dagian. Aelf is the wench with the long blond
braids, and Haesel is the youngest. None is weak or fragile, yet
he cannot get children on any of them. Men are wont to blame
a woman for their lack of son, but think you those four strong-
backed girls incapable of mothering children?"

"Nay," Wynne replied. "They seem fit enough, and you are
right that it seems odd none can conceive."

Caddaric's four women, walking together, now came deliberately abreast of Wynne and Ealdraed. The one called
Berangari spoke boldly.

"So, Ealdraed, this is the slave woman that our lord
Caddaric would have. A wild Welsh girl," she sneered. "And
fertile as a cow too, I see. You are fortunate, wench, that the
lord took you for himself, else I should have scratched your
eyes out myself."

"Have you tried a lotion of arum and bryony for the spots
on your face, Berangari," Wynne said sweetly. "If you have
none, I shall make it for you. You will not hold Caddaric
Aethelmaere's favor with a face as pocked as a worm-eaten apple."

Berangari gasped and her face grew red with her fury. The
women accompanying her drew back nervously. "H-H-How
dare you speak to me in such a fashion!" the Saxon woman
shrieked. "You are a slave! *A slave!* You have no right to
speak to me at all unless I give you my permission! I will go
to the lord! I will see that you are beaten!"

Unafraid, Wynne stepped forward so that she was directly in
front of Berangari. "You may believe what you like, Berangari,
and you may call me whatever you desire. You cannot, however, change the fact that I am not a slave, nor a slave born,
nor will I behave in a servile manner. I am Wynne of
Gwernach, wife to Madoc, prince of Powys. My blood and
that of my child is far better than any here! I will give my respect to Eadwine Aethelhard, for he is the lord of Aelfdene, and
a good lord too, I can see. I will give my friendship to
those who would have it, but I will not be anyone's slave. If
you ever address me again, do it with courtesy, or do it not at
all." Then Wynne turned her back on the four women and said

to Ealdraed, "What are these light tasks that my lord would have me perform?"

"Wait!" It was Berangari. "Can you really make me a lotion that would remove the spots from my face?"

Wynne turned back to her. "If I could gain admission to the pharmacea here, aye, I could."

"There is no pharmacea at Aelfdene," Berangari said.

"There should be," Wynne replied. "I will speak to Eadwine Aethelhard. Who makes your medicines and salves?"

"There is no one," Berangari replied. "There was an old woman once, but she died."

"Was not the lady Mildraed skilled in these things?"

"The lady Mildraed spent most of her time weaving and resting," Berangari said. "She was frail in her later years."

"And if someone is injured?" Wynne probed.

"Someone binds up their wounds and we hope for the best," Berangari answered.

"This will not do," Wynne told them. "Ealdraed, where is Eadwine Aethelhard? I must speak to him immediately! Light tasks can be accomplished by any hands, but I am a healer, and if there is none here at Aelfdene to heal, then that must be my task."

"The lord is in the fields. It is the day set aside for the gleaners," Ealdraed said.

"Take me to my lord," Wynne said firmly. "There is no time to waste."

Chortling to herself, Ealdraed led Wynne through the open gates of Aelfdene and down the road to the fields. There they found Eadwine Aethelhard, who sat upon his horse watching benevolently as the women and children belonging to his estate carefully gleaned through the mown stalks of previously harvested grain for the remaining kernels of oats, rye, and barley that could be salvaged. Whatever they found was theirs to keep and add to the winter allotment made them by their master. Successful gleaning could mean the difference between a comfortable winter or a lean, hard one.

As they approached him, Wynne studied Eadwine Aethelhard, for she scarce had time the previous night. He was very tall. At least as tall and as big as Einion. He sat his horse easily. The handsome face had a relaxed and pleasant look to it. There were laugh lines about his eyes and mouth. It was a

sensuous mouth, big, to match the rest of his body. She remembered the possessive kisses that mouth had pressed upon
her the previous night and felt suddenly warm. She forced herself to concentrate solely upon his physical traits. His nose had
an almost regal air to it, long and perfectly straight. Her eyes
strayed to the hands resting upon his reins. Although large and
in keeping with his frame, they were slender hands with long,
graceful fingers.

"Good morrow, my lord Eadwine," Wynne greeted him politely as she came to stand by his right stirrup.

The grey-blue eyes were instantly alert, and he looked down
at her, smiling. "Good morrow, my wild Welsh girl. Did you
sleep well?"

"I did, and I thank you for the rest, my lord, but it has come
to my attention that you don't have a healer at Aelfdene. Is this
so?" Wynne asked him.

"It is so. Why do you ask? Are you ill?" He was instantly
all concern for her.

Wynne shook her head. "I am in excellent health, my lord
Eadwine. I ask because I am a healer. While I remain at
Aelfdene I would be the manor's healer. Berangari tells me
you have no pharmacea, or medicine salves or ointment stored.
If a serious sickness were to strike Aelfdene, you would be at
a great loss."

Before he might reply, a shriek rent the air and a serf
woman set up a great hue and cry. The thegn turned his horse
into the fields, and Wynne hurried behind him to see what the
difficulty was. A sobbing woman knelt upon the ground in
midfield, clutching a small girl to her bosom.

"What has happened?" demanded Eadwine Aethelhard.

"My child, lord!" the woman wept. "My child has been injured. I cannot stop the bleeding!"

Wynne reached the little cluster of women and children and
pushed her way through to kneel by the frightened mother. "I
am a healer," she said quietly, her musical voice authoritative
and comforting. "Let me see the child's hand."

Fearfully the mother released her hold on her daughter's
hand and blood gushed forth, causing her to shriek once more.

"Be silent!" Wynne commanded her fiercely as she reached
beneath her skirts and tore a strip from her chemise. "You are
but frightening your daughter." She began to carefully and

tightly wrap the little girl's hand to stem the flow of the bleeding. "Will you take her to the hall, my lord?" she asked Eadwine Aethelhard. "I must prepare a medicinal paste for this wound." She turned to the mother. "Give your child to the lord, woman, and then follow along."

The thegn took the little girl from her weeping mother and turned his horse toward the manor house. Behind him Wynne and the other women followed.

"Ealdraed, I will need onions, salt, vinegar, rue, and honey, as well as a mortar and pestle," Wynne told the old woman. "Can you find these things for me? And clean cloth cut into strips, and a basin, and a kettle of boiling water as well."

Ealdraed nodded, all business, and said, "Aye, lady! At once." Then she began to run ahead of them on surprisingly agile legs for one of her advanced years.

When they had reached the manor house and entered into the hall, Ealdraed had already marshaled the house serfs into action. They scurried to and fro seeking the items she had asked them to obtain.

"Place the child on the bench by the fire pit," Wynne told Eadwine Aethelhard as he set the child gently down, standing back to watch her. "Comfort your daughter, woman," she told the serf mother. "You will make my job easier for me if you do."

"Will she die?" quavered the frightened woman.

"No, we have stopped the bleeding," Wynne told her quietly. "The salve I make will prevent infection and bad humors from setting into the wound." Wynne moved over to the high board, where Ealdraed was setting out all the ingredients necessary. "Peel the onions," she told a young house serf, "and then cut them fine." She quickly assembled the rest of what she would need.

The hall was quiet as, wide-eyed, the serfs watched Wynne pound the onions into a thick paste, which she then mixed with course, ground salt and a splash of vinegar. "Get me another mortar," she commanded. It was quickly brought to her. Wynne took the leaves of the summer rue plant and ground them into a fine powder. Next she added honey and carefully blended the mixture. When she was satisfied that the rue and the honey were well-mixed, Wynne added it to the onions, salt, and vinegar, combining all the elements of her salve neatly.

Satisfied, she asked that the child be brought up to the high board.

Gently she unwrapped her improvised bandage from the little hand, saying as she did so, "I am going to wash your hand, child, and then flush away all the evil humors with a bit of wine. 'Twill sting, but you will be brave, I know." Then Wynne smiled at the small girl and, as carefully as she could, cleansed her injured hand, cooing sympathetically when the little one winced. When the hand was cleaned to her satisfaction, Wynne said, "You were very brave, my dearie. Now I will put my good healing salve on your wound and handage you with a clean cloth." She worked quickly as she spoke. "Come to me tomorrow morning, and I will check to see how your injury is faring. There," she noted, finishing the bandaging. "You are done. Go back to your mother and tell her that I am well pleased with you."

The little girl ran quickly back to her parent, and the mother approached Wynne as she stepped down from the high board, falling to her knees. "Lady," she said. "I thank you for healing my daughter. May God bless you!" Then scrambling to her feet, she departed the hall with her child, the other serfs following behind her.

"Ealdraed, find me a stone jar and store the rest of that salve. I will need it tomorrow," Wynne told the servant.

"Aye, lady!" came the reply.

"You are indeed a healer," Eadwine Aethelhard said quietly, "and you know how to keep a cool head in a crisis. I think old Ruari Ban has done me a greater favor than he knew. You may have whatever you need to make your medicines, Wynne. There is a small room off the hall that has been used for storage. Ealdraed knows the place. You may have that as your pharmacea, and whatever you want to stock it."

"Thank you, my lord," she answered him coolly.

He turned about and went out again into the fields.

Wynne spent the remainder of the day cleaning out the little room that the thegn had given her for her pharmacea. The house serfs brought her a wooden table and a bench to furnish the room. Wynne, old Ealdraed by her side, sought out jars, bowls, and pitchers for the pharmacea.

"Where did you get the rue?" Wynne asked her companion.

"From the cook," came the reply.

They hurried to the cook house, where Wynne found that the child whose hand she had tended that morning was the cook's granddaughter, and the apple of his eye.

"I've herbs and spices aplenty, lady. Take what you need. I am grateful to have a healer at Aelfdene," he said.

Ealdraed shook her head in wonderment. "That old Heall is usually a bad-tempered creature. I held little hope of your getting what you needed easily."

"I will need far more than these few things," Wynne told her. "We will go out tomorrow, and I will see what I can gather myself. Though it is November, the weather is still fair, and the plants I need have not yet died back."

The dinner hour approached and Ealdraed said, "Come, lady. You must return to the Great Chamber to repair yourself," and when they had entered the room, she brought a basin of water that Wynne might wash her face and hands. Then she began to undo Wynne's thick, heavy braid.

"I have no brush or comb," Wynne said.

"The lord said you were to use those which belonged to lady Mildraed," was the reply, and Ealdraed began to brush out Wynne's long black hair, saying as she did so, "The lord has also had fabric brought from the storeroom, that you may choose several for your gowns. I will help you with the sewing." Then her gnarled old fingers began to rebraid Wynne's hair, cleverly weaving a bit of colored wool into the plait as she worked. When she had finished, she said, "We will return to the hall now. The dinner hour is upon us."

When they reached the hall again, Wynne saw that Eadwine Aethelhard and his family were already seated at the high board. She stood silently at the opposite end of the hall waiting, and finally the thegn, an amused look in his eyes, called to her. "Come, Wynne, and sit by me. Baldhere, give up your place and move down that Wynne may sit next to me."

"You would seat a slave at our table, Father? Have you gone mad?" demanded Caddaric angrily of his parent, his eyes all the while undressing Wynne as she came toward them.

"It is *my* table, my son," Eadwine Aethelhard said quietly, "and, aye, I would seat Wynne by my side. She has found favor in my eyes."

"By spreading her legs for you?" Caddaric replied insultingly. "Any whore would do that for you, Father."

Before the thegn might answer his son, Wynne said sweetly, "If I had spread my legs for you, Caddaric Aethelmaere, would that have made it all quite different? In future you will speak to me with respect. I have done nothing to merit your disrespect. You will also speak to your father with respect, for he is the lord of Aelfdene, and a good lord." With a swish of her skirts she seated herself at the high board.

"What is happening here?" Caddaric's voice was tight with his inability to wield any authority. "This woman has been here but a day, and you not only seat her at our table, I have heard that you have given her a place of her own. This Welsh witch has ensorceled you, Father!"

The thegn's booming laughter rang out, filling the hall with his merriment. "Caddaric, Caddaric! Your fears are groundless. As I have previously said, I bought Wynne because for the first time in many years I was stirred by a woman's beauty and I felt desire. If that is bewitchment, then surely all men have succumbed to such bewitchment at one time or another. As for the *place* your gossips have told you that I gave her, it is the small storeroom at the end of the hall. Wynne is a healer, and this afternoon I saw evidence of her skill when she tended to an injured serf child. We have not had a healer at Aelfdene in many years. I am grateful for her skill, which will be of value to the manor. A healer needs a place in which to have a pharmacea. Even you, my son, must understand that Wynne's skills may prove useless unless she can prepare and store her medicines, ointments, and lotions."

"I still think you set this slave above her station," grumbled Caddaric.

"And I think, my son, that you presume too much in *my* hall," his father replied with a warning tone. "Wynne is here because I wish her here. If you cannot treat her with respect, Caddaric, then you will no longer be welcome at my board."

For a time there was an uncomfortable silence. Aeldra Swanneck had a slightly disapproving twitch about her mouth, but she remained silent. Although she hoped that Aelfdene would one day belong to her infant son, Boc, she and Baldhere would eventually inherit her father's manor and leave here. For now this business with the new slave woman did not concern her. Eadgyth Crookback's eyes remained upon her plate, although she but picked at her food. Caddaric had been virtually unapproachable since yesterday when he had first seen the Welsh woman. He had been positively vicious with his four women last night in his frustration over losing the new slave to his father. Eadgyth had never seen him so filled with lust, and the knowledge that the object of his lust was now in his father's bed proved almost too much for him.

Eadgyth Crookback knew her husband well. He was a good warrior but a weak man. When they had wed, she knew that he took her only for her dowry of two and a half hides of land. Her father, no fool, had known his daughter's attraction was in her possessions. He had, in an effort to protect her further, promised that when he died, Eadgyth would inherit an additional two and a half hides of land. This bequest could only be effected if Eadgyth still lived. If she had predeceased him, then everything would go to his eldest son. With an additional two and a half hides of land, Caddaric Aethelmaere could attain the status of thegn in his own right. She knew how desperately he desired to be his own man. As her father was elderly, there was hope that Caddaric would attain his heart's desire sooner than he would inherit from his own father, who was in excellent health.

Eadgyth Crookback was by nature a sweet woman, but like her father, she was no fool. She had made her husband feel so comfortable with her that he had, to his own surprise, become her friend, and friends they remained even after ten years of marriage. Knowing her own physical weaknesses, she had encouraged him to take other women, even helping him to choose them, that her household not be unduly upset. As Caddaric gave her his respect and affection, so did his four lesser women, for it was impossible not to like Eadgyth Crookback. The Welsh girl, Wynne, had changed everything, however. She had never seen Caddaric so driven, and as she feared for him, so she feared for them all.

When the meal was finished, the women gathered about one of the fire pits gossiping, and Aeldra said to Wynne, "My daughter Willa has a cough. Can you give me something for her? If I cannot stop it, she will pass it on to her sisters, Beadu and Goda, and then the baby will get it. He is only six months old." She tried to keep the fear from her voice.

"Are there any cherry trees in the vicinity?" Wynne asked.

"Aye," replied Aeldra Swanneck. "Ealdraed can show you."

"Then I will be able to prepare something for your children, but it will take several days until it is at full strength and will do any good," Wynne told her. "Try and keep your daughter Willa from the others."

Aeldra nodded. "I will," she said.

"What about the lotion for my skin?" Berangari demanded.

"First I must set up my pharmacea," Wynne told her, "and gather all the ingredients that I will need. I have not half enough yet. Be patient," and she smiled at Berangari. "I will not forget you."

A pretty young girl with flaxen braids asked shyly, "Can you give me something so that my bowels will flow again? Between the child I carry and that, I am bloated and most uncomfortable."

Wynne looked at the girl. "What is your name?" she said.

"I am Denu, Baldhere Armstrong's lesser woman," came the reply.

"When is your child due?"

"In May, I believe," Denu answered.

"I can give you something," Wynne told her, thinking that Denu was already overlarge for a girl only a few months gone with child. Still, Denu looked healthy.

"I think it is a fortunate thing that you have come among us, Wynne," Eadgyth Crookback said quietly. "Not anyone can be a healer, I know. It is a rare and special talent."

"My mother and my grandmother taught me," Wynne told them. "My husband, Madoc, is a healer, *and*," she added wickedly, "a sorcerer of some renown. If I can find one amongst you who shows an ability toward the healing arts, I will teach her, that you are not without a healer when I leave."

The women about her looked distinctly uncomfortable at her words. The Welsh woman was a slave, and yet she neither behaved nor spoke like a slave. It was not unusual for captives who had been born free to become slaves. They had never heard of a slave, freeborn or otherwise, who would not accept his lot in life. The women of Aelfdene were so sheltered that it did not occur to them that such a fate could easily be theirs. They were basically simple women whose lives revolved entirely about their men and their home life. Having said what they wanted to say to Wynne, the wives and lesser women drifted nervously away into another part of the hall, leaving Wynne alone.

"You frighten them," Baldhere Armstrang said as he moved to her side. "You frighten them, and you intrigue both my father and my elder brother."

"And you?" Wynne replied. "I know I neither intrigue nor frighten you."

He smiled, and she thought he looked rather more like his father than did Caddaric. "Nay, I am neither intrigued nor frightened. I am fascinated. There is magic about you, lady. Who are you really?"

"There is no magic to me, Baldhere Armstrang, for if there was, I should not be here at this moment. I should be home at Raven's Rock with my husband."

"What is Raven's Rock?" he asked her. "Is it a manor like Aelfdene?"

"Raven's Rock is a castle. It sits upon the spine of a dark mountain between two valleys. It is the ancestral home of the princes of Powys-Wenwynwyn, who currently owe their fealty to Gruffydd ap Llywelyn, our king, who was my father's cousin," Wynne told him quietly. "Those princes of Powys are famed for their magic."

"If your husband is a man of magic, lady, then why has he not found you before now?" Baldhere Armstrang asked her most disconcertingly.

Before she might consider the answer to that question, Aeldra Swanneck was by her husband's side.

"I would return to our hall," she said sharply. "It is late, and I am tired." She did not deign to acknowledge Wynne now. The woman was a slave, whatever her manner, and besides, she did not need her at this moment. The elixir had been promised and that was enough.

"Good night, Baldhere Armstrang," Wynne told him, responding in kind, for she would not allow Aeldra Swanneck the upper hand. The woman had all the indications of being a bully, and Wynne did not intend to allow herself to be bullied by any of them. Turning away from the couple, she moved up the staircase to the privacy of the Great Chamber. There she found old Ealdraed awaiting her. "I want a bath," Wynne said.

"Are you mad?" Ealdraed replied. " 'Tis November, and it is night as well!"

"I am not used to being unwashed for so long a period of time," Wynne told her. "It is my custom to bathe almost every day. Since my abduction, I have only had one bath, in an icy stream."

"Foolishness! Foolishness!" grumbled Ealdraed.

"Have you a tub that could be brought up to this chamber?" Wynne persisted. "And I will need some hot water as well."

Ealdraed's brown eyes rolled in her head but, though she muttered balefully beneath her breath, she disappeared back down the staircase from the Great Chamber into the hall. Smiling to herself, Wynne began to look through the bolts of fabric that had been brought from Eadwine Aethelhard's storeroom that she might select some materials for her gowns. There were linens and silks and wools and brocatelles; all of good quality and in many colors. Eadwine Aethelhard obviously did not stint himself or his family.

Three additional gowns would be enough, she decided, to take her through the winter and into the spring, when her child would be born. Under tunics of yellow, red-orange, and deep green. Tunic dresses of indigo-blue, green-blue, and purple. All the under tunics and tunic dresses would be interchangeable with each other and with the gown she was now wearing. The under tunics would be silk; the purple and indigo-blue tunic dresses a soft, light wool; the green-blue tunic dress would be of an elegant brocatelle, upon which she would embroider gold thread and beads. Wynne also appropriated a small bolt of soft, natural-colored linen with which she could make her chemises and gowns for her newborn child.

Ealdraed returned grumbling, followed by several young boys, two of whom struggled beneath the bulky weight of a large oak tub; they were trailed by several others, each carrying steaming buckets of water.

"Well?" Ealdraed demanded irritably. "Where do you want it?"

"I think," Wynne said thoughtfully, "that we should set it down where it is to remain. There," she pointed, "in that corner."

"It's to remain?" Ealdraed sounded scandalized.

"Of course," Wynne replied calmly. "Why should the boys have to drag that awkward thing up the stairs each day when there is more than enough room here for it? Now only the water need be brought and afterward removed."

"Put it there!" Ealdraed snapped at the grinning lads. "Then dump yer buckets and get you gone!"

Wynne smiled sweetly at the old lady and said, "I have chosen the materials from which to make my gowns. We can begin tomorrow after I have returned from searching for herbs for my pharmacea. Have you brought me some soap?"

"Aye, I've brought you soap," Ealdraed said, and shooed the remaining boys down the stairs. "Noisy scamps," she groused.

Wynne swiftly removed her clothing and pinned up her braid, saying as she did, "This chemise is torn, for I took a strip from it to bandage the child's hand. I will use the material to make clothing for my son." She stepped into the tub and quickly seated herself. "Ahhhh!" she sighed gustily. "How good that warm water feels! Give me the soap and leave the toweling. I am capable of bathing myself."

"Then I'll find my own bed," Ealdraed said with a small smile at Wynne. "Bathing at night, and in November too!" She hurried off down the stairs.

As she departed, Wynne heard Eadwine Aethelhard's step upon the staircase, and he entered the Great Chamber. "Ealdraed told me you wanted a bath. I will join you." He began to remove his clothing. "She professes to be very shocked by the knowledge that you bathe almost each day."

"Do not the Saxons bathe regularly, my lord?" Wynne asked him. She was not certain that she should not be embarrassed, but the fact that on the briefest of acquaintance he had taken her the previous night seemed to abrogate any modesty on her part. She was a married woman. She knew what a man looked like.

"I suppose it depends on the Saxon," he answered her. "Some bathe with regularity, and others do not."

"Do you?" She raised her eyes to his.

"Aye," he said, and stepped into the tub, seating himself opposite her. "I find the strong scent of an unwashed body most repellent." His gaze, calmly meeting hers, was filled with amusement.

"Is there something that you find humorous, my lord?" she said tartly.

"Aye," he said, and a chuckle escaped him.

"What?" she demanded.

"You are a very bad slave," he told her. "In fact you are a terrible slave," he said, and another chuckle eluded him.

"I am not a slave!" she cried, her anger spilling over.

"You may not have been born a slave, Wynne, but at this moment you are legally a slave. *My slave.* And yet you behave more like a wife than a slave. You have taken my household in a firm grip, and the servants call you 'lady' I have noted. Even my younger son and the other women are respectful of you as they would be a wife."

"That, my lord Eadwine, is because I am a wife. I am Madoc of Powys's wife, and I am in your house against my will. Say what you want, and do what you want, you cannot change that, for it is the truth. I will never submit willingly to you. While I am in your house, however, you shall have my respect, for you are, as I told your elder son this evening, a good lord."

He ignored her emotional outburst and said in a matter-of-fact tone, "Wash me, sweeting. The water grows cold, and we will both catch a chill shortly." He turned himself about so that his back was to her.

Men, Wynne thought irritably. They would only accept what they wanted to accept, but it mattered not. *She was not a slave!* His or anyone else's! Still, she could not help but wonder as she washed him why Madoc had not found her yet. She had not forgotten Baldhere Armstrang's remark in the hall earlier this evening. That Madoc and his ancestors were men of magic and sorcery she had never doubted. Why then had he not come to her? Why was she caught in this benevolent cage, imprisoned by a man to whom she was, to her own surprise, finding herself increasingly attracted even upon their short acquaintance?

"Gently, sweeting," he cautioned her. "You are rubbing the skin from my shoulders."

Madness! It was all madness, Wynne reflected angrily to herself. How could this have happened to her? She had been happy and content as Madoc's wife. To suddenly find herself the slave of this charming man was ... was ... was infuriating! Why? *Why?* She splashed water over the soapy areas of Eadwine Aethelhard's shoulders and back. There was no point in her anger. She had brought this upon herself by refusing to accept Madoc's judgment in the matter of Brys of Cai; and she was certainly suffering for her insistence that she could reunite Madoc's family.

Suddenly the thegn turned himself about in the tub and took the cloth from her. "I will remember in future never to allow an angry woman possession of my person," he said humorously, his grey-blue eyes twinkling. "Why are you angry, and at whom are you angry, Wynne?"

"I am angry at myself," she replied, "for not believing Madoc when he told me that his brother was a totally evil man. If I had listened to my husband, I should not be here with you now. I should be safe at Raven's Rock." Then, unbidden, the tears began to slip down her cheeks.

Eadwine Aethelhard swallowed hard, when in truth he wanted to laugh. It had suddenly occurred to him how humorous their situation was, and then he sobered, for it was tragic too. Naked in a bath with a man other than her husband, Wynne wept for her past when the reality was her present and her future. He was that reality, and it astounded him that this girl should have such a grip on his heart. What did he really know of her? "You are tired," he told her, "and breeding women are given to fits of unexpected and irrational weeping. So it was with my Mildraed."

"I am not your Mildraed," she sniffled.

"Nay," he said, "you most certainly are not. You are my wild Welsh girl. I think, Wynne, if you will release your hold on the past, you will find your future a pleasant and happy one."

She pulled away from him and, standing up, stepped from their tub to towel herself dry. Eadwine caught his breath as his eyes beheld the lush beauty of her. Last night in their bed he had not been able to really see her, but now he could scarce take his eyes from her. His inspection of her in the hall had been to ascertain her general health, to be certain if he purchased her she would not die. He had seen she was lovely, but not how lovely. Never in all his life had he beheld a woman so fair. Her limbs were graceful. Her tall, slender body only beginning to ripen with the child she carried. He felt himself growing hot with his desire for her as, raising her arms, she undid her braid from atop her head where it had been pinned. Her breasts rose and thrust forward with the movement. He stepped from the tub and his aroused state was instantly apparent. Their eyes met, and Wynne turned quickly away from him, a flush upon her cheeks.

"I am cold," she said, and walking across the room, slipped beneath the coverlet of the sleeping space.

I will win her over, Eadwine Aethelhard thought to himself. I must win her over, for I am falling in love with her, and I cannot bear the thought that she might hate me. Slowly he dried himself, and then he joined her in their bed, slipping his arms about her and kissing the back of her neck softly. She lay perfectly still against him, and he was suddenly angry. "I want you," he growled at her.

"As you wish, my lord," she answered listlessly. "I am your slave, and you have the right."

"Aye!" he said furiously. "I am your master, and I have the right. I could have you killed if I so desired, Wynne!"

"Then do so," she cried, "for perhaps death is preferable to this bondage!"

His fury crumbled in the face of her pain. "Nay, sweeting, I want no harm to come to you or the child." He turned her about so that she was forced to face him. "Look at me, Wynne," he said gently. "You must accept what cannot be changed. If you do not, you will destroy yourself and perhaps the child as well."

"But life can change, my lord," she insisted. "A month ago I was the cherished wife of a prince of Powys; yet this night I lay in another man's bed, his slave. Who is to say that that cannot eventually change?"

Her eyes were green, he thought. He hadn't realized it until this moment, but her eyes were green. And her mouth was incredibly kissable; ripe and moist, the lips slightly parted in her fervor. His lips gently touched hers, and he murmured against them, "Aye, anything can change, sweeting, but for now can you not be content with me?" He could feel the blood roaring in his ears; the insistent throb of his manhood.

Wynne saw the desire in his eyes, and a mixture of sadness and despair overcame her. The child stirred within her, and she knew that for the baby's sake she must survive. Still, she could be no less than honest with him. "I do not know, Eadwine Aethelhard," she said, "if I shall ever be content without Madoc of Powys," and then she smiled slightly at him, "but I will try." It was the best she could do, she thought, and the words, spoken reluctantly, were half believed by them both. Wynne rolled onto her belly and carefully drew her legs up. "If you do not soon satisfy that lust of yours, my lord, you will do yourself an injury, I fear," she said.

He moved behind her and gently inserted his length within her woman's passage. "Some day you will welcome me," he said quietly.

Never, she thought, but she said nothing as he began to move upon her. His gentle, but firm attentions offered her a measure of satisfaction despite her resolve to remain unmoved. When he finally lay sleeping by her side, Wynne reached out as she had each night since her abduction and called Madoc. There had always been such a strong link between them, and yet now she felt that link blocked somehow. Still, she could not give up, nor would she ever stop trying.

Her plans for escape were never far from her mind. It had taken almost three weeks to travel the distance between Brys of Cai's castle and Aelfdene manor. Although she had ridden behind Ruari Ban, the pace had been a slow one because of the party of slaves the Irish slaver possessed. Therefore, Wynne concluded, she had to assume that it would take just as long if not longer for her to return to Raven's Rock. She wasn't even certain of the direction in which she should travel, but she would eventually gain that needed information.

She had to go soon. Before the snows came; while she was still able to travel. She would steal a horse! She could still ride, and if she dare not gallop her mount, at least she would walk it. A few days' time was all she needed. A few days in which to gather the knowledge she would need to make her escape successful. She had to be successful, for instinct told her there would be no second chance. The thought that she could soon be gone from Aelfdene comforted her, and Wynne finally slept.

In the morning the skies were grey and lowering. The day, however, was yet warm, and, encouraged, Wynne took a basket, setting forth with old Ealdraed to find what plants she could use for her pharmacea. They first visited the orchards, where Wynne removed some bark from the cherry trees, being careful not to injure the trees. They moved on out into the countryside, where they were delighted to find some bog myrtle. The bark could be used for dye; the leaves for flavoring ale; and the catkins when boiled yielded a fragrant wax that made particularly sweet-smelling candles.

Because there had not yet been a frost, there was much to be had from the fields and nearby marsh. There was wonderfully aromatic sweet flag, its yellow-green sword-shaped leaves rising from its root stock, which could be used in perfumes, for flavoring, and medicinally. Wynne found capers growing amid the stone ruins of some earlier structure, and an excellent supply of both acorns and chestnuts that had not yet been devoured by animals, nor were they riddled with worms. The acorns had a variety of uses. Pounded, they could be made into a paste by the simple addition of lamb fat. The paste was then used to cure inflammations. Finely ground, the acorns could be used in a vaginal pessary; and acorn tea was used to stop dysentery. Honey, however, was a necessary addition to the tea, for acorns were known to cause headaches. Chestnuts boiled in water and then eaten were an excellent stimulus for passion in a reluctant lover.

Much to Wynne's surprise, she found a goodly supply of pinecones that had escaped the birds. They stopped to hull the pinecones where they found them, for tiny worms were known to live beneath the scales. It was useless to take home such cones only to have to throw them out. The seeds in the cones were good for bladder and kidney difficulties, and no pharmacea should be without them.

As they walked on they found Betony and Hoarhound, and both field and marsh mint as well as pudding grass, which was excellent for repelling fleas. Wynne stopped suddenly and knelt down. Then she began to dig out several plants that were still quite actively growing. The plants were large, almost three feet in height, and the leaves quite hairy.

"What's that ugly thing?" demanded Ealdraed.

"Cheese rennet," Wynne told her, "though some call it lady's bedstraw. Although there are no flowers right now, the plant itself helps the sheep and goat's milk to thicken. I can get a yellow dye to color the cheese from the stem and the leaves, and a red dye which adheres particularly well to wool from the roots."

"I never heard of such a thing," Ealdraed told her bluntly.

"My family has been famous for their cheeses for many, many generations," Wynne said. "Our cheese is called

Gwernach's Gold, and the traders from Cornwall, Devon, and Ireland come to Gwernach regularly to get it."

They came upon a patch of chamomile and another of wormwood which had not yet died back. The latter was good for worming, and the former made a tea which was a cure for sleeplessness.

"Here's some elecampane for you," Ealdraed called, and dug it out. Dried and powdered, the elecampane root was mixed with honey and vinegar to make a tonic.

As they skirted about the other side of the little marsh where they had found the bog myrtle and the marsh mint, Wynne spotted some late-blooming wake-robin and hurried to gather it up. "If only I could find some bryony," she muttered to herself.

"There's some on the path back toward the manor house," her companion replied.

"I thought you knew little of herbs," Wynne teased her.

"I know bryony," Ealdraed said. "What is it for?"

"I'm going to make Berangari a skin lotion with the root of the bryony, this wake-robin, and some goat's milk. Lemon too, if I can get some."

" 'Tis a waste of time if you ask me," Ealdraed said. "Her face could be as smooth as a baby's bottom and Caddaric still wouldn't be able to get a child on her or any of the others. I've heard that he renders his women sore with his striving, for all the good it's done him."

"Perhaps Berangari wants smooth skin to please herself," Wynne suggested.

The day had suddenly grown cold, and the wind that had been gently blowing from the east was coming in stronger gusts now from the northeast. The grey clouds were darker, and Ealdraed announced, "There's snow coming. 'Tis been too warm for too long, and when it's like this in this valley, and the weather turns quickly, then it means snow."

"Please, God, no!" Wynne whispered.

"Put it out of your mind, dearie," the old woman said gently.

"What?" Wynne replied defiantly.

"Escape," Ealdraed said. "Be sensible, my lady Wynne. You are many days from your Raven's Rock, and you are with child. The winter is almost upon us. If you try and flee Aelfdene, you will be caught. If you are not caught, what chance has a woman alone of traveling all those miles? If you will not think of yourself, think of your child."

"I am thinking of my child," Wynne told her. "My son is a prince of Powys, conceived legitimately and lawfully, condemned to be born into slavery! How can I let this happen while there is breath in my body, Ealdraed? How can I allow my son never to know his heritage or his father, who mourns his loss? I cannot! Your master is a good man, and I am fortunate to be safe in his care; but I can already see that he cares more for me than he should. Despite his knowledge of my past, he takes me into his bed each night and forces himself upon me. He is a lonely man, and he would have a woman to love and be loved in return. I cannot love Eadwine Aethelhard, for I love Madoc of Powys, and I always will!"

"My lady Wynne," Ealdraed said patiently, "you must accept the fate that the good God has visited upon you. We are women, and what other choice do we have? I am a serf. You are a slave. It is God's will."

"And yet you address me as any of my own servants would, my good Ealdraed," Wynne told her. "There are other slaves in Eadwine Aethelhard's house, but you do not address them so. You do not think of me as a slave, any more than I think of myself as a slave."

"It is beginning to rain," Ealdraed said evasively. "Let us hurry home, lady," and she began to walk doggedly ahead.

Wynne smiled behind the old lady's back and followed after her.

When they reached the manor house Wynne gave Ealdraed her basket and, taking another, went off to the kitchen garden to gather what she could of the household herbs. If snow was indeed coming, there would be a frost and the plants would be useless thereafter, until spring, when they grew anew. Ignoring the light rain, she gathered sage for the nerves; fennel to aid with fever; mint for stomach ailments; and rue. The garden contained lettuce, parsnips, beets, and spinach, all of which could be eaten, but all of which were also medicinal in use as well. Lettuce for sleeplessness, parsnips for quickening desire, spinach for coughs and chest ailments. There were onions and leeks, which had many uses. Cabbages, marrows, and cucumbers. Wynne was astounded that no one in Eadwine Aethelhard's house understood the many uses and advantages of even the kitchen garden. Kneeling, she clipped dill, parsley, and caraway, whose seeds were also of value. She found plantings of sweet basil, rosemary, and marjoram as well as some garden heliotrope and yarrow, which were growing wild by the garden wall.

Heall, the cook, came out from his kitchens and said in a friendly tone, "I've lemons, should you need them, lady, and a good supply of apples and a few figs stored away."

Wynne rose to her feet, picking her basket up as she did so. "I cannot find any lavender," she replied. "I cannot imagine a proper household that does not grow lavender. It cannot have died back yet."

"Look behind the manor house," Heall told her. "The lady Mildraed had a small garden of herbs and roses. You will find your lavender there, lady."

Wynne thanked him and hurried off. She found the lavender exactly where he had said she would. The little garden was badly overgrown and had certainly gone unattended since the lady Mildraed's death. Obviously no one cared. The little garden had been allowed to run wild. There was plenty of lavender to be harvested. When she had finished cutting the fragrant stems, Wynne realized that she was beginning to feel quite tired, and she was very hungry as well. Her child was moving about quite actively, as if in protest, so she returned indoors.

Ealdraed had food for her, knowing Wynne hadn't eaten since early morning and it was now afternoon. There was cheese, fresh bread, crisp apples, and sweet wine that had been watered to render it less potent.

"You do not take care of yourself," grumbled Ealdraed. "Why do you not take better care of yourself? You have that babe to think about now, my lady."

"If I took good care of myself," Wynne teased her, "what would there be for you to do?" She sliced off a chunk of cheese and a slice of bread and began to eat hungrily.

"Heh! Heh! Heh!" the old lady cackled, well-pleased to be so appreciated. "When you have eaten, lady, we will get to our sewing," she said.

It snowed that night, as Ealdraed had predicted. Large, wet flakes that were half melted before they even hit the ground, where they melted completely, for the earth was still warm. It was a reminder to Wynne, however, that she dare not linger too long. She could learn nothing from the serfs or the other slaves as to the direction, for they did not know, such things not being of particular interest to them. She knew the dark hills to the west separated England from Powys, but there were no roads directly over them. If only, she thought wryly, Madoc had taught her the secret to changing one's shape, she could have turned herself into a bird long since and flown back home to Raven's Rock. She spent as much time out of doors as she could, wandering the fields in search of useful plants, searching the skies for the sight of old Dhu, for the certain knowledge that he had found her and would come to rescue her.

Eadwine Aethelhard watched her restlessness, easily divining some of her thoughts; knowing that she but sought a means of escape; and realizing that he must make her hate him if he was to save her from herself and the dangerous path she would take. In time she would come to see that he was right, and then perhaps she would not hate him. When Wynne had been at Aelfdene three weeks, he called her to him as he sat alone in the hall one evening, his family at long last departed.

"I have a gift for you," he said quietly, and unwrapped a cloth that lay on the table before him.

"What is it?" she asked, curious, but distressed that he would give her a gift.

He lifted the object from the cloth, and Wynne visibly paled.

"No!" she said, her heart thudding at the sight of the pale gold circle.

"Put it on, Wynne," he said. "It has been made especially for you and you alone. A mark of my high regard."

"It is a slave collar," she managed to gasp. "I will not wear a slave collar!" She felt near to tears and struggled to maintain her composure.

He arose and stood over her, the collar in his hands. "Look at it," he said. "It is of the finest gold and decorated with green agates that match your wonderful eyes." His hand reached out and stroked her slender neck. "I would not allow such a lovely neck to be encircled by an iron or leather slave collar."

"It will chafe me," she whispered desperately. "Surely you would not mark my skin?"

"It will rest upon your neck bone easily, and if it indeed chafes you, sweeting, then I will have it lined in lamb's wool." He gently slipped the gold collar about her neck, closing it and locking it with a small key as she sat frozen in shock, unable to move or to resist him. His lips kissed the back of her neck and he said softly in her ear, "Now, Wynne, you cannot escape me. Did you think I did not know of your plans to flee? Oh, sweeting, how far do you think you would have gotten? And if you had escaped me, do you think you could have escaped the other predators, both two-legged and four-legged, awaiting you along your long road home?" He knelt by her side, his arm slipping about her thickening waist. "I'm in love with you, Wynne, and I have been since the moment I first laid eyes on you. I would not be cruel to you, but I must protect you from your own foolishness. With this slave collar about your grace-ful neck, you cannot escape me. You are marked as a slave for all to see."

"I will never forgive you this," she said stonily.

"In time you will," he said with certainty, "and that collar will not remain upon your neck forever, Wynne. The day you become my wife, I shall remove it from your neck even as I have put it there."

"I cannot marry you," she cried desperately, leaping to her feet. "Why can you not understand? I am Wynne of Gwernach, wife to Madoc, prince of Powys!"

"Nay," he said. "You are Wynne, a Welsh slave belonging to Eadwine Aethelhard, the thegn of Aelfdene manor." Then he arose and looked down upon her. "You are Wynne, the most beloved woman of Eadwine Aethelhard."

"Call me whatever you will, my lord," she said proudly, "You cannot make me that which I am not, even by putting a slave collar about my neck. I will never be your wife." Then she turned and walked from the hall up the stairs into the Great Chamber.

She will love me in time, Eadwine Aethelhard thought stub-bornly. She will love me. She must, for I cannot live without her now!

Chapter 13

Madoc of Powys had returned home from the valley below his castle to find his servants hysterical with fear and grief.

"She went out riding early yesterday morning unescorted," Einion told him bluntly.

"Why weren't you with her?" the prince demanded, struggling to stem the violent beating of his heart. "Where is my wife?"

"I wasn't with her because I had no idea she intended to ride, my lord," Einion told him. "Had I known, I would have been with her. Have I not kept her safe from harm her entire life? She told the stablemen and the men-at-arms that she meant to go no farther than the bridge. They let her go believing her safe. Then everyone became involved in his daily routine, and no one thought to ask if my lady Wynne had returned until her horse reappeared riderless."

"You sent out search parties?" Madoc demanded, knowing the answer even before Einion gave it. *Wynne!* he cried in his heart. Where are you, dearling?

"I headed the search myself, my lord, but it was almost nightfall. The following morning we left at first light. We did not find my lady, but we did find her tunic dress and her chemise. They were torn and bloodied as if some wild beast had . . . had . . ." Einion could not go on.

"She is not dead!" the prince shouted angrily. How could this have happened? *How?*

"We did not find a body," Einion, now recovering himself, admitted. "Not even parts of a body. No shoes, no jewelry. Nothing but those two pieces of clothing. It is almost as if . . ."

"Someone were attempting to make us believe that Wynne is dead." Madoc finished the thought for Einion, his mind already filled with possibilities and troubled thoughts.

"But, my lord," said Einion, "you have no enemies. Who would do such a cruel thing?"

Madoc shook his head. "I do not know, my friend, but I intend finding out."

During the next few days the forest was carefully combed for the merest sign of Wynne, but none was found. There was no body. No bones. There was absolutely no trace of the lady of Raven's Rock at all. It was as if the earth had opened and swallowed her. Madoc then commanded that it be made known throughout all of Powys that his young pregnant wife was missing and feared abducted. The similarity between their previous life together and now did not escape Madoc. A reward was offered to anyone who could supply the prince with information leading to his wife's recovery.

His next move was to go to Cai, for he could still hear Wynne's voice importuning him to make his peace with his brother. Had she defied his authority and gone to see Brys? He would not have believed her so foolish, and yet, though old and wise in many ways, Wynne was yet a child in others.

"Why do you find it necessary to visit me with so many soldiers at your back, dear brother," Brys greeted his elder sibling. "Do you not trust me?"

"No," Madoc replied, "I do not. My wife is missing, Brys. Would you know where she is?"

"Do sit down, Madoc. Will you have some wine?" Brys inquired. "Your insistence in getting immediately to the point is really quite unnerving and most uncivilized, brother dear."

"And your evasiveness, Brys, is typical. Do you know where Wynne is?" Madoc demanded, his piercing gaze causing Brys a certain amount of uneasiness.

"Why would I know where Wynne is, Madoc? I am sorry that you cannot keep a better watch over your wife, especially as she is expecting your heir. Breeding women are fanciful creatures, I am told. Is it possible that she has gone to Gwernach? Have you sent your riders to her brother to inquire if she is there?" The bishop of Cai languidly lifted his onyx-studded silver goblet to his lips and sipped at his wine. Then setting the cup down, he smiled at Madoc and said, "If I knew where your wife was, brother dear, I should not tell you. Your obvious suffering is really quite delicious. I would have never thought your weakness would be a woman, Madoc. How pedestrian and common you have become."

Madoc of Powys's dark blue eyes narrowed dangerously. "Do not tempt me to rashness, Brys," he warned.

Brys of Cai laughed scornfully. "You will not harm me, Madoc. It goes against your kindly nature. You have always used your powers for good. Besides, I am your brother."

Madoc shook his head. "You are right, Brys. I cannot seem to destroy you. I will not jeopardize my immortal soul even for the moment of supreme pleasure that killing you would give me. Not now. Not at this moment in time. But there will come a day, Brys, when the Celtic warrior in me will rise up, and I will finally kill you, even if I be damned for it."

"That is where we are so different, brother dear, for I could kill you right now," Brys replied, smiling.

"Where is Wynne?" Madoc repeated.

"I do not know," Brys said, and he smiled again; but Madoc also knew that Brys would accept death rather than divulge what he did know.

The prince of Powys turned and left his younger brother's presence. In the courtyard of Castle Cai his men and their horses milled about restlessly.

"Well?" demanded Einion.

"I believe he knows where Wynne is, but he will not tell me," Madoc said.

"Give me a few moments with him, my lord," Einion begged. "He will tell me!"

"Nay, he will not," Madoc said. "He would die first," and the prince leaned against his horse wearily. "She was here, Einion. I can feel it!"

"Do you think she's still here, my lord?" Einion asked. "Perhaps he has her hidden away. We should search Castle Cai!"

"Nay, she is gone," Madoc said. "I sense it. We must go too, my friend." He mounted his horse, giving the signal to his men to do likewise.

They headed out along the road back to Raven's Rock. They had gone not much farther than a mile or two and were reentering the forest when they heard a voice calling from somewhere amid the trees.

"Let the prince of Powys dismount and come into the woodland alone. I will tell him of his wife."

"It is a trick of your brother's," Einion said grimly.

"Nay," Madoc said, sliding off his horse. "It is the voice of good fortune, I think," and he walked forward into the trees until the voice bade him stop. "Who are you?" he asked.

"Who I am matters not, my lord," the voice said. It was a man's voice. "I know of your wife's fate, and I would tell you."

"Why? How can I trust you? If you know what has happened to Wynne and to our unborn child, then you are certainly connected with my brother, who has hatched this plot and wishes me nothing good," Madoc said.

"That is so, my lord," the voice agreed, "but though I am in service of your brother, he has wronged me and my family greatly. I dare not defy him openly, for I am powerless before him, but I can be avenged upon him in this matter without his ever knowing. Your brother wantonly killed my younger sister. He beat her to death, for she tried to escape him after he had forced her into an evil, carnal bondage of a sort I need not describe to you, my lord. Your good wife attempted to save my sister, and when she could not, she held Gwladys in her own arms and prayed with her until she died. But for her, my sister would have died alone and afraid. For that great kindness I owe your wife a debt, and I am not a man to avoid my debts."

"Where is my lady?" Madoc inquired gently. How like Wynne to have tried to aid one of Brys's victims even to her own detriment.

"Your brother sent for a man named Ruari Ban, an Irish slaver. He sold your wife to this man, who I know went to England with her. I do not know where in England, my lord. I am sorry."

"You are certain of what you tell me?" Madoc said.

"I am certain, my lord. I was in the hall when the wicked business was done. Your wife was forced into silence by your brother by means of threats against your child. Your brother has dealt with Ruari Ban in the past. He is, strange to say, an honest sort for a slaver. If you seek for him along the roads into England, someone should know where he can be found, my lord."

"I would reward you, my friend," Madoc said.

"Nay, my lord. I have, I hope, but returned the kindness that your wife rendered to my sister."

"Surely there is something I can do for you," Madoc insisted, but there was silence now, and the prince realized that his informant was gone. Hurrying back to his own men, he remounted his horse and cried, "To Raven's Rock!" and while they rode, he told Einion of what the faceless voice had told him.

"You believe him?" Einion asked. "You are certain that this is no trick?"

"I am certain!" Madoc said grimly. "It is just the sort of evil that Brys would attempt."

"What will you do now, my lord?"

"I must think on this carefully, Einion. My decisions will affect Wynne's fate and that of our child."

When they had returned to Raven's Rock, Madoc locked himself in his tower room, considering the best course of action to take. One thing he was certain of, he had to speak with Nesta, for she was a part of this too. Flinging open the tower window, he said, *"Codam is ainm dom. Codam is ainm dom. Te se Codam!"* In his mind's eye he pictured a raven, old Dhu. Then he felt his wings flapping smoothly as they raised him up, and he flew through the window, catching the spiral of the wind as he headed southwest toward St. Bride's.

The day was waning quickly, and Madoc knew that he must reach St. Bride's before sunset or he would be forced to spend the night in the open, for it was the dark of the moontime. He flew over Gwernach and was pleased to see it so prosperous, its herds of fat cows grazing on the lush hillsides, sharing their territory with the deer. He could smell the salt of the sea long before he saw it, but when he did, the sun was fast sinking into a bright scarlet horizon. Then the turrets and towers of St. Bride's appeared, and the great black raven landed itself upon a fanciful stone balcony overlooking the dark sea.

"Madoc is ainm dom. Madoc is ainm dom. Te se Madoc!" he said, and was once again restored to his human form. The prince looked out over the sea, which was placid at the moment. He concentrated and called out in his mind to Nesta.

She came, joining him suddenly upon the balcony, her loose gown billowing gently about her, her swollen belly quite distinct. "Madoc! What is it? You would not have come were it not serious. Is Wynne all right?" She kissed his cheek.

"Wynne has been abducted and sold into slavery," he began without preamble.

"Brys!" Nesta said. "This is Brys's doing, isn't it?"

"Aye, it is. The time is drawing near, Nesta, when I must kill him. There is no other way."

"God will find a way, Madoc, but in the meantime, what of Wynne? Do you know where she is?" Nesta looked very troubled. "Poor girl!"

"We had argued the past weeks over Brys," Madoc said. "She could not believe he was so evil that he could not be redeemed. She wanted us to forgive him, that our family be reunited. She wanted that for her child and for yours, my sister. All I have been able to learn of her whereabouts is that she has been taken to England by an Irish slaver called Ruari Ban. I must trace him first before I can find my wife. I wanted you to know, Nesta, for I must begin my search immediately. I will most likely not be at Raven's Rock when your child is born."

"Does Wynne's family know of her abduction, brother? You cannot keep it from them. Her grandmother, the lady Enid, is coming to St. Bride's in a few days' time to help me when my child is born. I would be most uncomfortable, Madoc, keeping such news from her."

"You may tell her for me, Nesta," he said. "And tell her not to worry, for I will retrieve Wynne and get her safely home."

"Have you reached out for her?" Nesta asked.

"Aye," he said, "but it is as if I am shouting down a hollow tree. There is nothing, yet I know she is not dead. Death has a very different feeling to it."

"Perhaps it is the child, Madoc. Perhaps the child blocks your path to Wynne," Nesta suggested.

"You heard me," he replied.

"Aye," she nodded slowly, smiling, "but you and I have been together my entire lifetime, brother. Besides, you called me from within my own castle. You are trying to reach out to Wynne over a distance of many miles. She is undoubtedly frightened and very concerned for your child. Believe me, that fear for her baby is consuming her, and she cannot hear you, for she can think of nothing but the safety and the survival of her babe. All her energies are trained upon that, I know, for mine would be, Madoc."

"Surely you are right, sister, and I can certainly think of no other reason I am unable to reach Wynne," Madoc admitted. "It is so difficult, Nesta! I want to reach out and comfort my dearling, and I cannot."

"What of Brys?" Nesta asked. "What will you do about Brys?"

"Nothing for the moment, sister. All my efforts must be on finding Wynne. On finding Ruari Ban. I cannot be bothered with Brys."

"You cannot underestimate Brys, Madoc," Nesta warned him. "Though you know how evil he can be, you have always allowed him to take advantage of you. Why did you not set a watch on Wynne when you knew that her kind heart was determined to reunite us all?"

Madoc shook his head and sighed deeply. "Sister," he told her, "not for one moment did I ever believe that Wynne would actually seek Brys out. How could I have anticipated such goodness of heart?"

"You have never really known her, have you, Madoc? Heaven help you both! In that other time and that other place, she possessed the same loving kindness that she does in this time and place. You should have recognized that in her, but you did not," Nesta chided him.

"Nay, I did not," he agreed with her, "and once more my blindness has cost us dearly; but at least I have my own powers in this time and place. I will use them to their fullest to find her, Nesta! I will bring Wynne home, that we may at long last live out our lives together as we were meant to live them."

Nesta hugged him. "You must come into the castle and stay the night, brother," she said.

"What will you tell Rhys?" he said, smiling.

"That my brother has arrived unexpectedly," she answered him with a small twinkle. "Rhys is still much in awe of our family, Madoc, and will not require a detailed explanation of us."

Nesta was quite correct in her assessment. Rhys of St. Bride's was more than delighted to have his brother-in-law's company for the evening and offered whatever help Madoc would have of him in finding Wynne. If he was curious as to how his brother-in-law had arrived so suddenly and without a horse or an escort, he kept his inquisitiveness to himself. And even in the morning, when Rhys awoke to find Madoc already gone, he did not evince any strong curiosity. It was not his business, and his relations with his wife's kinfolk were one of mutual trust.

Madoc returned to Raven's Rock and, within the privacy of his tower room, he began to weave spells that might bring him a glimpse of Wynne, an inkling of where she might be found; but to his great surprise, his magic was useless in this matter. He sent riders into England to seek out the slaver known as Ruari Ban, who was traced first to Hereford and next to Worcester, where the trail grew cold, for no one knew of where the little Irishman was next headed, although the innkeeper with whom he had lodged had heard a mention of Brittany, or was it Byzantium? He was not sure. One thing was certain. No one remembered seeing a slave of Wynne's description amongst those belonging to Ruari Ban.

"He may have had a buyer in mind for her all along," Einion said, "and that will make it difficult for us, my lord. There is no direct road from here or from Cai to England. Ruari Ban would have had to go south first and then back north to Hereford and Worcester. We will have to travel the entire route that he took, and we will have to travel it slowly in order to investigate the surrounding countryside for an English thegn wealthy enough to have bought an expensive slave."

"How do you know he did not sell her to just anyone, Einion?" the prince asked his wife's servant.

Einion bared his teeth in a fierce smile. "I remember my own experience at the hands of slavers, my lord. My lady Wynne is a beautiful woman. In any land or culture, beautiful women bring a high price. Not only that, she was with child, proving her fertility and offering her buyer an extra dividend. Whoever he is, he would have to be a man of substance, and we will have to find him first before we can find my lady Wynne."

"We will leave in the morning," Madoc said impetuously.

Einion shook his head. "Nay, my lord. You and I cannot gain the information that we need to obtain. I am too imposing, and you, my lord, too regal. Simple people are afraid of men like us. Send out others who will blend into a crowd and quickly be forgotten should someone become curious as to their questions. You must divide the territory to be searched into sections, and into each section send one man."

"Who," said Madoc, quickly seeing the wisdom of Einion's idea, "will travel as a peddler; but not one man into each section, Einion, two. A peddler and his helper. They will travel the width and the length of their assigned section, learning which of the Saxons within that territory has the means to buy and own a prized slave woman. And when my wife is located, Einion, then one of those men can ride quickly back to Raven's Rock with the news."

"And then, my lord," Einion finished, "we can ride out ourselves to bring my lady and your child safely home."

"A map!" Madoc cried. "We must have a map! Go to the monastery in the valley, for they will have the maps we need. Tell my head shepherd he is to give the monks six young sheep as a gift from the lord of Raven's Rock."

"Shall I tell the monks why we need the maps, my lord?"

"Nay, I do not want my brother knowing what we do. Nesta is always warning me that I underestimate Brys, and she is right. We need eyes and ears within Castle Cai. The faceless voice who told me of Wynne's fate is a man-at-arms whose young sister was beaten to death by Brys after he had raped her. Find me that man and convince him to aid us, Einion."

"What shall I offer him, my lord? We cannot give him gold, for he would surely be found out," Einion said wisely.

"Tell him I would have him serve me here at Raven's Rock, and I will give shelter to his family as well," Madoc replied. "Should he believe himself in danger at any time before this is over, Einion, then tell him he is to come to me with his kin immediately. I want no innocent blood on my hands, but I need to know what Brys is doing before he knows it himself."

"Very good, my lord," Einion said, and bowing, he left the prince.

Madoc climbed to his tower sanctuary and peered out into the late afternoon twilight. It was beginning to snow. He felt a wave of frustration spilling over him. *Winter.* Winter was upon them, and it would be difficult with the bad weather to mount his search as quickly as he wanted. Somewhere over the mountains on the English side of Offa's Dyke was his wife. Was she afraid? Was she safe? Did she know in her heart that he longed for her and was even now seeking her? The thought that unless he was given a miracle, Wynne would undoubtedly bear their child alone, pained him. What if she died in childbirth? What would happen to their son? He angrily pushed the gloomy thoughts away.

Patience. It was a virtue of which he was not particularly fond, but one he had cultivated down through the centuries out of necessity. Had he not learned patience, he could not have survived. Once again he knew he would have to be patient. When he had the maps, he would divide the vast territory separating him from his wife into small sections. Each section must be combed carefully for any sign of Wynne. It would take patience. It would take time. It would take luck. Wynne was brave, and she must know that he would not desert her. She would know he would not believe Brys's shallow ruse. She would know that he sought her; would find her and restore her to her rightful place by his side. Wynne must cultivate patience too. She must understand the difficulties involved.

Time. Why was it that time passed so quickly when life was sweet, and so slowly when you wanted it to hurry? Wynne stared out the narrow window in the Great Chamber, watching the heavy grey downpour. It had been five months since her abduction, and yet she felt as if she had been gone from Raven's Rock for years. The winter had been cold and forever, and now on this long-awaited day of the Spring equinox, the rain came in discouraging torrents. She turned away from the window, a tear sliding down her cheek. Where was Madoc? Why had he not found her by now? Certainly he didn't believe her dead. He wouldn't! How could he have left her to bear their child alone?

She had been in labor since early morning, but she had said nothing to those about her. If Wynne could not have her husband by her side, she wanted no one else near her. Since the day Eadwine Aethelhard had put the gold slave collar about her neck, Wynne felt as if it were an enchantment of sorts to keep Madoc from her. There was no way in which she could remove the hated collar. Eadwine had set it about her neck, locked it, and carried the key himself. At first it had taken all the courage she possessed not to go mad, for the collar not only openly labeled her, but it was indeed the successful deterrent he had said it would be. She could go nowhere without being marked for a slave, which meant there was no escape from Aelfdene for her.

In the beginning she had raged against her fate, but then she realized that since Eadwine was the only person who could free her, she would have to convince him that she was content. Wynne knew how very much he wanted her to be his wife. After her child was born, she would agree to his proposal. There was no priest at Aelfdene, and therefore they could not be formally married until a priest could be brought to them. Her status would only change in the sense that he would legally free her. When she told the priest of her predicament, he would, of course, forbid any marriage between them. Eadwine would have no choice but to let her go home. In her desperation and naiveté, Wynne was convinced that the scenario could be successful, for although Eadwine Aethelhard was a stubborn man, he was also a very honorable man.

So over the past few months she had been sweet-tempered toward them all, despite the gold slave collar she wore about her neck. She never forgot that she was Wynne of Gwernach, wife to Madoc, prince of Powys. *"Madoc!"* she half whispered, and a hard pain gripped her, causing her to gasp aloud and double over. When the pain had passed, she straightened up and moved slowly across the Great Chamber to where the birthing chair with its open center had already been set up in anticipation of her child's birth. Wynne stripped off her yellow tunic dress and her indigo-blue under tunic, folding them carefully and putting them away in the large, carved chest that Eadwine had given her for her possessions.

Within the chest were the things she needed for the birth. She carefully lifted them out, spreading several thicknesses of cloth beneath the chair first and then laying out the baby's little gown, a cap, and the swaddling cloth, toweling, and finally a small flask of rendered lamb fat for gently cleaning her child free of the birthing blood. Another pain tore through her, and Wynne groaned loudly. The pressure was almost too much to bear. She seated herself in the birthing chair, legs spread, drawing her chemise up about her waist, and as she did so, a great gush of water issued forth from between her thighs. With a mutter of irritation, Wynne arose slowly from her chair and, kneeling down, removed the cloth beneath it, replacing it with fresh cloths. The soaking-wet fabric she lay carefully aside to be washed. Waste was an anathema to her, and, like most women of her time, she was frugal by nature. She returned to her chair.

Pain. And more pain overcame her. She gripped the arms of the birthing chair, struggling not to cry out too loudly. Eadwine, she knew, was surveying the rain-soaked fields, for the barley had been planted earlier in the week. His sons and their families kept to their own halls during the day, and Wynne had cleverly sent Ealdraed to the cook house to discuss with Heall her plans for the kitchen gardens this season. The cook had asked her to take charge of that small part of his domain. "That you may have all you need for your pharmacea, lady," he had said.

Her pains were coming quickly now, and the feeling of strong pressure was completely unbearable. She could not help herself, and with a great groan she pushed down once, twice, and a third time. For a dizzying moment she was free of pain. Then the agony and the straining began again. She was quite powerless to stop it now, for the birth was imminent. Unable to contain herself, Wynne cried out aloud, pushing down again as she did so. She found herself panting wildly. She could actually feel the child being born, but now she suddenly wondered if she could indeed birth Madoc's son without help. A shriek was torn forth from her again, and then, to her relief, she heard familiar footsteps upon the staircase.

Eadwine Aethelhard practically leapt into the Great Chamber and, hurrying to her side, knelt down, his hands sliding beneath the birthing chair. "The child is half born, my wild Welsh girl," he said.

"I don't want you here," she gasped unreasonably as another spasm gripped her vitals and she bore down once more. "I . . . I want Madoc!" Still, she was glad to see him, even if she couldn't admit it.

"Push again, and once again," he calmly instructed her, ignoring her sham anger.

"I hate you!" she cried out to him, but obeyed. Suddenly she realized that her travail was nearly over. From beneath the chair, she heard a small whimper which was almost immediately followed by a tiny bellow of outrage. Gasping and still overcome with small pains as she expelled the afterbirthing, Wynne watched in amazement as Eadwine tenderly cleaned the child off. Expertly he put the tiny gown on the infant, gently fit the tiny cap on the tiny head, swaddled it most efficiently, and handed it to her.

"You have a fine son, my wild Welsh girl!" he said approvingly. "What is his name to be?"

Wynne looked down at her son and tears sprang into her eyes. How much like Madoc he was, she thought sadly. They had planned to call a son Anwyl after that long-ago child from another time and another place; but she knew the circumstances of this baby's birth would not allow her to call him Anwyl. Someday they would be free, but she never wanted to forget Brys of Cai's wickedness, and so looking up at Eadwine Aethelhard, she replied softly, "His name is Arvel ap Madoc. Arvel means *wept over*, for this son of Madoc, the prince of Powys, is far from his heritage, and is to be wept over by all until he can be restored to it. By his mother, who has brought him into this slavery; and by his father, who has so longed for his coming and has lost him before he even knew him." She handed the baby back to the thegn. "Take him, my lord, and place him gently in his cradle while I attend myself."

"If you will wed with me, Wynne," Eadwine Aethelhard said, laying the infant in his cot, "I will raise your child as if he were my very own child."

"He will not be considered a slave?" she asked as she cleaned herself free of the traces of Arvel's birth. The heir to Powys-Wenwynwyn must not be a slave!

"Nay! From this moment of his birth he is free, and so I will affirm to all, my wild Welsh girl!" declared Eadwine Aethelhard passionately.

Wynne drew forth a clean chemise from her chest and put it on, adding her old garment to the pile of bloodied laundry. Slowly she crawled into their bed space. She was aching and suddenly very tired. "I am not certain that it is right, my lord, but I will be your wife," she promised, "if a priest, knowing of my history, will marry us."

He nodded. "We have no priest at Aelfdene now, and although I have applied to the diocese at Worcester for one, they have not yet granted us this blessing. Until such time as a priest is sent to us, Wynne, you will live with me openly as my wife. I will make it publicly known to all that I intend to wed with you; that you are to be treated with honor as the mistress of this manor; that all of your children are my children. There is nothing unusual in such an arrangement for a second marriage among our people. Rest now, my wild Welsh girl. You have done well this day. I will send Ealdraed to watch over Arvel, and you need have no fears for his safety." He bent down and kissed her gently, his crisp beard tickling her cheek. Then he left her.

She had done the right thing, Wynne thought sleepily. Arvel would never be a slave, no matter what happened. She would see that Eadwine fulfilled all his promises to her. As mistress of Aelfdene she would have even greater respect than she now had as Wynne, the healer. She was feeling giddy with happiness and filled with relief at having come through the perils of childbirth unscathed; of having a beautiful and apparently healthy son. Despite the rain, spring was here. Madoc would find them. It was the winter that had undoubtedly impeded his search. Now that spring was here, he would find them. Certainly before her six-week healing period was over, but if not before then, surely soon thereafter. Even if Eadwine was able to enforce his husbandly rights over her, it was a well-known fact that nursing women did not conceive. Everything would be all right. Madoc would soon find them and, in the meantime, her new status would protect her son.

And, indeed, Eadwine Aethelhard was true to his word. Several days after Arvel's birth he escorted Wynne into the hall. She was wearing a cream-colored tunic dress of brocatelle which had been embroidered with dainty gold thread butterflies. Beneath it was an under tunic of bright yellow silk. Eadwine had gifted her with it the day after Arvel's arrival, having instructed that it be secretly made for her. Upon her right shoulder Wynne had pinned a round gold brooch decorated with green agates. Another gift from this new *husband* she seemed to have acquired.

Eadwine Aethelhard had assembled his entire family, his servants, his freed men, and as many of his serfs as he could crowd into the hall. Wynne had to admit to herself that he was certainly a most attractive man in his scarlet kirtle. To celebrate the festive occasion, he had even perfumed his rich brown beard, and his brown hair curled gracefully just above his broad shoulders. Aye, he was a very handsome man with a commanding presence.

He led her to a high-backed chair that had been set before the dais at the end of the hall. Wynne sat as she knew she was expected to, and Eadwine Aethelhard stood by her side. "Today," he said, "I have freed this woman and her son from the bonds of slavery." He bent and unlocked the delicate gold slave collar from about her neck and put it in her lap. "It is yours to do what you will, my wild Welsh girl."

"I will send it to St. Frideswide's nunnery and ask that masses be said for the soul of your sons' mother, the lady Mildraed," Wynne told the assemblage.

A murmur of approval greeted her words, but Caddaric Aethelmaere glowered at Wynne, and she could feel his deep hatred.

"Today I have freed this woman and her son from slavery," Eadwine Aethelhard repeated, "and now I declare before all that I have taken her for my wife. When a priest is sent to us, we will formally seal this union; but you here know that in accordance with the old ways, I am within my rights to make the lady Wynne my wife by announcing it publicly before you all. Her infant son, Arvel, I adopt as my own child. Come now and pledge your fealty to the new lady of Aelfdene Manor."

"You would set this . . . this Welsh slave in our mother's place?" shouted Caddaric Aethelmaere. "How can you?" His fury caused him to redden unattractively.

"Wynne was a captive, Caddaric. She is of good birth," his father told him.

"How can you know that? Because she has told you so? I do not believe it for a minute! You are an old fool, my father! You have been ensorceled by this Welsh witch! You have already sampled her wares as is your right. Why must you wed her?" Caddaric demanded.

"Because I love her," Eadwine Aethelhard replied, his blue eyes hardening. "Because I am master here, and I choose to wed her. Now kneel before my lady and give your fealty, Caddaric, or I will disinherit you this day!"

For a moment it appeared that Caddaric Aethelmaere would defy his father, but Eadgyth Crookback gently tugged upon her husband's sleeve. Without even looking at her, Eadwine Aethelhard's eldest son fell to his knees before Wynne and hastily mumbled the required words of loyalty. Finishing, he looked up at her, and Wynne knew that Caddaric would never forgive her for this day. As he arose, Baldhere Armstrang took his place and, with a wink at her, swore his oath of loyalty to Wynne.

Rising, he asked mischievously, "Shall I call you Mother, lady?"

"Not if you wish to become an old man," Wynne replied sweetly.

Her humor broke the tension within the hall, and the others in the crowded room knelt, pledging their fealty in unison to the new mistress of the manor. Ale was passed about, and a toast drunk to the newlyweds' health. The hall then emptied of all but family. Eadwine picked Wynne up and returned her to her bed in the Great Chamber, for she was not yet fully recovered from Arvel's birth. Ealdraed followed behind.

"I am so happy for you, lady," she half wept as she helped her mistress to disrobe and return to her sleeping space. "I never thought to see the master happy again, but since the day of your arrival he is a young man once more! You will not be unhappy with him, and it will be good to have babies about this hall as in the past."

Wynne said nothing in reply, for she was distressed over the fact that her milk had not come in despite her own remedies to encourage it. She had reluctantly agreed to allow Ealdraed's granddaughter, who had given birth to a stillborn child the day of Arvel's birth, to wet-nurse her son.

"I know how disappointed you are, lady," Ealdraed had told her, "but the child must be fed to survive; and my poor Gytha must have a reason to survive also. Her child is dead and so is her man. She is young, healthy, and free of pox. Her milk is rich, for it began to flow a week before her child was born."

Wynne had had no choice but to allow the unfortunate Gytha to wet-nurse her son. The girl, younger than Wynne by two years, was pitifully grateful for having been given a reason to go on living. She cradled Arvel lovingly, and Wynne was ashamed to feel herself being strongly overwhelmed by jealousy. Gytha would have a sleeping space in the Great Chamber, the only servant in the house so honored, for Wynne would not allow her son from her sight.

Summer was near, and Wynne eagerly waited for Madoc to come, but he did not. She tried to be patient, for she understood that he must seek for her as one would seek for the very first flower of the spring. Not an easy task. Beltaine came, the anniversary of their wedding day, and Wynne went out into the fields just before sunrise to gather flowers before the dew was off them. She washed her face in dew, for it held magical properties. Her tears flowed silently, and she looked to the brightening skies above for a sign of old Dhu, but there was none. There were robins, and larks, and sparrows and cuckoos calling back and forth to one another, but there was no harsh, raucous cry of a raven. She tried to reach out to him in her mind, but she could not seem to concentrate.

His face. Madoc's fierce and handsome face was becoming harder and harder for her to focus upon. It seemed so long since she had seen him, and yet it was but seven months. So much had happened since they had been parted. She was beginning to wonder if she would ever see him again. It was becoming more difficult to resist Eadwine Aethelhard's persistent wooing. She had reached the point where she was not even certain she wanted to resist him. She was still not fully recovered from the ordeal of her son's birth, and susceptible to the Saxon thegn's loving kindness. There was no doubt in her mind that he loved her, and he treated Arvel as if the baby were of his own blood. Indeed she had come upon him in the Great Chamber the previous evening, Arvel cradled in his bearlike grasp, singing a lullaby to her son.

It was not fair! Wynne thought. Madoc should be the one holding his son, singing to him, but Madoc, prince of Powys, was nowhere to be found. Would he ever find her? How would she deal with the problem of Arvel's heritage as he grew? Would she tell him, or would she let him believe that a kindly Saxon thegn was his father? No, Caddaric would see that Arvel knew Eadwine Aethelhard was only his adoptive father. Wynne sighed deeply. She had thought that when she remembered that distant past and came to grips with it, they would all live happily ever after, but obviously that was not to be. Why must she and Madoc be so torn apart just at the moment when they had begun to live their greatest happiness?

"I am going to have to come to terms with my life as it now is," Wynne said to herself aloud. "I cannot go on like this forever! How long do I wait for Madoc to come? Why has he not come by now? *Is he coming?*" She sighed again and then bent down to gather up the sheaf of flowers she had set down when she had washed her face with the dew. Straightening up, she saw Eadwine Aethelhard coming across the field toward her.

"I awoke and you were gone," he called, waving.

She walked toward him. " 'Tis May morn," she said, not needing to offer any further explanation.

Reaching her, he gathered her into his arms and kissed her. "I missed you, sweeting," he said.

"Did you think I had run away, Eadwine?" she half teased him.

"You would not leave Arvel behind," he replied bluntly. "You are a good mother, Wynne. We should have more children."

She stiffened in his embrace, knowing what was about to come.

"Your healing period is over," he continued, "and I ache for you. I will wait no more!" His hand gently massaged her back in an attempt to relax her. "You are my wife, Wynne. I have said it before my sons, my family, my servants, and my serfs. None have denied you your rightful place at Aelfdene. Not even Caddaric. Now it is time for you to be my wife in the fullest sense."

There was no escape, she thought, her emotions mixed and confused. Looking up at him, she said, "Of course, my lord, it is your right. You are good to me, and I will deny you nothing." What else could she do?

"You deny me your heart," he said wisely, his blue eyes sad.

Wynne nodded. "Aye, I do, Eadwine, but perhaps it will not always be that way. I must have time. You have given me everything but that. Mayhap I will never love you, I do not know, but I will care for you, and I will respect you."

"I want a child by you, Wynne," he told her.

"If God will it, my lord," she answered quietly.

"But in your heart you hope he will not, for then you would have to release your hold on your memories," Eadwine said half angrily.

"I will never forget what has been, Eadwine Aethelhard, and you do not have the right to ask that I do. Arvel is part of those memories. Would you have me deny him and his father, that your conscience be clear? You could return me to Powys and to Madoc if you chose to do so, but you do not. Yet you know I speak the truth of my past life, for all your denial to the contrary.

"Mercia and Powys are allies. My king's wife is Earl Aelfgar's daughter. You would not suffer in any way should you return me and my son to our own people, but you will not. You recognize my small status by your actions, my lord. You have honored me by declaring to all that I am your wife, but I wonder if the Church would agree and marry us within their sacred precincts.

"You but desire a child to bind me further," Wynne said shrewdly. "What if Madoc comes after I have had that child you so desperately want? What if he comes before, and I am heavy with that babe? I will be torn apart by the two of you, and it is not fair! God, I wish I were back at Gwernach and an innocent girl once again!" She angrily pulled out of his embrace and, pushing past him, fled toward the manor house.

Eadwine Aethelhard watched her go, sadness and frustration overwhelming him. She was right. It wasn't fair, but the chances of Madoc of Powys ever finding her were slim. There was too much distance between their lands. He had purchased her honorably. Even if every word she had told him since her arrival at Aelfdene was the truth, he was not legally bound to return her to Powys. He loved her, and to do so would break his heart. Wynne was *his* wife now. He was not yet forty-four. She made him feel like a young man. A young man with a fertile young wife. There would be children! He was dissatisfied with his two sons. He wanted other children for Aelfdene, and he would have them!

▓Chapter 14

There was no trace of Wynne of Gwernach in England, or so those sent out to seek her reluctantly reported to their lord, the prince of Powys-Wenwynwyn.

"She's in England," Madoc said stubbornly. "I know it!"

"England is a large land, my lord," Einion replied. "Our people have traveled the entire countryside along the border, following the exact route of the Irish slaver, Ruari Ban, as his passing is always noted by those who live there, for he is unlike most slavers, being a kind and merry soul. He sold no slaves until he came to Worcester. In Worcester there are many to attest to his coming. It is said of him that his merchandise is always good, his slaves healthy and obedient. Ruari Ban is always welcomed in Worcester."

"And no one remembers a woman of my wife's description among his slaves?" Madoc was beginning to look distraught.

"No, my lord, no one remembers a lady to match my lady's description," Einion answered, "but that does not mean she was not amongst Ruari Ban's slaves. He may have kept her hidden because he felt he could obtain a higher price in a larger town. Such practice is common among slavers with an eye to a good profit. Ruari Ban may be a decent fellow, but 'tis said of him that he strikes a hard bargain. Or he may have sold her privately along his route, as we had previously discussed. There would be nothing unusual in his doing that. It may be harder to trace her under those circumstances."

"Why have we not found her?!" Madoc cried angrily.

Einion cast his lord a look of pity which he masked lest he offend Madoc. "My lord, it will take time. Each Saxon man who can amass for himself five hides of land upon which he builds a fortified house, a chapel, a bakehouse and a little bell tower with a bell, is elevated to the rank of thegn. In some parts of England a hide is equal to one hundred and twenty acres, but in others 'tis only forty acres. There are many thegns now, my lord. Any of them with enough silver could have possession of my lady Wynne."

"And our child!" Madoc burst forth. "My child has surely been born by now, and I know not if I have a son or a daughter. I know not if my wife has survived the rigors of childbirth or if the child was stillborn from the shock of their abduction! *I am Madoc of Powys!* A prince of the great family of Wenwynwyn, but for all my magic I cannot find my wife or my child! What good are these powers I possess if they cannot return to me that which I treasure the most in this life?"

"All is not lost, my lord," Einion told Madoc. "You must have patience. Your destiny will not play itself out any quicker for your impatience."

Madoc stared at the big man, and then he laughed. "Einion, Einion! How is it you are so wise? I am a man used to having what he wants when he wants it, for I am the prince of Powys-Wenwynwyn; but in this instance I seem to be no better off than a common peasant laboring in my fields."

"Perhaps there is a lesson to be learned here, my lord," Einion said, smiling back at the prince.

"Perhaps," Madoc agreed thoughtfully.

"We will continue our search, my lord," Einion said.

"Send more men out," Madoc told him.

"I would not advise it, my lord, lest anyone become unduly suspicious of our activities," Einion replied. "Although King Gruffydd's wife is English, the Saxons are not really our friends. England is not a stable place at this moment. Edward may be king, but Earl Harold has gobbled up most of the land, if not for himself, then for his equally greedy brothers. Only Mercia remains out of his grasp, although he has bitten off that chunk of it called Herefordshire. His only bishop, Ealdred of Worcester, has been consecrated Archbishop of York; although that wily cleric is being forced to give up his bishopric in Worcester to Wolfstan, Ealdred still remains the lord of Oswaldstow. He is the most important landholder in southwest Mercia, and he is Earl Harold's man, having given his sacred oath."

"Bishop Wulfstan is also," Madoc answered, "though his first loyalty is to his God, but you are right, my good Einion. Harold Godwinson has no love for the Welsh, and King Gruffydd in particular. Should he learn that Gruffydd's cousin is a slave prisoner in England, Wynne and our child could be in even greater danger. We must proceed with caution, as hard as that is for us all. If I am eager to find my wife and bring her home, then too must Wynne be as eager to come home." He thought a moment and then said, "Has the slaver's route been traced past Worcester yet, Einion?"

"Aye, my lord. He traveled onward to the coast, where he took passage with about twenty slaves for Brittany."

"Send someone to follow in his path asking after my lady. If they cannot obtain any information," said Madoc, "then they are to continue on over the water to Brittany. Find Ruari Ban and question him. Bring him back to Raven's Rock if necessary, but find him! In the meantime we will continue combing the countryside on the other side of Offa's Dyke for Wynne and our child."

Madoc turned away from Einion, and knowing that he had been dismissed, the big man hurried off to carry out his lord's new orders. Although Madoc could not know it, Einion understood his pain. Megan had recently given birth to their first child, a daughter, whom they had named Gwynedd, meaning *blessed one*. Einion knew that if his wife and daughter had been lost to him, he would find it difficult if not impossible to go on with his life. He admired Madoc, whom he knew loved Wynne totally and to the exclusion of all women. He realized what strength of will his prince must be imposing upon himself in order to remain calm in the face of this crisis. Like Madoc, Einion knew in his heart that Wynne was not dead; but he questioned whether they would find her again. And if they did, Einion considered, could these lovers be successfully reunited? Having suffered enslavement, Einion knew the fate of a beautiful woman far better than did his lord. Time was very much of the essence.

The year deepened, and England, for centuries wetter and colder than most places upon the earth, had begun to enjoy a period of sunny, warm summers. The fields were lush with ripening grain hurrying toward the harvest. Aelfdene was a prosperous estate with a good master who was canny enough to keep adding land to his holdings as it became available to him. Technically, Eadwine Aethelhard could not claim unconditional possession of his lands. He held lands at the pleasure of his lord, who in this case was the Mercian earl, Edwin. Aelfdene and its original land grant had been in his family since the days of the great Mercian king, Offa. Local legend said that it had been Eadwine Aethelhard's ancestor who had given King Offa the idea for his famous dyke and earthworks, which stretched for seventy miles along the border between his kingdom and the Welsh kingdoms, notably Powys. The original grant had been seven hides of land. By the time he had inherited Aelfdene and been confirmed in his inheritance by the previous earl, Aelfgar, the estate had grown to twelve hides of land. Eadwine Aethelhard had industriously added an additional six.

There was a distinct social order at Aelfdene, as there was all over England in the year 1062. Slaves and serfs were the lowest order. Slaves possessed nothing and owed their very lives to their masters. Serfs were only slightly better off, owing everything to their lord's bounty and bound to his land from birth to death. They, however, might accumulate a few possessions. There were few slaves at Aelfdene, and those who came as slaves were usually quickly elevated to the rank of serf if their behavior merited it. Troublesome slaves were as quickly sold off, for no thegn tolerated sedition upon his own lands.

Above the serfs were the cottars. Most of the cottars at Aelfdene were craftsmen. Among them was a blacksmith, a potter, a miller, two sawyers, and a tinker. Each was given a cottage by the thegn as well as a few acres to farm plus the tools and equipment with which to practice his craft. They owed Eadwine Aethelhard in return one day's work each week, and an additional three days a week during the harvest, when they were expected to go into the fields to reap the grain. Still in all, they were free men, and if they found themselves unhappy, they were able to move on to another village or another estate.

Every cottar aspired to become a gebura. Geburas could hold twenty acres of land from their lord. In general a man raised up to such a rank was given a good start by the lord in the form of livestock, tools, seed, and even some furniture for his home. A gebura was hardworking and reliable, a man upon whom his lord could totally depend. When a gebura died, his possessions, of course, reverted to the lord, but they were usually given back to the gebura's heir provided he was as reliable as his predecessor.

In exchange for his status, the gebura gave his lord two days of work each week as well as an additional three days a week during both the spring planting and the harvest seasons. He had to help with the plowing of the common land. He owed his lord tenpence at Michaelmas; two sacks of grain and two hens at Martinmas; a lamb at Easter; and one pig each year in exchange for the right to keep his pigs in the lord's forest, where they fed on whatever they could find. It was a great responsibility, and most geburas had large families to help them with all of their duties.

Eadwine Aethelhard was relatively free from agricultural duties, thanks to his cottars and his geburas. As thegn of Aelfdene he had other, more important duties. It was up to him to feed, protect, and escort any of Earl Edwin's messengers passing through his lands. Had the earl himself come his way, it would have been up to the thegn of Aelfdene to offer generous hospitality to Edwin and any who traveled with him. The thegn had not seen Earl Edwin since he was a very small child, when Earl Aelfgar had come with his son to see Eadwine Aethelhard. Aelfdene was not as easily accessible as other manors, nor was it on any heavily traveled track.

But nevertheless, Eadwine Aethelhard took his duties to his earl most seriously. He looked after the earl's hunting rights, hunted down and most vigorously prosecuted any poachers he could find, and saw that fences were built and maintained where they were needed. There was one stone bridge on Aelfdene lands that crossed a stream and led to a narrow track that ran down the hills to a main road. The thegn kept that bridge in good repair.

Once each month the thegn of Aelfdene sat in judgment with two other thegns in the local hundred court, where petty crimes and minor disputes were settled. Twice a year it was his duty to sit upon the bench in the shire court in Worcester, which heard more serious crimes and meted out judgments in the name of the king. Eadwine Aethelhard never shirked these duties, for he was a man of honor.

The most important duty of a thegn, however, was his military service. For two months of each year Eadwine Aethelhard was on call to Earl Edwin and to King Edward. His sons were on call as well. Men like these were the backbone of the fyrd, which was the army that the king or his earls could call upon

to defend England. In times of strife the thegns would raise
small troops of armed men to bring to the aid of their overlord.
They provisioned them and supplied their men with everything
they needed. Once each month the men at Aelfdene would
have weapons practice upon their village green. Offa's Dyke
did not always prevent the Welsh from cattle raids and general
mayhem.

Usually, however, one year passed another without the people of Aelfdene ever seeing a stranger but for the king's tax
collector, who always arrived regularly to collect the two hundred seventy shillings owed by Eadwine Aethelhard to the
crown. Each hide of his lands was assessed at fifteen shillings.
He raised the monies for his taxes from his rents, the sale of
his extra produce and livestock, and from his mill, which for
a fee ground grain belonging to some of his smaller neighbors
without mills.

Aelfdene was, like all English manors, fairly self-reliant.
They grew their own food, raised their own livestock, spun
their own wool, brewed their own beer, made their own butter
and cheese. It was not a very different life than Wynne had
lived at Gwernach, and she had not lived at Raven's Rock long
enough to become used to its luxuries. It was not difficult for
her to find herself becoming more and more comfortable as
each day passed.

When she had first come to Aelfdene, she had thought of
Madoc constantly. Now she found that her mind was full of
Arvel, and Eadwine, and her duties as Aelfdene's mistress.
Madoc, who had followed her through time and space to make
his peace with her, could not seem to find her on the other side
of Offa's Dyke. Perhaps he did not want to, or perhaps it was
their destiny to be separated now that they had resolved the
past. She could not seem to reach out to him, nor he to her.
Wynne did not understand why, but she knew that life would
go on nonetheless. She owed Eadwine some measure of happiness for the love he was lavishing upon her and upon Arvel.

He was a most passionate man, and it constantly astounded
her that a man in his forties could be so intensely amorous.
And he was thoughtful as well. On Beltaine, when he had told
her most firmly that her healing period was now past and that
he intended to exert his rights over her, she had been hesitant
for a number of reasons, but she had told him she would com-

ply with his wishes. There had been no one else but them at the high board that evening, to her puzzlement. The meal was a surprisingly delicate one and not at all what she had instructed Heall to prepare.

A basket of raw oysters had been served to Eadwine along with a goblet of heavy, rich-spiced wine. At her place, however, had been set a dainty breast of capon poached in white wine, as well as a goblet of the spiced wine. With a broad grin Ealdraed placed a platter of boiled asparagus and a dish of chestnuts which had been cooked with a single leaf of mint. Wynne flushed, embarrassed. The menu before them was one intended to arouse their passions and increase their sexual activity. She could barely nibble at the food, although Eadwine ate with gusto.

"I must bathe," she said finally when she could sit no more. "I have spent the day out of doors and am rank with my own sweat."

"The tub awaits you, my lady," Ealdraed cackled.

From the corner of her eye Wynne saw Gytha, Arvel in her arms, slipping from the hall. "Gytha!" she called sharply. "Where are you going with my son? It is much too late for Arvel to be out."

"I am taking him to the cottage that my lord Eadwine has given me," Gytha said brightly. "Oh, lady! 'Tis such a fine cottage, with its own fire pit and a sleeping shelf with a feather-bed!"

"I want no one else privy to our privacy, Wynne," the thegn said firmly before she could protest. "I would not put Arvel in any danger." Then he turned and smiled at the young wet nurse. "You may take our son and go, Gytha," he told her.

With a smile the girl curtsied and departed the hall. Ealdraed, too, seemed to have suddenly disappeared. Angrily Wynne arose and ran up the stairs to the Great Chamber. How dare he separate her from Arvel? Then entering the room, she saw it. *A bed!* A great, large bed with brass rings and brocade hangings! A bed with a mattress, and a featherbed, bolster pillows, and a down coverlet!

"*Ohh,*" she gasped, surprised, and felt the tears springing to her eyes. "Oh."

"You have spoken of a bed ever since your arrival here," he said, and she was surprised again, for she had not heard him come. "I know that you are uncomfortable with our simple sleeping spaces."

"But where did you find this?" Wynne asked him, touched that he cared for her that much, yet angry that his kindness made her own ire seem petty by comparison.

"I have traveled a bit in my life and knew what a bed was," he told her. "One of my sawyers is particularly clever at making furniture. I explained to him what it was I wanted, and together I think we have managed to get it right. The springs are deerhide for strength. They will not break beneath our combined weights. The mattress has been stuffed with a mixture of hay, straw, rose petals, and lavender. The featherbed and the coverlet will keep us comfortable, I promise you."

"And the pillows? Where did you obtain pillows?" she asked him.

"In Worcester when I went to serve in the shire court last month," he said with a grin. "I have surprised you, haven't I, Wynne?"

"You have indeed surprised me, Eadwine," she admitted.

"There will be other changes to come too," he promised her. "Two days' journey from Aelfdene is the manor of Aelfleah, whose lord is my distant cousin, Aldwine Athelsbeorn. His home has always been thought odd by all, for where the Great Chamber should be, Aldwine has instead built several rooms for privacy's sake. We will journey there one day soon and see exactly how he has done this. Then we will do it here at Aelfdene. Would that please you, Wynne?"

She nodded. "Aye, it would."

"Good! Now let us bathe, sweeting. I am anxious to try out our new bed. I have sent our nosy old Ealdraed off to spend her night with Gytha, so if you need help, it is I who will maid you."

The big tub stood awaiting them in its corner. Wynne undressed quickly, pinning her hair atop her head, and stepped into the warm water. Over the winter she had made several cakes of a fine soap which she had scented with lavender, that being the only dried herb she had that appealed to her in her pregnant state. She washed her face and was lathered and rinsed when he finally entered their tub.

Taking the soap from her, he turned her about and said, "Let me wash you, my love," and his lips nibbled lightly against the back of her damp neck.

He pulled her back against him, and immediately she could feel his persistent maleness against her. He was already engorged with his passion. His big hands, well-soaped, cupped her breasts and began to fondle them. His rough thumbs rubbed sensuously against her very sensitive nipples, even as bending over her his tongue licked about the shell of her ear.

"Do you know how much I desire you, Wynne?" he whispered softly to her.

"Aye," she said low. Oh, why were his hands so gentle and yet so provocative against her skin?

"I want you to desire me," he told her, and his tongue pushed into her ear to tickle it.

"No," she replied, but there was little conviction in her voice.

"Yes," he murmured, and while one hand grasped one of her breasts, the other slid lingeringly down her torso, his touch fiery and intimate. His lips kissed the side of her neck while a single finger slipped between her nether lips to find that sentient little pearl of her sex. Slowly, insistently, the tip of his finger stroked her, setting wildfires ablaze throughout her whole body.

Her upper teeth gnawed at her lower lip as she strove to maintain a control over herself; but her hips began to rotate seemingly of themselves, and she could not prevent a small groan from escaping from between her lips. She could feel him, hard and demanding, against her buttocks. "We will never finish our bathing," she managed to protest faintly, "and the water grows cold."

"Then wash me," he growled low, and turning her about, he kissed her with a hard kiss. "All of me!"

He held her in a light grip, an arm about her waist, as she began to soap him. Her breath was coming in short pants, for although she wanted to deny it, she was greatly aroused by this man who called himself her husband. Her breasts just touched his muscled, furred chest, and she blushed to see how thrusting and pointed her nipples were. "I cannot wash you properly if you do not release your hold on me, my lord," she finally said in an effort to regain some measure of self-control, and he instantly did.

"I do not want to impede you in your wifely duties," he teased, and chuckled at the pink flooding her cheeks.

Wynne tried to work with some sort of order. Unsmiling, she washed his chest and his arms, his shoulders and his neck. Taking her cloth, she washed his face and his ears, scolding him roundly as she did so. "Men! You are no better than little boys! Look at these ears, my lord! When on earth was the last time you washed them? Ears must be washed along with everything else!"

He chuckled at her, and his eyes were warm as he gazed down on her. This was what he had needed in his life. A young wife who scolded him, and whose passion—for despite her denials to the contrary, she was passionate—would keep him warm of a winter's night. He snatched the cloth playfully from her. "Let me see your ears, my lady wife! Ahh, yes, they are most perfect." He nipped at an earlobe and she shrieked.

"My lord Eadwine! You must behave yourself or I shall never get this done. The water is practically icy! Turn about that I may wash your back."

"Be gentle this time, lady," he begged her, remembering the last time she had washed his back.

Because this was a tub in which one could stand, and it had just been filled full, Wynne could not wash his legs and feet, and told him so. "You must do your own," she said, but he caught her hand in his and drew it down to his manhood.

"Will you not wash this randy piece of me, lady?" he pleaded softly, but did not release his hold upon her, even as with burning cheeks she dragged her cloth across his flesh. He held her gaze in his, willing her to touch him in a more intimate fashion. His lips brushed hers teasingly and, finally unable to help himself, he begged her with a single word, *"Please!"*

"Ahhh," she sighed, moved, unable to resist his plea, "you are cruel, my lord," and then her fingers closed over the great shaft of his manhood, fondling it gently, then stroking it until he thought he would expire of the simple pleasure she was offering.

"Tonight," he half groaned, "I will look into your face when I take you, my sweet wife. Do you know how very much I want to see your passion?" His arms wrapped about her and he kissed her hungrily, his lips almost tasting hers as he communicated his desire for her.

Wynne's arms slipped up and wound themselves about his neck. She sighed deeply as her breasts pressed hard against his chest. She was unable to help herself. She was eighteen years old and filled with the joy of life. Whether Madoc came or did not come, she could not deter this marvelous man in his intent. She didn't want to deter him. She wanted him to make love to her, and she wanted to make love to him in return.

"Not here," she whispered to him. "We cannot allow that wonderful bed to go to waste, Eadwine, my lord."

He climbed from the tub and, turning about, lifted her out, setting her upon the floor. He would have hurried, but Wynne would not allow it, explaining that if the bed were to get wet, it would take much effort to properly dry it. They dried each other carefully, and then Eadwine set her back that he might admire her natural beauty. Blushing, Wynne returned the compliment, her green eyes widening just slightly at the sight of his manhood, for he was certainly well-favored.

His hand reached out to caress her skin. "You are so fair," he said, his voice tender and filled with love. "I never knew a woman could be so fair." Reaching up, he loosed her long hair and it fell about her like a silken mantle. "It is as black as the night and as soft as satin," he observed. "Arvel has your hair."

"His father is also dark," Wynne said softly.

"I am his father," Eadwine Aethelhard told her. "Arvel is as much mine as he from whose seed he sprang. You cannot know, for not wanting to frighten you, I did not tell you, but when Arvel entered the world, the cord was wrapped about his neck. His color was good, however, but 'twas I who freed him and cleared his throat of mucus. 'Twas I who breathed the life into him."

Wynne stared at him, shocked. Her passion dissolved for the moment. "He might have died," she whispered, horrified not simply by his disclosure, but by the fact her stubborn determination to deliver her child alone might have cost him his life had Eadwine Aethelhard not come into the Great Chamber when he did.

"I was there to see him safely through the danger," Eadwine told her, correctly divining her thoughts. "I loved the boy from the moment I saw him. He will grow to be a strong and good man here at Aelfdene."

"Pray God he grows to be like you, my lord," Wynne answered him. "I could wish for no more than that." She put her arms about his neck and kissed his tenderly. "Thank you Eadwine, for seeing that my son lived when you could have as easily allowed him to die."

"I could never have allowed him to die, my wild Welsh girl," he told her. "Not when I love his mother so deeply. I will never make you unhappy, Wynne. *Never.*"

"Say it not, my lord," she told him. " 'Tis too great a promise to make."

He lifted her up in his arms and walked slowly toward their bed. "I will make you happier than you have ever been, my beautiful wife," he replied, setting her gently upon the coverlet, pressing her back amid the pillows, kissing her until she was dizzy with pleasure.

Happier than she had ever been. Was such a thing possible now? Once, oh it seemed so long ago, she had believed herself happier than any woman had a right to be. Once, long ago; but that long-ago time was gone; and she was beginning to realize, unlikely ever to come back. She caressed the back of his neck and felt his flesh prickle beneath her touch. Her fingers twined themselves through his thick ash-brown hair as once again his lips began to rain kisses upon her. His mouth was warm and just a little moist as he half kissed, half nibbled down the slender column of her throat.

She set his senses aflame. Her skin was like living silk beneath his touch, and perfumed with lavender. Her raven's-black hair was equally fragrant and soft. He could feel the blood coursing throughout her body wherever his lips passed. He moved to suckle upon her nipples, which seemed to push themselves at him, and he was selfishly glad her mother's milk had not come in, that he not be denied this pleasure.

His mouth upon her breasts all but destroyed her. Wynne could never remember her body being this sensitive, this attuned to a man; but perhaps it had just been so long, she reasoned guiltily with herself. She tingled all over with each tug of his lips, and a dull ache began to permeate her lower belly. She moaned low, and by the subtle slight movements of her body, urged him onward, but the thegn was not to be rushed. He had desired her from the first moment he had ever seen her, and their earlier couplings, when she had been pregnant with Arvel, had but whetted his carnal appetites.

Drawing himself level with her once more, they began to

kiss and caress each other simultaneously. Her lips were bruised with his kisses, but she did not want him to cease. Her fingers found battle wounds upon his skin as they passed teasingly over his flesh. She twisted from his embrace and kissed each roughened patch of skin, and he shivered at her touch. He rolled upon his back and lifted her atop him.

"You do not fear passion, do you?" he said, smiling up into her flushed face.

"Nay, not even from the beginning," she told him honestly, and leaned forward to nibble upon his lower lip, her breasts brushing the wiry hair upon his chest in a provocative fashion.

Unable to restrain himself, he stroked them, saying, "I want to prolong this time with you, my wild Welsh girl, but my own desires are near to bursting. Let me but have you once, and then I shall spend an eternity giving you pleasure!"

Wynne smiled down at him. "You are extravagant in your avowals of love, my lord," she teased him. "I, too, am eager to consummate this union!" Then to his great surprise she moved back just slightly, her green eyes half closed and glittering; and with a deep sigh she sheathed him languidly within her eager body. "You wanted to see my face when we mated this night," she said softly, looking down into his eyes. "Does this please you, my lord?"

"Nay," he told her, and then he quickly reversed their positions so that she now lay beneath him, "but this does! A wife should submit beneath her husband, my wild Welsh girl!"

Wynne laughed up into his face. "Why?" she demanded.

"Because a man is master of his household," came the answer, and he began to move upon her slowly.

"There will never be any peace between us, my lord, unless you learn that I am your equal within the privacy of our chamber," Wynne told him, and she forced herself to remain perfectly still.

"My equal?" He began to thrust with sharp, little movements of his hips and buttocks.

"In our bed," she replied, gasping softly, and then, pulling his head down to hers, she kissed him, her tongue pushing into his mouth to taunt him.

"My wild Welsh witch!" he groaned, and her tongue licked at his throat, her teeth nipped at his earlobe. His movements became faster.

"Your equal!" she persisted. She didn't know how much longer she could keep this up.

"Aye!" he half sobbed, and beneath him she returned his passion so that they moved in tandem, their bellies crushing at one another, their buttocks straining, their thighs slippery with their efforts.

Wynne felt the delicious remembered feelings of high passion beginning to catch at her. Releasing her grip on her self-control, she began to soar, following after the pleasure as it moved from plateau to plateau in search of perfect fulfillment. She could hear her own heart thumping wildly in her ears as the crisis neared for them both. Eadwine's handsome face was contorted with his raging desires and, as his passion burst, he howled a warrior's cry of victory, collapsing atop her.

Now Wynne could feel his own heart against hers. The sensation of his love juices flooding her was acute. She was but a moment behind him in ecstasy, sliding into a semiconscious state as satisfaction and delighted contentment overwhelmed her, rendering her weak with pleasure. For a long minute they lay together, and Wynne realized that she liked the weight of him upon her. There was something comforting about him; and even though this tumultuous coming together of theirs had occurred on the first anniversary of her marriage to Madoc of Powys, Wynne could feel nothing but happiness. Madoc was gone from her life as mysteriously as he had appeared in it; but in his place was a man who loved her.

She kissed the top of his head, and, looking up at her, he smiled. Wynne could not help but smile back, and in the many nights of passion that followed that first one, she came to realize that she loved him. Not with the same desperation or wild ardor as she loved Madoc, but with a quieter and deeper feeling. The autumn came and it was with joy that Wynne realized she was once again with child. Eadwine Aethelhard's child.

Her husband, for indeed she had grown to think of him as her husband, was delighted. Baldhere made wickedly bawdy remarks about his father's sexual prowess. The other women of the family were pleased for her, for it made Wynne truly one of them. Only Caddaric Aethelmaere was displeased and bitter.

"Are you certain she whelps your cub?" he demanded rudely of his father one October evening. "These Welsh wenches are said to be loose in their ways. You spawned but two children with my mother. Why should this woman now be ripening with your seed? It could be the bastard of some stableman or cowherd, and you in your dotage, Father, preen and prance about the hall like some young stallion trumpeting an accomplishment of which you are probably not capable."

Wynne, seated at her loom by the main fire pit, rose to her feet and moved to her husband's side. Her small hand snaked out to hit her stepson with a fierce blow. "How dare you?" she said to him. "How dare you insult your father so? And me as well? You do not have the right, Caddaric Aethelmaere. Your father, *my husband*, is more man at forty-three than you will ever be for all your women! Your mother, may God assoil her kind soul, was incapable of bearing children successfully after you and your brother were born. It happens sometimes with women. That is no reflection upon your father, who remained always faithful to her in her lifetime, else you should see familiar faces amongst the younger serfs.

"But she is dead now, and your father has taken me to be his wife. I am young, and I am fertile. I will give your father as many children as he will give me, Caddaric Aethelmaere! If you cannot keep a civil tongue in your head in future, then you may not come into our hall. I will not be insulted, nor will I allow your father to be," Wynne finished, and then she returned to her loom.

"She is overproud, your *Danish* wife," Caddaric Aethelmaere said, rubbing his cheek, amazed by the strength of her blow, which had come close to staggering him; but only, he reassured himself, because she had taken him by surprise. If he had her under him between his strong thighs, he would have had her screaming for mercy.

"*Danish* wife or no," replied Eadwine, "Wynne is my wife, and the child she carries my child, and the son she bore last spring mine by right of adoption."

The term *Danish* wife that his son had used referred to the fact that their union had not yet been blessed by the clergy. It was a common practice in England among many Saxons for the men of wealth to have two or more wives at a single time if they so chose, despite the reality of the Christian religion which was now dominant in the land. The old ways died hard, and there were many reasons other than children for a man to take a wife. Powerful men married for wealth and more power, rich men for more riches; but there was always love to consider. The *Danish* wife was the woman a man took sometimes for the sake of love. A wife taken under canon law was usually wed for more practical purposes. The children of a *Danish* wife, or indeed any of a man's concubines, were considered as legitimate as the children of the wife a man wed only for the sake of power and gold. Concubines, however, had not the prestige and status of a wife or a *Danish* wife. A *Danish* wife was as respected and as honored as any other wife.

From that night on, Caddaric Aethelmaere kept a guard on his tongue where his father's marriage and his father's wife were concerned. It was not that he felt any less bitter, but Eadgyth Crookback warned him that he endangered his own inheritance with his loose tongue.

"You are now legally entitled to inherit Aelfdene Manor as your father's eldest son," she warned him, "but if you continue to offend Eadwine Aethelhard, it is his right to divide his lands amongst whomever he chooses, or even disinherit you entirely. He has already adopted Wynne's son, Arvel, and your stepmother will give your father a child in the spring. It could be another male child. You call your father old, but he is not. Once we women teased Wynne about her *elderly* husband, and she blushingly confided to us that he is a vigorous lover. He uses her each night, and sometimes more than once, my husband! He could get half-a-dozen children on her before he tires of passion, Caddaric! Continue to offend Wynne and your father and you could find yourself without a manor house and but five hides of land only when my father dies."

So following his wife's advice, for Caddaric Aethelmaere had always respected Eadgyth Crookback's opinion, the thegn's eldest son ceased his attacks on Wynne and his father. The two men were at constant sword points, nonetheless, over the politics of the day. King Edward was more saint than ruler. The son of Emma of Normandy and Aethelred, called the "Unready," he had been raised in his mother's country and come to the throne only upon the death of two half brothers who numbered among his several predecessors. His wife was the daughter of the late Earl Godwin, also called Eadgyth; but the marriage was in name only, for Edward was a deeply religious man who would have entered a monastery had he not been prevented from it, being in the direct line of descent.

His celibacy, however, meant there would be no children of his union with Godwin's daughter. Edward had chosen as his heir his cousin, William the Bastard, duke of Normandy. Godwin did not approve the choice, but Godwin was now dead, and his son, Harold, took up where his father had left off. Edward was the last of Cedric's line. He would be the final king of the blood of Wessex. Royal blood did not run in Harold Godwinson's veins, and yet he aspired to Edward's throne once it became vacant.

Men like Caddaric Aethelmaere supported Harold. He was Saxon English, and the fact that royal blood did not run in his veins did not matter to them. Eadwine Aethelhard, on the other hand, believed that King Edward's choice must be honored. Besides, Eadwine had told Wynne, he did not believe that Harold could stem the tide of any invasion from the Viking north. William could. Harold would plunge England into one war or another, for men like Harold liked war. It was their business. William, on the other hand, preferred peace, although he was an excellent soldier. War cost a man his gold. Peace made a man more gold. So father and son argued back and forth nightly in a battle that neither could resolve.

Wynne enjoyed their disputes to a point, for she was learning all about English politics. She found it interesting, and wondered when Duke William claimed his inheritance someday whether he would be content to remain on the English side of Offa's Dyke, or whether he would come with his knights to invade Wales. Would Gwernach be in danger? Or St. Bride's? She often wondered how her family was getting on and hoped that one day Eadwine would allow her to go back to Gwernach for a visit. Would Enid still be alive?

She sighed, and then her hand went to her belly as the child moved. Two children in two years. She wanted to give Eadwine more babies, but she didn't want to become enceinte for at least another two years after this child was born. It was very wearing on her, for all her youth and vigor. To that end she was secretly making and storing vaginal pessary. Men were so silly about things like that.

Martinmas came. The cottars and geburas arrived to bring the thegn his rents. They celebrated with roast goose and baked apples. Arvel already had several teeth and gnawed happily upon a leg bone. He was a beautiful baby, with his father's blue eyes and dark hair. He was also a happy and secure child who made his needs easily known by shouting "Ba!" and pointing to whatever it was he desired. To Eadwine's delight, the baby would always call out "Da!" whenever he appeared within the infant's view. Arvel loved everyone with the exception of Caddaric Aethelmaere. He grew strangely quiet in his presence, as if sensing an enemy.

At Christ's Mass Wynne thought of Nesta, of whom she had given little thought over the past months. Nesta's baby would be a year old now. She missed Madoc's merry sister and wondered if Nesta ever thought of her. It was another lifetime, Wynne considered, for just the briefest moment saddened. She had been abducted more than a year ago, and yet despite the beautiful summer and the mild winter they were now experiencing, Madoc had never come for her. Sometimes she wondered if he were yet alive, or had he died of a broken heart as the wicked Brys of Cai had predicted. It didn't matter anymore. She was Eadwine's wife. Soon she would bear his child. She loved him.

■Chapter 15

On the fifth day of the month of April in the year 1063, two days after her nineteenth birthday, the thegn of Aelfdene's wife gave birth to a daughter. Eadwine Aethelhard was as delighted as Wynne.

" 'Twill save us difficulty," she said. "For all his silence, Caddaric remains jealous. He will not think of his half sister as a threat."

"I have a gift for you to honor this occasion," Eadwine told her. "I have built a new cottage and raised to the rank of gebura one of my cottars. He is, it seems, clever with bees, and we need a beekeeper at Aelfdene. The rents from the land the beekeeper hold of me are to be yours, my love. When our daughter marries one day, they will serve as part of her dowry."

"How wonderful!" Wynne said, and then she laughed. " 'Tis a sweet gift you have given me, my lord."

"Have you thought of a name for her?" he asked, looking down dotingly upon the baby who had his ash-brown hair and eyes he suspected would turn as green as her mother's. She was not all delicate like Wynne either, but a large baby, more a Saxon child.

"Averel," Wynne told him. "I want to name her Averel for the month in which she was born. 'Tis a pretty name, and she will be a pretty girl one day, for all her sturdiness. She is certainly your daughter, Eadwine. See! She has your nose and mouth, and her hands are very like yours."

He chuckled, pleased. "Averel Aethelhardsdatter. Aye, I like it too, my wild Welsh girl!"

"Da!" Arvel tugged at Eadwine's kirtle insistently. He was thirteen months old now and wise enough to know that another center of attention was taking this big man he adored away from him.

With a smile Eadwine lifted the boy up into his lap. "Look,

Arvel, my son. You have a baby sister. Her name is Averel and it will be your duty to protect her always, until she is wed one day and safe within another man's house."

Arvel leaned forward and peered at the swaddled infant. He found her singularly uninteresting, so, putting his thumb in his mouth, he cuddled back against his foster father. "Da," he sighed happily, content in the warmth of Eadwine's arms.

Baldhere Armstrang took in this most loving and domestic picture as he entered into the Great Chamber. "Old Ealdraed tells me I have a baby sister," he said, smiling at his father and stepmother. Bending, he looked down at the baby and then he chuckled. "She's got your stamp on her, Father," he said. "What is her name?"

"Averel," came the reply.

" 'Tis pretty. I'm sorry I won't get to see her grow up, but a messenger has just come to say that Aeldra's father is near death. We must leave Aelfdene as soon as possible. She and I will go this very day. The others will pack our belongings and follow with the children."

"Have you told your brother?" Eadwine asked.

Baldhere made a grimace. "I did, and what do you think he said to me? That Eadgyth's father persisted in living on, thereby robbing him of his rightful inheritance and the rank of thegn, while I, his junior, would now rank above him. How my good fortune irritates him." What Baldhere did not say to his father was that his elder brother had concluded that he would probably come into his inheritance of Aelfdene sooner than he would gain the remainder of Eadgyth's dowry, for Eadwine would surely wear himself out futtering his young wife, while his father-in-law cared for himself as assiduously as one would care for a newborn infant king.

"Come and bid us a final farewell before you leave," Eadwine said to his younger son. "I did well when I matched you with Aeldra Swanneck, Baldhere. She's a good breeder as well as a good wife. Remember what I have taught you about husbanding the land, and follow the wise example of our antecedents. Keep adding to your estate whenever you get the opportunity. That is the best advice I can give you."

"I will not forget, Father." Baldhere arose and departed the Great Chamber.

"I will miss Baldhere and his women," Wynne said, "but

then all of the women at Aelfdene are pleasant to be with, my lord. That is what I missed the most at Raven's Rock. I had only my maidservant, Megan, for company. At Gwernach I had my grandmother and my sisters. Although Caitlin and Dilys are difficult at best to get along with, my younger sister, Mair, was not." She yawned.

He could see how heavy her eyelids were, and said, "You are tired, sweeting. Birthing a babe is hard work, I know. Rest now." Rising, he lifted Arvel up into his arms.

"Aye, birthing is difficult work," she replied, "and well you know it, for you have been with me through both my labors, Eadwine." She smiled up at him, feeling a strong burst of affection for this man. She was certainly beginning to really accept him as her husband, although the Church still had not sent a priest to Aelfdene to look after the spiritual well-being of its people and to bless their union. It was really up to her to press the issue. Yet she had not. What would ecclesiastical opinion be on her status?

She was not fearful for Averel, for Eadwine claimed their daughter for his own child, and legally adopted Arvel. Although she was making peace with her situation, in the deepest recesses of her heart she still longed for Madoc and for their magical home at Raven's Rock. It saddened her that the prince did not know of his son. Oh, why had he not come to find her?

Eadwine bent down and kissed her brow, holding onto Arvel as the tiny boy leaned forward to hug her, planting a wet kiss upon her cheek at the same time.

"Maaa," Arvel said. He was such a happy, contented child.

"Sleep well, my love," the thegn told her, and took her son off.

She listened to his footsteps as they descended the stairs, Arvel's little voice chattering his baby babble which, to her amusement, Eadwine seemed to completely understand. Wynne smiled to herself, thinking how fortunate she and her son were to have fallen into Eadwine Aethelhard's hands. As for Averel, she was the thegn's daughter. Wynne looked down at the new baby. She was amazingly pretty for a newborn, with a head full of dark brown curls and healthy, rosy cheeks.

"What a lucky little girl you are, Averel Aethelhardsdatter," she told the baby. "You are your father's only daughter, and he will spoil you totally, I have not a doubt, for he is a kind man."

She heard footsteps upon the stairs and looked up as Caddaric Aethelmaere entered the Great Chamber scowling.

"So you've whelped the brat at last, have you?" was his greeting to her.

"You have a sister, Caddaric," Wynne told him in even tones, but her temper was close to flaring.

"Well, let's have a look at her," he said condescendingly, and Wynne lifted the edge of the blanket that protected her daughter's face. Caddaric stared down at the baby. "What's her name?" he demanded.

"Averel," was the short reply.

"She looks like Father," he noted dryly.

"Aye," Wynne answered in dulcet tones, but she was pleased. It was the closest Caddaric would ever come to acknowledging his half sister's legitimacy, but having done so, Wynne knew he would never deny Averel, for Caddaric possessed a strange sense of honor and a strong sense of blood ties.

"She should have been my child," he growled at her.

"You would not have wanted a daughter, Caddaric," Wynne said quietly.

"I would have given you a son," he said bitterly. "My father is old, and his seed is weak. I would have spawned a son on you had my father not stolen you away from me."

"When will you remember that it is your father who is lord here and not you, Caddaric? Your father did not steal me from you, for you never had me to begin with, and you know it to be so. Why do you persist in this fantasy?"

"I could get sons on you, Welsh woman," he said stubbornly. "My father did not need more children. He has two healthy sons and a host of grandchildren, thanks to my brother. He did not need a young wife and additional children. I, however, need sons, and the useless creatures I have shackled and surrounded myself with cannot produce even a feeble daughter! *I need you!* You are magic!"

She doubted that her stepson would ever like her, but Wynne realized that she had to make him face the reality of his situation, and now was as good a time as any. "Caddaric, answer me a question," she probed gently. "Have you ever in your life been seriously ill?"

He thought long, his broad brow puckering with his concentration, and then he said, "Once. Only once."

"Tell me about it," she pressed him.

"The year before I married Eadgyth," he said, "my cheeks became all swollen and ached. I looked like a frog when he courts his lady. I ran a great fever for several days. Afterward it was said that my mother feared for my life." He chuckled with his memory. "My cock became all swollen too, and God knows I have been more than well-endowed. Better than many, I am assured, but it was twice its size during my illness. I quite admit to being disappointed when it returned to normal," Caddaric finished with a leer.

"It is unlikely that you will ever produce children," Wynne told him bluntly.

"What?"

"I am a healer, Caddaric, as was my grandmother and my mother before me. The illness you have described to me is the swelling sickness. When a child becomes ill of it, there is little difficulty. The same is true of a young girl or young boy; but a man or an older boy can suffer greatly from the swelling sickness, especially if it affects their male organs, as the illness obviously did yours. The sickness burns the life from the male seed. I know this, for it is part of my healer's wisdom."

"You lie, Welsh witch!" he raged at her. His cheeks were scarlet above his beard.

"Nay, Caddaric, I do not lie, nor do I mean to be cruel to you," Wynne told him sympathetically. She could almost feel sorry for him, and she could certainly feel his pain. "It is a well-known fact among healers that the seed of men and young men is rendered virtually lifeless by the swelling sickness. It has always been thus, though we know not why."

"My childlessness cannot be my fault," he said stubbornly. "It is Eadgyth's fault, for she is frail and unable to conceive; but that loss is as much hers as mine. I do not blame Eadgyth. She is a good wife."

"What of the others?" Wynne asked him. "What of Berangari, Dagian, Aelf, and little Haesel? They are strong and healthy girls, yet they do not conceive, Caddaric. The fault lies with you, and yet it is not really a fault but a cruel mischance of fate that sent the swelling sickness to afflict you when it did. You are unlikely to give a child to any woman, even me."

"You are a healer, Welsh woman," he said grimly. "Can you concoct no potion or brew that would help me, if indeed you are correct in your assumptions?"

"There is nothing," Wynne told him bluntly. It was long past time someone was honest with this man. He had to make peace with himself for all their sakes.

"*Nothing?* I think you lie! No man with my appetite for female flesh could possess lifeless seed! It is the women who are responsible for my lack! *It cannot be me!*" Yet behind the open anger in his voice, Wynne could see the desperation and fear lurking in his eyes.

"Rarely, but only rarely," she told him, not wanting to arouse any hope in his heart, "a man who has suffered the swelling sickness does conceive a child. Perhaps some remedies that I know of for arousing the senses can help you to achieve the impossible, Caddaric. When I have recovered from Averel's birth, I will put my mind to it. I will dose your women as well; but now leave me. I am weary and would sleep."

He departed the Great Chamber without another word or even a backward glance at her or her baby. Wynne sighed deeply, feeling both sorrow and irritation toward Caddaric Aethelmaere. Men like Caddaric always measured their manhood by the number of men they killed; women they raped or seduced; and children, sons in particular, that they spawned. Caddaric's reputation was strong where killing, raping, and seduction were concerned. His complete inability to produce children of either sex was a glaring public failure that left, at least in his eyes, his personal stature in grave question. Still, she would see what she could do to help him, despite all his virulent unkindness to her. They would never be friends, but she knew it would please Eadwine if his wife and his elder son were not enemies.

Aye, she thought, sleepily. She did want to please Eadwine. He strove to make her happy. Did she truly love him? Aye, not as she had loved Madoc, but then she doubted that she would ever love anyone as she had loved her prince. *Madoc,* she wondered as she slid into sleep, *why have you not come?*

Wynne. She was never out of his thoughts. It had been a year and a half since she had disappeared. Sometimes in moments of dark discouragement he wondered if she was even still alive. If she had ever really existed. Wynne of Gwernach, with her long, black hair and her green, green eyes. It was as if the earth had opened up and swallowed her.

For over a year they had combed the countryside back and forth, over and over again seeking any word of her. Madoc had finally decided that his wife could not possibly be in England. Ruari Ban had obviously hidden her from public sight and taken her with him into Brittany. He called his men home and went about the painful business of waiting for Einion, who had personally followed after the Irish slaver, to return home to Raven's Rock. When he did, his news was discouraging.

"I followed Ruari Ban, my lord, first to Brittany, then to Italy, where I finally caught up with him about to take passage with his cargo of slaves to Byzantium."

"Did he tell you where Wynne was?" Madoc demanded eagerly. He had grown thin in the months that Einion had been away.

"She is not with him, my lord," Einion said gently. "At first he pretended to not even know what I was talking about. He would accept no bribe from me. It was only when I pressed the matter more strongly in a, ah, physical way, that he would admit to having had possession of my lady."

"Where is she?" There were great purple circles beneath Madoc's dark blue eyes. He hardly slept at all now.

"There was nothing I could do to make him tell me where, my lord. He lives in utter, total terror of your brother, Brys of Cai. He believes that should he betray him, the bishop can reach out and find him wherever he may be. He believes that your brother will kill him should he dare to break faith with him. I could have torn this Ruari Ban apart limb by limb and he still would not tell me what I wished to know. His fear is that complete, my lord.

"I did, however, in a roundabout way, discover one thing that will be of help to us. There was a young boy among Ruari Ban's slaves that the Irishman intended for some nobleman in Byzantium. The slave is, as his reputation has said, kind-hearted. The boy was allowed a certain measure of freedom. Overhearing my conversation with Ruari Ban, the boy came to me when I left him. He told me he had been with his master for many months as the slaver made his way eastward. He said if I would buy his freedom and help him to return to his home in Ireland, he would aid me in my quest."

"And did he?" the prince asked.

"Aye, my lord, he did indeed. His purchase cost me dearly, but 'twas well worth it. When they landed in Wales from Ireland, Ruari Ban left his men and his cargo about ten miles from Castle Cai. He had received a message to go there to see the bishop. When he rejoined them several days later, he had a beautiful dark-haired woman in his possession whom he treated with much care. The boy remembers this distinctly because Ruari Ban allowed the woman to ride behind him on his horse instead of walking her with the other slaves. Shortly before they were scheduled to arrive at Worcester, Ruari Ban departed his troop again, taking the woman with him. When he met them in Worcester, she was no longer with him. It is obvious to me, my lord, that the lady Wynne never left England!" Einion concluded triumphantly.

"But we have been unable to find her," Madoc answered him despairingly. "Where can she possibly be, unless, of course, the slaver murdered her and buried her body." He grew pale at the thought, hating his helplessness in the matter.

"My lord, she is here," Einion said firmly. "Our men have obviously missed her, for the territory in which they sought the lady Wynne is a vast one. Now we have narrowed it down to *somewhere* near Worcester. You and I will go together visiting each thegn in the area until we have found her."

The prince nodded slowly, a small bit of hope springing back into his heart. "We will consider Worcester the center of the circle," he said, "and we will work outward from the town. First to the north, then to the east, then to the west, and lastly to the south. We must start soon, Einion, for Earl Harold and Gruffydd, our king, have been skirmishing with each other like two stags fighting over a doe.

"Harold seeks to impress his own king, Edward, in hopes that Edward will change his will and name Harold his heir instead of Duke William of Normandy. Gruffydd will soon call out his liegemen; but if I am not here, I cannot answer that call. I care not for this battle of power between the mighty! I want only to find Wynne again; to bring her and our child home in safety."

"Will not Gruffydd ap Llywelyn be angry with you for ignoring his call to arms?" Einion queried.

"When I have my wife and child home again, I will explain to him why I could not be here for him. He will understand. Wynne is his kinswoman, however distant. Besides, why should we waste the summer playing these war games when it will all come to nothing in the end, as it always does? Why the Saxons feel that in their boredom they must harry the Welsh, I do not know," Madoc concluded.

"Perhaps," Einion answered him, "because we in our boredom harry the Saxons and steal their cattle, my lord." The big man's eyes were twinkling.

"The Saxons do indeed have fine cattle," Madoc agreed with a small smile, "but I will not let myself get swept up in this power struggle. Though my family and title be old, this small mountainous realm of Powys-Wenwynwyn is of little account to the mighty. Gruffydd will certainly survive without me."

In this conjecture, however, Madoc was wrong. The news was always slow in getting to Raven's Rock. The prince did not know that in early winter England's most powerful earl, Harold Godwinson, had raided into Wales, burning Rhuddlan, Gruffydd's estate. The king and his family had barely escaped with their lives, and Gruffydd was furious.

Gruffydd ap Llywelyn was the son of Llywelyn ap Seisyll, the king of Gwyndd, and Angharad, daughter of Deheubarth's king. As a boy he was not thought of as an impressive leader by those around him; but as a young man he grew into a great warrior, drawing men by the score to his banner, much to everyone's surprise. Gruffydd ap Llywelyn, the man, had a charm and magnetism about him no boy could have ever possessed.

He had been forced to fight for his inheritance of Gwyndd. In the same year he won it, he conquered Powys as well and defeated the Mercians in a decisive battle when they had dared to intrude on his territory. He then allied himself with Earl Aelfgar of Mercia, sealing their treaty by marrying Aelfgar's daughter, Edith. Gruffydd then went on to conquer Deheubarth, his mother's homeland; but all the while he maintained a fierce hatred of the Saxon earls of Wessex. First Godwin, who had sought Edith of Mercia for his own son, and now the son, Harold, who boasted that when he killed Gruffydd one day, he would take Edith for a wife.

With the coming of spring, Harold came into Wales again, traveling this time beneath a banner of truce; making peace and exchanging hostages with all who would meet with him. This had the effect of weakening Gruffydd's position, for the majority of Welsh lords did not want to fight. They wanted peace. Harold was offering peace even as Gruffydd sent out his messengers calling his liegemen to him for yet another assault on the Saxon men of Wessex.

Gruffydd realized immediately that Harold was attempting to take the threat of the Welsh from his flank, allowing him to concentrate totally on holding England against the Norman duke, William. When the time came, William would be swift to claim his rightful inheritance. Gruffydd did not know William of Normandy, but by his reputation as a great warrior. He knew, however, that William would have all he could manage, holding England against Harold and his ilk, to be bothered with the Welsh, and there were the Norse to consider as well. If the Welsh helped William by harrying Harold, Gruffydd knew there could even be something of value in it for them.

Harold, however, knew this too. He didn't want to have to fight the Normans and the Welsh at the same time. It would be a losing game. Gruffydd ap Llywelyn controlled most of Wales. By destroying him, Harold would take from the Welsh the only man capable of leading them as a nation. To this end Earl Harold went about his business of undermining Gruffydd's support among his jealous and petty nobles. He succeeded far better than even he had anticipated.

Madoc was not aware of this, for his holding was too remote for Harold to even be bothered about. The prince was wending his way into England even as Harold was coming to Wales. While Madoc spent the spring and summer of the year carefully combing the English countryside in a twenty-mile radius leading out from the town of Worcester, the Welsh king was fighting for his very life. It was a battle he lost in early August, when he was assassinated by several of his own men suspected of being in Harold's pay. The murderers did not live long enough to enjoy their ill-gotten gains. Gruffydd's sons took swift retribution. Harold capped his triumph by announcing that he was taking Gruffydd's widow, Edith of Mercia, as his wife.

Edith's younger brother, now Mercia's earl, was not strong enough to protest this breach of good taste, or even resist Wessex's earl. Harold's *Danish* wife, also an Edith, and the mother of his three sons, accepted the situation as one of necessity. Now Harold had virtually all of England beneath his control, after the king of course. All that was left was for Edward to die.

At Aelfdene, Eadwine and Caddaric quarreled even more virulently about the political situation. Eadwine continued to support the king's decision to name the Norman duke his heir. Caddaric continued to believe Harold should be king. As the summer days shortened and moved toward the autumn, there was hardly a meal that was not disturbed by the two men arguing the situation.

"Harold is a common Saxon berserker," Eadwine insisted one evening as the dispute broke out anew.

"He has the people's support," Caddaric returned.

"Humph," his father snorted. "The people. The people do not rule, and their support can be bought with a ha'penny's worth of ale, you fool! Harold cannot hold England against the Norse! They seem to believe that they have a claim on this land too. Do you think they will politely step aside when the day comes and support Harold? 'Tis an idiot's belief! Only William of Normandy can hold England. His reputation as a war lord is both fearful and to be feared. Once William is in firm control, the Norse will not dare to oppose him."

"The Norman duke is a foreigner!" Caddaric exploded. "You would support a foreigner over Harold? 'Tis treasonous, I tell you!"

"Treasonous?" Eadwine leapt to his feet. "You dare to call me treasonous, you ungrateful whelp?" The thegn reached for the dagger at his waist, but Wynne stayed his hand.

"Caddaric," she said angrily, "leave the hall and the board this instant! You are not to return until you have apologized to your father. I will not have this constant bickering at my table any longer!"

Caddaric opened his mouth to protest, but his wife hissed furiously in his ear, "Wynne is right, my lord! *Come now!*"

Eadgyth then threw Wynne a look of support and, with the other women, hurried Caddaric from the hall.

Eadwine slumped to his seat, and Wynne refilled his goblet with strong red wine, which he quickly drank down. "I want another son," he said in a determined tone.

"You have Baldhere, and Baldhere has two sons now," Wynne told him gently. "If Caddaric displeases you, then name Baldhere as your heir. It is his sons who will eventually possess Aelfdene at any rate, my dear lord."

"Nay," he replied. "I want a son of your loins for my heir!" He stood and grasped her tightly by the wrist. "Come, my wild Welsh girl. I am hot to fuck you and make a new son for Aelfdene!" He pulled her toward the stairs leading to the Great Chamber.

It was no good arguing with him when he got like this, Wynne knew. More and more, Caddaric Aethelmaere was getting on Eadwine's nerves. If only Eadgyth's father would die, that Caddaric might have his own lands and attain the rank of thegn in his own right. Then he would take his women and depart, leaving them in peace. The constant arguing wasn't good for Eadwine.

In the Great Chamber she twisted out of his grasp, laughing softly, one hand outstretched to fend him off. "Nay, my lord stallion," she said playfully, "you will not tear my gown as you have done in the past."

"My storeroom is filled with beautiful rich cloth," he replied. "I give it all to you, sweeting. You can make a hundred new gowns." He reached for her again.

Wynne danced out of his way. "Nay!" she said in the firm voice one would use with a recalcitrant child. "I have better things to do with my days than to sew meekly by the fire. Besides, you know I abhor waste. Let me disrobe for you, and then I will undress you, Eadwine." Her voice was now seductive and soft. She smiled enticingly at him, removed the gold circlet and the prim white linen veil from her dark head and laid them aside.

"Very well," he agreed, slouching back into an armed chair, a half smile upon his face. She knew well how to handle him, Eadwine thought, amused. He did not resent it, however, for everything she did, he realized, was for him and for the children.

There was no selfishness in her. She was a truly amazing
woman.

Wynne could see that the anger had now drained out of him,
and she was relieved. She slipped off her red tunic dress, laying it aside; her yellow under tunic and linen chemise followed. She wore no footwear within the house. Wynne raised
her arms to unfasten her ear bobs, putting them with her clothing. Slowly she undid her single, thick braid, combing her
black hair free of tangles with her fingers.

"Put your hands behind your head," he ordered her softly, and
then, sitting back, took in the lush beauty of her. Her firm young
breasts had grown fuller with childbirth, and their nipples had
darkened from coral pink to a deeper coral. Her belly was flat,
and yet there was a roundness to it that was most pleasing to his
eye. Her limbs were well-fleshed, but certainly not fat. He would
never tire of looking at her, he decided as, sensing his thoughts,
Wynne lowered her arms and came forward to stand before him.

Gently she pulled him to his feet and began to undress him.
First his kirtle with its decorated neck opening. Then his under
tunic and sherte. He kicked his house shoes off as, kneeling,
Wynne began to unfasten the cross-gartering on his braccos
and roll them down off his feet. Her hands teased at his thighs
and legs, sending shivers of hot anticipation through him; but
when she grasped his half-roused manhood in her hand and
brought it to her lips, he could not restrain the groan that burst
from his throat.

She held him firmly, her pointed little tongue encircling the
sensitive tip of his member. Her other hand reached beneath
him to cup and fondle his pouch. Then she took him into the
warm cavern of her mouth, suckling upon him strongly, even
as he began to shudder with the fierce passion she was arousing in him. His hands reached down, fingers tangling amid the
raven's-dark floss of her hair, kneading her scalp with more urgent motion until finally he managed to cry out to her,
"Enough!" As she loosed her grip on him, he dragged her to
her feet, his mouth finding hers in a scalding kiss.

Wynne slipped her arms about his neck, her naked body
pressing against his naked body, feeling the hard length of him
beating insistently against her thigh. He pressed her back onto
their bed, spreading her legs, which lay over the edge, wide;
kneeling before her to lean forward, that he might love her in

the same manner in which she had just loved him. Her love juices flowed almost instantly and she gasped, squirming beneath his tongue, which was never quiet; moving here and there with skilled delicacy until she was half mad with the pleasure he offered and she so greedily took. He pushed himself even farther forward, his artful tongue pressing into her very passage to stroke and tease her until she was whimpering with a desire that could not be assuaged.

"Please!" she begged him.

His tongue licked the warm flesh of her inner thighs, and he murmured, "Not yet, my wild Welsh girl."

She almost screamed as his tongue moved over her mound, over her belly, tickled at her navel and swept up toward her breasts. His own hard body followed, pushing her down into the mattress and the featherbed with his big-boned weight. "You're killing me," she half sobbed, and he laughed low.

"I want to consume you completely," he growled in her ear, kissing it, and then his mouth was on hers again, drinking in her kisses, tasting her, tasting himself on her tongue and lips. He forced her arms over her head, jockeying her between his two thick thighs, his free hand guiding his raging manhood to the mark.

With a sob Wynne thrust herself up to meet his plunging weapon, encasing him eagerly within her sheath, tearing her hands free of his grip that she might embrace him. Fiercely he plumbed her depths, and with each stroke Wynne felt herself whirling out of control. It had never been as wild between them before. Her nails raked his back, but he didn't even seem to notice as he thrust and withdrew, thrust and withdrew, his buttocks tight with his efforts. The passion between them was quite equal.

"A son!" he groaned in her ear. *"I want a son of you, my wild and sweet Welsh wife!"*

Wynne heard him and she understood his words, but her own desire was so great at this moment that she could but concentrate upon it. Her body began to respond violently to his loving, great racking shudders tearing through her even as she felt his own passion breaking, flooding her secret garden with his rich seed. It was sweet! Too sweet, and she was going to die of it she thought as she fell into the endless darkness; falling, falling, falling until there was nothing left of her, but then her eyes opened. *She was alive.* A marvelously satisfying feeling permeated her from the tingling soles of her feet to the top of her head. Eadwine lay sprawled by her side, panting. Reaching out, she took his hand in hers and, squeezing it first, raised it to her lips and kissed his fingers.

"I adore you, Wynne," he said quietly in response, and she heard the deep love in his voice.

"And I love you, Eadwine," she responded, knowing even as she said it that it was very true. How could she not love this kind and good man who had been so patient with her? How could she not love her daughter's father? It did not mean that she did not love her son's father, but it was almost two years now since she had been abducted from Wales; and in all that time Madoc had never come nor even sent a message to let her know he would come. She could not wait forever. She had made peace with herself at long last. Raising herself on an elbow, she looked down into Eadwine Aethelhard's bearded face. "Aye, my lord," she said softly, "I love you well," and her forest-green eyes were wet with tears; but she did not know if her tears were of happiness or sorrow.

"Wynne!" He cried her name joyfully, his whole face alight with his happiness at her words. "Ahhh, my wild Welsh girl, I will never make you unhappy, and I will love you forever! I swear it!"

Forever, Wynne thought as their lips met in a sweet kiss. Was there really such a thing as forever? Nay. There was but a moment in time, and those who were wise lived each moment to its fullest, for a moment gone could never come again. "And I will love you for as long as we live, my dear lord," she promised him, knowing how very much he needed to hear such words from her.

In the weeks that followed, all at Aelfdene remarked that they had never seen Eadwine Aethelhard so happy, and his happiness was infectious. Everyone but Caddaric seemed touched by it.

"She has woven a witch's spell about him," the thegn's eldest son complained to his wife.

"He loves her," Eadgyth Crookback patiently explained to her husband. "There is no magic in that."

"He never behaved that way with my mother," Caddaric grumbled.

"Your mother and father were of an age, my lord, and they

wed for expediency's sake, as we all do," Eadgyth replied, feeling pain for her husband, who had probably never loved anything in his life, including her. Caddaric was and always had been filled with bitterness and jealousy, though she could not say why. "Your father is in his late middle years. He skirts along the borders of old age. He did not expect to find love at this time in his life. Not only has he found it, but he has found it with a beautiful and kind young woman who has given him another child. Wynne will probably give him other children as well. You had best face the situation for what it is, husband, and make your peace with it," Eadgyth counseled wisely. "Wynne is not your enemy."

"She has said I will not father any children," Caddaric told his wife.

"I expect she is right," Eadgyth answered him quietly.

"She is wrong!" he shouted back at her. "I could get sons on *her*! I know it!" His look grew moody, and then Caddaric Aethelmaere told his wife darkly, "One day Aelfdene will be mine, and Wynne will be mine too! She will bear sons for me whether she wants to or not; *or I will destroy her!*"

Part IV

THE WHORE OF THE HALL

When love beckons to you, follow him,
Though his ways are hard and steep.
                    Kahlil Gibran
                    THE PROPHET

✷Chapter 16

The Feast of Christ's Mass was approaching, and a large wild boar had been seen in the woods belonging to Aelfdene. The thegn invited his eldest son to accompany him on the hunt.

"We'll have a fine boar's head on the table for the Yule," Eadwine promised Wynne, giving her a morning kiss, his hand sliding beneath her chemise to cup a plump breast.

"Stay abed awhile longer, my lord," she enticed him. "You'll have far better hunting here today than in the cold, dank woods." She pulled his head down for a longer, more leisurely kiss, her tongue licking most provocatively at the corners of his mouth.

With a deep sigh Eadwine buried his face in her perfumed hair for a long, sweet moment, but then he regretfully pulled away from her. "You, my wild Welsh witch, must await my pleasure. The boar, alas, will not," he said, half laughing. "If the creature goes beyond the boundaries of my holding, he will be someone else's prize."

"Are you so certain that I will *await your pleasure?*" she teased him mischievously.

"Aye," he said boldly, catching her back to him as, with a snort of pretended outrage, she leapt from their bed. He cuddled her in his lap for the briefest time and then, setting her on her feet, gave her bottom an affectionate spank. "See to my meal, wife!" he teased her back.

"We have house serfs to see to the meal," she told him loftily. "I think I shall go to my pharmacea and devise a potion that will keep you always by my side."

Instead, however, Wynne went to the cradle where their daughter was now very much awake and hungry. Quickly changing the baby's napkin, Wynne sat back down upon the bed and put the infant to her breast. Averel suckled greedily, and Eadwine had to look away. The sight of their child nursing at her mother's breast aroused him far more than he wanted

Wynne to know. Even now he could not quite believe his good fortune in his young and fair wife.

The servants came into the Great Chamber bringing water for washing, and, finished feeding her daughter, Wynne handed her to the young serf girl whose duty it was to watch over Averel.

At eight months of age Averel was a beautiful and healthy baby. She was plump, with her father's ash-brown hair and features. Only her eyes, which had turned from blue to her mother's forest-green, indicated her maternal heritage. Usually a sunny-natured infant, Averel's sweetness could quickly turn to rage at the most unexpected moments.

"She has a Saxon berserker's temper," Wynne would tell Eadwine when their daughter would howl and roar with anger. In those rare moments only he could calm her, and Wynne would shake her head in mock despair, saying, "She has already wrapped you about her tiny finger, my lord. I fear you will spoil her," which he, of course, would deny.

They washed and quickly dressed for the day ahead. While Eadwine and Caddaric went hunting for the boar, Wynne and the other women planned to decorate the house for the celebration. They descended to the hall below to break their fast with freshly baked bread, a hot barley porridge, a hard, sharp cheese, and newly pressed cider. Arvel and his nurse, Gytha, were awaiting them. Wynne's son still slept with his wet nurse in her cottage, for he was not yet weaned, and grew jealous when he saw his mother nursing his little sister. The rest of the family hurried in, and for once Caddaric was in a pleasant mood. He and his father bantered back and forth over who would be the first to sight the boar and, of course, who would have the honor of killing it first.

Shortly outside the hall the dogs were heard yapping and barking as they were brought from the kennels by their handlers. They would be joined by some dozen serfs who were assigned to the task of beaters this day. It was their job to drive the boar from his lair, out of hiding and into the open, where the bowmen, who were of the gebura class, might have a shot at him. Although the bowmen would defer to their lord and his son, if danger became imminent they would not hesitate to shoot. True, the kill must go to Eadwine Aethelhard or his son, Caddaric Aethelmaere, but all the hunters enjoyed the sport of the hunt.

The thegn, being a big man, had a large bow. It was made of the best yew wood and strung with the finest cord. The tips of the bow were of polished bone set in silver. With his mother's encouragement, little Arvel toddled up to his foster father, struggling beneath the weight of Eadwine's bow case.

Eadwine chuckled as, bending, he took the bow case from the tiny boy. "Soon," he said, smiling at Arvel and ruffling his black hair, "I shall have to teach you how to shoot, my small son."

Arvel's deep blue eyes lit up with pleasure, for he totally comprehended the words. "Daa!" he said, nodding his head vigorously.

"Does he say nothing else but 'Da'?" Caddaric asked sourly.

"He says what any child his age says, which is little," Wynne remarked sharply, "but how could you know that, Caddaric? You have no children." She handed Eadwine a bracer for his left arm. "For you, my love," Wynne told him. "I sent to Worcester for it."

He took the arm guard from her, smiling, pleased; turning the bracer, which was made of polished bone and set in silver, even as his bow tips were, over in his hand. " 'Tis a fine piece, Wynne," he told her. "I thank you!"

"The sun will be up before we get started if you do not leave this woman, Father," grumbled Caddaric.

"He is right," Wynne quickly said, forestalling an argument between father and son. "The day does not look particularly promising, and I smell snow, my lord. If it grows wet, return home. I have no wish to nurse you through a sickness with the Yule and Christ's Mass celebrations upon us."

Eadwine Aethelhard put an arm about her supple waist and gave her a hard kiss. "I'll return at the first flake of snow or drop of rain, my wild Welsh girl. Just remember that you are to await my pleasure." He chuckled.

"Indeed, my lord, and I will," she said softly and, standing on tiptoe, bit his earlobe.

The thegn roared with laughter. "Oh, vixen," he promised her, "I will have a fine forfeit from you this night for your boldness!" Then he kissed her a final time and exited the hall chuckling.

"He loves you well," Eadgyth said, a trace of sadness in her voice.

"And I have come to love him," Wynne told her friend.

"Do you ever think of the other?" Eadgyth asked curiously.

"Aye," Wynne answered honestly. "How can I not when Arvel is his father's very image?"

"Do you still love him?"

"I do." Wynne smiled a small smile, as if mocking herself, and then continued, "I do not think I shall ever stop loving Madoc of Powys, but at the same time I love Eadwine as well. Do not ask me, Eadgyth, for I do not understand it myself."

"You are very fortunate to love and to be loved," Eadgyth told her.

"Caddaric loves you," Wynne said. "Oh, I know you do not think him capable of it, but he does."

"Nay," Eadgyth replied, and tears sprang into her soft blue eyes. "He but remembers that my father promised him an additional two and a half hides of land if he treated me well. He needs that land to attain the rank of thegn in his own right."

"Caddaric loves you," Wynne repeated firmly. "He has never been unkind to you that I know of, Eadgyth. He comes to you for advice, and values your opinion. He is, although he would be astounded to know it, your friend. He should be lost without you."

"Yet he takes other women to his bed, and not just his four concubines, Wynne. There is not a pretty girl, serf or gebura, who is safe from his roving eye."

"It is his desperate desire for children," Wynne told her. "You know that is all it amounts to, Eadgyth. He does not confide in the others as he does in you."

"Caddaric says that you told him he will not father any children. Why did you say that to him? Was it in anger, to revenge yourself upon him for his unkindness?" Eadgyth nervously twisted a piece of her tunic dress. She was older than Wynne by several years, yet she stood in awe of her father-in-law's young wife. After all, Wynne was a healer, and healers were to be respected.

"Caddaric had the swelling sickness as a young man, he tells me. It attacked not only his face and neck, but his genitals as well," Wynne said. "It is well-known among healers that when that happens, a man's seed is rendered virtually lifeless. Sometimes, but oh, very rarely, such a man may father a single child, but it is quite unlikely. All this I have told your husband, but he will not believe me, Eadgyth."

Eadgyth nodded with her understanding. "I have always be-

-lieved myself incapable of having a child," she said slowly, "and frankly, Caddaric used me little before taking other women. Then Berangari came, and Dagian, Aelf, and finally Haesel. At first I was very jealous, but I hid it lest I displease Caddaric, for my lack was certainly not his fault. As each of these girls proved as barren as I did, we became friends. Like me, they would have moved heaven and earth for a child to call their own. I have suspected for some time now that the problem lay with my husband, and so, I believe, have his concubines; but none of us would dare to voice such a thing too loudly."

"Of course not," Wynne said. "Caddaric equates sons with his very manhood, as you well know."

"My poor husband," Eadgyth said, and Wynne could see she was near to weeping.

"The sun is up," she said briskly, pointing through the open door of the hall. "We must get our mantles and hurry outdoors to cut the pine, the rosemary, the holly, and the bay. These December days are so very short, Eadgyth. Where are the others? Surely they will not leave us to do all the work! Ealdraed, run and fetch the lord Caddaric's other women, who have so conveniently disappeared. We will meet them almost immediately where the bay grows."

"Aye, lady," Ealdraed replied. "I'll fetch the lazy sluts for you." She hobbled quickly off, muttering to herself beneath her breath.

"She grows old, yet is still feisty," Wynne said with a smile at Eadgyth, who had now managed to compose herself.

Fastening their mantles about them with elegant brooches of silver, the two women picked up woven baskets and hurried out of doors. On the nearby hill where the bay grew, the four other women awaited them. Their respect for Wynne was such that they had come at once when fetched by the ancient Ealdraed.

Wynne greeted them cheerfully and then said, "Haesel, you are the smallest. Gather the bayberries on the lower branches of the bushes, while Berangari, who is the tallest, will gather them from the topmost branches. When you have finished, cut some large and pretty branches for the hall. Aelf, you, I see, have been wise enough to wear a pair of mittens. Take your knife and cut the holly for us, as your hands will be protected. Dagian will come with Eadgyth and myself to cut the pine boughs."

"What of the rosemary?" asked Berangari.

"There is plenty in my kitchen garden," Wynne answered her. "We will pick it when we return."

The day had brightened somewhat, and there was little wind. In the woodlands beyond could be heard the occasional sound of the hunting horn and the barking dogs as they sought the wild boar. The women, however, hardly noticed. They were too much involved with their own tasks for the festivities. Their baskets were filled with bayberries which would add fragrance to the Yule candles. Their arms were ladened with branches of hay, holly, and pine with which they would decorate the house. Haesel ran back to the manor house to fetch several servants to help bring the branches back.

The greenery all cut and brought in, the women went to the kitchen house to begin making the holiday candles. Heall, the cook, grumbled and muttered at this invasion of his kitchens, but he sent his son for the tin molds the women needed. Sweet cakes drizzling honey and topped with poppy seeds mysteriously appeared atop a table next to a pitcher of cold, foaming cider. The bayberries were heated to free their fragrant wax, which was then poured off into another kettle already filled with rendered beeswax, for the Yule candles were always made of beeswax. The molds were neatly filled, the wick stands carefully placed over each row.

"I think they're the best candles we've ever made," declared Eadgyth. "I saw no bubbles at all to spoil the purity of our efforts."

" 'Twill be a merry holiday," Berangari replied, "and lucky too, thanks to the boar."

"Let us take our cakes and cider into the hall," Wynne said. "I think we deserve a respite before we begin decorating the house. The candles will not be set before tomorrow."

They adjourned to the hall and sat about the main fire pit eating and gossiping. Arvel toddled in and was roundly spoiled by them all. Now that Baldhere and his women had departed, he and Averel were the only children at Aelfdene whom they might indulge. Hungry for their own babies, Caddaric's wife and concubines could not help adoring Wynne's two children. Silently she watched them, actually feeling their pain, and wished it might be otherwise for them.

Finally, when they could delay no longer, the six women with the aid of Ealdraed and the serving women began to decorate the hall with branches. The room, normally plain and utilitarian, began to take on a bright and festive air. The fragrance of the pine was tangy and fresh. Finished at last, they stepped back to survey their efforts and smiled collectively.

"It is even better than last year," little Haesel said, clapping her hands enthusiastically, and the others laughed.

"She's right," Berangari agreed. "This will be the best Yule we have ever had! I just know it!"

The sun was beginning to sink in a tepid smear of washed-out color behind the western hills. In mid-December sunset came in what would have been mid-afternoon on a June day. Wynne looked anxiously through the hall door.

"The boar has obviously eluded them," Eadgyth said. "They will have to hunt again tomorrow."

"Wait," Berangari said, cocking her head. "I think I hear the dogs now."

"Aye," Eadgyth answered. "They are coming. Let us go out and see if they have caught the creature."

Wynne picked up her son and, with the others, hurried out of doors to greet the returning hunters. They could see them on the path leading to the manor house. But wait . . . There was but one horseman, and it was not Eadwine. Wynne thrust Arvel into Eadgyth's arms and began to run toward the men. It was then she saw behind Caddaric's horse the bearers with their burden. Her heart began to pump violently and she ran all the faster.

Reaching the hunters, she could quickly see that Eadwine lay injured upon his shield. "What happened?" she demanded fiercely of her stepson. "Tell me what happened, or as God is my witness, I will tear your heart from your chest with my bare hands!" Her face was a mask of unrestrained fury.

"Spoken like a . . . true . . . Saxon wife," Eadwine said feebly, a weak smile upon his lips. "I . . . will mend . . . sweeting."

"What happened?" Wynne repeated, glaring up at Caddaric, and then, before he could answer her, she was giving orders. *"You!"* A finger pointed at a hunter. "Run as fast as you can into the hall and tell old Ealdraed to bring hot water, wine, and my herb kit. Bandages too! And clear the high board. I want my lord laid upon it that I may examine him." Her gaze swung to the bearers. "Can you move no faster? But do not jostle my lord lest you give him undue pain! Caddaric, I am waiting for your explanation!" Dear lord, how pale Eadwine was, she thought fearfully.

They had reached the manor house now. As Eadwine was carried in and carefully laid upon the high board, Caddaric Aethelmaere told his tale, surrounded by his women. Wynne, even as she listened, was busy cutting away Eadwine's clothes, that she might get a better look at his wounds.

"We tracked the boar most of the day," Caddaric began. "Several times we even caught a glimpse of him, but we never got close enough for a kill. Finally, as the afternoon wore on, the creature made his stand in a briar thicket in the deepest part of the wood. Eadgyth, give me some wine. I am parched."

His wife quickly placed a goblet by his side, and swilling it down, Caddaric wiped his mouth with the back of his hand. "The wood was very dark and gloomy," he continued. "The dogs, however, were eager for the kill. They yapped, and howled and charged directly into that thicket after the boar. The first few were killed or injured, but then the vast numbers of the pack overwhelmed our prey. He broke from his cover and charged directly at us.

"I had the clearest shot, Eadgyth, but my foot slipped upon a stone and I fell. The creature was coming directly at me. I could smell his foul breath upon me even as I struggled to get out of his path. Then Father leapt forward and drew his bow. The beast was much too close for his own safety, yet he killed it with a single shot. The animal, in its death throes, however, gored father badly. He saved my life," Caddaric finished. For a moment the look upon his face was that of a young boy, and Eadgyth's heart went out to her husband.

The hall grew unnaturally silent as Wynne worked grimly, cutting away Eadwine's clothing so she might fully see his wound. It seemed to be located somewhere in the groin area. The thegn's lower body was covered in blood, some of it already dried and blackening, some fresh and oozing its bright red color. He winced as she was forced to peel away fabric that had already adhered to his skin.

"I am sorry, my love," she said, her mouth setting itself in a hard line.

"I feel so . . . light-headed," he murmured weakly.

"Ealdraed! Feed the lord some herbed wine," Wynne commanded the old servant.

Finally she had the wounds exposed to her sight, and they were fearsome to behold. The boar might have died, but he had done Eadwine cruel damage prior to his demise. There were at least three major slashes in the thegn's upper thigh and groin area. All were deep, but at least two had ceased to bleed. The third wound, however, was the most serious, for the animal's tusk had made a small puncture in the artery running through the groin. It was not a great hole, but the bleeding had not ceased.

Wynne stared at it and bit her lip in vexation. She was no surgeon, and a surgeon was what was needed here. If the puncture had been larger and more open, she might have sewn it up herself, but it was not. To reach the artery and close it successfully, she needed to open the wound up farther, that she might work at it. She didn't dare, and her lack of skills in this area frustrated her greatly. If she tried and cut too deep, she could do far more damage than the boar had. Eadwine would die. Yet if she didn't stop the bleeding, Eadwine would die anyway. He saw her indecision.

"What . . . is it?" he demanded, pushing Ealdraed's gnarled hand with the goblet away.

She must not worry him, Wynne thought, and then said, "I am debating the best method of treatment, my lord."

He saw the worry in her eyes, quickly masked from him, but pressed her no further. She would do her best for him, and if it was God's will that he not survive, then no amount of praying and hoping would change this.

"Drink the wine, my love," she counseled him. "There are eggs and strengthening herbs beaten into it. I must reassure your son before I begin my work." Bending, Wynne kissed his brow and then moved from the dais down the hall to where Caddaric and Eadgyth stood.

"Will he live?" Caddaric asked bluntly.

"I do not know," Wynne answered honestly. "There are three wounds, two quite deep, but they at least have stopped bleeding. The third wound just pricked an artery. It is not open enough for me to sew up, and I have not the skill to open it farther, that I may sew it up. I will try to stop the bleeding another way."

"If you cannot," Caddaric said, "then he will die. Is that what you are saying, Welsh woman?"

"Aye," she answered, and her green eyes filled with tears.

"Then you will be mine," he answered her cruelly, and Eadgyth gasped, shocked by her husband's brutal words.

"Never!" Wynne answered fiercely, and turning away from them, went back to her patient.

"Oh, Caddaric," Eadgyth half wept, "how can you voice such thoughts aloud, and your father on his deathbed?"

He led her to a bench by the fire pit and together they sat down. Eadgyth's blue eyes were fraught with her concern, but her husband put gentle fingers to her lips to stay her further words.

"She can give me a child, Eadgyth," he said in low, desperate tones. "*I know that she can!* As long as my father lived, I had no choice but to accept her status as his wife, but soon my father will be dead. Wynne will be mine to do with as I please." His eyes glittered with his anticipation.

"If God wills that your father dies," Eadgyth said in equally low tones, and she pushed his hand from her lips, "Wynne will be his widow and should be honored as such. Is that how you would honor her? By forcing her to your will? Oh, Caddaric! Never would I have suspected such dishonor in you."

"The Welsh woman was brought as a slave into this house. As such, she is a part of my inheritance and mine to do with as I choose!" he answered fiercely.

"Your father freed Wynne from her slavery, publicly, in this hall before us all!" Eadgyth cried softly. "She is your stepmother, and what you suggest amounts to incest! 'Tis a sin of the worst sort, my husband. Do not do it, Caddaric, I beg of you! We will find you a new and beautiful young concubine from a family of proven breeders; *but not Wynne!*"

"I do not want any other," he said obdurately. *"Only her!"*

Eadgyth's look was one of pity mixed with repulsion. "I will pray for you, my husband," she said helplessly. "There is little else I can do to aid you if you persist upon this course."

Wynne would not allow Eadwine to be moved from the hall. The servants lifted him gently up to lay a pallet beneath him, that he might be more comfortable. Wynne bathed, cauterized, and treated his wounds with all of the skill at her command. The larger of the wounds, though ugly, would heal easily if she could keep them free of putrefaction. The smaller, more dangerous wound, however, she was having difficulty with, for she could not seem to stop the slow bleeding. Several times by means of pressure she managed to stem the flow of the blood, but once the pressure was removed, the wound opened seemingly of its own accord and began seeping Eadwine's life force away. Toward the middle of the night,

Wynne crept into a dark corner of the hall and, for a few brief minutes, wept with desperation at the futility of her efforts. They needed a surgeon! She simply had not the skill to open the wound more fully and repair the damage done.

Eadwine Aethelhard drifted in and out of consciousness most of the night. Although he burned with fever, Wynne knew that it was just his body's way of fighting any infection attacking him. It was the loss of blood that was going to kill him. As the night ended, the thegn grew suddenly quite clear-headed for a brief time.

"Bring the family," he commanded Wynne, and she hurried about the hall waking them, for none had left them during the dark hours.

When they all stood about him, Eadwine said, "I am dying. I feel it. Caddaric, my son. You are my heir. Aelfdene is yours. I give you my blessing, but you must promise me this."

"Anything, Father!" Caddaric said, unable to conceal his eagerness to inherit.

A small bitter smile touched the thegn's mouth, and he continued, visibly weaker now. "Be good to Eadgyth. To your . . . women."

"I will, Father."

"Swear you will honor and protect your baby sister, Averel, my son."

"I swear it, Father! I will guard my sister with my life, and see she is well wed one day," Caddaric vowed, and in this he was quite sincere, for he had no malice toward the little girl.

"And Arvel too! I . . . have made him . . . mine."

"The boy will not suffer at my hands, Father," Caddaric said, perhaps a bit more evasively. No, Arvel would not suffer unless his mother proved uncooperative, which Caddaric knew she would not if the child's safety were in question. Wynne was above all else a good mother, and Arvel would be held hostage to his mother's behavior.

"Wynne!" Eadwine croaked, his voice beginning to grow weaker.

"I am here, my love," she said, bending to make it easier for him.

"I never loved any but . . . you, my wild . . . Welsh . . . girl," he told her. *"No other."*

"Eadwine," she half moaned, "I cannot bear that this should

be! I have been trained my life long to save lives, but I have not the skills of a surgeon. Forgive me!"

He smiled and nodded weakly. "I do."

"I love you," Wynne told him. "In the beginning I could not, but I came to it. How could I not love you? You are the kindest, the best man I have ever known!"

"Better than the . . . other?" he asked softly.

"Aye!" she answered quickly, and he smiled again, knowing she lied, but the very lie assuring him that she did indeed love him at least as well as she loved her prince.

The thegn spoke again. "Caddaric, my son!"

"Aye, Father?"

"Swear to me that you will honor, respect, and protect my wife and my widow. Swear you will watch over Wynne!" It took almost the last of his strength.

Caddaric Aethelmaere looked down at his dying father. The life was fading swiftly from his eyes. But a moment or two longer, he thought dispassionately.

A sudden and horrible realization sprang onto the thegn's face. Reaching out with a surprisingly strong hand, he grasped his son by the arm. *"Swear!"* he croaked, trying to keep the desperation from his voice as his very life ebbed to a close. *"Swear!"*

"Caddaric, my husband, in the name of God, I beg you to swear," Eadgyth Crookback pleaded.

"My lord! My lord!" His four lesser women were clustering about him, clutching at his sleeves with irritating fingers. He shook them off.

"Swear!" Eadwine Aethelhard's voice had sunk to a whisper, but still they all heard the word plainly said.

Caddaric Aethelmaere's cold eyes met those of Wynne's even as the death rattle sounded in Eadwine Aethelhard's throat.

Eadgyth and the others fell to their knees and began praying as the thegn's grip loosened on his son's arm and fell away. The coals in the fire pits crackled eerily. Old Ealdraed shuffled slowly across the hall, opening the door to the morning. A broad ray of sun splashed across the floor as the portal swung wide. Beyond, the clear song of the lark was heard, and then, his gaze never leaving Wynne's, the new thegn of Aelfdene manor said in a hard, harsh voice, *"Now, Welsh woman, you are mine!"*

▨ *Chapter 17*

*D*espite the bright December sunlight, the day was somber. Wynne moved away from Eadwine's body and over to Eadgyth.

"What are your customs for burying the dead?" she asked the kneeling woman. It was the day of the Winter Solstice, she thought. As good a day as any to die. Silent tears rolled down her beautiful face.

Drained, Eadgyth pulled herself to her feet. "In the old days," she began, "the custom amongst our people was cremation, although those to the south of us interred their dead in the earth with as many grave goods as the deceased was worthy of and could afford. Since the coming of the priests, we merely bury our dead. The cemetery is next to the little church."

"Will you help me prepare the body?" Wynne inquired. She was feeling tired, and she was shocked by Caddaric's words to her across poor Eadwine's fallen body. Her breasts ached terribly, and looking down, she could see the front of her tunic dress was stained with not only Eadwine's blood, but her milk as well.

"Of course I will help," Eadgyth said quickly, seeing Wynne's predicament, and she put a comforting arm about Wynne, "but first you should feed Averel."

"Do not begin without me," Wynne said grimly. "I owe Eadwine every consideration due a good lord by his wife." She moved away from Eadgyth's embrace and took her sleeping daughter from her nurse's lap. Wearily she climbed the stairs to the Great Chamber, where she changed Averel's napkin and then sat down, almost totally spent, to nurse her daughter. She cradled the baby protectively as the child suckled her vigorously. Slow, hot tears slid unchecked down Wynne's face as she considered her dangerous position at Aelfdene now.

Caddaric had made his position very clear, but she simply could not accept such a thing. Wynne knew she was in a far more difficult position than when she had first come to Aelfdene. Then she was simply carrying a child. Now she had two children born and dependent upon her for their very lives. If she fled, she could not possibly succeed with two children in tow. She therefore had no choice. She must remain at Aelfdene, but how she could remain and be safe from Caddaric's lust was another matter. She needed rest and time to think. Instinctively she knew that Eadgyth would help her.

She felt his eyes on her and looked up to see that Caddaric had entered the Great Chamber. How long he had been there she was not certain. He lounged arrogantly against the lintel of the door, and she longed to kill him where he stood. "What do you want?" she demanded in an icy voice that did nothing to hide her loathing and distaste for him. "It will distress your sister if you disturb her meal. Have you sent a messenger to your brother's hall yet?"

"If you are thinking of leaving Aelfdene," he said in a blustering tone, ignoring her question, "do not. It would displease me to have to brand you for a runaway slave."

"I am no slave, and you know it well," Wynne returned in angry but even tones. "I am your father's widow and the mother of his daughter. I would hardly be so flighty as to remove Averel from her home and the security of her brother's care. Remember that you promised your father on his deathbed to care for your sister and her half brother. I will never leave my children, Caddaric. Therefore, I will be here to be certain that you keep that promise to your father."

"You are not afraid of me, are you?" he said, coming next to her. He reached out and touched her head with his hand.

"Nay," Wynne said quietly. "I do not fear you, Caddaric. I despise you, for despite your name, you are a coward and a bully in my sight. If you should attempt to accost me in any manner, I will make every effort to kill you. I can be no plainer than that."

He laughed harshly, and his fingers gripped her braid tightly, forcing her face up, that he might look into her green eyes. "Despite our disagreements, Welsh woman, I admired my father, and I owe him a debt that I can never repay him, for he gave his life for mine. You may have a month in which to mourn my father properly, but then you will come to my bed. What sons you will give me, Welsh woman! I have waited all my life for a woman of fire and ice such as you. I care nothing that you will not love me, and I want nothing of you but children. Give them to me and I will treat you as a queen might be treated."

"And if I do not give you the children you so desperately desire, Caddaric Aethelmaere? What then?" Wynne demanded fiercely, and she raised her now sated daughter to her shoulder to burp her.

"You will, Welsh woman," he growled at her. *"You will,"* and then he leaned down and ground his mouth on hers.

Startled, Wynne still had the presence of mind to bite down sharply on the lips that assaulted hers, and when, with a roar of outrage, he pulled away from her, she spat full in his face. "That is all you will ever get of me, Caddaric Aethelmaere," she said, rising to her feet. "Anger and scorn! Nothing more. Keep well clear of me, *my lord!*"

For a moment he looked as if he would attack her where she stood, so filled with violence was his ruddy face. Then the rage gripping him drained suddenly away and the new thegn of Aelfdene burst out laughing. "By God, Wynne," he said, using her name for the first time, "what a woman you are! What a woman!" Then turning about, he departed the Great Chamber, leaving her shaken and, if it was possible, even more tired and drained.

She sat back down again for a few minutes, cradling Averel, who, warm and dry and well-fed, was nodding sleepily. Looking into her daughter's little face, Wynne felt the tears beginning to come upon her once more. How like Eadwine the baby looked. How like Madoc Arvel looked. Was she to be haunted for the rest of her days by the bittersweet memories of these two wonderful men? What was to become of them? Averel's head lay heavily on her arm now, and so Wynne rose to tuck the little one into her cradle once more, and departing the Great Chamber, returned to the hall where the others waited.

"Willa," she said, addressing her daughter's nursemaid, "go up and sit by your little mistress." Then turning to the women, she said, "Let us prepare my lord Eadwine for his burial."

Eadwine Aethelhard's body was stripped of its clothing and tenderly bathed. The wound that had killed him had ceased draining and was now merely puckered and discolored. Ealdraed climbed the stairs to the Great Chamber and returned bearing the dead man's finest clothing. First they put red-orange braccos, cross-gartered in yellow, upon his feet and legs, to be followed by pointed, soft leather shoes. A sherte of natural-colored linen was topped by an under tunic of yellow and a full-skirted kirtle of indigo-blue and gold brocade which was belted in gilded leather. His ash-brown hair was brushed thoroughly. It turned itself up naturally, curling under just below his ears.

Wynne gently brushed Eadwine's fine beard, noting here and there silver hairs she had not noticed before. Her tears flowed once more. Sighing heavily, she placed Eadwine's favorite gold chain about his neck even as the wooden coffin was being carried into the hall. "Where are his weapons?" she asked of no one in particular.

"I have them," Caddaric answered.

The body was laid in the coffin, and Wynne rearranged the garments so that they were straight. The thegn's sword was buckled to his belt, his bow and his arrow case placed on either side of him. Eadwine's arms were then crossed over his chest, his shield lain over them so that it appeared he was grasping it. Wynne stepped back and looked down at Eadwine. He looked quite well, she thought sadly.

The coffin was carried to Aelfdene's little church and left before the altar, that the manor's serfs might pay their respects to their fallen master. The widow repaired to her chamber to wash and dress herself in clean clothing, as her garments were all bloodstained. Then Wynne returned to the church to keep a vigil before Eadwine's coffin until its burial later that afternoon. The candles flickered brightly in the little stone church as she knelt numbly by the coffin's side, barely aware of the weeping serfs and geburas who shuffled by in solemn procession.

"He must be in the ground before sunset," Caddaric said. "I'll not have him haunting Aelfdene."

"Eadwine may be dead, and you may bury him this day," Wynne said sharply, "but he still knows what is in your heart, Caddaric. It was the last thing he saw in your eyes before he died. Not sorrow or filial piety, but his son's unbridled lust for his wife. May your own death one day be even crueler."

All through the daylight hours of the December day the people of Aelfdene passed before Eadwine Aethelhard's coffin, viewing their lord a final time. When at last they had all gone, Gytha brought Arvel. Wynne arose from her kneeling position and, taking her son in her arms, showed him the dead man in his coffin.

"Da dead," Arvel said. "Gytha say." A tear rolled down his fat little cheek.

"Aye, my son. Da is dead and gone to heaven to be with our lord Jesus," Wynne replied. "We must pray for him." Then a tear slid down her cheek as well.

Arvel looked at his mother with Madoc's serious look, his face a miniature of his father's, and pronounced solemnly, "Ric is bad man. I no like! Want Da back, Mama!"

"Da cannot come back, Arvel," she patiently tried to explain, "and you must not anger the lord Caddaric in any way, my son. Da would not like it. Do you understand Mama?"

The little boy nodded his head, but Wynne could see that he did not easily comprehend the situation in which they now found themselves. Why should he? He was not quite three. She turned to Gytha.

"From this moment on, Gytha, you must keep an extra watch on Arvel. Do you understand me?" Wynne asked the girl.

"Aye, lady," Gytha replied. "I'll keep the wee laddie out of the new lord's way, never fear. We'll give him no excuse to claim displeasure of us."

They buried Eadwine Aethelhard before the early sunset came, lowering his plain wooden coffin into its grave, which had been dug next to the grave of his first wife, the lady Mildraed. Wynne had closed the coffin herself, bending over it first to give him a final kiss. His lips were cold and stiff now, totally unlike the warm and loving man she had known. Her quiet tears began to flow once again as she followed the coffin to its final resting place, watching as the rich dark dirt was shoveled over it.

"In olden times wives were sometimes buried alive with their husbands," Caddaric Aethelmaere remarked, to the horror of the others.

Wrapped in her grief, Wynne did not answer him; and when they had filled in the grave, she remained.

"Let her be!" Eadgyth hissed at her husband, whom she saw wanted to force the widow back to the hall.

"She will catch her death of cold," he protested. "I cannot have her doing herself a harm. You know I need her!"

"Wynne will do herself no hurt as long as she has Arvel and Averel to care for and love," Eadgyth told him wisely.

When Wynne finally did return to the hall, she was pale and obviously chilled. She did not stop by the fire pits to warm herself, but rather went directly to the Great Chamber, calling a house serf to follow after her. Several minutes later she reappeared, the servant in her wake, struggling with a heavy wooden chest.

"What are you doing?" Caddaric demanded.

"I am removing myself from the Great Chamber," Wynne told him. "It is now yours and Eadgyth's by right."

"You are to remain," he said.

"I will not," she told him obdurately, and turning to the servant, said, "Take my things to the pharmacea."

The servant stumbled off beneath the weight of the chest.

"You are to sleep in the Great Chamber," he repeated. "There is no room in the pharmacea for you, my sister, and her nursemaid."

"With your permission, my lord, your sister and Willa can remain in the Great Chamber. I, however, will not. I will sleep on a pallet in my pharmacea. I am the manor's healer, and it is my right to be there." She then turned, and walking across the hall, entered into the little chamber.

"She has not eaten all day nor last night either," Eadgyth fretted. "I will have Ealdraed take her a plate of food."

"If she would eat," he said coldly, "then let her come to the high board with the rest of us. She is my father's widow and has a place amongst us."

"Caddaric, I beg you," Eadgyth said gently, a pleading hand upon his arm, "let me coddle her this night only. Her grief is greater than you can imagine."

"Then you take the food to her," he said. "You must keep a strict eye upon her for me, Eadgyth, and see she remains in good health, for she will give me sons before the new year is out."

Eadgyth sadly shook her head at his words. Wynne was not like any woman that they had ever known. Neither she nor her husband's other women would have ever considered refusing Caddaric anything that he desired; but Wynne would. Eadgyth knew that the beautiful Welsh woman was probably correct in her assessment of Caddaric's sad condition. There would be no children, and when Caddaric tired of forcing himself on Wynne, what then? What would happen to her, for Eadgyth knew that being faced daily with this particular failure would be more than her husband could stand.

"God and His blessed Mother help us all," she whispered softly to herself.

In the days that followed, Eadgyth watched with growing distress as Caddaric's eyes followed Wynne whenever she came into his view. She had never seen her husband like this before, and neither had his other women. He was totally and completely obsessed by Wynne.

"What if she gives him a child?" Berangari posed the question that was in all their minds. "What will happen to us?"

"Wynne assures me that there will be no child," Eadgyth tried to reassure them. "She says that Caddaric's bout with the Swelling Sickness just before our marriage destroyed his seed."

"What if he falls in love with her in spite of it?" Dagian asked.

"Wynne despises him," little Aelf spoke up.

"Aye," Haesel agreed. "I think if it were not for her children, she would have killed herself upon the lord Eadwine's death; but she absolutely dotes upon her babies."

"He is obsessed with her no matter," Berangari said.

"We must help her until we can cure our husband of this sickness that eats at him," Eadgyth told them. "We owe her that courtesy. Wynne has never been unkind to any of us, even when lord Eadwine made her his wife. It is not her fault that Caddaric desires her. She has done nothing to encourage him. She would be content to live out her life as Eadwine's widow and the healer of Aelfdene manor, raising her children, in peace with us all."

"How can we help her, Eadgyth?" Berangari inquired.

"Let me speak to her," Eadgyth replied. "She will tell us what to do."

"He has given me the space of a single moon to mourn Eadwine," Wynne explained to Eadgyth. "Then he tells me I must come to his bed. That I will never do, Eadgyth!"

"But what will you do?"

Wynne shook her head. "I honestly do not know," she said, "but it is good to know I may rely upon you and the others in this time of my trouble."

Caddaric, however, was expecting his helpless victim to attempt to outwit him. With a cleverness she would not have believed him capable of, he waited until his women were in the bakehouse one winter's morning, exactly five weeks after his father's death. Wynne, preparing a remedy for a serf's aching head, was seized in her pharmacea and carried kicking and struggling to the Great Chamber. A gag had been stuffed into her mouth almost at once in order that her cries not be heard. Wynne was lain upon the bed that Eadwine had had made for her, her arms and legs pulled wide and fastened to the bedposts by means of hempen rope. There she was left.

When her rage had abated somewhat and her heart had ceased to hammer so violently, Wynne considered her position, which was certainly a dangerous one. Gingerly she tested the strength of the ropes, but they had been made quite fast and cut into her delicate ankles and wrists at the slightest movement. The gag, though preventing her from screaming, was not unduly uncomfortable. She could breathe and swallow. Shocked, she realized that there was nothing that she could do to help herself. She would simply have to wait for Caddaric to make the next move, more than aware of what it would be.

She lay still for some time, her anger rising once more in the face of her helplessness. She had, she thought, been held prisoner like this several hours when she heard his step upon the stairs. Sauntering into the Great Chamber, he walked over to the bed and stood for a long moment gazing down at her. Finally he reached out and pulled the gag from her mouth.

"Aren't you afraid that I will scream, Caddaric Aethelmaere?" she demanded sarcastically.

"You may scream all you desire, Wynne," he told her. "I have sent Eadgyth and the others back to my hall for the time being. There is no one here who will help you now."

"How clever you are, my lord, to have prepared this rape so skillfully," Wynne murmured sweetly.

He laughed, at ease with himself because of her helplessness. "You are foolish to fight me, Wynne," he said. "You know I mean to have my way with you. What can you do to prevent me? Nothing! Would it not be better to come to me willingly? I know my women have told you that I am a magnificent lover," he bragged, and, bending down, pushed her head aside that he might kiss her neck.

"You revolt me," she said icily. "There is nothing manly in forcing a woman to your will, my lord." The wet touch of his mouth on her skin was totally repellent.

"Hate me if you so desire, Wynne, I will still have children of you," he told her. " 'Tis all I really want from you, your fertile womb."

"There will be no children, Caddaric," Wynne said quietly. "Why do you refuse to comprehend that? How many women have you poked with that weapon of which you are so prideful? And none has given you a child. *Not one.* Not a miscarriage nor a stillbirth. There has been nothing from all your efforts before, nor will there be anything now. You will labor in vain, Caddaric, shaming me before everyone at Aelfdene, and shaming your father's memory in the process. You violate the laws of decency and morality by your lustful and incestuous conduct toward me. Are you not ashamed?"

His answer was to take his knife from his belt and begin cutting her clothing away. Wynne lay silent now, for she could do nothing. It was fortunate, the thought passed through her head, that the garments he so heedlessly sliced and ripped were her work clothes and well-worn. When he had rendered her completely naked, he stood staring down at her, an almost glazed expression upon his face. Wynne felt a tingling in her breasts and almost laughed aloud.

"Loose me, Caddaric," she said in a hard voice. "My milk is beginning to leak and your sister must be fed. Untie me this instant and fetch Averel to me! I can go nowhere without my clothes, and you have totally destroyed mine with your mindless violence."

The new thegn of Aelfdene shook his head as a large dog might do, and his eyes filled with comprehension. Bending, he undid the ropes that bound her, and then he said as he departed the Great Chamber, "I will fetch my sister to you."

Wynne rubbed her wrists and ankles to take the soreness from them and then, standing up, moved across the room to where the tub stood, seeking the chamber pot. Her bladder was near to bursting, and she had truly feared she would wet the bed through with her water had he not given her this small measure of freedom. Relieving herself, she walked back over to the bed and, climbing into it, drew the coverlet over her nudity even as he returned to the room carrying Averel.

"She is a fine strong girl, isn't she?" he said in pleased tones. It amazed Wynne that he seemed to have a weakness for his half sister. "Give me hearty children like this, Welsh woman, and there will be no difficulty between us, I promise you!" He handed Averel over to her mother, ruffling the baby's curls affectionately as he did so.

Wynne smiled down at her daughter, giving her a kiss before putting the child to her full breasts. "There will be no children, Caddaric," she said grimly. "Why will you not understand?"

He would not answer her, and when she had finished feeding her child, he drew back the coverlet and lashed her ankles once again to the bedposts before she might protest. "Cradle my sister with but one arm," he commanded her, and when, puzzled, she did, he made fast her other arm, effectively imprisoning her once more. Then taking Averel from her, he said, "I will return to you shortly," and left the Great Chamber carrying the baby.

Wynne considered what to do. There was no time to use her free hand to unfasten her bindings. She could hear Caddaric turning Averel over to Willa at the bottom of the stairs. She could not seem to convince him of the futility of what he planned to do, and she was helpless to prevent his rape of her. There was but one thing she might use against him, and she realized now that she had no other choice. Eadgyth had told her in confidence that Berangari and the others had recently complained that Caddaric could not seem to complete what he so enthusiastically started. Though he bragged of his mighty prowess, Eadgyth remarked, he had always been over-quick to spill his seed. Recently, however, even that had changed. His manhood, raging and at the ready, too often withered before he might fully act. Wynne knew the power of suggestion could be a dangerous weapon, and now she must use it if she was to have any chance to save herself.

Caddaric sauntered into the Great Chamber again, a nasty smile upon his face. When he sat next to her upon the bed, Wynne lashed out at him with her free hand, but, laughing, he caught it, securing it as firmly as the other. Fully clothed, he clambered atop her and then, sitting back upon his haunches, he ran his big hands over her shrinking torso.

"That first night," he said in a rough voice, "when Ruari Ban displayed your charms for us all to see, I wanted you. I grew hard beneath my kirtle, and I longed to take you right then and there in the hall before all the others." Reaching out he squeezed her breasts, and a single bead of milk appeared upon one of her nipples. Caddaric leaned forward to lick it off, and then he suckled hard upon her.

"You spineless bastard," Wynne told him. "You will not have me!" She narrowed her eyes until they were but glittering green slits and silently willed him to look into her face. "I have tried to turn you from your folly, Caddaric Aethelmaere, but now you leave me no choice but to resort to the craft of sorcery which my first husband, Prince Madoc, taught me. Force me, and I will place a curse upon your manhood so that it cannot even lift its ruby head to salute me!"

Startled by her threats, Caddaric Aethelmaere raised his head from her breasts and looked into her face. "You cannot stop me," he said, but his tone was not particularly convincing. Her virulent words had already caused doubts to spring up in his eyes.

Wynne opened her own eyes wide now and stared hard at him. "Can I not, *my lord*?" Then she laughed. "Already it begins. In your mind you desire me greatly, but there is no passion in your rod, is there, *my lord*?"

The look he gave her was one mixed with anger and fear.

"Your manhood lies soft and shriveled between your legs, *my lord*," Wynne taunted him. She pushed him away from her, and he fell back surprised. By some miracle the ropes binding her arms had become loosened, and she was able to slide her hands free, to his further shock.

"Magic!" he gasped and crossed himself quickly.

Wynne quickly slid her hands down to her mont and pulled apart her nether lips, exposing her sweet secrets to his now bulging eyes. Mockingly she fondled herself, saying as she did, "Even I, at my most lewd, cannot arouse your puny worm, Caddaric Aethelmaere! Oh! Ohhhh!" She shammed at a passion she was certainly not feeling, but it was enough to drive him away.

Leaping off of her, he groaned. "Witch! Witch! You have

unmanned me! But though you be safe from me for the moment, I will return to you later. You will take my weapon within your reluctant sheath and beg me for more!"

Wynne laughed contemptuously at him. "Never, you fool! You will never have me! *Never!*"

Cursing violently, he bent to retie the ropes securing her, and this time Wynne knew they would not come unfastened, for they cut cruelly into her flesh. "Now, you Welsh witch, await my coming," he snarled, "and be prepared to service me well!" Caddaric stormed from the Great Chamber, his angry footsteps stamping angrily down the staircase.

Alone, Wynne began to shake uncontrollably. She had escaped him. But for how long she might play this game to keep him at bay she knew not. She was cold. So cold. The chamber was unheated, and the winter's day, though mild, was yet late January. She would not call out for help. She knew not if anyone would come, for they all lived in fear now of Caddaric's temper. Besides, she could not bear to be shamed before the serfs.

The day wore on, and in the hall below she began to hear the sounds of revelry. Listening carefully, she recognized Caddaric's voice becoming more and more bellicose as time passed. She could make out two or three young female voices giggling and laughing at first; growing more fearful and sullen as the afternoon waned. Serfs, Wynne realized, and as helpless to the thegn's will as she was at this moment. The Great Chamber dimmed and finally grew dark as Wynne lay there shivering. Finally she heard his footsteps upon the stairs again and braced herself for this new encounter to come.

He lurched into the room, half dragging a young girl with him. Carrying a candle, he stumbled about the Great Chamber lighting the lamps, then positioned himself at the foot of the bed, where she could clearly see him. He was clad in his sherte and braccos, and now drawing the sherte off so that he was nude, he commanded the girl, "Do as I have taught you, wench!" He was a big man and quite hairy, but his body ran more to fat than his father's had.

The girl, who was wide-eyed at the sight of Wynne bound and naked, fell to her knees. Taking her master's flaccid manhood into her mouth, she began to suckle it. She did not look as if she were enjoying her task. Her eyes were squeezed tightly shut, and her mouth worked earnestly to arouse him, as if knowing a lack of success on her part could lead to punishment.

Caddaric stood impassively as she struggled to fulfill her duty. "Prepare yourself, Welsh woman. When I have finished with you, you will truly know who your master is. Did you do this to my father, eh? You will soon pleasure me in that way. Enough, wench!" He shoved the girl away. "Get out!" he roared at her as she scampered most willingly away. He turned toward Wynne, his hand cradling his manhood. "My father's rod was surely not as fine," he bragged with a leering grin.

"Your father was twice as thick as you, Caddaric Aethelmaere, and at least an inch or more in length longer," Wynne said wickedly, and then she laughed. "There is little damage you can do to me with that poor excuse for a rod."

"Bitch!" he snarled, and flung himself atop her. "I will show you precisely what I can do!"

Her heart hammering, Wynne forced herself to laugh all the harder. Then quite suddenly, ceasing her mirth, she said, "I will place a curse upon your puny, feeble manhood, Caddaric Aethelmaere. May it wither and shrink even as you attempt your assault of me. *Look down at yourself!* Already you have begun to soften and grow limp!" She felt his big body upon hers, his hand desperately trying to insert his useless weapon into her. She squirmed just enough to foil him and assure his defeat.

He began to moan with frustration as he realized he was losing control of himself. He wanted her! He had to have her! Only she could give him the children he so hungrily desired, but she would not! *She would not!* He was unmanned by this Welsh witch, and that which had so delighted all the women he had used since he was eleven now lay feeble and worthless against her thigh, a victim of her sorcery. Almost weeping, he leapt off her and fled the Great Chamber wearing nought but his braccos.

Wynne began to shake once again. She was chilled to the bone and weak with her relief. Eadwine had always claimed that his eldest son was superstitious, even as the lady Mildraed had been. She had used that weakness against him this day, but how long she could continue along this path she knew not. Dear God, she was so cold, and her breasts were beginning to ache again. How long would he leave her here, she wondered, and then she heard the sound of soft footfall upon the stairs.

A female figure was silhouetted in the door for a moment, and Eadgyth said anxiously as she hurried forward, "Are you all right, Wynne?" Without waiting for an answer, she bent and untied the bonds that held Wynne fast. "Caddaric came raging into the old hall. He wore nothing but his under tunic and braccos. He demanded that Berangari and the others service him. What happened? He could do nought but mutter about curses and witches. When I left them he was preparing to beat poor Haesel for some imagined affront. Blessed Mother, you are frozen!" She pulled a chemise from the chest at the foot of the bed and pulled it over Wynne. Then she added a woolen under tunic. "There is no one in the hall," she continued, "but the fires are high. Come and we will get you warm."

Together the two women descended the stairs into the hall, and Wynne sat down upon a bench by the main fire pit while Eadgyth poured her a goblet of wine.

"Here," the new thegn's wife said, handing the goblet to Wynne. "You will feel better when you drink this."

Wynne swallowed the wine and, looking up at Eadgyth, said, "Did you know he planned to seize me this morning?"

Eadgyth shook her head in the negative. "I should have warned you had I known," she replied sincerely. "He did not have his way with you, did he?"

"Nay," Wynne answered, smiling slightly, "he did not. I am sorry poor Haesel must suffer for me though."

"What did you do to enrage him so?" Eadgyth inquired. "I have never seen him so angry, Wynne."

"I told him I was putting a curse upon his manhood," Wynne responded. "I remembered what the others had said about Caddaric's difficulties of late, and I remembered that Eadwine had told me that Caddaric was superstitious. Under the circumstances, I thought that I might succeed in unnerving him if I pretended I was cursing him."

Eadgyth nodded. "Aye, Caddaric is superstitious and 'twas a good plan, but now I fear what will happen on the morrow. He is not a man to take defeat lightly or well. Once when a young horse threw him, he caught the beast, remounted it, and rode it until he broke its wind. It was barely good after that for even the cart. My husband is a cruel man. He will not forgive you, Wynne. You have struck him in his most vulnerable spot."

Wynne was warmer now, and the blood was flowing hotly through her veins once more. "Eadgyth," she said, looking directly at her friend, "I do not care if Caddaric will not forgive me. All I ask is that he leave me be, and that he keep his promise to Eadwine regarding Arvel and Averel."

"Oh, he will keep his promise," Eadgyth replied. "I will see to that, but it is your safety I fear for, Wynne. Caddaric will find a way to revenge himself upon you, you may be certain. It will not be pleasant. We can but wait."

"I am his father's widow," Wynne said. "He cannot treat me badly. Today he tried and he failed. There will be talk amongst our people, and Caddaric will not want to remain the butt of their jokes for long. His ego is great. He will want the incident forgotten, and the quickest way to attain that goal is to pretend it never happened. To ignore it. If he does not react, the jest will be quickly over."

"I pray it be so, Wynne," Eadgyth said anxiously, "but I fear it will not. Caddaric will not forget."

Wynne felt saddened on the following day to see that poor Haesel had a blackened eye and Dagian was covered in bruises. "Come to my pharmacea," she told them, "and I will treat your wounds."

"It is not fair that we should have to suffer for your behavior," Dagian complained as Wynne stroked a soothing lotion on her aching arms.

"Nay, it is not fair," Wynne agreed, "but I cannot give Caddaric children, and I will not allow him to rape me because of this obsession. I am sorry you have been beaten, but 'twas not I who beat you. It was Caddaric Aethelmaere. Blame him, not me!"

Dagian sighed bitterly. "I know," she said.

During the next few days an uneasy peace settled about Aelfdene. The women moved nervously and quietly as they performed their daily tasks. Caddaric Aethelmaere scarcely glanced at Wynne or the others, and then one evening as they all sat at the high board, the new thegn said,

"For Aelfdene to remain prosperous, we must all pull our weight and contribute to the manor." His cold grey gaze fastened upon Wynne. "You, lady, you and your children take much but give little."

"I am the manor's healer, my lord," she answered him softly, in an attempt not to arouse his ire. Caddaric was more volatile these days than ever before. This was leading somewhere, but she did not know where.

"What do you do in your capacity as our healer?" he asked her, and his tone was almost affable now.

"I gather and grow herbs in season. I dig for medicinal roots and seek barks which can be used for healing lotions. I prepare all potions and brews needed, treat injuries and wounds, and generally care for the sick," Wynne replied. "It takes a great deal of time, my lord, to do these things. There is no time of the year when I am not busy."

His brow furrowed in mock concentration, and then he said thoughtfully, "You cannot gather and grow herbs after the growing season is over, lady. Neither can you dig for roots or seek barks except in the warm seasons. Is your pharmacea well-stocked with the provisions you need right now, Welsh woman? Are you well-prepared for any emergency?"

"Aye, my lord, it is and I am. There are a host of remedies that I must have on hand, and others whose ingredients but wait to be mixed and blended," Wynne told him truthfully.

"I see." Caddaric almost purred the words, and suddenly all the women at the table were alert and wary of what was to come. The new thegn smiled toothily. "You do little, it appears to me, to pay for your keep and that of your children, lady. My half sister Averel is my responsibility, and one I shall not shirk; but your son, lady, is another matter. He takes the serf, Gytha, away from the fields, thus costing me her labor. How will you pay me for his keep and the loss of Gytha?"

Wynne was shocked by his question. What was she to say to him? She was his father's widow, and by all rights should not have to account for herself, or her children, or her use of the serfs.

"You refuse to cooperate with me in my efforts to sire a child on you, lady," he continued. "You curse my very vitality with your witchcraft. Is it possible if I wooed you more gently you would come to me of your own free will?"

"Never!" The word was out of her mouth before she might even think on it. She quickly attempted to soften the harshness

of it with him. "Please, Caddaric Aethelmaere, please understand. I loved your father and, although I sympathize with your dilemma, to give myself to you would be a betrayal of Eadwine. I cannot betray a man who loved me, and who was so good to me, and whose daughter I bore."

"So be it," Caddaric said in a silky voice. "You have chosen your own fate, Welsh woman. If you will not be mine, then I shall make you the whore of the hall. You will pay for your keep and that of your son in this way." He smiled again, but his eyes were cold.

Eadgyth cried out as if she had been pierced with something sharp, and the others gasped, turning horrified eyes on Wynne. "Caddaric," his wife begged him, "do not do this thing, I beg of you."

"Be silent!" he told her, and then, turning back to Wynne, said, "Do you know who the whore of the hall is? She is the woman appointed by the lord to service his male visitors in whatever manner they so desire. There was no whore of the hall in my father's time, for he thought it a cruel practice to force a woman to such labor. I, however, see nothing wrong in offering my guests a full range of hospitality."

Wynne stood up and her voice was filled with distaste and loathing for the man. "I will do no such thing, Caddaric Aethelmaere. How dare you even suggest it? When I think that your father gave his precious life to save such as you, I grow ill with the memory of Eadwine's death."

"Disobey me and your brat will suffer for it," he told her dispassionately.

"Is this how you keep your sacred oath to your father to care for me and for our children, Caddaric Aethelmaere? You are dishonorable beyond the bounds of decency," Wynne told him furiously, her green eyes flashing.

"I did not promise my father that I should care for you, Welsh woman. I said I should look after my sister Averel, and that the boy would not suffer at my hands. He will not, but what is to prevent me from selling him to the first slaver I meet the next time I go to Worcester?" He laughed cruelly. "A pretty little boy like Arvel would fetch a handsome price and more than pay me back for my trouble. You will do what I tell you or I will take your son from you. How will you explain it to the boy's father when he comes someday to retrieve you both?" And the new thegn laughed again. "If indeed that story you told my father was truth, though I suspect it was not. How far will you go to protect your brat, Welsh woman? You are a good mother, aren't you?"

"I will take my children and leave Aelfdene," Wynne said quietly. "Somehow I will find my way back home."

Caddaric Aethelmaere rose to his feet shouting, "You will go nowhere, Welsh woman! You and your children will remain at Aelfdene, and you will whore for your son's keep! You might have been my woman, but since you find that so distasteful, you will be any man's woman. You will service the guests in my hall as the bitches in my kennels service the hounds. Do you understand me?" He grasped her upper arm, his fingers digging into the flesh hurtfully.

The rage boiling over in her, Wynne slapped him with her free hand, using every ounce of her strength. Then pulling away from him, she fled to the relative safety of her little chamber. It was there that Eadgyth found her, half tearful and frightened, yet angry and defiant. "I will kill him!" she said to her friend through gritted teeth. "I will cut his black heart from his hairy chest and eat it before his very eyes!"

"Do not fear," Eadgyth said calmly. "Caddaric may say what he wishes, but you will not be forced to whore for your living, Wynne. We will protect you. I promise you!"

"How?" Wynne demanded of Eadgyth. "You are all terrified of Caddaric. You will not defy him. I must leave here! There is no other way, and in that you can help me, for I will not leave my children behind."

"Caddaric need never know that we are helping you," Eadgyth explained patiently. "Calm yourself, Wynne, and think a moment. Few visitors pass through Aelfdene. When any do come and Caddaric offers you to them, we will see that the offer is not accepted. Trust us in this matter. We are your friends."

"How can you prevent a lustful man from his desires?" Wynne said. "And you cannot offer such a man another woman, for Caddaric would then wonder why his whore of the hall was not doing her duty. No, Eadgyth, it is impossible. I must flee Aelfdene!"

Eadgyth chuckled and replied, "Your fear is making you act irrationally. Think, I beg you! How did you stop my husband

and keep him from his vile purpose, Wynne? You frightened him and made him believe you had cursed his manhood."

"But that was simple given the fact that Caddaric is known to be superstitious, and given the fact that he was already having some difficulty in performing his manly duties," Wynne said. "I had but to play on his weakness, but the men who pass through Aelfdene will be lusty fellows, filled with energy and pent-up passions, and eager to fuck a pretty woman. I will not be able to deter them in their intent," she finished. "No, Eadgyth, it is impossible!"

"You will not have to frighten these men away from you, Wynne," Eadgyth told her. "*We will!* Berangari, and Dagian, Haesel, and Aelf, and myself. We will convince any man coming into this hall and offered your services that you are a sorceress. That you have rendered our poor husband useless, and if they value their own manhoods, they will not go near you. If there is one brave enough to attempt to breach your walls, we will drug his wine before he has the chance. Caddaric need never know of our deception. No man would dare chance the loss of his manhood, but neither will he admit to fear, particularly fear of a mere woman. And what can Caddaric do about it? He cannot force his guests between your thighs, can he?" Eadgyth laughed aloud. "It is really quite a good plan, I think. Don't you?"

Wynne nodded slowly. It was a good plan! "Eadgyth," she said, "why is it you are constantly amazing me?" She hugged her companion and then continued, "Thank you, Eadgyth! And the others too. You are truly the best friends I have ever had."

The winter drained away and the days grew longer as the springtime approached. The women at Aelfdene went about their daily tasks in a calm and orderly manner. There were no visitors, but they all knew that come the warm months there would be. It was simply a matter of time. Then one day a thegn, whose holding was farther to the northwest, stopped overnight at Aelfdene on his way to Worcester.

"May I offer you the services of the whore of the hall?" Caddaric said jocularly to his guest as they sat sharing a jug of wine after the meal. "She's a particularly toothsome and spicy wench. Wynne! To me! We have a guest in need of pleasuring."

"She is not Saxon," the thegn, whose name was Wilfred, re-marked.

"Nay, a Welsh wench. My father fancied her before his death," Caddaric replied, and then, looking up at Wynne, who now stood before the high board, he said, "Show our guest your breasts, Wynne."

It had been agreed amongst the women that Wynne would behave meekly in any situation like this where Caddaric was present, to allay any suspicions on his part when afterward he learned, if indeed he did learn, that she had not been used by a stranger. Expressionless, Wynne removed her tunic dress and then her under tunic before unlacing her chemise to bare her bosom.

"Are those not fine, big tits upon which to pillow your head?" Caddaric chortled, poking the half-drunk Wilfred, who, leaning forward, licked his lips with relish and leered suggestively at Wynne.

"Aye," he said, and his words were faintly slurred. "I would enjoy a tumble with your whore, Caddaric Aethelmaere. I dislike travel intensely, for I am a man who services *all* his women daily. When I am forced to travel, my energies become pent-up and I sicken. I have been on the road for three days now, with the prospect of another two days of riding before I reach my destination; not to mention the return trip. She looks like she'll be a juicy fuck."

"Wait at his bed space for our guest, Wynne," Caddaric ordered her with a pleased grin.

With a cold nod, Wynne restored her clothing to their proper mode and moved away from the high board. Berangari leaned over from her place at her husband's left and whispered something in his ear. Arising, he asked that his guest excuse him for a brief moment and moved off with his woman. Eadgyth slipped into her husband's place and said softly to Wilfred, "Do not use the woman Wynne, my lord."

"What?" Wilfred looked puzzled.

"She is a sorceress, my lord. My husband sought to have her after his father died. She cursed his manhood so that he has not functioned in a normal manner since. She has threatened to do so with any man who tries to mount her."

"This is truth, lady?" The thegn, Wilfred, looked distinctly worried regarding Eadgyth's revelations.

"Aye, my lord," Eadgyth said, nodding her head vigorously.

"Why does your husband offer such a woman to his guests then?" Wilfred contemplated aloud. "Why does he not just send her away?"

"He will not send her away because he promised his father to look after her. Wynne was the old thegn's favorite. She is our healer," Eadgyth explained logically. "My husband is a generous man, but somewhat shortsighted at times. He would be the best of hosts, you see, and foolishly offers the woman to you, hoping to please."

"You're certain the woman would curse me?" Wilfred asked, his eyes moving down the hall to where Wynne stood. She was a most toothsome female, and he was very reluctant to give her up.

"Did you see her smile, my lord? She never smiles. *Ever.* She had a soft spot for the old thegn, but she is a cold, hard woman with no heart. She wouldn't hesitate to hex you. I think she enjoys hurting men. Ahhh! The suffering she has caused us all!" Eadgyth sighed, her hand resting dramatically over her heart. "I would not wish such tragedy upon your wife and women. My poor Caddaric! He will never be the same again, although," and here Eadgyth lowered her voice so that the thegn, Wilfred, was forced to lean forward to hear her, "you must not tell him I told you of our mutual misfortune." And Eadgyth wiped a tear from her eye, or so at least the thegn, Wilfred, thought, sympathy rising in his breast for this gentle, good woman who but sought to save him.

"There, there," he sympathized with her, patting Eadgyth's hand. "Caddaric will not know that we have spoken on this matter, lady. As for the whore of the hall, tell her I have changed my mind. Caddaric need not know of that either."

The next morning the thegn, Wilfred, departed, promising to stop at Aelfdene on his way home, but he did not return. During the warm months of summer that year there were several visitors to Aelfdene, for Caddaric was foolishly involving himself in the politics of the day. King Edward was not well, and Harold Godwinson was lobbying hard for the English throne. None of these visitors, however, availed themselves of the hall's whore. Caddaric was at first surprised, but as the days went by and Wynne remained untouched by any other man, he began to grow angry.

"Is there no one who will help me to bring this proud bitch to heel?" he grumbled to Eadgyth.

"Perhaps, my husband, it is God's way of intervening in your cruel plan," she told him boldly. Eadgyth was the only one of Caddaric Aethelmaere's women who might speak to him without fear of reprisal. "I think God has saved you from yourself, and I thank him for it."

But Caddaric was not pleased by her words. Each day he watched as Wynne fed Averel, who was now toddling about the hall on fat, unsteady little legs. He watched her sit by the fire pit nursing her daughter, her son by her knee chattering up at her and stroking Averel's little head tenderly. The little boy adored his baby sister. How strange, Caddaric thought to himself. This small boy with his raven's hair and his deep blue eyes; this so obviously Welsh child and I have much in common. *Averel.* Averel who is both his half sister and mine.

Daily Caddaric Aethelmaere watched Wynne and her children, growing more and more embittered. Her womb was as fertile as one of his newly harvested fields. Yet she denied him its use. She denied him the children he so desperately desired. He had made her the lowest of the low in his hall; still everyone treated her as they had treated her in the days when his father had been alive. *Worse!* For some strange reason, no man who had come into his house as a guest would avail himself of her services. She remained cool and untouched. It was driving him mad. He wanted to punish her. He wanted to humble her. *He wanted to destroy her even as she was destroying him!*

He would give her to the first man who would use her in his very presence so that he could be certain she would be brought down and demeaned, he promised himself, and he waited for that man and that day.

≋*Chapter 18*

*A*utumn came once more and with it a peddler's cart that
rumbled down the barely visible path that led from a
poorly marked secondary track to Aelfdene manor. It was late
afternoon. The serfs and the geburas, curious, came from the
fields and from their houses, delighted for this pleasant intrusion into their otherwise dull lives. The cart was drawn by a
rather tired-looking dusty brown horse who ambled into the
manor house courtyard as if he were coming home and then
abruptly stopped.

Atop the cart's bench seat sat two men. One was large with
shoulder-length grey-white hair. Stepping down from the cart,
he announced in a rough voice, "I am Boda, the peddler. I
have come to trade, and I seek shelter for the night." Boda
walked with a most pronounced limp.

Caddaric Aethelmaere stepped forward. "I am the thegn of
Aelfdene," he said. "You're welcome to my hall. Let me see
your goods and we will talk."

"Very good, my lord," Boda said, and turned to the other
man with him, a gaunt shambling fellow with a half-vacant
look. "Display our goods, you fool!"

"Who is he?" demanded Caddaric.

"My son Tovi," Boda replied. "Since birth he has been slow
in his mind."

"Why do you keep him with you?" Caddaric asked.

"Why not? I do not have to pay him, and he is too stupid
to steal from me, aren't you, Tovi?" The peddler chuckled.

Tovi offered his audience a gap-toothed grin and nodded. He
had the definite look of a half-wit about him.

"A slave would have cost me money, my lord. With Tovi I
have but to feed him regularly and beat him occasionally. Or
is it feed him occasionally and beat him regularly?" The peddler chuckled loudly at his own humor. Then he said, "If you
have women you would favor and are of a mind to be gener-

391

ous, bring them forth. I have many pretties and geegaws that
will appeal to the ladies."

Caddaric did not know how generous he was of a mind to
be this day, but Eadgyth and his lesser women had been particularly accommodating of late. "Bring your mistress and the
others," he commanded the nearest serf.

The peddler and his son began to display their goods for all
to see. Caddaric was astounded by the variety of merchandise
laid out from the small cart which hardly seemed large enough
to hold half of what was presented. There were some fine iron
pots and attractive glass vessels, as well as the usual supplies
of salt and spices; but it was the extent of the luxury goods
brought forth that amazed Caddaric. He was unable to keep
from saying so.

Boda nodded as if pleased by the young thegn's astuteness.
"We are a large family of traders," he said chattily. "I have
nine brothers, and our business extends from England all the
way to Byzantium. It is there my eldest brother does the buying for us all, as it is cheaper to buy directly in Constantinople
than if we bought from some middleman here in England or
elsewhere. The goods are then shipped to us wherever we are.
I make my home in London during the winter months, but
once the roads are passable again, Tovi and I travel about in
our little cart, trading and selling as we go."

"Your *little* cart holds a great deal," Caddaric noted.

" 'Tis all in the packing, my lord," Boda assured him with
an airy wave of his hands.

The women had come from the house and were exclaiming
excitedly over the peddler's wares. The fabrics displayed on
wooden racks had them in raptures. There was fine linen from
Genoa; scarlet silk from Lucca; blue and white silks as well as
beautiful woolen cloth from Firenze. There were fine-tooled
leather belts, and leather belts that had been gilded in gold leaf.
There were silver and bronze buckles from Byzantium, and a
very beautiful silver dish from the same city, which particularly took Caddaric's fancy. Indeed, having seen it, he could
scarcely let it out of his hands.

The selection of jewelry was an excellent one. There were
beads of blue and white glass, and crystal beads and those of
garnet. There were gold and garnet disk brooches, and other
brooches fashioned from silver and decorated with moon-

stones. There were bracelets of both silver and gold; as well as decorative pins. A rock crystal pendant set in a silver sling took Berangari's fancy, but Eadgyth very much desired a beautifully engraved bronze work box. The others argued over simpler treasures such as small ivory boxes and packets of needles.

Wynne, however, fell in love with a fine-painted dower chest. "It would be perfect for Averel," she said wistfully. "It is never too soon to begin filling a girl's dower chest." She knew that had Eadwine been alive, the chest would have been immediately purchased for their daughter. She did not expect Caddaric, however, to buy it. So, turning away, she returned alone to the house, unnoticed by the others.

The peddler and his son would shelter in the hall for the night. Eadgyth knew that Caddaric would offer Wynne to them for their pleasure. His desire to break her spirit had not ceased, and the two strangers were the first visitors they had had in weeks. When Caddaric had finally gone back into the house, Eadgyth and the others clustered about the peddler. From a distance it appeared as if they were chattering, questioning him or seeking to bargain with him.

"My husband," said Eadgyth in a sweet voice, "will offer you the services of the whore of the hall tonight, sir. Do not, if you value your life, accept his offer."

"Why not?" Boda demanded in his rough voice, peering at her curiously with bloodshot eyes.

"She is a sorceress!" Dagian said dramatically before Eadgyth might even answer him.

"Aye," Berangari put in quickly, and lowered her voice, "she rendered our man useless when he sought to have his way with her. He has been no good to any of us since, though he blusters and pretends it is otherwise."

"There are no children here," Haesel said in an eerie tone. "None but those belonging to the Welsh witch herself. Her curse has denied us all our motherhood."

"Why does he not get rid of her?" Boda demanded suspiciously.

"She was purchased by the old master to be the manor's healer," Eadgyth answered him. "We have no other healer, nor anyone capable of it. That is why our lord will not let the girl go, though we have pleaded with him to do so."

"If she is the healer, then why is she also the whore of the hall?" Boda probed further.

"She was the old master's favorite woman. She bore him a child," Eadgyth said. "After his death, our husband sought to force himself on her, for he had a greedy appetite for female flesh. When he would not heed her objections, she worked her magic upon him. He punished her in return by making her the whore of the hall, but we have warned all to whom he would offer her, for knowing what we do, we cannot in good Christian conscience allow any man near her. She has threatened to curse any who would attempt her, and believe me, sir, she will!"

The peddler nodded his understanding of the matter. "I thank you for your warning, my lady," he told her. "I should not enjoy being crippled. I have a young second wife."

In the safety of the Great Chamber the women giggled over what had just passed between them and the peddler.

"He reeks of onions," little Aelf said. "I could smell them even from where I stood behind Berangari."

"At least he'll not bother Wynne," Eadgyth said in relieved tones.

"He's a big lout and ugly as sin," Berangari noted, "but it is his son who frightens me. Did you see him watching us from the sides of his eyes?" She shuddered. "I'd not like to meet him on a dark path on a moonlit night."

"He's just a half-wit," Aelf noted. "Do you think that half-wit men futter women? Do you think they even know how?" she wondered curiously.

"How horrible!" Haesel shrieked. "How can you think of such a thing?"

"Well, Caddaric will offer Wynne to the peddler, and he will refuse her," Aelf said. "What if he offers her to the half-wit? We did not speak to him, and besides, he would not know enough to refuse. What if he can fuck like any other man, despite his lack of wits? Did any of you consider that?" Aelf concluded, extremely pleased with herself for having thought it all out.

"The peddler will not allow his son near Wynne," Eadgyth said with firm assurance in her voice. "Even if the creature could function in a normal manner, the peddler will want to protect his offspring from any curse. Remember, the poor soul is free labor for his father."

At the dinner hour they adjourned to the hall to find Caddaric smiling and in a particularly good mood. Boda and his son were with him. At each of their places, but Wynne's, was a gift. For Eadgyth there was the beautiful bronze work box that she had so admired.

"Open it! Open it!" Caddaric chortled.

Inside Eadgyth found a packet of needles and a lovely gold and garnet disk brooch. "My dear husband," she said, and her eyes were filled with tears. She had never, since her wedding day when he had come bearing gifts, received such bounty from him. Why now, she wondered, delighted nonetheless.

Berangari, smiling, was clasping the rock crystal pendant in the silver sling about her graceful neck. She had never dreamed it would really be hers. Catching Caddaric's hand up, she kissed it in thanks, and Caddaric grinned.

There was an ivory comb in a matching case decorated with blue glass and moonstones, for Dagian, and a necklace of garnet beads for Haesel, the beads all strung on a gold chain. Aelf was in transports of delight over a silver and moonstone brooch. They fought over Caddaric in their efforts to thank him, which pleased him mightily, and he patted and pinched their buttocks in approval.

"Surely you have gifted yourself with something as well, my husband," Eadgyth said when the excitement had finally died down.

"After the meal I will tell you." He chuckled mysteriously.

It was a simple family supper. Rabbit stew, bread, cheese, and a sweet cake made with apples. There was newly brewed ale to drink, and Caddaric had more than his share. It was good, Eadgyth thought, to see him so happy. She could never remember ever seeing him so filled with the joy of living as he was this evening. When the dishes had been cleared from the board, Caddaric sat back smiling broadly. It was obvious he was quite pleased with himself.

"Eadgyth asked me before the meal if I had not purchased something from Boda that would give me pleasure," Caddaric began. "Well, I have!" Reaching beneath his chair, he lifted up the silver dish he had been so covetous of earlier and placed it on the table. "My father never had anything of such value in

this hall in his day," he bragged. "Boda says it is from the
workshop of Simon of Constantinople, one of the finest silver-
smiths in all of Byzantium. Look at the engraving, Eadgyth! It
is a bull fighting a lion. Boda says it is a lion, although we do
not have such beasts here. How I would like to hunt a lion!"
Caddaric's face was filled with pleasure and almost boyish excitement. *"And,"* he continued, "I have something else, my
wife." He drew a small vial filled with a reddish powder from
his pocket, whispering as he did so, "Boda says that this will
restore my vitality, Eadgyth. It is magical, and after I have
taken it all, which I must do over a period of seven days,
mixing it with wine, I will be able to give my women sons! Is
this not marvelous?"

"Caddaric," Eadgyth asked him nervously, "these items are
rare and of great value. What can you possibly have of equal
value that you could barter in exchange?"

"Boda wants a wife for his son Tovi," Caddaric said slyly.
"The half-wit has lately developed a lust for female flesh, and
Boda has already had to pay damages to two men whose
women Tovi used without permission. The fool knows no better." He laughed. "So Boda has decided to get a wife for his
son. In exchange for all your gifts, for the silver bowl, *and* the
magical powder, I have agreed to supply him with a bride."

"But what if the half-wit gives his wife children, Caddaric?
Think on it, I beg you, my lord," Eadgyth said. "Is such a
thing kind?"

"Do not fear, lady," Boda interrupted them, obviously worried that Caddaric would renege on their agreement if his wife
convinced him to do so. "Neither my wife nor I lacked any of
our wits, and we fathered three daughters as well, all sound.
Poor Tovi, our youngest and our only son, was so curst. My
young second wife has given me two boys as healthy as any.
My grandchildren are all full-witted. Any babies Tovi can sire
on a healthy woman will certainly have all their wits about
them, I am sure. The girl your husband is giving us will not
suffer. She will be well cared for, I promise you."

"The bargain has already been struck, Eadgyth," Caddaric
said firmly. "I want the silver bowl; but more important to me,
wife, is the powder which Boda assures me will overcome the
Welsh woman's curse. Do you not want me well and whole
again?"

What else could she answer but "Aye," Eadgyth thought. Her husband had purchased them all fine gifts by bartering away a serf girl. Eadwine Aethelhard would certainly not have done that, and then she pushed the guilty thought away. Caddaric Aethelmaere was a hard man, but he had always been good to her. What difference could one girl make? Knowing her husband's normally close ways, the girl would have some fault, Eadgyth was certain. The serfs were always spawning children. It almost seemed that they had nothing else to do. She smiled up at her husband and inquired, "Which girl is to go with Boda and his son, my lord?"

And the horrifying answer came. *"Wynne."*

"You cannot!" Eadgyth burst out as the others gasped in total shock, but Wynne rose to her feet, white with her fury.

"I am not some serf to be disposed of, Caddaric Aethelmaere!" she shouted at him. "I am your father's widow! Is this how you honor Eadwine Aethelhard's memory? By giving his widow to a low-bred half-wit?"

"I am the master of Aelfdene now, not my father!" he shouted back. "You will do as I tell you and go where I send you!"

"When Eadwine died, I wanted to take my children and return home to Gwernach, but you would not give me your help. 'Twas you who insisted I remain here that you might have free rein to attempt your rape of me; and afterward when you failed, you sought to demean me by making me the whore of the hall. You failed in that as well, Caddaric Aethelmaere! And you will fail in this shameful attempt too!" Stepping down from the high board, she called out, "Ealdraed! Fetch my children to me. I leave Aelfdene this night!"

Caddaric stood up and the muscles in his neck bulged darkly with his rage. "Aye, you Welsh witch, you have defied me at every turn, *but not in this*! I swore to myself that the first man who would agree to take you upon this board in my full view would have you for his own! The peddler has said that his son will have you for a wife, and that he will meet my conditions. *So be it!*" Then looking to Boda and Tovi, he told them, "She is yours."

Not even bothering to look back, Wynne turned away from her tormentor and walked swiftly down the hall. Suddenly the half-wit was before her, prancing foolishly and giggling. He repelled her totally, and she drew back as he reached out to grasp at her.

"Pretty lady," he chortled. "Father says you are now my wife."

Wynne slapped out at Tovi. "Get away from me!" she said in a low, tight voice.

It was like striking out at a persistent insect. Tovi moved agilely aside, and his surprisingly strong fingers closed about her slender wrist. Yanking her close, he grabbed at one of Wynne's breasts and squeezed it, repeating, "Pretty lady." He was drooling slightly.

Wynne struck out at him, but again he ducked her and began dragging her down the hall back toward the dais. She struggled fiercely, hitting out futilely at him. "Let me go, you idiot! Release me this instant! Caddaric, I will kill you for this! Do not doubt that I will wreak a vengeance upon you so terrible that you will live to regret your actions this night!" Standing stock-still, she managed to momentarily halt their progress and kicked Tovi quite hard on his bony shin. He grunted, but then quite easily yanked her up before the high board.

"My wife nasty," he whined at Boda. "Tovi no like, Father."

"There, my son, do not be distressed," Boda answered him smoothly. "What have I taught you makes a lady happy? You must fuck her. The good lord who has given you this pretty wife wants to see you fuck her."

"Caddaric, in the name of the blessed Jesu and his sainted mother, I beg you not to allow this thing," Eadgyth cried, and falling to her knees by his side, she took his hand. "Take back the work box and the other things, my lord. I do not want them if you will but substitute another for Wynne. Anyone, but not Wynne! What will Aelfdene do for a healer, my husband?" she attempted to reason with him.

"Aye, my lord," Berangari and the others said, and with little sighs they placed their own gifts upon the table. "Please spare Wynne."

"Aelfdene did without a healer for many years before the Welsh woman came," Caddaric said coldly. "We will survive without her. It is my wish she be given to the peddler's son. Boda, can your son do his duty by this woman? If so, then let him! *Here!* Upon my table before us all, because you, my dear wife Eadgyth, my lesser woman, will remain to see what happens to those who defy and displease me."

Caddaric snapped his fingers in a prearranged signal, and several serving men ran forward to roughly tear the clothing from Wynne's body. They held her firmly as they ripped away at her tunic dress, her under tunic, and finally her delicate chemise. Wynne struggled against them wildly, then, fear overcoming her, she began to scream as a mindless terror engulfed her. Her limbs became frozen, unable to move. They bore her up onto the dais, still resisting, but weakly, and placed her upon the high board. The half-wit, seeing her naked form, began to chortle and fondle himself lewdly. The servants held her arms and spread her legs wide as Tovi clambered up onto his victim, cackling with salacious excitement. Eadgyth and the others shrieked, horrified as the half-wit displayed a large and engorged manhood.

Wynne struggled uselessly against her captors. Her heart was pumping violently and she shrank back futilely as Tovi's body covered hers; unable to breathe properly, her head spinning, but totally capable of realizing what was happening to her. Tovi began to grunt like an animal as he settled himself atop her. She felt him begin to insert himself in her body, his hand guiding his great rod, pushing it slowly into her passage. Wynne began to scream helplessly beneath his assault, feebly trying to buck him off her. Tovi's mouth came wetly down on hers, but she quickly turned her head away in disgust. Then she heard a familiar voice whispering urgently in her ear. "Keep fighting me, dearling, else I cannot bring this deception off!"

It could not be! After almost three years? *It could not be!* Her fear subsiding somewhat, even though she howled like a scalded cat beneath the man atop her, Wynne focused her eyes and looked into the deep blue eyes of Madoc of Powys! She was going mad! That was it! She was going mad. Her head rolled about, and into her sight came the face of Caddaric Aethelmaere. It was filled with lust and sadistic pleasure. He almost slavered with his excitement, believing Wynne finally broken.

"That's it, half-wit!" he encouraged Tovi. "Hump her! Give her your all!" and he laughed even as he envied the fool the conquest he had so desperately desired.

Wynne's head rolled back to face her attacker. *"Madoc?"* she mouthed.

"Aye, dearling," he whispered in her ear as, to her shock, she recognized with absolute certainty the man violating her.

"No! No! No!" Wynne moaned, horrified by her own sudden reaction to him. It was simply too much to bear.

"Pretend to faint, dearling," he instructed her, but Wynne already had. Madoc forced himself to a quick conclusion. Then in his identity as the slack-mouthed Tovi, he climbed off the unconscious Wynne, chortling and wiping his limp weapon on his tunic as he pulled it down. "Lady nice now, Father," he said. "Tovi fuck her good."

Eadgyth and the others were weeping wildly. Little Aelf had vomited her dinner onto the floor. Rising, the women stumbled from the hall, supporting each other in their grief and their shame. Their continued sobs could be heard from above in the Great Chamber.

"Wine!" Caddaric called to his servants. "I would drink a toast to the bride," and he laughed uproariously.

The wine was brought and poured. The three men drank it down quickly. Wynne slowly began to regain consciousness, remembering at once what had happened and wondering if she had indeed heard Madoc's voice coming from the idiot's mouth.

"Take the bitch then," Caddaric said, slamming his heavy goblet down on the tabletop by her ear. "She's yours and good riddance!"

Wynne pulled herself up into a half-seated position and said bitterly to him, *"I want my children!* I'll not go without my children, Caddaric! If you try and keep them from me, I will somehow find a way to return to Aelfdene and kill you! *Give me my children!"*

"I got rid of the boy several days ago," he said with a cruel smile, and grasping one of her breasts in his hand, he squeezed it hard. "Did the half-wit service you well?" He leered at her.

"Arvel!" she shrieked. "You have killed Arvel!" Scrambling to her knees, she lunged at him, her nails going for his eyes, her teeth bared in almost feral fashion.

"I do not kill children," he said scornfully, pushing her away. "Ruari Ban, the slaver, came through here several days ago. You were out as usual, gathering your damned roots and berries. He said the man from whom he purchased you wanted your son. I sold the brat to him!" Caddaric laughed again. "I made a pretty penny too. Ruari Ban was very anxious to have the boy and made no secret of it."

"Arvel, my son." Wynne wept for a moment and then she snarled, "I will find my son, but you will not have my Averel, you devil!"

"Take the wench," he told her. "I won't have to provide for her or give her a dowry if you do. I owe my father nought, for had he not stolen you from me in the first place, you would have given me my children, and I would be a happy man. To hell with my promise!"

"Come, wife," Tovi said, and he lifted her off the table to carry her, protesting, from the hall.

"Where's the child?" Boda asked. "I don't want the Welsh woman unhappy."

"In the Great Chamber with her nursemaid. Willa will bring her to you at dawn before you go. You don't want the little wench in the way tonight, do you? I don't doubt that your son will be more than happy to share his bride with you," and Caddaric laughed nastily. Then he said sharply, "Get out! Our dealings are done. You will not be welcome at Aelfdene again. Do not come back."

"You need not fear, my lord," Boda said quietly. "There will be no need for us to come this way again." He bowed politely and then departed the hall, leaving Caddaric Aethelmaere to his wine.

In the courtyard the peddler's wagon stood silent. Boda climbed into the back of it, pulling at his dirty grey-white hair as he quickly clambered into the vehicle. Wynne lay, now clothed in a clean chemise, upon a narrow bench that served as a sleeping place. Her eyes widened at his entry, the wig in his hand, his red hair bright in the lamplight.

"*Einion!*" she half sobbed. "Oh, Einion!" and she sat up, relief pouring through her bruised body.

The big man enfolded her in his bearlike embrace and hugged her hard. "Lady! My lady Wynne. Thank God we have found you at last!"

"But you do not look like yourself," Wynne said, peering hard at him, "and yet I should know that fiery head of yours and your dear voice anywhere."

Einion chuckled. "My lord Madoc is a master of disguises, my lady Wynne. You did not recognize him in the repulsive Tovi, did you?"

"Nay," said Wynne softly, "I did not."

"My skin has been painted with bark and berry juices to resemble that of an older man, a man who spends half his year in a large town," Einion explained. "The shape of my nose has been altered by the use of clay. I hunch and I learned to modify my walk. I even changed my voice. It is a good disguise, my lady Wynne, is it not?"

"Very good, Einion," she replied, and then she looked at the other man in the wagon. "Is it *really* you, Madoc? I cannot see you through this deception. Yet for a moment in the hall, I thought I saw your eyes." She was beginning to shiver.

Madoc reached up, and drawing down a small length of soft wool, wrapped it about her shoulders. " 'Tis I, dearling, truly. I dare not remove my camouflage and restore myself to my own identity until we are well away from this place. This Saxon thegn would not be pleased to learn he has restored you to your own people. He seems to gain great pleasure in shaming you."

"This place is Aelfdene, my lord. It has been my home for three years now," Wynne said, and he immediately caught the reproving tone in her voice. "I have lived here longer than I did at Raven's Rock." Then she looked at Einion. "Where is my daughter?"

"With her nursemaid in the Great Chamber. He says he will give her to me in the morning."

"I will not leave here without Averel," Wynne said firmly.

"*Averel,*" Madoc said. "I thought we had agreed to call a daughter Angharad."

"Averel is not your daughter, my lord," Wynne answered him, and wondered why it was she felt a small bitter satisfaction in telling him this. His arrival here was certainly more than fortuitous, but the timing was all wrong and it rankled her.

Madoc's eyes darkened. "Is she the daughter of that animal who calls himself the lord of this place?"

"Nay," Wynne told him scornfully, "she is not. Her father was Eadwine Aethelhard; he was Aelfdene's former master. He died ten months ago in a hunting accident. He sacrificed himself to save the life of his eldest son, that pig who now rules in this hall."

"*And my child?* Did you safely deliver my child?" Madoc asked her.

"I did. You have a son, my lord. A fine, healthy boy. I called him Arvel, not Anwyl, for he was a child to be wept over in our captivity," Wynne told him. A captivity, she thought bitterly, that might have ended sooner if you had but come for us before now.

"Where is my son?" Madoc demanded. Indeed, she seemed far more concerned for her daughter than she was for her son.

"Did you not hear Caddaric Aethelmaere in the hall, my lord? He has taken my son and sold him to Ruari Ban, who is, as we speak, bringing my innocent child to your brother at Cai!" Her eyes were filled with tears. "Why did you wait all this time to come for us, my lord? *Why?* I waited and I waited, and I prayed and I prayed that you would rescue us; *but you did not come.* It was as if we had never existed for you, Madoc."

"That is unfair, Wynne," he told her, his own anger beginning to rise. She had had a child by another man, and from the tone of her voice when she had spoken of that man, she had cared deeply for him. Did she still love her Saxon? Had she ever loved him?

"*You did not come!*" Wynne repeated.

"We sought you from the very beginning, dearling," he began. Then he patiently explained to her as best he could his desperate search for her and for their child. "Until we could be sure that you even remained in the country," Madoc told her, "we could not be certain that we would ever find you. For the past eight months now Einion and I, positive you were still in this land, have traveled the Mercian countryside. We used Worcester as the center of our radius and stopped at each and every manor we came to, searching for you, Wynne."

"Almost three years have passed," Wynne said low. "Three years to the day, Madoc."

"Three years in which you managed to make yourself a new life and bear another man's child," he retorted, his anger spilling over. "How is it this Caddaric could steal my son away and you not even know of it, Wynne? Did you give my son as much love and care as you have given to your Saxon's daughter?"

Her hand flashed out, making hard contact with his face. "Do not dare to criticize my abilities as a mother, my lord. Where were you when Arvel was born? I was here at Aelfdene, and my son's life was saved by the very Saxon whose daughter I later bore. Arvel came into the world, the cord wrapped about his little neck. I had tried to bear him alone, without help, for I was frightened and proud, and yet angry that you had not found us. Eadwine heard my cries and helped me to birth Arvel. *Your son?*" She said scornfully. "He may have come from your seed, but it was Eadwine Aethelhard who was father to him! It was Eadwine Aethelhard who claimed him legally for his own; who watched him take his first steps; who sat up with me when he had a fever; whom Arvel called *Da*."

He was staggered by her vitriol as much as by the words she spat at him.

"You must not quarrel now," Einion said. "Not now that you have finally found each other. If you do, then you allow Brys of Cai the final victory over you both."

"Did you love your Saxon?" Madoc asked low.

"Aye," she answered him, "but not as I love you."

Love. She had said love! Not loved, but love! "Dare I hope," he said, "that you love me yet?"

"I thought I did," Wynne answered him honestly, "but the man I loved was someone I knew three years ago. I am your wife, Madoc, and that has not changed. Still, we must get to know each other again. I am not the same Wynne of Gwernach as you knew three years ago. I am older, and I hope wiser." She turned to speak to Einion once more. "In the morning when we have regained my daughter's custody," she said, "we must hurry directly to Cai. God only knows what evil Brys intends for my son, but we must save him!"

"What of your belongings?" Einion asked her.

"Caddaric does not have a good head for wine," Wynne said with a smile. "His women will see he is carried to his bed, and he will sleep until the morrow is half gone. I will be able to get my things and Averel's as well."

The dawn had scarcely broken when Eadgyth crept to the peddler's wagon, calling softly as she neared it. *"Wynne. Wynne! Are you there?"*

Wynne stepped down from the cart and embraced her friend. "It is all right, Eadgyth," she said. "I am well."

"But how can that be?" Eadgyth fretted. "I do not understand how you can be so cheerful after what happened to you last night. It was horrible! I will never, ever forgive my husband for his bestial treatment of you, Wynne. *Never!*"

Wynne put a comforting arm about Eadgyth and replied, "Do you remember how I always told you that my husband would one day come for me? Well, he has."

"*What?*" Eadgyth's blue eyes were huge with her surprise, and then she said, "Oh, Wynne! My poor, poor Wynne! This terrible night just past has driven you mad!"

"No, no, Eadgyth! I am as sane as you are," Wynne reassured her. "Boda, the peddler, is my own servant Einion, well-disguised, I assure you, for even I did not recognize him at first. As for his son, Tovi, 'tis my own lord, Madoc, and he is equally well-disguised. I will not go into the details of this, Eadgyth, but you must swear to me that you will not tell the others. None has been the friend to me that you have, dearest Eadgyth. I would not leave you to worry about me. Know that I leave Aelfdene today for my own dear land of Wales. I am going home, Eadgyth, as I always knew I would."

Tears of happiness for her friend slipped down Eadgyth's face. "I will miss you," she told Wynne. "The others have always been pleasant companions, but you have been my friend. I will miss Arvel and Averel too. Now there will be no children at Aelfdene."

"Why did you not tell me about Arvel?" Wynne queried Eadgyth.

"I did not know until last night myself," Eadgyth replied. "Do you think I would have ever allowed Caddaric to do such a thing if it had been in my power to stop him? Had I known his intent, I would have hidden Arvel from him. I went immediately to the serfs' village after I left the hall last night, and I learned that Caddaric had sold Gytha to Ruari Ban as well. She was to go with little Arvel and continue his care. Where has the slaver taken them?"

"To the castle of my brother-in-law, Brys of Cai. He is the most evil man in Christendom, Eadgyth. God only knows what plans he has for my son. We leave for Cai as soon as I have gathered my things and Averel's."

"Come now back to the house," Eadgyth said. "Berangari and I have packed everything, but perhaps you will want something from your pharmacea. All that is there is really yours, and your journey will not be either short or easy."

"Thank you, Eadgyth," Wynne said. "I will take a few basic things, but I will leave the rest for you. You must take my place as Aelfdene's healer, my friend. I have filled a small book with all my recipes and their uses. It will be yours now."

The two women returned to the house. Wynne gathered what she wanted from her pharmacea. Then, with the help of the others, Wynne's chest and the small chest containing Averel's things were brought out to the peddler's cart. Averel's nursemaid, Willa, looked most woebegone. Her little nose was red from her weeping.

"Would you like to come with us, Willa?" Wynne asked the girl, who had been born and lived her entire life at Aelfdene.

"If I could, lady. There is nought for me here," was the weepy reply.

As the others had returned to the house, but for Eadgyth, Wynne said to Madoc, "Give me a silver penny, my lord, that I may purchase this girl."

Digging into his pocket, Madoc drew forth the required coin and handed it to Eadgyth. "Tell your husband that Boda wanted the girl to continue looking after the child so that I might help with the wagon and the goods. That you refused to let Willa go for any less than a penny, believing Boda would not pay it," Madoc instructed her. "Your husband will undoubtedly be surprised you struck so good a bargain for her, and the little wench isn't even worth a ha'penny. He will, therefore, be pleased enough to ignore the fact you sold off his property."

"You are not the half-wit," Eadgyth replied slowly, her voice filled with wonder. She peered closely at the creature she knew as Tovi. Then she looked at Wynne. "Is he fair beneath his disguise, Wynne?"

"Aye," Wynne said shortly. "His face is fair."

"Will you keep our secret, my lady Eadgyth?" Madoc asked her gently. "I have sought so long to find my wife and restore her to my side."

"I will keep your secret, my lord," Eadgyth told him solemnly, "but you must not think it is because I do not love Caddaric Aethelmaere, or because I am a disobedient wife. I both love and honor my husband, though I know he is not the most admirable of men. Wynne is my friend, and Caddaric's actions toward her have been wrong. It is not my wifely duty, however, to tell my husband that he has returned Wynne to her own dear lord. Such knowledge, as you undoubtedly know, would not please him. Wynne has been like a fever in my husband's blood. The realization that he could not have his way with her hardened his heart and made him crueler than I have ever known him to be. It is better that he go on believing he has debased her and brought her low. Another defeat would be more than he could bear," Eadgyth finished quietly.

"The care you show for your husband's peace of mind is most admirable, my lady," Madoc told her sincerely. "I think you a most wise and patient woman."

Eadgyth smiled a small smile. "Go with God's good blessing," she said. Then she and Wynne hugged each other. "It is unlikely that we will meet again," Eadgyth said. "I am glad that this ends well despite Caddaric."

"If you should ever need my help," Wynne told her, "you have but to get a message to Raven's Rock. I can never repay you for all your kindness." She hugged Eadgyth a final time. "God watch over you, my friend."

Eadgyth turned away and reentered the house. To have stayed any longer would have caused suspicion. Wynne, her daughter in her arms, and Willa climbed into the cart while Einion and Madoc, in the disguises as Boda and Tovi, mounted the bench seat. Einion flapped the reins over the horse's back, and the cart lumbered out of the courtyard of Aelfdene onto the half-track that led to another obscured road that would lead them back into Wales. To the east the sky was beginning to glow with the promise of a bright new day.

◾Chapter 19

They had traveled five days from Aelfdene. Now certain that Caddaric had not followed after them in some warped change of heart, Madoc and Einion thought it safe to remove their disguises. Willa, who had been informed almost immediately of the truth, watched wide-eyed as they did so. Her admiration of Einion was ill-concealed. Wynne felt it necessary to tell the girl of Einion's wife, Megan.

"Did you have to tell her quite so soon?" he grumbled at her.

"It is not necessary that you seduce my daughter's nursemaid," Wynne told him tartly. "You have not stinted yourself of female company in the months you have been away from Raven's Rock, I am certain."

Einion's eyebrows rose in surprise. She had matured. The baby who had grown into the sweet and lovely young girl was now a full-blown woman; and a woman, he suspected, who would have to be reckoned with. He wondered if Madoc had realized it yet, or if the prince would continue to treat his wife as a restored prize possession. Einion grinned to himself. Life was becoming interesting once again.

"I'll not tell you I've been entirely true to Megan, except in my heart," he said plainly, "but then Megan is wise enough not to ask as long as I am a faithful husband when at Raven's Rock."

"It's a wonder you haven't been killed by some enraged father or husband by now," Wynne said, and then she chuckled. "You have not changed, Einion, and I am glad. Everything else has changed."

"Aye," he agreed. They sat before a small campfire in a sheltered glen where the little fire would not be seen by bandits. "You have changed," he told her.

"I had no choice," she replied. "It was a matter of survival.

It was not myself I thought of, but of the child I carried at the time."

He nodded. "You and Madoc are yet at swords' points. Can you not heal the breach between you?"

Wynne smiled at him. "I hope so, Einion," she said, "but Madoc refuses to understand how it was for me. Then there is the matter of our son which must be settled."

"What is he like, the boy?" Einion asked. "Averel is nothing like you."

"Nay, she is her father's daughter without a doubt," Wynne said with another smile, "and Arvel is his father's son. He is Madoc's mirror image. After a time I began to forget Madoc's face. I had but to look at his son to remember. He is healthy, and bright and quick for a lad his age. If Eadwine had been alive, he would have never let my son go, for he thought of him as his own," Wynne told Einion.

"If Brys of Cai wanted the boy, my lady, he would have nonetheless found a way to steal him," Einion remarked fatalistically.

"But why does he want my son?" Wynne wondered aloud.

"He wants our son," said Madoc, joining them, "because his mind is warped, and he has some nefarious scheme festering within him."

"How long will it take us to get to Cai?" Wynne asked.

"We are not going to Cai, nor to Raven's Rock, dearling," he answered. "I am taking you and Averel to Gwernach. If I return home with you, then Brys will quickly learn of it. He will know that we will soon be coming to regain our son. To our small advantage, I have never known Brys to harm a little child, and this child is his nephew, his blood. I believe Arvel is safe as long as Brys does not suspect that we have been reunited. If he learns that, however, our son's life could be forfeit. We must plan carefully, for there will be but one chance for us. This I know in my heart."

"Mercifully, you will not take as long to fetch our son as you did to fetch me," Wynne said sharply.

"You are not fair," he replied equally hotly. "I have explained over and over again that at first we did not know where you were, for Brys made it seem as if you had died in the forest. I did not believe that though but until I was certain, I did not know where to look. Then we spent months chasing after the Irish slaver, only to find that you had never left England. We were hampered by weather, and by the fact we had so much territory to cover. There are hundreds of thegns, and hundreds of halls in which we had to look for you. You could have been in any of them, Wynne."

"I almost lost hope that you were coming," she told him.

"You were quite safe it seems," Madoc said dryly. "Willa has gossiped to Einion the whole story of how your Saxon thegn fell madly in love with you at first sight. Did you fall madly in love with him?"

"I grew to love him," she told Madoc honestly, "for he was a good and kind man. Was it necessary for me to cease living because you had disappeared again from my life, Madoc?" Wynne demanded sharply. "I had Arvel to think of, and his safety was paramount. I think I probably would have died in those early months had it not been for Eadwine's patience and kindness; and the realization that I must go on for my child's sake if not for my own. Would that have pleased you? The tender memory of love lost? Would you have followed me once more into another moment in time that we be reunited again? Love, I have come to realize, is not all nobility and purity of passion, Madoc. Love is both laughter and tears. Sorrow and pain. Giving as well as yearning for. You must learn that if we are ever to be happy."

"You have changed so," he said, and then he smiled at her, his blue eyes growing warm as he drank in her beauty. "You have always been the older soul, Wynne, and I a step behind. Teach me, dearling, that I may at least in this life race evenly with you."

"I will teach you, my lord, but you must catch up with me, for I will not wait for you," Wynne said. Then she took his hand in hers and, raising it up, rubbed it against her cheek. "I have missed you, my lord. I am glad we are together."

Turning his head, he kissed the hand that caressed his face and then said desperately, "God, how I long for a little bit of privacy! I cannot even remember wanting you as much as I want you now."

Wynne laughed low. "There will be plenty of time for *that*, my lord," she told him, and leaning forward, she placed a sweet kiss upon his lips, "but let us find our child first."

Madoc looked somewhat startled. "Do you tell me, dearling, that you will not receive me in your bed until my son is safe?"

Wynne's smile faded instantly. "To you, my lord," she said icily, "Arvel is naught but an imagining, but to me he is flesh and blood. You speak so possessively of *my son*, but he is not your son but for an accident of birth. *Not yet!* Not until you have brought him home; seen his dear little face, which is so like your own; held him close; and gained his love and trust. Only then will he truly be your son. Do not your fleshly desires fade in the face of all of this? Mine surely do!" and she turned away that he might not see her tears.

Madoc arose from their campfire and walked away into the darkness.

"You are too hard on him, Wynne of Gwernach," Einion said to her sternly, "and you are wrong."

"You, who have been my shield and buckler from my earliest time, would say this to me?" Wynne wept, and her look was so tragic, it was all Einion could do not to comfort her, but he did not.

"He has given up much for you, my lady," Einion told her.

"What has he given up?" she sniffled.

"His magic," Einion replied.

"What?" Wynne's tears instantly ceased.

"Aye," Einion said. "Only I know of it, for Madoc knew if there were others who were aware of his sacrifice, they would use it against him. He is wise enough to realize that the strong stature the princes of Wenwynwyn have always enjoyed comes from their reputation for magic. This is a contentious time in which we live, my lady. If Prince Madoc's strength is thought to be his magic, then it follows his loss of that magic would be considered a great, if not fatal, weakness. Raven's Rock and its lands have always been secure from the covetousness of its neighbors because of that aura of magic. Even Brys of Cai is fearful of the prince for that reason."

"Not so fearful that he did not abduct me, and not so fearful that he has not stolen my son," Wynne noted.

"Brys is not as wise as he thinks himself. He plays upon the prince's love of his family and his reverence for life," Einion said wisely.

"You say Madoc has given up his magic," Wynne answered. "Tell me of this."

"Before I departed Raven's Rock to hunt down the slaver, Ruari Ban," Einion began, "the prince called me to him. He had sought desperately for you within his mind's eye, but he could not find you and was at a total loss to understand why. In his guise as old Dhu he had scoured the countryside, and again there had been no trace of you to be found. Magic in this instance, it seemed, was of no help. It came to him then, he told me, that perhaps the Creator was telling him that the time for magic was past. As the days flew by he became more strongly convinced of this. So after much soul-searching he decided that if he was to find you, if he was to find your child, he must make the ultimate concession to the Creator, even, he said, as you had once renounced your powers for love of him in another time and place. How, he asked me, could he do any less for you than you had once done for him? I did not understand him when he said that, my lady, but I think you will."

Wordlessly Wynne nodded, silent tears slipping down her face with her understanding of the enormous sacrifice Madoc had made for her and their child.

"Together," Einion continued, "we went to the chapel, and I stood witness as Prince Madoc renounced his powers before God's altar. Neither will he pass them on to your children, my lady."

"What of the shape-changer's art?" Wynne asked. "Surely he did not give that up too."

Einion nodded. "That he cannot so easily put away from him, for it is knowledge bred into his family by their descent from the ancient Celtic god, Cernunnos. The prince has sworn, however, never to use that art again; or to pass it on to his descendants. Although the ability to shape-change will lie within them all, without the proper magic that power will remain dormant for all time. So you see, my lady Wynne, Prince Madoc has given up much to have you back, when he might simply have accepted your loss and sought another wife." Einion arose from his seat next to her by the flickering fire. "I will seek my bed now, lady."

Alone, Wynne peered into the dancing flames. How could she have allowed herself to become so wrapped up in her own self-righteousness that she failed to consider Madoc's feelings as well as her own? She might have changed, but she wondered if she had matured. Perhaps it would not have mattered so greatly if she did not love him; but despite it all, she did love him. She had never stopped loving him, even when she had allowed herself to love Eadwine too. She sighed deeply. Why could life not be more simple? And then she laughed softly at herself for the childish thought, even as she sensed his return to her side.

He squatted next to her.

"Why did you not tell me?" she asked him.

"That you might feel sorry for me?" he demanded bitterly.

"Why," she said patiently, biting back a sharp retort, "would I feel sorry for you? When Rhiannon gave up everything for Pwyll, did he feel pity?" Wynne turned that she might see his face in the firelight. "What you have done is the most magnificent gesture of love that anyone could make for another. My feelings for Eadwine Aethelhard never lessened my feelings for you, Madoc of Powys. From the beginnings of time we have been two souls that somehow become a single entity while yet remaining separate. I wonder if I will ever understand it." Reaching out, she touched him and said softly, "Will you not kiss me, my dear lord?"

"If I kiss you again, dearling," he told her tightly, "I will want more." There was a look almost akin to pain etched upon his face.

"No more than I am willing to give you, Madoc," she replied quietly.

His sculpted face registered his surprise at her words, and he arose, drawing her up with him. Wynne reached out and touched his high-boned cheek. Her slender fingers moved over his proud visage as if relearning it. The heavy, bushy eyebrows that bristled above his smoky, deep blue eyes. The long nose and narrow lips that lay so sternly above the deep cleft in his chin. With a small smile, Wynne said, "You have the look of a brigand."

Returning her smile with one of his own, he caught her hand and, turning it over, placed a kiss upon her palm. "I will have to appear even fiercer now if I am to keep us from harm," he told her, and drew her against him.

Wynne's arms slipped up about his neck and she molded herself close against his lean, hard body. "Should I be fearful, my dear lord?" she teased him. Her lips were tantalizingly close to his.

With a groan his mouth closed over hers in a bruising kiss. Wynne felt her heart leap joyously within her chest at his touch, yet at the same time she had the sensation of being consumed by fire. Somehow it felt as if it were the first time with him, but it was also better. She was more aware of her body now than she had ever been, and wondered fuzzily what had brought this revelation about. Her breasts swelled and hardened while her limbs grew languid and weak. Her blood, it seemed, had turned to a stream of hot honey that dallied slowly through her body, wreaking havoc with her composure.

Madoc, however, appeared to be suffering from similar symptoms. There was no mistaking the reaction of his body to the sensuous stimulus of his wife's body. He groaned again, saying, "Alas, dearling, for a lack of privacy, else I should make love to you here and now!"

Wynne laughed low and replied, "You will find neither Einion nor Willa within a half mile of this site, my lord, for he knows me better sometimes than I know myself. Averel sleeps within the safety of the cart, and Einion will have taken Willa off to some secluded spot that he might have his way with her, though she will scarce refuse him, being a lustful wench. If you would have me, Madoc of Powys, we are free to indulge in our own passions," Wynne told him, and she began to undress before him.

He spread his cloak upon the ground in front of the fire and followed suit. At last they stood together, naked, facing one another and as equal as a man and a woman can be. He reached out and cupped one of her breasts, squeezing it tenderly. Wynne smiled into his eyes and caressed his muscled shoulder with gentle fingers.

"Undo your hair for me," he said, and she loosened her heavy, thick braid, combing her raven's-black tresses free with her fingers. It rippled down her slender back in lavish waves. He caught a small strand between his fingers and kissed it, inhaling its subtle perfume as he did so. "You are so fair," he told her. "Never has there been a woman like you, Wynne of Gwernach."

"Nor a man like you, my lord Madoc," she answered, her eyes brimming with her newly reawakened love for him.

Their lips met once more in a passionate kiss as Wynne slid her arms back around his neck. Madoc drew her close again, his hands clasping her rounded buttocks. They kissed frantically now, mouths wet against each other; hot and wet against the flesh of throats and shoulders and chests; tongues dueling wildly as they slid together to their knees upon his cloak. His head lowered, placing scorching kisses over her quivering breasts; licking sensuously at her nipples, suckling upon them so fiercely that he drew forth her milk and, half sobbing, could not cease for several minutes, so aroused was he by this clear sign of her fertility.

Wynne's head was whirling with a plethora of emotions as he made this leonine love to her. She had forgotten the depth of his passion, or perhaps she had simply not dared to remember it. His mouth upon her skin burned like a brand. He offered pleasure so great that she could not imagine how she would return that pleasure, but she nonetheless welcomed it as she had never welcomed it before. He had always had this wildly delicious effect upon her. His mere look could turn her into an unrepentant wanton.

"Look at me, dearling," he crooned at her, and Wynne realized that her eyes had been closed in her rapture.

She forced her lids open and looked directly into his beloved face, half drowning in his deep blue eyes.

He stared back into her clear, green gaze. "Do you doubt my love for you, my precious wife?"

"I never doubted your love, my husband," she returned.

Satisfied, he lowered his head once more and began to trail kisses down her waiting body. Wynne sighed happily, and Madoc smiled silently, his body moving to accommodate his actions. She was open to him, and he slid between her satiny thighs, placing burning kisses upon each one as he did so. His hands slipped beneath her, cupping the peachlike mounds of her bottom to hold her steady as she began to whimper in fevered anticipation of his desire. He nuzzled her, breathing in the pungent female perfume of her. Then he kissed the warm, soft flesh of her mound.

"Ahhh, yes!" she encouraged him and, reaching down, spread her nether lips wide for him.

His tongue snaked out to touch her lightly with just its pointed tip, and she quivered distinctly beneath the teasing caress. He let her wait a moment or two longer, and then he once again touched her delicately, and this time she shivered even harder than before. The small succulent bud of her womanhood seemed to take on a life of its own beneath his flickering tongue. Puffing itself up, it deepened in color, communicating its pleasure throughout her whole body in tingling waves of delight. She gasped and sighed as sensation after sensation pulsed through her. Carefully he sucked upon her little jewel, and Wynne shrieked softly, almost unable to bear the delight that he was giving her.

"I want you inside of me!" she cried low. "I can bear no more of this sweet torture, Madoc! Fill me full of you!"

Then his mouth was on hers again, and she could taste herself upon his tongue. His hard body covered her as she wrapped her arms about him once more. Pushing her legs up, he eased himself into her sheath and began to slowly pump her with deep, lingering strokes of his great manhood. With a cry of rapturous bliss Wynne wound her legs about his torso, her hips jerking furiously as she encouraged him onward.

"Ahhhh, 'tis sweet! So sweet!" she half moaned, and he held her tightly, for she was thrashing wildly in her ecstasy.

She could distinctly feel him pulsing and surging within her fevered body. Each new thrust of his ravenous lance brought her closer to perfection. Their mutual hunger for one another communicated itself. As she was attuned to him, so was he attuned to the deep tremor building up within her very core. It quivered and vibrated as, head thrown back, Wynne struggled for air. She was being totally and utterly overcome by the billowing, vibrating sensation that rushed up to overwhelm her.

Madoc groaned as if in anguish as his own heightened passions threatened to wash over him. "I can wait no longer!" he cried, and Wynne felt her parched and secret garden being flooded with his warm life force.

"Ahhhh, my dearest love," she whispered to him as her body eagerly received his lover's tribute and, after what seemed a long time, he shuddered with complete and total release even as she soared above him.

They lay sprawled together, replete with their fulfillment while the fire cracked sharply. Their contented bodies were wet with their efforts, and finally Wynne said, "We will catch our death of cold if we do not clothe ourselves, my sweet lord."

He kissed her neck softly, nipping lightly at the damp skin, and rolled off of her onto his hip. His fingers trailed down between her breasts, and then he said, "I had not realized how much I had missed you, dearling, until now."

Wynne laughed softly. "I, also," she admitted, sitting up and reaching for her chemise. "Cover yourself, Madoc, for if Willa sees you she will lust after you as she has for Einion."

He chuckled and began to dress himself. When they were both reclothed, they refurbished their fire and sat companionably next to it, holding hands.

"How are we to go about regaining our son?" Wynne asked him.

"I do not know yet," he answered her, "but as I have told you, it is best you secrete yourself at Gwernach, that Brys not know we are reunited."

"I will leave Willa and Averel at Gwernach with my grandmother," Wynne told him. "Although Willa cannot wet-nurse my daughter, there will be someone there who can. They will be safe at Gwernach. I, however, am coming with you. Can we count on Rhys of St. Bride's to aid us?"

"Rhys would, of course, aid us if I asked," Madoc responded, "but I will not. Cai cannot be taken by force of arms, especially where Arvel's life is concerned. We will have to regain our son through guile and great cleverness."

"You will have to kill Brys this time," Wynne said.

"You sound like my sister," Madoc replied.

"You cannot march yourself into Cai demanding your child, Madoc, and expect that Brys will acquiesce without a struggle." Wynne's look was a serious one. "Oh, Madoc, my love! You have given your brother every chance, but he cannot help himself. The destruction of your person and everything connected with you seems to be his ultimate goal; but I am convinced that even if he attained that goal, he would yet be dissatisfied. His hatred for you is a deep sickness of the soul that does not stem from the here and now. You know that as well as I do. We cannot spend the rest of our lives looking over our shoulders wondering what evil Brys is planning for us next time! *Kill him!* Put an end to it! Do not allow him to separate us as he did once before."

Madoc sighed deeply. "And if I kill him, will I not be in his debt? Will that hatred he harbors finally die, or will it be reborn anew in another time and place for me, for us to contend with, Wynne?"

She shook her head. "I do not know the answers to your questions, Madoc. I simply know that if we are to live out our lives in peace this time, Brys must be dealt with in a way that will leave him unable to hurt us anymore."

"He is my brother," the prince said helplessly.

"He uses that very tie of blood against you, Madoc!" she said impatiently. "He has cost us three years of our lives. He cruelly parted us in an effort to destroy you, forcing me into bondage, though God knows I was fortunate in that bondage. He has stolen our child. And for what purpose, Madoc? Why does he want our son? What wickedness does he now plan? This is the man of whom you would be compassionate? Your brother does not know the meaning of the word compassion. If you allow him to live on, the further misfortunes that Brys brings down upon us all will be your fault, my lord, for it will be you who will have let him wreak some new havoc."

"I know that the words you utter are right and true, dearling," the prince answered Wynne, "but do not fear. Though it will be hard to do, I will see that Brys never again hurts anyone." He made a small attempt at humor. "I think I should rather slay Brys myself than have to listen to you and Nesta scold me. My sister has never really forgiven me for not protecting you more thoroughly, Wynne."

Wynne smiled. "How is Nesta?" she asked him. "I thought of her often, particularly in the early days of my captivity, for she was near to term with her child. Was it a son or a daughter?"

"Nesta has two sons," Madoc told her. "The eldest is Daffyd, and the younger, Trystan."

"How I long to see her!" Wynne said, and then she frowned. "We cannot allow Nesta and Rhys to know we have returned until Arvel is safe," she told him. "Tell me of my grandmother, my sisters and Dewi."

"Your grandmother is well, though she has mourned you deeply, even knowing you were not dead. Dewi is almost a man now, and Mair is growing into a beauty. She is the only one of your sisters who will rival you."

"And Caitlin and Dilys?"

Madoc laughed. "They thrive, although the elder will not speak to the younger anymore."

"Why on earth not?" Wynne looked puzzled. "They were always friends, if one could call their odd relationship friendly."

"True, dearling, but remember, 'twas always Caitlin, the elder, who led the way. Now, however, the tide has turned in Dilys's favor. In the four years she has been wed, she has produced four children. Three boys and a girl. The girl is one-half of a set of twins. Caitlin, on the other hand, has had but one son, upon whom she dotes, and has miscarried twice of children too small to even sex. Although her husband treats her as if she were a queen, and she rules the roost at Coed without interference, she is discontent and furious that her younger sister has outstripped her."

"Does Arthwr complain of a lack of children?" Wynne asked him.

Madoc chuckled. "He does not. He would not dare."

Wynne laughed. She had not thought of Caitlin in a long time, but now her memories of her sister came flooding back. No, her brother-in-law would not complain. He would have learned by now Caitlin's long memory for a slight, and her uncanny ability to wreak revenge upon those who displeased her. "How unfortunate," she said, her face now smooth and serious, "that I shall not be able to invite my sisters for a reunion at Gwernach," and then she was overcome by a fit of giggles.

They reached Gwernach unannounced late on a grey afternoon.

Clasping her eldest grandchild to her bosom, Enid could only say, "I knew he would bring you home safe, my child!" Her eyes brimmed over with happy tears that ran down her worn face.

Wynne hugged her grandmother back. She was astounded by the change in Enid. Her grandmother had suddenly become an old woman who moved far more slowly than Wynne could remember. Her lovely visage was marred by lines. "I have brought you a great-grandchild, Grandmother," she said, and drew her daughter forward. "This is my daughter, Averel Aethelhardsdatter."

Enid masked her surprise and, bending, smiled into the little girl's face. "I like your name, Averel," she said. Then she lifted Averel up into her arms, kissing her cheek as she did so.

Averel regarded Enid with large eyes, debating whether she was ready to accept another new person into her life. So much

had changed for her in the last few weeks. She liked the giant
with the burning head who let her ride upon the wagon's bench
and hold the horse's reins. Willa liked him too. She was not
certain, however, of the dark man who always seemed to be
watching her mother and paid little heed to her.

Averel decided quickly. Putting her arms about Enid's neck,
she kissed her great-grandmother wetly. "Gama," she said,
sounding mightily pleased. The adults around her laughed.

"She is a dear child," Enid said delighted, "but she is not in
the least like you, Wynne."

"She looks like her father," Wynne replied. "His name was
Eadwine Aethelhard, and he was the thegn of Aelfdene Manor,
near the Mercian town of Worcester. He considered me his
wife, and I was treated as such by all there."

"Wynne!" A youthful but masculine voice spoke her name.

Wynne turned and saw a tall, black-haired young man. For
a moment she could not believe her eyes. *"Dewi?"* she said.
"Ohhhh! You have become a man! *Almost,*" she amended, and
hugged him.

"I am betrothed," he said loftily, "to Gwenhwyvar of
Clydach. We will be wed in two years' time. I made the match
myself."

"You did well," Wynne told him, remembering the family.
"They have a strong strain of milk cows. Your Gwenhwyvar
will be bringing cattle as part of her dowry, I trust."

"Aye," he said with a grin. " 'Twas her greatest attraction
for me."

"Villain!" his grandmother said, half laughing. "Do not tell
me her soft brown eyes did not attract you. She is a lovely
child with yellow hair. Her grandmother, on her father's side,
was Saxon, I am told." Then Enid smacked him lightly. "Have
you no word of welcome for your sister who has returned after
three years of captivity among the Mercians? Where are your
manners, Dewi?" She sighed and explained to Madoc, "They
are all alike. Gwernach first before all else."

"I'm glad you're home safe, Wynne," Dewi said, and then
he replied to his grandmother, "If I did not put Gwernach first
as Wynne taught me, where would we all be?" He wore a
slightly outraged look upon his handsome young face.

"He's right," Wynne agreed. "Dewi, I am so proud of you!"

"Who is the child?" her brother asked, his gaze moving to Wynne's daughter.

"Your niece, Averel," came the answer.

"She's a Saxon whelp," he replied, and Wynne explained once more Averel's parentage. Dewi took the little girl from Enid and smiled at her. "Hello, bunny," he said softly, and stroked her hair. "She's like a little brown bunny," he chuckled, "with that soft hair and those suspicious eyes."

Mair came into the hall, and again Wynne was astounded. Her littlest sister had grown taller, and had an almost coltish young woman's look to her. Madoc had been right. Mair was fast becoming a beauty. Her long brown hair was filled with golden lights, and her green eyes were like a forest lake, all dappled and mysterious. Shyly she greeted her sister, welcoming her home; but it was Averel who brought a smile to her lovely face. Mair immediately took her niece in hand, and Averel reciprocated, pleased to find someone young enough to understand her.

They sat down to the evening meal and, as they ate, Madoc explained to his in-laws that Wynne had borne him a son in her captivity; of how his brother had recently sent the slaver, Ruari Ban, for the child; and of how Caddaric Aethelmaere had sold the little boy to him. "I want Wynne to stay at Gwernach while I go to Cai to retrieve our son from my brother, and afterward we will all go home to Raven's Rock," he concluded. Then he added, "but no one must know that she is here. I have no wish for Brys to try another of his tricks."

"I have been thinking these past days as we rode," Wynne said. "I have already told you that I must go to Cai with you, Madoc. You cannot force Brys to give up our son, but I think I can. The one thing he will never expect is for me to beard him in his own hall once more. Besides, Arvel does not know you and will be frightened. I have thought hard on it. At first I thought we could do this ourselves. I did not want to involve others, but now I think you should go to St. Bride's and obtain Rhys's aid. With an army at our back, and me in Brys's hall, he will not dare refuse to return Arvel to us. He will simply have no choice in the matter."

"He could barricade himself within Cai with both you and your son as hostages," Dewi said to his eldest sister. "Have you thought of that, Wynne? I am not so certain that your idea will succeed."

"Nor I, dearling," Madoc agreed with his brother-in-law.

"Brys could indeed withstand a siege at Cai," Wynne said honestly, "but for how long? Cai is not Raven's Rock, for it can be approached quite easily from one side. Does it have an interior source of water, as does Raven's Rock? I know for a fact it does not, for when I was last there I saw servants bringing water in buckets across the drawbridge."

"Aye," Madoc said thoughtfully, "its water source is a spring which is located outside the castle, but still, I do not think it wise for you to go to Cai, my love."

"Think on it, Madoc!" Wynne persisted. "Can you not imagine Brys's surprise and shock when I come before him dressed in my finest clothing, bejeweled and exuding confidence? When I come before him to demand the return of my son, the heir to Powys-Wenwynwyn?"

"Aye, he will be surprised, but knowing my brother, he will quickly recover and order your imprisonment," Madoc told her. "No, Wynne, 'tis impossible!"

"It is not!" she shouted at him, and those about the table began to shift nervously in their seats. It was rare that Wynne lost her temper, but when she did . . . "Let Brys know that I have come not alone this time, but with an army at my back. He will understand he has no choice but to release Arvel to me. Oh, he may at first decide to withstand a siege, but he will quickly realize upon reflection that he has no other option, Madoc. Think about your brother, my lord. He never commits a crime openly. Secrecy is a part of him. He is like a creature one finds beneath a rock who cannot stand the light of day. Appearance is important to Brys. He delights in his ability to look charming and innocent, even as he delights in his own wickedness."

"That is true," Madoc admitted, "but it frightens me to think of you inside Cai again. There must be no more separations between us."

"Madoc, my own dear lord," Wynne said, "we have made our peace with each other. Somehow, I suspect, we will always be together."

"I am still not totally convinced of the wisdom of your suggestion," Madoc told her honestly, "but I will go to St. Bride's seeking my brother-in-law's help. We will return to Gwernach and discuss this again. Will you accept whatever decision Rhys and I make in this matter?"

"I will," Wynne agreed.

"And you will swear to me that you will not go tearing off to Cai while I am at St. Bride's? You will wait for us?" His deep blue eyes were half serious, half amused, for his request was clever, and the look upon Wynne's face one of a child found out in some anticipated mischief-making. "Promise me, my lady of Raven's Rock, or I shall instruct your brother to lock you in a cow byre until I return," he threatened her.

"Oh, very well!" she said with ill-concealed grace, and her family laughed with relief.

Madoc rode out the next morning for St. Bride's alone. He trusted his wife, but at the same time he realized her impatience to rescue their son might lead her to dishonor her promise to him. Einion remained behind to watch over his lady, as he had always watched over her, and if Wynne had had any thought to slipping away from Gwernach, she was not given the opportunity, for Einion's eyes were on her constantly.

"You could have gone with him," Wynne grumbled at Einion.

"He will travel faster alone," was the bland reply, "and time is important to us in this matter. We must lay siege to Castle Cai before the winter snows come."

Wynne nodded. "Let us hope the winter will be delayed, or at least a mild one, should it come early," she told him, and looked to the greying skies with their lowering moisture-laden clouds.

"The weather is still warm with false summer," Einion said. "There is time."

A week passed. A week in which Wynne renewed her ties with her family. Without Madoc she was free to speak of Eadwine, and she did.

"You loved him well, my child," Enid said. "I can tell it from the tender way in which you recall him. What happened to him?"

"Almost a year ago," Wynne began, "Eadwine went hunting for boar. A large one had been spotted rooting in his wood, and 'twas near the feast of Christ's Mass. He wanted a boar's head for the celebration. His eldest son, a discontented and unhappy man, rode with him. When the boar was finally run to ground, Caddaric leapt from his horse, eager to make the kill and shine in his father's eyes. The beast moved faster than they had anticipated. Eadwine put himself between his son and the creature, killing it, but being mortally wounded in the process. He saved Caddaric's life, but then toward the following dawn as my Eadwine lay near death, Caddaric refused his father's dying request to care for me. My poor lord died knowing he left me in danger."

Wynne then went on to explain to her grandmother Caddaric's obsession with her, and his unswerving belief that Wynne could give him the children that Eadgyth and the others had not been able to give him. Her brother and sister had now joined them and listened wide-eyed as she wove her tale. They all laughed when Wynne elaborated upon the scheme the other women concocted to protect her from the attentions of other men once Caddaric had condemned her to become the whore of the hall, of how finally, in anger and frustration, Caddaric vowed to give Wynne to the first man who would take her upon his high board in his presence; of Boda and his half-wit son Tovi.

"How wonderful that you were able to escape this horrible Saxon," Mair said earnestly, and she hugged Averel, who was comfortably settled in her lap. "How I should like to find a man someday who would love me as Prince Madoc loves you, dearest sister." Her green eyes grew dreamy with her secret thoughts and hopes for her future.

"He will be there at the right time, Mair," Wynne told her little sister. "You have but to wait, and Dewi, I know, will grant you the same grace and favor he granted me. You will only marry the man you love."

"Aye," Dewi agreed. "If he is suitable, and if he is available, Mair, he will be yours, I swear it!"

With a little smile, Mair took her niece and wandered off humming to herself. Dewi shrugged with amusement and, excusing himself, went back out into his fields to oversee his servants.

"And what of Madoc?" Enid asked her granddaughter. "Can you love him again, Wynne?"

"I never stopped loving him, Grandmother," came the answer. "I find it odd myself, but there it is, and though I puzzle about it over and over, I find no explanation as to how I can love two men at the same time. Each is different, and now, having lost one, I can love the other fully."

"What if your Saxon had not been killed?" Enid wondered aloud.

Wynne shook her head. "I do not know," she said. "Had I been faced with such a situation, I think I might have had to flee them both and live alone where neither could find me. It frightens me to even think about it. How could I possibly choose? Each has given me a child."

"Hmmmmm," Enid sighed, and her expression was a grave one. She had no answers to such a possible problem either. God was a far better architect than man in arranging such matters.

▓ *Chapter 20*

Madoc returned eight days after he had left them, bringing not only Rhys, but his sister Nesta as well. The two young women threw themselves into each other's arms, weeping happily.

"I never knew how much I missed you until now!" Wynne cried.

"Nor I, you," Nesta reciprocated. "Now let me see your daughter! Madoc tells me she is absolutely adorable."

"He said *that*?" Wynne was completely surprised. Madoc had not seemed too anxious to engender a relationship of any kind with little Averel. His attitude had pained her, especially when she remembered Eadwine Aethelhard's loving fosterage of Arvel.

Nesta immediately understood Wynne's thoughts. "He did indeed say Averel was adorable. He is quite taken with the child, Wynne. It is simply difficult for him to reconcile his feelings for her with his knowledge that she was conceived by another man upon his wife's body."

" 'Tis yet another wicked wound that Brys has done Madoc," Wynne said.

"Aye," Nesta replied, "but do not fear, dearest sister. Madoc will eventually reconcile himself to your lost years. The important thing is that we are now all reunited once more."

"Madoc must destroy Brys for all time," Wynne said suddenly.

"Aye," Nesta rejoined. "I agree with you. The defeat we are about to give Brys will embitter him far more than anything he has ever suffered before now. He is not a man to take such a defeat lightly. Left alive, he will seek new means of hurting us all. There is no choice but to destroy him first. Destroy him completely."

"Now you see, brother Madoc," Rhys of St. Bride's deep voice boomed out, "why I am not afraid to leave Nesta in charge of St. Bride's or Pendragon. She is the perfect mate for me." He chuckled, and took his wife's dainty hand as if to lead

426

her forth. "Look at her. She looks like a fairy princess, but she is as bloodthirsty as any berserker I have ever encountered!"

"Am I wrong in my assessment, my lord?" Nesta demanded of her husband, and she pierced him with a sharp look.

"Nay, my love, you are not. We must defang that snake who calls himself Brys of Cai once and for all." Rhys then smiled at Wynne. "Welcome home, Wynne of Gwernach!" he said, and enveloped her in a quick bear hug. Setting her back on her feet, he said admiringly, "I think you are equally as strong as my wife, lady, to have survived your captivity. Women of the Cymri race are, it seems, like well-tempered sword blades: both beautiful and strong."

"What a fine compliment, my lord," Wynne praised him, her cheeks pink with her pleasure. "I see you have learned well from Nesta how to turn a pretty phrase, but lest you turn my head with your flattery, I would know if Madoc has discussed my plan to retrieve our son, and if he has, what you think of it?"

"I think you are absolutely correct in your appraisal of the lord of Cai, sister," Rhys surprised her by saying. "He is a craven coward, and the best way to approach him is surprise."

"You agree with me?" Wynne was indeed astounded.

"I do," he replied. " 'Tis the best way to initiate our war against him. Surprise! And I can imagine the look upon his handsome face when you stride boldly into his hall demanding the return of your son!" Rhys's deep laughter echoed through Gwernach's hall. "He could easily choke on his own bile, and wouldn't that be a great pity! 'Twould save us the trouble of gutting him like the swine he is."

Wynne turned to Madoc and he shrugged in agreement. "I must bow to Rhys's wisdom and yours, it seems, dearling. I am no warrior, but a man of logic and reason."

"And you need not be responsible for killing the devil," Rhys said. "I will do it in repayment for the sin he attempted to commit against my darling Nesta when she was just a wee girl. Only an evil creature with perversion bred into his very soul could seek hurt against women and children."

Wynne paled. "Yes," she said, "Madoc assures me that Brys will not hurt Arvel. What if he already has?"

Madoc shook his head. "I know somehow that he has not harmed the boy," he reassured his wife. "If Brys wanted to harm or even kill our son, he would have done it at Aelfdene, making certain that we both knew. He did not. He arranged to steal the child away in secret so that you would not know immediately, and I would not know at all because I was not even supposed to find you, dearling. Nay, Brys has done no injury to Arvel."

"We must leave for Cai as soon as possible," Wynne said, and then she asked Rhys, "Where is your army, my lord? You have brought no armed force to Gwernach with you."

"My men left St. Bride's for Cai four days ago," Rhys said. "They travel by night only. Such a force as I am bringing would arouse suspicion, not only of our neighbors, but of Harold Godwinson over the hills in England as well. Now that he has seen to the murder of our king, he does well to fear us. Word might also reach Cai. Brys must not be warned of our coming, nor the English interfere with this family matter of ours. I sent a messenger to Raven's Rock instructing Madoc's men to travel by night as well. If we ride out tomorrow night, we will be in plenty of time to meet them."

"Will you go too?" Wynne asked Nesta.

"Aye, I must," Nesta told her. "I must see the end of this and know truly that Brys can never harm any of us again."

That evening Wynne and Madoc sought privacy in the peddler's wagon which had been placed neatly to one side of the courtyard of Gwernach's manor house. Emptied of its goods, it was quite spacious. A mattress filled with sweet meadow grass and fragrant clover had been placed upon the floorboards of the wagon to be topped with a featherbed and several sheepskins. The bleached linen that covered the top and sides of the cart gave them complete seclusion from prying eyes. Naked, they lay stroking each other's bodies to tender arousal.

"You are delicious," he growled low, nipping at the smooth curve of her hip.

"Villain!" Wynne smacked playfully at her husband. "Do I not feed you enough that you would attempt to feast upon my person?"

"I love feasting upon you," he murmured low. Then he rolled her onto her back, and pouring a little wine from one of two goblets they had brought into the wagon upon her belly, he lapped it up with his tongue. "I am drunk with my desire for you, Wynne of Gwernach," he told her passionately.

"And as randy as a stallion in heat too, my lord," she said, her heart beating a quick tattoo. How she loved him!

"Aye," he admitted, and rolling upon his own back, he begged her, "Love me, dearling! I need to feel your mouth upon me tonight."

Rising up upon her side, Wynne looked down at him sprawled upon his back, his manhood engorged and stiff as it thrust upward. She bent and rubbed her soft cheek against it, then placed a kiss upon the ruby tip, her tongue snaking out to encircle the smooth skin of the head, her fingers clamping firmly about it.

He groaned with pure pleasure when she took him into her mouth, reveling in the warmth of her tongue against his skin. "Dear God!" he exclaimed suddenly, "I am nigh to exploding with my desire for you, Wynne, my beautiful wife!"

Releasing him, she raised her head and looked into his eyes. "I feel no desire yet," she said frankly. "How quickly you men are ready to couple, fired by your own lusts, and by wine, no doubt. We women are not so quickly aroused. Alas, though I would give you all the pleasure that I could, Madoc, my dear lord, I am not ready to receive your wild and wondrous passion."

What other woman of his past acquaintance, he wondered, would have made so honest an admission? Other men, he knew, would have been angered by a wife's refusal to offer instant gratification, but then it had never been that way with them. Reaching up, he caressed her full breasts hanging like twin moons above him. Seeing the pleasure begin to creep into her eyes, he smiled slightly. One of his greatest delights in Wynne had always been her enthusiasm for making love. Lifting his head, he licked at her nipples, teasing at the sensitive pinkish-beige flesh until they contracted into thrusting nubs and she murmured with contentment. His hands closed about her waist, and Madoc buried his head in the deep valley between those soft breasts, rubbing his face against the perfumed skin. The fragrance of white heather, warmed by the heat of her body, assailed him.

Gently he tumbled her back onto the soft sheepskins, spreading her wide to him. His night-black head lowering, his mouth sought the honied sweetness of her. His skilled tongue began to stroke expertly at the sensitive coral-pink flesh. Beneath him she began to writhe and whimper with the familiar sound of pure pleasure. He felt his own desire beginning to rise as she cried softly, "Madoc! Oh, Madoc, my love!" with a building urgency he also recognized.

When he had brought her twice to a full and shuddering release by means of his tongue, he mounted her, filling her full with his throbbing passion; riding her furiously until they had both attained mutual pleasure a third and final time. Then rolling off of her, Madoc gathered Wynne into his strong arms.

It had begun to rain outside, and Wynne lay happily within the security of his embrace, listening to the sound of it against the tentlike top of the wagon, thinking her mixed thoughts. Tomorrow night they would leave for Cai. They would reach it in several days' time. Arvel, her precious son! *Their son.* How she longed to hold him once again within her arms. How proud Madoc would be of the little boy! Curiously she wondered what Brys wanted with the child. Brys with his angel's face and black soul. She would soon know.

The rain had stopped by mid-morning of the following day, but it had grown colder. Enid sought among the storage chests and found clothing that had belonged to Wynne several years earlier, before she had gone to Raven's Rock. Together she and Mair stayed up practically the entire night altering the garments, that Wynne would have warm clothing for the trip.

"They are not the elegant garments you are used to wearing at Raven's Rock," her grandmother apologized, "but they are clean and warm and will keep the wind and rain out."

Wynne thanked Enid lovingly and said, "I have not worn elegant garments for some years now, Grandmother. I am certainly not ashamed of my old clothes." Her fingers stroked at the soft wool fabric of her tunic dress. Both it and her under tunic, which was lined in rabbit's fur, were dark green in color and matched the heavy green mantle which was edged in wolf's fur. Wynne fastened the mantle shut with a pretty brooch of silver, a single piece of green agate in its center.

"Megan will be bringing Wynne's richer garments to Cai, that she may face my brother at her grandest," Madoc told Enid.

Averel was already in her cot sleeping when they finally departed Gwernach. The little girl fully understood that her mother would be leaving her for a time, but did not object as she was assured that Mair would be there with her. Hugging Wynne and placing a noisy kiss upon her mother's cheek, she had toddled from the hall that evening garbed in a little white chemise, her hand tucked securely in Mair's. Then suddenly she pulled away from Mair and, racing back across the hall, threw herself at Madoc.

He lifted her up into his lap and gently inquired, "What is it, Averel?"

"*Da?*" Averel said, and there was no doubt in anyone's mind that the word was posed as a question. For some inexplicable reason, Averel needed to identify exactly who Madoc was in her life; and she needed to know it now.

"Aye, bunny, I'm your da," Madoc replied, and looking over the little one's head, he almost wept at the look of gratitude in Wynne's beautiful green eyes.

"Da come back?" Averel asked.

"Aye, Da is coming back," he reassured her.

Averel wrapped her arms about his neck and hugged him with all her childish strength. Then climbing down from the prince's lap, she ran back to Mair, and together they left the hall.

"Thank you," Wynne said simply to her husband.

"Do not shame me any further," he answered her low. "Did not the Saxon, Eadwine Aethelhard, who was her father, take my son to his heart without question? In my pride I have been slow to act, but in the presence of our families I say now that I take Averel Aethelhardsdatter for my own true daughter. I will dower her, and never will I treat her with any less love or respect than I will treat my own natural-born children."

A quarter-moon lighted their way as they rode forth from Gwernach. Enid watched as they went, the six horses outlined darkly atop the hill. Dewi had insisted upon going, and there was nothing that either Wynne or Enid could do to dissuade him.

"He's fourteen and 'tis past time he had battle experience," Rhys agreed. "How do you expect him to defend Gwernach from attack, if it should ever be attacked, if he has no battle experience?"

"He also has no heir," Wynne protested.

" 'Tis unlikely there'll be a fight," Rhys said in an attempt to calm her fears. "Brys does not engender great loyalty among his men. 'Twill be a wee skirmish if anything at all, and we'll put the lad safely in the rear that he might observe and learn," the lord of St. Bride's soothed his sister-in-law, but he winked broadly at Dewi, who grinned back, delighted with the conspiracy.

When dawn came they camped in a secluded cave by a stream, taking turns at standing watch and keeping the little fire within their rocky shelter low that it not be seen by its smoke. Dewi trapped a hare in early afternoon and, after skinning it, broiled it. It was tough and gamy, but tasty. The weather remained clear as they began their ride that night.

"We're fortunate," Rhys growled. "I thought that rain the other night signaled the beginning of a wet spell. Nothing is worse than riding in the rain, unless it is riding in the snow."

"Where will we meet our army?" Wynne asked him.

"They will secrete themselves in the woods near Cai and await us. They must be careful that they are not discovered. Surprise is the key element to our victory," Rhys explained. "When a foe is surprised, he is less likely to act with either intelligence or instinct. In most cases he will react with fear, which is a breeding ground for ill-judgment."

"Rhys is a brilliant tactician," Nesta said proudly.

The lord of St. Bride's grinned, quite pleased by his beloved wife's appraisal of his abilities. "When you go into the castle, Wynne," he continued on, "you need have no fear. We will secure the drawbridge area immediately, and you will offer amnesty to any men-at-arms within the castle."

"If we are surprising Brys," Wynne asked, "why can we not secure the entire castle at once? You seem so certain that there will be little resistance."

"That is true," Rhys replied, "but we do not know where your son is, Wynne. Though we may secure the castle, there is no guarantee that we can capture Brys of Cai himself in a first assault. Without Brys in our hands, the boy could indeed be in danger. Better we stick to our original plan. Believe me, no one will be more surprised than the master of Cai to have you walk into his hall, proudly regal, and demanding that your son be returned to you." He chuckled. "Ahhh, Jesu, I wish I could see it!"

Wynne rode silently now, remembering the last time she had faced down Brys of Cai. This time, however, she would have an army at her back. This time she was fighting for possession of her son. This time she was wiser than she had been four years ago. Brys would not defeat her this time.

Another dawn, another bright day. They camped in a wooded thicket, unable to have a fire this time because, despite the density of the wood, they were in the open. Smoke from a campfire could easily give them away. Resigned, they ate cold barley cakes which were enhanced by thick slices of Gwernach's Gold, sweet, crisp apples, and drank a rich wine that warmed them before sleeping. Today Nesta and Wynne would take the first watch. The women insisted upon doing their part.

"Madoc tells me you have two sons," Wynne said to her sister-in-law. "Tell me about them. Do they favor you or Rhys?"

"Trystan, the younger, is Rhys reborn. He is a noisy, brawling child," Nesta told her. "As for Daffyd, he seems to be a mixture of us both, although he has my auburn hair. He's clever like Rhys, but more thoughtful. St. Bride's will not suffer when he comes into his inheritance. I shall give Pendragon to Trystan, however, for he would chafe beneath his elder brother's rule. But tell me of your Arvel."

Wynne smiled. "His father's image," she said. "He is a quiet lad, always watching and listening. He and Daffyd will be good companions for each other."

"Madoc was like that as a little boy, I remember our mother saying. He was so totally different from Brys, who was mercurial in temperament. Madoc thinks before he acts. Brys simply acts and considers not the consequences," Nesta told Wynne.

"That is what frightens me," Wynne said. "That Brys will act. For what purpose can he possibly want my son?"

Nesta shook her head. "Only in Brys's twisted mind can the answer to that question be found, dearest Wynne."

Once more the weather favored them, and they rode throughout the cold, clear night. The moon waxed fuller and silvered the landscape as they passed by. Slowly they traveled onward, drawing nearer with each passing hour to Castle Cai. Wynne pulled her mantle closer about her and was grateful for its fur-lined hood. The wind, though slight, was sharp and cutting upon her face. Her fingers were icy within her wantuses, which were well-tanned kid mittens lined with fur. She wondered if she would ever be warm again. How she longed for a well-built hall and a roaring fire to sit by and toast her hands and feet.

They rode for several more days, until finally one night as they rode along Madoc said, "We will reach Cai before dawn. Megan should already be there. You will have plenty of time in which to change your clothing, dearling."

Wynne nodded wearily. "Can we not rest the day?" she asked. "I am so tired."

"A hot meal will restore you, my lady," Einion broke in, and reaching over, he patted her shoulder.

"He is right," Madoc said. "We dare not linger any longer than necessary beneath Brys's very nose, for fear of losing our advantage with him, Wynne."

"A hot meal," Wynne sighed. "Do you think it will be venison stew? Or lamb?"

"If you eat too much you will want to sleep," Rhys counseled. "You may have just enough to revive your energy."

Nesta shot Wynne a sympathetic glance. She was as bone-tired as her friend was, but at least she would not have to stride into the hall at Cai and challenge her brother.

"Aren't you tired, Rhys?" Wynne asked him.

"Nay," said Rhys. "With each step we take toward Cai my energy rises. Battle, or the thought of battle, is like an aphrodisiac to me. I love it! It excites me! It sets my blood to raging and my heart to racing. I am never more alive!"

"Poor Rhys," Nesta laughed. "He has had little excitement but what he could find in our bed since our marriage. Is that not so, my dear lord? I will no longer allow him to go and play at war with the other little lordlings, unless, of course, we are attacked ourselves."

Rhys chuckled. "You have offered a multitude of sweet and infinitely delightful compensations, lady mine," he told her. "Still, I will admit to looking forward to this adventure. It will give me great pleasure to kill Brys of Cai, for never was a man more in need of killing."

"Of your skill with weapons, my dear lord," Nesta told her husband, "I have no doubt; but beware my brother, Brys. What he lacks in ability, he makes up for in cunning. Do not make the mistake of thinking that because he is nobly-born that he will act with chivalry. His sole intent when cornered will be to win by means fair or foul. He will care not which as long as he is triumphant. Give him no quarter!"

"It disturbs me that you have set yourself up as Brys's executioner," Madoc said. "I feel the task should be mine."

"Nay," Rhys replied. "Brys's death should not be laid at your door, not should his blood be on your hands, Madoc of Powys. It would, I fear, allow your brother the final victory. We will not give him that victory! He will go to his death knowing that he has lost totally. That his family has triumphed over him. Nay! He must not have any victory!"

▦*Chapter 21*

Brys of Cai had his private apartments within the north tower of Castle Cai. He liked facing north, for neither the sun nor the moon rose from that direction, and in their daily passage across the skies above, their light barely touched his rooms, which were usually cold with the harsh winds that blew from the north. The chill suited him. Even as a child he had disliked warmth.

The apartment was luxurious in its furnishings and scrupulously clean, for Brys could not tolerate disorder or dirt. Exquisite and very unique tapestries hung upon the walls. They offered scenes of erotic perversions totally unsuitable for a man who held a Church office. They were woven at a nearby convent by six nuns who relieved their tedium by occasionally gracing Brys's bed. The furniture was of heavy, well-polished oak. The apartments had another amenity known to few. Within the bishop's bedchamber was a small door behind one of the tapestries which led to the ramparts of the castle. From there Brys could get to any other part of the castle in the event of an emergency.

Such an emergency was now occurring even as a nervous servant shook his master awake.

"Your grace! Your grace!" the man gently patted at Brys's shoulder.

The icy eyes opened instantly. Brys sat up asking, "What is it? Be careful you do not wake the child, or you will suffer for it." The boy's face was still stained with the tears he had shed the night before, when Brys had whipped him soundly for whining that he wanted to continue to sleep with his nursemaid and not within his uncle's chamber. Arvel would learn quickly to obey his uncle, Brys thought with grim pleasure.

"Well?" he demanded of the servant. "Why have you awakened me at this ungodly hour? If it is not important, you will regret your lapse of sound judgment." He stared coldly at the man.

"My lord," the servant said, trying to hide his great and deep satisfaction at what he was about to impart to this vicious master, "we are under siege, my lord. I thought you would want to know." He bowed politely and quickly stepped back several paces that he might avoid any blow aimed at him.

Brys's eyes narrowed with speculation. "Who dares to besiege Castle Cai?" he wondered aloud.

"I could not say, my lord, but undoubtedly they will soon reveal themselves to you," the servant replied boldly.

"Get out!" Brys told him, swinging his legs over the side of the bed. Rising, he reached for his sherte, pulled it over his head, and, bending down, drew a pair of braies up his legs before stuffing them into his boots as he yanked them on his feet. Opening a chest, he took out a richly embroidered peacock-blue silk kirtle lined in marten and put it on. Then checking to see if the boy still slept, he lifted the tapestry and slipped through the little door. Quickly he mounted the steps, pushing open the trapdoor at the top of the staircase and climbing out onto the ramparts.

"My lord!" One of the men-at-arms came forward to help him.

Brys shook him off and, striding over to the battlements, peered down. The flat open space he had so carefully cleared before the front of the castle was filled with armed men standing shoulder to shoulder in line after line after line. The setting moon was strong enough to cast an eerie light that touched the tops of the assembled army's helmets, giving them an almost ghostly appearance. There was not a sound to be heard. Brys had absolutely no idea of who they were, and he hissed slightly in annoyance beneath his breath.

"What shall we do, my lord?" the man-at-arms asked him.

The bishop of Cai looked blankly at the soldier and said, "Why do you ask me? I am no soldier. Besides, they offer no hostile action toward us. They but stand before my gates." With a shrug he moved away from the battlements of the castle and returned down the staircase to his apartments. Squatting by the trundle, he woke Arvel. "Awake, my nephew," he said softly. "It is morning, or almost morning." Drawing the sleepy child to his feet, he quickly dressed him and then, picking him up, carried him from the apartments down into the hall.

The Saxon wench, Gytha, ran forward and took the boy from him. "I'll feed him his breakfast, my lord," she said, ducking her head to avoid his gaze.

He nodded and eyed her speculatively. She was a handsome creature with big, pillowy tits and broad hips. She would undoubtedly make a good fuck. He would amuse himself with her before he sold her off to Ruari Ban the next time the slaver passed his way. That would be time enough to begin erasing Arvel's happy memories of babyhood. His nephew must learn cold reality.

His thoughts turned to the boy as he watched Gytha spoon hot cereal into the child's open mouth. *Madoc's son.* Madoc's only son. *Only heir.* He had his hated brother's son in his possession! Brys smiled. He had taken Madoc's wife from him, but that had been but the beginning of his revenge. Madoc had not seemed to suffer greatly the girl's loss, and, indeed, a woman was easily replaced. A firstborn son, however, was not; and the best part was that Madoc did not even know of the boy's existence. There would be time for that, Brys contemplated, and he smiled.

He had sent Ruari Ban back to Mercia when he believed the baby would be weaned and could travel. "Fetch me the child," he had told the slaver. If the child were a boy, so much the better; but a little girl would do just as well. A boy he could raise as his own, teaching him to hate what Brys hated, and of course that meant Madoc. He would bind his nephew to him so tightly that Madoc would never be able to reshape Arvel's cold heart. And when the boy was old enough, say fourteen or so, he would bring him to Raven's Rock to displace whatever other children a second wife would have borne his brother. An heir who had been taught to hate and despise his father! An heir for Raven's Rock who would be schooled in pure evil; whose first task would be to kill his father and perhaps even his male siblings. It was such a perfect revenge!

But if Madoc's young wife had whelped a girl, then he had another plan in mind. He would lovingly raise the little wench, ~~introducing her to the~~ delights of the flesh as early as he dared. He would have her ~~virginity in due time, and~~ he would make the girl love him so desperately that she would ~~do whatever~~ he bade her to do. Hopefully she would look like her mother. Then one day when she was at her peak of perfection, he would introduce her into Raven's Rock. She would be instructed to seduce her father, not knowing, of course, that Madoc was her father. When she was well and truly ensconced as Madoc's lover and ripening with Madoc's child, he would tell his brother the truth. *That his mistress was his own daughter!* That the child she carried would be not only his offspring, but his grandchild as well! Brys almost laughed aloud at this scenario, and frankly, could not decide which revenge was best. He would have to rely on fate to choose, and fate had, bringing him a nephew.

Arvel was a strong child, healthy and intelligent. He would learn quickly once he could be forced from his babyish ways. He had allowed Ruari Ban to buy the boy's nursemaid and bring her along because, as the slaver had cleverly pointed out, the little lad would still need a woman's care. He would be more comfortable with someone familiar, and therefore less likely to sicken and die; or worse in Brys's estimation, to take a dislike to the lord of Castle Cai, whom he must be taught to love, trust, and fear implicitly.

Brys slowly sipped at his morning ale. He was a man skilled in patience, and he would need that patience now more than ever. It would be ten to twelve years before he could introduce his nephew to his father. He contemplated the story he would tell Arvel as to how he came to live with his doting uncle. He would not speak on it until the boy asked, and that, he knew, would be several years hence. Arvel would remember little of his first three and a half years by then. He would only recall the years lived at Castle Cai. Brys would tell his nephew that his father had cast both his mother and himself out of Raven's Rock when he fell in love with another woman and desired to make her his wife. As Wynne's loss had not killed Madoc with grief, Brys knew that he would have to remarry, and the sooner the better. After all, Wynne of Gwernach had disappeared almost four years ago. He might even pretend to make peace with Madoc and their sister Nesta, in order to be privy to their lives; in order to encourage Madoc's remarriage, something he knew their sister would approve of wholeheartedly. Aye, 'twas time for dear Madoc to remarry. Neither he nor Nesta need ever be aware of Arvel. Not until the time was ripe.

He smiled more broadly, and a small chuckle escaped him. Arvel would be taught to hate Madoc with a blind, unreasoning hatred. He would be told and retold of how he and Wynne were cast off, that his father might indulge his vices with other women. He would be mentally tortured with the picture of his half brothers and half sisters, all of whom were beloved of their father, spoilt and indulged by a doting prince who cared so little for his firstborn that he had cruelly cast him aside.

Siblings who were loved by their father, while he, Arvel, the most worthy of them all, was cast aside. Arvel would be taught to covet Raven's Rock so greatly that when the time came for him to meet Madoc, he would desire his father's possessions and title so passionately that he would be willing to kill to obtain them from the man who had deserted him and had been responsible for the death of his beautiful and gentle mother.

Brys stared out into his hall. *Wynne of Gwernach.* He could see her now standing before him. She was garbed in a magnificent tunic dress of grass-green brocatelle embroidered with gold thread in an acorn and oak-leaf design. Her girdle was of linked gold disks, and in the center of each disk was a polished round of green agate. A necklace of gold and pearl was hung about her neck, and in her ears were matching pearl drops. Her magnificent raven's-black hair was parted in the center, and the single, thick braid she always wore was woven with gold ribbons and small pearls. There would be thick, rich brown marten decorating the hem of her brocatelle tunic dress, and at its broad sleeves as well. She would have a jeweled band about her forehead.

Wynne of Gwernach. She was the most beautiful woman he had ever known. Even his sister Nesta could not hold a candle to Wynne. How often he regretted his lack of foresight that night he had held her captive. He would have enjoyed forcing her; showing her how much better a lover he was than his brother Madoc. It would have given him pleasure to hear her plead with him, but then she might have miscarried of the child, and his vengeance would have been quite incomplete. His self-control was to be commended, Brys thought. Ahh, beautiful Wynne of Gwernach. With a sigh of regret he blinked the vision away, *but it did not go away.*

Brys of Cai screwed his eyes tightly shut, but when he opened them again, she was still standing there, smiling at him. *It could not be!* He felt an aching tightening in his chest, and he struggled to draw a breath. She began to walk toward him, and Brys half rose, making the sign of the cross as if to ward off some evil.

Wynne's laughter bubbled up and tinkled throughout the hall. " 'Tis a wonder the roof does not cave in upon us, Brys," she mocked him. "What sacrilege that you should invoke the sign of the cross!"

"You are but a figment of my imagination," he managed to croak.

"More likely of your guilty conscience, but alas for you, I am quite real, dear brother-in-law. I have returned from Mercia whence you sent me, and I have come for my son, Arvel. Give him to me!"

"I know not of what you speak," Brys lied futilely, his icy eyes darting to where Gytha had been feeding Arvel. The Saxon bitch crouched nervously in the shadows, her arms wrapped protectively about the boy.

"Give me my son!" Wynne repeated, and now her voice was cold and hard. "I know not for what vengeful or perverted purpose you have stolen him away from me, but I want him back, Brys, and I mean to have him! Madoc is anxious to make the acquaintance of his heir."

"Where is my brother?" Brys demanded, and then his eyes lit with comprehension. "It is he outside my gates, isn't it?"

"Aye," she drawled. "It is."

"If he wanted the child so badly, my beauteous Wynne, why did he not simply use his vaunted magic to retrieve him? I would expect that of Madoc," Brys sneered.

"There will be no magic used here this day, Brys. This is not about magic. It is about you and your evil, which are about to come to an end. Now give me my son!" Wynne stood, determined now, before the high board.

"My lady!" Gytha called. "We are here!"

"Harry!" the lord of Cai barked, and immediately a hulking man-at-arms leapt forward. "Take the child to my quarters. As for you, my traitorous Saxon bitch," Brys turned his attention to Gytha, "you will leave Cai this day and thank God I do not punish you as you deserve! The lady here can tell you of my expertise with a whip upon the backs of bad servants."

The man-at-arms reached for Arvel, who immediately began

screaming, "Mama! Mama!" while Gytha gamely attempted to retain custody of her little charge. With a fierce yank, however, Harry tore Arvel from Gytha's arms and raced away with the boy, who was now howling loudly at the top of his small lungs. Gytha fled weeping to Wynne's side.

"It is all right, Gytha," Wynne gently soothed the distraught nursemaid. "Leave the castle now. You will find safety with my woman servant, Megan, outside the gates. I will shortly bring Arvel back to you."

"Do you think she can so easily walk through my gates?" demanded Brys arrogantly as Gytha ran from the hall.

"Your gates have already been secured by my husband and the lord of St. Bride's," Wynne told him. "You should also know that your men-at-arms, but for those within this hall, have all surrendered to us." She turned and spoke to the remaining few of Brys's men. "We offer amnesty to any of you who will join your mates and go in peace."

Brys laughed bitterly as he watched his remaining retainers flee his hall. "Vermin! Lice!" he shouted after them. "I will yet win this day, and you will come crawling back to me for your places! Do not, for I will kill with my bare hands any who do!"

"You are beaten, Brys of Cai," Wynne told him. "Come now and face your death like a man and not some craven, ignoble thing."

"My death?" Brys looked truly astounded. "What do you mean, face my death? You have won. What more can you want of me?"

"We want your life," Wynne said solemnly.

"My life? You want my life?" Why did he keep repeating everything she said? Brys wondered irritably.

"Your life, devil!" the deep voice of Rhys of St. Bride's thundered through the hall, and the great lord strode forward, armed and ready to do battle.

"I will not fight you," Brys said petulantly. "I am no warrior as you!"

"You will fight me, coward, for I offer you no other choice but to die on the end of my sword like the dog you are!" Rhys said. "Before this day is over, Brys of Cai, you will be in Hell, where you surely belong, and never did a man deserve to suffer more for his sins than you do."

Brys looked down the hall. It was slowly filling with heavily armed soldiers. He edged himself nervously along the high board. "Where is my brother Madoc and my sister Nesta?" he whined, childlike.

"You will not see them again," Rhys told him.

"You would deny a condemned man this last request?" Brys bleated piteously, forcing his icy eyes to fill with tears.

"Hah, charlatan! Think not to elicit my sympathy with your false tears," Rhys replied. "There is no pity in me for the likes of you!"

"Wynne, I appeal to you?" Brys pleaded, holding out his slender, long hands.

"I owe you nothing, Brys," she answered him coldly. "You abducted me from my husband, sold me into slavery along with my unborn son. You have caused Madoc and me pain far greater than you will ever know. I owe you nothing, for this is not the first time you have come between us, and I think you know it well."

"You do not seem to have suffered so greatly the wretched experience you claim I forced you into," he said with a sneer.

"No thanks to you, Brys of Cai!" Wynne snapped angrily.

"Enough of this talk," Rhys said harshly. " 'Tis time, coward!"

Brys broke from the cover of the high board and, dashing across a corner of the hall, fled through a small door that had been hidden behind a tall-backed chair. With a roar of fury Rhys leapt after him, followed quickly by Wynne. They found themselves within a small interior hallway whose only other exit was up a stone staircase. Above them they could hear Brys's footsteps as he ran from them. Rhys began to swiftly mount the stairs with Wynne behind him.

"It probably goes to his apartments," she shouted after her brother-in-law. "He'll not trap himself. There will be another exit."

"Fear not," Rhys replied. "I'll have the miserable devil's hide and send his soul to Hell before the hour's out!"

At the top of the staircase they encountered a locked door, but in no mood to be denied his quarry, Rhys of St. Bride's quickly and methodically battered the barrier down. They found themselves within an antechamber. Ahead of them a door slammed shut. They hurried to open it, but once again

Rhys was forced to smash through the oaken portal, which easily gave way beneath his mighty blows just as Brys and his lone remaining henchman rushed out another door; but as there was no time to close off this door, their pursuers were immediately behind them.

Up another narrow flight of stairs they ran, Rhys puffing from the weight of his battle gear, but nonetheless game. Wynne could hear her son crying ahead of her, and Arvel's desperate sobs almost broke her heart. Dear God, she silently prayed, keep my baby safe! Don't let us lose him now. She hurried around another turn in the stairs and saw before her a trapdoor, already open, as Brys and Harry scrambled through it. As the hapless man-at-arms attempted to slam the trapdoor shut on them, Rhys, teeth bared, roared loudly, "Do so and you're a dead man!" Harry, still grasping Arvel about the waist, drew back, quite intimidated.

Then they were all outside upon the roof of Castle Cai. Rhys drew a deep breath to clear his head and said, "Now fight me, you whoreson, and let us be done with this farce!"

"I have no weapon," Brys whined piteously.

"Give him your sword," Rhys commanded Harry, and the man-at-arms successfully struggled to free his arms, which he then passed to his master.

Brys glared angrily at him and complained, " 'Tis not the weapon of a nobleman."

" 'Tis your only chance, you cowardly, sniveling devil," Rhys told him coldly, and raising his own weapon up, he aimed a blow at his enemy, who staggered, but blocking the blow successfully, backed away.

With grim precision the lord of St. Bride's drove his enemy across the roof of the castle and toward the battlements along the edge. There, silhouetted against the bright blue afternoon sky, the two men fought upon the heights of Castle Cai. Metal clanged fiercely on metal as the well-forged blades of the broadswords met again and again with a noisy ringing tone that echoed in the otherwise clear silent air.

Below, all the inhabitants of the castle, along with the army of Rhys and Madoc, clustered in groups staring upward, hypnotized by the fascinating yet terrifying spectacle going on above them. This was a life and death struggle, and the soldiers were open-mouthed for the most part. Megan and Gytha knelt, praying fervently for the lord of St. Bride's safety and eventual triumph over the wicked lord of Cai. Nesta, however, had full faith in her husband's ability to overcome her evil brother.

"It is but a matter of time," she said quietly to Madoc.

"Do you feel no remorse or sadness for Brys?" he asked her.

Nesta shook her head. "Nay," she said, "I do not. How can I, dearest brother? How can you? Yet I realize that in your kind heart you do feel pity for Brys despite all he has done. Perhaps you are a better soul than I am. I understand it not, but I do know that Brys must die for any of us to be safe. There simply is no other way."

"Will he learn from this, I wonder?" Madoc said aloud.

"That I cannot tell you," Nesta answered her brother honestly. "He is so filled with envy and anger and bitterness. Until he can purge himself of those evils, I feel he will always be a danger to us and to himself. Perhaps in time." She let her eyes stray back up to the battlements where her husband and brother fought their duel to the death.

Wynne, from her greater vantage point upon the roof, watched the battle. If she was afraid, she was not aware of it, for her mind was devoid of everything but her son. She looked to Harry.

"Give me Arvel," she said softly.

He shook his head. "I dare not, lady, until this is finished," he replied, and she felt sorry for him, caught between them all. Arvel would be safe. Instinctively Wynne knew that the man-at-arms would not harm her child.

"Cease your weeping, Arvel," she told the little boy. "Mama is here, Harry has you safe, and we will soon go home."

Arvel sniffled, but reassured, he stopped howling and regarded his mother with round, solemn eyes.

Wynne's gaze moved back to the battle.

Slowly and quite deliberately Rhys fought against Brys of Cai, raining blow after punishing blow at him, pushing him back and to his limit, wearing him down for the eventual kill. Rhys's own great heart was hammering with the exertion of the battle. The sweat ran in hot rivulets down his face and in cold rivulets down his back. Neither Rhys nor his opponent wore mail, for the lord of St. Bride's would have considered it dishonorable to fight well-armored when his enemy was not.

Rhys relied upon his own skill to overcome Brys. He had to admit to himself that Brys was a skilled swordsman, for all his disclaimers to the contrary. He could see, however, that Brys of Cai's soft and sensual life, with its overabundance of fine food and even finer wines, had rendered his stamina less than that of a hardened veteran as himself.

I want to put an end to this quickly, Rhys thought suddenly. He knew that the longer their conflict raged on, there was always the chance that a lucky blow struck by his enemy could seriously maim or even kill him. He wanted to live a long and happy life with the beautiful Nesta, and his sons were far too young to be orphaned. With a sudden, wild battle cry that startled them all, Brys in particular, Rhys showered a series of fierce blows down upon his adversary, forcing Brys to his knees.

With the terrible realization that death was indeed staring him quite directly in the face, Brys of Cai sought to save himself in a most dishonorable fashion. With an instinct for survival and an agility that surprised even himself, he quickly scooped up a handful of dirt and pebbles from atop the castle walls and, with an unfailing aim, flung them directly into Rhys of St. Bride's face. Blinded temporarily, Rhys could only flail helplessly as Brys of Cai struggled to his feet and raised his own broadsword to deliver the lord of St. Bride's his death blow. Horrified by this sudden turn of events, Wynne screamed helplessly in desperation.

The day had waned while the two men fought, and now from out of the sunset-stained sky, a large black raven swept down, screaming his raucous cry as he dove directly at Brys of Cai's head and face. Startled, Brys was forced to drop his weapon in a vain attempt to defend himself from the huge bird. The creature, however, would not be deterred from his apparent purpose, which seemed to be Brys of Cai's destruction. Against the background of a flaming orange-gold sky, the great black raven deliberately forced Brys backward, all the while screaming fiercely, his sharp beak scoring several open, bloody wounds upon the handsome face and the hands which were raised to shield himself. The bird's large wing span beat upon his enemy. There was nowhere for Brys to go.

In a shrieking final assault upon Brys of Cai, the great black bird drove his victim over the battlements of Castle Cai to a

screaming finality below. The body landed with a loud, unpleasant thump upon the wooden drawbridge. It was spread-
eagled and faceup, allowing those near it a glimpse of Brys's
face, which was contorted in rage, surprise, and terror.

"Madoc!" Wynne whispered as the raven flew up into the
burning scarlet sky, cawing triumphantly. Then she whirled
about and said fiercely to Harry, "Give me my child!"

Without another word the man-at-arms thrust Arvel into his
mother's care, and Wynne, her son clinging to her, climbed
back down through the trapdoor and hurried down the stairs.
She flew through Brys's chambers and down the next flight,
back into the now empty hall. Her feet barely touching the
ground, she raced out of Castle Cai, skirting Brys's dead body,
and looked back up. Above her the great black bird flapped his
wings noisily, still crying his triumph.

Then to the horror of both Wynne and Nesta, a voice was
heard to say, "Damned impudent bird!" and an arrow flew
from somewhere within the ranks of the standing army to find
its mark within the raven's chest. The bird plummeted to the
ground. With a shriek Wynne pushed Arvel at Gytha and ran
to where the raven had fallen. Kneeling upon the ground, she
cradled the creature in her arms and heard his voice weakly
saying, *"Madoc is ainm dom. Madoc is aimn dom. Te . . .
se . . . Madoc!"*

About them the startled soldiery drew back with a single
gasp of surprise. " *'Tis the prince!"* she heard them saying.

"Oh, my dearest love," Wynne wept, the tears pouring down
her pale cheeks. "What have you done that it should end like
this?"

"I have killed my brother," he said weakly, "but alas, dearling, there was, it seems, no other way."

"Arvel is safe," she told him as a shudder ripped through his
body.

Madoc's smoky blue eyes grew bright for a brief moment
and he whispered, "Show me my son!"

"Gytha! Bring Arvel!" Wynne cried, and when Gytha hung
back afraid, Nesta took her nephew from the Saxon girl's arms
and brought him into Madoc's sight.

Madoc's gaze feasted upon his son, and he said in a satisfied
voice, "He is me. It is good, dearling." Then the light began to
fade swiftly from the eyes, and Wynne cried out, seeing it.

"*Madoc!* My lord and my love! Do not leave me!" She cradled him tightly, her dark hair, which had come loose in her pursuit of Brys, now falling about them like a curtain. Her tears, flowing copiously, wet both her tunic front and his kirtle.

"You will survive, dearling," he said, his voice so weak that she was forced to bend even closer to hear him. "*You must!*" Then his soul pulled free of his body and he was gone from her.

"*Madoc! Madoc!*" Wynne cried desperately. "Do not go, my love! Do not go! You must get to know Arvel! And there is the other! I have not yet told you of the new child I am to bear you, the child now growing beneath my heart! The child created of our reunion! *Madoc!*"

Nesta, having returned Arvel to Gytha, now bent and gently helped her sister-in-law to her feet. She, too, was weeping at the sight of her beloved brother's body. Rhys stumbled out onto the drawbridge, still half blinded with the grit his dishonorable opponent had thrown at him.

"What has happened?" he demanded.

"Did you not see it?" Wynne said tonelessly.

"See what?" Rhys said. "I had Brys of Cai all but beaten when the dishonorable whoreson threw dirt in my face, and I was blinded for a time. All I could hear was the flapping of wings and a bird's cry. I saw nothing."

"Madoc saved you," Wynne told him. "Although he had sworn never to use his shape-changer's powers again, he did so in order to defeat Brys and save you, Rhys. Now he is dead! Shot through with an arrow by one of our men." Her tears flowed briefly and hotly for a moment, and then she said, "Come, my lord. I must prepare an herbal wash for your poor eyes. I doubt there is any serious damage to your sight, but your eyes are most likely scratched and will need my attention. Nesta, take your husband into the castle."

"She is so cold of heart," Rhys said to his wife as they reentered Cai. "Her husband is dead, and she weeps but a moment, and then says she will treat my wounds. Thank God I have you, my angel!"

"Dearest Rhys," Nesta told him gently, "you have never understood Wynne of Gwernach. She loved my brother with every fiber of her being. She will mourn him until she dies, and she will never, I promise you, remarry. She will raise her son

Arvel, and this new child she is to bear, to know their father as if he were there with them and not just a memory. Her grief will always be a private grief, as her love for Madoc was a private love. She is not cold of heart. Indeed, her heart is broken; but she will go on as Madoc wanted her to go on, and she will survive to raise her children to man- and womanhood. Madoc will always be in her heart, and in her mind and in her daily thoughts. What they have, have had, and will one day have again, is a love that time cannot destroy. Dearest Rhys, my darling lord! I love you so very much!" And Nesta of Powys flung her arms about her husband and kissed him passionately. "I shall never be able to thank Madoc," she said, and Rhys knew exactly what she meant. Madoc had saved his life.

Gently he disengaged himself from his beautiful wife's embrace. "We must help Wynne," he told her.

"You must offer to help, but let her have the decision whether to accept or not," she told him, and he nodded his agreement.

Outside, Brys of Cai's body had been lifted from the drawbridge.

"What shall we do with it, lady?" the captain of the guard asked her helplessly, there being no other authority in his sight.

"Lay him out upon the high board in his hall," Wynne instructed. "After I have treated the lord of St. Bride's eyes, we will leave here. Before we do, fire this castle. It must be totally destroyed."

"But the night is upon us, lady," the captain protested.

"Would you seek shelter here?" Wynne demanded of him, and he shook his head.

"And my lord Madoc?" the captain asked nervously.

"We will take my lord back to Raven's Rock," she answered. "Prepare a litter for his body that it may be carried with the honor and the dignity it deserves."

"Shall I look for the archer, my lady?"

Wynne's green eyes looked bleakly at the soldier. "Why? He knew not what he was doing. I want no one punished. I forgive the archer, whoever he was. I never want to know!" She turned away from the captain and reentered the hall to minister to Rhys's eyes.

Her wishes were immediately carried out. When she had finished treating the lord of St. Bride's, Brys had been placed upon his high board, cold and stiff. They piled furniture and other combustibles about him. On the floors above, flaming brands had already been placed in each nook and cranny of the castle. Now Wynne took a torch and lit Brys's funeral pyre. The scarlet flames leapt upward, casting dark dancing shadows on the walls. Wynne stood for several minutes watching, unable to leave until she saw the fire beginning to consume Brys's body. Then finally at a touch of Rhys's hand on her arm, she turned and walked slowly from the Great Hall of Castle Cai. Outside, and on the other side of the drawbridge, she paused and again stood watching as the castle, now fully engulfed in flames, burned. It stood as a beacon against the dark night sky, yet Wynne felt not the warmth of the fire.

Madoc was dead. The words burnt into her consciousness like a brand. She had lost him again even as their reunion had allowed her to believe that their difficulties were behind them, and that they would be together forever. Yet the choice had been Madoc's. He had not, of course, chosen to relinquish his life; but he had simply been unable to allow his friend to do so. Rhys, whose own sense of honor would not permit Madoc to destroy Brys, now owed his very existence to the prince's great sacrifice. And Madoc's actions had certainly included her and Arvel as well, Wynne thought sadly. Whatever sins he had committed against them in that other time and place had been surely expiated by the unselfish surrender of his own life in this time and place. It was a bitter comfort, but she understood.

Suddenly a small hand slipped into her cold one, and she heard her son's voice saying, "Where is my uncle, Mama?"

Wynne looked down at him. "Your uncle is dead, Arvel," she told the little boy. "He will never hurt you again."

Arvel nodded at her with Madoc's look, and Wynne's heart contracted most painfully. "Can we go home, Mama?"

"Aye, my lord prince," she told him.

Arvel's smoky blue eyes widened at her words. "Am I a prince?"

"You are the prince of Powys-Wenwynwyn, Arvel ap Madoc," his mother told him.

"My home is not at Aelfdene?" Arvel was suddenly possessed by a new awareness.

"Nay, my lord prince," she answered.

"Where is my home, Mama?"

"You are the lord of Raven's Rock, my son," she told him.

Rhys came and said, "Whatever you want, Wynne of Gwernach. Whatever help you need, ever. It is yours in return for a debt I can never repay, as well as for the kinship between us."

She nodded. "I thank you, my lord," she answered him, and then she said to Arvel, "This is your uncle, my son. He is Rhys, the lord of St. Bride's."

Rhys bowed solemnly to the little child, saying, "I am always and ever at your service, my lord prince. Is there any way in which I can now serve you?"

"Take me upon your horse, uncle," the little boy answered. When they were all mounted, Arvel commanded Rhys to the head of the line of soldiers. "I would go home now," he said. "I would go home to Raven's Rock."

They moved away from the burning castle, the little boy upon his uncle's great horse leading them. Behind, the bearers surrounded by men-at-arms carrying lighted torches bore the body of Madoc of Powys-Wenwynwyn. They were followed by the women and the small army as they wended their way into the forest. Above them the night sky was lit by a bright, full moon now. Wynne looked up at the moon. It shone pure and white against the blackness.

Then suddenly the pristine beauty was marred a moment by the shadow of a raven as it flew across the moon. Wynne thought that perhaps she might even hear the bird's cry, but had she, it would have been a different cry. Madoc was dead. Once again they had been separated by a cruel moment in time. That they would be reunited again one day she had not a single doubt; and next time ... oh, next time, it would be even better!

She was unaware of the tears that were flowing quickly down her beautiful face; unaware that her mouth had turned itself into a secret, small smile at her thoughts. Nothing mattered now but the children. Arvel, and Averel, and the new child growing within her. The children, and Raven's Rock, and her memories. Aye! Her memories. *And what memories they were!*

Epilogue

WALES, 1805

Forget not that I shall come back to you.
A little while, and my longing shall gather
dust and foam for another body.
A little while, a moment of rest upon the
wind, and another woman shall bear me.
                                    Kahlil Gibran
                                    THE PROPHET

▓Epilogue

"*I* am not certain; no indeed, I am not certain at all that we were wise to allow our young people to go off without a proper chaperone," Lady Marcella Bowen fretted to no one in particular. A large, handsome woman in her mid-forties, she wore a purple gauze scarf wrapped in turban fashion about her graying locks that bobbed with her uncertainty as she peered myopically after the departing riders.

"Nonsense, m'dear," her portly husband, Sir Rumford Bowen, replied jovially. "Summertime . . . informality here in the country, y'know . . . not to worry."

"Yes, indeed!" echoed Sir Rumford's good friend, Sir William Thorley. "Informality quite the order of the day here at Tretower Wells."

"We should have gone to Bath," muttered Lady Marcella.

"Bath is out of fashion now, m'dear. Brummel himself has said so, and the ton is quite scattered this summer," Sir Rumford told his spouse.

She glowered at him and said acidly, "And to what purpose, I should like to know, sir? Every eligible male of good breeding in London is God only knows where, instead of in one central place, *Bath*, where they may be properly inspected and assessed by the families of young ladies of equal breeding. Mr. Brummel has rendered the natural order of things into chaos. If he were a decent man he would be quite repentant. Knowing him, however, I expect he finds all of this quite amusing, the wretch! How shall we ever find a husband for Honoria, I should like to know?"

"Now, now, m'dear," Sir Rumford attempted to soothe his wife, "there are several fine young men here at the spa, and others expected as the summer passes."

Lady Marcella sighed with the air of one martyred. How did one explain to a man about these things? Tretower Wells was not Bath. It could not even compare to Bath. It was a new watering spot, just opened to guests this summer, in which her husband, Sir William, and several other gentlemen whose wealth and titles stemmed from their success in trade, had invested. With Brummel's declaration that Bath was passé, these gentlemen and their families had all flocked to Tretower Wells, much to the distress of their ladies.

The wives of the investors were all of one mind. That their sons and daughters marry young women and gentlemen higher up on the social ladder, not each other. What good was money if it could not buy you what you most desired? Now, alas, months of careful planning was gone awry, for Tretower Wells, in the Black Mountains of Wales, was hardly a hub of society. Indeed, it was quite at the ends of the earth.

"Thank God Olympia is already betrothed or we should completely be ruined," Lady Marcella declared. "Honoria is, after all, only seventeen, and we have at least another year before I must really worry."

"You need never worry about Honoria where men are concerned," her husband remarked wryly. "She attracts them like bees to a flower."

"Do you not also have the responsibility of your orphaned niece, Miss Katherine?" ventured Sir William's mousy wife, Lady Dorothea.

"Honoria must be considered first," Lady Marcella replied firmly with maternal interest. "Dear Kitty is an heiress, after all, and despite the fact she is an American, a most desirable catch for any young man of good breeding. Actually," Lady Marcella continued archly, leaning over to confide in Lady Dorothea, "I am considering her as a possible partie for our eldest son, George. Perhaps, however, I should seek a wife with English wealth for George. He and Kitty do not seem particularly enamored of each other."

"Do they not like each other?" queried Lady Dorothea, eager for a bit of juicy gossip.

"Oh, indeed they do, for cousins," Lady Marcella said, "but I am not certain they would make a good match as a husband and wife."

"What about matching her with one of your younger sons?" asked Sir William, getting into the spirit of things. He and his wife were childless, but they took a great interest in the Bowen children.

"Impossible!" Lady Marcella replied. "Anscom is studying for the church. It will be some time before he can take a wife. Darius is in the army. His regiment is to be posted to India soon. An American wife would not do for Darius at all. As for Nestor, his career with His Majesty's navy almost precludes his having a wife, although he may someday take one; but he is several years younger than dear Kitty. No, it will be either George or some other acceptable gentleman, but alas, we are not at Bath. There are no acceptable gentlemen I might consider for either Honoria or Kitty." She sent her husband a black look. "I vow they will wither on the vine here this summer, poor dears!"

"It appears to me that none of them are withering at all," Sir Rumford replied spiritedly. "They were, in fact, quite looking forward to their outing."

"Where are they off to?" Lady Dorothea inquired curiously.

"Up the mountain," he told her. "There is some sort of local legend about a ruined castle atop the ridge, and they are to meet up with several of George's friends from Oxford who have been riding about the countryside. They will return with the children later for a stay of several weeks here at Tretower Wells. Quite nice young fellows, they are. Olympia's betrothed, Sir Halsey Halstead, and two others, Sir Frederick Galton and Sir Thomas Small. Perfectly eligible, both of them, m'dear, or had you forgotten?" he grinned at his wife.

"They are indeed eligible! You are correct, Rumford! I had quite forgotten that Freddie Galton and Tom Small were coming to Tretower Wells." Lady Marcella had brightened considerably.

"Sir Thomas Small? Isn't he Baron Lindell? Why, he came into his money when he was just five years old. Raised by a spinster aunt. I went to school with Emily Small," Lady Dorothea said excitedly. "He's fabulously wealthy, y'know! Has properties in India and the Americas as well. The money comes from tea, and furs, I'm told, not to mention huge holdings in land."

"Indeed?" Lady Marcella said, almost purring, her blue eyes dancing with interest. "We have only met him twice. Once at Oxford, and once when George brought him home between terms. He is a handsome young man, rather dramatically so, I thought. I was not aware of his most excellent background, my

dear Dorothea. How kind of you to enlighten me. He is certainly a very possible match for our Honoria. He is not betrothed, is he?" she asked anxiously.

"I have not heard of it if he is," Dorothea Thorley replied, delighted to have known something that her formidable friend did not.

"Then perhaps it is better I did not send a chaperone along with the children," Lady Marcella decided out loud. "They will feel freer to get to know one another in a more informal setting. Oh, I do hope Honoria will not do anything unseemly to put this worthy gentleman off," she fretted.

"Do not distress yourself about Honoria, my dear," her husband said. "She is just a bit high-spirited. Most gentlemen find that charming in a young girl."

Lady Marcella looked once again in the direction that the riders had gone, but the shaggy little Welsh ponies were long out of sight. She frowned.

"Why, I vow I can actually feel Mama worrying that she has let us go without a proper chaperone," Miss Olympia Bowen said as they trotted along.

Her siblings laughed, and then her brother Anscom said, "I believe I should censure you for such an unfilial thought, my dear sister."

"You're no parson yet, Anny," Olympia replied tartly.

"And I should not be at all had not George been so discourteous as to be born before me," Anscom Bowen replied mischievously.

"Do not blame me," George Bowen replied. "Have you any idea at all the difficulties involved in being *the heir*? I should just as soon study for nice quiet Holy Orders, Anny, as be responsible for Bowenbrooke House in London, and Bowenwood Manor in Worcestershire, and of course, first and foremost, by appointment to His Majesty, Bowen's Best, the Tea of Royalty."

The riders laughed again, and then Miss Honoria Bowen said, "And do not forget, Georgie, that Mama is counting upon you to marry some wickedly rich and fecund young heiress."

"Rich and fecund heiresses are usually horse-faced. I must have a pretty wife, or none at all," he told them. "It's only fair."

"I am quite insulted, George," their cousin Miss Katherine Williams said. "I am most wickedly rich, although I do not know if I am fecund, but I am certainly not horse-faced."

"Then marry me, Kitty, and put an end to all our troubles. Mama will be looking for a husband for you as soon as she has settled Honoria, I warn you!"

"Dear George!" Kitty reached out and patted his hand with hers. "You deserve a girl who loves you unabashedly, and I deserve a man whom I can love forevermore. Neither of us is that person for the other, and well you know it."

"You are a most unrepentant romantic, dear Kitty," Olympia told her.

"Do you not love Sir Halsey then, cousin?" Kitty probed.

The Honorable Miss Olympia Bowen blushed to the roots of her short chestnut-brown hair, but said boldly, "I most certainly do love Halsey! He is the best of men!"

"Then will you not allow me the same good fortune as you yourself have found?" her cousin asked.

"Love! Love! Love! Is that all you silly creatures are going to talk about?" demanded Lieutenant Darius Bowen, of His Majesty's Bengal Lancers. "This castle we're off to see was, I am told, in a most perfectly and naturally fortified setting. It was, so legend says, never successfully captured in a war."

"Then why is it deserted, little brother?" George Bowen asked.

"I've absolutely no idea," Darius answered with a shrug. "The family probably gained properties in the lowlands, and decided to come down off their mountain in a safe century. Why on earth live in such an out-of-the-way place if you didn't have to, I say!"

"Mr. Tretower, the original owner of the wells, says that the castle once belonged to a family of sorcerer princes," Honoria told them. Honoria, like her father, and youngest brother, was a blond with huge, ingenuous blue eyes. Her hair, as her elder sister and cousin's, was cut fashionably close to her head, à la Grecque. Her tiny ringlets were most appealing. She was petite in a family of tall women, which was considered most odd.

"Mr. Tretower says," Honoria continued, "that his great-grammy was always talking about the sorcerer prince, and his beautiful wife, and some terrible tragedy that separated them."

"The usual Welsh fairy tale," Olympia said dryly.

Ignoring her, Honoria continued, "Mr. Tretower's great-grammy used to cry whenever she told him the story. She said she could just feel the sadness in the very stones of the ruins. Isn't that just simply wonderful!" At seventeen, Honoria was wildly romantic.

"Mr. Tretower," Olympia said, "has a Celtic flair for the dramatic. I expect he tells that Banbury tale to every gullible young girl who comes to the spa. Then he rents her one of his ponies to go off trekking for a day. A most profitable business, I think."

"It is not a Banbury tale!" Honoria said indignantly. "You believe me, Kitty, don't you?"

Katherine Williams did not hear her cousin, however. She was far too busy struggling with the strong sense of familiarity sweeping over her. *I know where I'm going*, she thought. *I know precisely where I am going!* Though a slightly startling revelation, it was not a particularly frightening one, for she had had such feelings of déjà vu before.

"Kitty!" Honoria's voice pushed insistently into her thoughts.

"What? Yes, Honoria, what is it?"

"Mr. Tretower did not tell me a Banbury tale just to rent us all ponies, did he? His story about the prince and his wife are true. I am certain it is!"

"Of course it is!" Kitty assured her, and then wondered why she had said the words with such conviction.

The ponies trotted across an ancient stone bridge spanning a rocky little river below, and Kitty felt her excitement mounting as they began their climb up. The narrow tract of a worn stone path that nature had definitely not fashioned was covered with lichens.

"Why, bless me! This seems to be a road of sorts," Olympia said, surprised.

"See!" Honoria crowed, kicking her pony's fat sides to hurry him forward that she might be first to the top.

The others followed her up the increasingly steep path that twisted and wound until finally, rounding a bend, they came upon what appeared to be the remains of some long-ago habitation in a clearing. The black stones soared in some places, lay tumbled in a forlorn heap in others. In some ways it almost seemed a part of the mountain itself.

"Mr. Tretower's great-grammy was right!" said Honoria, laughing, and she leapt from her mount.

Her siblings followed and began to walk about, chattering with surprise. But Kitty was strangely silent and thoughtful. There was sadness here, even as Mr. Tretower's great-grandmother had predicted, Kitty thought, but there was happiness too. Great happiness, and so much more!

"Oh! Oh!" Honoria said almost worshipfully. "Is the view not simply divine? Why, the castle seems to have been built on the spine of the mountain itself. You can see into two valleys from here."

"I am not certain your Mr. Tretower has not misled you after all, Honoria," Olympia said tartly. "There is no castle here, nor was there ever one here. It is simply the ways in which the stone formations are set here on the mountain that give the impression of a former dwelling."

"You are quite mistaken, Olympia," Kitty said quietly in an odd, little voice, and they all turned to look at her. She walked slowly about, to the astonishment of her cousins, as if she were looking for something specific, and then her green eyes lit up. "Rock formations do not create stairs, Olympia. Look here!"

Amazed, they watched as Kitty walked regally up a moss-covered, lichen-encrusted stone staircase.

"By Jove!" George exclaimed. "Kitty is quite correct. It is certainly a staircase."

"Oh, very well," Olympia admitted, and then she shivered. "It is a staircase, George, and Honoria is correct too. It is a castle, but I am catching a chill. Now that we have all agreed, may we please return to Tretower Wells?"

"We must wait for the others, dear sister," he told her. "Do you not remember that your beloved and two gentlemen of my acquaintance are to join us here?"

Before Olympia might reply, however, the sky above them, with typical British perversity, suddenly darkened. There was an ominous rumble of thunder, and large droplets of rain began to drive down upon them. With a collective shriek the Bowen sisters cast about for some sort of shelter, and were quickly herded by their three brothers into a recess in one of the castle walls. Kitty, though, took shelter in an alcove atop the staircase where she had been standing.

She felt strangely safe and secure. It was as if she actually belonged here. As if she had stood in this very place before. She sighed with a sudden overwhelming sense of happiness, and for a minute everything else about her was gone but for the feeling she felt at this moment in time. Then below her a movement caught her eye at the very point where they had come into the castle clearing. She watched, amusement bubbling up in her, as three fashionably dressed young men, mounted upon quite superb horseflesh, trotted quickly, laughing and whooping, into the clearing. Dismounting, they dashed across the grass seeking their own escape from the very wet storm.

After a few more minutes of rain, which came in thick, silver sheets accompanied by spectacular lightning and noisy thunder, the storm passed over them, moving on into the valley below. The sun burst forth over the mountaintop, gilding the lush, wet summer greenery, touching the stone ruins with a golden light and bringing a new warmth to them. A red kite, catching a whorl in the wind, soared out over the valley to her right.

Below she could hear introductions being made. Honoria was laughing her most flirtatious laugh. It was a sound peculiar to her cousin, that Honoria always seemed to make when she found a gentleman who interested her. Kitty allowed her eyes to stray out over the densely forested valley below. A light breeze ruffled her black curls, but she was simply in no hurry to leave her little niche and join the others. She sighed deeply with a feeling of total peace and contentment, even as she suddenly sensed another presence by her side.

"Your cousins have sent me up here to escort you back down the stairs, Miss Katherine," a rich masculine voice said at her ear. "I am Sir Thomas Small, and actually having observed you from below, I do not think you can possibly be related to the Bowens at all. I think you are the magical lady of this tower."

Kitty turned to look up at the gentleman, a clever sally upon her rosy lips, but it died in her throat as her green eyes locked onto a pair of deep, smoky blue ones. *You have found me at last!* Her heart hammered violently in her chest even as the words flew through her brain. *I know this man*, she thought wildly as her more practical nature struggled to assert itself, assuring her that she had never seen this handsome man before in her entire life. *I know this man!* both her heart and her soul insisted, and struggling no more against her deeper instincts, she gave in to the wonderful feelings sweeping over her.

Sir Thomas Small smiled warmly into Katherine Williams's face, and taking her dainty hand in his, he said quietly. "Yes, I feel it too, dear Miss Katherine. You must not think me mad, although I am not certain I have not gone mad. Will you believe me when I say, beautiful lady of the tower, that I believe we are fated to marry? Will you believe me, my darling one, when I tell you that I intend making you my wife as soon as your guardians will allow us to wed? God!" He ran an impatient hand through his wavy, dark hair. "What must you think of me? I swear I am not a lunatic. I have never before behaved in such a manner with a woman!" His fingers squeezed hers gently. "You will marry me, won't you?"

Kitty nodded slowly, mesmerized by his eyes, her gaze anxiously scanning his face for something, but she knew not what. "I do not think you mad at all, sir, for I, too, am beset by emotions familiar, and yet quite unfamiliar to me. Still, I know in my heart that what you say is true, and I will gladly marry you."

He raised her hand to his mouth and kissed it lingeringly, the warmth of his lips filling her with a delicious heat. It was all so strangely right, she thought, losing herself in the depths of his wonderfully smoky gaze. For a sweet brief moment she saw this place as it had once been; the fireplaces blazing in the Great Hall below, colorful silken banners hanging from the rafters, the servants hurrying to and fro. Then as suddenly her vision cleared and he was smiling at her.

"Shall we join the others, my darling?" he asked her, and without waiting for an answer, he led her down the flight of wet stone steps from the ruined tower to join the others.

As they went, Kitty suddenly realized that she had been waiting all her eighteen years—no!—she had been waiting centuries for this tall, dark-haired stranger who was not really a stranger at all. They had been fated since time began to be together in this time and place. Yes! They would be married, although she knew that her aunt, in particular, would be most shocked. But she and Tom, Kitty knew, would have a marvelously happy life together. An instinct she had never even known she had assured her of that. For an instant she wondered if it were possible to expire of pure, sheer happiness. She had never believed such joy possible.

As they reached the bottom of the staircase she heard a bird cry above them, and looking up she saw a large, black raven soaring in the bright blue sky. *Remember!* Kitty heard the word as clearly as if someone had whispered it into her ear. *Remember!* Yes, she would indeed remember. How was it possible to ever forget this wonderful moment in time that had brought them together—reunited them, she was certain—*once again*; but deep within the very core of her being she knew that this time it would be *Forever*.

▓Author's Note

R eincarnation. A most controversial subject, yet many people and cultures believe in it. I have read it was even taught in the early Christian church. A practice quickly discontinued when it was realized that the early converts, simple people for the most part, were taking the attitude that they might be less than good in their current lives because they could always repent in the next incarnation.

That, of course, is not the purpose of reincarnation. It is believed we reincarnate in order to perfect our human souls, that we may in time aspire to a higher level of existence. If you accept the Christ it seems quite obvious, for who among us can believe we might attain in a single lifetime that which God incarnate, in the persona of Jesus of Nazareth, attained in his single lifetime? I leave it to the reader to decide. Faith is a deeply personal matter, which is as it should be.

The simple premise of *A Moment in Time* hinges on those single moments in time when we make decisions, some important, some not so, which affect us for our entire lives. Its ending is admittedly a very different one for a Historical Romance novel, but I like to think it offers the reader the reassurance of better things to come. I hope you have enjoyed this book as much as I have enjoyed writing it.

Next year Ballantine Books and I will bring you the sixth and final book in the O'Malley Saga. It is the tale of Yasaman Kama Begum, the lost daughter of Velvet de Marisco. It will, I promise, be a great deal of fun when Yasaman, rechristened Jasmine, arrives in England, and havoc ensues among the members of her loving, if somewhat surprised, family there. You'll meet several old friends, but don't assume anything, dear readers, because you know how very much I enjoy surprising you!

In the meantime I hope you will write to tell me how you

enjoyed *A Moment in Time*. Until next year I remain your most faithful author,

Bertrice Small
P.O. Box 765
Southold, NY 11971

*Lovely Nyssa Wyndham, fair and proud as her
mother Blaze, is lady-in-waiting to
Henry VIII's fourth wife in*

Love, Remember Me

by bestselling author
BERTRICE SMALL.

Henry's marriage is annulled, for the Queen
cannot meet the bawdy desires of the insatiable
king. Henry seeks a spirited new wife and it is
clear that Nyssa is favored. But in a land rife
with conspiracy and rebellion, there are those in
secret power determined to thwart Henry's
intentions. A drugged Nyssa awakens in the
arms of the notorious rake Varian de Winter.
Her virtue is destroyed, and the outraged king
orders them to wed.

Varian de Winter dares to conquer his spitfire
bride. But the intrigues and dark side of the
court intrude upon their happiness as Nyssa is
trapped in a devious plot and witness to the
deadly wrath of Henry Tudor. For as the
Reformation spawns ruthless ambition, as jealousy and revenge become bloodthirsty, all
Nyssa holds dear is suddenly in dire jeopardy....